D1919139

THE BEST HORROR OF THE YEAR

VOLUME TEN

Also Edited by Ellen Datlow

A Whisper of Blood
A Wolf at the Door (with Terri Windling)
After (with Terri Windling)
Alien Sex
Black Feathers: Dark Avian Tales
Black Heart, Ivory Bones (with Terri Windling)
Black Swan, White Raven (with Terri Windling)
Black Thorn, White Rose (with Terri Windling)
Blood is Not Enough: 17 Stories of Vampirism
Blood and Other Cravings
Children of Lovecraft
Darkness: Two Decades of Modern Horror
Digital Domains: A Decade of Science Fiction and Fantasy
Echoes: The Saga Anthology of Ghost Stories
Fearful Symmetries
Haunted Legends (with Nick Mamatas)
Haunted Nights (with Lisa Morton)
Hauntings
Inferno: New Tales of Terror and the Supernatural
Lethal Kisses
Little Deaths
Lovecraft Unbound
Lovecraft's Monsters
Mad Hatters and March Hares
Naked City: Tales of Urban Fantasy
Nebula Awards Showcase 2009
Nightmare Carnival
Nightmares
Off Limits: Tales of Alien Sex
Omni Best Science Fiction: Volumes One through Three
Omni Books of Science Fiction: Volumes One through Seven
OmniVisions One and Two
Poe: 19 New Tales Inspired by Edgar Allan Poe
Queen Victoria's Book of Spells (with Terri Windling)
Ruby Slippers, Golden Tears (with Terri Windling)
Salon Fantastique: Fifteen Original Tales of Fantasy (with Terri Windling)
Silver Birch, Blood Moon (with Terri Windling)
Sirens and Other Daemon Lovers (with Terri Windling)
Snow White, Blood Red (with Terri Windling)
Supernatural Noir
Swan Sister (with Terri Windling)
Tails of Wonder and Imagination: Cat Stories
Teeth: Vampire Tales (with Terri Windling)
Telling Tales: The Clarion West 30th Anniversary Anthology
The Beastly Bride: And Other Tales of the Animal People (with Terri Windling)
The Best Horror of the Year: Volumes One–Ten
The Beastly Bride: Tales of the Animal People
The Coyote Road: Trickster Tales (with Terri Windling)
The Cutting Room: Dark Reflections of the Silver Screen
The Dark: New Ghost Stories
The Del Rey Book of Science Fiction and Fantasy
The Devil and the Deep
The Doll Collection
The Faery Reel: Tales from the Twilight Realm
The Green Man: Tales of the Mythic Forest (with Terri Windling)
The Monstrous
Troll's Eye View: A Book of Villainous Tales (with Terri Windling)
Twists of the Tale
Vanishing Acts
The Year's Best Fantasy and Horror (with Terri Windling, Gavin J. Grant, and Kelly Link)

THE BEST HORROR OF THE YEAR

VOLUME TEN

EDITED BY ELLEN DATLOW

NIGHT SHADE BOOKS
NEW YORK

Night Shade books may be purchased in bulk at special discounts for sales promotion, corporate gifts, fund-raising, or educational purposes. Special editions can also be created to specifications. For details, contact the Special Sales Department, Night Shade Books, 307 West 36th Street, 11th Floor, New York, NY 10018 or info@skyhorsepublishing.com.

Visit our website at www.nightshadebooks.com.

10 9 8 7 6 5 4 3 2 1

Library of Congress Cataloging-in-Publication Data is available on file.

Interior layout and design by Amy Popovich
Cover art by Chenthooran Nambiarooran
Cover design by Amy Popovich and Mona Lin

Print ISBN: 978-1-5107-1667-4

Printed in the United States of America

Thanks to Gardner Dozois, Priya Sharma, Jonathan Strahan, and Stefan Dziemianowicz for their recommendations.

Than you to all the magazine and book publishers who sent me material for review in a timely manner.

Thanks to Kristine Dikeman, who helped me in my reading. And special thanks to Jason Katzman, my editor at Night Shade.

Table of Contents

SUMMATION: 2017

Here are 2017's numbers: There are twenty-one stories, novelettes, and novellas in this year's volume, ranging from 1,500 words to 17,900 words. There are almost 20,000 more words this year than there were last year. The material comes from anthologies, collections, magazines, webzines, and eBook-only publications. Eleven of the contributors live in the United States, five in the United Kingdom, three in Canada, and one in Australia. Eleven stories are by women (two stories are by one of them) and ten are by men. The authors of nine stories have never before appeared in my best of the year series.

Awards

The Horror Writers Association announced the winners of the 2015 Bram Stoker Awards® April 29 on the Queen Mary in Long Beach, California. The presentations were made during a banquet held at the organization's second StokerCon. The winners were as follows:

Superior Achievement in a Novel: *The Fisherman* by John Langan (Word Horde Press); Superior Achievement in a First Novel: *Haven* by Tom Deady (Cemetery Dance Publications); Superior Achievement in a Young Adult Novel: *Snowed* by Marie Alexander (Raw Dog Screaming Press); Superior Achievement in a Graphic Novel: *Kolchak the Night Stalker: The Forgotten Love of Edgar Allan Poe* by James Chambers (Moonstone); Superior Achievement in Long Fiction: *The Winter Box* by Tim Waggoner (Dark Fuse);

Superior Achievement in Short Fiction: "The Crawl Space" by Joyce Carol Oates (*Ellery Queen Mystery Magazine*, March/April); Superior Achievement in a Screenplay: *The VVitch* by Robert Eggers (Parts and Labor, RT Features, Rooks Nest Entertainment, Code Red Productions, Scythia Films, Maiden Voyage Pictures, Mott Street Pictures, Pulse Films, and Very Special Projects); Superior Achievement in an Anthology: *Borderlands 6* edited by Thomas F. Monteleone and Olivia F. Monteleone (Borderlands Press/Samhain); Superior Achievement in a Fiction Collection: *The Doll-Master and Other Tales of Terror* by Joyce Carol Oates (Mysterious Press); Superior Achievement in Non-Fiction: *Shirley Jackson: A Rather Haunted Life* by Ruth Franklin (W. W. Norton); Superior Achievement in a Poetry Collection: *Brothel* by Stephanie M. Wytovich (Raw Dog Screaming Press).

The Specialty Press Award: Omnium Gatherum.

The Richard Layman President's Award: Caren Hanten.

The Silver Hammer Award: James Chambers.

Mentor of the Year went to Linda Addison.

Life Achievement Awards: Dennis Etchison and Thomas F. Monteleone.

The 2016 Shirley Jackson Awards were given out at Readercon 28 on Sunday, July 16, 2017, in Quincy, Massachusetts. The jurors were Nadia Bulkin, Robert Levy, Helen Marshall, Robert Shearman, and Chandler Klang Smith.

The winners were: Novel: *The Girls*, Emma Cline (Random House); Novella: *The Ballad of Black Tom*, Victor LaValle (Tor.com Books); Novelette: "Waxy" by Camilla Grudova (Granta); Short Fiction: "Postcards from Natalie" by Carrie Laben (The Dark); Single-Author Collection: *A Natural History of Hell* by Jeffrey Ford (Small Beer Press); Edited Anthology: *The Starlit Wood*, edited by Dominik Parisien and Navah Wolfe (Saga Press) and the Board of Director's Award to Ruth Franklin in recognition of the biography, *Shirley Jackson: A Rather Haunted Life.*

The World Fantasy Awards were presented October 30, 2016, at a banquet held during the World Fantasy Convention in Columbus, Ohio. The Lifetime Achievement recipients, Terry Brooks and Marina Warner, were previously announced. The judges were Elizabeth Engstrom, Betsy Mitchell, Daryl Gregory, Juliet Marillier, and Nalo Hopkinson.

Winners of the Best Work 2016: Best Novel: *The Sudden Appearance of Hope*, Claire North (Redhook; Orbit UK); Best Long Fiction: *The Dream-Quest of Vellitt Boe*, Kij Johnson (Tor.com Books); Best Short Fiction: "Das Steingeschöpf," G.V. Anderson (*Strange Horizons* 12/12/16); Best Anthology: *Dreaming in the Dark*, Jack Dann, ed. (PS Australia); Best Collection: *A Natural History of Hell*, Jeffrey Ford (Small Beer);

Best Artist: Jeffrey Alan Love; Special Award, Professional: Michael Levy & Farah Mendlesohn, for *Children's Fantasy Literature: An Introduction* (Cambridge University Press); Special Award, Non-Professional: Neile Graham, for fostering excellence in the genre through her role as Workshop Director, Clarion West.

NOTABLE NOVELS OF 2017

Chalk by Paul Cornell (Tor.com Books) begins with a brutal act perpetrated on a bullied British teenager, accidently awakening an ancient power that becomes the embodiment of revenge against those who wronged the boy.

The Bone Mother by David Demchuk (ChiZine Publications) is a series of related vignettes about monsters and magical creatures trying to survive in three villages on the Ukrainian/Romanian border in a time of war. Moving, horrifying, terrifying. A quick, enjoyable read.

Mormama by Kit Reed (Tor) is a marvelous southern gothic about a cursed ancestral home with three elderly sisters living within. When a divorced relative and her young son move in and an accident victim with no memory hides out in the basement the haunts become active, whispering ugly secrets.

The Dark Net by Benjamin Percy (Houghton Mifflin Harcourt) is an entertaining ride into the dark side of the internet where all sorts of things can be acquired and where awful secrets reside. Demons are intent on using the dark net to create havoc in the world by infecting everything digital. A reporter in Portland, Oregon, stumbles on the plot by accident, and her blind niece—using a new device that enables her to see—might be the key to stopping it. What's most interesting about the plot is how it dovetails nicely with our dependence on and anxieties about the ubiquitous technology that inextricably links us worldwide.

The Boy on the Bridge by M. R. Carey (Orbit) takes place in the same post-apocalyptic world as *The Girl with All the Gifts*, the terrific 2016 novel and movie. However, it's not a sequel—it's been called a "sidequel," which seems about right. A fungus that mutated from insects has turned most people in England into "hungries"—mindless creatures with a craving for fresh meat—animal or human.

A group of scientists, soldiers, and a brilliant fifteen-year-old boy who is the only survivor of a hungries attack embark on an expedition to Scotland from the last human holdout in England in an attempt to find caches of *Cordyceps* cultures spread around the countryside by an earlier expedition to test whether specific environments might be less hospitable to the pathogen—or better yet, contain a cure. Initially, the relationship of the boy and the epidemiologist who has taken care of him since he was orphaned plus the road-trip plot seem to indicate a trajectory similar to that of *The Girl with All the Gifts*, but oh, does it move along.

Carey's characterizations make this book pop. It's fascinating to watch the relationships evolve, and characters who initially only appear in the background begin to emerge into the light. Because the reader really cares about most of them, the book is edge-of-your-seat suspenseful—and agonizing. Despite what you *think* is going to happen, there are plenty of surprises. Highly recommended.

Under a Watchful Eye by Adam Nevill (Macmillan) is about what happens when an old, unwelcome acquaintance inserts himself back into the life of a horror writer, imposing his disgusting, debased presence into the writer's comfortable existence. With him, he brings mysterious and threatening creatures, acolytes in thrall to a cult leader dead almost thirty years. It's a real challenge to keep readers engrossed in a novel with a horrible, disgusting character playing a dominant role in the first third of the book, but Nevill manages to do so.

The Changeling by Victor LaValle (Spiegel & Grau) takes the reader for an emotionally wrenching rollercoaster ride when a horrific act destroys the seemingly idyllic life of a New York couple and their infant. Apollo Kagwa's father disappears, leaving him with strange dreams and a box of books. Apollo becomes a rare book dealer and a father himself. When his wife, Emma, starts behaving oddly, he's alarmed, but before he can do anything she does something horrible and unforgivable—and disappears. The story becomes a dark fairy tale about Apollo's odyssey into a world just beyond our ken, with magic that can empower or destroy.

Hannah Green and Her Unfeasibly Mundane Existence by Michael Marshall Smith (HarperCollins) is a charming dark fantasy about a preteen whose parents split, leaving her perplexed, angry, and feeling betrayed—especially when she's sent to her grandfather's home in Santa Cruz, California. The Devil discovers that his sacrifice machine, used to convert evil deeds into energy, is not working properly. There are certainly horrific aspects—the Devil plays a major role, as does a consciousless criminal and his gang. But there are also many fun and funny bits, including the regular appearance of a stupid, but well-meaning "accident" imp who usually looks like a giant mushroom.

Devil's Day by Andrew Michael Hurley (Tartarus Press) follows the author's celebrated, award-winning debut novel *The Loney*, and again uses his ability to create a sense of place that overpowers the reader in an atmosphere of dread. This dread emanates from the secrets of the Lancashire moors, where the Devil might (or might not) come calling and the inhabitants find it necessary to propitiate him. John Pentercost and his pregnant wife return home for his grandfather's funeral. John wants to stay. His wife does not. Engrossing but not as satisfying as *The Loney*, and the end is somewhat confusing. Worse than that, though, is the character of John, who appears to be a jerk caring little about his wife's wishes or needs, only his own. Has he always been a selfish jerk, or is it the influence his childhood home exerts on him the longer they remain there?

The Wardrobe Mistress by Patrick McGrath (Hutchinson) is the deservedly celebrated writer's ninth novel. He's written a marvelous story haunted by a ghost and by the persistence of evil. It takes place in the theatrical world of post-WWII London, which is still reeling from the devastating bombings and privation. A celebrated actor in his prime dies unexpectedly, leaving his widow grief-stricken and in shock. When she accidently discovers an ugly secret about her late husband her state of mind—and the plot—takes a darker turn.

The Child Finder by Rene Denfeld (HarperCollins) is by the author of the acclaimed first novel *The Enchanted*, published in 2014. Is *The Child Finder* horror? Probably not, although it *is* a crime novel about child abduction and abuse. A young woman, herself a former child abductee who remembers little of her experience yet is haunted by it, has taken it upon herself to find other lost and abducted children. The book is brilliant, suspenseful, heartbreaking, and thought-provoking. One of the best novels of the year.

Black Mad Wheel by Josh Malerman (Ecco) is the author's second novel and is very different from his first, the acclaimed *Bird Box*. Post WWII, a washed-up band from Detroit is asked by the US Army to go on a secret mission to a desert in Africa from where a mysterious sound emanates. Their job is to find discover the source of that sound—a sound that neutralizes atomic weapons and negatively affects those who hear it. A second thread of the novel is about one band member who is recuperating from awful, life-threatening wounds he suffered in that desert, while the Army questions him. Suspenseful and chilling.

Also Noted

The Night Ocean by Paul La Farge (Penguin Press) is a clever novel about a woman whose husband has disappeared while researching a mysterious period in H. P. Lovecraft's life and the writer's relationship with a young fan named Robert Barlow. Not horror, but it's fun and might be of interest to those interested in Lovecraft as a character and in imaginings about the science fiction's Futurians. *Come to Dust* by Bracken MacLeod (Trepidatio Publishers) is about what happens when—for no apparent reason—dead children come back to life. *The Grip of It* by Jac Jempc (FSG Originals) is about an urban couple who move into a haunted house in rural Wisconsin. *Bad Magick* by Steven L. Shrewsbury and Nate Southard (Weird West Books) is about Aleister Crowley, an ex-Confederate guerilla, and a group of Jesuits fighting evil in 1901 El Paso, Texas. *Universal Harvester* by John Darnielle (Farrar, Straus, Giroux) takes place in late 1990s Midwest, in which several residents discover that parts of the video tapes they rent contain alarming bits of stray footage of possible criminal behavior. This is a strange novel, more weird than horror. Every time it threatens to edge into horror, it never quite makes it. *Shadows on the Bayou* by Patrick Malloy (Bedlam Press) is about a man who ignorantly sells his soul in what he thinks is a tourist attraction in New Orleans and finds himself unable to leave the city. *The Vampire Years* by Eric Del Carlo (Elder Signs Press) has vampires winning a war against humankind, sending survivors to reservations in an uneasy truce. *Borne* by Jeff VanderMeer (Farrar, Straus, Giroux) is a marvelously inventive novel told from the point of view of a scavenger living with her partner in a no-man's land of feral children and monstrous bear-like killing machines. It's not quite horror, not quite science fiction, but might be the quintessential work of the weird. The scavenger discovers a small . . . object—plant, animal, machine-mysterious something that she dubs Borne. As Borne grows and their relationship deepens it becomes a threat to the status quo of the couple's survival. *The Time Eater* by Aaron French (JournalStone) is about a man unexpectedly forced to confront his past when a dying college friend asks him to visit. *Last Man Screaming* by Steve L. Shrewsbury (Weird West Books) is a Lovecraftian Western set in 1899 El Paso, Texas. *A Summer with the Dead* by Sherry Decker (Elder Signs Press) is about a woman taking refuge from her abusive husband on her aunt's farm, only to be plagued by terrible dreams about the farm's history. *The Devil Crept In* by Ania Ahlborn (Gallery Books) is about the disappearance of a young boy from a town where history seems to be repeating itself. *See What I Have Done* by Sarah Schmidt (Atlantic Monthly Press) revisits the case of Lizzie Borden, who infamously murdered her parents by whacking them with an ax. *Behind Her Eyes* by Sarah Pinborough (Flatiron Books) is about a single mom becoming involved with a married man who turns out to be her new boss. Her relationship with him and his wife take a dark turn in this thriller. *Sleeping Beauties* by Stephen King and Owen King (Scribner) is a novel about what happens when most of the women in the world fall asleep, leaving only men awake. *The Adventures of the Incognita Princess* by Cynthia Ward (Aqueduct Press/Conversation Pieces) is about Lucy Harker, daughter of Dracula and Mina Harker, who, as a spy for the British government, is assigned to guard a military officer on the way across the Atlantic—on the *Titanic*. *Ubo* by Steve Rasnic Tem (Solaris) is about a group of humans trapped in a mysterious place called Ubo by roach-like creatures/scientists who force them into scenarios where they play violent men from human history. *Hounds of the Underworld* by Dan Rabarts and Lee Murray (Raw Dog Screaming Press) is a supernatural noir set in New Zealand about a room full of blood but no body, and the consulting detective (accompanied by her troublesome brother) assigned to the case. *In the Valley of the Sun* by Andy Davidson (Skyhorse Publishing) is a Supernatural Western noir, with a brutal killer on the loose. *Corpselight* by Angela Slatter (Jo Fletcher Books) is the second in a dark fantasy series about an investigator of the weird who acts as guardian for her city, Brisbane, Australia. *Little Heaven* by Nick Cutter (Gallery Books) is about three mercenaries hired to check on someone who might have been taken against their will to a cult enclave in New Mexico. *The Lovecraft Squad: Waiting* edited by Stephen Jones (Pegasus Books) is a multi-authored novel based on the idea that H. P. Lovecraft's novella *The Shadow Over Innsmouth* was real, and that a group of stalwart men and women joined together to investigate and defeat other-worldly invaders. *Volk: A Novel of Radiant Abomination* by David Nickle (ChiZine Publications) takes place about twenty years after the author's previous novel, *Eutopia*, and once again features eugenicists and parasitic monsters doing their best to destroy humanity as we know it. *Moriah* by Daniel Mills (ChiZine Publications) is about a former army chaplain of the American Civil War who, nine years later, is sent to an isolated village in Vermont to investigate possible supernatural occurrences. *The Greenwood Faun* by Nina Antonia (Egaeus Press) is a beautifully produced hardcover weird fiction debut, with a foreword by Mark Valentine.

Magazines, Journals, and Webzines

It's important to recognize the work of the talented artists working in the field of fantastic fiction, both dark and light. The following created dark art that I thought especially noteworthy in 2017: Sandro Castelli, Joachim Luetke, Tran Nguyen, Vince Haig, George C. Cotronis, Richard Wagner, Vincent Chong, J. K. Potter, Armando Veve, Greg Chapman, Sam Dawson, Luke Spooner, Ilona Reny, Dusan Kostic, Daniele Serra, Natalia Maroz, Yaroslav Gerzhedovich, Kim Bo Yung, Allen Koszowski, Tara Bush, Mikio Murakami, Psychoshadow, Erik Mohr, Jason Zerillo, Galen Dara, Jason C. Eckhardt, Douglas Klauba, Paul Lowe, David C. Verba, and John Stanton.

Tim Lucas's lovingly produced, long-running, digest-sized movie magazine *Video Watchdog*® stopped publication with its 184th issue, published in June 2017. RIP. It will be missed by genre movie aficionados everywhere. *BFS Journal* edited by Allen Stroud is a nonfiction perk of being a member of the British Fantasy Society. It's published twice a year and includes reviews, scholarly articles, and features about recent conventions. In 2017 there were articles about Religion in Fantasy, *Bladerunner*, shapeshifting vampires, and a variety of other topics of interest. *BFS Horizons* is the fiction companion to the journal; #5 was edited by Phil Lunt. There was a good piece of fiction by Steve Toase in the issue. *The Ghosts & Scholars M. R. James Newsletter* is published annually and edited by Rosemary Pardoe. It contains mostly nonfiction articles and reviews, with an occasional piece of original fiction. *Lovecraftian Proceedings 2* edited by Dennis P. Quinn (Hippocampus Press) is a journal that published some of the academic papers presented at the Henry Armitage Symposium held at the 2015 NecronomiCon, in Providence, Rhode Island. In addition to those papers selected for inclusion, there are abstracts of all the other papers presented that year. *Dead Reckonings: A Review of Horror and the Weird in the Arts* edited by Alex Houstoun and Michael J. Abolafia is an important journal filled with reviews and articles about fiction and film. It's published by Hippocampus Press and two issues were published in 2017. *The Green Book: Writings on Irish Gothic, Supernatural, and Fantastic Literature* edited by Brian J. Showers brought out three issues in 2017. In those issues there was an article about the insect literature of Lafcadio Hearn, a fragment of an unpublished book by Irish mystic and poet, A. E., the introduction by Elizabeth Bowen to *The Second Ghost Book*, published in 1952, an article exploring the influences of Ireland on Caitlín R. Kiernan's writing, plus other articles and reviews of books, magazines, and theater. Issue #10 concentrated on Lord Dunsany's place among his Irish peers, featuring reviews of Dunsany's work written by his contemporaries A. E., Elizabeth Bowen, Forrest Reid, and Austin Clarke; introductions by W. B. Yeats and Padraic Colum; and reminiscences of the author by Katharine Tynan, Oliver St. John Gogarty, and Seán Ó Faoláin.

Black Static edited by Andy Cox is still the best, most consistent venue for horror fiction. In addition to essays, book and movie reviews, and interviews there was notable fiction by Eric Schaller, Bonnie Jo Stufflebeam, Danny Rhodes, Ian Steadman, Scott Nicolay, Charles Wilkinson, Tim Lees, Ray Cluley, Kristi DeMeester, Tim Casson, YZ Chin, Ruth J. Booth, Sarah Read, Ralph Robert Moore, Mark Morris, Carole Johnstone, Mel Kassel, Carly Holmes, and Mike O'Driscoll. The Read and the Morris are reprinted herein.

Nightmare edited by John Joseph Adams is a monthly webzine of horror. It publishes articles, interviews, book reviews, and an artists' showcase, along with two reprints and two original pieces of fiction per month. During

2017 there were notable stories by Andrew Fox, Jenn Grunigen, Kathleen Kayembe, Eric Schaller, Nate Southard, Cadwell Turnbull, Caspian Gray, Silvia Moreno-Garcia, Caroline Ratajski, and Carrie Vaughn.

Supernatural Tales edited by David Longhorn is a regularly published repository of excellent supernatural fiction, in addition to book and movie reviews. In the two issues from 2017 there were notable stories by Tom Johnstone, Jane Jakeman, Gary Fry, Helen Grant, and Charles Wilkinson.

Tales from the Shadow Booth Volume 1 edited by Dan Coxon is the debut issue of a new journal (that looks like an anthology) of mostly new dark fantasy and horror fiction. The magazine looks promising, with strong stories by Sarah Read and Stephen Hargadon.

Mixed-genre Magazines

Mythic Delirium edited by Mike Allen, is a quarterly magazine of fantasy fiction and poetry. In 2017 there was notable dark work by Maura McHugh, Jennifer Crow, and Jane Yolen. *Weirdbook* edited by Douglas Draa brought out three issues in 2017. The long-running magazine publishes both prose and poetry. The strongest work in 2017 was by James F. Mabe, Christian Riley, Charles Wilkinson, Chad Hensley, Gillian French, Chris Kuriata, Clay F. Johnson, Patrick Tumblety, Tom English, and C. R. Langille. *Not One of Us* edited by John Benson is one of the longest-running small press magazines. It's published twice a year and contains weird and dark fiction and poetry. Issue #50 was especially good. In addition, Benson puts out an annual "one-off" on a specific theme. The theme for 2017 was "Care." There were notable stories and poems throughout the year by Sonya Taaffe, Billie Hinton, Tim Major, Michael Piel, Rose Keating, K. S. Hardy, and Gillian Daniels. The Major is reprinted herein. *Shimmer* published by Beth Wodzinski, edited by several people, comes out every other month and usually contains a good mix of fantasy and dark fantasy, with the occasional science fiction story. During 2017 there was notable dark work by Malon Edwards, Martin Cahill, Heather Morris, Lina Rather, Sonya Taaffe, Maria Haskins, and Ashley Blooms. *The Dark*, edited by Silvia Moreno-Garcia and Sean Wallace, is a monthly webzine dedicated to dark fantasy and horror. It publishes new stories and reprints. During 2017, there were notable new stories by Kristi DeMeester, Suyi Davies Okungbowa, Carlie St. George, Ian Muneshwar, Octavia Cade, and Kelly Stewart. *The Magazine of Fantasy and Science Fiction* edited by C. C. Finlay is one of the longest running sf/f/h magazines in existence. Although it mostly published science fiction and fantasy, there's usually a few healthy dollops of horror during the year. During 2017 the strongest horror stories were by Cat Hellisen, Marc Laidlaw, David Erik Nelson, Rachel Pollack, Robert Reed, James Sallis, Shannon Connor Winward, Rebecca Campbell, G. V. Anderson, Leah Cypess, Nina Kiriki Hoffman, Lisa Mason, R. S. Benedict, Amy Griswold, and Justin C. Key. The Nelson is reprinted herein. *The Stinging Fly* is a biannual magazine of Irish writing, mostly mainstream, but issue #35 guest edited by Mia Gallagher was subtitled "Fear and Fantasy" and included notable dark fiction and poetry by Lucy Sweeney Byrne, Gerard Hanberry, Roisín O'Donnell, Natasha Calder, Dawn Watson, and Oliver Arnoldi. *Gamut* is a new monthly online magazine edited by Richard Thomas, focusing on crime and dark fiction. It publishes new and reprinted stories and poems. The strongest new work in 2017 was by Mel Kassel, Holly Goddard Jones, Stephen Graham Jones, Chloe N. Clark, Andrew McSorley, Mercedes M. Yardley, Kate Jonez, Damien Angelica Walters, Maria Haskins, Lina Rather, Judy Jordan, S. L. Coney, Eric Reitan, E. Catherine Tobler, Letitia Trent, and Cassandra Khaw. *Dark Discoveries* edited by Aaron French only brought out one issue in 2017, with a good, new story by Paul Tremblay, book and movie reviews, and interviews with Kelly Wilde, Peter Levenda, Paul Tremblay, and Ellen Datlow. *Apex* magazine edited by Jason Sizemore is an online magazine that publishes a variety of genre fiction. There were notable dark stories published in 2017 by John Hornor Jacobs, Lyndsie Manusos, Annie Neugebauer, Rich Larson, and Ursula Vernon. *Lamplight: A Quarterly Magazine of Dark Fiction* edited by Jacob Haddon brought out three issues in 2017. It published originals and reprints. The strongest stories were by Nate Southard, Andrew Reichard, Noelle Henneman, and Morgan Crooks. Tor.com publishes new sf, fantasy, and horror weekly, and the acquisitions and editing is done by several in-house editors and several consultants (I'm one of the latter). In 2017 there were notable horror and dark fantasy stories by Lucy Taylor, Cassandra Khaw, Kelly Robson, Max Gladstone, Sunny Moraine, and A. C. Wise. The Robson is reprinted herein. *Uncanny* edited by Lynne M. Thomas and Michael Damian Thomas publishes both nonfiction and fiction. The fiction veers toward the weird, and sometimes is quite dark. In 2017 there were notable stories by Maurice Broaddus, T. Kingfisher, Mary Robinette Kowal, S. Qiouyi Lu, and Catherynne M. Valente.

Anthologies

Horror Library Volume 6 edited by Eric J. Guignard (Cutting Block Press) is an excellent, un-themed anthology of twenty-seven stories. More than half the stories are notable, particularly those by Marc E. Fitch, Thomas P. Balázs, and Carole Johnstone. The Fitch and the Johnstone are reprinted herein.

Halloween Carnival Volume 1–5 edited by Brian James Freeman was published by Cemetery Dance's new e-book imprint Hydra. It's a series of mini-anthologies to be published for Halloween, with new stories and reprints. There are notable new stories by John R. Little, Lee Thomas, Kealan-Patrick Burke, Lisa Tuttle, and Norman Prentiss.

Dark Screams Volume Seven edited by Brian James Freeman and Richard Chizmar (CD-Hydra) contains six stories, four of them new. The best originals are by Kaaron Warren, Bill Schweigart, James Renner, and a novella by Brian Hodge. The Hodge and the Warren are reprinted herein. *Dark Screams Volume Eight* had six stories, all new but one. The best was Glen Hirshberg's oddity "India Blue" about cricket.

Nights of the Living Dead edited by Jonathan Maberry and George A. Romero (St. Martin's Griffin) is an anthology of twenty new stories taking place on the night that the infamous zombie apocalypse began. Unfortunately, only a few entries bring much new to the table, but there are some notable stories by Mira Grant, Brian Keene, Joe R. Lansdale, Mike Carey, and David Wellington. The Grant is reprinted herein.

In the Footsteps of Dracula edited by Stephen Jones (Pegasus Books) is an all-reprint anthology of stories featuring Count Dracula throughout history.

Terror Tales of Cornwall edited by Paul Finch (Telos) is the first new volume in the series since 2015. Telos has taken over publication from Gary Fry's Gray Friar Press, which shut down in 2016. This new volume continues with the same editor and same format, with brief historical vignettes breaking up each story. All but two are new. There are notable stories by Ray Cluley,

Mark Morris, Reggie Oliver, John Whitbourn, DP Watt, Mark Samuels, Sarah Singleton, and Steve Jordan.

Darker Companions: Celebrating 50 Years of Ramsey Campbell selected and edited by Scott David Aniolowski and Joseph S. Pulver, Sr. (PS Publishing), features twenty new stories honoring the great Ramsey Campbell. The strongest stories are by Cody Goodfellow, Kaaron Warren, Orrin Grey, Adam L. G. Nevill, Jeffrey Thomas, Alison Littlewood, Gary McMahon, Michael Griffin, Marc Laidlaw, and Christopher Slatsky. The Grey is reprinted herein.

Shadows and Tall Trees Volume 7 edited by Michael Kelly (Undertow) epitomizes the idea of, and is the most consistent venue for weird, usually dark fiction. This volume features nineteen varied stories, covering a wide range of themes. Well worth your time. There were notable stories by Brian Evenson, Harmony Neal, Michael Wehunt, V. H. Leslie, Laura Mauro, Charles Wilkinson, Robert Levy, Simon Strantzas, Malcolm Devlin, Robert Shearman, M. Rickert, Conrad Williams, and Manish Melwani.

Hellfire Crossroads 6: Horror with Heart edited by Trevor Denyer (Midnight Street Press) has twenty-two stories, most of them horror, some dark fantasy, and a few mainstream. There were notable stories by Len Dawson, David Penn, Alex Zivko-Clark, Steve D. Hamilton, Andrew Darlington, Neal Privitt, and Tony Fosgate.

The Dark Half of the Year: By the North Bristol Writers edited by Ian Milstead and Peter Sutton (Far Horizons) focuses on the ghostly in these eighteen stories by regional writers. The best are by Madeleine Meyjes and Clare Dornan.

New Fears edited by Mark Morris (Titan Books) is an excellent all-original un-themed anthology with nineteen stories. Most of the stories are really, really good. The Gallagher is reprinted herein.

Black Feathers: Dark Avian Tales edited by Ellen Datlow (Pegasus Books) is an anthology of fifteen dark stories and one poem about various kinds of birds, all but two published for the first time.

Haunted Nights edited by Ellen Datlow and Lisa Morton (A Blumhouse Book/ Anchor Books Original) is the most recent Horror Writers Association anthology and features sixteen new stories about horror's favorite holiday, Halloween, and others' cultures celebrations held around the same time. John Langan's novella is reprinted herein.

Wicked Haunted: An Anthology by the New England Horror Writers edited by Scott T. Goudsward, Daniel G. Keohane, and David Price (NEHW Press) is an all-original anthology of twenty-four stories and poems about hauntings, with interior art by Ogmios, Judi Calhoun, and Kali Moulton. There are notable stories by James A. Moore, Trisha J. Wooldridge, and KH Vaughn.

Witches: Weirdbook Annual #1 edited by Douglas Draa (Wildside) is the first in a project annual series. It has twenty-one stories and twelve poems. The best was by Matt Neil Hill.

California Screaming edited by Danielle Kaheaku (Barking Deer Press) has fourteen new stories that take place in California. The strongest are by Sarah Read, E. S. Magill, and Aaron C. Smith.

A Breath from the Sky: Unusual Stories of Possession edited by Scott R. Jones (Martian Migraine Press) is an anthology of twenty-one stories, five reprints. There were notable stories by Jonathan Raab, Megan Arkenberg, Gordon B. White, Cody Goodfellow, Premee Mohamed, and Aaron Vlek.

The Beauty of Death II: Death by Water edited by Alessandro Manzetti and Jodi Renee Lester (Independent Legions Publishing) is a big anthology of thirty-nine stories. Eleven are reprints. There are notable original stories by John Langan, Nicola Lombardi, Lisa Morton, Michael Arnzen, Michael Bailey, Simon Bestwick, Daniele Bonfanti, Daniel Braum, Marge Simon, and Lucy A. Snyder.

A Suggestion of Ghosts: Supernatural Fiction by Women 1854–1900 edited by J. A. Mains (Black Shuck Books) features fifteen ghost stories never reprinted after their initial publication. Cover art by Les Edwards. Interiors by Mike Mignola.

Great British Horror 2: Dark Satanic Mills edited by Steve J. Shaw (Black Shuck Books) is a solid annual anthology showcasing modern British horror (with one international author). This volume of eleven stories and novelettes has notable work by Charlotte Bond, Carole Johnstone, Andrew Freudenberg, Cate Gardner, Marie O'Regan, and Angela Slatter.

Unspeakable Horror 2: Abominations of Desire edited by Vince A. Liaguno (Evil Jester Press) features twenty LGBT horror stories, all but three new. There are notable new stories by Gemma Files, Stephen Graham Jones, and Marshall Moore.

Imposter Syndrome edited by James Everington and Dan Howarth (Dark Minds Press) is an all-original anthology of ten stories about doppelgängers, changelings, and other types of duplicates—real or not. There are notable stories by Georgina Bruce, Ralph Robert Moore, and Timothy J. Jarvis.

Now I Lay Me Down to Sleep edited by P. D. Cacek and Laura J. Hickman (Necon Books) is a charity anthology with all proceeds going to the Jimmy Fund/Dana-Farber Cancer Institute. The book is in tribute to the late Bob Booth, known as Papa Necon. Included are thirty-four short stories, poems, and a comic. Nine are reprints. The best of the originals are by Doungjai Gam, Tony Tremblay, and Marianne Halbert.

Tales from Miskatonic University Library edited by Darrell Schweitzer and John Ashmead (PS Publishing) has terrific cover art and end papers by J. K. Potter. Most of the thirteen stories are a bit too close to mythos pastiche for my taste, but there are two notable contributions by P. D. Cacek and A. C. Wise.

Black Wings VI: New Tales of Lovecraftian Horror edited by S. T. Joshi (PS Publishing) features twenty-two stories and poems (all but one new). The best are by Ann K. Schwader, Donald Tyson, Steve Rasnic Tem, Jonathan Thomas, and David Hambling.

Shadows Over Main Street, Volume 2 edited by Doug Murano and D. Alexander Ward (Cutting Block Books) is an enjoyable volume of seventeen stories (all but two new) combining Lovecraftian horrors with small-town living. There were notable new stories by Max Booth III, Suzanne Madron, James Chambers, Michael Wehunt, and Lucy A. Snyder.

The Children of Gla'aki: A Tribute to Ramsey Campbell's Great Old One edited by Brian M. Sammons and Glynn Owen Barrass (Dark Regions Press) has contributors writing in response to a Lovecraftian story written by Campbell in 1964. That story is reprinted in the volume, along with seventeen new tales. Most are too narrowly focused on the one creature, but there are notable entries by John Langan, Pete Rawlik, and Tim Curran.

Looming Low Volume 1 edited by Justin Steele and Sam Cowan (Dim Shores) is a good anthology of twenty-six weird, mostly dark stories. There are notable stories by Gemma Files, S. K. Miskowski, A. C. Wise, Brian Evenson, Michael Wehunt, Daniel Mills, Livia Llewellyn, Kaaron Warren, Lisa L. Hannett, Kristi DeMeester, Jeffrey Thomas, Richard Gavin, and Nadia Bulkin. The Miskowski and the Wise are reprinted herein.

Tales from a Talking Board edited by Ross E. Lockhart (Word Horde) contains fourteen new stories about Ouija boards, tarot cards, and other mechanisms of divination. There are notable stories by Nadia Bulkin, Scott R. Jones, Wendy N. Wagner, Matthew M. Bartlett, J. M. McDermott, S. P. Miskowski, and Kristi DeMeester.

Another anthology inspired by Ouija boards is *Intersections: Six Tales of Ouija Horror*—no editor listed (Howling Unicorn Press), with stories by six crime and horror writers.

Dark Places, Evil Faces compiled by Mark Lumby (PS Publishing) benefits a British cancer facility—it has twenty-five stories, reprints and originals.

Sycorax's Daughters edited by Kinitra D. Brooks, Linda D. Addison, and Susana M. Morris (Cedar Grove Publishing) has forty-two gothic and horror stories and poems by African American women. Most are new. The strongest are by Eden Royce, Vocab, Tanesha Nicole Tyler, Zin E. Rocklyn, Nicole D. Sconiers, Tracey Baptiste, and Regina N. Bradley.

The Mammoth Book of the Mummy edited by Paula Guran (Robinson) has nineteen stories about mummies, three new. The best of the new ones is by Stephen Graham Jones.

Several best of the years covering horror were published: *Year's Best Body Horror* edited by C.P. Dunphey (Gehenna and Hinnom) includes more than forty very short stories, several reprints from between 2002–2016, and the rest new stories published for the first time. It's intended to be an annual. *Year's Best Hardcore Horror Volume 2* edited by Randy Chandler and Cheryl Mullenax (Comet Press) promises to have the best extreme horror fiction of 2016 that breaks boundaries and trashes taboos, with lots of blood and gore. *The Year's Best Weird Fiction Volume Four* edited by Helen Marshall and Michael Kelly (Undertow Press) contains fifteen stories from a variety of venues including *Granta Online*, *Nightmare*, Tor.com, *Interzone*, and other magazines webzines, anthologies, and collections. *The Year's Best Dark Fantasy and Horror 2017* edited by Paula Guran (Prime Books) has thirty-seven stories from magazines, webzines, anthologies, and collections. Three choices overlap with my own best of the year.

Mixed-genre Anthologies

Through a Mythos Darkly edited by Glynn Owen Barrass and Brian M. Sammons (PS Publishing) describes itself as "steampunk" Mythos-inspired anthology, but it's not steampunk at all. So if you pick it up expecting the trappings of that era, you'll be disappointed. Nonetheless, of the seventeen new stories, there are some notable ones by John Langan, Damien Angelica Walters, Konstantine Paradias, Tim Waggoner, and Don Webb. *Ride the Star Wind* edited by Scott Gable and C. Dombrowski (Broken Eye Books) is filled with new stories combining space opera with cosmic weird, and I admit that it's not my cup of tea. Not much horror in it. The only stories that really got to me were by Brian Evenson and Deserina Boskovich. Each story is illustrated by a different artist, in black and white. *Blood Business: Crime Stories from This World and Beyond* edited by Mario Acevedo and Joshua Viola (Hex Publishers) is an anthology of twenty-seven crime stories: half supernatural, half not. The best are by Stephen Graham Jones, Patrick Berry, and Jason Heller. *Adam's Ladder* edited by Michael Bailey and Darren Speegle (Written Backwards) contains eighteen new stories of dark science fiction exploring the course of evolution. The strongest horror stories are by Laird Barron, John Langan, and Mark Samuels. *Mixed Up: Cocktail Recipes (and Flash Fiction) for the Discerning Drinker (and Reader)* edited by Nick Mamatas and Molly Tanzer (Skyhorse Publishing) contains more than two dozen recipes and stories by writers including Maurice Broaddus, Jeff VanderMeer, Ben Percy, Elizabeth Hand, Carmen Maria Machado, and many others. There are a few notable darker tales by Hand, Machado, and Percy. The Machado is reprinted herein. *Nightscript III* edited by C. M. Muller (Chthonic Matter) is an interesting, varied volume of twenty-three new stories. There are notable tales by M. R. Cosby, Charles Wilkinson, Rebecca J. Allred, Adam Golaski, David Surface, Stephen J. Clarke, Clint Smith, Inna Effress, M. K. Anderson, Christi Nogle, and Daniel Braum. The Effress is reprinted herein. *Boundaries and Other Horror Stories from Finland* edited by Matti Järvinen and translated by Jukka Särkijävi (Nysalor-Kustannus) features ten stories published in English for the first time. They're more dark fantasy than horror. *Darkly Haunting* edited by Robert Morgan (Sarob Press) is a mini-anthology of five, all-new, intriguingly weird tales by Rhys Hughes, Peter Holman, James Doig, Colin Insole, and D. P. Watt. *Eight Ghosts: The English Heritage Book of New Ghost Stories* edited by Rowan Routh (September Publishing) features new stories (some dark) by eight British writers who were given time to explore, after hours, their chosen heritage site and write a ghost story about it. The best of them are by Sarah Perry, Mark Haddon, Andrew Michael Hurley, and Kamila Shamsie. In addition to the stories is a brief overview of how the castles, abbeys, and houses of England inspired ghost stories, plus a gazetteer of English Heritage hauntings. *The Scarlet Soul: Stories for Dorian Gray* edited by Mark Valentine (The Swan River Press) is an interesting anthology of ten new weird and dark stories inspired by Oscar Wilde's novel *The Picture of Dorian Gray.* There are notable horror stories by John Howard, Timothy J. Jarvis, and Lynda E. Rucker. *Mrs Rochester's Attic: Tales of Madness, Strange Love and Deep, Dark Secrets* edited by Matthew Pegg (Mantle Lane Press) feature twenty-two stories inspired by the fate of Mrs Rochester in *Jane Eyre.* All but seven are new. The stories never really gel around the theme, but there are notable ones by Josh Jones, Grace Haddon, and Douglas Ford. *Pacific Monsters* edited by Margrét Helgadóttir (Fox Spirit) is the fourth volume in the publisher's series of monster stories from around the world and features fourteen stories and comics taking place in Antarctica, Hawaii, New Zealand, Guam, and Australia. The strongest were by Michael Grey, Rue Karney, and Bryan Kamaoli Kuwada. *Behold! Oddities, Curiosities & Indefinable Wonders* edited by Doug Murano (Crystal Lake Publishing) has sixteen stories, two reprints. The best of the darker ones are by John Langan, Lisa Morton, and Patrick Freivald. *Murder Ballads* edited by Mark Beech (Egaeus Press) is a rich anthology of seventeen weird and/or horrific dense stories and novellas inspired by classic ballads. The best of the dark ones are by Stephen J. Clark, Philip Fracassi, Lisa L. Hannett, Timothy J. Jarvis, Angela Slatter, and Colin Insole. *Mad Hatters and March Hares* edited by Ellen Datlow (Tor) is an all-original anthology of eighteen stories and poem inspired by Lewis Carroll's *Alice in Wonderland.* The stories are mostly fantasy and dark fantasy, with some horror. The darkest stories are by Stephen Graham Jones, Matthew Kressel, Katherine Vaz, and Angela Slatter. *Strange California* edited by Jaym Gates and J. Daniel Batt (Falstaff) is a mixed bag of twenty-six science fiction, fantasy, dark fantasy, and horror stories about the Golden State. There was notable horror by Patricia Lundy and Melissa Monks. *From Ancient Ravens* by Mark Valentine, Ron Weighell, and John Howard (Sarob Press) is a mini-anthology with each of the three weird, dark tales dredging up the past to bad end. *Hellboy: An Assortment of Horrors* edited by Christopher Golden (Dark Horse) features sixteen new stories related to Hellboy and his friends. The balance of the anthology seems weighted toward dark fantasy rather than horror. Each story has an illustration by Mike Mignola. If you're a *Hellboy* fan and not expecting horror stories, you're the audience for this fun anthology.

Collections

It, Watching by Elizabeth Massie (Dark House Press) is an overview of Massie's work over thirty-three years. This seventh collection contains seventeen stories and a poem. Three of the stories are new.

And Her Smile Will Untether the Universe by Gwendolyn Kiste (JournalStone) is a debut collection of fourteen stories, five previously unpublished, by a promising new writer.

Nights of Blood Wine by Freda Warrington (Telos) is a collection of fifteen stories, ten of them set in the world of her vampire series *Blood Wine*. Another five are fantasy and horror. Four stories are new.

She Said Destroy by Nadia Bulkin (Word Horde) is a smart, powerful debut collection with thirteen stories of horror and weird fiction, one of them new. Three of them were nominated for the Shirley Jackson Award.

Ornithology by Nicholas Royle (Cōnfingō Publishing) is a fine new collection of sixteen dark, sometimes uncanny stories about birds, two published for the first time.

Cthulhu and Other Monsters by Sam Stone (Telos), the author's second collection, features sixteen horror stories, six published for the first time.

Made for the Dark by John Llewellyn Probert (Black Shuck Books) is the author's sixth collection of stories and brings together stories eighteen pieces published since 2010. Three stories appear for the first time.

Behold the Void by Philip Fracassi (JournalStone) is a strong debut collection with nine horror stories, five previously unpublished. Laird Barron provides the introduction. One of the originals is reprinted herein.

13 Views of the Suicide Woods by Bracken Macleod (ChiZine Publications) is another strong debut collection, with twelve stories, three new.

I Will Surround You by Conrad Williams (Undertow Publications) is the author's powerful third collection and features fourteen dark stories, two of them new.

Seven Strange Stories by Rebecca Lloyd (Tartarus Press) is the author's excellent fourth collection of eerie dark stories and novellas. Two are reprints. The original "Where's the Harm" is reprinted herein.

The Carp-Faced Boy and Other Tales by Thersa Matsuura (Independent Legions Publishing) is a strong second collection, with ten horror stories, several of them inhabited by creatures from Japanese folklore. All but two of the stories are new. With an introduction by Gene O'Neill.

The Night Shop: Tales for the Lonely Hours by Terry Dowling (Cemetery Dance) is the Australian, multi-award-winning author's fourth horror collection (his non-horror fiction has also been collected) and it's a terrific sampling, with eighteen disturbing stories, three of them new. Dowling's at the top of his game.

The Fiddle is the Devil's Instrument and Other Forbidden Knowledge by Brett J. Talley (JournalStone) collects thirteen Lovecraftian tales, five new.

The Prozess Manifestations by Mark Samuels (Zagava) is the author's sixth collection. It's a slim volume of six, somewhat related stories, some horror, at least one Kafkaesque.

Strange is the Night by S. P. Miskowski (Trepidatio Publishing) is better known for her award-nominated novellas, but her short stories have been published in a variety of magazines and anthologies in the past few years. This is the first time they've been collected, with thirteen stories, three of them new.

The Dreamer in Fire and Other Stories by Sam Gafford (Hippocampus Press) is another debut. It contains seventeen stories (six new) heavily influenced by H. P. Lovecraft.

Perfect Little Stitches and Other Stories by Deborah Sheldon (IFWG Publishing) has twenty-one dark fantasy and horror stories, ten of them new.

Inferno: Tales of Hell and Horror by Angeline Hawkes (Elder Signs Press) is a series of linked stories about twenty-five sinners, their sins, and their punishments. Introduction by Robert Weinberg.

Infernal Parade by Clive Barker (Subterranean Press) is a beautifully produced little hardcover of six interrelated stories comprising a novella originally published in 2004. The jacket art and interior illustrations are all by Bob Eggleton. A gorgeous collectible for Barker fans and readers.

Goblin by Josh Malerman (Earthling) is the press's annual Halloween offering. The six novellas make up a novel, set in the town of Goblin.

Exploring Dark Short Fiction #1: A Primer to Steve Rasnic Tem edited by Eric J. Guignard (Dark Moon Books) celebrates the four-decade-long career of an underappreciated master of horror and the weird. This introduction to Tem's work includes six stories, one especially creepy new one, an interview, bibliography, and commentary throughout by Michael Arnzen. With illustrations throughout by Michelle Prebich.

Disexistence by Paul Kane (Cycatrix Press) has twenty-one stories, five of them new. With an introduction by Nancy Holder and story notes by the author.

Hasty for the Dark by Adam LG Nevill (Ritual Limited) is a self-published collection of ten stories (two new). Included are excellent story notes. Two of the stories were reprinted in previous volumes of my Best Horror of the Year series.

Mixed-genre Collections

Fire. Plus by Elizabeth Hand (PM Press) is number eighteen in the publisher's "Outspoken Authors" series. The mini-collection features three stories (one new), one autobiographical piece from 2004, several nonfiction essays and reviews, and a new interview of Hand by Terry Bisson. Hand is one of several contemporary writers who slides effortlessly between genres, most recently writing a dark, occasionally supernatural-tinged crime series. The new story "Fire" is short, intense, mainstream, yet dark. *Singularity* by Melanie Tem (Centipede Press) collects sixty of the late, award-winning writer Melanie Tem's most important short fiction, highlighting her diversity and mastery of her art. With illustrations by Jessica Fortner and an afterword by Caitlín Kiernan. *Strange Weather* by Joe Hill (William Morrow) features four impressive novellas, three new. "Snapshot" was originally published in two issues of *Cemetery Dance*; "Aloft" is a fantasy about a grieving young man who when jumping out of a plane to skydive, magically lands on a sentient cloud that would like him to stay to keep it company; "Loaded" is a terrifyingly believable story of easy access to guns, revenge, and psychosis; "Rain" is about a mysterious and deadly rain that begins its fall in Colorado. *The Unorthodox Dr. Draper and Other Stories* by William Browning Spencer (Subterranean Press) collects ten years' worth of Spencer's most recent stories, which includes nine stories and one poem. His work is surreal, funny, horrific, and very well written. *Tales of Falling and Flying* by Ben Loory (Penguin Books) is this quirky writer's second collection of forty very brief tales and vignettes. Strange, sometimes unsettling, sometimes funny, but always entertaining. *Wind Through the Fence: And Other Stories* by Jonathan Maberry (JournalStone) collects twelve stories by the bestselling author of the Joe Ledger series of thrillers. The selection demonstrates Maberry's versatility in the fields of sf, dark fantasy, crime, and horror. One story is new. *Written in Darkness* by Mark Samuels (Chômu Press) adds four reprints to an earlier collection with the same title originally published by Egaeus Press in 2014. *You Should Come With Me Now: Stories of Ghosts* by M. John Harrison (Comma Press) is the author's first collection of short fiction in fifteen years and contains forty-two stories and flash fiction pieces of surrealism, fantasy, and a wee bit of horror. A few appear for the first time. *The Wish Mechanics* by Daniel Braum (Independent Legions Publishing) includes twelve stories of science fiction, dark fantasy, and horror. Five are published for the first time. *Her Body and Other Parties* by Carmen Maria Machado (Greywolf Press) is the celebrated author's debut collection, and has made quite a splash in the literary world, having been nominated for the National Book Award. Although usually more weird than dark, several of her stories over the years have been horror, including "The Husband Stitch," reprinted in this collection. *You Will Grow Into Them* by Malcolm Devlin (Unsung Stories) is a strong debut collection of ten stories by a new writer of dark fantasy, weird fiction, and horror. Four of the stories are published for the first time. *Speaking to Skull Kings* by Emily B. Cataneo (Trepidatio Publishing) is another debut by a new writer. The collection contains twelve stories of fantasy and dark fantasy, two of them new. *Behind You* by Ralph Robert Moore (self-published) is the author's fourth collection. Among the eighteen mixed-genre stories are four new ones. Most of the stories are mainstream, a few are dark. Next are two mainstream collections that skirt the dark but don't actually delve very deeply into it: *The Doll's Alphabet* by Camilla Grudova (Coffee House Press) is the author's first collection of thirteen very short stories. Most are surreal and bizarre, with hints of fairy tales and an edge of darkness. *The Dark Dark* by Samantha Hunt (Farrar, Straus, Giroux) is also a debut, this with ten stories, mostly new. Weird doings, some dark. *The Dream Operator* by Mike O'Driscoll (Undertow Publications) is the author's second collection of stories. In it are eleven science fiction, dark fantasy, and horror stories. Three are published for the first time. *Holidays From Hell* by Reggie Oliver (Tartarus Press) features fourteen stories, one new in this seventh collection. With a gracious introduction by Robert Shearman. *The Echo of the Sea & Other Strange War Stories* by Paul StJohn Mackintosh (Egaeus Press Keynote Edition III) is a lovely little hardcover book containing four WWII stories (one reprint) that deal with Nazi attempts to harness supernatural forces to their cause. None is horror. *Anthony Shriek* by Jessica Amanda Salmonson (Centipede Press) is a gorgeous new edition of this 1992 novel, originally published in the Dell Abyss line. It's illustrated by David Ho and has an introduction by Eileen Gunn. In addition to the novel, the volume features a number of reprinted stories and poems published between 1975 and 1997, plus two new prose pieces and seven new poems. *Haunted Worlds* by Jeffrey Thomas (Hippocampus Press) is another varied and imaginative collection of reprints and five new stories by the creator of the world of Punktown. Thomas often mixes sf and horror and weird fiction to good effect. With an introduction by Ian Rogers and story notes by the author. Thomas had a second collection out from Lovecraft eZine Press: *The Endless Fall and Other Weird Fiction*. This one collects fourteen stories, one new. *Naked Revenants and Other Fables of Old and New England* by Jonathan Thomas (Hippocampus Press) is the fifth collection of weird and often dark tales by the author. This volume has twenty-one stories and poems, nine new. *The Lay of Old Hex: Spectral Ballads and Weird Jack Tales* by Adam Bolivar (Hippocampus Press) is a collection of thirty-three reprinted and new tales, ballads, and vignettes about a man with a silver key that takes him on many a weird journey. Not much horror. With an introduction by K. A. Opperman. *Telling the Map* by Christopher Rowe (Small Bee Press) is the author's debut collection and contains ten stories, all but one reprints. Although most of his work is science fiction or weird fantasy, there's the occasional strain of darkness running through it (three of the stories were originally published by me). *Call for Submissions* by Selena Chambers (Pelekinesis) features fifteen stories reprinted from a variety of anthologies and small press magazines. One was nominated for a 2016 World Fantasy Award. *Dis Mem Ber and Other Stories of Mystery and Suspense* by Joyce Carol Oates (The Mysterious Press) presents seven dark suspense stories originally published in magazines and anthologies, including one from my avian horror anthology, *Black Feathers*. William Meikle had two collections out in 2017: *Carnacki: The Edinburgh Townhouse & Other Stories* (Lovecraft EZine Press) is an entertaining collection of ten new tales about William Hope Hodgson's creation Carnacki, the ghost-finder, and his friends, often plagued by the supernatural. In *The Ghost Club: Newly Found Tales of Victorian Terror* (Crystal Lake Publishing) we have another entertaining collection of fourteen inventive new stories written in the styles of Bram Stoker, Jules Verne, Madam Blavatsky, Rudyard Kipling, and ten other illustrious writers of the period. *The Big-Headed People and Other Stories* by D. F. Lewis (Eibonvale Chapbook Line #2) consists of an expanded version of the title story plus four shorter stories. *Old Hoggen and Other Adventures* by Bram Stoker (The Swan River Press) is a lovely little hardcover book that collects nine stories by the author of *Dracula*, with a preface by Brian J. Showers and an introduction by John Edgar Browning and Brian J. Showers. *My House Gathers Desires* by Adam McOmber (BOA Editions) is an excellent literary mix of horror and fantasy of fifteen stories, all previously published in various small literary magazines. *Black Pantheons: Collected Tales of Gnostic Dread* by Curtis M. Lawson (Wyrd Horror) is a debut of mostly dark fantasy with eleven stories, all but three new. *A Flutter of Wings* by Mervyn Wall (The Swan River Press) has eleven pieces of fiction from throughout Wall's writing career and includes both satire and darker material. *Tales from Harborsmouth* by E. J. Stevens (Sacred Oaks Press) contains four stories and novellas about a supernatural detective. *Dear Sweet Filthy World* by Caitlín R. Kiernan (Subterranean Press) is the author's fourteenth collection of short stories and vignettes. All twenty-eight were originally published in her subscription-only *Sirenia Digest*. One was reprinted in an earlier volume of the Best Horror of the Year series. *Up the Rainbow: The Complete Short Fiction of Susan Casper* edited by Gardner Dozois (Fantastic Books) is a lovely memorial to the late author of speculative fiction and horror and includes twenty-four stories written solo and in collaboration (one original). The volume also features seven of Casper's fascinating trip reports and an afterword by Andy Duncan. *Writing Madness* by Patrick McGrath (Centipede Press) is a big deluxe hardcover collection of this expert in the macabre's short stories, introductions, essays, and reviews. *Blood and Water*, McGrath's first collection (and the work that first piqued my own interest in his short stories), is reprinted in its entirety, as is McGrath's most recent, three-story collection, *Ghost Town*. Joyce Carol Oates introduces the book. Danel Olson edited it and wrote the afterword. Jacket and interior illustrations are by Harry Brockway.

CHAPBOOKS/NOVELLAS

Agents of Dreamland by Caitlín R. Kiernan (Tor.com Books) is a wonderful, darkly disturbing cosmic horror story about a cult that believes aliens have come to liberate their bodies, a secret agent tasked with tracking down their missing leader, and a terrifying mystery woman who travels back and forth in time. *Mapping the Interior* by Stephen Graham Jones (Tor.com Books) is a vivid, dread-inducing supernatural ghost story about a teenage boy who believes he sees his dead father haunting the house where he lives with his mother and younger brother. Over time, the supernatural begins to subsume the everyday world of Junior and his family. *Paymon's Trio* by Colette de Curzon (Nightjar Press) was written in 1949 and this is its first publication. Even back then, its plot—about the discovery of a demonic piece of music and its effect on those who play it—would have been old hat. Despite this, it's well-told. Other Nightjar Press titles (the press is run by writer Nicholas Royle) published in 2017 were *The Automaton* by David Wheldon, a weird story about a young boy in pre-WWI England whose family theater hires an impresario with a chess-playing, elegant automaton; two stories by Claire Dean: *Bremen*, an uncanny tale of identity, loss, and marzipan people and *The Unwish* about fairy tales, two sisters, and their uneasy relationship. *Gwendy's Button Box* by Stephen King and Richard Chizmar (Cemetery Dance) is a Castle Rock tale about a twelve-year-old girl who is given a box full of buttons and levers to care for by a mysterious man. *I'll Bring You the Birds From Out of the Sky* is a terrific novella by Brian Hodge (Cemetery Dance), whose short fiction keeps getting better and better (and longer). This one is about a young woman with roots in rural West Virginia who brings a piece of art by her great grandfather to the city to be appraised by a dealer of folk art. Hodge is great at building a sense of dread in his stories. *The Twilight Pariah* by Jeffrey Ford (Tor.com Books) is about a group of friends who meet up during a break from college and what they discover when they excavate an abandoned outhouse on the edge of town. *The Murders of Molly Southbourne* by Tade Thompson (Tor.com Books) is about a woman whose blood creates new versions of herself that are bent on the original's destruction. *How I Learned the Truth About Krampus* by Tom Johnstone (Eibonvale Press) is a chiller about a man's belief that his missing baby son has been taken by his real father, the ancient evil precursor to the contemporary jolly Santa Claus. *The Book Club* by Alan Baxter (PS Publishing) is about a man whose wife disappears after attending one of her book club meetings. Under suspicion by the police and devastated by the idea that she's been abducted and murdered, he discovers even worse possibilities. *In the Country of Dreaming Caravans* by Gerard Houarner (Bedlam Press) is a beautifully told story of a little girl, sold by her parents to a desert caravan, who tells stories in order to save her own life. *The Teardrop Method* by Simon Avery (TTA Press) is about a woman who, after someone close to her dies, discovers she can hear music in those who are dying. *Sacculina* by Philip Fracassi (JournalStone) is about a fishing boat crew facing sea monsters. *Liars, Fakers, and the Dead Who Eat Them* by Scott Edelman (Written Backwards) is a good-looking chapbook consisting of two new zombie stories. With an introduction by Brian Keene. The Borderland Little book chapbook series continued with Joe Hill's *A Little Silver Book of Sharp Shiny Scissors* featuring a miscellany of nineteen snippets of fiction and nonfiction within a beautiful silver hardcover. David Morrell's *A Little Gold Book of Protector Tales* includes three stories about people willing to sacrifice their lives for strangers. Jonathan Maberry's *A Little Bronze Book of Cautionary Tales* presents four of his own favorite stories. *The Doll House* by Edward Lee (Necro Publications) was originally published 2015 as *A Little Magenta Book about a Dollhouse* by Borderlands Press. Quite unlike Lee's usual blood and guts work, this was written in homage to one of Lee's favorite writers: M. R. James. *Pretty Marys All in a Row* by Gwendolyn Kiste (Broken Eye Books) is a tale told by a ghost named Resurrection Mary about various other "Marys" from urban legends, all existing in one house. *Festival* by Aaron J. French (Unnerving) is about a young couple who stumble across a cult while on their romantic getaway at an isolated camp with hot springs. *The Process (is a Process All Its Own)* by Peter Straub (Subterranean Press) is an expanded version of the story originally published last year in *Conjunctions* (and reprinted in *The Best Horror of the Year Volume Nine*). The signed limited hardcover is a beauty, with its jacket illustration by Susan Straub and designed by Michael Fusco-Straub. *Small Ghosts* by Paul Lewis (Telos) is about a recent widower who returns to where he grew up to help his mother deal with her dying father. The dying man was a policeman who years earlier was the investigator in an undisclosed series of child murders that haunted both him and his wife throughout their lives.

POETRY JOURNALS, WEBZINES, ANTHOLOGIES, AND COLLECTIONS

When the Night Owl Screams by Michael H. Hanson (Moon Dream Press) contains over one hundred brief poems, with an introduction by Alessandro Manzetti. *Visions of the Mutant Rain Forest* by Robert Frazier and Bruce Boston (Crystal Lake Publishing) is a powerful collaborative collection of poetry and fiction, using the world the two authors created decades ago. There are five new poems and two new pieces of fiction. *Diary of a Sorceress* by Ashley Dioses (Hippocampus Press) is a volume of almost one hundred weird and dark poems, most previously published in small press poetry journals. *PseudoPsalms: Sodom* by Peter Adam Salomon (Bizarro Pulp Press) is the author's third collection of poetry and includes almost one hundred short poems. *Escape Claws* by Angela Yuriko Smith (self-published) is a combination of about thirty pieces of poetry and text about the author living in haunted houses when growing up. *A Collection of Nightmares* by Christina Sng (Raw Dog Screaming Press), with thirty-one poems, is the author's first full-length collection of dark poetry. *The 2017 Rhysling Anthology: The Best Science Fiction, Fantasy & Horror Poetry of 2016* selected by the Science Fiction Poetry Association edited by David Kopaska-Merkal (Science Fiction Poetry Association) is used by members to vote for the best short and long poem of the year. The volume includes ninety-eight short poems and fifty-four long poems originally published in eighty different publications and venues in 2016. *Horror Writers Association Poetry Showcase Volume IV* edited by David E. Cowan has been supporting its poet members by publishing a juried anthology of new poems for the last four years. The 2017 edition features more the fifty horror poems. There are some especially notable ones by Stephanie M. Wytovich, Robert Perez, Megan Hart, and a collaboration by Marge Simon and Alessandro Manzetti. *Fungi from Yuggoth* by H. P. Lovecraft (Hippocampus Press) is a good-looking hardcover edition of a thirty-six sonnet cycle Lovecraft wrote in a little over a week. This annotated edition is edited by David E. Schultz and illustrated by Jason C.

Eckhardt. *No Mercy* by Alessandro Manzetti (Crystal Lake Publishing) is an excellent collection of eighteen horror poems (all but one new). *Sheet Music to my Acoustic Nightmare* by Stephanie M. Wytovich (Raw Dog Screaming) is another excellent collection of more than one hundred poems, several about murder, all dark. *Selected Poems* by A. E. (The Swan River Press) has been published to commemorate the 150th anniversary of the Irish poet George William Russell's birth. It includes poems written and published throughout his career, essays by W. B. Yeats and other of his contemporaries, and a bibliography. *'Til Death: Marriage Poems* by Janice Leach and James Frederick Leach (Raw Dog Screaming Press) is a collaborative collection of more than seventy poems about the joys and horrors of a long marriage. *Love for Slaughter* by Sara Tantlinger (Strange House) has about one hundred horror poems lovingly laden with violence. Good show.

Nonfiction

This Spectacular Darkness by Joel Lane (Tartarus) came out in late December 2016 and I missed it. It's a collection of critical essays by the late British author, written for various dark fiction journals, and also includes appreciations of Lane's poetry, essays, and fiction by other writers. *Confrontation with Evil: An In-Depth Review of the 1949 Possession That Inspired The Exorcist* by Steven A. LaChance (Llewellyn) is by a true believer who claims he was a victim of demonic possession himself, and thus is less skeptical than most previous accounts. *Hail to the Chin: Further Confessions of a B Movie Actor* by Bruce Campbell with Craig Sanborn (Thomas Dunne) is the actor's "Act II"—his passage into middle age and all that entails for a human being and an entertainer. *Spanish Gothic: National Identity, Collaboration and Cultural Adaptation* by Xavier Aldana Reyes (Palgrave Gothic) is an introduction to the broad history of the Gothic in Spain. It focuses on key literary periods, from the Romanticism of the late-eighteenth century through the fin-de-siècle, spiritualist writings of the early-twentieth century, and the cinematic and literary booms of the 1970s and 2000s. Aldana Reyes elucidates how the Gothic mode has been a permanent yet ever-shifting fixture of the literary and cinematic landscape of Spain. *Giant Creatures in Our World: Essays on Kaiju and American Popular Culture* edited by D. G. Mustachio and Jason Barr (McFarland) is a collection of new essays about this subgenre of monster films. *Consuming Gothic: Food and Horror in Film* by Lorna Piatti-Farnell (Palgrave Macmillan) is an analysis of the relationship of food and horror in post-1980 film. (From the publisher's description.) By looking at food consumption within Gothic cinema, the book uncovers eating as a metaphorical activity of the self, where the haunting psychology of the everyday, the porous boundaries of the body, and the uncanny limits of consumer identity collide. It discusses such movies as David Cronenberg's *The Fly*, *The Machinist*, *Se7en*, and *The Human Centipede*, among others. *Paperbacks from Hell* by Grady Hendrix (Quirk) is an entertaining, profusely illustrated history of the very pulpy looking (for the most part) paperback cover art generated in the '70s and '80s. Many of the books and their authors are forgettable, but some are excellent and continue to be read and their authors continue to write. It didn't matter whether the content was literary or not, the covers were unremittingly lurid. The book includes some story summaries and overviews of various horror subgenres including satanic rituals, creepy and demonic children, haunted houses, animals attacking—you get the idea. *Why Horror Seduces* by Matthew Clasen (Oxford University Press) is an attempt to answer the question so many horror aficionados, writers, and editors are regularly asked. The book claims that horror entertainment works by targeting humans' adaptive tendency to find pleasure in make-believe, allowing a high-intensity experience within a safe context. The book is organized into three parts identifying fictional works by evolutionary mode—the evolution of horror, evolutionary interpretations of horror, and the future of horror. *H. P. Lovecraft Letters to C. L. Moore and Others* edited by David E. Schultz and S. T. Joshi (Hippocampus Press) is Volume 10 in the series. Much of the volume consists of Moore's letters to Lovecraft, as only fragments of his letters to her survive. Lovecraft apparently introduced her to Henry Kuttner, Moore's future husband and writing partner. There is also a fascinating correspondence between Lovecraft and Jonquil and Fritz Leiber. *Demons, Devils, and Fallen Angels* by Marie D. Jones and Larry Flaxman (Visible Ink) is a fun book to dip into, covering the beliefs of ancient cultures up to contemporary Satanism. Generously illustrated. *Dawnward Spire: The Letters of H. P. Lovecraft and Clark Ashton Smith* edited by David E. Schultz and S. T. Joshi (Hippocampus Press) is massive, more than seven hundred pages plus bibliography and index. The volume covers fifteen years of correspondence and 330 letters. *The Crow's Dinner* by Jonathan Carroll (Subterranean Press) is the admired and lauded fabulist's first collection of essays. The generous, five hundred plus page volume includes fragments, musings, and reflections on life. It's perfect for fans of Carroll or anyone who enjoys dipping into the mind of one of our most creative contemporary fantasists. *Cannibalism: A Perfectly Natural History* by Bill Schutt (Algonquin Books of Chapel Hill) is a fresh and remarkably entertaining look at the subject by a zoologist who surveys the latest scientific research on this long-held taboo. Illustrated by Patricia J. Wynne. *The Annotated Frankenstein* by Mary Shelley, edited with a foreword and notes by Leslie S. Klinger (Liveright Publishing), emphasizes the broad cultural significance that *Frankenstein* has achieved in the realms of science fiction, feminist theory, modern intellectual history, as well as film history and pop culture. The volume includes nearly one thousand notes with information and historical context on every aspect of *Frankenstein* and Shelley's life. Profusely illustrated, with an introduction by Guillermo Del Toro and afterword by Anne K. Mellor.

Odds and Ends

The Weight of Words (art by McKean) edited by Dave McKean and William Schaefer (Subterranean Press) is an anthology of eleven new pieces of text inspired by McKean's art, creating a highly collectible package to be savored. The stories are a mixed bag of science fiction, fantasy, and horror, the best dark piece by Maria Dahvana Headley.

The Rooms by Stu Horvath and Yves Tourigny is a fascinating little puzzle book made up of a horror novelette by Horvath and the amazing paper/design work of Tourigny. It's a kind of choose your own adventure. If you're a game player and patient (I'm neither), you'll love it.

The Grief Hole Illustrated: An Artist's Sketchbook Companion by Keely Van Order (IFWG Publishing) is a beautiful complement to multi-award-winning Australian writer Kaaron Warren's acclaimed 2016 novel, *The Grief Hole*. The original novel contained illustrations and cover art by Van Order. Consider these—as Nick Stathopoulos, who provides the introduction does—the extras on a Blu-ray disc

Some Notes on a Nonentity by Sam Gafford, illustrated by Jason C. Eckhardt (PSI Books), is a fascinating rendering of the life of H. P. Lovecraft as a graphic novel. The 120-page book covers his life from birth to death. The title is taken from an autobiographical essay that was published in 1963.

BETTER YOU BELIEVE

CAROLE JOHNSTONE

Maybe true
Maybe not true
Better you believe
—Old Sherpa Saying

It's all downhill on a descent. The oldest climbing joke of the lot, but only because it's true. If I like any bit of it at all, it could never be that slow, painful climb down from the highs of before and the bone-deep exhaustion of after. People make mistakes on a descent because everything's against them: altitude, time, their bodies. And always their mind. No one gets excited about survival—not like they do about standing on the top of the world. And no one gets a good write-up in *Nat Geo* or *Time* for managing to get back down a bloody mountain in one piece. Unless they're Jean-Christophe Lafaille, I guess.

The air is raw, thin, dry. Acke Holmberg's cough is worse; when ice walls throw up rare shelter, I can hear it rattle up from his lungs hard enough to start doing damage. Nick likes to tell me about the gross stuff when we're in bed, warm and lazy, blissed out. One guy he climbed with ruptured his esophagus on Nanga Parbat, a few thousand feet above base camp. The blood spray froze in mid-air, Nick said with a grin, before pulling me back under the covers and him.

The wind is a demented banshee. *Only fifty k,* Nick said maybe twelve hours ago; on the summit it beat around our heads so hard we had to crouch. Some of the Swedes were convinced they were going to be yanked off into the swirling white void. *As if they'd be fuckin wheeched off,* Nick said with usual scorn. *As if* it had never happened, when I know just how many dozens of times it has on this peak alone. But he's earned the right to be scathing, I guess. Until today, Annapurna was the only eight-thousander he hadn't summited.

But things are different now—I know that without being able to either see or hear him, somewhere further down the Lafaille line and attached to the same fixed rope. It's dark and growing darker. It's too late—much too late—I can barely see the low sun beyond Gangapurna's peak, some 7,000 meters above the Marsyangdi River. The weather is moving. And the mountain is getting jittery; I feel its hackles under my frozen feet, like we're ticks that just won't quit. We've been inside the Death Zone for too long, but we're too slow, too tired, and have too far to go.

Bad Things, I think, in Nick's lesser spotted concerned voice, as I battle on down through the white and the wind, putting one boot in front of the other in the kind of trance that's both helpful and dangerous. Bad Things are about to happen.

By the time they do, I've managed to convince myself they won't. The wind has died again; the flag cloud west of the summit tilts up and sharp against the dying sun. Up is good, flat is bad, down is fucked. I remember the big poster tacked alongside prayer flags in the med tent, and Nick laughing with one of the American doctors that it was a far more reliable indicator than any other base camp forecast. The mountains make their own weather, and it's rarely kind.

Even though I'm still descending through the French Couloirs, the snowpack is harder, the incline less steep. I'm surprisingly warm, but I know much of that is a cocktail of O and illusion—I last felt my feet at Camp IV. I don't feel bad, I don't feel good. I don't feel much of anything at all. Not even afraid.

There's a subtle but sudden shift in the air around me, like a hush, a breath too close to my ear; my heart stutters a little to feel it through my hood and balaclava. And then Jakub Hornik appears from the gloom behind and above—maybe ten feet east, no more—face-first and flat on his belly, anchored to nothing. He doesn't flail or shout as he slides down the snowfield; he makes no sound at all save the fast friction of his suit against ice. And he makes no attempt at self-arrest either, even though he's holding his ice axe up like any moment he's going to let it fall. His eyes are wild. They find my light and grow wilder, wider—holding onto it right up to the moment that the gloom swallows him back down and I'm left alone, literally frozen, the dropping wind washing out my mouth.

There's a tug on the rope from below. Nick. *Are you all right*?

Not really, not at all, but what use is there in saying so; in being either one or the other up here? I'll still be up here. I'll still be needing to get down fucking there. A big shudder goes through me, it cricks my neck and finds a home in my belly. It's never a good idea to puke more than halfway up a mountain. I think of Jakub's eyes, his silent slide. I remember Kate renaming him The Horn, after he spent the whole first month at base camp trying to hit on her. My belly squeezes hard again.

Bad Things.

Because they're never ever singular.

The last Bad Thing was Felix Garcia. There are always deaths on a climb. Climbing seasons are short, summit windows shorter; at any one time there can be dozens of teams within a few hundred meters of each other. But the threat of actually seeing someone die is surprisingly low, as easily dismissed as the threat of dying yourself. You hear about them, on the short wave or the satellite phone, or when you reach a camp: falls, accidents, strokes, disappearances. People go crazy. People get the shitty end of the stick. People just die. There are lots of ways to do it. And pretty soon those muttered summations become nearly routine, like all the frozen landmarks and trig points that used to be people. *Red Legs. Green Boots. North Col.*

Felix was different. Mountains attract arseholes; eight-thousanders attract Olympic-level arseholes. He and Nick clashed before we even left Everest base camp. Felix was a solo-climber, and that's pretty hard to do on a mountain as rammed as Everest. Nick doesn't like taking them on because they're glory hounds and crappy team players, but he's had to get a lot less picky now that he's competing with Nepali companies for business. It was to be my third summit, Nick's seventh, but we didn't even get close before the weather doubled down and Pasang advised Nick to turn us all back and fast. Felix suffered the final indignity of being geared up with me and three Koreans on the snow fields at the foot of the Lhotse Face as we scrambled over crevasses on shrieking ladders, a snow storm blinding us, deafening us, making us stupid.

By the time I heard his scream, I was already being dragged so fast along the ice I couldn't get my axe free. Our belaying had been too clumsy, the Koreans behind too quick, the rope too slack—Felix plummeted so hard and so fast down the hidden crevasse that by the time anyone managed to arrest our screaming progress along the glacier, I was flying over its edge too. The pain I didn't feel. The horror of all that silent blue dark after howling white space, I did. I looked down at a still screaming Felix and didn't see him, only the hard tight swing of the rope between us vanishing into black. The air prickled against my skin like blunted pins. I looked up at the shouting beyond the ice-rimmed circle of white, and I thought, *they can't hold us both. They can't save us both.*

And they didn't.

I feel another yank on my harness. I've been standing still for too long; the fixed rope is taut, impatient. The wind has grown high again. The darkening sky looks heavy with snow, and when I squint west, I can't see the flag cloud any more. I start moving.

Nick won't have told the other Slovaks about Jakub. They were last to leave the summit, despite Nick and Pasang's warnings about the time. They're far too far behind us to attempt any kind of rescue, but they'd want us to try because the four of them were tight: Jakub and Hasan were as close as brothers. They wouldn't accept that there's no point; that at the edge of this snowfield is a short rock buttress and then a drop of over a thousand feet. I don't want to think about that: about Jakub's wild eyes staring at my light as he slid away from me toward the plummet of black, empty space that he must have known was coming.

Jakub's silence; Felix's high screams. Dark, cold yawns of nothing. What it feels like to fall, to be alone, to feel it coming, to *know.* I can't think about shit like that. We're still nearly a thousand feet inside the Death

Zone—thinking about shit like that is for messy Khukuri rum nights in Pokhara or Kathmandu. Or if you're Nick, never. Easier just to pretend things didn't happen at all.

⊸⊷

The snow starts heavy and doesn't stop. It slows my efforts to catch up to Nick. Even though I know he's already got his hands full with the Chinese couple who arrived at The Sanctuary with no equipment at all, and the always determined Tomie Nà from Hong Kong, who started showing signs of altitude sickness as low as Camp II. And Kate, of course. Following him around like a bad smell. Nick always does the babysitting, while Pasang rounds up the stragglers, the hardcore *just-another-five-minuters*. It's always been this way, even though Pasang is the tolerant one, and Nick couldn't be patient if he tried. But Pasang is the better climber too; certainly, he's the better guide. Nick is the guy in charge, the guy people write the checks to, and even if that's the kind of responsibility he'd sooner shirk than have to suffer, it lets him climb mountains. For that he'd babysit an entire busload of Sunday hikers and Olympic-level arseholes.

I wonder what he'll tell Jakub's family. I remember an evening in The Sanctuary, one of those rare pre-climb nights of excitement and camaraderie not yet spoiled by the reality of weeks of acclimatizing in close, cold quarters. Pavol and Hasan were drunk and red-cheeked, laughing about Jakub's wife, and how pissed off she'd be when she found out how much their trip was costing. That Nick will be the one to tell her what has happened, I have no doubt, but he won't say how it really was: how long Jakub suffered knowing he was going to die on that hard, fast slide; that we were all still on that mountain, but he was already lost, already gone before he was gone.

Climbers have their own rules, their own language, their own religion. And these take years to earn, to learn, to understand. Climbers believe in dreams, as long as those dreams have a purpose, a summit. They believe in God, if God is a mountain, because they worship nothing but the climb—the endless, soulless, merciless demand of it. They believe in trying to help, in trying to save, until they can't. Until they don't. They believe in the individual: in their own strength, their own will, their own survival. And they also believe that mountains can hate, that the weather can be cajoled, that the spirits of those long dead can provide comfort to the dying and lead the living to safety. Even Nick believes—scornful, pragmatic, ever practical Nick—like a liar crossing his fingers, or a fisherman never setting sail on a Friday, or like Pasang leaving offerings to the mountain at the end of every day, while muttering low to the friends whom he has lost.

I trip on a rock under growing drifts of snow and stumble against the fixed line. It's too much snow too fast. Anything over an inch an hour is bad news, and this is much, much more. Visibility is getting worse: I can no longer see the setting sun at all, and my headlight shines through a kaleidoscope of dense monochrome. I'm starting to wonder if we'll make it back down to Camp IV today at all, and that is bad—worse than bad. Bivouacking in the Death Zone is never a good idea, but on the South Face of Annapurna, it's pretty much suicide. I try not to think of all the stats that Nick—and so many other climbers—take such solemn glee in. The summit-to-death ratio on Everest is one in twenty-six. *On Annapurna*, he said, sliding a cool palm down my naked back and along my flank, making me shiver even though then I was warm, *it's one in three*.

The first stirrings of real fear find me then, and it's followed by a strange, slow sense of unreality. I should *already* be frightened. I should have been frightened when the Slovaks weren't ready to leave Camp IV at midnight, or when we finally summited at 5 p.m. instead of 3. I should have been frightened when Nick started moving folk back down the mountain so fast there was barely any time to celebrate our victory; when Acke started sounding like he was coughing up a lung; when the wind, then the night, then the snow started closing in, the mountain began trying to buck us off, and our descent became a disordered, scattered scramble. And I should have been *shitting* myself when Jakub slid past me on the way to his silent death.

Denial. A mountain climber's best and worst friend.

Acke, I think. Acke should be behind me, higher up, but not so far that I can't hear him. Only I can't remember the last time I did hear him; the last time I remembered that I *should* be able to hear him.

"Acke?"

The wind screams back at me.

"Acke! Are you there?"

Maybe I hear him, I don't know. Something hits my face: a stone or some ice carried on the rising wind, and when I press a glove against my cheek, it hurts; the balaclava sticks warm and wet to my skin. "Acke!"

Though I don't want to, I start back up. Not far, I won't go far. Just far enough to ascertain that he's still there, still alive, still descending. In this direction, the wind batters at me hard enough to nearly drop me to my knees.

"Acke!"

There are different kinds of numb in the Death Zone, and denial is only one. Is my heart rate and breathing fast because of altitude or fear? Or because of cerebral oedema? Are my actions, my responses still rational? Do I *think* they are? Climbing above 7,500 meters is the same slow asphyxiation suffered in the *Nightmare-Age* of heavy-curtained four-poster beds. When we climb, we have night terrors, paranoia, depression. When we descend, the euphoria of returning oxygen levels can just as quickly cause psychosis. We're not supposed to function up here; we're not *designed* to function up here. Nick once saw a man launch himself off the Hillary Step like he was dive-bombing the deep end of a swimming pool.

I nearly stumble over Acke before I see him. He's sitting in the snow, legs splayed out, trying to take off his gloves.

"Don't!"

He stills, lifts up his face, winces against the wind and flying debris, but what he says is in Swedish; the only word I recognize is *allena*. Alone.

"You can't stop. You have to get up. Where's Bosse? Is he still behind you? Acke!" I'm shouting hard enough to hurt my throat now. "We *can't* stay here."

He shakes his head, resumes the removal of his gloves, and once he's done that, his frostbitten fingers move to the carabiner connecting him to the fixed line.

"Acke, no!"

He pays me no mind. There's a ring of blood around his mouth like old lipstick, and a brighter slash of it running into his frozen beard. And if he already has pulmonary oedema, then he's probably not too far behind dive-bombing the deep end of a swimming pool either. Because disengaging from the line in a snowstorm is what you do if you're crazy. It's what you do if you want to die.

He grins and his teeth are bloody. "Stay with me," he says. Shouts. But he's not looking at me, he's looking all around me—at the stone, the snow, the nearly night sky.

And then I hear it. The worst Bad Thing. The thing I've been trying the hardest not to think about on our painfully slow descent down this 2,500 meter gulley in a snowstorm; this funnel for spindrift and debris and worse.

By the time Acke hears it, I'm already turned around and running. *Trying* to run. The noise is terrific. My heart thunders in my ears, as I try to seek out somewhere—anywhere—to hide. But there's nothing, nowhere. Because there never is. You're fucked or you're lucky, and that's it.

I know when it's about to hit me because Acke screams high and short, and I feel a cold wall of air rushing against my back, shoving me forward with invisible hands. An impossibly high shadow that eclipses even my own light. I think of Jakub. Dark, cold yawns of nothing. I think of Nick.

And then the avalanche steals away any sense I have left.

Climbing is lonely. You think it won't be. You imagine that the endeavor will be mutually achieved, an ordeal always shared, but the truth is, on some sections, particularly on a disorganized descent, you can go a whole day without setting eyes on another soul. I've learned if not to love, then to appreciate the stark, stripped isolation of those days. The very opposite of the long, crowded intimacy of lower camp life, or the breath-stealing wonder of the summit—whether your vista is the golden curve of Earth and low, white mountain peaks in a sea of clouds, or a whiteout of raging wind and snow. But that other isolation—that other *allena*—is what you dread while never allowing yourself to think of it. It's the realization that you're fucked. Like Jakub. That you're still alive, still on the mountain, but suddenly you're on the other side of a two-way mirror and you won't ever be coming back. *That* is the worst Bad Thing. The only one. Whichever way it happens.

When I open my eyes, I think I'm inside that terrible crevasse again; the horror of all that silent blue dark after howling white space. Blunted pins and the hard tight swing of the rope vanishing into black. An echo of *they can't hold us both. They can't save us both.*

The cold is too cold to feel. I'm not in the crevasse because I can't move. My limbs are folded tight and trapped; my lungs struggle to find space enough to breathe. Too much weight presses down on me. Panic starts crushing me from the inside out. Not this. Not this.

The circle of my arms around my head has allowed for a small air pocket, but it won't last long. My wrist strap has snapped; my ice axe has gone. I think of Nick's face: the dimple in his left cheek, the chip in his right incisor, the always paler circles of skin around his eyes. I think of *his* weight on me, pressing me down, filling me up, and it calms me a little. It calms me enough.

I breathe. I breathe. And then I spit. It dribbles down my cheek along the length of my right eyebrow. Upside down. Maybe 160, 170 degrees. I don't know how deep I am, and the small space I have left isn't enough to find out. Slowly, slowly, I burrow my hands down toward my torso. The snow is like cement. By the time my knuckles bump against the axe, I'm already hyperventilating again. I have cobalt blue boots, I think. The legs of my suit are black with red stripes.

I make myself remember the night we first met in a dark tavern off the main Kathmandu drag in Thamel. Me, pissed on Mustang Coffee and home-brewed Raksi, dancing among dozens of other sweaty gap year tits just like me. And Nick, sitting in a darker corner, disinterested, his mouth curled into a routine sneer until I asked him if he'd dance with me too. The first time we fucked, he gripped me tight enough to leave bruises and told me that he'd never come so hard in his life. The first time we summited—close to the end of season on the Northeast Ridge of Everest—he swung me up to that golden curve of Earth and told me that he loved me; laughed when I said I was on top of the world.

I make myself think of the warm flat of his hands against my skin; the low and steady timbre of his voice, whether he's talking about clove hitches and belay points, or about those spirits that save only people like us: explorers on the edge of the world. Stroking my hair and reading aloud from Ernest Shackleton's *South*: the treacherous glaciers, icy slopes, and snow fields of his doomed Trans-Antarctic expedition; the fog, the dark, the blank map; the exhaustion, starvation, hopelessness. And the spirit—the voiceless, faceless Third Man—that had led him down to the safety of the whaling station on Stromness. Nick's solemn eyes, his slow smile; quoting T. S. Eliot in a tickling whisper against my ear—

Who is the third who walks always beside you?

Where is my *third*? I wonder now, and my eyes sting. Where the hell is the bloody spirit that's going to lead *me* down to safety? My tears feel hot and my throat tries to close up. I stop trying to think of anything at all.

Me. Just me. My own strength, my own will. I am all that can save me.

Slowly, slowly, I manage to turn around now, to bring the axe around. At first I can only twist and shimmy it against the hard-packed snow; I choke and try to turn my face away from what little I manage to hollow out. I feel panic rising again. I don't want to be on the other side of that mirror. I don't want to be a frozen landmark. A trig point. I don't want people to take selfies next to my frozen corpse. My cobalt blue boots. My red-striped suit.

When the way becomes abruptly easier, I nearly sob with relief. I choke more as my axe excavates more, but now I don't care. I'm reaching out of that dark blue echoing silence, up toward that ice-rimmed circle of white. I can nearly taste the mountain's thin air; see its clear, starry sky.

But in the instant before I break through—in the instant before I know I'm *going* to break through, I hear Acke's scream. No longer high and short, but long and horrified. And oh God, so, so much deeper. I have enough room now to clasp my left hand hard over my mouth. I can't feel the press of its glove against my lips, my skin, my teeth.

And then I'm free. The snowstorm has died. My headlight is dead. The only remaining light comes from a half-crescent moon, hanging low over the Nilgiri Himal range to the northwest. I shuffle onto my knees, pushing away from my already collapsing escape shaft. After moving no more than ten feet, I look down at the hard-packed snow between my hands and knees. Acke. *Acke.* I don't shout his name, don't even say it out loud. If he hears me, he might think that I can save him.

Two months ago, in a trekkers' lodge close to the edge of The Sanctuary, he laughed and sang along to Fernando while mixing terrible Brännvin cocktails. He had a boyfriend in the Swedish navy who'd bought him a house, but wouldn't tell anyone he existed. He struggled to grow a beard, always trying: every morning he'd roll his eyes and tug on it, *still sexy ass fluff, my friends.*

So I stay. In the disorientating white-dark, I kneel in the snow over where I think Acke is, and I keep him silent company. I hear him coughing again. Maybe he'll drown instead of suffocate; which is worse, I don't know—don't *want* to know. I reach round for my O. I don't know when I last drank or ate something either. These are the things you must fight: numbness, confusion, lethargy. Mercy. What good will staying here do? How can Acke know he's not *allena*, and what does it matter if he does? But I think of him shouting *stay with me* to the mountain, the snow, the sky, and so I stay.

I'm always exactly where I'm supposed to be.

It's no longer snowing. It's no longer gloomy either. It's dark. Night. I can't hear Acke anymore. I wonder how long he fought. How long he pretended. If he's pretending even now. Because denial has to be better than acceptance, if one side of the coin—the mirror—is death and nothing else. I shudder hard enough to again crick my neck.

When I try to get up, it feels as if I no longer exist below my waist. It takes too long to locate and change out my headlight, and the reward does not justify the effort: the thin revived glow casts only slow and frightening shadows. The drifts are high, unwieldy; the terrain is entirely changed as if I haven't made it back through the mirror at all. The couloirs are gone, their scars and fissures hidden under the weight of so much new snow.

I shine my light down on my harness. Its main carabiner is bent and twisted out of shape, probably when the avalanche wrenched me free of the line. It takes another long time to replace it with a spare; my fingers are slow, my mind slower. Finally, I move the light wider, over smooth swathes of black and white, searching for the way down. It takes the longest time of all for the truth to sink in. The fixed ropes are gone.

My panic is too slow. There's even something close to relief in it. The thin air whistles around me like I'm an obstacle, a rock in a stream. *Now* I'm fucked, there's no way I'm not. How can I ever negotiate my way out of the Death Zone alone and with no fixed lines? This is my worst Bad Thing. After years of dread, of anticipation, this, here, is how it happens. This is the *way* it happens for me.

"Sarah? Why you here?"

I swing around, slow like an astronaut; at the same time assuming the voice is inside my head. It's a not unfamiliar question.

Pasang is standing less than ten feet away, looking none the worse for wear at all. He's half-crouched, as if readying himself for a starter's gun. He doesn't look afraid *or* fucked—more startled. Because he never expected me to make it this far? I feel the pinch of familiar resentment when I should only be feeling relief. Pasang will help me. He has to.

"Jakub Hornik and Acke Holmberg are dead," I say, and my voice sounds strange, thin, like the air. It's very quiet, I realize. Nearly silent. After the storm and the avalanche, it's still enough that I wonder if I'd hear one of those blunted pins drop.

Pasang doesn't react. Chongba isn't with him, so he must have left him behind with the Slovaks, while he's come down the mountain to see how bad it is; if they can still make it down without having to bivy or call for an evac that'll probably never come. How long did I stay kneeling in the snow waiting for Acke to die? It must have been hours. Pasang's eyes scan the terrain ahead and then he looks back at the mountain behind. He never wears goggles and he never carries O. I sometimes wonder if he even needs to eat, shit, or fuck either.

He asks, "Who was higher than them?"

"Holmberg means Island Mountain. Did you know that?" I feel numb, but I no longer know which kind of numb. Something tugs at my mind, puckers my skin. Makes me remember to be afraid. I don't know what the fuck I'm doing here.

He blinks. "Sarah. Who was higher than them?"

I know why he's asking. It's because I'm the first person he's seen. And everyone else between us is gone.

"Bosse. Benoit and Savane. The Australians, I think. I don't know."

Pasang curses. This will be the end of the *8000er Experience*, I think, and I feel a guilty spark of hope that must show in my eyes because Pasang straightaway narrows his.

"Why you here?"

"What the fuck does that mean?" I look down at the snow under my boots, my crampons. Already my escape route has filled in as if it never was.

"You hate the mountains. Always." His voice is not cold, though his words are. They sound angry. "Why you come back, every time?"

I swallow because even if I understand the question, I don't understand why he'd ask it now.

"You don't belong here." His gaze grows softer. "You never belong here."

But I don't want to argue with him, because he'll never understand. He's never understood why any of us keep coming back, not really. Most of the time he manages to hide his contempt. Just about.

"You know why. I'm here for Nick."

The way is treacherous, of course. I'm clunky, *a functional climber*, Nick has always said, though I've never taken offense. It's true. But now, clambering down barely settled snow, with no protection beyond my own gear, my own judgment, I wish that I loved it, I wish that I felt it. I wish that I could reach Nick by sheer force of want, of will.

Instead my descent is anything *but* functional: I stumble and I fall and I fuck up my handholds, my footholds. My rope snags and burns; my overhangs and hitches and anchors are poor—I move too slowly because I have as much confidence in my abilities as I do in the new ground beneath me. I only have the distant lights of Camp IV and Pasang's directions to guide me, and I keep thinking of that cold, blue space and blunted pins, but I'm still doing it. I *am* doing it. And whether that's down to his help or his scorn, I suppose hardly matters.

I knew Pasang would never come with me, but when he turned back to the dark shadow of the mountain, my belly clenched all the same, and I wanted to beg him to stop. Though I didn't. His job is to look after the Slovaks. The fucking Slovaks who didn't manage to get out of their fucking sleeping bags until 2 a.m. He has to trust that I can look after myself, and that Nick can look after his group. Alone. Just as I have to trust that Pasang will be okay, even if that suffocating dread behind thick, heavy curtains suspects better.

Nick. He's all I can think about now. Not me or Pasang, Jakub, Bosse, the French Canadians, the Australians—not even Acke. Except to wonder if Nick has suffered the same terrible fate. I don't think about the others in his group either. I don't care about any of them—these idiots with too much money and too little of everything else. In that, I understand Pasang's contempt. If my reasons for being here are stupid, then theirs are moronic. Nick despairs of their inexperience: their lack of knowledge, training, equipment; their sheer bloody self-entitlement. They've paid Nick and Pasang to get them to the summit and back, and nothing less will do. They haven't paid for any kind of *Experience* at all. They've paid for a photo-op, a flag; Nick even prints them out a certificate. When Tomie Nà refused to stop after the docs at Camp II told him he could die if he climbed any higher, Nick rubbed his hands through his hair, spat into the snow, and then carried on preparing for the next section.

For all his faults—and I'm aware of them all, despite what everyone, including Pasang, believes—Nick loves these few places high above the rest of the world with a passion that could never be faked. And that's why he's here too. That's why he puts up with everything else, all the other shit that he hates. Because he has as much choice as I do.

But it isn't Nick I find first. It's Kate. Her sobs creep up through the darkness like the wind around ice pillars; I only realize it's her when I see headlights less than fifty yards below. I don't know how long I've been descending now, or how much longer before I leave the Death Zone behind me. The lights of Camp IV look hardly closer, though the moon has moved far enough to disorientate me completely. I'm struggling to breathe, and my O is getting too low. That slow, creeping paralysis is back; a numbness inside and out that's nearly seductive. It makes me want to stop asking myself if I'm about to dive-bomb the deep end of a swimming pool. It makes me not want to care if the answer is yes.

Kate's sobs are nearly hysterical. I shout, but she doesn't hear, doesn't stop, barely draws breath. I try not to move too quickly as I edge down over still-shifting snow. The drifts are higher here, creating precarious peaks of their own, but overall the terrain is flatter, more glacial. Here is where most of the avalanche came to rest, I think. Here is where deep, dark crevasses will be hiding, waiting, beneath all that treacherous new snow. I try not to hesitate, to stop, to look for Nick, to waste precious breath of my own in more shouting. Instead, I carry on descending, descending, fucking descending, and praying a little too, for good measure. He *has* to be all right.

"We can't go! How can we fucking go?" After an avalanche, mountain air gets thicker and sounds flatter; Kate's voice is a hysterical monotone. "What about Tomie and—"

"Tomie, Jìng, and Lì are already gone, and you know it."

I allow myself the luxury of stopping, of staring at the second headlight. His voice still echoes. *Nick.*

"Jesus, how can you be so cold?"

"We're both pretty cold, Kate. And getting pretty fucking colder. It's not them you care about. It's the fucking serac between us and fucking freedom, and I can't help you with that."

By the time I reach them, I'm close to collapse. I can't feel my legs, but I know it all the same. I feel hot when I should feel cold—or nothing at all. And all I can see is Nick. He's hunkered down under a high overhang of rock, head low, gloved hands dangling between his legs. Kate sits close alongside him, and I try—and fail—not to care about that. They've been there too long, I care more about that; about the stiff, tired threat in their bodies, their voices.

"We can't free-solo around a fucking serac with fuck knows how many tons of snow weighing down on it!" Kate's digging in. Her voice is calmer, stronger. Once she makes her mind up about something, that's usually it. "We need to stay here, wait for an evac. You've phoned our position in. We can't—"

"We're still in the Death Zone. No one will be coming for us." Nick's voice is just as calm, as confident, but I know he's horrified. I know he's blaming himself. Even though it's the fault of the bloody Slovaks.

"We *can't*—"

"I *will* leave you behind, Kate," he says.

"You're a bastard."

"No," I say. "He's what'll keep you alive."

Kate gasps, looks in my direction, and her breath catches formless in the air. I wonder if she can read something in my expression that I'm usually better at hiding. I've been free-soloing since Acke, but it would be pretty petty to say so. Though I want badly to bask in Nick's uncommon approval.

Nick's head drops further between his knees, and I hear only his chattering teeth. Still none of us move. Up here, we're statues: half-frozen, half-thawed; half-numb, half-crazy. Half-alive, half-dead. It's a miracle we feel anything at all.

Nick gets back on his feet with grunted effort. He swears again; coughs. The latter rattles down inside his chest. "Let's go."

The serac is a block of glacial ice as big as a three-story townhouse. Near to the start of our summit ascent, the route alongside was lit by flare lamps and set with fixed ropes. Now, its threat is magnified by darkness and formless new terrain. And all the death and weight that we've brought back down the mountain with us.

Nick wedges a metal nut into one of the rocks close to the serac's beginning. He clips a quickdraw to the wire, threading the rope through it and his own carabiner before feeding it backwards in generous loops. "We're not decking out, okay? Not fucking today."

Some color has returned to Kate's cheeks. She picks up the rope, locks into the belay. I do the same—muscle memory triggering too many other less welcome memories: me and Nick, Kate and James climbing rock faces, ice pillars, mountains. Trekking and hiking and camping all over the world. Getting shit-faced in dodgy bars and on deserted beaches. At James' funeral, Kate clung to Nick as if he was the only anchor on a Grade V vertical climb. She and I had been friends since high school, but she never again dragged me to karaoke bars or treated me to spa weekends in wanky Essex hotels, as if she'd lost me over the same sheer cliff as her husband. When I asked Nick how I could help her, he told me I'd be best leaving her alone until she came to me. And she never did.

The serac radiates a different kind of cold than the mountain. It's breathless, sharp, and thin. Fragile. Silent blue dark looking up into an icy white space and sky. Endless shadow.

Nick edges along the base of the serac too slowly. The ledge is narrow—less than a foot across in some places—and the drop on the other side is big; even in the dark it has the power to squeeze my stomach, water my eyes. And it's always been Nick's cautiousness that frightens me, never his selfish recklessness. He feeds back more rope in slow turning loops, but he doesn't look around. "Don't stop," he says.

Close to the halfway point, Kate falters, one gloved hand getting caught in the gear as she tries to navigate Nick's hastily improvised line. I dilute my impatience with the memory of the couloirs, the dread and relief of *now I'm fucked, there's no way I'm not* when the avalanche stole the fixed lines. It's too easy to stop thinking past doctored routes, too easy to start shitting yourself whenever you have to unhook from their security for even a few seconds.

Kate goes on fumbling, hesitating, trying and failing to free herself, to move. Powdered snow falls through the gap between us. The serac was never stable, but now fuck knows how many tons of avalanche threaten to overload it to the point of collapse. And if that happens, it doesn't matter how careful and slow we're being; how many ropes and anchors we do or don't have.

"I'm scared," Kate whimpers, and her hands still, shoulders hunch.

Nick is far enough ahead to be nearly out of sight, so she can only be talking to me. I remember the *puja* twelve hours before we left base camp: a Lama and two skinny monks bent over a stone altar, the smell of juniper reminding me of the gins from the night before; equipment spread around us and waiting to be blessed: harnesses, crampons, ice-axes, and helmets, even our expedition flag. Pasang chanting alongside the monks, placating the spirits, making his offerings of yak milk and chocolate and rice as the Lama talked to the mountain, asked it to let us climb to its summit. Kate, hungover and dull-eyed, her smile scornful as she stifled a yawn: *Mountain says no.*

She doesn't know I hate her. She doesn't know that less than six months after James' funeral, Nick got down on his knees and told me how many times they'd fucked; that he held onto me so tightly I was nearly glad that they had. She doesn't know that he would never leave me. She doesn't know him.

"It'll be all right," I say, and her shoulders drop, she finally tugs her glove free, clips back into the line.

And at the halfway point, I start to think it might be. That maybe—just maybe—the sheer number of Bad Things that have already happened are enough. But then I feel it: the air changing just like it did before Jakub came sliding out of the gloom on the other side of that mirror—a hush, a breath too close to my ear—and I know that I'm wrong. Again.

I unclip myself from the line, and I'm no longer slow, no longer afraid. My crampons find little purchase; my left foot slips off the ledge into dark space more than once, but I keep on going, faster, faster. Until I reach Kate.

"Go!" I push her so hard she shrieks—but either she can sense the danger in my voice or in the slow deadly shifts of the wall of ice against us, because she immediately obeys, abandoning the fixed line even as Nick is screwing in another anchor up ahead.

"Go!" I scream again. "Nick! Go!"

He turns just as my headlight finds him, his face slack and pale, and then he looks up at the serac in the very moment that *it* starts to scream.

We run. And run. And the world collapses around us.

Kate is who I hear first. She's sobbing again, but she can't catch enough breath—the result is an oddly comforting squeak. She only stops to shout Nick's name, and a sob comes out of me too when, finally, he answers in a hoarse shout.

I sit up, struggle to get to my knees. When I look back, the line is gone, the ledge is gone, the serac is gone. I'm finding it hard to breathe myself—I hear the thin air wheeze through my lungs—but my O is gone too.

I stand up and sway, but there's nothing to hold onto. When Nick struggles to his feet a few meters further down, his headlight glancing off Kate's helmet, her suit, I see a long streak of blood running from his temple to his jaw.

"Oh my God, Nick," she says. She sounds exhilarated and broken at the same time. "Oh my God."

He doesn't answer, just keeps staring up at all the destruction behind us, eyes still wide and wild and black.

And I stare back, but even though we're the closest we've been since the summit, I know I can't reach any closer. My dread is exhausted, heartbroken. He's safe. He's alive. But it isn't enough.

"You felt her too, right?" Kate grabs hold of his upper arms. "I know you fucking did. She was there! She was—"

"Don't touch me," he says, but he's already shrugged her off, already backed away. He keeps on looking, looking, *looking*, and something in him finally breaks as he drops to his knees, as he howls into the black, the vast ocean of white.

I look away from Nick and back at the summit. The low moon throws light and shadow against the rock, the snow, the ridges and fissures, the pillars and gullies. I think of Jakub and Acke and all the others who'll be left on this mountain, frozen in time and in place; disappeared, or dragged away from the path to become a landmark, a trig point, a cautionary tale. I think of Pasang and Chongba and the Slovaks trapped inside the Death Zone with no fixed lines, and an avalanche and collapsed serac between them and Camp IV. They may as well be on that moon.

And I think of them all sitting around that stone altar, laughing and eating. Smearing grey sampa flour on their faces; the promise that they would live to see each other become old and grey. *Mountain says no.*

Because the view from the other side of the mirror can so often look the same. Even when you know exactly what it feels like to fall, to be alone. Even when you know—as you look up out of silent blue dark into howling white light and life; as the air prickles against your skin like blunted pins—that it's already too late. Like a slow-suffocating nightmare inside thick, heavy curtains. A leaving that never feels like going anywhere at all. To be gone, but not gone.

They can't hold us both. They can't save us both.

And they didn't.

The shocking agony of plunging into that silent blue dark, Felix's weight pulling me down faster, harder, the snapped rope showering snow. To feel it coming, to *know*. A breath, barely long enough to scream, but stretching out into infinity.

Denial: a mountain climber's best and worst friend. Better to believe. Except we never do—those of us already on the other side of that coin, that mirror. Because then there really is no going back at all.

Nick still howls even as the wind picks up again and the night gets colder. But he'll come back. He'll always come back. Because this is where Nick lives. Not in our shitty Catford maisonette. Not even in base camps or trekking lodges. Only up here, in the clouds and violent snowstorms and hurricane-force winds; on the rock faces and ice fields and stony summits; in the gullies and crevasses, the ridges and jet winds and dancing tails of white snow. Up here, where people can't survive; where we start dying faster the moment we start to climb. This is Nick's home.

And mine. Because what I told Pasang will always be true. I think of Acke shouting *stay with me* to the stone, the snow, the sky. I am here because Nick needs me to be here. And so I stay. I will always walk beside him. It's the only reason I've ever climbed any mountain at all.

LIQUID AIR

INNA EFFRESS

In the pickup, Kris pulled down the visor, tousled her sandy hair, and reapplied the Carmex. Sharkey had instructed her to stop off at the sign shop to collect a repair—a giant flashing arrow—to be placed high on a post visible from the road. It would be her second time meeting the sign-maker. Why was she so concerned with her looks? *Just habit*, she thought.

At Wild River Paper Mill, she turned, and tires crunched against gravel. The Mill was a sprawling brick building. Its stink hung like rotten cabbage over the Neches River, the unmistakable odor of sulfur from the chemical pulping of wood chips, what locals termed "the smell of money." On the top floor, the dark windows seemed liquid, in each of them a rising moon reflected a coin floating in melted mercury.

The parking lot was empty besides a hauling truck, and on the far side, in shadows, the sign-maker's van. His bumper sticker read, "The beginning is in small things."

On the stroke of eight, a fizzing sputtered from up high. Lights flickered, then strobed. Up on top of the industrial building beamed Vegas Vic, the sign-maker's most famous restoration job, forty feet of cowboy looming over the roof's lip. His ten-gallon hat grazed the sky, blazing red. Eyebrows, thick and fiery, a comic strip version of wisdom, the red-embered tip of his cigarette dangling from his lips for a touch of mystery. Years ago, the mill owner had unearthed Vic at a neon boneyard in Nevada, but to Kris, the sign was a misfit, an alien, condemned for life to flash its loneliness and deformity, like an immigrant imprisoned in his crumbling memory—his mind's snapshots of a dacha paneled with driftwood along the Volga River, of mushroom-picking in rubber boots in the darkness before a fleeting dawn, the river lapping at the bank, where the only inkling of a road was two tracks of dirt through long, grasping grass.

With a timid knock, Kris let herself in the shop where the van was parked.

"Hello?" she said, and a muffled voice responded, "Be right with you."

The shop had been one of those old shotgun houses, the kind inhabited by logging camp gypsies who vanished with the final thud of the last tree standing.

It was dark. On the far side, orange flames flared. She pivoted and blinked. Parts and valves, machinery and cables crowded every shelf and surface, along with giant sketches of reverse lettering like looking at one's tattoo in a reflection, as long as the tattoo said Bar, Espresso or Pawn.

"Hi, it's Kris Church?" She couldn't recall the man's name. It was something exotic. "I was here last week. The order for the Roadhouse?"

Her sight adjusted. He sat on a stool behind a metal table littered with four-foot glass tubes. Some of them were already bent, so the pile looked like a den of glass snakes. A live hand-torch like a wishbone roared ice blue in his one hand, while he manipulated a melting glass tube with the fingertips of the other. No protective gloves.

One end of a skinny yellow hose dangled from his mouth, as from a hookah. It slung around the back of his neck, coiled down and attached to glass he was warping. For a moment he stopped blowing, the hose still drooping from his lip, so his consonants were distorted when he spoke.

"Have a seat."

A scowl formed behind his goggles, probably directed at her.

"Okay, um, will you be a while?"

No answer. Whatever it was she'd felt coming here was snuffed out, though not quenched, by his obvious indifference.

When he looked up, the glass in his grip began to buckle and he quickly resumed blowing, his thumb alarmingly close to the torch. At his elbow, a burner labeled "crossfire" stood ignited, a series of brass nozzles streaming blue flames, all of them aimed at the same point from two sides, like six lasers meeting at an optical center and refracting.

Kris pushed aside some clutter on a dusty loveseat, and settled into a clearing by a copy of *Signs of the Times* magazine, addressed to Tertullio Ramone. No wonder she couldn't remember.

What was she doing here again, in this backwards place of her childhood? Sometimes it didn't feel anything like civilization. She pictured her husband, with his glazed expression, his enigmatic condition, holed up in the barn, confiding in his dolls, dressing them, grooming them and giving each one a story of her own. I wish I'd never seen what was out there, she thought. At least then this life would be more bearable.

"Your sign's not ready yet. Electrode problem. You can wait here or come back tomorrow evening."

With the hose out of his mouth, his speech had a trace of an accent, sharp and unexpected, like hail on a sunny day.

"It's not for me. It's for my boss—Sharkey."

"Like I said—it's your call."

He placed his goggles on his hair, so black it looked blue. The lines on his wide forehead deepened and for the first time, he directed an unflinching gaze at her. Kris swallowed. His eyes were the consistency of tar, dissecting and remaking her, the eyes of any cannibal or Picasso, himself. Her mouth was dry. It was as though she were ensnared in quicksand, trying to avoid any frantic movements that might suction her further and swallow her whole.

"Listen, Tertullio? Did I say that right? I'll be back tomorrow."

He shrugged and replaced the protective glasses. As she pushed the screen door, he said, "Come earlier. I'll show you how it's done."

Kris tilted her head in a question mark, but he was already intent on angling the twelve converging flames of the crossfire to a particularly tricky twist.

Out on the asphalt, sulfur particles chafed her throat. Vegas Vic's waving arm reminded Kris of the way her widowed mother would pull on the slot machine, her torso slumped, driving the lever again and again in a mindless void of feeling, those fruit reels spinning and flashing her into a numbness, deeper and deeper.

⟜

It was just after ten when she got home. A mist hung low over the patchy lawn, a molten wax globule in a lava lamp, and it descended over the small blackjack oaks fanned out in the soil, their bark cracked into black rectangles with orange fissures. Droplets clung to the peeling shutters of her childhood house. Inside, she set her bottle opener key ring on the kitchen table and listened. Opaque silence. From the window, she could see light shining from the open barn door below. Kris stepped onto the stone path and broke into a trot, welcoming the pain of small acorns stabbing at her bare heels. Inside, her husband had his back to the door, still in his pajama bottoms, and nothing else. He was whispering to the two dolls he called the Blackwood sisters.

"Women don't know when they look their best," he was saying as he teased an auburn wig with a comb.

The remaining seventy-eight dolls were posed around the room, in various stages of dress, like contestants in a child beauty pageant. Some wore cardboard signs displaying a name or anecdote. The walnut faces of the sisters were lacquered with smoky eyes and dripping red lips, and the short corduroy dresses that he had hand stitched himself, were unbuttoned down to the navel, the lewdness of their exposed bodies incongruous with cultured pearl chokers. All the dolls were forty-nine inches tall, the height of an eight-year-old girl, eyes cast sideways for the effect of sullen loneliness, with lashes so thick and drooping, it was impossible to make contact. Their breasts were fully formed, the breasts of a grown woman, pink-brown nipples, explicit and obscene, down to the goose bumps and darkened areolas. Kris had to look away.

"Wit." Her tone was loveless, a dried bouquet of baby's breath disintegrating at the slightest touch.

He seemed puzzled, as if he only vaguely knew her, as if she had no business being there, in his domain of dolls. His condition seemed to have deteriorated over the past few weeks.

"Who is Wit?" He had a fit of hissing laughter, like an angry goose defending her eggs, then lowered his voice as if he was going to confide something, "What is Wit?"

"Why do you talk about yourself in third person? Is this one of your riddles?" Kris shook her head. "It's late. I just don't think I can do this tonight."

She turned to leave. In a bound, her husband was at her side and squeezing her upper arm.

Kris tried to pry his fingers loose, but his will was the to-the-death sort. He held his nose to her and made loud sniffing noises like a dog smelling a tree, then inhaled deeply and sensually.

"Oh, will you stop." When she rolled her eyes in disgust and jerked her body backward, the whites of his eyes enlarged and he crushed her tighter in a wringing motion. She slapped her free palm on his shoulder and pushed, making small grunting sounds. Even when she hit his chest, he did not ease up, but pressed himself against her and nibbled on her ear.

"What are you doing! I don't want—not this." They continued to scuffle until he tore the front of his pants down and urinated on her bare feet, humming with spurts of laughter, his lips pursed in ecstasy. Satisfied, he abruptly sat, his back to Kris, cross-legged on the wet floor, and cradled a doll's headless torso, caressing it once before inserting a large black spring from an old screen door.

"An artist must be cruel long enough to implant a spine," he said, lecturing to his miniature, wooden women.

⊸

The sky was a light gray when Kris pulled herself out of bed. She was unclear whether she'd even achieved sleep. Her muscles ached. Sometime in the night, Wit had made his way beside her, a rare occurrence lately. As Kris watched her husband's relaxed breathing, she imagined standing over him, clutching a pillow at both ends, pressing it squarely over his face, and watching his legs thrash, his stripped belly thrusting in agony, while his convulsions spaced out farther and farther between, the last popcorn kernels exploding in the pan.

⊸

In the waning light at the Mill, the wind kicked up. Kris braced herself. She gulped the dust that came hurling at her. Stepping into the sign maker's world of fire and color, she felt her body relax. Over the speakers, some drawn-out bars of a symphony rippled with a cello pizzicato, giving her the sense of bubbles rising from the depths of the sea. Harps and violins produced the hollow tones of slithering winds. The day was not cooling down. If anything, it was getting hotter.

"Tertullio? It's me, Kris." Until her eyes adapted, he was a faceless silhouette, a contrast to flames of orange and blue. "I came back. For the sign."

"Ah, Kristine. Good. I have prepared something for you. Please, come closer. And call me Tullio."

His accent flooded her ears and echoed. She approached the cluttered table. In a chipped vase stood a lush bouquet of roses, the petals perfectly black.

"Those are for you." His stare was blunt, forceful. Again, that impenetrable tar of his eyes threw her and she reached out for the back of a stool.

"Well, thank you. I don't know that I've ever seen black roses. How unique."

"It's a trick of the light," he said. "Under ordinary light, they would be ordinary."

It seemed to her that his subtlety had layers of meaning. She was charged and spellbound, two opposing sensations that stunned her, a vacuum between repelling magnets.

"That blue light you see shining on the flowers is argon laced with mercury. Argon is from the Greek for 'the lazy one.' It's one of the noble gases, along with neon, the one that makes red. A funny name. Noble. Long ago, scientists determined that these gases resisted combining with other elements. That's where their so-called nobility comes from."

He was welding two glass tubes together, searing the ends with his hand torch, but she was only interested in the sound of his voice.

"So, how does neon make red?" she asked.

"In its natural state, neon gas is unremarkable. It's colorless. No odor." He smiled tersely. "But it's all around us. It's a component of liquid air. We extract it by liquefying the gas and distilling the air."

Kris nodded. She was watching his mouth more than listening.

He ran a blade across the surface of a glass, and snapped it. The methodical heartlessness of the scoring and severing sent a shiver of pleasure through her.

Tullio handed her a pair of goggles, and she hesitated, searching his face for a sign.

"There are three risks. Cutting yourself, burning yourself and electrocuting yourself."

He took the end of the yellow hose that had been in his mouth and slipped it inside her bottom lip. She studied his face. His attention was trained on the glass he was holding to the torch.

"Now, breathe out."

In nervous anticipation, she took a heaving breath in, instead of out. The glass imploded.

"I'm so sorry." There was a swell of music from the speakers above and she wondered what he really thought of her. It was impossible to mine any information from those thick pits.

Tullio gave her an unmarred tube.

When the melting and bending was complete, he stepped in close behind her, guiding her hand. Together, they fastened electrodes to the ends.

A steel cooler-shaped box thrummed, the sound of a strained motor on a drill. Two glass insulators grew out of its lid, like antennae from a black and white Frankenstein movie.

Next, she heard the sound of an old steam engine.

"This is the pumping heart of my workshop," he yelled over the noise. "We must incinerate and suck out all impurities before the noble gas is injected."

High current passed through the tube. Illumination was instant, but anemic, pale. Gradually, color seeped in, its cool glow warming to red in stages.

"Neon is a dying art, Kristine. I don't know how much longer I'll be creating words and images. But each time I prepare to pack up and leave, a job or two trickles in."

He turned the pumping off, and in the sudden void of that rhythmic pulse, the radio station swept back through the air with the moaning of a tortured sea. Violins surged, their tempo that of blinding strikes of lightning.

Kris felt his hot breath on the back of her neck. She peeled off her cardigan, which had dark sweat stains on the underarms, and wondered if he could see the beads she felt forming on her back, above the dip of her tank top.

"Let's take a break," he said, "and cool off. The swimming hole is nearby. It will be refreshing, no?"

"I—I don't have a suit."

"Darkness will cover you." He opened the screen to see outside. Fog swathed Vegas Vic and smothered the reach of his light, actually swallowed and internalized the light, as if the fog were a lead apron. "Clouds have rolled in. Our night is perfectly starless."

In the abandon of darkness, Kris had no sense of the cliff's edge, until there was no more earth under her feet. For a sliver of time, they hung suspended, midair. Then, her outside arm flapped in tiny circles, her stomach dipped, and, hands still interlaced, they dropped through thirty feet of nothing. A prolonged yell, part exuberant, part terrified, escaped her and rang out to the treetops. Then a cold, hard splash. There was barely time to close her mouth before the water engulfed her, then curbed the freefall, like a net below a tightrope. They paddled up and bobbed. Kris pushed the clinging hair back from her face and unleashed a whoop, long and piercing, which curved into a kind of throaty grunt, the kind a javelin thrower releases as she takes her delivery step and transfers her momentum into the spear, her body a whip from toe to arm.

Veins of lightning throbbed above them, followed by a crack like a splitting tree. She clasped his neck, and entwining their ghostly, weightless legs, she grazed his jaw with shivering lips. The smell of him was masked by the film of water cellophaning his skin.

Holding their shoes and exhaling the last tendrils of adrenaline, they dressed and walked to his van, an arm slung casually around the other's waist. Ahead of them, a man was walking. For a sinking moment Kris wondered if it was possible, somehow, that Wit had followed her.

Don't be ridiculous, she thought, and shook her head. *Farfetched, even for me.*

A fat rain drop stung her shoulder, then another, until they heard plunks smashing to the ground in all directions, slow at first, and gaining speed, as does a train pulling of its station.

In the shadows of the little shop, by the red light of the bar signs and flames of orange and blue, they faced each other, dripping puddles at their feet. Kris stripped his sopping shirt from him, tearing it at the collar. Neither one blinked, not even when she kissed him, or when she pushed him back onto the loveseat and straddled him, unbuckling his jeans with one hand, and skimming her free fingers over and inside his mouth. They stayed that way for two nights and a day, she waking him whenever the hunger washed over her again, until the rains gushing onto the roof finally relented to a steady drum track, looping and isolated.

When Kris stopped at the gas station on her way home, her head was swimming with a long-forgotten sensation, of discovering herself in another, of going all-in, the idea that if she stepped into the void, an answer in a form she never expected would be waiting for her.

The convenience store was empty aside from a toothless cashier, who spat a squirt of tobacco into his spittoon, fashioned from a Styrofoam cup, ragged and stained, and lined with leaves from days-old chew. Squirt-plunk, went the brown sludge.

"Good Lord willin', the worst is over. Best we can hope for, now."

Kris sprinted from the driveway, into the house. Wit wasn't in there. No surprise. He was probably back in the barn, she thought. But when she squinted out the window, past a fresh burst of rain, she saw the barn was gone.

In the end, the river rose a record eleven feet. There was flash flooding everywhere. As the sky dumped an endless stream, floodwaters were strong enough to derail a freight train, lift cars and force animals into trees. People paddled in boats on streets underwater. On the sixth morning they awoke to find the sun illuminating the Neches River, and dozens of caskets drifting downstream. The dead had been disturbed, disinterred from their plots, coffins gently bumping each other—a jumble of corpses, coasting with the steady pull of nature, the formaldehyde used in the embalming process leaching into the soil, into the river, a bright greenish oil forming a skin on the river's surface, a potion of formaldehyde and melted flesh. As temperatures rose, the odor entwined with the sulfur.

Dozens of volunteers showed up to sort the bodies, with Kris among them. They were given cloth respiratory masks as they waded out into the slime, to heave coffins onto shore. It wasn't until mid-morning that a child-sized body came floating at them, facedown, about fifty feet up-stream from where Kris was positioned. Those around her stopped what they were doing. They held their breath.

The child's Medusa hair snaked out, and, in the contaminated water, each strand had the green and purple hue of a snakelocks anemone, its tentacles tapering, flexuous, and rippling gracefully in the current. Following that one, there was another, and another, until a tangled sea of girls, soiled, lifeless, wooden, all of them the same size and shape, appeared, lashed together with fabric and debris, and conjoined at the limbs like a mass of defective births, in one, long raft, bobbing languidly, high to low, and up again, from around the river's bend toward the frozen onlookers, and joining the coffins in their lurid parade, a drifting canvas of gray earth tones, blacks and browns, a dark vision welling up, unchecked, blotting out the light and spilling its ink out into the poisoned waters.

From the peculiar vessel's center rose an obtuse pyramid built from dismembered parts, a contortion of limbs, torsos, mouths and eyes, its capstone a half-sitting girl, straining upward in salvific longing and desperation, a shredded blouse sleeve flapping from her outstretched arm, like a flag hoisted in truce on its mast.

The dolls' faces were vacant, emotionless, their sideways eyes neither tormented nor satiated, painted lips pressed against navels and buttocks and necks, their unclothed places teetering between nudity and the innocent nakedness of children.

As it neared, the raft seemed to extend outward, into Kris, drawing and engaging her as a participant in the wooden contraption that seemed on the verge of fracturing apart.

She stood shuddering. A figure—a man with a charred-looking face—rested along the rear of this deranged pageant boat, pulled along by his head and shoulders, floating carefree as a monarch whose kingdom has been threatened, or an ant colony's queen in a flood, her majesty kept safe by her larval ant brood.

At first, the man looked like a massive, polyurethane balloon character. His inflated thighs and bloated arms trailed in the water, bulging with unnatural strength. His blackened head twisted, confronting Kris, beckoning her with his open, putrefied palm, his stretched arm exposing a triangular gaping wound beneath his ribs, the blood-tinged froth about his nose and mouth taunting her, his eyeballs protruding in their sockets, between his teeth, the heel of a headless doll.

A gnarled branch in the water caught the hem of the man's pants. The collision disturbed his balance, dislodged him from the interstices of doll parts. His distended form slid from the raft and flipped over in the muck, the tarnished-bronze rag of him, macerated, broad shoulders slumped forward, his head now vanished underwater, acting as ballast. He released a sigh. The decomposing gasses produced by bacteria in his chest cavity and gut—methane, hydrogen sulfide and carbon dioxide—erupted from him as he began to deflate, until diving, groaning, a ship in distress, he was swallowed up whole by the Neches, with all that remained on the surface only bubbles, gas molecules rising upwards through the air.

HOLIDAY ROMANCE

MARK MORRIS

Skelton could hear the sea from his room. As a teenager he had found the breath of the tide more soothing than a lullaby, but now, with disappointment filling up the years in between like accumulated grime, it seemed like nothing more than the death-bed respiration of a sick old man, struggling to draw air in to atrophied lungs.

The springs inside the old-fashioned mattress creaked so loudly as he sat up that it might have been the same one he had slept on over thirty years before. By contrast, the carpet that he crossed to the window was thinner and coarser than he remembered, and the Ikea wardrobe was nothing like the one he had once imagined might lead to Narnia—at least during the day, before the darkness transformed it into a shape that loomed with such sinister intent that he couldn't close his eyes until his head was beneath the covers.

The promenade, and the beach beyond, looked as lifeless as an old postcard, which was not how he remembered them at all. Viewed through the shifting warp of rain on the window, the sea, sand and concrete seemed to smear together into a grey substance barely more substantial than mist. When Skelton blinked, the fist of the pier, with its overlong finger pointing out to sea, hovered into focus for a second before slithering back into murk. Was the dark blob that seemed to twitch half-way along the pier's length a person? Was someone leaning over the railings, having braved the November squall? Or was it merely a huge gull perched on the upper rail?

Skelton leaned forward for a better look, but was closer to the glass than he had anticipated, and the sudden cold shock of it against his forehead made him flinch back with a gasp. He recovered almost at once, but by then the dark blob was gone—or at least he could no longer locate it.

He drew back from the window, unsettled by the notion that the figure—if it *had* been a figure—had darted out of sight because it had seen, or sensed, him watching it. Frowning, he crossed to the chair, also from Ikea, to the left of the bed, across which he had casually tossed the bulky waterproof jacket that Janice had bought him in the hope that if they spent every Sunday walking together in the country it would give them the time she felt they needed to save their marriage. As he zipped himself into it, he heard a scuff and a thump from the room above his. He looked up instinctively, even though he knew he would see nothing but his own ceiling, and thought about his parents.

They had had that room. Number 12 wasn't it? He had a vivid memory of opening the glossy, pale-blue door at the end of his landing each morning and ascending the twisty staircase to the floor above. As he had climbed, the door had swung slowly shut behind him, like a door in a ghost story, trapping him momentarily in stuffy, creaking gloom. He had run up the remainder of the stairs, a little breathless and deliciously spooked, and had scuttled along the landing to tap lightly on his parents' door.

"Yes?" It had always been his father who had answered, his voice stern and a little irritable, as if he had been interrupted in the middle of some fiddly task. It made Skelton wonder whether his parents had been happy here, whether the holiday had been as enjoyable and memorable for them as it had for him.

The instant the question occurred to him he was surprised by it. As a child, or indeed since, he had never really given a thought to his parents' feelings. They had simply been his parents. A fixture. Unchanging. They hadn't shown their emotions; they hadn't expressed affection towards each other, or to him. It wasn't that they had been cruel or unkind. On their holiday here they had bought him things – ice cream; a stick of rock; a Frisbee to play with on the beach; a paperback book to read. They had indulged his teenage enthusiasms, as much as they were able, and had allowed him his freedom.

Thinking of his parents made him sad. The fact that he had never really got to know them was something he would now be unable to remedy. It was one of many lost opportunities in his life, the majority of which had slipped away due to his own reticence, his inability—to coin any number of clichés—to step up to the plate, take the bull by the horns, put himself in the firing line.

Janice had found this aspect of his personality appealing at first. She had thought him "mysterious." A challenge. "Still waters run deep," she had used to say, with a smile that had seemed to suggest she alone was privy to some great secret. But as time, and their marriage, had dragged on, she had become increasingly disenchanted and disillusioned with his refusal to open up. She had craved affection, and had been unable to find it. "Getting a reaction from you is like trying to squeeze blood from a stone," she had told him once—another overused analogy.

The thing was, Skelton *had* loved her. He *did* love her. He just hadn't been able to find a way to show it, or even articulate his frustration. His own emotions were as inaccessible to him as . . . as his foetal memories. And much as he had wanted to, he could no more save his marriage than he could carry out brain surgery, or build a car engine from scratch.

"You're not going out, Mr. Skelton?"

Mrs. Derry, the landlady of the B&B (though she referred to it as a 'hotel') sounded almost disapproving. Perhaps she was thinking of the effect his wet shoes and dripping clothes would have on her carpet when he returned.

"Just a quick ramble, Mrs. Derry," he replied. "Reacquaint myself with some old haunts."

She pursed her lips. She was a tall, angular, large-boned woman, whose tightly curled hair only served to accentuate, rather than soften, the squareness of her jaw.

"I'm afraid you won't find the town displayed to its best advantage in this weather."

"That's all right. I'm wearing my rose-tinted spectacles."

She peered at him as though he was being facetious, or at best obtuse, which only served to remind him that he had never been able to make jokes. His face and voice seemed unable to conjure the knowing hint of jollity that generally accompanied their delivery.

After a moment she said, "Dinner will be at seven."

"I won't be late," he assured her. "I'm looking forward to it."

When even this display of enthusiasm seemed not to flatter her he decided to withdraw. With a final nod, he stepped smartly out of the house, pulling the door closed behind him.

As soon as he turned to face the wind it sprang forward to slap and tug at his hair and clothes like an angry child, or perhaps one that was eager to show him something. Hunching his neck beneath the level of his collar he hurried towards the promenade, pausing on the wide road not to avoid a car, but to allow a fish and chip wrapper, blotched with grease, to flap past him at head height. The iron railings that stretched the length of the promenade for as far as he could see in either direction curved from the pier's entrance like a pair of outstretched arms welcoming him into an expansive embrace.

He broke into a stumbling run not because he was starved of the affection this seemed to promise, but because he thought the glass ceiling that stretched across the central cluster of cafes, stalls, shops and takeaway food emporiums—all locked and shuttered now for winter—might provide him with temporary shelter from the rain. And so it did, though the wind angling in from the sea cut along the unprotected length of the pier like a ceaseless flurry of cold, sharp arrows, each of which struck him with unerring accuracy.

Though the pier remained accessible to whoever might wish to stroll along it, the fact that it was deserted made Skelton feel like an intruder. With every one of his clomping footsteps, across wooden boards worn smooth by the passage of countless feet, he expected to hear a sharp cry of reprimand at his back.

His apprehension couldn't prevent memories that felt like magic from stirring within him, though. As a boy he had eaten candyfloss here; indeed, he had bitten into one of the most delicious things he had ever tasted, a fat hot dog that oozed fried onions smeared in ketchup over his hand. He had fed money into a Lucky Dip machine that had coughed up a flesh-coloured egg containing a yellow plastic car; he had wandered among an exhibition of mediocre waxworks; he had held on to the metal railings and turned his face up to meet the warm sun.

He had met . . . the girl.

What was her name? Skelton was appalled that at some point over the past three decades the information had eluded him. He had realized on the drive up, when he had been trawling through his old memories, that he could no longer remember.

He had the *flavour* of the girl's name in his head, though. It had been a soft, almost dull sound. Gail? Bernie? Norma? It had been full of blunt letters, not sharp ones. She hadn't been Tracey, or Susan, or Kate. Her name had been non-threatening. Almost bovine. It had partly been this that had drawn him to her.

Rain spattered on the glass ceiling above him, making it squirm. Stepping out from beneath the protective canopy at the end of the arcade, he scrunched up his mouth and eyes and rammed his hands into his side pockets as he angled his body towards the end of the pier. As the wind gnawed and slashed at him and the icy rain caused his scalp to contract like an over-tight cap, he wondered why he was here. He knew that he was running away, seeking solace, giving Janice the space and time she'd demanded in order to 'reassess' her life. But what he didn't understand was why *here*, of all places. Was this run-down little seaside town *really* the location of his happiest memories? Had a ten-day holiday with his parents when he was fourteen *really* been the pinnacle of a life spanning almost five decades?

"Excuse me. Are you all right?"

At first, when Skelton turned, the woman seemed composed almost entirely of hair. It flapped and snapped around her head like ragged black wings, or thrashing tentacles, providing little more than glimpses of her face.

He felt too melancholy to be startled, though his hands did tighten on the upper rail, the metal so cold that it seemed to burn his palm. What surprised him, initially at least, was not that the woman was here, but that *he* was; Skelton had been so preoccupied with his thoughts that he had no recollection of having reached the end of the pier, or of removing his hands from his jacket pockets to grip the uppermost rail as the sea raged beneath him.

Realising that some response was called for, he said, "Fine." And then as an afterthought: "Thank you."

The woman raised an arm and used a black-gloved hand to scoop the unruly mass of hair from her face. Now Skelton could see that she was roughly his age. She was not conventionally pretty, but attractive all the same. Her fleshy, sensual lips were half-parted as though to form a question as her green eyes held his in a steady gaze.

At last she said, "Forgive me for intruding, but . . . well, you look as though you've been crying."

"Do I?" Surprised, he unpeeled his hand from the rail and touched his cheek. Of course it was wet; he was drenched with rain. He barked a laugh. "Must be this wind, making my eyes water."

She smiled with him, but in a way that suggested sympathy rather than mutual mirth. He broke the connection between them by looking out to sea.

"Have you just arrived?" she asked.

His head snapped back to regard her. "Yes. How did you know?"

"I think you're staying where we're staying." She wafted a hand towards the shore. "Mrs. Derry's?"

"Ah." He nodded. "Are you here with your family?"

"My husband."

"Didn't he fancy braving the elements?"

Now it was her turn to break eye contact. Turning her face to the sea, she gripped the upper rail with both gloved hands as though it was the safety bar on a fun fair ride. Released from her constraining arm, her hair began to thrash wildly again. "He's not well," she replied. "He's confined to bed."

"Oh dear. I'm sorry to hear that. I hope he makes a speedy recovery."

Her reply was non-committal and after a moment Skelton slid her a sideways glance. For the first time it struck him as odd that she was here. Was it coincidence or had she followed him? But why would she? Perhaps she had sensed a kindred spirit in him? Perhaps her husband's illness was taking its toll and she was desperate for someone to talk to?

He was toying with the idea of suggesting they retreat to a café for a cup of tea when a voice called his name.

He turned. With rapid, bow-legged strides, a balding man in a dark grey overcoat was emerging from the open-ended glass-ceilinged tunnel. As he approached he scowled fiercely, as if he intended to give whoever was responsible for the weather a piece of his mind. Skelton might have guessed he was a policeman even if he hadn't spotted the distant white car with the central yellow stripe parked opposite the pier entrance.

Instantly he felt his stomach tighten, his extremities tingle, as though with the onset of fever. His immediate thought—his *only* thought—was: *Janice.*

"Yes?" he said, both admitting his identity and enquiring why he was being hailed.

"Mr. *Marcus* Skelton? Of-" The balding man gave Skelton's full address, which made Skelton—particularly in front of the woman—feel unaccountably vulnerable.

"Yes," he said again.

"Mr. Skelton, my name is Detective Inspector Parr. Might I have a word with you?"

"What about?"

DI Parr glanced at Skelton's partner. "A *private* word, if you wouldn't mind?" And then, to the woman, he said less officiously, "I'm sorry to intrude."

The woman waved away the apology. "We were merely passing the time of day." She startled Skelton by placing a hand on his arm. "Perhaps I'll see you later? At dinner?"

Skelton nodded and she left—though her touch on his arm, light and warm despite the chill of the day and the thick jacket he was wearing, lingered.

On tenterhooks, his stomach crawling with apprehension, Skelton followed DI Parr back to the promenade's entrance. Shouting into the wind and rain he asked again what it was about, but Parr only muttered something about finding somewhere warmer.

"Is it Janice?" Skelton asked.

"Who?"

"Janice. My wife. Has something happened to her?"

"Not as far as I know." Parr forged ahead, either to prevent further conversation or because he was eager to get out of the rain.

Reaching the pier entrance, Skelton was surprised when Parr, instead of requesting that Skelton get into the car, swivelled like a radar dish to face a fish and chip restaurant across the road and suggested that the two of them speak over lunch. Although Skelton was not hungry, he was too intimidated to say no, and so found himself following Parr across a road that gleamed like polished steel in the rain.

"You're not squeamish, are you?" Parr said when the two of them were seated on opposite sides of a sea green Formica tabletop. As he asked the question he rocked forward on his elbows so that Skelton could hear his low voice above the big front window beside them, which shuddered at every gust of wind.

"Why?" Skelton asked, staring at Parr through the steam rising from their plates. "Is the food here that bad?"

He was too nervous to make the joke sound like one, which was perhaps why Parr failed to smile. Instead, as he subjected his Friday Feast—extra large haddock, chips, mushy peas, bread and butter, pot of tea—to a barrage of salt, vinegar and ketchup, the DI shook his head.

"It's an odd one, that's all. Early this morning a dog walker made a discovery on the west beach." He stuffed a forkful of chips into his mouth, as if by way of a dramatic pause. As Parr chewed, Skelton helped himself to a chip from his own small portion, nibbling at it while he waited for the bulge in Parr's cheeks to transfer itself to his throat.

When it had, Parr said, "It was body parts, Mr. Skelton."

At first Skelton thought the DI was referring to the crispy end of the fish he was sawing into.

"What was?"

"The discovery. The dog walker. She found a freezer bag with a seal to keep it watertight. It contained human body parts. A hand and an eye."

"How horrible."

Parr nodded. He crunched on fried batter and washed it down with a swill of tea. "We ran DNA tests." A row of chips, speared on the tines of his fork and smothered with mushy peas, dripped greenly onto his plate. "They're yours."

"I beg your pardon?"

Parr popped the food into his mouth, chewed, swallowed. His face adopted an expression of compromise.

"At least," he continued, "that's what the results told us. We made enquiries, and when we found out you were staying at Derry's Hotel . . ." he shrugged " . . . well, naturally we feared the worst." His cutlery still clutched in his hands, he threw up his arms, causing ketchup to fly off his knife blade and fleck the window like blood. "But here you are! Larger than life! Which leaves us with something of a puzzle."

Skelton stared at the DI. "What do you mean they're mine?"

"DNA match," Skelton said around a mouthful of fish.

Skelton continued to stare, unable to shake off the impression that the passersby on the other side of the window were covertly awaiting his reaction.

"Everyone's DNA profile is unique," Parr explained. "And according to our results, those body parts belong to you."

"Then there must be some mistake," Skelton spluttered.

"Well, *obviously*. Bit of an odd one, though, eh? I mean, especially with you staying here as well. Are you a frequent visitor to our little enclave, Mr. Skelton?"

"No. The last time I was here I was fourteen. Over thirty years ago."

DI Parr tilted his head to one side. "Curiouser and curiouser."

Skelton sat back. He could no longer even maintain a pretense of wanting his chips. "Why are you telling me this, Detective Inspector?"

Again, Parr fixed his eyes on him. "Isn't it obvious?"

Skelton's mind was whirling, but the DI's scrutiny suddenly focused his thoughts. "You think I'm an imposter?"

Parr shrugged as though in apology. "It's a natural assumption, you must admit."

"But I'm not!" Skelton said. "I'm me. I can show you ID."

"Which you could have stolen from the real Marcus Skelton."

"But I *am* me!" Skelton was aware his voice had risen to a bleat that was causing heads to turn. He controlled himself with an effort. "How can I prove it to you?"

Suddenly Parr was all business-like. Although his meal was less than half-eaten he picked up his napkin and dabbed at his greasy lips. "If you'll come down to the station with me, Mr. Skelton, we can take a DNA sample, run tests." He smiled, though it didn't reach his eyes. "Don't worry. I'm sure this is nothing but a computer glitch. Records getting mixed up or some such. We may live in an age of technology, but that doesn't mean our systems are not still prone to human error."

He put his napkin down, took a final swig of tea and stood up.

"Shall we go?"

Skelton might have foregone dinner that evening if he hadn't already told Mrs. Derry how much he was looking forward to it. Despite having not had any lunch, the afternoon's ordeal had unsettled him so much that he was still struggling to muster an appetite by 7 p.m.

He was ready for a drink, though, and ordered a bottle of Merlot from the admittedly limited wine list. He sipped his first glass as his gaze shifted between the slithering greyness of rain on the long windows of the hexagonal dining room and the murky oils depicting various boats on stormy seas, which adorned the walls. It was almost certainly the proliferation of water, both real and artificially rendered, which made him think of the room's floor space as a sea of crisp white tablecloths and gleaming silver cutlery. Even the sound that filled it seemed to swell and dip like the waves, an almost ambient murmur of low-key conversation interspersed with the chink and scrape of china and metal.

Preoccupied by the efforts of the melting grey landscape outside the window to maintain a sense of itself, he sensed a presence beside him. He turned, expecting to see the spotty, painfully shy girl with braces on her teeth, who Mrs. Derry employed as a waitress, leaning forward with his chosen starter of leek and potato soup.

But it wasn't the waitress, it was the woman from the pier. From his seated position she looked impressively statuesque, her black hair, tumbling in waves over her shoulders, framing the creamy swell of cleavage above her low-cut, off-the-shoulder burgundy dress.

"Are you dining alone?" she asked.

In less than a second, Skelton's gaze ricocheted from her cleavage, to her plump lips, to the unoccupied place setting opposite him. "Er . . . yes."

"Would you care for some company?" She held up a hand, whose nails were as crimson as her mouth. "Please don't be afraid to say no if you'd rather be alone with your thoughts. I won't be offended."

When Skelton glanced beyond the woman, he gained an immediate impression that the rest of the room's occupants were hastily averting their eyes.

"Won't you be dining with . . . ?"

"My husband? No. He's too ill to join us." She sounded almost vehement.

In truth, Skelton *would* have liked to be left alone, though not because he didn't find the woman attractive. In fact, he felt drawn to her, though the effect she had on him unsettled him, made him nervous, jittery even. However he felt trapped by her request. If he refused her he would be acutely aware of the two of them dining in isolation, and of the thrumming tension that that gulf would create between them.

And so, fixing a smile on his face and waving at the opposite chair, he said, "In that case . . . by all means . . ."

A heady, musky fragrance billowed from her as she sat down. Almost involuntarily Skelton felt his prick stiffening in his pants. Adjusting his position slightly, he cleared his throat. "Would you like some wine?"

Her eyes seemed to dance. "Only if you allow me to buy the second bottle."

Again Skelton felt his smile was enforced rather than natural. He felt a muscle jerk involuntarily in his cheek as if pushed beyond its limits. "Perhaps one will be enough."

"Perhaps." Her own smile seemed to come easily. "But the night is young."

Once she had ordered her food—smoked salmon for starter and pork medallions for main course—she asked, "How was your afternoon?"

It was clearly a loaded question, which she acknowledged by chuckling throatily. "Please feel free to tell me to mind my own business."

He gulped wine and found that his answering smile was easier this time. "It was . . . interesting."

"Good interesting or bad interesting?"

Reluctant thought he initially was to respond, he was surprised by how liberating he found it telling her what had occurred with Parr, and afterwards at the station. She was an attentive and sympathetic listener, and as he spoke, haltingly at first and then more easily as he lubricated his throat with wine (she matching him sip for sip), he felt his spine straightening, the stiffness in his neck and shoulders fading away.

"Poor you. What an ordeal," she said when he had finished.

"So you believe I'm not an imposter then?"

Although they had only just finished their starters, they were already on their second bottle of wine and her eyes had become dewy. "Of course I do."

"Why? You don't know me from Adam."

"I pride myself on being a good judge of character. You're a good man, Marcus. A gentle man. I know it."

He blushed. "I'm not sure my wife would agree."

"Then she's an idiot."

He blinked in surprise, and immediately she looked contrite.

"I'm sorry, that was uncalled for."

He felt as though he should be leaping to Janice's defence, but as usual his response was half-hearted, almost apologetic. "She's had a lot to put up with . . ."

"I'm sure you both have. It takes two to tango, as they say."

He grunted non-commitally, then asked, "What about your husband? How long have the two of you been together?"

"It seems like forever." Her laughter was brittle. "Sorry again. I shouldn't be so mean. But illness does get wearing. On both partners."

"What does he suffer from?"

She wafted a hand, as if to say, *Who knows?* "He's wasting away, poor dear." She snatched up the bottle and refilled both their glasses, which all but drained it. "One more with our main course?"

Again his response was half-hearted. "I don't normally drink that much . . ."

"Me neither. But let's push the boat out. We're on holiday."

When their pork medallions arrived—they had both ordered the same thing—the woman picked up the bottle and waggled it at the girl with the braces, who looked instantly alarmed. "Another one of these, dear."

As the girl scuttled away, Skelton was struck by a sudden revelation.

"I'm sorry . . . I still don't know your name."

The woman pouted her plump lips. "Perhaps I'd prefer to maintain my air of mystery." Then she rocked back in her chair with a laugh so shrill that heads turned. "Your face! I'm sorry, it's mean of me to tease. My name's Belinda."

She reached across the table, offering a jokey handshake, which he accepted automatically. The touch of her skin on his sent pleasurable ripples through him. Her name seemed to ripple too, as if it was echoing out from the past. He felt fuzzy-edged memories becoming more solid, slotting into place. He stared at the woman, then averted his gaze when she met his eyes with her own. There was something in the look she gave him; something candid, knowing.

"Say what you're thinking," she said.

"I'm sorry?"

"I can see the cogs whirring away, but you're keeping whatever you're thinking bottled up inside. Why not just say it? I won't be offended. And I'm fairly unshockable. In fact, my reaction might surprise you."

He felt his face getting hot. He took a gulp of wine. What was she *expecting* him to say? He put down his glass a little too heavily. "I'm just . . . well, it sounds weird, but . . . we haven't met before, have we? Before today, I mean?"

Her face was almost avid. "When were you thinking we had?"

"I don't. That is . . . I'm probably mistaken. Have you been here before?"

"Not since I was a girl."

His heart leaped. "How old were you?"

"I don't remember. Twelve, thirteen . . . perhaps older. Why? Do you think we might have been teenage sweethearts?"

He reddened. He knew it was silly, but he couldn't help feeling disappointed that she didn't remember. He cut into his pork with a vigour he hoped would suggest that the thought was nothing but idle conjecture.

"I came here when I was fourteen. I met a girl who I think was called Belinda."

"You think?"

"I'm pretty sure. She . . ." he glanced at her, then quickly away. She was staring at him again. The wine had stained her lips dark red. His voice dropped to a mumble. "She meant a lot to me at the time."

He pushed meat into his mouth and chewed. For the next few seconds he pretended to remain preoccupied with the vegetables on his plate. There was silence from the woman. From Belinda. He wondered what she was thinking.

Finally she said softly, "Life is full of might-have-beens, isn't it?"

By the time they had eaten dessert, finished their third bottle of wine, and washed it all down with a pot of coffee, the dining room was almost deserted. Even so, they left separately, at Skelton's suggestion.

"We don't want people to talk, do we?" he mumbled.

"Let them," Belinda said, throwing a withering glance around the room. When she turned back her face immediately softened. "You're very gallant, Marcus. A knight in shining armour."

"I don't know about that," he said, blushing.

"You put yourself down too much. You know that?"

He shrugged.

"I'll go first, shall I?" she said, standing up. Despite the amount of wine they had drunk she seemed remarkably sure-footed, which led Skelton to wonder, perhaps uncharitably, whether her husband's illness had caused her to gravitate towards the bottle a little too often. She stepped around the table and leaned towards him. He looked up at her instinctively and she kissed him on the side of his closed mouth.

"Good night," she murmured. "Thank you for a lovely evening."

"Good night," he said, his throat tight.

Back in his room, he stripped off, lay on his bed and masturbated, thinking of her. He felt sordid and ashamed, though not enough for it to affect the uncharacteristic strength of his orgasm, his semen spurting as high as his throat. He cleaned himself up using tissues from the box beside the bed, then fell into a doze, still naked and spread-eagled on top of the covers. He woke once in the night, hearing thumps and bumps from the room above him, possibly even a sharp but quickly stifled cry of pain. But his mind was thick with wine and sleep, and after dragging the duvet over his cold body he fell quickly asleep again.

The next morning he was showered and dressed before any of the other guests had stirred. He sneaked downstairs and was out of the house without alerting Mrs. Derry or any of her breakfast staff, all of who were clattering about in the kitchen. After last night he needed to clear his head, and not only because of the wine. He couldn't stop thinking about Belinda, couldn't stop analyzing her body language and everything she had said to him—which, in his muggy, befuddled state, seemed laden with significance.

If she *was* the girl he had met over thirty years ago, was she aware of the past link between them and was simply being coy by pretending not to remember? But how *could* she be the same person? The coincidence was too great to be acceptable, unless she had manipulated the situation in some way.

But if so, it suggested not only a prior knowledge of his life, but of his movements and intentions, which was clearly impossible. How could she have known he was coming here? He had told no one—indeed, his decision had been made on a whim—besides which, hadn't she said that she and her husband had checked into Derry's Hotel before him?

Of course, she could have been lying—in fact, she may not even *have* a husband—but why would she? Was she merely a stranger who had fixated on him? Was she mentally unstable? Or was she what she claimed to be—a lonely, perhaps sexually frustrated woman with a sick husband, who was seeking a little freedom from the daily grind by way of companionship, perhaps even intimacy?

Skelton had half-expected her to be waiting by his door when he had followed her up the stairs last night. When she hadn't been he had felt half-relieved, half-disappointed. He had been unable to help wondering whether he had fallen short of her expectations in some way, whether he had been deemed somehow unsuitable. He had dreamed of her last night. In the dream she had prowled around his bed, enticing but forever out of reach.

It was the sight of the police cars that dragged him from his reverie. There were four of them, in a line beyond the pier entrance, parked alongside the promenade. Uniformed officers were milling about, preventing sightseers—not that there were many at this hour—from descending the steps to the sands. A further deterrent were the flimsy barriers of yellow tape printed with the words POLICE CRIME SCENE DO NOT CROSS, which had been erected across every potential access point to the beach.

Skelton, who had been walking towards all this activity without initially registering it, came to an abrupt halt. When DI Parr suddenly appeared at the top of the stone steps and ducked beneath the tape barrier he considered turning round and heading in the opposite direction. But then, as if Skelton had given off some sort of signal, Parr looked up and spotted him. Skelton had no choice now but to approach the Detective Inspector; anything else would have looked odd or suspicious. Resisting the urge to raise a hand in greeting, he walked across, trying to keep his movements as casual as possible.

"Good morning, Mr. Skelton," DI Parr said with a hint of smugness, as if he had caught Skelton out in some way. "This is quite a coincidence."

"I was out for a stroll and saw the cars," Skelton tried not to mumble.

"Bit early to be out, isn't it?"

Skelton gestured at his head. "I needed some fresh air. I had a bit too much wine last night."

"Celebrating, were we?"

"Not at all. Just . . ." Skelton couldn't think what to add. Parr stared at him, as if alert for any sign that might incriminate the other man.

Skelton looked away, nodding towards the police tape stretched across the entrance to the steps and the uniformed officers standing guard. "What's going on?"

"Developments, Mr. Skelton," Parr said. "I trust you have no immediate plans to leave our fair town?"

Skelton shook his head. "I'll be here for a few more days, at least."

Parr bared his teeth in a grin. "Glad to hear it. Plenty of time to chat then before you go."

"Will we need to?" Skelton asked, and immediately wondered whether his question made him sound facetious.

"Well, I assume you'll want to know the results of your DNA test?"

"Oh. Yes. Though I know they'll confirm I'm me."

Although Parr smiled with apparent warmth, Skelton found himself repressing a shudder. "I'm sure they will, Mr. Skelton."

Without knowing why, Skelton had been half-dreading encountering Belinda at breakfast, though when she didn't appear that morning he was disappointed. He wondered whether she was avoiding him. Perhaps she felt that the wine had made her too indiscreet last night, though he couldn't specifically recall anything either of them had said that they needed to be embarrassed about. He worked his way with stolid efficiency through his full English, then trudged upstairs. He ought to make plans for the day, though just now his room felt like a refuge.

Once in it, though, he felt nothing but restless. He crossed to the window, then back again to the bed. He perched on its edge, bouncing gently on the springs, and stared up at the ceiling.

All at once he came to a decision. He stood up, crossed the room and stepped out on to the landing.

As he approached the door at the end—as glossy as he remembered, albeit cream now rather than pale blue—he told himself it was perfectly reasonable of him to check up on her. If her husband was there he would simply explain that he and Belinda had been chatting last night over dinner, and that when she hadn't turned up for breakfast that morning he had become a little concerned, given her husband's illness. He would ask if the two of them needed anything, if he could help them in any way. Surely Belinda's husband wouldn't be suspicious of his motives? He had nothing to be suspicious *about*. If anything, he would almost certainly be grateful. Perhaps he and Skelton might even become friends.

Even so, he felt nervous as the door to the room once occupied by his parents, and now by Belinda and her husband, came into sight. The twisting staircase and upper landing were just as he remembered them; even the door at the bottom of the stairs had creaked shut behind him, as it had always used to. He raised a hand, hesitated a moment, then knocked on the door.

"Yes?" said his father sternly—though only in his imagination.

In reality his knock was answered with silence. Skelton leaned forward and put his ear to the door. He knocked again. Did he hear a shuffling thump from inside the room—or was it from elsewhere in the house?

"Belinda?" he said, and immediately wondered whether he was being too familiar. If he and Janice had been in that room, and an unknown man had knocked on the door and spoken *his* wife's name, how might that make him feel?

He tried to remedy the situation—if, indeed, it needed remedying. "It's Mr. Skelton from downstairs. We met yesterday. I just thought I'd pop up to see if . . . if you were both all right."

If there *had* been a sound from the room, it had faded to silence now. Suddenly an image came to Skelton's mind: Belinda crouched on the other side of the door, facing a vague figure who was half propped up in bed, a finger pressed fiercely to her lips. It was so vivid a picture that Skelton felt unsettled by it. He waited a moment longer and then tiptoed away, taking the twisting stairs slowly so as not to make them creak.

Although it had started to drizzle again, he decided to go for a walk. Leaving the B&B he turned right, away from the pier and the police activity beyond it. After a quarter of a mile the town's buildings petered out, as did the beach, the strip of grey sand squeezed increasingly thinner between the incoming tide and a jumble of craggy rock formations until it disappeared altogether. The rocks, black as fire damage, swelled gradually into a curving cliff face that enclosed the bay. A coastal path, edged with spiny marram grass and tangled clumps of tough, springy bracken, formed a deep groove that meandered across the top of the cliffs. The path sloped uphill for at least two miles before levelling out at the top, from where, Skelton supposed, you could turn to see the town spread out below you. Despite the weather, he decided to walk as far as he could, in the hope that the psychological baggage he carried with him would become increasingly lighter the more distance he put between himself and civilization. His eventual hope was that if he walked far enough it would become entirely weightless, leaving him free.

It was a fanciful notion, but it was nice to entertain it nonetheless. It was nice to be surrounded by the drizzle too. Although it was an isolating experience, he felt protected by it, rather than besieged. Perhaps being alone was his natural state; certainly he felt calmer, less anxious, when he had no one to answer to. What was that old saying? Hell is other people. Much as he loved Janice, perhaps the biggest mistake of his life had been to allow himself to become involved. By doing so, he had ruined not only his life, but Janice's too.

Had it come to that? *Were* their lives ruined beyond repair? Skelton felt guilty about the fact that in the early days of their marriage, Janice had expressed a desire to have children; a desire which had subsequently dwindled and died, perhaps due to his lack of enthusiasm.

Was it too late for her now? Was it too late for both of them? How old was she? Forty five? Struggling up the path, he glanced ahead of him, and saw a standing stone at the crest of the slope, silhouetted against the murky sky.

Suddenly his right foot, coming down on a nub of rock slick with lichen, slid from under him. He stumbled, would have fallen on his knees if he hadn't put his hands out to break his fall. Within seconds he had regained his balance. He straightened, rubbing his hands together before holding them palm-up to the drizzle to clean them. Then he froze.

The standing stone had gone.

Coldness prickled through him, as if the drizzle had seeped into his body. But almost immediately his mind clicked back on to its rational course. He must have been mistaken; it must have been a person, not a standing stone, he had seen. He had only glanced at it, and the reason it had seemed featureless was because the sky was so murky it stripped light, and therefore detail, from everything.

And now that Skelton recalled, hadn't he subconsciously thought of the stone as womanly? He had assumed it was because he was thinking about Janice, but perhaps that wasn't the case. Scrambling up the slope, he called out, "Hello?"

Only the hissing of rain in the undergrowth greeted him. But when he reached the top of the slope, didn't he glimpse a dark blur of movement on the path ahead, just before it bobbed behind a protruding thicket of bracken at the next corner?

"Hello?" he shouted again. "Anyone there?" It occurred to him that if the figure *was* a woman, then she might be alarmed by his presence, and more particularly by his apparent over-eagerness to make her acquaintance.

He paused on the path, breathing hard. He had thought he might hear her brushing through the undergrowth as she progressed up and along the muddy path ahead of him, but the persistent white noise of drizzle muffled all other sound.

Should he actively pursue her? If he did, it would only be to satisfy his curiosity. And then would come the awkwardness of explanations and apologies, of exchanging comments about the terrain and the weather simply to be polite. Plus, of course, they'd be faced with the prickly question of how they should proceed from this point—together or singly? If together they would be forced to converse, because silence between strangers is always embarrassing; and if singly, it would be like a mutual snub, each of them making clear that neither relished, nor desired, the other's company.

Skelton told himself that none of this should matter, and yet somehow it did. As a result, he decided to wait a few minutes, give the woman time to move ahead. Because the foliage grew to chest height on either side of the path, and because frequent outcroppings of jagged black rock rose up to form mini valleys along the route, Skelton was not entirely sure how close he was to the summit of the cliffs.

As it turned out, he was closer than he thought. After waiting for five minutes, he began walking again, and a few minutes after that he emerged from between clumps of bracken to find the sky, grey and marbled like old cheese, expanding before him. He clenched his teeth as the drizzle, propelled by a wind now unencumbered by obstacles, flew at him almost horizontally, stinging his face. To his left, in his peripheral vision, he glimpsed movement.

He turned, squinting against the rain, and saw a figure standing at the edge of the promontory a hundred or so metres away. The figure was silhouetted against the mist-grey sea that seemed to merge seamlessly with the sky on the horizon. Though the figure had its back to him, Skelton felt an instant jolt of recognition at the sight of the masses of wind-swept black hair that flapped and writhed around its head.

"Belinda!" he shouted, moving towards her, but his voice was snatched away by the wind.

He was still fifty metres from the woman when she spread her arms out wide and dropped forward, disappearing over the cliff.

Skelton screamed and broke into a run, though all at once his legs felt as if they were made of loosely connected splints of wood. He couldn't have seen what he thought he had seen. It was a mistake, a trick; perhaps the woman (*Belinda?*) had known he was there, and simply wanted to shock him for some reason.

He reached the promontory and fell to his knees, shaking as if with fever. He felt so faint, so uncoordinated, that he couldn't trust himself not to stumble forward and follow the woman over the edge. Experiencing a sudden attack of vertigo, he dropped on to his front and crawled the last few metres, using his fingers to drag himself across the soft, wet ground. Craning his neck, he peered over the cliff, dreading—and already flinching from—what he might see.

There was nothing. Nothing but white, foamy waves swirling around the black rocks far below.

Had he been somehow mistaken? Or had the woman's body already been dragged out to sea? He looked further out, fearful of glimpsing something dark and shapeless bobbing in the water, but the sea beyond the shoreline was like grey, unbroken skin.

After a few moments he slithered back from the cliff edge and pushed himself, with difficulty, to his feet. He swayed and shuddered like a drunk, his upper body hunched over. What he had seen—thought he'd seen—had sapped the energy from him, turned him into a shambling wreck. He began to stumble back the way he had come, desperate to fetch help, or at least alert the authorities. He wished now that he hadn't consistently and stubbornly refused to buy a mobile phone, despite Janice's exhortations.

How he managed to get back to town he had no idea. It seemed to take an age, and he spent the majority of the journey slipping and stumbling, half-falling down the path, his eyes blinded by rain and tears, his ability to think obliterated by the pulse of shock filling his head.

Eventually, however, he made it, and ran all the way along the promenade until he reached the place where he had spoken to Parr several hours earlier. There was only a single panda car there now, and two uniformed officers guarding the steps, one of whom was taking shelter beneath the awning of a seafront café, sipping tea from a Styrofoam cup. He emerged only when Skelton pounded to a halt in front of his colleague and doubled over as if about to be sick. In truth, Skelton thought he *was* going to be sick; it was only when he stopped running that he realised how exhausted he was. His head was pounding, his lungs were burning, and beneath his several layers of clothing his body was pouring with sweat. When one of the officers spoke to him—he had no idea which—the voice seemed to reach him through a long, echoing tunnel: "Are you all right, sir?"

Pulling himself together with an effort, Skelton spat out his story in disjointed segments, as if they were chunks of glass. He had to repeat himself several times, and answer a great many questions, to make himself understood, but at last, at his behest, the two officers agreed to inform Parr.

By the time the DI arrived, Skelton was sitting at a table inside the café whose awning the police officer had been sheltering beneath, his hands curled around a mug of strong hot coffee. Steam rose from his hair and clothes as he dried out beside a wall-mounted heater, but he was still shivering. Though his thoughts were mostly turned inward, he knew that the café owner was eyeing him suspiciously, and had only allowed him to take refuge in the café on the condition that one of the police officers remain on the premises. What he must look like to alarm the café owner Skelton had no idea—not that he really cared.

DI Parr sat opposite him and spoke softly. "Mr. Skelton?"

Skelton's eyes flickered to regard him.

"Mr. Skelton, I understand from my officers that you've had a very distressing experience. Now, I know you've already told them your story, but I'd be grateful if you could repeat to me what you claim to have seen this afternoon."

Skelton told his story again, quietly and more coherently this time. When he had done Parr excused himself and went away to inform the coastguard and make enquiries. Eventually he returned and sat down. Without preamble he said, "Mr. Skelton, you claim that this woman, *Belinda*, is staying in the same hotel as you?"

Skelton nodded. "With her sick husband, yes. They're in the room above mine."

"And you're quite sure about that?"

Skelton stared into Parr's eyes. "Yes. At least . . . it's what she told me. Why?"

Parr sighed and sat back. "According to Mrs. Derry, the owner and manager of the hotel, the top floor is currently unoccupied. Furthermore she says that there is no woman matching the description you gave us staying in the hotel, with or without a sick husband. Neither did Mrs. Derry recognise the name 'Belinda'." He shrugged. "It seems you've been hoodwinked, Mr. Skelton."

Skelton felt as if something was unwinding inside him. "But . . . I had dinner with her last night."

"That's as maybe—but the woman you describe is not a resident at the Derry Hotel."

Skelton felt panicky; he had to resist an urge to grip Parr's sleeve. "But you do believe me, don't you? You do believe she exists?"

"I have no reason not to," Parr said carefully.

"Even though you still think I might be an imposter?"

Parr shook his head. "The results of the DNA test came through earlier today. I'm satisfied that you're who you claim to be."

"So what about the . . . things you found on the beach?"

Parr grimaced. "Currently unidentified. The earlier results must have been wrong. As I suggested before, a computer error."

Skelton thought of the uniformed officers outside, of the police tape stretched across all access points to the beach. He was still struggling to fight down the feeling of panic inside him. "What about this morning? What did you find?"

Parr looked at him shrewdly, narrowing his eyes. Then he shrugged and said, "More male body parts. Sealed in plastic freezer bags like before. There was a foot in one. A tongue and a . . . a more intimate part of the anatomy in another."

"So who do they belong to?"

Again Parr shrugged. "I wouldn't like to speculate. The inquiry is ongoing."

Skelton slumped in his seat. He clenched his fists to stop shudders from rippling through him. "I'm cold and wet," he said. "I'd like to return to my hotel now."

Parr looked surprised, but he raised a hand and gestured vaguely towards the door. "Certainly, Mr. Skelton. You're free to go whenever you like."

Back at the B&B Skelton went up to his room, stripped off his jacket and dropped it on the floor. Grabbing his towel from the rack over the radiator he sat down on the edge of the bed and rubbed at his wet hair. He felt so sapped by all that had happened that even this simple yet momentarily vigorous action enervated him. Allowing the towel to slip limply to the floor, he sank back on to the bed, arms stretched out like the woman (*Belinda?*) who had dropped like a diver off the edge of the cliff.

He stared up at the ceiling, watching the remains of a cobweb, clotted with dust, quiver on the light fitting. From the room above he heard three deliberate thumps, as if someone was trying to attract his attention, followed by a groan.

Echoing the groan, he pushed himself into a sitting position. His heart thumped hard, as if even this amount of activity was putting a strain on him. He stared up at the ceiling until his eyes started to ache, but the sound was not repeated. With another groan he rose to his feet and clumped heavily across the room to the door.

The B&B was so silent as he stepped out on to the landing that he might have believed he was the only person in the building. Slowly, as if moving underwater, he plodded along the landing to the cream door at the end. After opening it he began to ascend the twisting staircase that lay beyond, his breath rattling at the base of his throat, his leg muscles straining. The door slowly swung shut behind him, enfolding him in gloom. A minute later he reached the upper landing. He crossed to room 12 and raised his hand to knock on the door.

Before he could do so, he heard a sound coming from inside. A sigh? Or perhaps a whispered invitation to enter? Unclenching his fist he lowered his arm, wrapped his hand around the door handle and twisted. There was a grinding clunk as the latch disengaged. He pushed the door inward and stepped forward.

The room beyond was wreathed in shadow, only a few slivers of light leaking in around the edges of the closed curtains over the single window. The window was directly opposite the door through which Skelton had entered, but the main focus of the room was to the right of that, tucked into an alcove. Here was a bed, and what appeared to be a figure in it. Skelton could make out a dark hump of bedclothes, and the blurred shadowy oval of a head creating a depression in the centre of a faint glimmer of white pillow. Reluctant to relinquish his grip on the doorknob, he leaned forward.

"Hello?" he hissed.

The bedclothes shifted. From the oval of the head came an inarticulate groan.

Skelton took another step into the room.

"Are you all right? Do you need help?"

Another rustle of bedclothes. Another groan. Heart thumping, Skelton crossed to the window, tugged back one of the curtains.

The light was grainy, as though flecked with dust motes. The air was thick, stale. Trembling, Skelton turned from the window to confront whatever was in the bed.

It was a man, and he was shuddering as though with fever. A bandage wrapped around his head was slanted down on one side to cover his left eye, from which a brownish liquid had seeped, staining the white gauze. From the neck down the man's body was covered with a thin white sheet, which was smeared and splotched with dark stains. With a mounting, dream-like sense of horror, Skelton crossed to the bed and pulled the sheet aside. Though he opened his mouth to scream, the shock that seized him rendered him unable to do so.

The man was naked, and incomplete. Blood-stained bandages covered the stump of his left hand and right foot. More bandages were wrapped around his mid-riff and upper thighs to create a sort of nappy, the front of which, where the bulge of his genitals should be, was dark with blood. The sheet beneath him was similarly blood-stained—sopping in places. Clearly the man's horrific wounds had been bandaged not in the hope that he might recover from them, but simply so that he wouldn't die from them too soon.

Sickened with horror and pity, Skelton returned his attention to the man's face. The man opened his mouth and gave another gurgling, inarticulate groan, and now Skelton could see why he had been unable to form words, to call for help.

His tongue had been cut out.

Skelton opened his mouth to offer words of comfort, of reassurance, but before he could say anything the man suddenly reached out with his remaining hand—his right—and grabbed Skelton's wrist. Skelton's instinctive response was to jerk away with a cry of revulsion, but he forced himself to remain where he was, and even reached out to place his own right hand over the man's.

And then he froze. He stared at the hand that was gripping his wrist. As a boy he had fallen from a tree and sustained a gash on his hand that had eventually become a ridge of white scar tissue, shaped like a question mark, beneath the knuckle of his third finger. Impossibly the man had an identical scar in the same place. Slowly, with a sense of dawning realization, Skelton raised his head and peered at the man's face once again.

Because of the bandage wrapped around the man's head and eye, Skelton hadn't seen it at first, but now it was so evident that it couldn't be *unseen*. The man's face might be pale and etched with pain, his lips and chin flecked with blood from his mutilated tongue, but Skelton was in no doubt whatsoever that the man in the bed was him; that he and this poor creature were one and the same.

He could see from the expression in the man's remaining eye that he knew Skelton had finally realised the truth—and not only that, but that he was grateful for the fact. The victim opened his mouth and gave another gurgling groan, and this time Skelton heard an appeal in it, a plea—not for help, but for something else, something more merciful than mercy itself.

All his life Skelton had shunned responsibility, and even now his instinct was to fetch someone who might be better equipped to deal with this situation: DI Parr or Mrs. Derry.

But there *was* no one better equipped. This was *his* life. *His* decision. And it was time that he finally faced up to that.

Carefully, gently, he slid the pillow from underneath the man's head.

"It's all right," he told him. "The pain will be over soon. I promise."

Then, with love, he placed the pillow over the man's face and pressed down as hard as he could.

FURTHEREST

KAARON WARREN

As kids we'd dare each other to go further and further into the dunes each day. You couldn't come back until you found something, some proof you were there: A cigarette butt, a page from a book, a shoe, a ribbon. We always found something. I cheated often, tucking things into my swimming costume so I wouldn't have to travel too far. I didn't want to stumble on a dead boy, but I didn't want anyone saying I couldn't do it because I was a girl.

We'd been going to this beach every year since I was seven. There were four houses lined up, with pathways of sand between each one. The houses were raised, enough so we could squeeze under there on really hot days and drink lemonade and eat the icecreams our dad bought for us from the van.

We were called House 1.

All four houses were identical; painted blue, full of glass, open and airy. It was like a second home to us and the families in the other houses our second neighbours.

Good and bad.

Four houses, four boat houses, four families, lined up.

From the beach you'd think *isn't that nice.* You'd think *lovely families getting along.*

That's what you'd think.

Some years there were dozens of us there. Other years there were just a few. It was always a mix of fun, boredom, fear, and fast food. Sun and sea. Just the smell of suntan lotion can evoke those early years, when things were simple and your only responsibility was to wash the sand off your feet before you went inside.

We got ours cheap because those two boys were murdered in the dunes and no one wanted their kids nearby. Dad was a cop and taught caution and self-defence; no one would get hold of us. But the dunes still terrified us. The way you were blocked off, alone. No one could hear you.

We'd tell stories of murderers and lost boys, of ghosts that made you blind, or made you so sad you wanted to go to sleep forever. Jason thought he knew more than the rest of us because his dad found the bodies, but we'd all heard the story. His dad would tell us if he was drunk on the beach and none of the mums were there to stop him. I first heard the story when I was 8.

Jason and his dad were House 2. He always told it the same way but each time, as I grew older and more worldly, I understood more.

At 8, all that made sense were the boys and their bodies and the dunes.

The Vietnam War was on, but he didn't go, even though he was 20, nearly 21. He'd dropped out of Uni, finding himself, he said. His eyesight was poor and he was woefully overweight, like Jason. Cruel children (me. My brothers Bernard and Gerard) called them The Beach Balls. I loved my brothers and did everything they did. Bernard, the oldest, known for acting without thinking which wasn't fair because really he thought too much. And Gerard, only 18 months older than me, was funny as fuck from the moment he realised sticking his toes in his mouth made people laugh.

Jason's dad didn't care who listened. He told the story word for word, every time. "There were three of us that day. Me, my best mate Nick, and Kate." Kate was House 3. "I wouldn't normally have got a girl like Kate. She thought of me as a brother. A nuisance. But so many of them were shipped out. We had what? Three mates die over there. Two of her brothers were there. They were fit. Not shit like me. Shitness runs in our family, sorry, Jason. So I was 20, she was 17, and she'd barely have a bar of me. She was hanging out though because my mate Nick was heading over and that made him a hero. I tried to get him to do the conscientious objector thing, keep him home. But he wouldn't. And he was fit, strong. Kate liked him but she was too girl-next-door for him. Too boring. We'd been smoking, but not much, and we'd had a few beers. The beach was crowded and Nick and I were getting 'the look'. People gave it to you when they saw you having fun. Because we had mates. They had sons over there fighting, and we were having fun. So you got the look.

"We piled a few more beers and a ton of ice in an esky (even at the beach you gotta have cold beer) and Kate chucked in some leftover sausages and we headed out into the dunes where no one went.

"There were ghosts in there or kiddy-fiddlers, depending on who warned you, so people kept away.

"We went in. We walked until we couldn't hear voices anymore then plunked ourselves down. Kate had a towel and Nick sat on it with her, so I sat on the esky, facing the direction of the water.

"At first I thought it was a pink crab. Four legs poking out of the sand. A pretty big crab. Nick and Kate were sitting close and that shat me so I thought I'd dig out the crab, drop it in between them.

"I scrabbled in the sand, but realised quickly it wasn't a crab.

"It was a hand.

"A boy's hand.

"I swore and Kate and Nick noticed at last. I'm scrabbling in the sand and they're just laughing at me, cacking themselves at my fat arse in the air, and I'm sweaty and gross.

"They stopped laughing when I dug the boy's body out.

"Nick was the one who fell apart, chucking up all over the place, crying like a little baby.

"He ran off, left us there, scared of ghosts or that the killer was still around. I guarded the bodies while Kate went for help. We knew they'd believe her over me and we didn't want the birds to get at the bodies. They were already squawking overhead.

"You've never heard silence like it, once the birds took off. Not just silence but the negative of noise. The sea, I could hear that, like a heavy-breathing giant, and another breath, I thought behind me, someone watching me, but there wasn't anyone.

"We found out later the boys swallowed weed killer. Stole it from the Hardware Store, hid in the dunes and swallowed it."

And he said, "That night me and Kate gave each other what comfort we could."

I didn't figure out what he meant by that until years later.

He always ended with, "So don't go into the dunes, kids. You never know who's lurking in there."

Then one of the other adults would bring him a beer (men) or try to get him to go inside (women) and we'd be left to scare each other stupid with stories of murder and our parents would read us *Winnie the Pooh* to help us sleep without nightmares.

His friend Nick survived the war but drowned on our beach a few years later. Suicide, some people reckoned, so all our parents were terrified of it, *are you all right*? if you spent five minutes of solitude. The thought never crossed my mind. "I was too busy stuffing my face," Jason's dad liked to say. "Sitting there. Eating Spag Bol. I didn't even notice he was gone. All they found of him was his shoes on the beach. His dog tags tucked into them."

Jason's house was always overgrown. The other men would be out the front, round the side, keeping on top of things, but Jason's dad let his weeds grow. No one cared except Mr. White, the old man in House 4.

He was a man of habit and routine. He wore same clothes every day; dark brown thigh length shorts, a pale green stripy polo shirt. A panama hat he never took off.

The beach almost killed him, with its relaxation of time.

The other adults loosened up when we were there, some of them too much. Jason's mum Kate was always in swimmers, tiny bikinis that made us all feel uncomfortable, although I had fantasies for years about her pubic hair peeking out.

The dads joked and played and rarely shouted at us.

Mr. White started coming a couple of years after we did. He didn't have a wife. Rumour had it she'd died in childbirth. His son only came once, I think, and had no interest in any of us. He was about my age but far more independent, heading out for hours up the beach, into the water. Mum said it was because he had no mother and his father wasn't much. We called the old man Grandpa Sheet because he was pretty old to be a dad and he was white as a sheet. White as a ghost. He was the one who taught us the dune game. "Go further in," he'd say. "See what you find. There might be treasure in there, washed up. A reward for the one who goes the furtherest." But he never gave out any rewards, and we never found treasure. Once (and the parents deny this but it did happen) he put a sheet over his head and appeared around our boatshed, where we were hanging out, smoking. The boys from House 3 had jobs before the rest of us and were generous with their money.

Grandpa Sheet appeared, pretending to be a ghost and nearly died laughing as we scattered like cockroaches.

I was the one who found the first memorial, when I was sixteen, there with friends. My parents still owned the place. Mum and Dad didn't mind me and my friends using it; I guess they thought I was safer there than the streets of Sydney.

Probably true.

We were there most weekends and it probably did save my life. Not because of the damage I could do myself, but because of the damage others could do to me.

It was off season so mostly no one else was there except Jason's dad, who was always there, and bloody Jason, who wasn't as fat as he used to be but annoyingly clingy and boastful.

Jason's parents were long since split up. His mum was on TV, presenting a beauty segment on afternoon TV. She never came any more. His dad spent most of his time on the beach, making shell necklaces and researching the great Australian novel, he reckoned, a crime novel. Jason looked more like his dad that his mum which was a shame for him because his mum was gorgeous.

House 3 only ever came in the holidays. They took it in turns; it seemed like there were hundreds of them. They were the most normal people you'd ever meet. The worst thing that ever happened to them was Jason's mum Kate having him when she was a teenager. All the kids my age were doing well, so normal. Married, kids, and you see them here, running around like we used to. Generation after generation, rolling in like waves. Venturing towards the dunes but lacking our bravery so mostly hovering on the edges. "It's like going back in the past," Mum said. "Like no time has passed at all."

And Grandad Sheet in House 4 was always there. No one liked him much. He was one of those too-friendly old men, always carrying coins and shit, handing things out. You'd watch him carefully. Dad taught us to watch everyone carefully and be polite. We warned each other not to go into Grandad Sheet's boathouse. It was full of ghosts, we told each other. You could see the shine of them through the window some mornings and light where it shouldn't be some evenings.

One morning, after we'd taken a quick dip in the chill water to wash away hangovers, Grandad Sheet stood waiting for us on the beach, wearing his usual uniform; brown shorts, stripy polo, panama hat. I almost felt sorry for him but not so much I would talk to him.

He waved to us. "You're old enough to help me finish this wine," he called out, but we'd rather stay sober than that. Anyway, Jason's dad bought us whatever we wanted. It didn't make us like Jason any more, but it meant we let him hang out with us whenever he showed up. We had to listen to Jason's dad's stories, though. The dead boys one, and the when Nick died one, and the *why I lost my job* one, and the *why I left Jason's mother* one.

"A case of beer for the one who goes furtherest," Grandad Sheet said, nodding his head at the dunes.

The boys went off, because we were all out of money and this was beer without obligation or story. I followed, calling for them to wait. Part of the fun of the dunes was you had to be scared going in, so I reminded them about the murders, the bodies, the maybe ghosts.

"That's all bullshit," one of my friends said. I don't remember his name; I don't remember any of them.

We went further ('furtherer,' Grandad Sheet would say) than I'd been before. I felt safe with these friends; they lacked the imagination to be really scared, and were funny whenever they could be. Jason hung back. He hated the dunes (maybe because of times my brothers had threatened to bury him out here) but wasn't going to miss out on anything.

Then we saw it.

We knew it was a memorial rather than a grave, but that didn't stop any of us from imagining a body there. We could see the affect the weather had had on the cross, the flowers, and we imagined bleached bones buried beneath the sand, looking more like driftwood each day.

The wooden cross must have been bright purple, once. It was very straight; buried deep in the sand to keep it upright. The paint had all peeled off, leaving just the stain of its colour on the wood, which was peeling splinters.

There had been decals, once, on the three outward reaching edges of the cross. Only the glue was left, petrified against the wood; the shape of a flower, perhaps, and a ball-shaped thing which could have been the world, and something which may have been a bird.

Remnants of the name were there, but like Piglet's "Trespasser's Will," the original meaning was obscured.

"Got Her," Jason read. "Got who?" which was the funniest joke he was capable of making.

A plastic basket of mottled, ugly flowers sat crookedly in the sand. Smooth stones surrounded the cross, and these confused us; were these being replaced when they washed away or covered with sand? They looked dirty somehow, sticky.

There was a jar of some thick, yellow, viscous liquid. We couldn't think what it was.

"I told you," I said, and no one said it was all bullshit this time.

We left it there; no one wanted to touch it. It felt bad to leave the memorial as it was, disrespectful somehow, as if death was dirty but we couldn't be bothered to spend a few minutes to clean it up.

A shadow fell over us, strange on a cloudless day, and I shivered. Someone spying on us? Standing over us, wishing they were part of our group?

There was no one there, and the shadow lifted. Something had passed between me and the sun, that's all.

One of the guys picked up a stone.

He held it in his palm, then tucked it in his pocket. He wasn't bothered by gross things. He'd been known to throw dog poo, bare-handed. He took the stone over to Grandpa Sheet who examined it and nodded. He handed over a six pack of beer.

"He asked what we saw. That's all he wanted. And he said something about the poor boys."

"Someone must have set it up for the boys I told you about," I said. "The one's Jason's dad found."

Grandpa Sheet seemed full of life, hopping up and down the stairs like a puppy dog wanting to play.

"You see?" he called out. "Reward for the ones who go the furtherest."

That night I dreamt my pubic hair was matted and massive, like seaweed. I woke to find Jason down there, trying to get a fingerhold, his hair balled against my stomach, greasy and damp.

I pushed him off and he whined, "I thought we could give each other what comfort we could."

"Yeah, well," I said. I left him on the corner of my bed and went to have a shower, to wash the nightmare and him away.

We all sat on the verandah, eating the last of the cereal. Dry, because there was no milk and no one wanted to go buy some. Money was tight and we'd lost track of who'd spent what. I'd lost track, anyway, because I never had any money to spend.

Grandad Sheet sat in the shadows on his verandah. I heard clinking, like glass, and he stood up and walked towards us.

"You hungry?" he said. He carried four jam jars, clink clink. "Teenagers are always hungry. It's jam," he said, lifting it to the light. "Blackberry jam."

"Thanks," one of my friends said, because Jason and I wouldn't.

He set the jars on the verandah railing, nodded, walked away.

"Must have been a sale on jars," one of my friends said. Because they were the same.

The same as the jar we'd seen at the memorial.

The surf was high and the day bright, so the beach filled up quickly. The others went for a swim even though the jellyfish warning flags were out, but I didn't have the energy.

Instead I went to the memorial. It was tucked away in the dunes where hardly anyone went, is why it lasted so long.

Someone had been there. I could see drag marks in the sand, and there were six sets of weirdly perfect footprints pressed deep next to the jar of sticky yellow liquid.

But I didn't see a ghost until Grandad Sheet died.

I didn't go back for a long time after that. My life progressed, sort of, or at least I didn't fuck it up, and there never seemed to be time to go to the beach just for the sake of it.

It was fifteen years later before I went again, with Mum, Dad, my two brothers. None of us wanted to be there much but Bernard was depressed. Gerard had found him in the shed, with a glass and a bottle of weed killer. Seriously. Weed killer. We gave him shit about that, non-stop, because weed-killer? Could you be more obvious? But Gerard found him, anyway, sitting there trying to write a suicide note but not really knowing WHY, thus proving me right and every one else wrong; he thought too much.

Luckily.

So Gerard saved him and now we were all there to pretend we were kids again and the worst thing that could happen was Dad cooked dinner and made raw hamburgers.

We arrived in two cars. I'd packed wine, cheese, fancy snacks from my local gourmet store. Mum and Dad had a carload of food, stuff we'd lived on as kids. White bread, sausages, sweet cereal. Custard in cartons. They'd brought cricket gear and new table tennis bats, because there was a table in the boatshed. It was surely ruined but that wouldn't matter.

Dad got the key from under the front mat and opened the front door. The place was stuffy but open windows would let the sea breeze in and we'd soon feel relaxed and healthy. That was the plan.

Dinner first night was Fancy Chicken Salty Bucko. Mum called it that, trying to pretend she wasn't showing off. Dad was getting pissed with Jason's Dad, so Mum banned him from the barbie.

It was delicious. Mum always was a great cook.

"I picked the sage myself. There's a gorgeous batch behind Jason's house. I don't think they even know it's there."

"Sage is good," I said. She was making a point but I wasn't sure what it was yet.

"If you pick twelve leaves at midnight you'll see the ghost of your future husband," she said. She knows I'm gay and doesn't ban me from the house, but secretly, it seems, she thinks I just haven't met the right man.

"Doesn't that mean he'd be dead? You can't have the ghost of a living person," Bernard said, and we all got stuck into our Salty Bucko and bottles of wine and it felt okay. Mum kept squeezing Bernard, watching him, as if she couldn't believe he was real. He's been missing a long time, gone from us, and she'd say, it's like we have no son, as if he didn't exist when not in our presences.

Dad made us pull out the table tennis table and set it up. It wasn't too bad. Buckled and mottled but reasonably sturdy when you shoved the legs in the sand.

Then he knocked on Jason's dad's door. Gerard and I exchanged looks of relief; now he'd stop trying to make conversation with us. Bernard was already on the beach, heading for the dunes. We'd spoken of little else but the memorial, because they'd seen it but we hadn't been into the dunes together for years. And the dead boys. We talked about the dead boys and gave Bernard shit about the weed killer. He planned to ask Jason's dad for the story again, because you have different ears as an adult. I don't know what he was hoping to hear.

Gerard and I followed him, leaving Mum to fuss with the windows and the beds and to put a cuppa on.

We always left someone at the foot of the dunes, just in case. They could run for help.

This time, though. My brothers and I wanted to go in together, find the memorial that was periodically covered up.

Bernard had a hip flask of Bundy Rum and we drank that as we plodded on.

"We used to run in this sand, don't you remember?" Gerard said. "As if it was a footpath."

"We were a lot lighter then. Didn't sink to our ankles." Bernard was skinny as a stick, far too thin. Our brief hugs made me cringe, because I could feel his bones.

"I'm as svelte as ever," I said, "Like a blade of grass," and that set them off mocking me for a while, which was good.

"Is this thing actually here?" Gerard said. "It was, but I haven't seen it in years."

"Let's give it another five minutes, then we'll head back," Bernard said. We weren't going to argue.

At the moment he was living in these small increments of time. Five minutes. Half an hour. One afternoon. The more increments of time that passed, the further he was from that moment when he was prepared to drink the weed-killer.

What we didn't know.

What we should have known.

Was that time goes forward to a thing as well as away from another.

We finished the rum, and I made them sing stupid songs, and then Bernard said, "There it is."

Only it wasn't. It was a different one. White-painted wood hammered into a cross and imbedded with sea-softened glass pieces.

We stared at it for a while, chilled even though the sun burned down.

Gerard bent over, digging in the sand. He revealed a small glass jar, filled with the viscous yellow liquid I remembered so well from the other memorial.

"Did someone make a new one?" Gerard said, but Bernard had already walked on, and called out, "Here's another one."

The one Bernard found could have been the original but wasn't. It was a wooden cross but not as aged; some weather-damage but it seemed to have been made of that 'outdoor' wood, paint thick, with chains dangling off it, held in places by notches in the wood. One fine chain with a butterfly pendant, one thicker one with fake dog tags.

"We should take these back and hang them over the verandah at House 2. Freak out Jason's dad."

Even now he still got shit for not going to Vietnam. Every now and then, especially on Anzac Day.

We found the original memorial next, collapsed now, with few stones remaining. And we found two more, looking even older, that we thought must have been there all along but we never walked that far.

The next memorial was built of rusted metal, with words scratched in. We couldn't read beyond a few letters. F and H and T

Bernard kept on walking. "There might be more," he said. I hoped not each one meant that someone had died.

We wouldn't have recognised the next one if we hadn't seen the others. This one was a mound of stones, perfectly placed, with a surround of large rocks to keep them in place. Each letter on a different stone.

We pulled them out carefully and laid them on the sand, shifting them around until we found a word.

FURTHEREST

All of the memorials hosted a jar, filled with that yellow stuff.

We stayed until the sun started to dip then headed back. Bernard didn't want to come but we dragged him. Night fell dark and fast at the beach and we didn't have torches or food or anything but an empty hip flask.

Dad had the BBQ out when we got back. The boys stopped with him, drank beer, and I went inside for a shower.

Mum and Dad are getting on, now, but they're sticking to the plan. Eggs for breakfast, leftovers for lunch, BBQ for dinner, cooked by Dad even though he can't see in the dark well anymore and insisted on BBQing out there on the beach.

We told them what we'd seen, all those memorials.

"No names on them?"

"Nothing but the word 'furtherest'."

"Like Grandad Sheet always says," Mum said. I didn't think she knew about all that. "Maybe he made the memorials for his wife and son. And his parents. Who knows?"

As we talked I could hear children laughing, and someone squealing as they dipped into the water, and the pop of a champagne cork.

We all looked over the House 4. It was dark; no squatters tonight. Grandad Sheet had died five or six months earlier. No one went to the funeral. I don't even know if there was one. His son was long dead and there was only one grandson who wanted nothing to do with him or the house. He'd never even been.

No one shut the house up, or put it on the market. The dads looked after the outside, weeding when they did their own, clearing off dead birds that periodically made it to the verandah.

No one touched the inside.

You could easily imagine him there, watching as he always did.

"There's usually a party of some kind going on in the house. They're always at it. Leave a great pile of shit behind," Jason's dad said. He still walked for hours and actually looked better than he had in years. He made shell necklaces to guard against the evil eye and handed them out to anyone he saw. Even now, he sat with his beer, threading.

"Maybe I could move into his place for a while," Bernard said. "Keep the squatters out."

"Yes! You could!" Mum realised straight away she'd been too excited but couldn't rein it in.

"We'd have to get in and clear it out. He was house-proud, you could say that for him. He'd be turning in his grave to see the state it's in."

We'd gone off track. "What about the crosses? The stones?" I said, and my brothers said *yeah*, agreeing with me. The grownups (yeah, we were grown up now but not like they were. Not like kid-producing, home-owning, holiday house-owning adults) nodded.

"We'll call the police tomorrow," Mum said, and she did it, too. They never did come, though.

Not about that.

"I should get Jason to come back, give us a hand to clear the place out." Jason's dad said.

We rolled our eyes (yeah, adults).

"He's overseas, isn't he?" Mum said. "For his job?"

"He's doing bloody well. They love him on the TV over there."

He was actually a bit of a spunk now but he was still gropy-fingered Jason to me.

"He thinks of you all as cousins. He'd love to be here."

The verandah at House 4 sat in shadows, darker than anywhere else, I thought.

The dads were up early to start the big clear out.

They wanted us to help but I wasn't going in that place. It always gave me the creeps. Grandpa Sheet wasn't someone you wanted to go near. He was so desperately lonely, so needy, it felt like he'd grab on and wouldn't let you go.

He had been married; they said it lasted a week. Long enough to make a baby (the son who died) and we never saw the wife. Someone said she was a geologist and one of Gerald's jokes was, "She must have had rocks in her head to marry him."

Jason's dad said, "I'm glad you're all here. You anchor me. Not long before Grandpa Sheet died I wasn't feeling the best. I shouldn't tell you this. But Jason says it helps to talk. I was pretty low. I was hearing voices or something, telling me what I should do. End it all."

"I don't know if that's the best topic," Mum whispered to me.

"You can't say anything. It'll be really awkward and embarrassing and obvious if you do and Bernard will hate it," I whispered back.

"I almost did it. I'd gathered rocks and rope and I was going to swim out and let the rocks drop like an anchor, you know. I was so close."

"So what stopped you?"

"It's stupid. But the smell of something BBQing wafted over. Sausage and onions. And I was suddenly starving and I thought, *I can't die on an empty stomach*. I went home and ate, then Jason rang and I went to bed and just . . . forgot about it.

"The next morning I found Grandad Sheet hanging in his boathouse. The door was banging in the wind so I went to shut it and there he was, hanging. I wondered if he'd taken my place. That someone had to die that night and it turned out to be him.

"It wasn't as bad as finding the boys. Nothing could be as bad as that. But it was still a shock. So you have to ignore the voices. If they're telling you what to do. Shut them out whatever way you can."

"Come on you lot, help," Dad said. Bernard had been hard at it, carrying out loads of rubbish, whistling, running into the surf for a dip every now and then.

Not even his family went near the place, so why should we? We did take drinks and snacks over to them, though.

Dad and Jason's dad stayed over there for hours with Bernard, making a big pile of rubbish, getting drunker by the minute. They chucked out any wrecked furniture, shouting out, "Executive Decision" each time. It was actually pretty funny and we all set up beach chairs to watch the show. Even Mum, who angled her chair so she could watch all of us, too. I couldn't be a mother. I couldn't cope with that level of love. Too painful. I can't even cope with a dog, too needy, too easily saddened.

They found mostly crap, like the embroidered wallhanging that said, "The furtherest you go, the better the place."

The dads finished in the house. "What about the boatshed?" Gerard called out, then whispered, as Dad called back, "I'll boatshed you!"

But they did go in there, torches out because all the boatsheds were filled with years of crap that blocked the windows.

They were in there for a bit so we turned our chairs around to watch the sea instead, and a group of teenagers down there making a bonfire, swearing as loud as they could, throwing bottles.

"Don't throw the fucken bottles," Bernard roared. You'd have to call it a roar. That stopped them. He walked down there and pointed; *stack 'em there*, he said, and *we'll clear them up in the morning. Don't leave broken glass on the beach.*

He bent to pick up some of it and the kids helped, and he was back soon, smiling to himself. I nearly cried to see it, that pure, happy smile.

I was thinking of going inside when I heard a dragging sound. I turned to see the dads coming towards us, both dragging shop mannequins.

Shop mannequins.

We gathered around as they set the mannequins back on their feet. They were taller than me, dressed in clothing from, what the sixties? Mum said so; *you had a shirt like that*, she said to Dad.

"There are four more," Jason's dad said. "All standing there in his shed behind a stack of corrugated iron."

The boys helped drag them all out and we stood them up on our verandah. It gave me the creeps, as if six strange men stood there, staring at us, watching us too closely.

Each was dressed differently. One had black pants and a white singlet. One had black shirt, white singlet, open orange shirt. One had brown shorts, green polo, panama hat. One had grey pants, blue shirt. One had faded pink shorts, towel around neck, hat. One had white pants, white hat, light jacket, blue singlet, towel under arm.

The clothes were moth-eaten, dusty, stained.

The mannequins were made of pink plastic that made me think of silly putty. They were all damaged; dents and cuts. Cracks and fissures. And they leaked, oozing thick yellow sticky stuff that was too slow to be fluid.

"That's the stuff in jars in the dunes," I said.

And I thought of the jars of jam Grandad Sheet gave us years ago, and of the jars at the memorial, and of this yellow sticky stuff.

"This is too weird," Gerard said. "Was he a tailor or something?"

"Fashion designer, darling," I said, modelling for them.

"I think they must be the police dolls. Don't you remember?" Jason's dad said. "After I found the boys?"

"We weren't here then," Dad said.

"There were six men who didn't come forward. Others saw them at the time they thought boys disappeared, but they never spoke up. So the police dressed these doll things up in the gear people remembered them wearing and paraded them all over the state, hoping to get a clue, *did you see something? Is this you?* But no one ever did. No idea how Grandpa Sheet got them. Maybe they were left on the beach."

Bernard stood up, looked at them from different angles. Then he said, "That's Grandad Sheet," and jeezus he was right. Brown shorts, stripy shirt. Panama hat. Why had no one ever seen it? He'd moved in to the area after the murders, maybe? So no one knew him?

Sand coated the feet of the mannequins. I walked down to where the dads had first stood them up and saw the weird, perfect footprints they'd left behind.

I'd seen these at the first memorial we found. Someone had dragged the mannequins to the memorial and let them stand there, casting shadows.

I shuddered at the thought.

⊸

The Grandad Sheet one leaked the worst of all. I was tempted to collect it. In the end I set up a bucket and listened to the slow, solid, regular drip in the night.

⊸

We set the six of them up in front of the houses. They all cast a shadow but one cast a shadow longer than the others. I couldn't figure out why; I shifted it from place to place and still the shadow was long, dark and cold. It was cold in the shadow, colder than it should be and darker than the middle of the night.

⊸

We went for a walk, all of us, heading away from the dunes.

Birds circled overhead, squawking so loudly we could hardly hear each other. I covered my head, worried they'd let loose a sea of shit and I did feel a spatter of something but it was the first drop of rain. The sky blackened and we tried to make it home but were caught in a great downpour.

The house lay ahead so we laughed, because soon we'd be warm and dry.

Running from the rain, laughing, but it fell so hard it actually hurt and when I made it inside there were red marks across my arms, face, chest, legs; any exposed skin was striped. I stopped laughing but someone still did, I could hear the echo of it. Or not the echo but an actual laugh, one of those men's laugh when they think the women aren't listening.

The Grandad Sheet dummy stood in front of the door. We'd set him at the end of the verandah, a sentinel, but here he was blocking the way.

Bernard stripped his own clothes off, dressed in the dummy's clothing, leaving the dummy anonymous, sexless.

I said, "It's bad luck to wear the clothes of a man who died at sea."

"He didn't drown."

"He drowned in his own blood. That's what happens after you hang yourself."

He gave me a chuff on the shoulder, then a harder one on the chin. "Help me shift my stuff," he said. He hardly had anything; just a couple of duffle bags, a guitar he never played, his surfboard.

I carried the board to the front of House 4 but I wasn't going in.

"There's no one here," Bernard said, but I could hear footsteps inside, for sure. "I think this is a better place," he said, and he sat himself down in the shadowy verandah to look out.

⊸

Later, I sat on our verandah and watched Dad cooking the BBQ. He stooped over the hot plate, looking so very old. Tired. It was dark out there, darker than usual. In the shadows I thought I saw a figure. Did Dad have a buddy out there? A beach friend? He always made friends, loved to chat.

He looked up suddenly as if just noticing the person there, then he pulled back, raising his arms to his face.

Then he fell.

"Dad!" I'm saying as I'm running down the steps, calling to the boys because I wanted them there to get the person who'd hit our dad.

They were slow to respond as ever. Bernard hated to move fast, even though as a kid you could never stop him. On the rare times Dad tried to whack his bum for some wrongdoing he'd scoot out of the way so fast hand never laid on bum cheek and we'd all end up laughing.

Now his feet fell flat and sluggish.

We made it to Dad who was on his knees, moaning. Bleeding from the nose, but he said he'd bumped that, falling. There'd been no one standing over him, he said.

But I knew there had.

Bernard and I helped him up and inside while Gerard finished the cooking (everything was burnt anyway; Dad's idea of BBQ perfection) and Mum panicked. Dad said, "I'm fine. Stop fussing. I fell," but he had a look in his eye, a slight shiftiness. I'd seen it in older people who were starting to lose their memory, or bodily control, and didn't want anyone to know. Their minds race, wanting to cover up a lapse. That's what he was doing.

"I thought I saw someone out there with you," I said, close to his ear.

He shook his head. "There was no one."

We settled Dad in bed, against his will, and made Mum cups of tea because she was freaking out.

"I can't be on my own," she whispered to me. "I just can't."

"You can come and live with me," I said, although no way. I couldn't do it. Better she goes into a home, she'd be fine. Never alone, at least.

That night was the first time I thought I heard someone outside, carrying a metal bucket *clank clank*. I heard weird things all night. The bucket being dragged or something, and a deep male laugh, a single laugh, a man alone.

I got up to check on Dad and Mum twice in the night; they both happily snored away.

Next morning Bernard's eyes were bright, set deep in dark bags that made him look older.

"Waffles for breakfast?" Mum said, bright and desperate, so 'let's pretend' I had to go along with it. So I started a fight with Gerald and the two of us ran hollering bloody murder around the house, with the others inside laughing their arses off at us.

A thin layer of yellow ooze lay at the bottom of the bucket. I set jars out to collect from the rest of the mannequins as well.

That night Bernard asked us all 'for drinks' at his house. At Grandad Sheet's house. He'd set up chairs on the verandah, and found glasses, and he had wine. It was nice. I stayed there longer than the others, not wanting it to end. It was peaceful, Bernard calmly smoking, pouring wine, neither of us talking. The mannequins stood forward over there in front of our house, casting shadows by moonlight. I thought I saw one man walk to the water, keep walking until he disappeared. And another vanish into the dunes, then there he was, back on the verandah, then into the dunes again. It was tiredness, my eyes aching from sun-on-sand reflection.

Bernard didn't want to go inside. He liked it on the verandah, No man's land, he called it, neither in nor out. I had a last glass of wine out there with him then left him to it. He was snoring gently and I thought that anyone who slept so easily must be feeling okay.

When I looked back I saw him lift his arm to wave at someone.

I went inside.

I went inside.

The only thing I feel okay about is that I didn't do it because I was tired, or cold, or bored. I did it because I thought he wanted to be alone. He seemed peaceful, barely affected by the things I saw.

So I went inside.

Sometime in the night, Bernard walked into the dunes. He went past the last memorial, using a big old torch to guide him.

We knew where he was because of the note he left. It said, "He says it will be all right. That he'll take me the furtherest I can go."

Gerard and I went to look for him, and Jason's dad came with us. That shat me, later, as if he thought he had a monopoly on finding dead people.

Bernard had cut his wrists with broken glass, sliced his arms carefully long ways from wrist to inner elbow.

The sun was well up and he looked so pale, as pale as Grandad Sheet. His arms were flat beside him, legs stretched out, and the sand dark and damp all around him.

Gerard said, "You fucking idiot," and took my hand so we could go close together, look into his face, looking for a beat in his eyelids, touch his throat hoping for a beat there.

Nothing.

"I'm sorry." Jason's dad. A lot of people would say that over the coming weeks, but I thought he really meant it.

Bernard wore a dozen of those damn shell necklaces and I wasn't sure what made me the saddest; the fact he thought they'd help, or the fact they didn't.

We built a memorial for Bernard. Jason's dad wanted to use the shell necklaces; I thought Gerard was going to kill him. Instead we laid Bernard's surfboard down, anchored it with rocks, and every time we went back we took something for him. A bottle of wine, or a new piece of music, or a book.

We didn't give him a jar of the yellow stuff because we'd burnt all the dummies and their clothes. The smell of them. They left a terrible pink mess, a sludge that set into a hard rock, so we left that on the surfboard, too.

The memory of them. Me, Gerard, and Jason, with the adults, those alive and those who were ghosts, all watching from their verandahs, The families from House 3 would arrive in the next holiday, in whatever variation, blissfully unaware.

Lucky them.

Mum and Dad wanted to sell up the house or just abandon it but Gerard and I wouldn't let them.

"I need this place," I told them. Although it wasn't a safe place. There were too many voices. But it made me feel strong to resist them and that was worth a lot.

Some days it was just me and Jason's dad on the beach, and he talked. He told me his stories; the meanderings of a broken mind. The dead boys one, the when Nick died one, the how I lost my job one, the why my wife left me one, the when I nearly killed myself one.

And the Granddad Sheet one. He reckoned Sheet thought of those dead strangers memorialized in the dunes as his family. His friends. That's how alone he was. He always felt excluded. "We never let him into our perfect world," Jason's dad said, and that's how deluded he was.

"I think he did it," he said. "He wore those same clothes every single day. The police doll clothes. Maybe he wanted someone to identify him and no one ever did. Maybe he had something to feel guilty about. That why he wanted us to go into the dunes. To find the memorials. To do something about it. To stop him. We never did. I reckon he blamed us for that. Blamed us for all the memorials, all the . . . things he has to feel guilty about. He still blames us."

Because we always felt him over there. In his house. And I could hear him whispering in my ear as I walked along the beach, the feel of it somehow driving my mood down, making me need a drink. Grandad Sheet could get through walls. Maybe that's why he killed himself; so he could get to us in more ways than one. There was no privacy. He was always there and I saw him down on the beach, amongst the families down there. Trying to lead them into the dunes. He wasn't always alone; sometimes there were the shadows of others around him.

He chilled me cold.

"We should have stopped him," Jason's dad said.

You should have I thought. And something else.

Jason's dad should have died two, three, four times over. Each time, someone had stepped in for him; his best friend. Grandad Sheet. My brother.

They all died in his place.

Jason's dad shakes his head as if he was trying to clear water out of his ear, but he rarely goes swimming. "The call of the deep is stronger when I hit the surf," he always says. He's shaking his head to stop the voices, looking at me sidelong as if sizing me up.

Some nights the ghosts come scrabbling at my door, they crawl up the hallway, they hover over me.

And I'm starting to think thoughts that aren't my one. *There is a better place.* It's like a whisper. I'm starting to think, *this is shit, life is shit*, and I haven't thought that before.

I never had that feeling before.

I sniff a bottle of sunscreen, to get that feeling back that memory of childhood when we were all safe and happy. Trying to get rid of the bad thoughts. The thoughts of dying. I could leave. I should leave. But I have to stay until I've done one thing.

I'm keeping Jason's dad well fed. I make sure he's never hungry.

There's only the two of us here now and it isn't going to be me, so when the ghosts come knocking again, I point to him at House 2. I say, *his turn.*

At last it's his turn.

WHERE'S THE HARM?

REBECCA LLOYD

When we first arrived back home to fix our parents' house, we were eager for the money we'd make on it; my brother's latest venture was going bust, and I was despairing of ever making a living from my photography. We reckoned the house could fetch a handsome sum even though it was a bit out of the way down the wooded lane. Our plan was to re-decorate, fix the garden, replace parts of the veranda, put the thing on the market, and get back to our normal and very separate lives in Holesville Nine—my brother and I had never learnt how to get on together, he drank too much and gambled too often to be any real use to me as a brother. At my cruellest I used to describe him as one of those guys who are overly proud of themselves, the type that endlessly pontificate about their honourable natures.

We'd agreed to complete each room before we moved onto the next. Eddie was to remove layers of wallpaper, fill in the gaps and holes beneath it all, then wash the walls down and paint them in some pastel colour that the eye could ignore and that a buyer would not be offended by. I was to remove many years of chipped paint from the skirting boards and the window frames, and re-paint them in simple white gloss.

The evenings had turned chilly and we'd taken to lighting the old log burner in the kitchen. Apart from its heat, it gave us something to focus on because conversation between us was so difficult. Being younger by five years, Eddie felt a peculiar impulse to compete with me, but I had no interest in being drawn into whatever crazy infected jumble was going on in his mind, and whenever I suspected he was attempting to manipulate our interactions, I clammed up. But I have also to own up to the fact that when we were kids, I scared him a lot and he was, deliciously for me, dead easy to scare. It's how I kept him under control, I now realise. I often wonder just how cruel I really was to him, but he'd be the last person I'd ask.

Each morning, before starting our work in the house, we walked down the lane into the beginnings of the wood, to collect supplies for the log burner. There was one other dwelling that we knew of for certain further on from ours, and in it lived a very ancient man, who, even when we were kids, looked far too old to still be alive. Mr. Ratchetson—that was the name, and I used to tell little Eddie that he was a night-creeper who crawled up the wall and stared through our window while we were asleep. He didn't believe me until I told him about the noises Mr. Ratchetson made as he clung to the side of our house and moved disgustingly in and out like a fire bellows.

"What noises does he make, Ross?" Eddie asked, wriggling down further into his bed.

I had to think quickly, so he didn't see my lie. "Like the noise Mum's door makes, Eddie. Just like that . . . squeaking and groaning at the same time."

"What does he do it for?"

"It's Mr. Ratchetson's way of talking to you."

"What's he saying?"

"How would I know, it's a different language, silly."

Eddie gazed at me for a long time that evening, his eyes steady on my face and widened, and the next morning I saw that I'd convinced him, and felt the grim pleasure of my deceit. Because we now live in the same town, we come across each other every so often, and he still looks at me that way sometimes, so I like to *think* anyway—but perhaps the uneasiness is mine for my cruelty towards him back then. I don't know.

As we drew level with Mr. Ratchetson on one of our wood gathering trips, he was at his gate looking away from us towards the darkness of the trees. "Oh God, look! That's old Ratchetson, isn't it? Must be way past a hundred by now," Eddie whispered.

"More like two hundred, and still peeping through windows," I said.

"Thank you, Ross. I don't want to be reminded of that stuff. And by the way, I never did believe you."

"Like hell you didn't."

"You don't know, do you?"

"What?"

"That to keep you happy, I perfected a certain way of looking that convinced you I'd fallen for your crap."

"Yeah?" I half-turned to look at him, but my attention was on Mr. Ratchetson. "Why do old people do that?"

"Do what?"

"Stand and stare into the distance like that?" I said.

"They've got nothing better to do, I expect."

On hearing our approach, Mr. Ratchetson turned his head slowly towards us, tortoise-like and blinking. "Why are you down here?" he asked. "Town is the other way, up on the tarmac road."

"We're the Marshall brothers," I explained. "We've come here to sell Mum and Dad's house."

"Marshall kids?"

I nodded, and he inspected Eddie and me closely. "Selling your mother's house?" I nodded again. "Why, what's the matter with it?"

Eddie laughed. "They've passed on, you know. Died . . . and someone has to do something with the house."

"They died," Mr. Ratchetson said, and I couldn't tell if it was a question or a statement. He turned his head to the wood again and I had the distinct impression he was waiting for something, or at least thought he was—maybe something out of his long and very distant past.

"Do you have relatives yourself, Mr. Ratchetson?" Eddie asked in a nice voice.

"They died."

"Ah, of course they did."

I wanted us gone now and I tugged at Eddie's arm, but remembered suddenly something my father once said which I'd found so intriguing that it'd become a fixture in some part of my mind. "We're going into the wood to get fuel for our log burner. It's chilly in the evenings now, isn't it, Mr. Ratchetson?" I began, thinking to lead him gently towards my question.

"It is."

"What's the best wood to pick up do you think?" I asked.

"Ash if you can find some. Most of it's further in towards the middle of the wood, though. Did you have it in mind to go right inside there?"

"Yes. We were never allowed as kids, so it's time we did."

"Right inside," Eddie repeated, and I could hear an echo of the night-whisperings of our childhood in his voice.

"You might find a house in there," the old man muttered. "But if you come across it, you should move on in haste."

"What house would that be Mr. Ratchetson?" I asked trying not to show my interest, for here was the point of my questioning.

"The last one along this stretch," he answered, raising his thin arm into the air for emphasis.

"I thought *yours* was the last," Eddie said.

"Lots of folk did," he answered.

"Dad spoke about that house to me once," I said. "He reckoned it got swallowed up by the encroaching wood, and when I asked if Eddie and I could go and see it, he said if we did, we'd be swallowed up by the wood too, and never find our way out again."

"You didn't tell me that when we were kids," Eddie said, frowning at me.

"I didn't think there was any point."

"Dad liked to know exactly where we were, you see, Mr. Ratchetson," Eddie explained, and I could hear a tiny scraping of anxiety in his voice.

"You're the Marshall boys, you say?" the old man asked. "Ann Marshall was your mother?" We nodded. "She had glorious hair, but I'm glad she cut it off; it put my mind to rest. Mightily to rest."

"I remember Mum's hair when it was long," Eddie said. "It used to swing about when she had it loosened on Sundays. I really loved it; I was heartbroken when she had it all shorn off."

Mr. Ratchetson shifted from one slippered foot to the other. "Wisest thing to do, son; it was attracting a great deal of attention."

I glanced at Eddie and was startled to find myself moved by the emotion on his face. I too had been sad when Mum cut off her hair. I'd asked her what she did with it and was puzzled when she whispered that Dad had taken it into the field behind our house and burnt it. She wouldn't say anymore, and Eddie and I could tell by our parents' faces that we were not to ask about it, and not to stare at Mum's raggedy shorn head, or at the hundreds of little cuts on her arms and neck.

"So, the house, Mr. Ratchetson?"

"Try to sell it to decent people," he answered, "if there are any such left in the world."

"The other one; the one inside the wood."

"To collect the ash, you mean?"

"Yes, exactly . . . where we can get ash."

"I know where a big old oak has fallen down," he said, turning his head first and then by small shaky movements, his body, in the direction we'd come from. "Walk along the railway to the old shoe factory. Whole tree down just there." He stared at us for a short intense moment, and then, without saying more, turned, and made his way to his open front door.

"Wow," Eddie said, "did you see the way the pulse on his skull was twanging?"

"I want to find that house," I murmured, somehow fearful of the words as I spoke them. "I've been curious about it all my life."

Eddie shrugged. "Let's not waste more time then; half the morning's gone already."

Moss had formed vivid green pillows along the route into the deeper wood, some of them huge and glistening with moisture, and although we didn't see fungus poking out anywhere, I could smell it above the odour of wet rotting leaves. As we walked on, the tree trunks began to take on an unfamiliar slimy look and I was disinclined to reach out and run my palm over them, as had always been my way with trees.

"It's a little ecosystem all of its own in here," I said, "moist and dripping."

"What's that stuff growing in the rock crevices with black stems?"

"Maidenhair fern, Eddie. Or Venus's hair." We could see that it had grown lushly and undisturbed for a long time, and it made me shiver despite its beauty.

"Quaint," Eddie whispered, and walked towards it. "It'd make a great shot, or have you given up nature photos?"

"Let's not stop," I said. Time's getting on, and we've got stuff to get in town later. As I spoke, just at the corner of my eye something attracted my attention. "How weird is that?" I whispered, pointing it out. "Who do you think did it—kids?"

"Must be, I suppose."

"It's on both sides of that path, look." We stood close together, and stared; the vegetation and wood grasses on a small side track off the main path had been neatly plaited and their ends bound together with some kind of delicate twine. "Shall we see what's further on?" I asked.

"Let's just stick on this path and find the ash," Eddie said.

I've never forgotten those words of his, and each time I think of them, my heart seems to plummet downwards and fall away into a great void of pity, and longing, and grief, for I said, "No, come on, let's just take a quick look down there. Where's the harm?"

We turned off the main track and walked down the tiny dark and plaited pathway before us. We came to a bend pretty soon and as we rounded it, both of us cried out. We'd found the house, and it was huge with many shabby, grey glinting windows.

"Abandoned ages ago by the looks of it," Eddie murmured.

I could understand why he thought so; trees and spindly saplings had grown right up against the peeling walls of the house and across what once would've been a handsome pathway to the front door. But some of the windows on the upper floor were curtained and they weren't in ribbons or covered in filth, but clean-looking and made of the same shiny fabric that the haberdasher in town kept on a roll at the front of his shop.

We stood in silence for a long time and gazed. I was just thinking how distracting the wind was, when I saw movement. "Eddie," I said, gripping his arm tightly, "that place is not abandoned. I've just seen someone in the top room on the left."

A while later, the same figure moved across a different window.

"Whoa!" Eddie said loudly, "it was a woman. How can she be living out here? Look, no cars in the front, no road down here *anyway*."

There comes a strange pricking sensation, almost like a weight has settled on your shoulders. It's not a sensation I've experienced a great deal, but as Eddie fell silent, I was compelled to turn around, and in the dappled shade of a large tree behind us on the track some thirty yards away, two women were watching us. The smaller one had her arms crossed and was balancing on one foot. The other had her hands on her hips and was stooped forward slightly, the better to see us, I felt. Eddie had turned too, and joined me in my scrutiny. The wind had whipped up the leaves of the tree the women stood beneath and caused changing patterns of moving light on the path, so that we had to blink and look away several times. No words had passed between the four us, and perhaps it was that small oddness more than anything else which alerted me to the peculiar nature of our situation.

It was Eddie who brought an end to the staring. He moved forward a pace or two, and put his hand up in greeting. "Hi there," he began. "I'm Eddie and this is my brother, Ross."

The women looked at each other and moved slowly out from the shadows. What I'd taken to be cloaks of an old-fashioned kind draped around their shoulders, were no such thing. Their hair hung about them concealing much of what they wore, and it stopped a few inches only from the ground itself. I felt quickly nauseous and assumed, knowing Eddie's sensitivities that he would too. But he walked straight over to them and although they would not take his outstretched hand, they were, within minutes, smiling up at him. I hadn't moved and it was as if I was irrelevant, and that unsettled me further.

I stayed put and studied them for several minutes, before Eddie beckoned me over. My very guts seemed to have shrivelled and my breathing was shallow and raspy. Absurd thing to describe, I dare say, but I was acutely alert and conscious of a vague but persistent danger of some indefinable type. I can't remember what Eddie said to them, the tone of his conversation, or its subject matter. I'd never come across women like them before and I quickly concluded that they were part of a cult. They had that same quiet and thoughtful look that religious women sometimes have. Most of the women I knew laughed too loudly and talked for too long about nothing of interest and in squeaky voices. They had fussy hairstyles and fidgety hands, and were always far too eager to agree with what I thought. These women had a curious melancholic air about them that wasn't exactly a state of sadness, more as if they—and this is crazy—carried within them a sense of all the isolated places on the earth.

I would describe them as beautiful, the smaller one in particular, the one Eddie could not keep his eyes off, but I can say for certain that I didn't like those faces. Several times I squeezed his elbow to try to get him to come away. He glanced at me once and frowned. His eyes were literally shining, and I shivered.

"We were just *talk*ing, Ross. You were standing right there!" Eddie said on our way home. "How could you not hear us?"

"I wasn't paying attention to their words, but their hair . . ."

"Fantastic wasn't it?"

"Freakish," I replied. "Freakish."

Eddie laughed. "Not your kind of women, eh?"

I moved my sack of wood onto my other shoulder and quickened my pace. We'd wasted a good part of the day and I was irritated and feeling shuddery. "Did you see their clothes?"

"A bit Amish, I agree, Ross. But so what?"

"Not the kind of women who're asking to be touched," I replied, "and you're a bit keen on that, aren't you?"

"Does that mean you're not coming?"

"Huh?"

"They invited us to that old house tomorrow afternoon."

Our argument when on into the night. I couldn't persuade him not to go. He suggested we both take a day off as we'd been working on the house for a couple of weeks with no breaks, and were beginning to get fatigued. In the end, I decided I was going to walk around town and see if I could find anyone I knew from when we were young, and he could do the hell what he liked. I watched him go. I watched him walking fast down the wooded lane, and when he disappeared into the first of the trees, I picked up my coat and headed for town.

I spent the rest of the day arguing with myself. I sat in the park for a while and then followed our old route through the back streets. I didn't meet anybody we used to know, although the place itself hadn't greatly changed. It was only when I became aware that I was walking aimlessly and with very little interest in anything other than what was in my mind that I returned home.

A great jumble of contradictory thoughts battered my head. The most part of me was seized with horror made more terrifying because I had no idea how such a powerful reaction had come about. I could almost feel the reasoning voice I'd conjured up as Eddie walked away that morning fading into silence: so, my brother had met a couple of deadly strange women and found them to be charming, while I thought they were grotesque. Was it not just evidence of how differently we saw the world? Maybe . . . but what had they done to him in those moments that we stood with them that he should be so eager to return? I tried repeatedly to bring their faces to mind so I could search for expressions on them that would explain something . . . explain anything. All I remembered was a curious blandness of expression, while Eddie's face was alight with interest and pleasure. The bloody fool.

I left the kitchen and went to stand on the veranda, dusk was falling and the local frogs were beginning to get noisy. Eddie had not returned. God damn it! I wasn't going after him. What was the point? Soon it would be pitch black. Just as I was thinking that, I saw him.

He was wandering towards the house, taking his time—and he was whistling.

"For Christ's sake, where the hell have you been?" I shouted at him, and I realised by the expression on his face, that I'd badly over-reacted.

"I told you. You know. You were invited too. What's the matter with you?" he asked, almost whispering at me and with such as dismissive expression on his face, that I felt curiously ashamed of myself.

"Sorry," I said, following him into the kitchen.

"I've eaten already. Have you?"

"No. I'm not hungry."

"I ate with them."

"What?"

"I said I ate with them."

"Those women?"

"Don't call them those women."

"What did you eat?" I asked, moving around the table to get a better look at him.

He seemed startled all of a sudden, and he frowned. "Hey, guess what? I haven't a clue, Ross; isn't that strange? They are so . . . engaging, I don't think I noticed the food."

"You must be joking!"

He seemed tired, and before I could get anything much out of him, he edged towards the door. "I'm whacked, Ross. See you tomorrow," he said, and closed the door extra quietly, and was gone.

I remember shaking my head in frustration about him for some few minutes after he'd left; he'd seemed so calm, almost luminous, as if he'd risen slightly above the normal dirtiness of human life. I made the decision not to talk to him about it the following day. We'd just get on, each with our separate work, and stop for short coffee breaks when the time seemed right. But I didn't sleep that night, only roamed about in my thinking, ricocheting from one awful thought to another.

⊸

We were working on the living room the following morning and I had a lot of shabby-looking window frames to deal with in there. Eddie was priming the opposite wall. We hadn't spoken at breakfast, but every time I glanced at his face, he seemed perfectly normal, as if somehow he'd come down to earth during the night. I well knew that if I brought up the subject of the women directly he'd take pleasure in thwarting me. Back in Holesville Nine he had a girlfriend. She was as different from the women in the wood as could be. Her clothes were ill-fitting and badly chosen and often garish, she walked with little tittering steps as if about to topple, in shoes that looked as though they'd been deliberately designed to harm the wearer. Yet, her face was childish and kind of sweet and I know she adored Eddie.

"Cherie doing okay?" I asked after some time.

"She's good. She's doing good. Yeah. Thanks."

"She'll be glad to see you back," I suggested. "I was wondering if we should forget the upstairs. Sometimes people are keen to get hold of places they can do up themselves."

"Not what you said when we first talked about it."

"Yeah, but how long have we been here now, three weeks isn't it?"

"Ross, I think we should do what we planned to do. What've you got to get back to in Holesville Nine?"

"Nothing in particular," I agreed. I turned my head to look at him and was surprised to find that he was no longer priming the wall, but standing facing me with his arms folded and his face pale in the poor light. "Nothing," I said again. "Hey! How about asking Cherie to come and visit us? She could cook for us; I'm tired of scrabbling about trying to make our meals." Eddie stared at me with an expression so hostile, that for the first time in my life I felt afraid of my little brother. "It was just an *idea*, Eddie. I mean, she used to help out in Cygnet's Café, didn't she?"

Eddie shrugged and seemed to relax. "I'll tell you what, Ross. How about, after this wall, I start on the upstairs. I'm way ahead of you now anyway, since you've got those windows to tackle."

"So no Cherie, then?"

"She wouldn't like it here. She doesn't care for trees."

"No?"

"Insects, mosquitoes, things like that. She's a woman, after all."

"Are you serious about her?"

Eddie laughed, and stooped down to move his painting gear further along the wall. "I can see where this is going, Ross. D'you think I'm an idiot?"

I turned my back on him and stepped up to the window. The wood was of course no closer than it had been before we stumbled upon those women, but now it was omnipresent in my mind.

"It was gritty stuff," Eddie said suddenly. "It came in little balls."

"*What*?" I turned about again.

"I don't know what it was. And then we had fruit of some kind . . . sour."

"Sour?"

"Like gooseberries or something. They grow their own stuff behind the house; they've even got a stand of corn. They'd like to see you too, Ross. Why don't you come with me?"

"Look, Eddie . . . they gave me the creeps."

"You should open your mind to them."

"Fuck off!"

"You're so closed. They thought you looked like a mean and sad person. Are you a mean and sad person, Ross?"

"What the hell would they know? They're freaks, Eddie. How long have they been living there?"

"The family has been there for some generations. People in town know about them, but no one bothers them. And that's as it should be. Free country, you know."

"Fuck!"

We left it on that note; he'd taken my breath away. I had no idea what to say to him. He took his stuff upstairs in the early afternoon, and from time to time, I could hear him whistling.

I moved Mum's old radio into the living room and listened to whatever jumble came out of it and worked on. I'd stripped all the outer frames, and the paint was coming off well with my tungsten blade, before I became aware of the quietness upstairs.

I knew even before I pushed the door open that he wouldn't be there, and sure enough, he wasn't. Eddie must have climbed out of the window, slid down the little tiled roof below, and jumped to the ground, just as we both used to do as children.

I didn't know how long he'd been gone for, and although I was sure I could find my way to the house in the wood again if I wanted to, I didn't fancy the idea of turning up there unexpectedly. I was really angry with him; he was beginning to fuck up our work plan. So I sat on the step of the veranda and stared down the lane, and it was exactly then that I discovered we had woodworm. When I understood the extent of it all along the veranda on the east side of the house, I knew we had to get it treated immediately, or we'd have a lot of trouble selling up. So while Eddie hung out with the hairy forest women, as they had become in my mind, I went into town to see what could be done about the house.

He turned up late-afternoon shortly after I'd arrived back.

"What the hell?" I said.

"She called me," he replied, "and I went."

He looked peaceful—slightly disengaged. I shook my head slowly at him. "We've got woodworm in the veranda, and no one can get here to treat it for two months," I told him, as if it was his fault.

He didn't laugh, but I could see some sly calculation on his face about it. "Oh!" he said. "Now, that's a shame. How much will it cost us?"

I shrugged. "We have no option, we can't sell the place untreated, so it doesn't matter what it's going to cost. So, what have you been up to?"

"I was helping Domescia and Carboh turn some earth over."

"No kidding; so our work just becomes nothing because of those women?"

"I've asked you before, Ross, not to call them those women."

"What did you say their names were?"

"Domescia and Carboh."

I realised I was trembling, but I didn't think Eddie could see it. He was standing some fifteen yards away. "God damn it, Eddie, what's going on with you?"

"No. What's going on with you, more like. Carboh says you're haunted by your own meanness."

"Which one was that, Eddie?"

"The smaller one."

"I thought so. The one you kept staring at."

"The one I'm going to be joined with, Ross."

"God *damn*, Eddie, God *damn*! What the *hell* has gotten into you?"

I could not speak further. I stared at my brother, and if I'd thought all along that I never really knew him, I could not have wanted a heavier, more sinister conviction of that fact now. I turned and went inside. It was getting towards early evening and I set to lighting the kitchen stove with shaking hands, when a thought struck me. Eddie had come in and was looking in the fridge for something to eat.

"What d'you mean she called you?" I asked. "You don't have a mobile and the house phone is disconnected."

"Hard to explain, Ross."

"Try me," I replied.

"I don't think you'd get it, and I don't want to make you madder than you already are with me."

"Damn right, I'm mad with you. What about Cherie?" I asked.

"Well, *now* you bring her up. But really, you've always been dismissive of her in the past."

I could feel my face heating up and I rubbed my hands over it to control the redness; he was right. "Yeah, that *was* mean of me," I murmured.

"There you are you see—*mean*."

"Hey now, look here, Eddie, have you gone crazy or something, you've only met those women a couple of times, you can't be thinking of marrying one of them. You hate the idea of marriage, you've always said that."

Eddie looked at me evenly and I could tell he was enjoying my dishevelment. "Come and dine with us tomorrow night, Ross. Domescia is going to prepare a grand feast, the five other sisters will be there, and their mother will be joining us for a short while too."

"Dine with *us*?" I repeated, "come and *dine* with *us*?" I could do nothing but laugh.

"You've been invited, and the other sisters really want you to come; they want to see you," Eddie explained.

So far I'd understood there were a whole bunch of women in that scratchy old house and somehow living off the land. Who the hell lived like that in the twenty-first century? "The others—have you met them?" I asked, trying for all I was worth to stay calm.

"Yes, Carboh took me to them. They were in one of the upper rooms."

"And?"

"And nothing, Ross. They were engaging. Really engaging."

"Engaging, Eddie? Where are these weird words coming from all of a sudden?"

"Well, are you coming or not? I mean where's the harm?"

"Where's the harm, you say?"

"Loosen up, big brother, why don't you?"

Domescia and Carboh were to meet us on the bend of the main track, by the plaited path at around nine. We found Dad's old heavy duty torch and set out in good time. I was frightened and angry, and could not bring myself to look at Eddie or talk to him. I was intent on examining these curious women and looking for evidence of cultism, so I had some ammunition to lob at the stupid jerk who was my brother.

When we reached the stopping place, I really did not see the two of them standing there although I'd shone the torch all around slowly. But they were there all right. I think their hair must have made them resemble the trunks of trees. As we approached, they turned abruptly and made their way down the plaited path, with us in the rear. I kept the light from the torch on the ground, not wanting to shine it on all that swaying hair. Nobody spoke, and it wasn't until we stepped into the hall of the house that the atmosphere between us all changed. Domescia and Carboh turned to face us and bobbed a neat little curtsy, and Eddie inclined his head gravely in return. I stared at them and then at my brother and I must have been frowning hard, as finally Carboh said: "Ross, you will frighten my sisters if you look that way at them, it is not friendly; it is mean."

Caught by some faint movement on the wide and elegant staircase behind us, I looked up and saw, standing in a line, five women of different sizes, all of them sheaved in curtains of hair that gleamed in the faint light as if they'd dressed it with something oily. The sight of them was worse than the thought of suddenly disturbing a snake's nest and discovering a coiling mass of vigorous young when you least expected it. I stared upwards in horror and my heart began a shuddering thump that I could not make quiet for a good while, although later, I believe the women connived in rendering me calm.

Eddie raised his hand and showed his palm to them, and in return, they each curtsied as the first two had done, and as they did, they made a flurry of small noises—squeals and sighs and whisperings that pitched my stomach over.

I turned to look directly at Domescia and Carboh to find them studying me with keen intensity, and at that moment my impulse was to run from the house, but as much as I despised Eddie, I could not leave him there alone.

The five at the top of the stairs shifted away and us four moved through a wide doorway and into a large, poorly-lit room. The windows in there were tall and curtain-less, and through them I could see the moving forest trees and the different ever-changing shapes they were making. I kept close to Eddie on one side and was aware that Carboh was sticking close to him on the other, while Domescia guided us to the centre of the room and had us all sit down together in a nest of cushions. I could see no other furniture, and its absence alarmed me further.

I decided that Eddie was getting off on the novelty of the situation, it being so opposite to his normal life of bars and drinking and gambling with men who had big opinions but led sloppy, repetitive lives—and the whole woeful mess propped up by restless, troubled women who waited vainly for the men to morph into guys they could admire.

Domescia was touching my arm. I cringed, and she saw that, and took her hand off me. But I felt the imprint of her fingers all through that evening.

"Domescia was asking you if you were hungry, Ross," Eddie told me.

"We have plenty of food tonight," Carboh said.

I looked from my brother's face to that of the woman beside him and could not abide the closeness I felt there. Her hair was now arranged so that very little of her was visible. In the shadows of the room it was like looking at a mask-like disembodied face.

"It certainly is hungry work fixing that house," I exclaimed, attempting to smile at her. "Eddie had thought of asking his girlfriend, Cherie, to come and help us out with the cooking."

Although she regarded me steadily, it wasn't consternation that flickered across Carboh's features, but pity. It was as if I was very far behind in this game. She knew about Cherie and didn't care, perhaps. Ross laughed in a light and happy way, and taking Carboh's hand in his, he played with her fingers, while she gazed at me with what I took to be distain.

"Our mother will come to meet with us later," Domescia announced. "She doesn't eat any longer, so she does not attend when we gather, but she was concerned you might think badly of her if she was absence at our feast."

I found myself shrugging in a surly kind of way. "But this is the first I've ever heard of her," I said, " . . . and she doesn't have a clue who I am."

"But we have talked to her about you at length," Carboh said, "and she has a great desire to meet you."

"Me?" I asked, "to meet me?"

"In particular, you."

"Why?"

"You don't know our ways. She would like to help you with them."

"And Eddie does know your ways?" I asked, pointing at him.

"He senses them rather than knows them; in that regard he is generous."

I could feel a surge of fury rising in me at her words. Eddie senses them? Eddie is generous? I clenched my jaw and studied my own hands so that I could get a moment's relief from looking at the faces of those women.

Before I could think of what next to say to them, the door opened and the other five entered, and with them came a perfume—a scent—so exquisite and lingering, that I could scarcely help myself, I threw my head back and inhaled deeply and the long drawn out sigh that I heard came from my own lips.

I try to remember the moment often. The women came in, walking one behind the other, and arranged themselves, cross-legged on the floor in a circle around the cushion nest. At what point Domescia and Carboh shifted to join the outer circle, I cannot be sure, but it ended up with Eddie and me facing each other within the circle of women. The drowsiness that overcame me was utterly delicious, and the only other time I can remember smelling a scent as compelling, was when I was taking photographs in the concrete suburbs of Tangiers, and the scent of the Night Queen wafted across the neighbourhood. Someone told me that on the night the single flower blossoms, dogs and quarrelling lovers become silent in the hypnotic miasma. I tried to read my brother's face through my curious other worldliness, because surely it was happening to him as well. He seemed very composed, but nothing about his expression told me he was wallowing in the same way I found myself to be.

We ate things; how and when it happened, I do not know, but we ate things. We ate sticky messy unidentifiable stuff, and I found myself so ravenous that I didn't care to question what it was I was putting into my mouth. Eddie and I were talking, I know we were, and from time to time, one of the women made a remark, or someone laughed behind us. But I don't remember the details. At a certain point, a change occurred; the mother entered the room, and however mesmerised I'd become, her presence demanded utter attention. I sat up properly on the cushions and looked above the heads of the daughters to a tall, gaunt woman in dark clothing. She had no hair. I glanced at Eddie who was smiling up at her in an obsequious way that made a flare of anger arise in my belly.

"You should be happy for your brother, Ross," the mother whispered as if she could see instantly what I was feeling. "He has discarded his earth bonds so he can forever float."

After that, I *know* a conversation took place, and I believe it went this way with me replying: "You've just said something that means diddly-squat to me, Mam."

"That is no more than I expected," the mother murmured, "I was told about you."

I looked quickly at Domescia and Carboh, the only two of the seven weird sisters I had met. They smiled benignly at me between their curtains of hair. "You will forgive me, Mam, but I cannot see how it could be any concern of yours what and who I am."

"But my daughter Carboh is winding with your brother, so of course you are interesting to us!" She laughed then, and it really, really frightened me. In my panic, I wanted to claw my way out of the cage of scent, because that's how it seemed to me then.

I grabbed hold of Eddie's arm, but he shrugged me off. "Don't do that, Ross," he whispered.

"Stand up Sissiol," the mother said, "where you can be seen." One of the seven arose and walked around the outside of the sitting women until she was facing me. Like the others, she was sheathed in hair, and hers was the colour of river mud. Her face was angelic, her lips embarrassingly sensual. I glanced at the other women, at their glinting eyes, their white brows, their delicate hands. Each was smiling at me, in the way a woman does at a baby, full of warm love, openness and delight. Sissiol slowly extended her hands through her hair and held them open to me in a manner that suggested that I should rise and go to her.

I stood up suddenly, and kicked my brother on his ankle as hard as I could. "For Christ's Sake, what've you got me into here, Eddie?"

The women swayed and sighed and seemed to me to squeak, almost. Sissiol lowered her arms and turned her mouth down in a parody of disappointment and went to lay her head on the breast of the bald-headed horror.

Eddie stood up too, and gestured to Carboh to stay where she was, and then something between him and the mother took place, some unspoken understanding, because the circle of women parted, Eddie pushed me forward, and we were outside the . . . enchantment. It was as if the extraordinary perfume had surrounded us in a bubble that we'd broken out of. Sissiol and the mother shifted away from us into the far corner of the room, and I, with my brother, headed for the door. Outside the nest of cushions and the circle of women, the change in temperature was startling—inside had been beautifully warm, outside it was cool, and I was thankful for it because my brain began to awaken from whatever mesmerism had taken place in that company. We did not speak on the way home through the wood, and it didn't even occur to me to use Dad's torch to guide us back.

I stayed in bed in my old room the next day. Fuck the decorating, I thought. I stared upwards at the familiar crack in the ceiling that, as a child, I used to imagine was a road that would take me on wonderful adventures. I would visit as many countries in the world as there were to visit. I'd yearned to be a traveller, but I'd ended up struggling for money no more than forty kilometres from this house in Holesville Nine, a pit of a town. As I reached my arms out from beneath the blankets, I noticed a yellow-coloured indentation on my arm. Rubbing did not change it, and I realised it was where Domescia had gripped me the night before.

Eddie came into my room with coffee and doughnuts. I could scarcely look at him.

"I thought you're like Sissiol," he said, putting the tray on my bedside table. "She's really intelligent you know. You like intelligent women, don't you?"

"Eddie, they're not women," I answered, "what is the *matter* with you?"

"What is the matter with you, more like? Do you know how rude you were last night?"

I sat up and stared at him. "How the hell did you get involved with them, and so quickly?"

Eddie smiled at me and then frowned as if he was dealing with a wayward but much loved child. "When we were with the sisters, Ross, were you aware of time passing?"

I shrugged. "No, I can't say I was."

"So, what did you feel like, until Mother came in?" I didn't want to tell him. I wanted to remind him that our mother was dead and that bald-headed freak woman was not "Mother." "Did you feel *good*, Ross?"

I swung my feet out of bed and began to dress. "Yes, damn and blast you to hell. I felt ecstatic. I felt as if I could be there forever in that . . . perfume. Where did it come from, Eddie?"

"Where did what come from?"

"That perfume. Is it something those women put in their hair?"

"They don't put it in their hair, Ross."

"What then—was it some kind of incense?"

"No. It is their hair."

I repeated him, stupidly. "Their hair does that?" I sat heavily back on the bed.

"Wonderful isn't it?" my brother whispered.

"How about we change plans, Eddie? How about we sell the house as it is and split the money. Get back to normal life, eh? Don't you miss Cherie just a bit?"

"I don't care what we do with the house in all honesty, Ross. And as for money . . . ." He sighed and stretched as if delirious with pleasure.

"What about all your debts you were so intent on paying off with your share?"

"Ah! That was before."

"Before you met those women, you mean."

"Please don't call them that, Ross. Anyhow, didn't you say they're *not* women?"

"I've never met women like them in my life before! And what was going on with that one called Sissy?"

"Mother wanted you to meet her, to see her beauty."

"Fuck off, Eddie! Just fuck off!"

I left the house, got in my jeep, and headed for town. I found a café with hardly anyone in it and ate a good breakfast. I didn't know what to do, and I found myself crying without caring if I was seen or not. The night before I'd experienced the most pleasurable dream-like sensations I could ever have imagined. I could've stayed and stayed and stayed. I could've given myself; I could've gone with that ghoul of a woman with hair the colour of mud. Yet in me, deep and powerful, was some instinct that must've been entirely missing in my brother. I feared for him. Yet, I argued to myself that he was a grown man and he could do what he liked.

I stayed away from the house for most of the day, and when I got back, Eddie was there, in the kitchen, cooking something. "Well, little brother, you're full of surprises!"

"I went to the new shop on the tarmac road, they sell pies and stuff, thought we could do with a good meal."

I set about lighting the old stove as the air was getting cold in the falling light. I glanced at him; he seemed relaxed and cheerful, the slightly troubled look he habitually had was gone, and it came to me in a rush of feeling that I loved him . . . after all and after everything, I loved him. "Thanks for doing that, Eddie," I said.

He shrugged and laughed, and turned his head to smile at me. "So, are we okay?"

"Yes," I whispered. "Let's get back to work, eh? Let's finish the house, and leave. I'll come back for the woodworm guys, you don't have to worry."

"Whatever, Ross. I'm happy."

I straightened up and stood looking at him. "You look it."

"It puts everything in perspective, you know."

"What does?"

"Being happy; feeling content with all about you, feeling . . . blithe."

I laughed. "Blithe? I couldn't have guessed you even knew a word like that."

"Well, one of the things living and working together has shown us, is how little we *do* know about each other, Ross."

I turned away to check the stove. "How about when we get home, we make an effort to do things together from now on . . . like we could meet for a meal once a week. You could bring Cherie. You're wrong to think I don't like her, Eddie. Actually, I find her heart-breaking the way she adores you."

"I'm not going back to Holesville Nine, Ross. I couldn't take Carboh there, could I?"

I curbed the impulse to fling insults at him; I laughed as if we were engaged in pleasant chit-chat instead. "Hey!" I said, maybe you could buy my half of Mum and Dad's house and move in there with your . . ."

"No. The sisters must be together. They must not be separated. I'm moving down into their house. There's plenty of room and they struggle a bit with chores and so forth, and now that Mother is ill, it's very hard on everyone." He laid one bowl on the table, broke up some bread pieces and invited me to sit.

"You not eating, Eddie?"

"No. I look at it and don't quite see it as food. I cooked it for you."

"Thank-you, then. It looks good. So, tell me, are you really planning to marry Carboh?"

"I'm winding with her, that's what they call it."

"Ah! You mean that's what they call it where they come from?"

"I guess."

"So, where *do* they come from?"

A moment of discomfort moved across his face, and a flicker of the old Eddie was visible. "They've been in that house a very long time, so they're more connected to this area than anyone else around here. They know Mr. Ratchetson well."

"I didn't mean anything by it, Eddie, it's just that their ways of doing things are so different. "So when you *wind* with Carboh, am I invited to the ceremony?"

Eddie shook his head. "I'm afraid not, it's intensely private."

"Really?"

"You could wind with one of them yourself, Ross. You could wind with Sissiol; she's ready."

I felt my stomach lurch, and I put down my fork and drank some water. I glanced at my brother over the rim of the glass. It was as if all his anxiety had vanished; he seemed almost noble. "When are you going there again, Eddie? I need to know because we did have a plan once about how we were going to deal with this house."

"You needn't worry, Ross. I've discussed the matter with the household, and they've agreed I should carry on with the work, and visit them at night time."

"They've *agreed*, did you say?"

"Yes, Ross. They're generous like that."

I stared at him. When did I lose him? What happened that I didn't see?

⟜

I stood in the hall for a long time with Mr. Ratchetson as if he couldn't quite bring himself to lead me into one of the rooms. In the end, we went to the kitchen, where he, with painful slowness, prepared some foul-smelling coffee. I was happy to see him reach for a bottle of whiskey and with badly shaking hands, pour a tot into each chipped mug.

"I could see from the outset that your brother was in danger," he told me. "He's the anxious type, isn't he?"

"You were telling me how long those women have been down there in the wood, Mr. Ratchetson, and I didn't quite catch what you said. I think you might have been joking, but seriously, has the family been there a long time?"

"Family, you say?"

"Yes, mother, father, children," I said loudly.

Mr. Ratchetson shook his head. "That's not the way it is with them."

"Well . . ."

"It's just women always."

"A cult of women, then."

"What's that?" he asked, turning to face me.

"Just women in the cult," I repeated. "You say my brother is in danger. Can you tell me why?"

"My guess would be that they've already got to him. I don't know how close you two are; you were always together when you were boys, so he might let you in on a few things."

"Eddie said the women knew you, is that right?" Mr. Ratchetson drew in a deeply-wheezing breath and laughed, and at the end of it his mouth was still open. "It was their house you told us to avoid when we first met you, wasn't it?"

He nodded and his reptilian eyes blinked and stared, blinked and stared. "Your brother will be for a winding," he whispered.

"He is, Mr. Ratchetson. He's going to be wound . . . winded . . . to one there called Carboh."

"So, it's her turn now, is it?"

I stood up, and taking my mug to his kitchen window, looked out at the dark line of trees and the track that led down to them. I felt as if I was getting nowhere with the old guy. "You knew my parents, Mr. Ratchetson, right?"

"Nice pair."

"Yes."

"She was in some danger though."

"My mother?"

"Lovely woman."

"How in danger, Mr. Ratchetson."

"Billy."

"Pardon."

"You're old enough now to call me Billy."

"Okay, Billy. My mother . . ."

"All that hair, you see."

"She cut the whole lot of it off, one day."

"I know. It was my advice. Lovely woman."

"You advised her to cut her hair off?"

"Competition with those in the wood, you see. They were taking too much interest in her. Following her to the brink. I used to see them hankering to get at her. She started going in there to pick berries and fungus. I told her. I said they feasted their eyes on her."

"The brink?"

"The wood's edge. They don't come out farther."

"But she was okay, my mother?"

"One time they chased her hard. She came hurtling out of there and fell down by my garden gate. I thought she was going to explode with terror. I looked over yonder and the one called Domescia was standing as boldly as you please just under that first tree with the split trunk. They think they're camouflaged you see. They think if they stand against the trunks, they can't be seen. But I got used to picking them out, living here so close by."

I went to the old man's cupboard and brought out the whiskey. He was shivering badly and I was feeling nauseous. I poured a good glug-full into our mugs and sat down opposite him at the table. "It would seem," I said, "that Domescia has a daughter or granddaughter also called Domescia. I've met her, her and Carboh, the one my brother is interested in."

"No. There's just one Domescia. You say he likes the one called Carboh?"

"Yes, and when I was in their house . . ."

I saw Mr. Ratchetson blanch. He swallowed hard several times with an alarming amount of effort, and lowered his head. "I told you to walk on *by* if you came across that house, you stupid young idiot."

"We found it by accident down a plaited path, and Domescia and Carboh where there watching us from the shadow of a tree. My brother was drawn to them more or less on the instant."

"Thought he would be," the old man murmured, "he's just the type."

"What type, Mr. Ratchetson?"

Oh, you know; a wastrel with big ideas and a lot of self-regard. They're the ones who fall the fastest. But I'm warning you, they can get just about any man if they're minded to."

"How would you know what my brother's like, Mr. Ratchetson?" I whispered.

"Well, it's plain on his face and in his expressions, is it not?"

"I didn't think it showed," I answered. "Anyhow, are you saying other men have got themselves involved in that cult?"

"Cult, you say—what gives you that notion?"

"Weird stuff happened when we went to visit them," I mumbled. I wanted to talk again about my mother, and it was as if Mr. Ratchetson realised that. He stared at me for a while, and reached his ancient hand across and rested it upon mine lightly.

"Your mother, Ann, was stubborn, that was the trouble. I believe she even befriended those creatures for a while. I think they laid in wait for her and wanted to play with her hair. But she got frightened of them, especially the mother, whose own hair dragged along the ground for a foot or so behind her. There was a time when your father had to go in and pluck her back from them—the winders had set about her on the forest path one afternoon when she'd gone in there for wood, and they were lashing her with thorny branches until she bled."

"Christ Almighty, Mr. Ratchetson. . . . Christ Almighty."

"That's what I used to say too. Not that church would've done any good where the winders are concerned."

"Winders?"

"Yes, because of what they do . . . the foul stuff they do in the wood."

"Do other people round here know about them?"

Mr. Ratchetson shrugged. "I don't go talking to people in town, so I couldn't tell you. Maybe some do, and maybe some don't. You should get your brother to leave."

"I've tried. He doesn't want to. I can't force him. If that sort of life is what he wants, why should I stop him anyway?"

I sat bewildered at Mr. Ratchetson's table, and for a good while neither of us spoke again. "But my mother was okay in the end, wasn't she, so maybe Eddie will be too," I said finally. I stood up to go, as I sensed rather than saw the coming of the dark and the walk back to our house was a bit of a stretch. I was feeling frightened. Mr. Ratchetson looked upwards into my face, but all I could see in his eyes was pity.

I cursed myself on the way home; I'd asked the old guy far too many questions and come away with hardly any answers. " . . . because of what they do . . . the foul stuff they do in the wood," is what he'd said, and I hadn't pressed him on the point. I stopped on the track and looked back at his weathered old house, but could not bring myself to return and bother him further.

Eddie was on the veranda reading the local paper when I arrived home. The air had darkened and the first bull frogs were beginning their rasping croaks. I felt utterly forlorn and deeply troubled; it was as if I was watching my brother teetering on the edge of a cliff. I'd considered contacting Cherie myself and asking her over to spend some time with us, but she'd have wanted to talk to Eddie, and I could see only confusion and anger as a consequence.

Eddie patted the seat beside him and I went to sit with him gladly and in the hope he'd changed his mind about Carboh. "Anything in the papers?" I asked.

"No. There never is. I was just whiling away some time, waiting for you to come back. Wondering where you'd gone, actually. This business with the house isn't really working out too well is it? We've got three rooms finished, that's all, and those windows in Mum and Dad's room will take a fair bit of work, won't they?"

"Let's pack up and leave, Eddie. We can hire some painters to do the work for us, it'd be worth the money and we've got to pay the woodworm people anyway. I say let's skedaddle and get back home."

"So where did you go, Ross?"

"To Mr. Ratchetson's." I paused, but saw immediately how I could use the moment. "He told me about the time Mum cut her hair off."

"Oh, wow! I never thought of asking him that."

"Yes, well it's a pretty terrible story and you should know that it directly involves the women that you're intending to hang out with."

Eddie shook his head. "That was, what? Thirty odd years ago, so you're talking rubbish, Ross."

For a moment, I was floored. "Well it was the same family, at any rate," I said.

"Carboh and the others can't be responsible for things that went on in the past. You're being illogical and really mean to them."

"Mean," I repeated. "Look, I'm worried about you, Eddie. You're behaving as if nothing you've ever known before matters now."

"You've got it in one. That's exactly how I *do* feel."

"So when's the wedding?"

Eddie laughed and slapped his hand down hard on my knee. "You won't let up on that one will you?" he asked.

"The winding, then?"

"Windings happen at dawn, and I don't think Mother has decided the day yet. Carboh will let me know."

"Will there be a party afterwards?"

"The winding itself is the big celebration, they tell me. But I've already said, Ross, it's a private affair, and you're not invited."

"So, supposing I get in some drinks and a bit of food, sandwiches or something, pizza slices, and you both come back here afterwards?"

"Yeah. Maybe. But where goes one, goes all."

"Huh?"

"The sisters and Mother, you should invite them."

I could not bear to turn my face and look at him, so I stood up and turned to go inside. "Of course," I answered over my shoulder, "of course."

I believe that it was only by chance that I awoke as the sun came up on the morning of my brother's winding. He was using Mum and Dad's old room while he prepared to paint his own, and the squeak of that door had never been dealt with. I think I heard it in my sleep and woke up on the instant. I heard the soft click of the front door and went to the window. Sure enough, Eddie was out there heading towards the wood. I knew I could easily lose him if I didn't move swiftly and by the time I was also on the path, he'd just disappeared into the first line of trees. I sprinted. My shoelace was untied and whipping itself around my bare ankle.

Once I was in the wood proper, I stood for a moment to catch my breath and listen out for sounds. There was nothing but the whispering of wind through leaf. I stuck to the main path for a good while, hurrying, then slowing down, then hurrying again. My heart felt wretched and I knew I was badly frightened, yet just as it was when we first encountered Domescia and Carboh, I couldn't describe the nature my terror or explain the reason for it.

I made my way towards the plaited path, supposing that I might be able to locate them in the surrounding area, as surely, if they were having a version of a wedding no matter how peculiar, there'd be noise, and particularly if the activity was as foul as the old man had said. I stopped and started many times, wanting so badly to call out to my brother, but not daring to. I could hear nothing, no birds even, and it was only the sight of some broken stems that sent me off down a meandering track to the left of the main pathway. I blundered along it, suddenly convinced it was the right way, and sure enough, I came to a wide circular opening in the forest with few trees, and there they all were. When I try to tell Cherie this . . . when I try to describe it to her, she starts her uncontrollable sobbing, and yet, she is so fierce to know about it that she never gives up making me describe it. She often says, "you say Eddie had no clothes on, Ross. Are you sure?"

"I could see his legs sticking out under that mess."

Fact is, after I'd both seen and understood it, I retreated to Mum and Dad's house and holed up there for many days, and it was only when Cherie arrived noisily by car, that I tried to connect again with the outside world. I came out to the veranda to meet her.

"Hey, Ross! How's it going?" she asked. She had on those shoes poised on a mountain of cork that some women are drawn too, and she was trying to see where best to put her feet as she made her way towards me. "I got this idea you might like someone to cook for you while you're doing up the house, I mean where's the harm? So I came over," she said, just as she read something on my face that alarmed her.

"Where is he?" she asked.

I shook my head. "You know Eddie. He's gone off, Cherie. He suddenly took it into his head he wanted to go travelling. He's gone."

"You're kidding me," she said. "The fucker."

"Yes. In any case, I'm not sticking around either."

"Why do you look like that, Ross?"

"Like what?"

"Like the whole world's gone to shit."

"Do I?"

"I think you know you do. Something's happened, and if you try and bullshit me and say it hasn't, I'm going to shoot you, right there on that veranda."

However wrong it was of me to involve someone as child-like and innocent as Cherie, I couldn't help myself; I didn't want to carry what I'd seen around with me by myself any longer, and so I think I was brutal in the way I handled her.

I told her as much as I knew before saying anything important, before describing what I actually saw. I thought I could limber up to it, if in the end I had to tell her, and it would be easier that way . . . and I cannot say at what point I did begin explaining what happened to my brother in that clearing—at least what I could see of it.

"He'd been really restless and snappy before he left Holesville Nine," Cherie declared. "He was worried about working with you because he reckons you always look down on him."

I shrugged. "You know yourself what he's like, you're forever bailing him out of one situation or another."

"Yes, but I love him, so it's my job."

"Don't you ever worry about yourself, Cherie, instead of about my brother?"

"You think I'm such a small person that I don't have enough of what it takes to worry about the both of us?"

"No. Of course not; I didn't mean that at all. I'm talking about the futility of it."

"That's just mean of you, Ross. Who exactly were the women you say you saw anyway?"

"A bunch of weird women with very long hair who lived in an old house in the wood, Cherie. That's all I know."

"Hippy types?"

"Well, I had the idea they were part of a cult at first."

"Are you saying Eddie got involved with them or something? You can tell me, I don't mind; I'm used to him. What you don't realise about your brother is that he knows he's got a soul, so he's always interested in anything that he thinks shows him the meaning of life."

Which of the sisters was sitting astride my brother's chest was difficult to see at first, but after some long minutes standing there at the edge of the clearing, I saw that it was Carboh. She was sitting astride his body with her head close to his face, and her hair, all the long length of it was wound, cocoon-tight around his neck and upper chest. I could see my brother's face, pale and slack. Below Carboh, and also sitting on his body, facing in the opposite direction, was Domescia, and she had her hair wound tightly around his middle section. I could see the top of his bare thighs. Domescia kept yanking her head up in little jerking motions, although there were no sounds. Sissiol was attached to one of his legs, her hair wound down the whole length of it, and she was lying face up with her head near his bare feet. Likewise, one of the others was attached to his left leg, and at his two arms, women had wound their hair round and round him. The seventh of the sisters was rocking backwards and forwards a few feet away in the arms of the hideous mother. Beyond my terror and revulsion, I registered that this seventh was not yet ready to feast.

Eddie looked like a gigantic brown cocoon, and I knew he was dead by the striking whiteness of his feet and face. "Let's just stick on this path and find the ash," he'd said on the first day we ventured into the wood proper, and I'd said, "No, come on, let's just take a quick look down there. Where's the harm?"

WHATEVER COMES AFTER CALCUTTA

DAVID ERIK NELSON

It was late in the day when Lyle Morimoto saw the hanged woman and almost crashed his Prius.

He was somewhere between Calcutta, Ohio, and whatever the hell came after Calcutta. For hours he'd been sipping warm Gatorade and cruising the crumbling two-lane blacktop that sliced up the scrubby farmland separating Calcutta, Cairo, Congo, Lebanon, East Liverpool, East Palestine—in southern Ohio, apparently, you could circle the globe without ever crossing the state line.

He understood that he was not thinking clearly, but that seemed okay, since it also meant not thinking about his ear, or his wife, or Detective Jason Good, or the gun in the pocket of his suit jacket.

Lyle's day had begun in court. He'd had every reason to assume it would end there, as would the next day, and possibly the day after that. But midway through jury selection, his client had pled guilty to the charge of fifth-degree arson, despite the fact that she'd demonstrably not set the fire. Before being led away, she had leaned in close to Lyle's ear and whispered that she *hadn't* torched that trash can, but *had* murdered two girls that no one knew about, so she figured this "evened things up." She'd looked enormously relieved, almost radiant.

As the court officer led the defendant back to holding, Lyle had struggled to feel something about this—frustration at the System, disgust with humanity, pleasure at escaping the dingy hearing room, hope that an unexpectedly free morning might allow him to make a dent in the mountain of paperwork surrounding his desk, even just relief that he wouldn't have to eat lunch out of the vending machines again.

At the very least, he should *say* something—if not to the judge or court officer, at least to his client, who would spend no more than a single year in prison, then walk out having absolved herself of double murder.

But Lyle felt nothing in particular, and so did nothing in particular.

Lyle had only been planning to stop at his house long enough to change into chinos and microwave some noodles. But when he opened his bedroom door he froze, wondering if they'd been robbed. He and Olivia had left the room pin neat that morning: tidy bed buried under a small mountain of varicolored throw pillows, curtains drawn back to let in the morning sun, closet and bathroom doors closed, not a dust mote in the bright air. The room he saw before him was a mess: dim, curtains drawn, bathroom door ajar, mountain of pillows littering the floor, bed in disarray.

But what half-witted burglar left a $3,000 flat-screen TV in the living room in favor of trashing the bedroom?

Then the sheets burst with sudden movement. Olivia scrabbled to cover herself, cowering against the bedside table and lamp. The man with her leapt in the opposite direction, coming to rest as far as he could from the bed, arms extended, palms out.

Lyle riffled through the range of emotions he thought he should feel—rage, wrath, indignation, embarrassment, sorrow—but none of them were there. He didn't even feel particularly surprised. Not that he'd suspected—he'd suspected nothing—but just that this sort of monumental, senseless slap in the face seemed, in its randomness, entirely predictable. If working in the justice system had convinced him of anything, it was that while there was indeed a System, there was no Justice.

The naked guy who'd just leapt out of Lyle's bed was remarkably good-looking. Pale, yes, but well-muscled through the arms and legs, with *Men's Health* abs and pecs, and that little muscular pelvic V-thing all the guys had in that *Magic Mike* movie Olivia loved. But he had a kind of weird dick. Nothing earth-shattering, just more emphatically curved than Lyle would have thought comfortable. It reminded him of the big Koegel's hot-dog billboard he passed every day heading into the city, which showed an enormous, bun-less, upthrusting wiener proudly surmounted by the words *SERVE THE CURVE.*

Out in the kitchen the microwave beeped; his noodles were ready.

"Hey there," the naked man panted, and Lyle realized he knew him: this was a detective with the local PD, Jason something.

"Jason Good?" Lyle asked, recalling that, the one time they'd met, he'd made some crack about being glad to finally meet that "Good Cop" he was always hearing about. The detective had laughed genuinely at the joke. He'd seemed like a legitimately good guy.

"Yeah," the Good Cop said, open hands still outthrust. "We met one time, at a fundraising thing. Listen, I know this looks—"

Then the world exploded, a sound so loud that it was more light and heat than noise.

Then darkness.

Lyle's hearing cleared quickly but his head continued to ring like a struck bell. He found himself on the floor, his face numb, as though he'd gotten a dose of Novocain. He felt no urge to move or speak or continue living.

"—SHOT HIM IN THE HEAD, Olivia!" Jason Good cried. "Whyd'ya do that, Olivia?"

"I don't know!" Lyle's wife shrieked back.

Bleeding to death in an awkward jumble of decorative pillows, Lyle thought of a number: *4.5*. He'd read it on a poster in his doctor's waiting room: You're 4.5 times more likely to be shot if you keep a gun in the home. He had scoffed at that number once. Shame on him.

The gun had been in the bedside table. He'd put it there himself. The district attorney had advised getting something for "home protection" immediately after Lyle joined the public defenders' office. "You'll be in court," she snuffled, sounding like a cartoon bulldog. "People end up behind bars—despite your best efforts. People are unhappy. People have family. Doesn't matter that you were technically on their side. If these people were good at thinking things through, you never would have met them to begin with."

"Okayokayokayokayokay . . . ," Jason Good's words floated around somewhere above Lyle. He heard the man drop down and start tossing pillows around. "Get dressed," Good said, his voice full of both confidence and urgency. "We've gotta clear out. Where the fuck is my other sock?"

"What? We have to call nine-one-one!"

"You shot your husband in the head, Olivia! With a stupid hand-cannon as loud as a goddamn A-bomb, Olivia! Some neighbor has *definitely* already called nine-one-one. Responders will be here in under seven minutes. We need to be as far and deniable from here as possible in seven minutes, Olivia."

Lyle heard her leap from the bed. The bang of the headboard against the drywall reverberated, as though he was in a long metallic hallway. *Oh*, he thought. *I'm dying now.*

"Go where?" Olivia shouted, hangers clattering in the closet.

"I don't—" Good stopped throwing pillows. "What about that place you share with your sisters, that cottage near Calcutta?"

"What about it?" she asked, her voice momentarily muffled as she pulled on a sweater. "Calcutta is to hell and gone!"

"Exactly—" Good began, but Lyle missed the rest as he finally succumbed to blood loss.

⊸

Lyle Awoke. It was painfully apparent that he was not dead. There were no cops or EMTs wandering around trying to figure out what the hell had happened, so he assumed he'd been unconscious for under seven minutes. As his vision cleared, Lyle found himself staring under the bed, the dust ruffle tickling his nose. Just inches away lay a detective's badge on its leather belt-clip placard, J. GOOD emblazoned across the bottom. And on the far side of the bed, just in front of the bedside table, was a nickel-plated revolver, the Taurus .45 Public Defender he'd bought, put in the bedside table, and not thought of since.

He reached under the bed for the forgotten badge, then carefully circled around for the pistol. Lyle didn't particularly want these things, but leaving them lying there seemed fundamentally wrong.

He caught his reflection in Olivia's vanity mirror and was astounded by how bad he looked.

There was a long lash-mark across his left cheek where his wife's bullet had grazed him before mostly tearing off his ear, which now dangled upside down from the still-attached lobe. He carefully reached for the ear with his left hand, then thought better of it and instead vomited on the thick cream carpeting. His face was numb, not the roaring mask of pain he expected. Maybe that was a good sign?

The one time Olivia and Lyle had gone to her family place near Calcutta, they'd attended a rodeo and seen an amateur bullrider almost lose an ear while trying to last eight seconds on the back of a speckled bull named "Hot for Teacher." The bull had thrown the kid in just under two seconds, hooking the rider's helmet in the process and tossing it into the bleachers, despite the straps staying steadfastly buckled. The waiting EMTs—neither of whom had looked a day older than the gawky bullrider they were patching up, all three of whom seemed ready to puke—had glued the torn ear back in place using generic superglue. Not twenty minutes later, Lyle had seen the dazed kid wandering the midway with his buddies, drinking a large Pepsi from a paper cup, his hat pulled down low at an odd angle so the hatband could hold his ear in place while the glue set.

Lyle stumbled to his kitchen. He pawed through the junk drawer, found an expired bottle of Tylenol 3 with codeine, washed one down with a warm slug of Gatorade, pocketed the bottle, pawed further, came up with a tube of superglue, and went to the bright half-bath just off their entryway.

A week ago, his wife had hung one of those little framed inspirational "Footprints" poems next to the mirror. It was the one about Jesus, where the speaker recounts a dream where she's walking down the beach, two sets of footprints trailing behind her. But during the worst passages of her life she looks back and there's only one set of prints, and she feels totally abandoned.

Lyle considered this as he twisted the cap off the glue and leaned toward the mirror. The poem suddenly felt portentous—although he wondered how much of that was due to the cocktail of codeine, Gatorade, and adrenaline stewing in his guts.

To his surprise, reattaching the ear was remarkably similar to reattaching a teacup handle—which was what he'd bought the glue for originally. Afterward he opened the hall closet, grabbed a Toledo Mud Hens stocking cap, and pulled it on, pinning his loose ear to the side of his head.

Lyle heard the approach of distant sirens. He hustled into his Prius and out of his neighborhood. He didn't want to go to the hospital, or to file a police report. For that matter, he didn't particularly want to go chasing after his wife and Detective Jason Good.

But he'd walked in on them having sex and, in contradiction to every country or blues song ever recorded, *he'd* somehow been the one who got shot over it. This felt fundamentally unfair.

Now he had a gun in his pocket and a full tank of gas. It looked an awful lot like the Universe might be trying to give him a nudge in the right direction.

At the very least, he deserved an explanation.

And that explanation was headed to Calcutta.

After several hours, Lyle had finally begun to accept the possibility that the Universe had no particular plan, and he'd likely never find his wife's family's cottage.

Then he glanced up from tuning the radio and saw the bucking woman dangling from that neglected field's single misshapen tree. Arms bound at her waist, she threw herself against the crisp spring air, her spasms both frantic and hopeless.

"Olivia?" he said, absolutely certain—illogical as it was—that he was seeing his wife being hanged in a fallow field next to a slouching barn.

He hit the brakes and veered onto the soft shoulder. The loose gravel sucked at the wheels, but he managed to bring the car to a shuddering stop rather than flip it into the deep drainage ditch. Lyle was out before he knew what he was doing, vaulting the culvert, charging across the stubble, the heavy pistol battering his hip.

It was almost immediately obvious that the woman was not his wife. Even as a distant silhouette, she was clearly too old, too scrawny, her hair all wrong. But Lyle did not flag. He was moving on instinct, and moving on instinct felt okay—or, at least, it felt better than feeling nothing. He'd slowly realized that feeling nothing felt *terrible*.

Racing closer, Lyle saw the aluminum A-frame ladder tumbled beneath the hanged woman. He poured his last ounce of panic into a sprint, and without thinking—he would certainly have botched it if he had—Lyle vaulted from the ground to the fallen ladder's side rail, took a wild leap, grabbed hold of the cord a good two feet above the old woman's head, and held on for dear life. The branch sagged a few inches, landing the woman's feet firmly on the ladder rail. Then the limb snapped with a soggy crack, dumping them both onto the hard earth.

Lyle immediately rolled on top of the thrashing woman, trying to worm his fingers between the noose and her throat. Her face was a swollen purple caricature. One of her arms had come loose in the fall, but the other remained lashed to her waist by a complicated set of thin leather straps and buckles. Their hands bashed and stumbled over each other as they struggled to loosen the noose. It wasn't even rope, Lyle discovered, but instead a length of salvaged Ethernet cable, sticky with age.

They finally got the knot to budge a single gasping inch, and then another, and then they were yanking the cord freely. She immediately rolled over and crawled blindly away on elbow and knees, hacking and grinding like an engine full of sand, one arm still bound. Lyle had a single panting moment to notice how clean the soles of the woman's feet were, soft and seashell pink as a toddler's, before he heard a throat clearing behind him.

"Pardon me?" someone asked. "No offense or nothing, but what the heck do you think you're doing?"

Lyle rose slowly, sliding his hand into his jacket pocket as he did so, finding his pistol and the "Good Cop's" badge. The owner of the twang was clear-eyed and amiable. He wore a filthy mesh-backed Marlboro cap and a similarly grimy work jacket, the cuffs black and chewed up from long years spent elbow-deep in engines. EARL was embroidered over his heart in red floss.

There was a crowd of very surprised people behind Earl, standing or sitting in lawn chairs shaded by the collapsing barn. To Lyle's eye, they were prototypical rural Ohio: white people, men and women, mostly dressed like they'd just got off from work, mechanics and Subway sandwich girls and schoolteachers and farmers. There were even a few kids, seated cross-legged on a wide, flat board to keep their pants clean. The youngest looked confused by what had been—and was still—happening, but the older kids were keenly, sickeningly thrilled, both by the spectacle of the hanging of the woman and by the action hero antics that had interrupted the show.

Lyle immediately understood how he'd managed to miss the spectators: He'd been focused on the woman fighting the strangling line in the blazing light of the sunset. They'd been sitting quietly in the barn's deep shadow, as quiet and watchful and unobtrusive as birds on a wire.

He glanced at his watch. Fewer than five minutes had passed since he'd looked up from his car radio.

Behind Lyle, the woman hacked and retched, dragging her breath down her throat like a blade scraping a dry whetstone.

"You could have killed this woman," he panted.

"Well, yeah," Earl said. "Duh. If you hadn't messed it up. Now we gotta start from scratch. She ain't even a little dead." Earl paused, giving Lyle a once-over: rumpled suit, blood-stiff shirt collar, puffy face, mangled ear held in place by a Mud Hens ski cap. "Not to be rude or nothing, but what happened to your face?"

Lyle fought the urge to reach up and check whether his ear had torn loose. Instead, he pulled his hand from his pocket and discovered he was holding the badge, J. GOOD embossed in clear blue lettering across the banner along the bottom of the shield.

Earl squinted at the badge in Lyle's hand. "Officer J. Good?" He read. "Like 'Johnny B. Goode' in that song?"

"*Detective* Jason Good," Lyle heard himself say. "I'm asking the questions."

They waited. And waited. A distant dog barked.

"You said you wanted to ask questions," Earl nudged, like a preschool teacher encouraging a shy show-and-teller. "Ask away."

A large bearded man in one of the folding chairs raised a finger. "Um, Earl, shouldn't we do something about Leighanne—"

Earl answered with a shrug and a shake of his head. "Naw. She's not flying off anytime soon. Just look at her?" They all looked at her for a moment, including Lyle, who had to turn to do so. She'd stopped crawling, having only made it about a yard, and was resting her head on the dirt. Her jackstraw hair—a dull blonde with dark roots—was snarled in the scrub like dog fur caught in Velcro.

"So," Earl said, "Detective Good, whatcha wanna know?"

Lyle wanted to know a lot of things: *Why had his wife shot him? Why was he chasing after her? Why was Jason Good's dick so crooked? Why had he just lied about being that crooked-dicked cop?*

Earl could help Lyle with none of these.

"What," Lyle finally asked, "what are you people doing?"

"Executing this witch," Earl answered. Many of the gathered observers were nodding.

Lyle had no idea what to say to that.

"I'm not a fucking witch," the woman croaked from the dirt. "Jesus, you dumb fucking bumpkins."

Earl shook his head and rolled his eyes. "We been through this, Leighanne. Things were no good since you moved out here, and then . . ." His mouth twitched in an involuntary grimace. "All that other stuff. We convened a Common Law Court, tested you, and . . . well, and here we are."

"Tested?" Lyle asked. He'd returned the badge to his pocket but left his hand there, sandwiched between Good's shield and Lyle's revolver.

"Yup," Earl nodded. "Tested. And she failed."

"We made a witch cake," a woman seated in a beige plastic folding chair volunteered. She looked like a generic Ohio schoolteacher: heavyset, dark hair cropped short and teased out, vaguely cat's-eye-shaped glasses on a beaded neck chain, cardigan sweater with seasonal bunnies-crosses-and-pastel-eggs motif. She looked eerily like Lyle's own third grade teacher, who would have to be at least ninety now, and presumably still back in Schaumburg, Illinois.

"Which cake?" Lyle asked, feeling like the straight man in a rejected Abbott and Costello routine.

Everyone shifted uncomfortably.

"It's like a regular cake," the schoolmarm hedged, "but for testing witches. We used plain box cake from the superstore. Yellow cake. You make it like regular, but mix the batter with the, uh . . . ," she girded herself for the next word, "*urine* of an individual, or individuals, hexed by that witch."

Lyle stared at her as he reviewed this in his head, trying to find some reasonable way to understand what she was saying.

"I Googled it," the woman offered apologetically.

Bile simmered at the back of Lyle's throat. "You made her *eat* a cake you pissed in?"

The teacher lady grimaced in shock. "Good Lord, no! We fed it to a dog—"

"My dog Chet," the fat man who had been concerned the witch might slither away interjected.

"—and the witch, Leighanne, got sick," the schoolteacher continued. "You see, the hex is passed in the urine. Any harm it comes to reflects back on the witch." She paused, then added, "I Googled it."

"And that means this woman's a witch? Because you think she got sick after that guy's dog ate a cake someone peed in?"

"I Googled it," the woman reiterated, her mouth firm.

"I had the shits from an expired can of Hormel chili!" the accused witch cried from the ground. "From the goddamn food pantry! Not 'cause Albert's dog ate piss-cake!"

"What kind of a person—" Lyle began, intending to ask what kind of a person bakes a cake with her neighbors' pee in it, but he was cut off by a fuming bald man with a white walrus mustache and bright red suspenders.

"Oh, that is *it*." The mustachioed man spoke firmly. Earl rolled his eyes, an annoyed martyr with his cross to bear.

"*She* is not a '*person*,'" the Great White Walrus thundered, pointing at the piss-baking schoolteacher. He then pointed at Earl: "*He* is not a '*person*.'" He jabbed himself in the chest: "*I* am not a '*person*'!" He flailed his pointing hands, indicating the gathered mob. "There are no '*persons*' here!"

Lyle looked around, bewildered.

"We—" he gestured at the gathered crowd "—are *sovereign citizens*, not 'persons.'"

A heavy man in a red MAKE AMERICA GREAT AGAIN ball cap piped up: "Flesh-and-blood asseverated private individuals!"

The Walrus nodded. "Article 4 free inhabitants, fully redeemed via duly filed UCC-1 statement!" The mob nodded and grunted their assent.

Despite being a lawyer, Lyle could follow little of this, even as that phrase—"sovereign citizen"—set off bells in his head. His face and ear ached like a bad tooth; not terrible, but promising more to come.

"For the purpose of this interaction," the Walrus fumed, "I am the authorized representative of JOHN ROBERT DOE." He paused, then carefully enunciated, "I am the live flesh-and-blood man Doe: John-Robert, *sui juris*. That's *Doe-FULL COLON-John-DASH-Robert, sui juris*. So don't hang your straw man B.S. on any of us!" He spat. "We. Are. *Asseverated!* I did the paperwork myself! And if you federal stormtroopers can't—"

"Settle down, J-Bob-D," Earl said soothingly, "he didn't mean nothing by it."

"He appears under color of law here!"

"He ain't under color of law; he just wandered—"

"He presented a *badge*, Roberts: Earl-James! That's—"

Earl was holding up his hands soothingly and kept repeating the words "misunderstanding" and "simmer down."

The Walrus shifted his attention back to Lyle, pointing viciously as though casting a hex of his own. "I do not wish to create joinder with you!"

"He ain't creating joinder, J-Bob-D; he just wandered in at the wrong time and has misunderstood this entire situation."

As all this played out, the alleged witch had slowly gotten to her feet, although she was still stooped over and panting, hands planted on her knees.

"Listen, Detective Good, work with me." Earl locked eyes with Lyle, then continued portentously, "You aren't here in honor of, or under jurisdiction of, any admiralty courts or their agents, *are you*?"

Lyle finally noticed that although Earl was not obviously armed, many of the gathered "private individuals" wore guns at their hips. A lone assault rifle leaned against the sagging barn. The phrase "sovereign citizen" finally clicked: He'd come across it while reading a report on domestic terrorism and anti-government groups.

Earl continued, "Nor are you appearing on these privately held lands under color of law to create joinder in any manner?"

The right answer to Earl's questions was fairly obvious:

"No," Lyle said, "of course not."

"Satisfied?" Earl asked the Walrus. The man crossed his arms above his belly, leaned back in his folding chair, and looked away, then nodded once.

"Nonetheless," Lyle said, "what's happening here isn't right. Adulterating a cake with bodily fluids is not right, regardless of intent." The schoolteacher reddened but held firm, refusing to drop her gaze. Lyle could see the words *I Googled it* forming in her mouth, although she didn't dignify his criticism with an actual response.

"That witch-cake business," Earl said reasonably, "was just the last straw that broke the camel's back. Whole thing was practically said and done by then. Our Common Law Grand Jury had already issued a True Bill of charges."

"Charges?"

"Of her witchiness. She came here and blighted our whole situation." Again, grunts and grumbles and head-nods rippled through the crowd.

Lyle glanced at the fallow field around him, the sagging barn, the fact that these many gathered "private individuals" didn't appear to have more pressing business on a weekday afternoon than sitting in a muddy field and murdering an old woman. He expected he'd now hear tales of failed crops and joblessness and bankruptcy. But that was not the case.

"She made me kill six people," a frail, elderly woman in a powder-blue camp chair and matching tracksuit offered. Nodding and affirmation again riffled the crowd. "Two big fellas that had broke into my barn in October, and then a family of four in a brand-new minivan last week. They were lost, trying to get back to the interstate. And they were *Hindus*." She looked around with mild astonishment as she added this last, although her tone was less *I can't believe I murdered an entire Indian family!* and more *I can't believe I ate an entire footlong Subway sandwich!*

A hand went up. Lyle shifted his gaze, acknowledging the hand-raiser. It was the heavy man whose red ball cap proclaimed his intent to MAKE AMERICA GREAT AGAIN. "She made me throw battery acid in some girls' faces in Pittsburgh." Again, commiseration throughout the mob like a made-for-TV AA meeting.

More hands were raised, and more voices chimed in:

"She made me poison a bunch of the formula they give out at the hospital in East Liverpool."

" . . . made me Krazy Glue razor blades all over the playground equipment out in Canton . . ."

" . . . made me mail roadkill to a daycare . . ."

"This is crazy talk," the woman muttered to Lyle, not raising her head, her moving lips concealed by her hanging hair. "You can see that."

" . . . burn down eleven churches—Jew and Islam ones, mostly . . ."

" . . . violate graves . . ."

" . . . defile . . ."

" . . . torture . . ."

" . . . corrupt . . ."

" . . . children . . ."

" . . . rode us . . ."

" . . . she rode us hard, rode us fit to make our hearts burst . . ."

" . . . rode us cruel . . ."

"Please," the hanged woman whispered. "You gotta help me. Please."

But still the voices continued with their earnest accusations. Not with the enthusiasm of a witch-hunt, Lyle thought, but the oddly resigned admissions of the bewildered and contrite.

"And there was the sex stuff."

"Yeah. That stuff."

"A lot of bad, weird sex stuff. Copulations with things you shouldn't, animals, dead stuff. . . ."

"And with things that shouldn't even exist. Nightmare stuff."

"Uh-huh. Total nightmare stuff."

"Yeah." Earl nodded with finality. "A lot of bad stuff. Me, too. No need to rehash it. All was sworn into the record as testimony before the CLGJ. We didn't just get up pitchforks and torches, Detective. This is a done deal."

"You're saying this woman took control of you all?" Lyle said carefully.

"She rode us," Earl specified, "like ponies. Came in the night, bridled us, and then rode us off to do the things she wanted done." Earl frowned. "Nope. That ain't right, 'cause she can't just hop on your back and go against your will. It has to be something there's already a glimmer of in you, even just the dimmest middle-of-the-night curiosity. She finds that glimmer and focuses a bright, bright light on it, making it flash and shine bright in you. Dazzling bright."

Lyle glanced back at the frail woman, terrified, red-rimmed eyes peeking out from her scraggled hair. He was struck by the absurd image of this woman riding piggyback on the fat man who'll MAKE AMERICA GREAT AGAIN, cackling madly and waving a cowboy hat with glee.

"Once you're being rode, the shame is gone. It feels good when it occurs to you to do it—when you're pouring the acid out of an old tractor battery into a Ball jar, or whistling down the aisles at the Dollar Store looking for superglue and razor blades, or twisting the wire around a kitten's neck. And you feel good doing it. It feels . . . ," Earl paused, and Lyle was shocked to see tears pooling in the hard, lean man's eyes. Earl sniffled, then rubbed at his eyes with one hand, index finger and thumb pinching the bridge of his nose. He loosed a long, slow breath. "It feels wonderful to do it, like it's the thing you been waiting to do all your life, like sinking a nothing-but-net three-pointer or winning a big prize or sliding into bed with a beautiful pair of gals. But then, after that bitch lets up on you. . . ."

He shook his head, grimacing, breathing slowly and with effort.

"It's like meat that goes rancid in your mouth. It's fucking awful. You never felt so low."

Again the nods. Quietly, someone said, "It's okay, Earl; you tell your truth," and others murmured their support.

"That's what's delicious to her: that you choose to damn yourself. She's like a fucked-up kid who finds it hilarious when the frog chooses to jump out of the pot and into the fire."

"You hear how nuts this is," the woman behind him hissed desperately. "This is nuts. These people are nutbags. My name is Leighanne Halloway. I moved here at the end of October, 'cause it's all I could afford with my Disability. These people are fucking insane, and they have a shit-ton of guns."

"Anyway," Earl said with a sigh, "point is, there's no problem here, sir. We finally have this situation under control. You can move along."

"Plus it's getting late!" a voice added from the crowd.

Earl nodded. "Yup. And she gets damn tricky once the sun's down. New moon tonight, too. That's the worst." Earl was looking up into the tree now. "'Course, you totally trashed the easy branch." He worked his jaw ruminatively. "Nathanial," he called over his shoulder. "You figure you can shimmy as high as that one?" Earl pointed into the canopy. "Lash the noose back up?"

A dark-haired boy, his face a spray of freckles, sprang to his feet even as the schoolteacher frowned.

"I don't know about that, Earl," she said. "It's *awful* high."

"I can do it, Ms. Everly," the boy insisted.

"Jack, Ethan, you wanna get the ladder back up?" Earl went on, not acknowledging Ms. Everly's objection. "And lash Leighanne's hands again; she got 'em loose somehow."

"Shit," Leighanne hissed, grabbing hold of Lyle's jacket and pulling herself tight to his back, face buried between his shoulders, like a toddler hiding behind Mom rather than meet a new babysitter. "No. No." Her voice was hot and frantic and awful on his neck.

Lyle had a brief but powerful intuitive flash: This groveling woman was somehow like the badge and the gun, something very useful for today.

"No," Lyle said, his voice clear and calm. "This woman is coming with me." All faces turned to him, as though he'd said something unintelligibly absurd—"*No, I'm a kangaroo*" or "*The toilet injured my lunch.*" Everyone stopped. Earl looked at him quizzically.

Only the Walrus in Red Suspenders appeared to take it in. He rose to his feet with ponderous rage.

"I told you," the Walrus announced. "I said he was here under color of law, and you jackaninnies just brushed me off—" Now that the Walrus had risen, Lyle saw the short-barreled submachine gun dangling from a tactical sling circling the man's beefy neck and shoulder. The Walrus pawed for the pistol grip as he continued his diatribe.

Lyle drew the Public Defender from his pocket, finger already on the trigger, and pointed it at the droopy mustache. Everyone froze. Not a word or breath or rolling drop of sweat even quivered. Not a cicada sang in the field. The dead tree gave no shelter. The setting sun, red and blazing, paused in the sky.

Lyle wondered if the gun had a safety, and if the safety was on. He'd only fired it once, at a shooting range, immediately after buying it. That had been six years ago. If he hadn't been shot by the gun that morning, he'd have wondered if it was even loaded.

Everyone else was frozen, but Lyle was sweating freely, his palm growing slick on the heavy revolver's rubber grip.

"So," Earl said carefully, "you're taking possession of her, then?"

"Yes. I'm taking her into my custody."

"*Possession*," Earl repeated cagily. "You're taking her in *your possession*."

"Yeah," Lyle reiterated. "I'm taking her in my possession."

As soon as the magic words left Lyle's mouth, Earl stepped back, hands up. "All yours, then, Detective."

The Walrus blustered, "Just wait a damned—"

"No," Earl said, "you heard him, J-Bob-D: she is *his* now. In *his* possession. Not *ours*. Not a member of our community. Not our problem." There was a moment, and then a palpable ease swept through the crowd.

Lyle was already carefully backing up across the rutted field, his free arm out wide to his side, herding the cowering woman behind him in the direction of the Prius, his gun pointed toward the crowd. But this had no apparent impact on them. They were thoroughly desensitized to guns.

"Yeah," one man marveled, "I can feel it."

"Uh-huh."

"Yeah," Earl said. "I think we can rest our case."

The Walrus frowned, but nodded.

"C'mon," Earl said, "everyone grab a chair," then added, "Hope your face heals up quick, Detective Good."

Lyle tentatively reached up and checked his ear. It screamed when his fingers brushed it but stayed firmly attached.

Lyle kept guiding the woman back, but no one appeared to care. They bustled around like families after a church picnic, folding chairs and hauling them into the barn, wrestling with the aluminum ladder. Before Lyle and Leighanne were even halfway across the untended field, cars were already pulling off, truck springs creaking as they eased along the mostly washed-out gravel driveway. Lyle was still walking backward, gun up but pointed at nothing in particular. The mob had dispersed.

"I think," the woman offered hesitantly, "this might go faster if you just, like, put the gun away and walk regular. I don't think they're coming after us."

The last of the trucks pulled off with a jovial "*See ya!*" double-toot on the horn. A lone figure, tall and lean—maybe Earl?—picked his way across the yard separating the barn from the white clapboard farmhouse. Hands in pockets, shoulders stooped, he looked exhausted and unmistakably relieved.

Lyle did as Leighanne suggested, then turned to look at her. She was finger-combing her hair as they walked, running out snarls, catching twigs and grass and hay, pulling these free to flutter to the ground, then smoothing it all down and repeating. The movement was precise and compulsive, like a dog in too small of a cage licking its paws raw. She did not look at Lyle, but instead at their destination.

"What's your name?" she asked, eyes on the car.

"Lyle Morimoto," Lyle answered without hesitation or thought.

"Not Detective Jason Good?"

"No."

"Okay," she said. "I appreciate your help back there."

"One good turn," Lyle said, then trailed off. She did not ask what his one good turn might deserve.

They got in the car. Lyle started it, checked his mirrors, checked his blind spot, turned on his left blinker, and eased back into the roadway.

"Where to?" he asked. In his peripheral vision, Lyle saw her stop worrying her hair. She pulled it back, twisting it at the nape of her neck.

"I have no clue," Leighanne Halloway said. "They set my place on fire after they arrested me yesterday." For the first time that day, he wondered about tomorrow, and the day after that. The sun was setting now, garish and cruel. The woman didn't appear to feel anything about her ordeal, no fear or outrage or sadness. Lyle, for that matter, had been shot in the face just before lunch, and he didn't feel anything much about that, either. They made a good pair that way.

His face ached, and he considered taking another painkiller, but then thought, "*Why bother?*"

"Maybe I could drop you off with local law enforcement?" he suggested. "So you can file charges?"

She laughed once, hard as a backhanded slap. "Sheriff's Earl."

"Oh," Lyle replied.

"Where are you headed?" she asked. Her voice wasn't sounding as rough. That was probably good, he thought. Lyle knew well the havoc smoke inhalation wreaked on the trachea—it had come up when he was prepping for that morning's court appearance—but had no idea what strangulation with Cat-5 cable might do to one's windpipe. He didn't imagine it was good.

"My wife's family cottage," he answered. "It's somewhere around Calcutta."

"Where?"

"I'm not sure," Lyle admitted. "I thought I might recognize something once I drove out here."

"Don't worry, sweetie. I'll get you there. What happened to your ear?"

He glanced over at her. Now that her hair was smoothed back from her face, he saw that she was a good deal younger than he'd assumed, her skin clear and pale in the savage dying light.

"It's a long story."

"We got time," she said.

And so he told it, told it all as they drove into the setting sun. He didn't particularly want to, but he didn't particularly *not* want to, either. The words flowed the way water pours out of a jug. She made conciliatory noises as he spoke, but also occasional suggestions—right, left, turn here, watch this curve coming up—and they wended their way further from the highway, deeper into the darkness that separated Calcutta and whatever came after Calcutta. Every time she made a navigational suggestion, she reached over and brushed the back of his hand with her fingertips. And each time, Lyle noticed something new: the softness of her fingers, the smoothness of her skin, her delicate manicure. When they'd been in the bright field together, wrestling with the ligature around her neck, her hands had felt hard, ground with dirt, the nails chewed to the quick. Now they reminded him of the slender satin gloves you saw in old movies. The image gave him an electric, erotic thrill, embarrassing and enthralling.

When he finished his story, Leighanne said, "So we're going to visit your wife and the Good Cop?"

"Yeah." Lyle sighed. He didn't know why he was so certain the two were still together, let alone in the cabin near Calcutta—nor how Leighanne might know this—but it was clearly true.

"Why?"

Lyle didn't know. But as he'd told the story, the pain in his face and ear had steadily subsided. He'd begun to feel lighter, almost giddy.

"To kill them?" the girl asked. *Had she sounded this young before?* He wondered. *This fresh?* He glanced over, and she was much younger than he'd thought. Not teenager young, but close. Thrillingly so.

"No," he said, surprised it was true, and somehow disappointed.

"You know—Oh, slow down, left up here." Lyle obeyed. "There you go. You know, lots of times folks think of killing as a form of taking away. And they don't like to think of themselves as thieves. Thieves are low things. But maybe we've got something to share with your wife and the Good Cop. Maybe there's some things about the world we can show them, together. Killing them right off would be a waste."

Yes, Lyle thought. He suddenly had a lot to share. What had been sludgy and cool and dim in him for so long was now kindling bright and liquid and joyous.

"Later on, killing them might prove a mercy. Which maybe they'll deserve." She paused, smiling in the dark. "Or maybe not."

Lyle'd never had an affair, but he'd worked in the public defender's office long enough. He understood an essentially dark human tendency, not for pleasure so much as for *intensity*: grappling and pulling hair, a kiss that scrapes teeth, a hard pinch, a scratch, a twisted nipple, a bitten earlobe.

And then there was *real* intensity: a scream in a locked trunk, a wire coat hanger looped around an elbow or ankle—or somewhere more private—and twisted tighter and tighter with a pair of pliers.

Lyle smiled. He felt Leighanne next to him, a hot summer musk wafting off of her as she leaned close, setting one smooth hand on his hand, and the other on his thin slacks.

"Almost there," she said.

He thought of blood swelling beneath the skin as wire wound tight, the ecstasy of release when that skin is finally pricked with a blade. The long scream, screaming the throat raw, then screaming some more, until the voice cracks and disintegrates like a car window in a collision.

Lyle sighed. "I know what you're doing," he said, "but you can't get in my head, because I don't have what Earl said, not even a glimmer. I really, truly, and honestly *do not* want to hurt my wife, or even that Good Cop."

Leighanne looked at Lyle prettily, and did not respond.

Lyle sighed again, then added, "But I sure as hell *want* to want to hurt them."

Now she smiled. "That, my buddy boy, we can work with."

And then, just for a moment, her glamor slipped.

Lyle gasped in shock, and the breath he drew in was choked with her mildewed stink. Leighanne was not a withered crone, nor something young and petite. She was lean and tall and mottled and pale. She hunched to fit in the small car. She was naked, bristle-haired like a boar, her breasts numerous and pendulous as a dog's that's whelped countless pups. Her noseless face was many-eyed as a spider, lipless and tooth-full as something from the bottom of the sea.

But grinning.

The witch was *awful*—in that she filled him with awe—and *wonderful*—in that she was full of terrible wonders, an ambulatory torture chamber, a lightless and all-swallowing heat.

Lyle threw his arm wildly, reflexively recoiling from Leighanne's touch. He needed to be much farther from her than the cramped confines of the Prius allowed. He jerked the wheel toward the edge of the road.

This time the soft shoulder got the best of him. The Prius dug in, slewing out to the left. The wheels skidded, screaming against the crumbling blacktop. One side bit in, the other began to lift. The car rose, then came down with a tumbling crunch.

Darkness.

For a long time. Or a little.

When Lyle finally awoke to himself, he was walking toward a small house standing alone in the dark fields. His back was to the road. There was a high metallic tang to the air. Lyle wondered if the car's big hybrid battery had cracked. He tried to remember what the warning sticker inside the doorframe said. Something about a fire hazard, he thought, but he couldn't be sure.

Then he smelled burning plastic and rubber, and supposed it didn't really matter one way or another.

The gas tank burst with a *phooooom!*

A gout of hot, noxious air washed across his back. Leighanne laughed. Not a crone's cackle, but a teen's burst of champagne glee. She walked beside him, and his heart was light. She was everything—the pretty young thing, the old crone, the stooped awful wonder. He felt good and purposeful walking next to her, alive and joyful.

"Here." She handed him something, a complex arrangement of leather straps and buckles, a brass bar. It was whatever had been lashing her hands to her waist as she hanged, back in the field. He'd never held a bridle before, but had seen them in cowboy movies and museum displays.

"Put it on," she said.

He did so willingly, placing the brass bit between his teeth. It dug into the corners of his mouth, pulling back his cheeks, splitting his lip where the bullet had grazed him. He tightened the buckles, then tossed the reins over his shoulder. Leighanne grabbed hold of these, planted one foot on his hip, and swung up onto his shoulders. He wasn't a large man and had never been strong. He should have buckled under her weight. But the weight felt good and solid. *He* felt good and solid, strong, his muscles flexing and releasing under his skin, beautiful in their smooth inexorability.

He thought about the kitschy poem hanging next to the mirror in his guest bathroom. The last verse hung in his mind:

My precious child, I would never leave you;
during your times of trial,
when you see only one set of footprints in the sand,
that was when I carried *you.*

At first, it seemed the poem had it dead wrong: Maybe during your times of trial, you felt so damn heavy because God was perched up on *your* shoulders, kicking you in the ribs, driving you forward and cackling all the while.

But maybe that wasn't it at all. If Lyle was the one doing the carrying, maybe that made *him* God. He liked that idea quite a lot, as his muscles flexed and the void new moon rose, as he stalked the dark, abandoned fields, steed to this great and unbounded rider.

He liked that because God got to pass judgment, and make that judgment real in the world.

Lyle could see the cabin, his wife's family place. The windows glowed warmly through the thin curtains. There were two cars in the driveway. The lights switched out, one by one. Bedtime.

"C'mon, big fella," the witch cajoled, her heels digging into his flanks. "This is gonna be some fun."

Inside the house, in the shadows under the sink, there were tools: stout wire, pliers, a dull saw, a hammer, a steel nail punch. Lyle didn't know how he knew this, but he did, the same as a hawk can count the mice in a field by their fluttering heartbeats, the way God knows the content of your heart.

The gun felt inevitable in his hand. And that felt good. That good feeling was all the better, knowing that an awful lot could happen between *now* and the *inevitable*.

For the first time in a long time, Lyle Morimoto was really looking forward to something.

A HUMAN STAIN

KELLY ROBSON

Peter's little French nursemaid was just the type of rosy young thing Helen liked, but there was something strange about her mouth. She was shy and wouldn't speak, but that was no matter. Helen could keep the conversation going all by herself.

"Our journey was awful. Paris to Strasbourg clattered along fast enough, but the leg to Munich would have been quicker by cart. And Salzburg! The train was outpaced by a donkey."

Helen laughed at her own joke. Mimi tied a knot on a neat patch of darning and began working on another stocking.

Helen had first seen the nursemaid's pretty face that morning, looking down from one of the house's highest windows as she and Bärchen Lambrecht rowed across the lake with their luggage crammed in a tippy little skiff. Even at a distance, Helen could tell she was a beauty.

Bärchen had retreated to the library as soon as they walked through the front door, no doubt to cry in private over his brother's death after holding in his grief through the long trip from Paris. Helen had been left with the choice to sit in the kitchen with two dour servants, lurk alone in the moldering front parlor, or carry her coffee cup up the narrow spiral staircase and see that beauty up close.

The climb was only a little higher than the Parisian garret Helen had lived in the past three months, but the stairs were so steep she had been puffing hard by the time she got to the top. The effort was worthwhile, though. If the best cure for a broken heart was a new young love, Helen suspected hers would be soon mended.

"We had a melancholy journey. Herr Lambrecht was deeply saddened to arrive here at his childhood home without his brother to welcome him. He didn't want to leave Paris." Helen sipped her cooling coffee. "Have you ever been to Paris?"

Mimi kept her head down. So shy. Couldn't even bring herself to answer a simple question.

Peter sat on the rug and stacked the gilded letter blocks Bärchen had brought him. For a newly-orphaned child, he seemed content enough, but he was pale, his bloodless skin nearly translucent against the deep blue velvet of his jacket. He seemed far too big for nursery toys—six or seven years old, she thought. Nearly old enough to be sent away to school, but what did Helen know about children? In any case, he seemed a good-natured, quiet boy. Nimble, graceful, even. He took care to keep the blocks on the rug when he toppled the stack.

She ought to ask him to put the blocks in alphabet order, see how much his mother had taught him before she had passed away. But not today, and probably not tomorrow, either. A motherless, fatherless boy deserved a holiday, and she was tired from travel. The servants here were bound to be old-fashioned, but none of them would judge her for relaxing in a sunny window with a cup of coffee after a long journey.

They *would* judge her, though, if they thought she was Bärchen's mistress. She would be at Meresee all summer, so she needed to be on good terms with them—and especially with Mimi.

"We traveled in separate cars, of course. Herr Lambrecht is a proper, old-fashioned sort of gentleman." Helen stifled a laugh. Bärchen was nothing of the sort, but certainly no danger to any woman. "The ladies' coach was comfortable and elegant, but just as slow as the rest of the train."

Still no reaction. It was a feeble joke, but Helen doubted the nursemaid ever heard better. Perhaps the girl was simple. But so lovely. Roses and snow and dark, dark hair. Eighteen or twenty, no more. What a shame about her mouth. Bad teeth perhaps.

Helen twisted in her seat and looked out the window. The Meresee was a narrow blade of lake hemmed in tight by the Bavarian Alps. Their peaks tore into the summer sky like teeth on a ragged jaw, doubled in the mirror surface of the lake below. It was just the sort of alpine vista that sent English tourists skittering across the Alps with their easels and folding chairs, pencils, and watercolors.

The view of the house itself was unmatched. Helen had been expecting something grand, but as they had rowed up the lake, she was surprised she hadn't seen Bärchen's family home reproduced in every print shop from London to Berlin, alongside famous views of Schloss Neuschwanstein and Schloss Hohenschwangau. Schloss Meresee was a miniature version of those grand castles—tall and narrow, as if someone had carved off a piece of Neuschwanstein's oldest wing and set it down on the edge of the lake. Only four storeys, but with no other structure for scale it towered above the shore, the rake of its rooflines echoing the peaks above, gray stone walls picked out in relief against the steep, forested mountainside. Not a true castle—no keep or tower. But add a turret or two, and that's what the tourists would call it.

No tourists here to admire it, though. Too remote. No roads, no neighbors, no inns or hotels. From what Helen could see as she sat high in the fourth floor nursery window, the valley was deserted. Not even a hut or cabin on the lakeshore.

She'd never been to a place so isolated. Winter would make it even more lonely, but by then she would be long gone. Back in London, at worst, unless her luck changed.

When she turned from the window, Peter had disappeared. The door swung on its hinges.

"Where did Peter go?" Helen asked.

Mimi didn't answer.

"To fetch a toy, perhaps?"

Mimi bent closer to her needle. Helen carried her coffee cup to the door and called out softly in German. "Peter, come back to the nursery this instant." When there was no answer, she repeated it in French.

"I suppose Peter does this often," Helen said. "He thinks it's fun to hide from you."

Mimi's lips quivered. "Oui," she said.

"Come along then, show me his hiding places."

The nursemaid ignored her. Helen resisted the urge to pluck the darning from Mimi's hands.

"If I were newly orphaned, I might hide too, just to see if anyone cared enough to search for me. Won't you help me look?" Helen smiled, pouring all her charm into the request. A not inconsiderable amount, to judge by the effect she had on Parisian women, but it was no use. Mimi might be made of stone.

"To hell with you," she said in English under her breath, and slammed the nursery door behind her.

It was barely even an oath. She knew much filthier curses in a variety of languages. Her last lover had liked to hear her swear. But no more. That life had cast Helen off. All she had left in Paris were her debts.

The clock chimed noon. When it stopped, the house was silent. Not a squeak or creak. No sign of Bärchen or the servants, no sound from the attics above or the floors below. She padded over to the staircase and gazed down the dizzying stone spiral that formed the house's hollow spine. Steps fanned out from the spiral, each one polished and worn down in the center from centuries of use.

"Peter," she called. "Come back to the nursery, please."

No reply.

"All right," she sang out. "I'm coming to find you."

Who could blame the child for wanting to play a game? Peter had no playmates. She could indulge him, just this once. And it gave her a good excuse to snoop through the house.

By the time Helen had worked her way through the top two floors, it was obvious that the servants were outmatched by the housekeeping. The heavy old furniture was scarred and peeling, the blankets and drapes threadbare and musty, the carpets veiled with a fine layer of cobwebs that separated and curled around her every footstep. The surfaces were furred with a fine white dust that coated the back of her throat and lay salty on her tongue. After a half hour of wiggling under beds and rifling through closets and wardrobes, she was thirsty as if she'd been wandering the desert.

In old houses, the worst furniture was banished to the highest floors. As Helen descended, she expected the furnishings to become newer, lighter, prettier, if just as dusty. In the main rooms, the ones Peter's mother would have used, the furniture was the same: blackened oak carved into intricate birds, fish, and beasts. The sort of furniture that infested Black Forest hunting lodges, but raw and awkward, as if one of the family's great-uncles had taken up a late-in-life passion for wood carving and filled the house with his amateur efforts.

Still, if she could get the servants to clean it properly, she might adopt the large sitting room as her own. She could teach Peter just as well there as in the nursery. It would save her from climbing up and down stairs all day long. And though the sofa was backed by a winding serpent with a gaping maw, it was still a more likely setting for seducing a nursemaid than a drafty nursery window seat.

Under one of the beds she found a thin rib from a rack of lamb, riddled with tooth marks. Somewhere in the house was a dog. She'd have to take care to make friends with it.

Still no sign of Peter. Perhaps he was a troubled child, despite his placid looks. If so, this summer wouldn't be the holiday Bärchen had promised. She'd found him in a booth at Bistro Bélon Bourriche, downing himself in cognac. Within five minutes, he'd offered to pay her to join him for the summer at his family home and teach his nephew English. It would be easy, he said. Bärchen knew how badly she needed money. He was always so kind—famous for his generosity among the boys of Montparnasse and Pigalle.

Helen tapped the rib in her palm as she descended to the ground floor. There, the staircase widened and spread into the foyer, forming a wide, grand structure. At the back of the foyer, the stairs continued through a narrow slot in the floor. To the cellars, no doubt. Exploring down there would be an adventure.

Helen's trunk still sat by the front door, waiting for the steward to bring it upstairs. On the near side of the foyer, tobacco smoke leaked from the library. It smelled heavenly. She hadn't been able to afford cigarettes for months. She'd almost ceased yearning for the taste of tobacco, but her mouth watered for it now. Bärchen would give her a cigarette, if she asked for one. But no. She wouldn't disturb him. He had kept a brave face all through their journey. He deserved some time alone with his grief.

She padded into the murky parlor opposite the library and pulled aside the heavy green drapes, holding her breath against the dust. The sun was high above the mountains. The lake gleamed with light. Dust motes swarmed the air. The sunlight turned the oak furniture chalky, the heavy brocade upholstery nearly pastel. The walls were festooned with hunting trophies—stuffed and mounted heads of deer, wild goats, even two wolves and a bear. Their glass eyes stared down through the cobwebs as if alarmed by the state of the housekeeping.

She skated her finger through the dust on the windowsill. P-E-T-E-R, she wrote in block letters. When she began the boy's lessons there'd be no need for work books and pencils. Any flat surface could be used as a slate. It might embarrass the servants into doing their work.

Stepping back from the window, her foot jittered over a lump on the floor. Two tiny bones nestled under the carpet's green fringe—dry old gnawed leavings from a pair of veal chops. She tucked them in her pocket with the lamb bone. Then in the dining room she found a jawbone under a chair—small, from a roast piglet. She put it in her pocket.

Helen found her way to the kitchen at the back of the ground floor. An old woman chopped carrots at the table, her wrinkled jowls quivering with every blow of the knife. Beside her, the steward crouched over a cup of coffee. He was even older than the cook, his skin liver-spotted with age. They watched as Helen poured herself a glass of water from the stoneware jug.

"Peter likes to play games," she said in German. "I can't find him anywhere."

The cook began fussing with the coffee pot. The steward kept to his seat. "We haven't seen the boy, Fräulein York."

"I hardly expected bad behavior from him on my very first morning at Meresee."

"The boy is with the nursemaid. He is always with the nursemaid." The steward's tone was stern.

"How can you say that? He's certainly not with her now." She brushed cobwebs from her dress. "I've searched the house thoroughly, as you can very well see."

"You must continue to look for him, Fräulein," the steward said.

The cook bit into a carrot. Her jowls wobbled with every crunch.

They were united against her, but it only made sense. They were old country people and she was just an English stranger in a dirty, dusty dress. Raising her voice would win her no friends.

"Could you bring my trunk up to my room?" She smiled brightly. "I'd like to change out of my traveling clothes."

"Yes, Fräulein York," the steward said.

The cook went back to chopping carrots. The steward sipped his coffee. Did they expect her to retreat now?

"There is still the matter of Peter," Helen said.

The cook's knife slipped. Carrots scattered across the floor.

"The French girl takes care of the boy." The cook's words were barely understandable, some kind of antique form of Bavarian. "He's not allowed in the kitchen."

The steward's mouth worked, thin lips stretching over his stained teeth.

"Is that true?" Helen asked the steward. "Why not?"

The steward covered the cook's hand with his own. "The boy's welfare is your business now, Fräulein."

Helen found Peter at the back of the freezing cellar, hunkering in front of a door set deep into rock. The walls were caked with frost. The boy's breath puffed like smoke.

"Aren't you cold?" she asked. "Come back upstairs now."

"*Bitte*, miss," the boy said. He wedged two fingers under the door, then crouched lower, head bobbing as he worked them deeper and deeper. His hair was neatly parted, two blond wings on either side of a streak of skin pale as a grub.

Whatever he was up to, whatever he thought he was going to find on the other side of the door, he was fully engrossed by it. Helen let him have his fun for a few minutes while she poked around the cellar, ducking under the low spines of the vaulted ceiling. On the wall opposite the door, bottles were stacked into head-sized alcoves in pyramids of six. She wiped the dust off a few labels. French, and not that old. Champagne, Bordeaux, Burgundy. More than three hundred bottles. Enough to last the summer.

The cellar smelled salty. It must have been used for aging and preserving meat, in the past. The cold air's salty tang flooded her dry mouth with spit. What she wouldn't give for a piece of pork right now, hot and juicy. Her stomach growled. Perhaps the cook could be persuaded to let her explore the kitchen larder.

Helen wandered back to the boy. "Come along, Peter, that's enough. Mimi is waiting for you."

The light from her candle jittered across the brass plate bolted to the door's face. The tarnished metal was crusted with frost. She stepped closer, lifting her candle. It was a shield—griffins, an eagle, a crown.

She nudged Peter's foot with her toe. "Time to go back upstairs." He was stretched out on his belly now. "Peter, come along this instant." An edge came into her voice. She was tired of being ignored by everyone in the house.

He pulled something from under the door and put it in his mouth.

"Stop that." She grabbed Peter's collar and hauled him across the cellar to the stairs. He pitched forward onto his hands and knees. The object popped out of his mouth and bounced off the bottom step.

Helen picked it up and turned it over in her palm. It was a tiny bone, slender, fragile, and wet with spit.

She stared at Peter. "That's disgusting. What are you thinking?"

"Mama," he sobbed. His thin shoulders quivered under the velvet jacket. "Mama."

Remorse knifed through her. She tossed the bone aside, scooped him into her arms, and hauled him upstairs. "Hush," she said, patting his quaking back as he sobbed.

Tobacco smoke leaking from the library had turned the air in the foyer gray. Her trunk still crouched by the front door.

Helen lowered Peter to his feet. He was heavy. She couldn't possibly carry him up to the nursery. She'd be gasping.

Helen squeezed his bony shoulders. "You're a good boy, aren't you?" He wiped his nose on his sleeve and nodded. "Good, no more crying."

She lugged the trunk upstairs and dropped it in her room. Then she took the boy's hand and called up the spine of the staircase for Mimi.

When her pretty face appeared at the top of the spiral, Helen shooed the boy upstairs.

"Take care of him, won't you?" Helen said. "There'll be no lessons today. Not tomorrow, either. Then we'll see."

"Oui," Mimi said.

⊸

When Bärchen came to dinner he was already drunk. The scarlet cheeks above his brown beard were so bright it looked like he'd been slapped.

"So many letters. My brother's desk is stuffed to bursting." Bärchen offered

Helen a cigarette. "I can't understand them. I have no head for business, Mausi."

Helen blew smoke at him. "You always say that, but you seem to manage your own affairs well enough."

"I must go to Munich for advice. I'll be back soon, I promise. Two days at most."

"Don't stay away too long. You'll come back to an empty wine cellar and a pregnant nursemaid."

He giggled. "If that happens, it must be God's will."

Helen opened her mouth to make a joke about the furniture, but managed to stop herself in time despite the free flow of wine. The dining room chairs were particularly awful. Each one was topped by a sea serpent, thick and twisting, with staring eyes faced with mother-of-pearl. Under it was a rudely-rendered pair of human forms, male and female. And beneath them were thumb-sized lumps the shape of fat grubs. They dug into the small of Helen's back.

Portraits glared down at the table from the surrounding walls. Wan blond children with innocent, expressionless faces. Handsome, smiling men and women, brown-haired and robust just like Bärchen. And sickly-looking older people, prematurely-aged, with smooth gray skin and straggly black hair framing hollow, staring eyes.

When the clock struck seven, they were halfway into the third bottle of claret. Bärchen was diagonal in his chair.

"Time for me to play *pater familias*." He called out, "Mimi! *Ici!*"

Mimi appeared at the door, clutching Peter's hand.

"Now, Mimi," Bärchen slurred in French. "Is Peter behaving well? Is he in good health?"

"Oui," said Mimi.

Helen watched close as the girl spoke. Yes, some of her teeth were missing, but how many? Helen pretended to yawn, making a dramatic pantomime of it and sighing ecstatically.

Mimi's eyes watered as she tried not to yawn in response. When her lips curled back Helen caught a quick glimpse into her mouth. Her front teeth were gone, gums worn down to gleaming bone. Candlelight glinted on metal wire twisted through her molars.

Mimi clapped her hand over her mouth. Helen reached for a cigarette and pretended she hadn't noticed. Poor girl. Nothing more sad than young beauty in ruin.

"Peter, come here," Bärchen said.

With rough hands, he examined Peter's fingernails and scalp, looked into his ears, then pried opened his mouth and poked a finger along his gums.

She knew what that felt like. Her father had done the same. His fingers had tasted of ash and ink.

One of Peter's front teeth was loose.

"You're losing your first tooth," he said. "Does it hurt?"

Peter shook his head.

Bärchen wiggled it with the tip of a finger. "Let's pluck it out now, and be done with it."

Peter ran to Mimi and hid his face in her skirts.

"Oh come, Peter." Bärchen laughed. "I'll tie it to the doorknob with a bit of string. It'll be over in a moment."

Peter clutched Mimi's waist.

"No? Then we'll get an apple and you can bite into it like this." He mimed raising an apple to his mouth and chomping down. "You can do that, can't you?"

"No, Uncle." Peter's voice was muffled against Mimi's hip. The girl had backed against the wall and was inching toward the door. Bärchen was taking this too far.

"It's late, Herr Lambrecht," Helen said. "Let the girl take Peter to bed."

"Well then. The tooth with fall out on its own and then this will be yours." Herr Lambrecht put a silver coin on the table. "Miss York will keep it for you."

Mimi and boy slipped out the door.

"How was my performance?" Bärchen asked. "Was I convincing?"

"Very. I can hardly believe you never had children."

"God forbid." Bärchen shuddered and drained his wine glass. "Did I ever tell you about my nursemaid? Bruna was her name. She was devoted to me. You would have liked her. Very pretty. But like Mimi, not much of a talker. Not like you."

"Nothing can keep me from saying what I think." Helen reached into her pocket and set the bones on the stained tablecloth. "For example, your servants are lax," she said.

He shrugged. "What can be done? They're old. Who would choose to live here, if they could be anywhere else?"

⊸o⊷

After dinner they took their wine out the front door and onto the wide front terrace. Evening stars twinkled above looming mountains and a lakeshore veiled in mist. The three sides of the terrace stepped straight down into the water, like a dock or jetty. The skiff bobbed alongside, tied to an iron ring.

That morning, the water had been an inky sapphire, the color so brilliant it seemed to cling to the oars with Bärchen's every stroke. Under the darkening sky it was tar black and viscous. In the distance, a dark object broke the surface, sending lazy ripples across the water. Helen squinted.

Bärchen followed her gaze. "Just a log, that's all. I have a present for you."

He pressed a silver cigarette case into her hand. It was her own—she'd pawned it for rent money three months ago. And it was full—forty slender cigarettes, lined up with care.

She grinned. "If we were back at the Bélon Bourriche, I could put on a pair of tight trousers and sing you a song, as many a young man has done. But you don't want me sitting in your lap any more than I want to be there. So I'll just say thank you."

"It's nothing. Will you be happy here, Mausi?"

"Of course. It's so beautiful. Though I'm not sure how long I can stand to live in a place where nobody appreciates my jokes."

He laughed. "Meresee is beautiful, but it can be a little confining. I'll show you." He led her to the edge of the terrace to peer around the side of the house. Its walls jutted straight down into the water, raising the house's profile far beyond the shore. Behind, the steep mountainsides advanced on the lake, threatening to topple the house into the water.

"You don't want to fall in. It's deep, and so cold it'll knock the breath right out of you." He braced himself against the wall with an unsteady hand.

"I suppose this was a fortress, once," said Helen. "Holding the border of some medieval Bavarian principality."

Bärchen patted the wall. "A fortress, yes, but it never protected a border. It protected the salt."

"Your family had salt mines?" Helen asked. No wonder Bärchen was wealthy.

"The mines belonged to the Holy Roman Emperor. The crown owed much of its wealth to Meresee. More precious than gold, once, this salt. My family protected it."

Bärchen peered over the edge of the terrace. The water clung to the sides of the house. A shadowed stain crept up the foundation.

"Don't fall in," he repeated. "In winter it's somewhat safer. When the ice forms, you can ski across the lake, or skate, if the snow has blown away. But even then, you must be careful."

She laughed. "You've convinced me. I'll be careful to be far, far from Meresee by winter."

"Of course, Mausi." Bärchen forced a chuckle. "Naples for the winter. Neapolitan widows like tall Englishwomen like you. Or Athens, if you please. The world is open to us. We are rich, happy, and at liberty."

Bärchen was trying too hard to be jolly.

"Your new responsibility is eating at you, isn't it, Bärchen?" She threaded her hand through the crook of his arm and drew him gently away from the water's edge. "Why worry? Send Peter away to school. In England, many boys are sent away at his age."

"Maybe you're right. After the summer, if you think he's ready. I'll take your advice."

"What do I know about children? Next to nothing—I told you so in Paris. You couldn't find a less experienced fraud of a governess."

Bärchen patted her hand. "You're a woman. It will come naturally to you."

"I doubt that very much." Helen pulled her hand away. "But how much damage can I do in one summer? I'll teach him a little English at least."

"That's fine, Mausi. Do your best."

She grinned. "Are you sure you're not his father? Peter favors you."

"A family resemblance." The last trace of dusk drained behind the mountains, and Bärchen's mood darkened with the sky. His gaze fixed on the floating log. "If you think I'll develop a father's feelings, you're wrong." Bärchen's deep voice rose to a whine. "It's not fair to shackle me to a child that's not mine. And it's not fair to the child, either. He should have a mother's love—devoted and selfless."

"What happened to his mother?"

"It was grotesque. She swelled larger than this." Bärchen held his arms out, encircling a huge belly. "How many babies can a woman's body contain?

Twins are common, triplets not unheard of. I can't imagine how women survive even one, can you?"

Helen shook her head. Sour wine burned the back of her throat.

"My brother's fault. He should have been more careful than to get so many babies on his wife."

"I don't think it works that way," Helen said.

"It does in our family. One is fine. They should have been content with Peter and stopped there. But no, they had to have more children. And now they've all joined our family in the crypt."

Bärchen stared at the house's foundation stones. Helen followed his gaze.

"Do you mean there are tombs in your cellar? The door in the cellar leads to a crypt?"

He nodded. "I'll go there too, eventually. Not soon—I'm still young." He shrugged his broad shoulders. "I try not to think about such things. Paris makes it easy to forget."

A chill breeze stirred the water. She put her empty wine glass down and chafed her arms. "And your brother?"

"My brother couldn't live without his wife. He had to join her."

"Let's go in, it's getting cold." Bärchen shook his head. "I can't leave you out here alone," she insisted, pulling on his elbow. "You're too melancholy."

"Don't worry about me, Mausi," he laughed. "I have no urge to join my family. I love my life in Paris too much to give it up yet."

At the door she stopped, half in, half out of the house.

"Do you know what happened to Mimi's mouth?" she asked.

"I heard it was an accident," he said, and turned back to the lake.

⊸

Bärchen left at the first light of dawn. Helen's pounding headache woke her just in time to spot him from her bedroom window, rowing across the lake in the skiff, pocking the water's surface with each frantic pitch of the oars. She'd never seen him move so quickly, put so much of his bulky muscle to work. It was as though he were escaping something.

Anxiety wormed through her breast. If she called out to him, he'd turn around and row back. But the window latch was stuck, the claw cemented into the catch with years of dust and grit. She struggled with it for a minute, and then gave up. Her head throbbed, her mouth was coated in grit, and her eyes felt as though they'd been filled with sand. She crawled back to bed and shoved her head under her pillow.

When she finally ventured up to the nursery in the afternoon, Mimi was sitting in the window seat, needle and thread idle in her lap. The boy was nowhere to be seen.

Helen joined Mimi in the window seat. "How long have you been caring for Peter, Mimi?"

The girl shrugged.

"I suppose when you first came here, you ransacked the house every time he hid from you."

"Oui," said Mimi.

"But you're tired of it. He's older now. He should know better."

Mimi hung her head. One lone tear streaked over the rose of her cheek and dropped to her collar, staining the cotton dark.

Helen longed to wipe her knuckle along that soft cheek, lift the dregs of the tear to her lips as if it were nectar. But no. That might be fine in a sodden Pigalle bistro, but not here. She'd only frighten the girl.

She rested her palm on Mimi's knee, just the lightest touch. "Stay here, I'll get him."

Helen found Peter sitting on the edge of the terrace, legs extended, trying to reach his toes into the water. He leaned back, balancing on his arms, and squirmed closer to the edge.

Helen's heart hammered. She bit the inside of her cheek to keep herself from calling out—a sudden noise might startle him. She crept closer, poised to run and grab him if he fell. When the boy turned his head toward her, she kept her voice low and calm.

"Come here, Peter."

He ignored her. She slowly edged closer.

"Come away from there, please."

When he was within reach she snatched him up, hauled him to the front of the house and set him down on the doorstep. She gripped his arms firmly and bent to look him in the eye.

"Peter, you can't keep running off, do you understand? It's dangerous. What if you'd fallen into the lake?"

"*Bitte*, miss." The boy scuffed his foot. The light bouncing off the lake seemed to leach the color from his skin.

"*Yes, Miss York.* That's your first English lesson. Repeat after me, *Yes, Miss York.*"

"Yes, Miss York," he said.

"Good," she said.

He raised his hand to her cheek. He gave her one brief caress, and then snaked two of his fingers into her mouth.

Helen reeled backward. Her arms pinwheeled. She grabbed for the door handle but missed. When she fell, she raked her shin along the doorstep's edge.

Peter stood over her and watched as she keened in pain, clutching her leg and rocking on the ground like a turtle trapped on its back. She rolled to her side and wadded her skirt around her leg to sop up the blood.

When she could stand, she grabbed his hand and yanked him upstairs, lurching with every step and smearing blood in a trail up the steps. Mimi met her on the upper landing. Helen shoved the boy into her arms, dropped to the floor, and raked up her skirts. Blood poured down her leg and into her shoe. Her shin was skinned back, flesh pursed around gleaming bone. She fell back on one elbow, vision swimming.

Mimi guided her to a chair and lifted her skirts. Helen flinched, but Mimi's touch was soft, her movements quick and gentle. She ran out of the room for a moment, then returned with rags and a jug of water. As Mimi cleaned her wound, Peter cowered in the window seat. Helen kept a close eye on him. He was crying again, silently, his mouth forming one word over and over again. *Mama.*

Mimi put the final tuck into the bandage, then squeezed Helen's knee and looked up, her brown eyes huge.

"*Merci,*" Helen breathed.

Mimi smiled. Lips peeled back over gaping gums. Wire wormed through pinholes in her back teeth. Helen recoiled. She grabbed the edge of the table and hauled herself to her feet. She stumped over to the window seat, grabbed Peter's shoulders and shook him hard.

"That's enough," she yelled. "No more games. No running off on your own. Understand?"

The boy sobbed. She lowered her voice, trying to reach a source of calm, deep within her. "Don't be afraid, Peter. I'm not angry anymore. What do you say?"

"Yes, Miss York."

"Very good. I understand you miss your mother and father. It hasn't been very long since they died, but it will get easier, with time."

"*Bitte*, miss," the boy said. "Mama and Papa died many years ago."

The cook and steward blocked her questions. In between their one-word answers, they commented to each other in an impregnable Bavarian dialect, gossiping about her, no doubt, as if she weren't even there. And why shouldn't they? She was acting like a madwoman, limping around the kitchen, waving her arms and yelling at them in every language she knew.

Helen took two deep breaths, and tried again.

"A few days ago, in Paris, Herr Lambrecht told me his brother had just passed away. He had to travel to Meresee and take responsibility for his nephew, the house and the family finances. Is that true?"

"Yes, Fräulein," said the steward.

There. Everything was fine. The knot in Helen's chest loosened. "But Peter just told me his father and mother have been dead for years."

"Yes, Fräulein," said the steward.

"How can you say that?" Helen longed to grab him by the throat, shake him until he rattled. "How can both those things be true?"

The steward ran his tongue over his stained teeth. "It's not my place to contradict either Herr Lambrecht or his nephew."

It was no use. She stumped up to the nursery. Mimi and Peter stood in the middle of the rug, waiting for her.

"Peter, play with your blocks. I want to see them in alphabet order when I return." She pointed at the blocks. "*Ah—bey—tsay.*"

He knelt on the carpet and began stacking the blocks, obedient for the moment. She didn't trust him, though. She wedged a chair under the handle of the door, trapping them both inside. Then she stumbled downstairs to the library. It was locked, but one stubborn shove and the lock gave way.

The desk was abandoned, cubbyholes dusty, drawers empty except for old pen nibs, bottles of dried ink and a silver letter opener shaped like two entwined sea serpents. *So many letters, I can't make sense of them*, Bärchen had said. Had he taken everything away to Munich?

It made no sense. Why would Bärchen lie to her? He knew how desperate she was. No more friends to borrow from, nothing left to pawn. She would have followed him across the world. She had no other option.

She lit a cigarette and pulled hot smoke deep into her lungs. By the time it had burned down to her knuckle, she was sure the mistake was nobody's but her own. It was typical of her—always too busy searching for the next joke to listen properly. Bärchen had said his brother was dead, but not newly dead. He said Peter's mother had died in the spring, but not this spring. She'd made assumptions. Hadn't she?

There was one way to find out.

"The crypt key." Helen held her hand out to the steward, palm up. "Give it to me, please."

"I don't have it, Fräulein."

"Of course you do. You're the steward. Who else would have it?"

He flipped his jacket open and turned his pockets inside out. "I only have this." A blue and white evil eye medallion spun at the end of his watch fob. "You should have one of these, Fräulein. It keeps you safe."

Helen ransacked the house for keys and limped down the cellar stairs. Her mouth began watering as soon as she smelled the salty air. She lit a cigarette. It dangled from her lips as she tried each key in turn. None fit the crypt's lock. She leaned on the door with all her weight but the heavy iron hinges didn't even shift. She squinted through the keyhole. Only darkness.

She lowered herself to the floor and threaded her fingers under the door. A feathery shift of air drifted from below, ruffling her hair. It smelled delicious, sea-salty and savory, like a good piece of veal charred quickly over white-hot coals and sliced with a sharp knife into bleeding red pieces.

Her fingers brushed against something. Forcing her hands under the door, she caught it with the tips of her fingers, drew it out. It was a tiny vertebra, no bigger than the tip of her finger. Helen held it close to the candle flame, turning it over in her palm. It was brown with dried blood. The canal piercing the bone was packed with white crystals. She picked at them with her fingernail. Salt.

There was something else under the door, too—a tooth coated in a brown blush of blood. A tendril of frozen flesh hung from its root.

Helen limped upstairs. The chair she'd leaned against the nursery door was wedged so tightly the feet scratched two fresh scars into the floor as she dragged it away.

Peter waited in the doorway. Mimi was curled up in the window seat.

"Is this yours?" She showed him the tooth.

"No, miss." He skinned his lips back. His loose tooth hung from his gum by a thread.

"Where did it come from, then?"

He blinked up at her, eyes clear and innocent. "*Bitte*, miss, I don't know."

Tall as he was, in that moment he seemed little more than an infant. His voice was quite lovely. The effect of a slight childish slur on those German vowels was adorable.

"Do you know where the key to the crypt is?"

"No, miss."

"Have you been inside the crypt?"

"No, miss."

He was just a child; children had no sense of time. Did he even know the difference between a month and a year? She'd gotten herself worked up over nothing. The steward and cook had taken a dislike to her, but it was her own fault. She should have taken care to make friends with them. But no matter. Bärchen would be back in a few days, and the summer would continue as planned.

Helen brought Mimi and Peter their dinner, barricaded them in the nursery, then helped herself to a bottle of claret from the steward's pantry. She set it on the dining room table beside her dinner plate. No corkscrew, and she hadn't found one while searching through the house for keys. The steward must have had hidden them. She hadn't seen any cigarettes, either. She'd have to ration the ones in her cigarette case until Bärchen came home.

She called for the steward. When he didn't come, she fetched the silver letter opener from the library and used it to pry the cork from the bottle. She lifted the bottle to her mouth like a drunk in a Montparnasse alleyway. The wine burned as it slipped down her parched throat.

Helen put the letter opener in her pocket and took her plate and the wine bottle out to the terrace. The air was fresh with pine. The first evening stars winked overhead between clouds stained with dusk. A hundred feet off the terrace, the floating log bobbed. Slow ripples licked the terrace steps.

She had almost drained the wine bottle when the log was joined by another. The breeze carried a whiff of salt. The two logs seemed to be moving toward her, eel-sinuous. Starlight glistened off their backs as they slipped through the water, dipping under and then breaking the surface in unison like a pair of long porpoises.

The bottle slipped from her hand and smashed on the terrace. Shards of glass flew into the lake.

The logs turned to look at her.

Helen scrambled into the house and slammed the door. She ran to the parlor and began dragging an oak chest across the floor, rucking up the rug and peeling curls of varnish from the floor. She pulled it across the foyer, scraping deep scars across dark wood. By the time she'd barricaded the front door, she was dripping with sweat. Her wounded leg throbbed with every shuddering heartbeat.

She crept to the parlor window and peeked between the drapes. Only one creature was visible, floating just beyond the edge of the terrace. It looked like a log again, but she knew better. She'd seen them. Two long, inky serpents raising their heads from the water, their maggot-pale eyes hollow and staring.

Just a log, that's all.

The log flipped. Water poured across its back. Its mouth split open. Starlight revealed hundreds of teeth, wire-thin and hooked.

Just a log, that's all.

Bärchen was a liar.

The cook and steward sat at the kitchen table, heads down over their dinner, one candle burning between them.

"I suppose you'll tell me there are no serpents in the lake. Herr Lambrecht says they're logs, and it's not your place to contradict him." She threw her arms wide. "If one of those monsters bit off your leg and Herr Lambrecht said it hadn't, you'd agree with him."

"Would you like another bottle of wine, Fräulein?" the steward asked.

"Always." She pounded her fist on the table, rattling their dinner plates. "But I'd rather know how badly Herr Lambrecht lied to me, and why."

The steward shrugged and turned back to his meal.

Helen ransacked the kitchen drawers and piled instruments on the table—knives, forks, even a slender iron spit—everything she could find that was long and slender and strong. She wrapped them in a rag, grabbed the candlestick from the table, and lugged everything downstairs.

Delicious, salty air roiled out from under the door, stronger than before. Helen's stomach growled. She lit a cigarette and rolled up her sleeves.

The white coating on the walls and door wasn't frost; it was salt. She scraped the crust off the eye of one of the griffins. It wadded up under her fingernail, dense and gritty.

Helen licked the salt off her finger and slipped a filleting knife into the keyhole. She could feel the latch inside, and bumps that must be a series of tumblers. They clicked as she guided the knife tip back and forth. The blade sawed at the corners of the keyhole, carving away fine curls of brass. But the knife was too wide, too clumsy.

She tried the iron spit next. It left a patina of sticky grease on her palms. She attacked the lock with each instrument in turn, whining with frustration. She knocked her forehead on the door, gently, once, twice.

A chill played over her bare skin. Gooseflesh prickled her arms. Sour spit flooded her mouth.

Finally, she drew the letter opener out of her pocket and fed its tip through the lock, leaning into the door as if she could embrace its whole width. She peeked into the keyhole, hand by her cheek like an archer with a drawn bow.

She licked salt from her lips. The lock clicked. The door opened an inch, hinges squeaking.

A little wet bone bounced across the floor and hit her foot. She turned.

Peter was right behind her.

Candlelight flickered over his round cheeks and dimpled chin, the neatly combed wings of pale hair framing his face. He was just a child. Orphaned. Friendless. She'd already given him her sympathy. Didn't he deserve her care?

"Hello." She kept her voice gentle. "How did you get out of the nursery?"

"*Bitte*, Miss York. The door opened."

The chair must have fallen. She hadn't wedged it hard enough.

Peter stared at the crypt door. She should take him back upstairs, tell Mimi to put him to bed, but he would just come down here again. And wasn't this his own home?

"Do you know what's behind this door, Peter?"

"Mama," he said.

"Yes, that's what your uncle told me. Not just her, but your whole family—all of your ancestors, in their tombs. Do you know what a tomb is?" He shook his head. "A big box made of stone, usually. Or an alcove in a stone wall, sometimes. Usually family crypts are in cemeteries or churches. But your family—"

She hesitated. *Your family is strange,* she thought. She needed to find out exactly how strange.

"Are you sure you want to see your mother's tomb?"

Peter nodded.

The air that rushed out as she opened the door had a meaty, metallic tang. Her stomach roiled with hunger; her vision swam. She shielded the candle flame with her body. Peter took her hand and led her into the crypt.

Helen had seen crypts before. They didn't frighten her. At age five she'd seen her mother shut away in a Highgate Cemetery tomb. She'd kissed her first girl in the crypt at St Bride's, after stealing the key from the deacon. And she'd attended parties in the Paris catacombs, drank champagne watched by thousands of gaping skulls.

But this was no crypt.

The passage opened into a wide cavern, its walls caked with salt crystals and honeycombed with human-sized alcoves, rough indentations hacked out of the rock with some primitive tool. Some were deep, as if they might be passages, some gaped shallow and empty, and others were scabbed over with a crusted mess the color of dried blood, leaking filth down the crystalline walls. One of these was just over her left shoulder. Tiny bones were embedded in the bloody grime. It smelled like fresh meat.

A few—just a few here and there—were furred over with cobwebs the same bloodless pale pink as Peter's skin.

At the bottom of the cavern, a wide pool of oily water quivered and sloshed.

"Mama," Peter said. "Papa."

"I don't think they're here, Peter," she whispered, pulling him back toward the door.

His hand slipped from her grasp. He ran to a cobwebbed alcove and plunged his hand deep inside. She grabbed his jacket and pulled him away. The strands clung to his arm, stretched and snapped. When his hand appeared, he held tight to a squirming grub the size of his head. His fingers pierced its flesh; the wounds dripped clear fluid.

Its eyes were dark spots behind a veil of skin. Its tiny, toothless maw opened and closed in agony.

"Brother," Peter said. He raised the grub to his lips and opened his mouth.

Helen swatted it out of his hand. The grub rolled across the floor of the cavern and plopped into the pool.

She ran, dragging Peter behind her by his elbow.

Helen slammed the door and braced it with her shoulder, throwing her weight against it as she jabbed the lock with the letter opener. Getting the door open had been sheer luck. She'd never get it locked again, not if she worried at it for a hundred years.

She couldn't believe her stupidity. Opening doors that should stay shut. Going places she didn't belong. Trusting Bärchen, as if she actually knew him. As if he were human.

"Stupid, stupid, stupid," she said under her breath.

The lock clicked. She fell to her hands and knees, weak with relief. Pain shot up her leg. Her vision darkened.

Peter lifted the candle. "Yes, Miss York?"

She sucked air through her teeth and wrenched herself around to sit with her back against the door. She would get away from Peter, run as fast and as far as possible. Into the mountains, into the forest, anywhere but here. But she didn't think she could stand. Not yet.

"Do you remember your mother? Your father? Do you know what they are?" Monsters, with hollow staring eyes. Her voice rose to a shriek. "Do you know what you are?"

"No, Miss York. I know you."

He sat at her feet and slipped his hand into hers. His fingers were sticky with fluid from the grub. It stank like rot, like old meat turned green and festering with maggots. Her gorge rose once, twice. She took two convulsive gasps for air and then the stench changed. Her stomach growled. She raised Peter's fingers to her mouth and licked them clean, one after another. Then she sucked the last of the juice from his sleeve.

There was more on the other side of the door, puddled on the stone floor. She could open the door again. But Peter looked so tired. His eyelids were puffy and the skin under each eye was stained dark with exhaustion.

"Come here," she said, and the boy climbed right into her open arms.

Helen watched Mimi undress Peter and tuck him into bed. When the nursemaid tried to leave the bedroom, Helen stopped her.

"No. We're staying here. Peter can't be alone. We have to take care of him."

Mimi hung her head.

"Do you understand?"

"Oui."

"I don't think you do. You let Peter go—every time. You don't even try to stop him. Why don't you care for him? He's just a child."

The boy watched them, hands folded between cheek and pillow. Mimi stared at the floor. A tear streaked down her cheek.

"We have to keep Peter safe, you and I, so he can grow up healthy and strong like his uncle. And then like his parents, out in the lake." Helen sighed. "I wish we could talk properly, you and I."

"Oui."

"Wait here," she said.

Helen ran to fetch a pencil and paper. When she returned, Peter was asleep.

"Tell me why you let him go."

Mimi fumbled with the pencil. She couldn't even hold it properly, and the only mark she could make on the paper was a toppling cross inside a crude shape like a gravestone.

Mimi's lower lip quivered. A tear dropped onto the paper. Helen took the pencil from Mimi's shaking fingers. "It doesn't matter," she said.

Mimi climbed onto the bed and lay beside Peter.

Helen pulled a heavy chair in from the hallway and slid it in front of the door. It might not keep him from getting out, but if he tried to drag it away the noise would wake her. Then she kicked off her shoes and climbed onto the bed, reaching around Mimi to rest her palm on Peter's arm.

The girl was crying. Her back quivered against Helen's chest.

"It's all right," Helen whispered, holding her close. "Everything is going to be all right."

Mimi cried harder.

Helen expected to be awake all night, but Peter was safe, the room was warm, the bed cozy, and Mimi's sobs were rhythmic and soothing. Helen slipped into sleep and tumbled through slippery dreams of inky shapes that writhed and grasped and tore at her skin. When she woke, the moon shone through the window, throwing the crossed shadows of the windowpanes over the rug. Her leg throbbed. The clock struck four. And Peter and Mimi were both gone.

On the pillow lay two bright pieces of copper wire, six inches long, worried and kinked, their ends jagged. The pillow was spotted with blood.

Helen ran down to the kitchen and fumbled with a candle, nearly setting her sleeve on fire as she lit it on the oven's banked coals. She plunged downstairs, bare feet on the freezing steps, and when the smell hit her she stumbled. She slipped on a bone and nearly sent herself toppling headfirst.

She panted, leaning on the wall. The smell pierced her. It coiled and drifted and wove through her, conjuring the last drip of whiskey in her father's crystal decanter, the first strawberries of summer, the last scrap of Christmas pudding smeared over gold-chased bone china and licked off with lazy tongue swipes. It smelled like a sticky wetness on her fingers, coaxed out of a pretty girl in the cloak room at a Mayfair ball, slipped into a pair of silk gloves and placed on a young colonel's scarlet shoulder during the waltz.

The smell was so intense, so bright it lit the stairwell. The air brimmed with scents so vast and uncontainable they poured from one sense to the next, banishing every shadow and filling the world with music.

Helen fell from one step to the next, knees weak, each footstep jarring her hips and spine. Her vision spun. The cellar brimmed with haloes and rainbows, a million suns concentrated and focused through a galaxy of lenses, dancing and skipping and brimming with life.

The only point of darkness in the whole cellar was Mimi.

The nursemaid crouched in front of the crypt door. She humped and hunched, ramming her face into the wood as if trying to chew through it. The threshold puddled with blood.

Mimi's jaw hung loose. It swung against her throat with every thrust. Her nose was pulped, upper lip shredded, the skin of her cheeks sloughed away.

The remains of her teeth were scattered at her feet.

Helen grabbed her foot with both hands and heaved, dragging her away. Mimi clawed at the floor, clinging to the edges of the stones with her shredded fingernails.

"Miss York?"

At the sound of Peter's voice, the air cottoned with rainbows.

Peter stood at the head of the stairs, lit by a euphoria of lights. It cast patterns across his face and framed his head in a halo of sparks.

Mimi threw her head back and screamed, her tongue a bleeding live thing trying to escape from a gaping throat, a cavitied maw that was once the face of a girl.

Mimi lunged up the stairwell. Helen chased her.

"Peter, run!" Helen howled.

Mimi threw her arms around the boy. The huff of breath through her open throat spattered the walls with blood. She lunged down the hall, dangling Peter like a rag doll. Helen pitched after her, grabbing at the nursemaid's hair, skirt, sleeves. In the foyer she caught hold of Peter's leg and yanked the boy away.

Mimi dug her fingernails into the heavy chest and pulled. It scraped over the floor, throwing splinters across the foyer. She yanked the door open and turned. Blood puddled at her feet. Her tongue wagged from deep in her throat. She raised her arms, as if yearning for Peter to enter her embrace.

Helen clutched Peter to her chest. She forced his head against her neck so he couldn't see his nursemaid's pulped face.

Mimi yowled. Then she plunged out the door and clattered across the terrace. At the edge of the water she teetered for a moment, arms wheeling. In the moment before she fell, an inky shape welled up from the water. Its jaws welcomed her with barely a splash.

The boy knelt on the nursery window seat beside Helen, his nose pressed to the window pane. Two sinuous forms floated in the lake, lit by the pale rays of dawn poaching over the mountaintops.

"Come sit over here." Helen patted the stool in front of her.

When the sun broke over the peaks, Peter's mother and father were gone, sleeping the day away at the bottom of the lake, perhaps, or in the crypt pool, keeping watch over their precious, delicious children.

Helen kept Peter by her day and night. She barely took her eyes off him, never left his side. To him she devoted all her care and attention, until her lashes scraped over dry and pitted eyeballs, her tongue swelled with thirst, and her ears pounded with the call from below.

The scent slipped into her like welcome promises. Lights spun at the edge of her vision, calling, guiding her down to the cavern.

At night, the serpents tossed back and forth in the waves, dancing to the rhythm shuddering through the house. She didn't have to look out the window to see them; every time she blinked they were behind her eyelids. Beckoning.

Helen made it three days before she broke. When her pen turned clumsy, when her handwriting dissolved into crude scratches, she was past caring. The crypt was all she could think of. Hunger gushed through her, overflowing and carrying her down each flight of stairs as if floating on a warm river to the source of everything left in the world worth wanting.

Her hands were too clumsy to open the door, but it didn't matter. She could eat her way through it. The scent itself was nourishment enough. Every bite was a blessing. She drowned herself in it. Gave herself over until her mind hung by a thread.

Her world collapsed into pain when Peter pulled her out of the cellar. She resisted, a little, but she couldn't fight him. Not if it might hurt him. When he got the wires through what was left of her teeth and jaw and twisted them tight, the light abandoned her, the call receded, the house darkened.

"Will you be all right now, Miss York?" Peter asked.

"Oui," she said.

THE STORIES WE TELL ABOUT GHOSTS

A.C. WISE

Growing up in Dieu-le-Sauveur, my friends and I told stories about ghosts—the Starving Man, the Sleeping Girl, and the House at the End of the Street. The summer I was twelve, I saw my first ghost for real. That was the summer my little brother Gen disappeared.

The first official day of summer, the day after school ended for the year, we gathered in Luke and Adam's clubhouse—me, my little brother Gen, and Holly and Heather from across the road. Luke and Adam lived next door. By the time Gen was born, Luke and I had already spent years passing through the hedge between our houses.

That didn't change immediately when Gen was born, but it changed when he got old enough to walk and my parents insisted I take him with me any place I wanted to go. Luke didn't mind, but he was the younger brother in his relationship, the one used to tagging along. He couldn't understand why I could be annoyed, and yet protective of Gen at the same time, the first to rush to him if he got hurt, or stand up for him if someone else gave him trouble.

This is what I couldn't explain to Luke: It didn't matter that I loved Gen or not, because I did; it didn't matter that he was actually pretty cool for a little brother. What mattered was I didn't have a choice anymore. I used to be just me, but for the last seven years, I'd been Gen's big brother. I would always be Gen's big brother, with all the weight and responsibility it entailed.

"This is that game I was telling you about." Adam pulled out his phone. All week while we waited for school to be out, he'd been talking about an app called Ghost Hunt! where you collected virtual ghosts and stored them in a scrapbook. He already had twenty-seven unique ghosts, including the Bloody Nun.

"I found her behind the church. There used to be a cemetery there, but they dug up all the bodies and moved them somewhere else."

He turned his screen to show us the Bloody Nun's picture. The clubhouse was really a cleared-out garden shed, but Luke and Adam's mom had put in a carpet for us and a mini fridge with an extension cord running to the garage. I reached to grab a soda, popping the tab before I looked at the picture on Adam's phone.

The colors were washed out and strange, like one of those filters had been applied to make it look like an old photograph. The grass had a peachy tone, but I recognized the lawn behind the church, but not the woman, who wore an old-fashioned habit, with a wimple and a big silver cross. Her face was jowly, making me think of a bulldog, and at first I didn't even notice her feet until Holly pointed it out.

"She's floating." Holly pointed at the screen.

Even though she was closer to Luke and mine's age, Adam had a crush on Holly. Even though he hadn't said as much, I'm pretty sure recruiting me and Luke to play Ghost Hunt! was Adam's way of trying to impress her.

I leaned in for a closer look. Holly was right, below the nun's full skirt, her feet just sort of vanished. Instead of standing flat on the ground, she hovered, casting a dark stain of shadow.

Gen jostled my shoulder. I glanced back, moving so he could see better, but he edged away from the screen as Adam continued to scroll. Heather looked doubtful, too. She and Holly were only eleven months apart, practically twins. Like me and Gen, they came as a set. Wherever Holly went, her sister followed.

"Certain ghosts show up more in certain places." Adam continued flicking through his catalogue. "Like the Nun and the church, but regular haunts and ghouls can show up anywhere."

He paused on the picture of a haunt, a black and white photograph made to look all harsh and full of contrast, so the boy in the picture appeared to have no eyes, only dark staring pits where his eyes should be. The ghouls Adam showed us looked like they'd been shot in night-vision, emerald-tinted blurs hinting at tooth-filled mouths and legs bending the wrong way.

"We should all play together." Holly searched for the app on her phone, setting it to download, and Adam sat a little straighter. "I know some places where I bet we'll find ghosts."

Even though I didn't know Holly all that well, I knew she considered herself an expert on ghosts. I looked back at Gen. He had his phone out, but he hadn't downloaded the app yet. Our parents had gotten him his own phone just this year. They didn't care if he used it to play games and watch videos as long as he kept it with him in case of emergency.

"It won't be scary. I promise," I said, taking his phone.

Gen scrunched up his mouth; I hadn't played the game yet, so I had no way of knowing if it was scary, but I could tell he wanted to believe me.

"There are add-ons," Adam said. "EVP Mode, Night Vision, Auto Detect, but they cost extra. The game's still fine without them."

He led us outside, and we swept our phones around the yard.

"I don't see anything." Holly sounded impatient.

"Ghosts don't appear everywhere." Adam put his phone away. "Anyway, I have soccer practice now, but we'll go on a proper hunt tomorrow."

He tried out a grin, seeing whether anyone would challenge his self-appointed role as our leader. Holly fake-pouted a moment, but no one else said anything, other than agreeing we would meet up again tomorrow. I couldn't tell whether Holly liked Adam the way he liked her, or just considered him a means of finding ghosts. I couldn't tell whether I liked Holly, not as a girl, but as a person. But the best place to hang out was Luke and Adam's clubhouse, which probably meant I'd have to put up with her either way.

I ducked through the hedge, pausing when I realized Gen wasn't following me. He stood framed by the gap we'd made over the years, the ground worn by our feet so the grass didn't grow. I crouched, so I could see him fully. He had the look of concentration he got when he was trying to solve one of the math problems my parents gave him to practice while I was doing my homework, so he wouldn't feel left out.

"What's wrong?"

"What if I don't want to see a ghost?" Gen fidgeted with the pack around his waist. It held his phone and his inhaler; he wasn't allowed to leave the house without it.

"You don't have to play."

"But then you won't play with me if you're all doing it and I'm not."

Gen pushed his lower lip out. Guilt stung me, making the hope that flared for the briefest of moments feel ugly and cruel. I couldn't help the thought: would it really be so bad if Gen stayed at home and played with his own toys some days while I played Ghost Hunt! with Luke and Adam? At the expression on Gen's face, I tried to push the thought away.

"Hey." I crab-walked through the hedge and put my arm around his shoulders.

His bones poked at my arm, even through the fabric of his shirt. He'd always been small. Reminding myself that Gen needed my protection chased away the last bit of hope so that I could almost convince myself I'd never felt it in the first place.

"It's just a game." I tightened my grip into a one-armed hug. "If it gets too scary, we'll both stop playing, okay?"

"Promise?" Gen looked up at me through his lashes.

I held out my hand. Our dad had once sealed a promise to take us out for ice cream if we cleaned up the yard with a handshake. Gen had been three years old, and the idea of a handshake had stuck with him as the gold standard for a really serious deal you couldn't ever go back on.

"Promise." I said it loudly and clearly, making sure I believed it, too.

"I have a good one," Holly said.

The six of us sat shoulder to shoulder in the clubhouse. We'd been hunting ghosts all morning, but only Holly and Adam had caught anything, a regular haunt and a ghoul each. After a while, it had gotten too hot out, and we'd retreated to the shed with a fan run from the same extension cord as the mini fridge, and freezies from the corner store.

"It's one you haven't heard."

At the edge in Holly's voice, I looked up. She was looking straight at me and I blushed, realizing I must have rolled my eyes. She held my gaze for a moment longer, then launched into her story.

"Before Dieu-le-Sauveur was a real town, it was just a bunch of houses and a general store. A man named Martin St. Jean lived in the last house at the end of town, and everything after that was fields and forest. Everyone knew everyone back then, and neighbors looked out for each other, except for Martin St. Jean.

"He didn't go to church on Sundays. He would grunt instead of saying hello to his neighbors. His wife was even worse. If she came to the general store with him, she would sit in the wagon and wait, or walk behind him with her head down, never looking at anyone. She never spoke at all.

"The last time they came into town together, Martin's wife was pregnant. They were there to get supplies before a big snow storm. The shopkeeper's wife tried to talk to Martin's wife about the baby while their husbands loaded up the supplies, but Martin came back into the store and grabbed his wife's arm saying they were done."

Holly paused, looking around to make sure we were all paying attention. Seeing nobody was looking away or playing with their phones, she gave a half-smirk of satisfaction, and continued.

"When the storm came, all of Dieu-le-Sauver was snowed in for weeks, but no one thought to check in on Martin St. Jean and his wife, even with the baby on the way. Or maybe they did think of it, and they chose not to go because he didn't smile and nod at them and because his wife looked so small and afraid all the time.

"Once the snow thawed, people started to feel guilty. They got a party together to check on Martin St. Jean. No one answered when they knocked, but they heard a sound like a wild animal inside his house. It took three men to break down the door."

Holly dropped her voice, leaning forward. I found myself leaning forward, too, and Gen's shoulder brushed mine.

"When they got inside, they found Martin St. Jean crouched in the corner, covered in dirt and blood. He snarled, and when one of the men spoke to him, Martin St. Jean tried to bite him and tear out his throat.

"Another man tackled him, and they dragged him outside. That's when the men who were still inside found Martin's wife. She'd been tied to the bed, and pieces of her had been carved away. In the fireplace, they found bones. Some were too small to belong to anything but a baby, and they all looked like they'd been gnawed on."

Beside me, Gen flinched. Holly grinned.

"Martin claimed a wolf got into the house. He said he killed it and survived on its remains, even though he was too late to save his wife and child. No one believed him. They locked him up and he howled night and day, never stopping except to say how hungry and cold he was. In the end, they couldn't take it anymore, and they strung him up from a tree without waiting for a trial."

Holly paused again, making a point of meeting each of our eyes before delivering her last line in a dramatic whisper.

"And that's how the Starving Man was born."

I caught my first ghost in the high school parking lot after we'd been playing for a week. The six of us rode our bikes over together, then split up. I went to the far side of the lot near the trees, Gen sticking close as my shadow.

There was nothing, nothing, nothing, then suddenly a girl crouched on the asphalt right in front of me. When I looked away from my screen, I couldn't see her, but through my phone she looked as real as Gen. She wore a bathing suit. Water ran from her skin, pooling beneath her and soaking into the ground. I didn't remember animations from Adam's phone, but then he'd only showed us the still pictures. I wasn't prepared for how real she looked, the dripping water, or the way her lips seemed tinted blue.

"She's talking," Gen said.

I'd almost forgotten he was there. The girl's lips moved, but I couldn't hear anything.

"It's okay." I didn't look away from my phone.

I centered the girl and clicked the app's camera button. The girl's blue-tinged lips and the multi-color stripes of her bathing suit resolved into a black and white picture like the ones Adam showed us. I breathed out.

"I got one!" I raised my voice.

"Where'd you find her?" Holly was the first to reach me, everyone crowding around.

I pointed. Holly lifted her phone, but her screen only showed only asphalt and painted lines.

"Spawn must have timed-out." Adam shrugged. Holly looked annoyed.

"She was talking," Gen said.

A small line dented the skin in-between his eyebrows, his math problem look again.

"If you download the EVP add-on, you can play that back. Sometimes you can make out words," Adam said. "Here. Listen."

He tapped a button and held out his phone out. A garbled sound emerged.

"What's that?" Heather's eyes widened.

"Ghost voices." Adam played it again.

"It's just noise." Holly's mouth crimped, and Adam's shoulders slumped.

"I'm going to keep looking." Holly followed the border to some trees to the left, Heather trailing after her.

"Why was she dressed like that?" Gen asked.

Adam was still close enough to hear and answered.

"There used to be a swimming pool here. Maybe she drowned."

"Seriously?" I couldn't tell if Adam was messing with us, but he didn't have that look.

"I took swimming lessons here when I was really little. They filled it in right before Luke was born. I'm sure hundreds of kids drowned here."

Gen made a small noise, and I leaned down to whisper in his ear. "It's okay, we don't have to play anymore today."

I straightened, pitching my voice louder so Holly and Heather would hear, too. "We have to go home now. Our aunt is coming over for dinner."

I put my hand on Gen's shoulder, squeezing so he wouldn't give away my lie. I was a proud of myself, not for the lie, but for keeping at least part of my promise to Gen.

Later that night, I downloaded the EVP add-on, and pulled up the picture of the ghost girl in the bathing suit. Green lines scrolled across the screen, jittering up and down with the volume. I didn't have the add-on installed when the ghost girl's lips moved, so there was no way I could have captured real sound.

Even though I knew it was just a trick to make the game feel more real, I couldn't help the tightness in my chest as I listened. The noise on Adam's phone sounded like someone talking with marbles in their mouth, or a recording slowed way down so you couldn't make sense of the words. The sound on my phone was nothing like that at all.

It reminded me of how when we visited our grandparents, Gen and I would sink to the bottom of their pool and take turns saying words and trying to guess what the other was saying. Gen was always better at it than me. The sound on my phone was like that, a wet sound. I listened five times in a row, and after the fifth, I crept down the hall. Gen's door was open a crack; he lay on top of the covers with his back to me, the lights off.

"Hey. I downloaded the EVP mode. Will you help me figure out what the girl is saying?"

His shoulders might have twitched, but it might also have been a trick of the shadows as a car passed by outside. I waited, listening to his breathing, but I couldn't tell if he was really asleep or faking.

"Gen?" I tried one more time. No answer.

Before I could decide whether to barge into his room anyway, the screen lit up on Gen's phone. Wavy green lines scrolling, just the way they had on mine, the wet sound, but louder so I could almost make out a word.

I stepped back. Gen hunched his shoulders. I couldn't hear his breathing at all now, but I couldn't make myself move. Was he holding his breath, waiting for me to go away? Trying to pretend I hadn't seen anything at all, I retreated to my own room, closing the door behind me.

I woke to the sound of Gen's screams. Disoriented, my legs tangled in my covers and I hit the floor with a crash trying to get up. I made it into the hall at the same time as my parents.

Gen stood at the top of the stairs, his heels hanging over the top step like he was about to do a back flip off a diving board. His eyes were blank, his mouth a perfect circle of darkness. He looked like one of the ghost pictures on Adam's phone.

No one moved. Up until he turned five, Gen had suffered night terrors. The sleep specialist my parents took him to said to let Gen wake up on his own, no matter how bad it seemed. I never understood that, and my mom looked doubtful now, too.

"Gen, honey?" She took a cautious step, one hand out like she was trying to catch a nervous dog. "It's okay. You're safe."

Her fingers sketched the air near his arm, but she didn't touch him.

"Gen?"

He turned toward her, his mouth widening impossibly, and let out another shriek. He leaned back, like he was trying to get away from her, and his arms pin-wheeled as gravity snatched him. My mother threw her arms around him, yanking him back. They hit the floor together, Gen's limbs flailing in panic and hitting my mother in the nose.

"Get his inhaler." My father spoke without turning around.

I found it in his bedside drawer. My father still didn't look at me as I handed it over, concentrating on Gen. When Gen's eyes finally focused, he reached toward my mother's face.

"Mommy, you're bleeding."

"It's okay. Just a nosebleed." She smiled, her eyes bright with more relief than pain, but it still made Gen cry.

He buried his face against her shoulder, exhaustion and fear coming out in a rush. She held him, rubbing his back and reminding him to breathe. My dad stayed nearby, watching them. There was nothing else I could do, and everyone seemed to have forgotten about me.

I crept back to my room and opened Ghost Hunt! thinking of the green wavy lines scrolling across Gen's screen. I hadn't seen him download the EVP app, or take a picture of a ghost. As far as I knew, he hadn't caught any at all. I pulled up the ghost girl again. Nothing had changed. Some part of me expected to see Gen's picture instead, his mouth open like a circle of darkness, bruised eyes staring at me from the screen.

⟜

The next morning, I looked up the swimming pool before I went down to breakfast. Adam hadn't lied, but he'd exaggerated. Hundreds of kids hadn't drowned, just one. Her name was Jenny Holbrook, and she lived right behind the pool so she could get there by cutting through her backyard. I read through the stories about her, piecing together a narrative. Gruesome as it was, I had a vague idea in my head that the next time we all gathered in the clubhouse, that would be the ghost story I would tell.

Jenny used to sleepwalk when she was little. She hadn't done it in years, but one night when she was almost twelve, she got up, put on her swimsuit, and went outside. She cut through the yard and somehow got inside the fence around the pool even though the gate should have been locked. A lifeguard found her floating in the deep end the next day. Jenny had climbed the high dive board, jumped, and hit her head on the way down. She might not have even woken up before she drowned.

Another story published a few months after Jenny died said how she'd been planning to try out for the diving team. She'd been practicing for days. In the follow up report, the coroner revealed Ambien had been found in her system during the autopsy. Jenny must have been so nervous that she wouldn't sleep before the tryouts, she'd taken a pill.

The scent of my dad making banana pancakes wafted up from the kitchen, Gen's favorite, but it made me feel sick. I abandoned the idea of telling the story in the clubhouse, imagining the hungry expression on Holly's face if I did. Jenny Holbrook had been a real girl, and she'd died in Dieu-le-Sauveur. Why would the makers of the Ghost Hunt! who had probably never even heard of our town, have put her in the game?

"I have a story," Adam said.

He slid a glance sideways at Holly. She put her phone down, and Adam struggled with a smile. I wondered if he'd been reading up on ghosts and the history of Dieu-le-Sauveur.

"In the 1960s, there was a girl in Dieu-le-Sauveur named Candace Warren. She disappeared and no one knows what really happened to her. Candace lived in the House at the End of the Street."

Adam grinned, waiting for the startled look of recognition. Of course we all knew the House at the End of the Street. There's a cul-de-sac at the end of our street, and a set of wooden steps leading up to street running parallel. At the end of that street is the House. There's an empty lot beside it, and a park with a big willow tree, but nothing else around.

"There used to be another house there a long time ago, and that's the house where Martin St. Jean lived." Adam's grin widened, and Holly smacked his arm.

"Shut up. That isn't true."

"It is."

Holly crossed her arms; she was supposed to be the expert on ghosts. Despite her frown, it was clear she was still interested. After a moment, she relented.

"Okay, keep going."

Adam took a breath and continued.

"Candace spent most of her time with her babysitter, Abby. Her parents fought a lot and sometimes Candace would have bruises on her arms. She never talked about it with Abby, but Abby knew what the bruises meant. Because of that, Abby and Candace spent a lot of time away from the house, and one of their favorite places was the park across the street. They would have picnics under the willow tree, and Abby would tell stories."

It had taken him a few moments to recover from Holly's interruption, but he'd fallen back into a rhythm. In fact, it was the same rhythm she used, like he'd been studying the way she told her stories. I caught movement out of the corner of my eye. Gen looked uncomfortable, like he was trying hard not to squirm. I'd taken him away from the parking lot, and after his night terror, I thought for sure he'd want to stay home, but he'd crossed through the hedge right after me. I'd briefly considered turning back, but a nagging voice in the back of my head spoke up—why should I have to give up my summer and my friends just because he was scared and too stubborn to stay home?

Gen met my eyes, and I looked away, concentrating on Adam's story.

"One day while they were having one of their picnics, Abby showed Candace a secret. There was a certain spot under the willow where if you squinted just right, it looked like winter on the other side of the branches even in the middle of summer.

"Candace asked how it worked, but Abby said she couldn't tell her. The magic wouldn't work if it was explained. Instead, she told Candace to close her eyes until her lashes and the willow branches made a crosshatch pattern. When everything was hazy and glittery, Abby took off her shoe and threw it. They saw it pass through the branches, but they never heard it hit the ground. They made a full circle around the tree, but Abby's shoe was gone. When Candace asked where it went, Abby would only say one word: winter.

"That night, Candace disappeared."

"That's not a ghost story." Annoyance edged Holly's tone. This time, Luke was the one to answer her.

"Shut up. He's not done yet."

Holly opened her mouth, but Luke and I both shot her a look, and she closed it.

"This is the part with the ghost," Adam said. He glanced at Holly as if for approval. She didn't say anything, and he went on.

"A couple years after Candace disappeared, another family moved into the House at the End of the Street. Everyone had forgotten about Candace by then, and even Abby had moved away. The new family didn't have any kids, but people would sometimes see a little girl standing at the upstairs window. Then one day, a whole pile of drawings appeared around the oak tree in the House's yard.

"They were a kid's drawings, in bright crayon, hundreds of them. They showed a stick figure family—a mother, father, and little girl. The parents always had red smiles, but the girl's face was blank, with no mouth or eyes at all. There were also pictures of a tree that looked like it had been drawn over something else, and a house with its windows scribbled out.

"No one could figure out where the drawings came from. They thought it was a prank until they noticed something weird. Every picture had a figure in black ink somewhere on the page. Sometimes it was so small you could barely see, and sometimes it would fill the entire page, like it hadn't been there before and suddenly spread. It was a tall, thin man, so thin he looked like he was starving. He had no eyes or nose, but he always had a mouth, full of sharp teeth, and it was always open."

Adam sat back; he wore a satisfied look, but he looked at Holly while trying to pretend not to.

"Was it the Starving Man?" Heather asked. "In the pictures?"

"Yup." Adam nodded.

"How do you know it's true?" Holly asked.

"How do you know your stories are true?" Luke countered.

A low-level argument broke out. I ignored it, turning toward Gen. I felt guilty for looking away before, pretending I couldn't see he was upset. I caught my breath. Tears rolled down Gen's cheeks, his shoulders hitching. I grabbed his pack, which he taken off, and dug out his inhaler, but he shook his head.

"Come on, let's go," I whispered.

Luke and Holly were still arguing. Gen took my hand and squeezed it so hard I felt my bones shift, but I didn't pull away. I let him hold onto it as we crossed through the hedge and back home.

Gen forgave me. When I asked, he said he'd never been mad, but he also didn't want to talk about it. I tried to make it up to him by staying away from

Ghost Hunt!, and from Adam and Luke's house for a whole week. Everything went back to normal for a bit, and Gen didn't have any more night terrors. I started playing Ghost Hunt! again on my own without mentioning it. If Gen knew, he didn't say anything.

Three weeks after Adam told the story about Candace Warren, Gen and I were on the swings in the park near the school. I'd just finished baseball practice, and we were waiting for our parents to pick us up to go to our grandparents' for the weekend.

"Push me?" Gen asked.

I dragged my feet to stop my own swing.

"Think I could push you all the way around?"

I asked as I pulled his swing back.

"Don't!" He squealed as I let go, kicking his feet, but laughing. It was an old game between us. I pushed as hard as I could.

"Higher!"

I pushed again and as the swing came back toward me, Gen's phone pinged. It was the Auto Detect sound Ghost Hunt! made. Gen yelped, jumping. The swing's chains jangled as he hit the sand.

"Hey! You okay?" I caught the swing before it cuffed him.

His phone had fallen when he did. Green lines scrolled across the screen. I froze. The sound coming from Gen's phone was cold wind and the rattle of chains.

Gen whimpered. I inspected his hands. No scrapes. I brushed dirt off his palms.

"You're okay."

The sound from Gen's phone changed. The chains rattled more violently, and underneath came a noise like someone struggling to breathe.

I reached for the phone, and Gen yelled, "Don't!"

I rocked back, startled. I pulled out my own phone. Gen shook his head.

I ignored him, and opened Ghost Hunt! panning across the park. In the empty swing at the far end of the set, a girl sat with her hands wrapped around the chains. Her lips moved, breath trickling out in a cloud despite the summer day.

Gen turned to look over his shoulder, leaving his phone where it lay. He scrambled back, almost knocking me over.

"Gen!"

I reached for him, and he twisted away. Grabbing his phone, I ran after him. At that moment, our parents pulled around the corner. If they saw him running, I would be the one to get in trouble. Gen slowed at the park's edge, and I caught up. His breath rasped, but he wasn't having an attack.

"What happened?" I touched his shoulder, but he shrugged me off, climbing into the car.

He tucked his fingers in his armpits; goosebumps rose on his skin. I held his phone out and he shoved it into his pack without looking at it.

"Everything okay?" Mom glanced in the rearview mirror, looking between us.

Gen's face was pale, but blotchy with high points of color. He pressed his lips together. I shrugged. Her gaze lingered, doubtful, but she pulled away from the curb.

That night, I lay awake for a long time, watching the unfamiliar shadows slide across the ceiling of my grandparents' spare bedroom. I woke to Gen peering over the side of my bunk bed with no memory of falling asleep. I always slept on top, because Gen was afraid of falling off.

"What's wrong?" I sat up.

Gen didn't answer. I made room for him, and he scrambled up. A nightlight by the door gave off a bluish glow, and orange-tinted streetlights seeped through the window. Gen had been crying. He shoved his phone into my hands, the case damp like he'd been clutching it in sweaty palms. Ghost Hunt! was open to the scrapbook page.

It took me a moment to recognize the girl from the park. On Gen's phone, the swing she'd been sitting on hung from one chain, empty. The other chain had been cut, a length of it wrapped around the girl's throat so she dangled from the crossbar, her bare feet high above the ground.

"She can't breathe." Gen touched his throat.

I dropped the phone, then picked it up again, stabbing the button to close the app. It didn't feel like enough. I turned the phone all the way off, and shoved it under the pillow. Then I pulled Gen closer. He shivered against me. I imagined the sound of cold wind and chains, the sound of someone struggling to breathe.

"We should go to the House at the End of the Street for real and hunt ghosts there," Holly said.

Gen drew his knees up against his chest. After what he'd shown me at our grandparents' house, I'd thought for sure he would stay home when I mentioned going over to the clubhouse. I don't know why I'd suggested it, why I was still playing Ghost Hunt! when I'd promised him we'd quit.

I hadn't even been playing that much since catching the first ghost in the parking lot, but no one else had quit yet, and I didn't want to be the first. If it wasn't for Holly, I'm sure Adam would have quit long ago. Same thing with Heather. But there was no way Holly was giving up.

As for Gen, I don't know if he was being stubborn, or in some weird way he was trying to shame me into keeping my promise. Surely, if he got scared enough, I would quit, right? Until then, he wouldn't stop, no matter how miserable he was, which left us in a weird standoff. Every time I didn't shut the app down, or suggest doing something else, it made me angry at myself, which inevitably turned into being angry at Gen. Why couldn't I have this one thing? Why'd he have to be such a baby about it? When I wasn't looking at the pictures on his phone, or hearing the sounds, I could forget how terrible they were. I could convince myself it really was just a game.

"We should go tonight," Adam said.

"Mom and Dad would never let us." Heather spoke without looking at her sister, but Holly still turned to glare at her.

"So we don't tell them."

"I know how we could do it," Gen said.

As small as the clubhouse was, his voice was almost lost. I stared at him, but he ignored me, looking at Holly and Adam instead.

"All our houses are on the same security system. If we trick them into doing a maintenance cycle, we can sneak out and our parents won't know we're gone. I saw how to do it on the internet."

It was simple once I thought about it, but I hadn't thought about it, and Gen had. How long had he been planning this? Gen finally looked at me. Some trick of the light made his eyes as dark as the ghosts in my scrapbook, a stranger staring back at me.

Maybe Gen's asthma made him vulnerable, or maybe it was his night terrors. Maybe being afraid is what let the ghosts in. Martin St. Jean's wife was afraid. Jenny Holbrook was afraid. Candace Warren was afraid, too.

Or, what if Candace Warren's parents did more than just leave bruises one day? What if Jenny's parents gave her the Ambien because they just couldn't take her nerves and wanted her to shut up? What if there's a reason we tell so many stories about ghosts?

What if we need an excuse.

Or maybe, Dieu-le-Sauveur really is haunted. Maybe a bad thing happened here long ago, and it keeps happening, and there's nothing anyone can do to stop it. It's a comforting thought in its own way.

Every town has their version of the Starving Man, The Bell Hook Witch, the Weeping Woman, Drip, Drip Drag. Ghosts have always known how to get inside people's mouths, using them to tell themselves over and over. Before everyone had smartphones and creepypasta, and Normal Paranormal, they had nursery rhymes, and clapping games, and campfire tales.

There have always been ghosts.

And even if there weren't ghosts, kids would still disappear all the time.

It's not my fault. Just because I wanted Gen to quit the game. Just because he got more attention than me because he was sick and small and afraid.

There's a reason we want to believe in ghosts. We need them.

Luke, Adam, Holly, Heather, Gen, and I gathered in the middle of our street and walked together to the cul-de-sac. At the top of the stairs, we turned right. Shadows jittered through a stand of trees, and Heather's phone pinged. She jumped, but stopped and snapped a picture. I didn't look at her screen. I didn't want to see. Holly whispered something in her sister's ear, and jabbed her with her elbow.

We kept walking, stopping at the edge of House at the End of the Street's lawn. The streetlights threw harsh patches of darkness across the empty lot next door. I imagined the Starving Man folded away in one of those patches, waiting.

The House looked perfectly normal, even in the dark. It was two stories, painted a pale yellow like cold butter, the door and windows edged in white trim. The yard bore a scar where the oak tree had been pulled up, roots and all. The worst thing about the House was that it felt empty—hollow all the way through—the kind of loneliness that goes with a place where no one has lived for years.

"Well?" Holly nudged Adam. "You're the leader."

Adam didn't move. I could just make out the willow in the park across the street, its branches swaying even though there was no wind. A glimmer of light showed through the leaves, sparkling and hard-edged, then it was gone.

"Gen, let's go." I caught my brother's sleeve.

Gen glared at me, but didn't move. It was my fault he was here, and he wanted me to know. I wanted to tackle him to the ground like my mother had when he was gripped with a night terror. I wanted him to bloody my nose. It would be easier than admitting I was wrong, saying I was sorry. Gen spun on his heel, brushed past Adam and Holly, and kept walking right up to the House's front door.

It shouldn't have opened, but it did. I can't remember whether he looked back before he stepped over the threshold, daring me to follow, giving me one last chance to keep my promise.

From where I stood, it looked like he fell into a solid wall of darkness, visible one moment, then gone. I hesitated; it was only a split second, I'm sure. My chest tightened; my heart kicked against my ribs. I hated Gen for everything he had and hadn't done, then I loved him again, and I sprinted up the porch steps.

I caught myself on the doorframe. Must and still air greeted me. My upper body leaned inside, while my feet stayed planted outside the door.

A staircase stretched up to my left; a hallway receded to the right. Doorways opened in either direction, revealing furniture-less rooms. Blank walls, nowhere for Gen to hide.

I must have shouted his name, because it echoed back to me. I caught a flash of movement, a small face peering over the railing at the top of the stairs, but it wasn't Gen.

I took the stairs two at a time, wheezing the way Gen did in the middle of an asthma attack. In room after room, my feet kicked up dust. My footsteps overlapped until it seemed like a whole herd of ghosts running with me. I searched, going through more rooms than the house should have, but Gen wasn't in any of them.

Finally, I pulled out my phone. Fumbling, I got Ghost Hunt! open. Nothing. Nothing except green lines briefly skittering across my screen, accompanied by a sound like snow ticking against windows, building up and sealing away the inside like a tomb.

I shouted Gen's name over and over, but no one answered me. In the end, I folded myself onto the top step. I wrapped my arms around my legs, my knees pressed against my chest, and struggled to breathe.

Before we moved away from Dieu-le-Sauveur, before my parents got divorced, one more thing happened. On a rainy day, I crossed through the hedge and knocked on the clubhouse door. Moisture spotted my shirt and dampened my hair. I heard shuffling inside, hesitation, then Luke opened the door. An uncomfortable glance passed around the room like they'd just been talking about me. I didn't blame them.

Luke sat back down, and I sat beside him. Holly put away her phone, her expression guilty. I suspected they'd been comparing ghosts like nothing happened.

No one said anything. It was clear they wished I hadn't come; everything would be so much easier if I'd just disappeared along with Gen. I didn't disagree. The truth was, I didn't know why I was there either. Except it was better than listening to my parents shout or staring at the walls while my eyes stung.

In that awkward silence, while everyone searched for something to say, my phone pinged.

I hadn't opened Ghost Hunt! since Gen disappeared, but the sound was unmistakable—Auto Detect kicking in. It was so quiet I could hear everyone breathing. Then Holly spoke, her voice barely more than a whisper and rough around the edges.

"Aren't you going to look?"

Her eyes were bright, but for once it wasn't with eagerness. She looked like she regretted her words, but couldn't stop herself.

I picked up my phone. Green wavy lines scrolled across the screen. At first, all we could hear was wind blowing and an old house creaking. Then the sound of breathing. Louder than any of us, and getting more strained. Someone struggling, someone running out of air. I thought of Gen touching his throat. I wanted to scramble in his pack for an inhaler that wasn't there.

Before I threw my phone against the clubhouse wall. Before it shattered and tears gathered in my eyes and my own breath hitched in response to the terrible noises coming out of my phone, one more thing happened. We heard a voice.

It was a bare whisper, but I would recognize it anywhere—Gen saying my name.

ENDOSKELETAL

SARAH READ

The figures are drawn in yellow ochre, their limbs overlong, their faces drawn as skulls—white with crushed calcite, eyes carbon black with a spark of red ochre inside. Each figure holds an orb-like jar beneath its chin. Umber shadows trail behind them as they march the length of the chamber, deep into the small spaces at the back of the cave, where there is the monster. A mass all in soot bone black, large as the cave wall, covered in a hundred lidless eyes. The eyes are not drawn, but etched into the stone itself.

Ashley looked from the cave wall back to her sketch and smoothed her thumb over a figure's shadow, blending her pencil lines. Henri's camera flashed, blinding her. When her eyes adjusted, pupils wavering into equilibrium, her LED lantern seemed dimmer than before, the figures drawn on the cave walls harder to make out.

"Can you wait a minute, please?" She didn't temper the edge in her voice. She'd asked him this a hundred times already—at the office as she checked her daypack, along the Alpine trail as he led the way at a pace she could not possibly match. *You must get used to the altitude if you want to study here,* he'd said as she caught up, panting, the thin air heavy in her lungs. *You're not ready to study here*, is what she heard. What he probably wanted her to hear.

"I *am* studying here," she'd puffed between shallow gasps. "And you can't outrun altitude sickness. Don't they teach that to guides here?" She'd planted herself on a rock and made him wait.

His camera flashed again. "We don't have time." Another photo. "We've waited half the day away. Your drawings are too slow. We don't do it that way anymore."

Ashley shifted; the cold of the cave floor had crept through the sweater she'd folded into a cushion. She counted to ten, her eyes squeezed shut against the flashes. "I'm not just sketching to record them, Henri. I'm learning them—studying them."

"You can do that in the lab, unless you want to hike back in the dark. You're wasting time. We don't even know if you'll be allowed to study these."

She stood then, clutching her pencils in her fist. "What do you mean?"

"You came to study bears? These aren't bears. There are bears in the other chamber you can study—we have enough of those to share. But this is special. This is weird. They will want a Swiss archaeologist for this."

Ashley hadn't considered that. When she'd proposed the expedition to explore the new chambers exposed by the receding glacier, she'd counted on finding either cave bears or nothing. Instead she'd found a national treasure. The specters from the camera flash danced in her eyes as she added notes to her handwritten report. He hadn't convinced her to hurry. Now her notebook was more important than ever—it might be the only proof she'd have of the discovery, if the site was seized.

The cave painting showed at least twenty figures confronting the shadow covered with eyes. The skull-faced figures threw bones at the shadow, though it wasn't clear if they were fighting it or feeding it. Ashley paced the length of the chamber, back toward where she had to bow her six-foot-seven frame to fit beneath the mineral-slick stone. The eyes of the monster seemed to follow her, their charcoal-darkened shadows shifting in the weak light. It made the hair on her arms rise, made it difficult to look away from the creature—as if it would move closer when her back turned.

A dozen skeletal remains filled shallow alcoves that lined the walls beneath the drawings. Beyond the alcoves, two narrow openings split the back of the cave. One led to nothing but a cavernous sinkhole. The other led to the much-trafficked cave chamber containing the remains of several cave bears. No one had known that the loose rubble wall of the cave bear room had concealed the entrance to another chamber. No one had wanted to disturb the stones and risk a cave-in. But with temperatures rising, the ice on the opposite slope had melted away, and the true entrance to the cave had opened its dark eye over the valley below.

She looked back to her sketch and darkened the space inside of an eye socket, layering the charcoal until there was no hint of cream paper beneath. She leaned farther over the skeletal remains in an alcove. The bones of the legs and arms were broken, but Ashley could tell from the growth plates that he died young. *The bones are in bad condition—fragmented and overgrown with mineral deposits that will be difficult or impossible to remove without destroying the specimen . . .*

The skulls, though, were all complete. Each one with its jaw pried apart and a jar shoved between its teeth. *The jars are clay or stone, perhaps dug from the cave walls? Smooth and yellowed. They're undecorated, sealed with fine leather. They are some form of canopic jar perhaps, or an offering to the dead or the afterlife?* She reached out a finger to touch the fragile leather, then pulled back. *The leather remains intact despite no apparent organic matter left on the bodies themselves. It will need to be tested for ancient preservation techniques.*

There wasn't much known about Paleolithic funerary rites. Because sites like this were never found.

Most of the jars lay in shards—the pieces tumbled toward the back of the skeleton's throats, the jaws left gaping—only fine dust remained of their contents. But there were five jars whole and tempting. Her hands kept returning to the space above the skull, hovering, as if to stroke its brow. She had never before been tempted to touch a specimen, to violate every rule that she herself had repeated incessantly to students and assistants at her sites.

"We're taking one back with us," Ashley said, tucking her book into her pack.

The camera flash paused and Ashley felt Henri's eyes scolding her through the darkness. There was something in the way he looked at her that made her skin prickle.

"I don't think we should," he said.

Ashley pulled another kit from her pack—a small plastic crate filled with chunks of polyethylene foam, and rolls of gauze and tape. She began assembling a nest that would protect the specimen as they hiked back to the research center.

"Dr. Knochdieb won't like it. You'll lose your post for sure if you disturb this site."

"Isn't that what you all want, anyway?" She was done with their bureaucracy—she'd come here to work. And the thought of leaving without something more to study—without some way to begin answering the thousand questions storming in her brain—was torture.

Henri's scoff echoed off the walls, the drawings, the bones. "It'll be dark before we get back as it is. It'll be dark before we leave if we wait much longer. *I* can hike that trail in the dark, but you're going to get hurt if you try." He mumbled to himself in German as he changed the camera's memory card. It sounded like a prayer. His hair was the brightest thing in the cave—the sort of blond Californians paid good money for. Perhaps he'd be her beacon in the dark. She imagined she'd disappear in the dark entirely, invisible against the sky, though Henri had earlier said that her height made her impossible to lose. She felt the telltale ache in her shoulders as she'd unconsciously slouched ever since.

He was right, though, about all of it. She could picture the red-faced spluttering of the department head when he learned she had touched an unknown burial site. It would be several shades darker than when he learned she'd be studying there to begin with. The program hadn't accepted any foreign students since the dawn of digital record keeping. They weren't keen to break the record. And, of course, they hadn't known what she would find in the cave. Henri, in particular, was upset to lose what would have been *his* project—what now would be, at best, a third-author credit, behind her, if she stayed—and her behind the soon-to-be-furious Dr. Knochdieb.

But he'd be mad tomorrow. Tonight was her chance to learn what she could and put together a proposal to convince them to give her the project—this project, instead of the bears—or at least allow her to stay involved. An underling, even. She'd bring them coffee, up the mountain, if she could work on-site. Anything to stay with the bones.

Now gloved, she did risk a touch. Just a fingertip, above the teeth, where the lips would have been stretched back around the bulbous jar.

She draped sheets of gauze over the skull as carefully as if wrapping a newborn. Its face—its gaping jaw and strange jar—vanished behind the layers of soft white. She set the bundle in a ring of foam inside the crate and layered more around it. She scoured the alcove for any small pieces or artifacts she may have missed. *Nothing. Not even a bead. All they have is their jars.*

The camera flash had returned, throwing her shadow in front of her, up the cave wall and across the skeletal drawings, as if she were another soot monster swallowing the stick-like figures whole.

But Henri wasn't documenting the remains anymore. He was documenting her. Just as he'd probably been told to do from the beginning. More of a spy than a guide and assistant. But he didn't have the authority to stop her. And even if he went straight to Dr. Knochdieb, she'd have a few hours to study her sample and make her case. There was little hope either way. But at least she could learn something about the bones.

Ashley's body ached as they reached the foot of the mountain. Every knuckle was skinned and bleeding, the tendons in her wrists and ankles throbbing from every twist and fall. But the specimen was safe, its crate wrapped in her blanket in the padded compartment of her pack. She'd been careful to pitch her weight forward when she fell. Her palms, elbow, even her face took the brunt of her falls. After the first few, Henri had stopped helping her up, leaving her to the natural consequences of her decision to keep them in the mountains past dark. The mountain dark of the Alps was as black as the inside of its caves, and her dimming lantern hadn't shown every peril on the path. She'd embarrassed herself. But she tried to focus on her project—the specimen in her pack—her future.

She nearly wept at the sight of the single lamp post that illuminated the door to their isolated research center. It was tucked in a folded valley between steep hills, along the path of an old glacier flow. The scars of its ancient passage could still be seen from the hills above. At least, in the light they could.

She wanted the close space of her drafty clapboard dorm. The antique, Alpine barn conversion had been anything but welcoming, but she'd make a home of anywhere with Tylenol and a hot bath. And a private lab.

Henri flashed his keycard at the sensor and held the door for her as she limped across the threshold. "Do you need first aid? There is ice in the kitchen."

"No, thanks." His offer seemed sincere, though she thought he might be mocking her. His accent made it difficult to discern. "I'm going to drop this off at the lab," she said, holding her pack in front of her like a baby. "We'll need to meet with Dr. Knochdieb in the morning."

"I think he'll come in early for this. I'm going to call him now."

"There's no need to wake him. The bodies have been there for thousands of years; they aren't going anywhere."

"*They* aren't. I suggest you start packing, Miss Alesso. I'm sorry."

Ashley watched him strut down the hall toward the dorms. His machismo didn't hide his own limp as well as he doubtless hoped it would. She felt a mixture of shame and wicked glee. She'd forced him to risk his neck on that trail. Her hopes of winning the friendship of her young assistant were in ashes, but at least she could count on him habitually underestimating her.

The halls were dark, empty. The few other researchers and students who shared the facility had long since gone to bed. The lab was hers for as long as it took the director to climb down from his fancy chalet.

—○—

The browned bones of the face appeared through the gauze as if surfacing through a sheet of melting snow. She leaned over it as she worked, the muscles in her back and neck knotted and angry. The soft brush feathered over the skull, sweeping away the dirt and fine white threads into the nest of packing gauze.

She studied the protrusions that lined the brow. Under the bright lights of the lab, she saw that they were a part of the bone itself—not cave deposits or applied funerary decorations, but some sort of cancer or deformity. Her heart pinched for the people of the cave. The spurs must have hurt.

She ran a gloved fingertip around the perimeter of an eye socket. They were like toothy hills crowned with needles that snagged at the latex of her glove as she pulled back.

Her fingertip trailed to the jaw and the jar wedged inside the mouth. She could see, then, that it was stone—carved from a solid piece. The walls eggshell-thin. Ashley brushed away all traces of debris and slid her fingers past the long teeth, deep into the mouth, and cupped the bottom of the jar with her fingertips. She lifted gently and felt it give, the stone scraping against the ancient teeth like squeaking chalk. An uncomfortable shudder moved down her body. The jar worked free, intact, and she set it on a pillow of foam on a tray. The skull, its mouth unnaturally stretched, appeared as if it screamed, or laughed. Its empty eyes seemed accusatory in their darkness. She covered the face with a fold of gauze. The empty eyes reminded her of the eyes on the cave monster.

The walls of the jar were thin enough that she could see the glow of light behind it, and the silhouette of a lumpy shadow inside. She photographed every angle, every detail, and made sure the pictures were uploaded and saved before grabbing her scalpel and tweezers. She both hated and wanted this part. Her pulse grew distracting, a pounding in her sore joints, and it would continue to rise until the beautiful thing in front of her was destroyed. And destroying the sample would destroy her career, or make it. Her hair stuck to her sweaty brow.

She cut away the cord that secured the flap over the opening and gathered the flakes of leather as they fell, dropping them into a jar of her own—bright glass, sterile, but otherwise little had changed in twenty-five thousand years.

The leather scrap was thin and fine like the tender skin of a rodent. It had dried to something almost like vellum. *It shouldn't exist at all.*

Once the seal was pulled away, odor overwhelmed her. Sweet and rancid like cherries and old cheese. She clutched her wrist to her nose until the wave passed. She hadn't dealt with fresh remains in years. This specimen shouldn't be fresh. Shining more light inside revealed dark clumps clinging to the illuminated walls. She dipped her scalpel inside and scooped out a trace of the substance, sending a fresh wave of odor down her throat. It stuck to the blade as she tapped it onto a glass slide. It was crumbly and clumpy like wet, purple sand. She took more photographs, brightened them, and saw purple, red, gold, brown. Perhaps a desiccated organ. Or maybe the tongue, considering the placement of the jar.

Magnified under the microscope, it was a brilliant lattice of blood cells—platelets, red and white cells, stem cells, and fatty deposits. Myelorytes. Fragments of vessel. Bone marrow.

Ashley turned back to the crate with the skull and peeled back the gauze. She ran her fingers over the blossoms of bone again, ignoring the sharp snags, searching for a perforation in the bone. Then she remembered the arms and legs, each broken on every body. Not from the brittleness of millennia, perhaps, but as part of this strange funerary ritual. She wanted to get the rest of the bones—make a full layout of the body and examine the breaks. Look for manmade trauma. But she needed to finish her work with the jar. She grabbed the jar and held it directly above the light, peering into its mouth, trying to gauge the quantity of marrow collected, presumably from the man whose mouth it had filled. Though it was astoundingly preserved under its ancient seal, some evaporation had to have occurred. A slow concentration. She couldn't tell how much marrow was there, but she didn't want to disturb the whole sample.

There needed to be something left intact for her report—and some evidence that she'd be dedicated to the proper handling of these artifacts, despite her hasty removal of the sample.

She was beginning to like the smell. She breathed it in and felt certain, then, that the gaping skull smiled.

The tightness in her neck made it difficult to lift the crate onto the high shelf in the storage fridge. Her hands shook and fresh blood had slicked the inside of her gloves. She felt the altitude again like a punch in the gut.

The ache in her body had deepened by morning, but she couldn't stop pacing. She limped from one end of the conference room to the other, her eyes sweeping over the board that she'd papered with her sketches. She paused, pulled a pencil from her hair, and fixed a sketch. Deepened a shadow. Added texture to the rough fracture of the bones.

She ran her fingers through her hair and pulled another sliver of shale from the dark curls. She hadn't managed a bath, yet. With any luck, she'd be coated in dirt again by the afternoon, anyway.

The meeting wouldn't start for an hour, but she needed time to prepare. They'd be looking for the first excuse to kick her out, contract be damned. But she wouldn't let it go without a fight. This was the find of a lifetime, and it was her discovery. She wasn't likely to ever see anything like this again—but if she got her name on this study, it could change the trajectory of her whole career.

Her knees gave and pain shot up her legs. Her body contorted on the floor, folding over as the cramps arced across her body. Pain twisted through her hips and up her back before it faded, leaving her sweating and panting on the floor.

She had been distracted and preoccupied on the way down the mountain. She must have pulled a tendon. Pinched a nerve. Her breath evened, and she pulled herself up into one of the rolling desk chairs. Black spots receded from her vision. She poured herself a drink of water from the pitcher on the table, spilling as she did, her hands unsteady—her fingers weak and trembling. She choked on the water, coughing splashes down her front.

Dr. Knochdieb burst into the room, Henri behind him.

She wiped her dripping chin on her sleeve.

Dr. Knochdieb stormed past her to the board covered with her sketches and photographs. His tie was slightly off-center. *He must have rushed.*

"Quite the find," he said, pausing to look at the sketch of the shadow monster. "We were of course aware of Stone Age human settlements near the lake, but we hadn't yet found any in the high hills. Not in any of the dozens of caves. So tell me, scholar, why they are there?" He pulled her sketch of the cave paintings from the board and sat in the chair to her right. From this angle, she could see that he had also failed to press down his silver cowlick. The spike of hair at his crown was usually plastered with gel—a feature Henri had nicknamed The Oberaletsch Glacier.

Ashley's voice caught deep in her chest. She'd had a speech prepared, but it didn't account for this sort of question. She'd been expecting more "who do you think you are," not "what do you think." Hope made it hard to think at all.

"Well, the bones show significant funerary preparations. They're laid out, and the stone jars are inserted into the mouths. The jars contain bone marrow, which I suspect came from the arms and legs, which have all been broken—"

"How do you know that?" Dr. Knochdieb and Henri both turned to her at that, their faces masked with twin looks of alarm.

Ashley felt the cold water creeping back up her throat. "I examined the specimen last night. I wanted to provide a full rep—"

"You tampered with it?"

Here was the tirade she'd been expecting. His eyes roved over her in a way that made her feel inside-out. As though she was raw to his judgment.

"I felt it was my responsibility to report my findings in full. To provide enough information to justify a continued excavation and protection of the site." Her jaw stiffened as she spoke, so that her last words hissed past her teeth, sounding more impertinent than she meant them.

"Of course it will be excavated. And protected. But it's not your job to tell us that." Dr. Knochdieb's hands shook with indignation. The color of his face rose to match his tie.

"I meant to justify *my* continued excavation. Just . . . please. Please, let me work on this with you." This wasn't her script—she hadn't intended to beg. But her head was spinning. She couldn't remember what she was supposed to say—her jaw felt sealed against her words. Something about her past experience under her mentor in Peru. Something about global cooperation. She could only think of the bones—of getting back to them. *Remind them why you're here—why they said yes.*

The black spots were returning to her vision. She held herself firm in her seat, upright, eyes closed.

She caught the word "dismissed," then stumbled out of her chair, sending it rolling into the board, knocking sketches into the air. She ran from the room as Dr. Knochdieb scolded her rude departure.

Her legs buckled awkwardly as she raced down the hall to her office. She slammed the door shut behind her and sank to the cold floorboards.

Her fingers ached as though they'd been jammed. It reminded her of her adolescent growing pains—of soaking, curled, in hot baths and the aftertaste of Advil bitter on her tongue, her mother's long fingers pulling through her wet, curly hair, reassuring her that the boys would catch up to her height, that she wasn't a "freak." She felt the familiar itch of the stretch marks that lashed across her back and around her thighs—a crossed dark lattice. She remembered the eyes on her, everywhere she went—the staring, their gazes tickling up her neck. She remembered waking at slumber parties to find games of tic-tac-toe played in the crosshatch of her scars. Every dry itch of that pull of skin brought fresh humiliation. And now she felt it on her hands, her face, and neck. It felt as though her flesh was a shrinking glove, curling her fingers to her palms and holding them there.

Panting, she held her hands up to the light. Her knuckles twisted as the skin pulled tighter. The grooves of her knuckles split, the fissures like small gaping mouths from which erupted bone upon bone. She shrieked at the sting of it and tried to close the split flesh by straightening her fingers, felt the pressure grow, pulsing under her nails—saw the white of bone pale like blisters at the tips of her fingers. She stretched her fingers further and the skin burst, springing back along the protruding shafts of bone, curling back like a blooming flower. Her fingernails scattered around her. Each breath, deep and ragged, felt as though it contained less air than the one before.

There's something in those jars. Something wrong. She remembered the prick of the bone spurs, the blood in her gloves. *Careless.*

She struggled, shaking, to her feet. Blood dripped from her twisting fingers to the dingy floor. She reached long, tender, bone-tipped fingers into her pocket, moaning as the rough fabric scraped against the exposed nerves, and pulled her lab keycard out. *This hurts, hurts, this hurts . . . but not as much as it should.* Half her brain was a hum of panic, while half observed, fighting the adrenaline for scraps of logic.

The hallway was empty. It was still early—no one was in their offices yet. She limped around the door and down the hall, catching herself against the wall as she stumbled, crying out when her bones clacked against the plaster. *What is happening to me?* The metatarsals of her feet strained against the leather of her shoes.

She fumbled with the keycard at the lab door, dropping it, scraping it from the tiles with her bone-tips. *The bones; I need the bones; I need the marrow.* She brought the card to her mouth and used her lips to hold it to the sensor. The light flashed red. The door handle stuck, unmoving.

They've changed the locks. Dread washed over her, almost enough to erase the pain in her hands, her face, her feet and knees. There was only one other place she could study the jars. Only one place that might have an answer about what was happening to her.

The thought of the cave was like an endorphin balm. She needed the cave.

Her knees left damp patches of blood along the trail behind her. She held her lantern clenched in her teeth. Her long fingers slid through spaces between the rocks, gripping them, hauling herself more easily than she had the day before—all her weight pivoting on the levers of her long bones. The pull of the cave was so strong it felt as though it lifted her up the mountain. When she reached the top of the rise where the cave gaped open, her bones had grown so tall that she had to fold herself unnaturally to enter. She rolled inside and lay on the floor, shaking violently, shrieking as more bones popped out of her jaw and hips, spraying blood across the ancient amber bones and ochre drawings. *I'm contaminating the samples.* She nearly laughed at her impulse to preserve the cave art. *Die somewhere else. You're making a mess.*

Her hands, feet, face continued to erupt—her legs and arms extending until they were difficult to place. She tried to stand and fell over her own long legs, as she had when she was fifteen, trying to dance.

She felt eyes on her, then—angry and hungry—and turned toward the cave entrance, expecting to see Henri, maybe even Dr. Knochdieb. The opening was hidden in shadow, as if night had fallen as she lay on the floor. Shingles of bone growing from her face obstructed her view. But still she felt watched. Then the darkness moved toward her. She scrambled back, long limbs flailing against the rock and pushing her farther away from her lantern. As she squirmed toward the back of the cave, the neon white light disappeared, as if draped in cloth.

She skittered deeper into the cave, tapping with her long bones to find her way. She passed an alcove, and remembered the painted figures marching on the monster. She grabbed for the bones on the shelf and hurled them into the shadow. The pressure abated—drawing back, a flinch—a blink. The pile dwindled till she came to the skull, and remembered the jar. The sacred marrow. She reached into its mouth, to the intact orb of stone, and slipped it free—clutched it to her chest as she threw the skull, the final bone, into the shadow. It fell back, just enough to free the glow of her lantern. She crawled toward the openings at the back of the cave. She remembered the chamber maps, vaguely—what Henri had let her see of them. One chamber led to the bear cave and exited onto the southern slope above town. The other led to a chasm. She couldn't remember which was which. *I can't think; why can't I think anymore.* It was as if the bones pulled the thoughts from her head.

She slid her long legs into the hole just as darkness drowned the lantern again, and the shadow moved toward her, all thousand eyes fixed on her bone helmet as she dropped from the chamber into the narrow passage beyond.

She slid, fell, branching fingers clutching at empty air, then landed on a haystack of bones in a frenzy of fracture and splintering. Dry, ancient bones shattered against her armor. Three of her long fingers snapped. The stone jar had crushed against her chest, the sticky paste inside smearing her with its scent. She coughed a scream.

The eyes were all around her, stripping her, driving through her armor, under her skin. The old dry bones did nothing to slow it. These weren't ritual bones. They weren't marrow bones—these bones had already been drunk dry. She found the warm twigs of her broken fingers, phalanges five inches long—she could smell the meat in them, rich and fatty. Life itself, reborn over and over, the factory of longevity. She slid the bones through the small holes in her skull mask and wrapped her lips around the jagged edges, felt the needle-like texture of their surface prick at her lips. She sucked at the marrow. It slid over her tongue, thick and creamy. Her pain faded. Her eyes began to adjust to the darkness on all sides. She threw her empty bones at the shadow and it fell back, giving her room to see and breathe.

The sinkhole was a trash heap of abandoned remains. Eyes were etched deep into the walls as far up as she could see, as though the monster slept here under its own watch. Above her, the shadow swirled like a cloud of bats, all pupil, wide and dark. She slid her long fingers into the carved grooves and began to climb. Her overlong arms and legs quivered under the stone weight of her growing bone armor. They gave, and she plummeted back to the bottom, snapping more protrusions.

She sucked more marrow from her freshly broken digits, and her strength increased—the pain faded further. The fragments continued to drive back the shadow. The marrow from the jar smeared across her chest made her itch again, and she felt more stretching, more calcium armor growing with a deep bass rumble deep in her core. She began to climb again. When she weakened, her body growing too heavy even for her strengthened hands, she put a finger in her mouth and bit down, breaking it off with her teeth and sucking at it, drawing more strength, more ammunition against the monster. When her fingers were stumps just long enough to press into the grooves of the stone, she broke away pieces from her face—thick wings of bone from her eyes and jaw, 'til her head was free again but for the jagged edges of broken bone at the tattered eruption points. Her face a mask of ivory needles.

She reached the top and slithered back through the opening into the catacomb chamber. Her lantern was there, the monster no longer between her and the exit. The exposed nerves in her body sang with pain again in the open air of the chamber.

The beast emerged from a crack in the rocks. Its gaze buckled her knees and dropped her to the cave floor as she turned to face it. It bubbled up through the narrow vent, its vision multiplying as it filled the cavern.

Ashley's bones bled from fragile, ragged fractures. There was nothing left to throw. Her bones weren't growing fast enough.

She edged to the cave wall and reached into an alcove, running her fingers over the ritual skeletons till she felt the familiar curve of a skull, a jar. She pried it out of the jaw and brought it to her mouth. The neck of the jar shattered between her teeth and she drove her tongue into the opening, lapping at the gritty paste inside. Her body quaked. She screamed as bones burst from her, jutting from her hands, feet, and face. The shadow lurched, and she pitched an alcove bone at the monster. It hesitated, rushed forward.

Ashley scrambled back. She reached into the next alcove and claimed another jar, sucked its contents down, and grew again. Sheets of bone from her eye sockets crept into her periphery, growing across her face. She raked long fingers toward the shadow, swiping at it. She felt it blink—a momentary release from its boring gaze.

She danced on long toes across the narrow chamber to the other alcoves, and the last jar. More marrow, more bone, less darkness. Her ribs crisscrossed in front of her, a shield over her soft, bleeding center. She charged the monster. She glared into its gaze, eye to eye to eye, until it sank back through the crevasse, back to the eye-walled pit, its vision winking out, leaving her in only natural darkness. She drove her ossified fist into the stone above the fissure, pounding it into grit, her hardened hands like hammers glancing off the slick stone till it crumbled. The opening gave and the ceiling fell, thundering, sealing the side chamber shut—like the jars, like the bone closing over Ashley's face.

Her rapid breath flowed back at her in the confines of her outer skull. Her vision narrowed to the width of a single finger. She reached through the small hole and tried to pull at the bone, to break herself free. The skull mask clamped shut on her fingertip, growing over it, trapping it, shutting out all but a little light. She screamed inside her skull and the sound bounced around her ears. The expanding lattice of her ribcage lifted her off the floor.

Her breathing slowed. Cradled in her bones, with her own soft breath against her face, her panic settled into calm. It was quiet inside her bones, and no one could see her. Not the monster with his thousand eyes or Henri through his camera lens, or the thousands who had stared over the years at her height, her scars. She was hidden. Shielded by armor of her own making.

They'd find her, though, she knew. Later. Long after her life was gone. She'd be a curiosity—a national treasure: the woman inside of a bone cave inside of a cave of bones. A freak. They'd take her bones away and seal them in jars. Study them. But the monster was gone. And so was the sacred marrow. Except for the sample in the lab. The open jar with its rich odor, its inescapable pull toward the cave. Perhaps, exposed, it would fall to dust. Perhaps, exposed, those who laid eyes on it would become monsters. Maybe covered with bone, maybe covered with eyes.

The last seams of her skull plates squeezed tight—only slivers of light slipping through and dancing across the inside of her skull like figures on a cave wall. All she could see was her own darkness, her own shadow, and the only eyes were hers. Nothing and no one looked back.

WEST OF MATAMOROS, NORTH OF HELL

BRIAN HODGE

It was the photographer's idea, get some shots of them in the city before heading west into the countryside. He'd done his homework. Good for him. Good for Olaf the photographer. He'd read up on how one of Mexico's biggest shrines to Santa Muerte was here in Matamoros. So they might as well take advantage of that, right? The shots they'd already planned for, they wanted afternoon light for those, didn't want that glaring vernal sun directly overhead. There was time.

Sofia thought it was cheesy and wasn't shy about saying so. Sebastián was all for it, but then, he would be. More pictures meant more pictures of *him*. Enrique didn't care either way. You choose your battles wisely. No point in getting into one here inside the airport terminal.

And see? The idea was a done deal anyway. Olaf had run it past the PR guy on their flight down from LA, so Crispin had arrived pre-sold. Crispin was all about the enthusiasm. That was his job: make cheesy things sound like a good idea. The label must have paid him well for enthusiasm.

Besides, Crispin reminded them, they had to stay in town long enough to find a *carniceria* for the pig's heart. There had to be one close to a Santa Muerte shrine. They practically went together, right?

Crispin turned to Morgan, who looked all of a hundred pounds, half of it hair and the rest of it camera bags. "Maybe we can put you on that."

She looked queasy and stammered something about not speaking the language.

Olaf wasn't having it anyway. "If you want an assistant, maybe you should've brought your own."

So. These three in from LA Plus the crate they'd shipped along in cargo. Plus Enrique and Sebastián and Sofia, fresh off their puddle-jumper flight up from Mexico City. Twenty minutes later, all of them were packed into their driver's SUV. This was how it was going to be for the rest of a very long day. At least it was a long SUV.

Crispin sat up front, taking the only other bucket seat for himself so he could play captain, give the orders. After a few moments of idling beside the curb as their driver scrolled his phone, Crispin slapped his fingertips on the back of the man's headrest, bap-bap-bap-bap-bap. "Come on, let's get rolling. We're not paying you to check Twitter."

"Yeah you are," Enrique said. "Back home, all you got to check is traffic reports. Where we are now, before you go anywhere it's a good idea to check that you're not gonna be heading into somebody's shootout."

"I'm sorry, señor," the driver said. "He is correct."

Sofia perked up from the very back. "Crossfires don't ask to see your passport."

Hector, that was their driver's name. A middle-aged guy, big thick moustache, and you could just tell, this spotless SUV meant everything to him. It wasn't all that long ago Enrique would've laughed at the idea of a guy like Hector, where Hector found his pride. And had, probably more times than he wanted to admit. It took a while to grow up and find the respect again. The man was somebody's father.

Hector spent a few more moments on his phone, then looked up happy and put the SUV in gear. They were rolling.

Next to Enrique, Morgan was still looking queasy, but in a whole new way, like she didn't know what she was doing here and was two seconds from jumping out and running back into the terminal. They'd ended up seated together in the middle because he was so big and she was so small, so they evened out. And what was wrong with this Olaf guy, anyhow, he does his homework but doesn't bother telling her what to expect.

"It's okay. We'll be okay." Enrique leaned in close, kept his voice to a soothing murmur. "Just a little precaution, that's all. Nothing bad is gonna happen."

She took a deep breath and smiled at him. Tried to, at least.

"And remember this: *Tiene usted un corazón de cerdo?*" he told her. "That's how you ask for a pig's heart. Just in case."

Growing up, Enrique knew who Santa Muerte was. No secret about her. She was around. You just didn't see much of her, not then. She was a back room kind of saint, for the kind of altars you never got to see as a kid, because they were private, kept by people who fucking meant business.

Now, though? Now you didn't have to look hard at all to find her. Santa Muerte was everywhere, never more so than during the last decade, ever since the cartel wars erupted into a never-ending series of bloodbaths and massacres. Saint Death, Holy Death, had really come into her own.

In hindsight, it seemed inevitable. There were things you took for granted as a kid that took being an adult to see how strange they really were. That, and being lucky enough to gain perspective, to see past your own borders. And he had. Enrique had seen enough of the world to know now. The band had given him that much. Every tour made it that much clearer:

Here at home, people found death a lot more interesting than life.

Santa Muerte—she might look different in a hundred details, but was always the same simple figure: a skull in a dress, a skeleton where a woman used to be. She might look like a nun. She might look like bride. She might look no different from Santa Maria, except for that face of bone. Sometimes she might be holding a scythe. Always, she held your fate.

Here in the southside neighborhood in the Colonia Buenavista, Enrique knew they were getting close without anybody having to say a thing. It was the population explosion on the other side of the SUV. People on their own. Families. Mothers and fathers carrying sleepy babies, crying toddlers, to introduce them to the Saint of Death. The slow-goers made it up the street on their knees, not because they had to, but to show humility and devotion. They brought offerings. They brought photos and needs. They brought sorrows no one would ever hear about except the saint.

It wasn't a proper sanctuary, not like a church or a mission. The shrines never were. It just happened, grew up here like a tree from a seed. Some family starts it in their home, puts up the saint in their front window, and that's all it takes. They built it, and people came. Eventually they moved the saint farther inside, where there was more room, once their shrine took on a life of its own.

Hector wheeled as close as he could, then cut over to the side of the street and shut down. He stayed with the SUV while the rest of them went ahead, stepping out into the clamor, the laughter and the tears and the numb despair of people who didn't know where else to turn.

Along the way, Crispin bought a bouquet of droopy flowers from a kid on the street. "Why not?" he said, and waggled them at Enrique and Sofia and Sebastián, petals sifting to the street. "Maybe we can get her to bless this next album."

Sofia perked up again. She was like that—you never knew when she was tuned in and listening. Looked hard and wiry and ready for combat, muscles like taut cables, drummer's muscles, her thoughts a thousand miles away, yet she was onto you. She shouldered past to squeeze up close to this PR guy who was always coming off like the band's biggest fan, like he'd never heard genius until he heard Los Hijos del Infierno.

"Don't joke," Sofia told him. "I know you're only joking, but don't, okay? You stop a minute and think what it takes to push people, good people, everyday people, to revere what's inside there. It makes sense the *narcos* would pray to her, sacrifice to her. She's made for men like that. But these folk? Jesus and Mother Mary . . . people still believe, they've just given up. Jesus and Mary don't deliver anymore. Or they can't. Or maybe they stopped listening. But Santa Muerte does. She's the one who listens now. She's the one who loves them. She's the one they look to for healing. So remember where you are and think what it's taken to do that to them."

Crispin was a clean-cut Anglo who looked beyond shame, but he wasn't above looking chastened. Good to see.

Did these people in the street know who they were? Many looked, some stared. A few, maybe, might have recognized them. The six of them weren't your average half-dozen people out here, that much was blatant. Three gringos and three Mexicans, but even as locals, more or less, he and Sebastián and Sofia stood out. The black clothes and boots, the hair. No other guys out here had a need for eye makeup. Sebastián drew the stares most of all, the way a front man should—a head taller than most, crazy thin, with a spiked black leather pauldron belted over his left shoulder, like a gladiator on his way into the arena.

Equals, though, in spite of it all. Death turned everybody into equals.

The closer they got to the pink shrine house, the more crowded it got. After a minute of conferring with Olaf, Crispin squeezed his way inside and found the owners, used the power of dollars to get them to close off the inside for a private audience. After passing through a couple of arched doorways, the walls close and the ceiling low, they had the place to themselves.

Santa Muerte came in all sizes, and this one was as big as a live woman—on her pedestal, even a little bigger than that. She wore pale patterned robes, purple and white, with a sky blue cowl over her head. A wreath of dried-out flowers circled her brow. Her scythe was enormous, the blade oversized and stylized, six inches wide in the middle, curving over her head from outside one shoulder to past the other. It was way bigger than anything you'd want to swing in the fields, with a smaller skull mounted where it angled away from the wooden shaft.

Her teeth were white and even, her eyes a pair of empty voids.

She swam in wavering shadows, lit by a forest of candles. The rest was like every shrine he'd ever seen, gaudy and colorful and beautiful and sad. Flowers, from fresh to withered, lay everywhere, more bouquets than they had vases. A plate of tortillas sat at the bottom hem of her robes. Petitioners' notes were pinned to her robes. Pictures were taped to the walls, propped against the candle jars, stacked on tables—the sick and the dying, the dead and the missing, and somewhere in between them, the lost. Those who were simply lost.

Morgan was on it, in her element now, setting up a tiny, stubby-legged tripod with the efficiency of a soldier field-stripping a rifle—a tabletop tripod, but down on the floor. She set out a couple of Nikons, then unfolded a pair of circular reflectors, one silver and the other gold, and put them off to one side, and then went scurrying about with a light meter.

Olaf moved the three of them around, had them hunker and squat while he sprawled in the floor with his camera mounted on the pygmy tripod, the lens angled at them, shooting up from below. You could see his bald spot from here, a circular patch the size of a drink coaster missing from his white-blond hair.

He sounded happy with what he was seeing.

He'd positioned Sofia in the middle, the way photographers often did. Balance, Olaf was probably after, but there was something else he may not have been consciously aware of. The way Sofia looked, her features were a hybrid of the polarities on either side of her. In Sebastián, what you saw was a fine-boned European strain, the face of a Spanish conquistador. In Enrique, the broad peasant face and long, coarse hair of what the conquerors had found waiting for them, like he'd stepped out of some arid canyon that time forgot.

You looked at their faces and saw the whole of Mexico's history in them.

And now, behind them, Santa Muerte looming over them all.

A couple hours later and one pig's heart heavier, the SUV rolled west out of Matamoros, through that zone where the city frayed apart and unraveled into the countryside, a stark land seared by the sun and sprinkled with small farms, small ranches, tiny hovels. Twenty miles into it, Hector hooked a right onto a dirt road and headed north, until they were only a mile or so from the river. One mile away, Texas, but still, a whole other world.

Hooray for GPS. It wasn't like there were signs pointing the way here.

They stretched their legs again across the scrubby, hardscrabble ground and listened to Crispin be confused.

"There's nothing here," he said. "I thought there'd at least be some buildings left."

"Not for a long time," Sebastián told him. "After the investigation, the police brought in some *curanderos* to cleanse the spirit of the place, then burned everything."

"Then what's the point, may I ask? For all that's going to show in the photos, you could shoot them literally anywhere."

"Because the point is here. *Here* is the point." Bas sidled up to him and threw an arm around Crispin's shoulders, a rare moment of salesmanship for him instead of flat-out telling how it's going to be. "You can't cleanse away something like what happened here. You can't get it all. You don't feel it? You will. It'll come through." He patted Crispin on the back. "The fans, it'll mean something to *them*. They'll appreciate the effort. This place called to us. We heard it loud and clear, and we had to answer."

"What's this *we* shit?" Sofia muttered, only loud enough for Enrique to hear.

She was right. This was totally a Sebastián thing. Not a bad idea, necessarily, as image went, because image mattered, but still . . . this was kind of out there even for Bas.

"Half the songs on this next album are about here, and what came out of here. What they did here opened the gates to Hell and the gates never shut. If you don't get that, you don't get us." Sebastián, closing the deal with their alleged number one fan. "Where else *could* we shoot?"

Rancho Santa Elena, this place had been called, back when it was somewhere that somebody wanted to live. A generation ago it was the headquarters of a family business moving marijuana from the south up into the States. Different era, same old shit. Problems with the DEA, problems with rivals. They'd hooked up with this good-looking Cuban guy out of Florida who was making his own religion—part voodoo, part Santeria, part Palo Mayombe, and the rest, his own sick craziness. An isolated spot like this, with an outbuilding to repurpose as a temple, nobody close enough to hear the screams, human sacrifice seemed a reasonable price to pay for keeping their traffic routes safe. Eleven shallow graves' worth. Body parts for their cauldron, necklaces out of bones. There was power in it. It made you bulletproof. Made you invisible.

And nobody knew, nobody cared, until the Cuban decided he needed the blood of a young gringo who would die screaming. So they nabbed a college boy down on spring break, he and his buddies coming over the border for a change of scenery after they got tired of things on South Padre Island. Poor guy went off for a piss and never came back. They gave him twelve or so really bad hours before they got down to the serious business and took off the top of his head with a machete to get at his brain.

Enrique had to get a little older to learn the less obvious lesson: where he and his parents and sisters and everyone he knew ranked in the North American scheme of things. If it had been another dead Mexican, those people would've kept getting away with it. You want to wreck your shit, kill a gringo. That's when people start noticing.

By now, Hector had opened up the SUV's back door, and they moved in to help slide out the long, bulky crate that had flown cargo class from LA. Real wood, you didn't see that much anymore. Pride in your work, right there—the props company had packed this thing for *survival*. Hector took a tire tool and pried off the lid, and after they pawed aside the foam peanuts, they lifted the thing free.

Plenty of *wows* and *holy shits* all around. Those props people knew their stuff, how to take fiberglass and make magic. The statue was lighter than it looked, sturdier than it felt, and even when standing right next to it, looked exactly like stone that had weathered for centuries. They'd even painted it with stains.

"What is it?" Morgan asked, the only one of them who didn't know.

"It's called a *chacmool*," Sebastián told her. "It's a really old design, pre-Colombian. Aztecs, Mayans, maybe even older. Up at the top of a pyramid, that was one place they might go. See that platter in the middle? That was for holding sacrifices." He grinned, a needling meanness behind it. "Didn't have to be a heart, but if you got one laying around loose, why not."

The same as the likenesses of Santa Muerte, *chacmools* might differ in little details, but the core was always the same. A strange design, blocky, the way so much of that ancient Mesoamerican sculpture was carved. The basic template was a man, feet flat, knees up, leaning back on both elbows, while balanced on his middle was a receptacle to receive offering—could be a platter, could be a bowl. His head was turned to the side, like he was challenging anyone who approached him to give until it hurt.

For their replica, they'd opted for a platter. They all three liked the look of the bowl better, but its sides would have blocked the view, in pictures as well as onstage. Sebastián's idea—for the next tour's stage show, he was going to mime a self-sacrifice three songs in, cut out his own heart with a fake obsidian knife and present it to the audience on the *chacmool*. It would continue beating the whole time, and eventually start gushing blood again.

Every tour, the show just got messier.

And why shouldn't it. So was everything else in the land of their birth.

Olaf and Morgan and Sebastián conferred on where to set up for the shots. Crispin kept trying to offer suggestions and was tolerated, but otherwise got frozen out. Looked like it would be awhile, so Enrique wandered the property, scouting for cues as to what might have happened where. Where was the temple, where were the graves?

It was easy to be distracted in a cluster of people bickering and chasing the best light. Get off by yourself and you could feel the weight of what had happened here.

No . . . not *happened*. That made it sound like an accident. Everything that went on here had been *done*. It had occurred to human beings to *do* this to other human beings. Sodomize them. Chop them up. Lop off the top of their heads. Scoop out their brains. Wrap wire around their spines before they buried them, and leave the end sticking out of the ground so that after the worms and beetles and decay had their way with the corpses, they could pull the wire and haul up a nice new spinal column to use for making necklaces. Save them the trouble of digging again.

Shit like that did not just *happen*. Something got inside you, or was there all along and got loose from its cage, and told you that doing these terrible things was a good idea. Told you that was how business needed to get handled from now on. Same as it told the Aztecs: This is what it takes to keep the corn coming up in the fields, to keep the sun moving across the sky every day. This is what it takes to keep your world intact. Blood, and lots of it.

"You feel it too, don't you?" Sofia, coming up behind him.

"It leaves a stain, you know?" he said. "Like it's sunk in. You'd have to dig this place out fifty feet down and haul the dirt to an incinerator, and maybe even then you wouldn't get it all. It's like, whatever the *curanderos* thought they were doing, all they managed was to sweep the porch."

Somebody had died here. Right here. On this spot. He was sure of it. The whole plot of earth, saturated with fear and betrayal. Maybe it was the little boy. That was the one that really haunted him—how one of the guys doing this killed his own nephew. Decided he needed to snuff a kid, so somebody else went off and snatched him a kid. Brought the boy here, tossed him on the ground. The guy with the machete went right at him—just a boy with a bag over his head. It wasn't until the kid was dead that the guy started thinking, hey, that green football sweatshirt sure looks familiar.

But it's okay, you did right, the malignant thing inside him must have said. *This is what it takes to keep your world running.*

"Come on." Sofia reached up to rub his shoulder. "You're not doing yourself any good over here. Let's get back to the van so I can fix your makeup. Doesn't that sound like fun?"

"No," he said, like it was the silliest question she'd ever asked, and the exact right thing to do at the time, because it broke the spell. And he loved her for it. Loved her anyway, but sometimes it was good to be reminded of reasons.

They found that Sebastián and the photo team had decided where to take the shots. They had the *chacmool*—complete with the pig's heart now—set against a backdrop of gnarly scrub. Off to one side was a hummock of earth that, if they insisted it was a grave, the fans would say, oh, right, sure. A grave, still there after all this time. I totally buy that.

Olaf positioned them in different configurations, shuffled them around, with the sun dipping low enough that the natural light was coming in from the side. Morgan held the gold reflector to bounce the light back from the other side, give the scene a warm tinted glow, like the whole place was simmering.

Every few shots it was a different motivation. Look angry. Look disinterested. Look like you're grieving. Look hungry. Look dead. Anything but look like you're having fun. The only one of them enjoying the process was Sebastián. His idea, after all, the only one of them who could conceive of this. Who could think they could come here and evoke the spirits of this place where so much misery and evil were done, and then go away untouched.

Hector, though—Hector knew better. Once they'd unloaded the *chacmool* and got it set up, he was back in his SUV and hadn't left. Probably going to burn his shoes tonight because of what they'd touched, so he didn't track it into his home.

Be like Hector, Enrique told himself.

When they wrapped it up, packed it up, he'd never been more ready to leave a place. It was fitting that the last image he would take away from this little spot of Hell on earth was the heart of some poor pig, tossed aside now that they were through with it, left in the dirt for scavengers and blowflies.

Then they were in the SUV again, backtracking along the dirt road, halfway to the highway. He was slumped into the door with his head against the window when he perked up at the sight of something shooting out of a bush ahead of them. Thinking in that instant, holy shit, it was the biggest snake he'd ever seen, even though he knew that wasn't right.

An instant later came the sound of blowing tires, a double bang in front, another double bang in the rear. Enrique swiveled his head to follow the sound, and saw the not-snake slithering back into the bushes. No snake was triangular like that. No snake had spikes sticking up from its spine.

Hector was all instinct now, fighting the steering wheel and stomping the brake as the SUV slewed back and forth until he brought it to halt, skidding across the loose dirt as a churning cloud of dust caught up with them.

Just the worst feeling ever. Knowing, on one level, exactly what was happening, the rest of him denying it, no no no, this can't be real, Morgan's hand almost breaking his fingers she was squeezing them so hard, and he didn't even know when she'd grabbed him.

The driver's window blew inward and Hector's head went with it, a blizzard of glass and blood and brains and hair and bone and eyes spraying into the windshield. In the front passenger seat, Crispin got showered with some of it and had no idea what it was, turning with a look of pissed-off disgust on his face, like he was thinking what next, first the flat tires and now somebody had thrown a pot of stew at him, and the next dumb thing out of his mouth was going to be *Who's going to pay for this, do you have any idea how much this shirt cost?*

Outside, more guys than Enrique could count at once were converging from every direction, and he couldn't conceive of where they'd come from. This place was so poisoned that people like this came bursting out of the ground. If from the comfort of home he'd envisioned something like this, they would have been wearing masks. But they weren't. They had faces and didn't care who saw them, and that was the most frightening thing he could imagine.

They began yanking open the SUV's doors, and if they found one locked, would either aim through the window and scream until the person on the other side got the idea, or bash out the glass with the butt of a gun and reach in to unlock it themselves.

Everybody was vacating, stumbling out on their own or getting dragged. No say in it, Enrique hit the road hard and tasted a mouthful of hot, dry grit. A few feet away from him, Crispin was finally up to speed, groping for his pocket and pulling out his ID to flash like it was going to matter to someone: Oh, it's you, sorry for the mistake.

"Americano!" he screamed. *"Americano!"*

Nobody could've cared less. Nobody wanted to deal with him other than right then, right there, on the spot. They could just tell, the scariest judges of character in the world. You hear about someone getting blown out of his shoes and think no way, that's Hollywood bullshit. But it happened. Steps away, Crispin was hit with gunfire so hard he bounced off the fender and left a dent as he went down barefoot.

All Enrique could think of was Sofia, Sofia, because she'd gone out the other side and he couldn't see her any more. He'd forgotten how to pray, too, something about Santa Maria, but it wasn't there anymore.

Santa Muerte, full of grace, was the only thing he had left. *You don't want us now.*

Vans came roaring up from the south, the direction of the highway, this entire operation going off with military precision. Someone's knee dropped into the center of his back and emptied his lungs with a whoosh. They twisted his arms behind his spine and he was so confused and paralyzed he let it happen, let some guy squat on top of him like a goblin and lash his wrists together with a nylon zip-tie before he realized that was happening too. Then everything went dark and stuffy when they yanked a black hood over his head, and now the world was reduced to bad sounds and worse sensations.

They hauled him upright, slinging him around like a bawling calf destined for a branding iron. Once his feet were under him, two pairs of hands rushed him stumbling toward whatever was waiting next. Then he was cargo, banging into the hard floor of a van as other bodies landed around him. Doors slammed, then the blackness shot into high-speed acceleration, and whenever any of them said anything somebody up front yelled for them to shut up, no talking, and it was a long bumpy ride before the last person was too tired to cry any more.

The only thing Enrique was sure of was that they hadn't gone north. Whatever was coming next, they hadn't been driven into Texas for it. No, they'd gone a long way south, or west, or both. The air felt dryer and hotter on his arms.

After hours of motion, the van finally stopped and guys hauled them out and rushed them across open ground, hardpacked earth under his wobbly boots. Then it was doorways and a fresh feeling of claustrophobia—a hallway. That opened into an expanded sense of space, the noise around them no longer confined. Wooden floors, he knew from the sound.

The ties were cut and the hoods came off and they were shoved forward. Behind them, doors slammed and locks turned. Then they were on their own in a big dark emptiness, still nothing to see because the night had followed them inside.

Head count: Sofia. Sebastián. Morgan. Olaf. Himself. In spite of the hours in the van, he hadn't been totally sure. Free to move, Sofia hugged him. Morgan hugged Olaf. Sebastián was on his own for the moment, and that wasn't right, so Enrique pulled him close and wrapped him up too. Everybody stank of sweat and fear, and he didn't care, he'd never been so glad to smell anything in his life.

They weren't alone. From the darkness came a sound of somebody stirring.

"Who's there?" he asked. "Who is that?"

"Solamente nosotros los muertos. Acostúmbrate a la idea y cierra tu puta boca para que lo demás podamos dormir," came the sullen answer.

Just us dead people. Get used to the idea and shut the fuck up, so the rest of us can sleep.

They staked their claims in the floor, and if he could've folded himself all the way around Sofia like a fort, he would have.

The two of them had known each other too long to feel like anything other than brother and sister, but there were times he wondered, man, what if, huh? They'd come into each other's orbits as a couple of nerdy kids from bad neighborhoods, the kind it was easy to beat the shit out of, so that's what other kids did. The kids that listened to that thing inside, telling them, *This is what it takes to make your day more fun.*

They listened a lot, the cruel ones. Like they knew already, nothing had to tell them anything.

And keep at it, okay? There's a future in this. We got plans for you.

A couple of nerdy school band kids—they had targets on them early. It wasn't much of a band, and the instruments weren't much, either. Sofia liked to hit things, so they put her with a snare and a marching bass drum and a tom, but she never got to hit them as hard as she would've liked because she was scared of breaking a head, and then where would she be?

Enrique they'd fixed up with a leaky trumpet, but every spare moment he let the gravity of the out-of-tune piano in the corner pull him over to its yellowed keys. He could play more than one note at a time, plus if he held down the sustain pedal, he could pound them out and they'd keep ringing, a tapestry of overlapping noise that never had to end. The same thing he was doing now, just that with Los Hijos del Infierno he was doing it electronically, with synthesizers and sequencers and samplers, and it was way harder and louder and a lot more caustic.

So no, it wasn't much of a school band, and the instruments weren't much, but he always figured that without them, he and Sofia would be dead. Dead for real, or as good as dead, or wishing they were, or maybe worst of all, dead on the inside and not realizing it. There were all kinds of dead.

And Santa Muerte loved each and every one.

The dark bled out with the dawn.

He stirred awake at the first sign of it, sitting up in the floor so he could put an environment around them as things took shape. Get that much figured out, at least.

The first light came slanting in through windows set up high, near the roof. It lit up rough, bone-white walls and a gently peaked ceiling with wooden beams arching overhead, plus a few square pillars near the front and back. The windows on ground level started to brighten next. All of them were barred—no surprise.

It looked like it may have been an abandoned church or mission that had outlived its usefulness as anything but a prison, in some dusty little village where the good cops, if there were any to start with, were all dead. The mayor, dead. Anybody who'd ever said one wrong word, dead.

It was gutted of everything that might have marked it as a holy place. The pews were gone, the altar was gone, the font for holy water was gone. All that was left was a raised platform at the front where the altar would've been, and empty alcoves in the walls where statues of saints would've stood.

They shared the place with twenty-odd other people. Most were curled up on the floor, still asleep. A few others sat with their backs to the walls, looking ring-eyed and dazed, like they'd forgotten what sleep was. Men, mostly, gone grubby and unshaven. A couple of hard looking women.

"We don't belong here."

He turned and found Sebastián was awake now. He'd seen their singer looking this bad before, but it was only hangovers, or too many days speeding catching up with him. Nothing like this, like now he wasn't expecting to get better.

"This is cartel shit, man. We don't have anything to do with that. Why would they grab *us*?" Bas stopped a moment, getting a freshly horrified look on his face. "You don't think it has to do with the pictures during the show, do you?"

That was something new the past couple tours, since they'd put out the last album, *La máscara detrás de la cara*. They'd always gone for a projected multimedia assault whenever they played, and Sebastián had decided it was time to forget about the chaos of the world at large for their imagery and tap currents events closer to home. All the photos of carnage you could want were a few clicks away online. The aftermath of massacres and assassinations and messages sent in buckets of blood splashed across pavement. Severed heads and arms hacked off at the elbows, and death sentence by blowtorch, and rows of butchered bodies hanging from train trestles. Film clips, too, that the anonymous murder teams had posted online. *This is who we are, this is what we do, this is what it takes to keep our world turning.*

He never knew how Sebastián could do it, comb through the ugliest shit in the world and arrange it in a sequence that whizzed by at four frames per second. From the audience perspective, there wasn't time to linger on any one thing, so you couldn't be sure what you'd just seen, you only knew it was terrible and probably real. Bas, though . . . he had to linger over it.

"No, I don't think it's got anything to do with that," Enrique said. "That's free advertising for them, is all."

He looked down at Sofia, still asleep, the kind of sleep that becomes the only self-defense you have left. Same with Morgan. Olaf too, only he looked like could just as easily be unconscious as asleep, all that dried blood down one side of his face and caked in his white-blond hair. He must've really taken a beating during the grab.

Sebastián was trying to look hopeful but it came off looking queasy. "Maybe they're gonna ransom us, that's what this is about. It's part of the business model now, you know."

He was right on that much. Used to, the people might see cartel crews rolling in their convoys of pickup trucks, and as long as everybody kept out of their way, they'd leave the people alone. Not anymore. Times were tougher, even for the cartels. Every time a boss got killed or captured, organizations fractured and the chaos ramped up. Plus anybody who said the Federal police and the American DEA weren't having an impact wasn't paying attention. Whenever they lost another tunnel to the north side, or another supply route, that was another fortune lost.

But all around them were people too scared to fight back. And people who loved those people. Some of them even had a little money to pay to get their loved ones back in more or less one piece. It wasn't drug-sized cash, but $40,000 for a few days of no-risk work wasn't a bad sideline.

Only Enrique wasn't seeing it. Not here.

"I don't know, Bas," he said. "They didn't have any interest in Hector. They didn't give him a chance. And Crispin, he was the one looking like he could buy his way out of anything."

Go back to the site now, what would be left? A lot of nothing. The SUV would've been towed to a chop shop in Matamoros or Reynosa. For Hector and Crispin, graves no one would ever discover, or maybe an acid bath.

"What I can't figure is how they knew where to find us at all. They shouldn't have known that. Nobody was following. Where would they have picked up on us?"

Oh god, that look on Sebastián's face—like his eyes were falling back inside the cold black emptiness of his head, and his skin was on too tight.

"What did you do, Bas? What the fuck did you do?"

It came from somewhere so far inside him he could barely squeeze out sound: "I sent out a tweet. Right after we got to the airport."

Enrique's breath left him all at once. Twitter. Sure, why not. Because Sebastián couldn't wait to get a jump on the image thing. Tell the whole world what lonely, godforsaken, evil place they were going to. Look at us, everybody, see how edgy we are. Never guessing who might be paying the wrong kind of attention.

"The airplane didn't kill us, so you figured you would?" Enrique whacked Sebastián across the face, open-handed but with heft behind it, to knock him off his ass and send him sprawling across the dingy wooden floor.

A few of the dead people, *los muertos*, looked up at the commotion, decided they'd seen it all before, and tuned them out again.

Near tears, Sebastián scuttled a few feet away and put his head between his knees. Sofia roused, coming awake, feeling the disturbance in the air.

"What?" she said, her tongue thick with morning, then she jolted into high alert as everything hit her all over again. "What's going on?"

"Nothing." He couldn't think of a single good result that could come from telling her. Not now. Later, if there was time for it to matter. "Just nerves."

She looked around, taking it all in and liking none of it. He noticed, for the first time, a pair of five-gallon plastic buckets in the farthest corner—the communal toilet. Currently in use.

Meanwhile, Sebastián had gotten brave enough to have a look out one of the barred front windows flanking the pair of main doors, big slabs of wood and iron that looked solid enough to withstand cannon fire.

Up. Sebastián was looking *up*.

He backed away from the window then, one slow foot after another, so tense his tendons were going to pop if he wasn't careful. His fingertips went to his lips and he stopped, something inside shutting down.

They took his place at the window.

Not far beyond the front doors was the biggest Santa Muerte he'd ever seen. She stood fifteen feet tall, easy. Her blue robes were voluminous, enough material there for a festival tent. She seemed too big to have found her a scythe that wouldn't look like a toy. Yet they had. Somebody must've made it just for her, a scythe big enough to cut the moon in half. And somehow . . . somehow the skull was at scale.

"That can't be real," Sofia said.

No. It couldn't. It just looked real. The yellowing of age. The uneven teeth. The *missing* teeth, random gaps in the jaw. They'd had it made, that was all. Same props company that made the *chacmool*, maybe. Wouldn't that be a kick in the head.

A sight like this, the biggest thing around, your eyes would naturally go to it, linger on it. So it took a while for them to notice the rest, the bits and pieces scattered around the hem of Santa Muerte's giant robe. Never mind the skull. *These* were real. Arms and legs, hands and feet and heads. They were as real as real got.

"Do me a favor," Sofia said, quiet as a butterfly. "If it looks like that's where I'm headed, kill me. If I ever got on your nerves and you wanted to break my neck, that would be a good time."

After everybody was awake and moving, there was only one person who would talk with them, a graying, droopy-jowled *viejo* who said he was a priest. Everybody else, Enrique figured it was like that guy in war movies—the tight-faced veteran with the thousand-yard stare who's been around the longest, and he doesn't want to get to know the new recruits transferring into the unit. Doesn't even want to know their names. They'll be dead in a week, so why bother.

"What's a priest have to do to get a cartel mad at him?" Enrique asked.

"Exorcisms," Padre Thiago said. "I cast out the devil from the ones who let him in but don't want him dwelling in them any longer. He doesn't like that, and neither do his servants." The old man looked out in the direction of the towering Santa Muerte, then grinned and spread his hands as if to bless his flock. "But you see how God works. He brings me here where prayers of liberation are needed most."

Enrique had all kinds of things he could've said then about God and deliverance and working in mysterious ways, but there would have been no upside to any of it. You choose your battles wisely. And you don't drive off your allies.

"Who are his servants here?" he said instead. "I don't know what this is about. I don't know who took us, or why."

"That group of men over there?" The priest pointed with discretion at a sullen cluster occupying the farthest corner opposite the toilet buckets. "They say they are with the Sinaloa Federation. This would probably make it the Zetas who have you."

"Just me," Enrique said. "Not you?"

"Wherever I am, I am only God's."

Knowing *who* still didn't explain why. The Sinaloa Federation controlled the northwest. The Zetas, once they'd turned against the Gulf Cartel, took control of the northeast and the coast all the way down to the Yucatan. There were others, but these two were the gorillas, fighting for as much turf as they could take, with strips of contested no-man's-land running down the center of the country.

"And there's that one, too." Padre Thiago meant a stocky man milling about on the Sinaloa periphery, as though he didn't belong but was allowed closer than most. "Do you recognize him?"

The man looked to be in his upper thirties, and like the rest of them, he'd been at least a week without a razor, so his beard was catching up with his moustache. Enrique gave it his best, trying to see who he was under the whiskers and the unruly, unwashed hair.

No," he had to admit. "Should I?"

"You don't recognize Miguel Cardenas? I thought one music person might know another, but what do I know."

Enrique never would have gotten it on his own, but now he had enough for the connections to link. Different music, different look, different everything.

He knew the name, ignored the rest. Miguel Cardenas was a traditionalist, singing dusty songs for the provinces. Enrique could picture the man in his cowboy hat, holding an acoustic guitar, in front of a backup band of brass and accordion, tasteful drums and upright bass. He still wore a white dress shirt, dingy now, and black slacks with silver studs down the sides. What had they done—nab him after a show?

"I bet I can guess," Enrique said. "The idiot did a narco ballad about one of the bosses in the Federation."

Padre Thiago gave a sad nod. "If you seek favor by flattering one side, the other may not turn a deaf ear to it."

Enrique couldn't help but stare. He was looking at the deadest man in this room. A guy like that, there would be no ransom for him. He was an insult that couldn't be forgiven. He was the pet dog that got killed to make a point.

And it was one more reason why this didn't make sense. The three of them, Los Hijos del Infierno, weren't on anybody's side. They sang nobody's praises. It would've been like asking whose side you were on between lung cancer and heart disease. They were on the side of life, end of story.

That was the thing people never got about them. The look, the sound, the lyrics, the stage show . . . all of it left people who couldn't look or listen any deeper thinking they must've been on the side of death. What else could they be? Because look at them. Look at the freaks. Never once considering the band was another symptom, the world getting the art it deserved.

You only screamed that loud when dying was the last thing you wanted to do.

⟜

It was the middle of the day when they came for Olaf and Morgan.

A squad of armed guys burst in shouting for everyone to get on the far side of the room, and everybody else knew the drill already. It seemed to be the way the cartel guys handled everything here. They either brought what they wanted or took what they wanted, and did it at gunpoint with lots of yelling.

If you wanted to die quick, here was your chance. Whatever they said, do the opposite. Go straight at them, screaming for blood. It had to be a better end than you'd get under that giant Santa Muerte. There was every reason to believe whatever happened there would go a lot worse.

So why didn't anybody do it? Most of these people had been here for days or longer. Padre Thiago had been here over two weeks. They all knew what was going on.

The only thing that could've stopped them from rushing into gunfire was hope. They still hoped someone cared enough to buy their release. That's what kept them docile. That's what would keep them docile one day too long.

Then again? Forcing a quick end was easy to dream about, but when they came in that first time, all stormtrooping and chaos, the only thing Enrique could do was scuttle to the wall with everyone else and try to wrap the adobe around him. Ashamed, because the thing he wanted most in the world right then was to be invisible. Don't see me, don't pick me, don't act like you even know I'm here. He folded himself over Sofia and that was all the altruism he could muster. When he saw it was Olaf and Morgan they wanted, he'd never been more with disgusted with himself for feeling relief.

Olaf was still feisty. They had to pry Morgan from his arms and knock the wind out of him with the butt-end of an AK-47 to the gut. He dropped to his knees, gasping, then they dragged him by the shoulders. Morgan went easier, stumbling along with her eyes popped wide and her mouth open in a silent scream, like she'd hit a place of panic so overwhelming she froze there.

As quickly as they'd come, the extraction team was gone, and everyone unglued themselves from the wall. Enrique drifted up to the front window, forcing every step, because someone who knew them should bear witness. He would watch as long as he could.

Only they didn't reappear. Santa Muerte continued to stand alone.

That was life here, the terrible erratic rhythm of it. Long stretches of boredom and soul-eating dread, waiting for something to happen, and when it did, you shit yourself with fear.

Within hours, he and Bas and Sofia had become fixtures the same as the rest, subject to the same pecking orders and probing. Even in captivity, the Sinaloa guys had their own mini-cartel going. They'd been watching, taking the measure of the newcomers, and an hour or so after Morgan and Olaf were taken, one of them decided he wanted a woman and wanted one now, and made a move on Sofia.

Enrique went tense, ready to go off if needed, and he figured he would be before it was over. One on one, though, the guy didn't have a chance.

Sofia had been fending off grabby assholes for years. She'd gone through a phase when she cut her hair short and choppy, thinking it might discourage them, but it didn't, so she'd grown it out again and instead worked on preemptive strikes.

This one she kicked in the balls, and when he doubled over, gripped him by the curly ringlets of hair on the back of his head to steady him for a knee to the face. He was on the floor before his buddies saw it was going to happen. A few of them moved to step in, so Enrique came forward for the intercept.

He'd already guessed how they had him pegged. That they saw him as someone for whom size didn't matter, whose mass they could dismiss. He'd accepted years ago that he was always going to have the round, moonfaced look of some lumpen guy too big and slow to do anything other than let bad shit happen to him.

Sometimes it was good to leave the wrong impression. When all they saw was freaks with smudged, day-old makeup, you could do a lot of damage before they caught on.

The first one who got close, Enrique hooked a punch into the side of his neck that landed with the sound of meat slapping onto stone. It sent him staggering until he dropped a few steps away. The next, Enrique stomped a kick into his belly to fold him in half, then brought a hammer-fist down like an anvil to the back of his skull. Another he picked up and threw at two others, a carnival game of pins and balls. It took them by enough of a surprise that one of them stood there stupid long enough to let Sofia break his wrist, and all at once they were backing away, changing their minds, no fresh pussy was worth this.

He'd have to sleep light from now on, but was probably going to anyway, if last night was any indication.

Awhile later, Olaf and Morgan were brought back, neither of them worse off than before. The cartel guys, Olaf said, had only sat them down and grilled them about who they were, what they did, where they came from, who did they know with money. Mainly it was about the money.

Nobody was more relieved to hear this than Sebastián. He turned giddy, going on how it was only a matter of time before somebody came through, somebody had to—they made other people money, didn't they? They were an investment somebody would want to protect. Bas couldn't wait to help their captors out, give them names. Manager, label people, promoters. They had fans, so maybe a Kickstarter, bring the whole world in on getting them home safely.

Sebastián was everything hope looked like when it came unhinged.

The longer the day went on with nobody asking them anything, the farther Bas fell again. By dusk, he was making such a fuss at the barred windows, shouting to anyone who'd listen how ready he was to talk, that Enrique dragged him back before someone decided they were sick of listening to him squall.

It wasn't happening.

Whatever they were here for, it was something other than money.

Later that night they got their first look at how things ultimately went here. It was just late enough for people to start getting drowsy, this holy prison filling with the sounds of people dropping off and snoring, one of them muttering from someplace deep inside a bad dream. Then reality intruded, as bad or worse, everybody rousted by the extraction team as they burst in and went straight for one of the Sinaloa guys he'd scrapped with earlier and dragged him away screaming.

Straight to Santa Muerte.

Maybe they'd picked him because he'd outlived his usefulness. Or because it was a good time to grab him, since he was fucked up from earlier and couldn't struggle as well. Or because he'd lost a fight with a big chubby guy and this left him looking weak. Maybe it was random and there was no reasoning behind it at all.

Enrique's nerves were too shredded to settle on how he was supposed to feel about this. Relieved? One less enemy to worry about, after all. Hours earlier he could've killed the guy himself. He'd *wanted* him dead, wanted him humbled and suffering.

Just not like this.

Enrique was the only one at the window—everybody else must have seen it all before—until Sebastián joined him like it was the last place he wanted to be except for everyplace else here.

"Don't watch, boys," Padre Thiago called out to them. "Why would you watch?"

Good question. With that cartel snuff footage he'd combed through online, at least Sebastián was better equipped to handle it. As for himself?

Could be he needed an unfiltered look at where this could end for them. All the motivation he would need to push the schedule and make it quicker, when the time came.

The crew had enough stark white lights burning out front that it wasn't hard to see. It took eight or nine guys to handle things—three to get the victim into place, the rest standing guard to enforce compliance if needed, then one more coming into view when the others parted and the light caught him.

"Oh shit," Sebastián breathed. "I know that one, I've seen him . . . seen him in pictures, I think."

This newest guy didn't need the machete in his hand to look like walking death. He had the part down already. Tall, thin as a broomstick and without a shirt, bone and ropy muscle standing out in equally sharp relief across his tattooed skin. They covered him, maybe 20% of his hide left uninked for contrast. The rest was monochrome designs in black and dark green, cheap ink. Or maybe he hated color.

"How can you be sure?" Enrique said.

"The ones on his face. I only ever saw one of them looking like that."

The skin around his eyes had been shaded into dark ovals. The sides of his nose were blacked out too, along with his lower cheeks and parts of his chin. His head was shaved. From a distance, and probably close-up, too, the effect was like a living, decorated skull.

"I think he's MS-13," Sebastián said. "They don't even try to blend."

Funny thing—he thought he was at rock bottom already. No more room left to feel worse about their chances. But hearing this was a reminder: There was always room to go lower.

Some may have been as bad, but nobody was worse than MS-13. Salvadorans from Los Angeles, originally, but over time they'd spread, exported, colonized, let others in. Worked with the cartels, some of them. Salvadoran, Mexican, Guatemalan . . . nationalities didn't matter as much when the big thing you had in common was the ability to bury your humanity so deep you could never find it again, leaving it to rot with the worms. When you could do what they did without feeling anything more than that it had to be done. That this was what it took to get business taken care of. No different than guys who clocked in at the meat plants. They all had two eyes, two ears, and a mouth, same as the pigs and cows, but were still the ones holding the chainsaws.

The Sinaloa guy was stripped to his boxer shorts, then stretched out flat on the ground as somebody stood on each arm to keep him there. The Skull started by taking off his hands. As somebody else moved in with a propane torch to cauterize the stumps, he picked up the hands and flicked the blood from them into the dirt as he carried them over to Santa Muerte. They hacked off his feet next and made offerings of those, too. The men weighting him down stepped off to let the guy roam at will because how far could he get now, down to four stumpy limbs, nothing but charred nubs at the ends.

They seemed to find it entertaining. Nothing funnier than watching a guy in that condition try to flop away.

The Skull opened a big wooden box then, pulling out every kind of knife there was: military knives, hunting knives, fish knives, kitchen cutlery. He took his time, sticking one in and leaving it in place like a plug, because pulling the blade out would free the wound to bleed, and the Skull didn't want that. Soft tissue, areas that wouldn't be immediately fatal—those were his targets, and he found them one by one.

There seemed no end to it, a harder thing to watch than the amputations because of the calm, casual progression, the guy on the receiving end mindlessly trying to wallow away every time another blade skewered him, until he could no longer manage even that much, and could only lie there and take it, more and more bristling like a porcupine. The only way Enrique was certain he was still alive was because of how the handles rose and fell with each ragged breath. Every now and then, his whole carcass shuddered.

Enrique wouldn't have thought so until now, but he found this ordeal worse to contemplate than coming apart at the joints. He had more soft tissue than anybody here, enough to keep the Skull busy for hours.

He watched when he could, turned away when he couldn't. But he never left the window. *This is what it takes to be glad to die.*

Sebastián, though, had checked out a long time ago, sliding down the wall and holding himself together with both arms wrapped around his knees. Maybe it was easier to watch when it was on video. Bas could always pretend it was special effects in a movie. All he had to do was turn off the sound.

Sound was the giveaway, he'd explained once, how you knew when something was real and when it was staged. Terrified people, dying people, people in agony, made sounds that nobody could get to under any other circumstances. Once you'd heard the difference, there could be no confusing the two.

Just as there were sights you couldn't unsee, there were sounds you couldn't unhear, and this poor fucker out there out had made them all.

So when they finished it, the Skull tugging a wicked looking military knife free of the guy's groin and using it to saw off his head, the sound was more a part of it than anything Enrique could see. The angle was bad, too many bristling knife handles in the way. But he could hear it, that soul-shredding crescendo of mortality the guy had been holding in reserve.

Enrique didn't know when it happened, only that at some point Nietzsche's old warning came to mind: *If you gaze long into an abyss, the abyss will also gaze into you.* This was the feeling he got every time the Skull looked up from his work and peered straight at him in the window, as if making sure Enrique was still watching.

Good. You need to pay attention, the Skull seemed to be saying. *I know it's rough, but this is what it takes to get where we're going.*

He lost track of time, didn't know if it was an hour after the slaughter or an hour before sunrise. All he knew was that he was lying on the floor next to Sofia, their arms hooked around each other's at the elbow. He remembered seeing somewhere that otters slept this way, holding hands so they wouldn't drift apart on the river. If he had a next life coming, that was how he wanted to be reborn. Come back as an otter, sweet-faced and sleek and holding hands while he slept, and life would be simple.

"We should have never gone to Matamoros," Sofia said to him in the dark. "You and me, we should have voted Bas down. We should never have agreed to go to that ranch." She moved her head closer and kept her voice low, everything just between them. "It had us then. It reached out from the past and took us."

That was how it felt, yeah. They'd raised their heads high enough to be noticed by the dreadful thing that claimed this land, and it decided it wanted them. It opened its jaws to gobble them up and the cartel guys were its teeth.

"I was going to tell you earlier, when we were there, but I didn't want the place listening to me, you know?" she said. "Hearing about what happened at that ranch was my first memory. The first one I can pin down."

So much worse was going on around them, but this still hurt him straight to the heart. "That's awful."

"I was three," she went on. "Something like that, kidnapping, human sacrifice, you don't understand it when you're that little. And you shouldn't. You shouldn't ever have to understand it. At the time, it was more about the effect it had on my mother, and me seeing how she reacted. Not just to what they'd found, but what they hadn't, too, because there was talk of them maybe taking kids that never did turn up."

Lying there, he wished for an arm of iron that they could never break if they came in to drag Sofia away.

"I didn't understand it, but my mother did. I could see how much it scared her. How afraid she was for me. That there were people out there who would do these things. That's what came through. And I could tell, she was afraid she couldn't protect me, not from people like that. Because they had the devil behind them. Once that settled in, I don't know if I ever felt totally safe again."

"I'm sorry," he whispered, and meant it for everything he hadn't been able to do for her, then or now.

"I should have never stopped believing in the devil."

The next afternoon, at the height of the heat of the day, they came for Sebastián.

At first, weirdly enough, it was just an order, almost deferential compared to their usual methods, threat behind it but no force. When he didn't want any part of it, only then did things get rough, Bas taking a knee to the groin so hard it brought up his meager lunch. The bones went out of his legs, the fear so overwhelming every muscle went loose.

Sofia was screaming, reaching for Bas as they dragged him across the floor. It took both of Enrique's arms in wraparound to hold her back. Had it been just him and Bas, he would've done it, rushed them, made these savages shoot them both, let them bleed out quick from twenty bullet wounds apiece. But with Sofia here, he couldn't bring himself to do it, not as long as they didn't want her yet, and he hated himself for being like the rest of the docile herd, buying into the desperation: that as long as there was time, there was hope.

When they got Sebastián out the door, they surprised everybody by coming back for one more. Miguel Cardenas this time, the country balladeer who'd written one *narco* ballad too many, in his filthy white shirt and black pants with the silver studs down the sides. With him, there was no deference at all, the cartel team back to their usual routine of brutality first, orders later. Once he got over the shock, he begged all the way out the door.

You could follow their path outside by the sobbing. After Sofia hunkered on the floor with her hands squashed over her ears, Enrique forced himself to the window and saw two guys waiting near Santa Muerte, holding sledgehammers like firing squad riflemen waiting for the order to aim.

Both, as it turned out, were for Cardenas. They took out his knees first, and after he was down they smashed his elbows, then went to work on his hands and feet. They left him plenty alive, just nothing to crawl with, fight with, grab with, resist with. They reduced it all to pulp and compound fractures.

At the first couple of blows, Sebastián buckled to the ground as if he'd been hit too, going fetal as the hammers rose and fell. When the guys swinging the iron backed off, the Skull took over, squatting next to Sebastián, doing no worse than laying a hand on his shoulder, but Bas flinched anyway.

This was beyond figuring out, as long as he couldn't hear what the Skull was saying—and there *was* a conversation going on. One minute, two minutes, three. He wasn't treating Bas cruelly, only patting him on the shoulder a couple of times, as if telling him, *There, there, it'll be all right.*

Then the Skull had somebody bring his box of knives and it looked to be last night all over again. Until he took one for himself and gave another to Sebastián. He pointed at Cardenas and his pulverized joints, lying on his back and howling at the sky.

Enrique clutched the bars over the window as Bas began shaking his head, *no no no no.* The Skull went first, sinking his first knife to the hilt into Cardenas' thigh, then glaring at Sebastián: *Your turn.*

When he couldn't do it, the Skull's voice got louder, yelling now, discernible.

"You don't hate him? You don't hate his music, everything a hack like him stands for?" the Skull shouted. "Come on, man, you're ten times the singer he is. Let it out! You sing about hate all the time! Is that just an act? What good is the hate if you don't let it out!"

Sebastián gave Cardenas a half-hearted poke, sufficient to scratch the skin, but not good enough. The Skull badgered and threatened, then told him he'd better do it right this time or maybe Santa Muerte would get one of his eyes. He didn't need both eyes to sing. Didn't need either of them, for that matter.

It snapped him. Bas wailed from the ground and with a sob plunged the knife into Cardenas' belly.

Back and forth then. *One for you, one for me.* It came easier each time, Bas sticking in every subsequent blade with less hesitation and more resolve. *This is what it takes to crawl away.* It was like watching a little more of him going dead inside each round.

Ten or twelve knives later, the Skull called a break to confer, voices too low to hear again. He had somebody bring another wooden box—like a small, low crate—and hefted something out of it, treating it with obvious care. Enrique couldn't tell what it was, only that it looked flat and heavy and as black as outer space. It was lost from view as the Skull put it on the ground and the two of them hunched over it.

Minutes of this, while every so often, Cardenas wailed and moaned and tried to move in some way that his smashed parts wouldn't allow.

Until it was back to the knives. Just the Skull this time, looming over Sebastián in a posture of challenge, authority. Bas kept trying to back away but was too cracked to get anywhere, head hanging at the end of a neck gone limp as he used up the last of whatever he had in him to say no. Not that. Please no. Every time he did, the Skull merged another knife with some part of Miguel Cardenas.

"I can do this all day!" the Skull told him. "You gonna let that happen? Gonna let me keep doing this until I run out of knives? All you got to do is cut him once. It would be an act of mercy."

And that was how you broke somebody for good: made him do a thing like this.

"You tell me no one more time, the next thing you get to do is pick which one of your people you get to watch me gut in front of you. Your choice."

Took one piece of his soul at a time.

Bas must have quietly acquiesced. The Skull handed him a knife, one of the big, mean looking ones, maybe the same go-to blade he'd used to finish things last night. And the finish was the same. From this angle, Enrique couldn't see much, Sebastián in a kneeling position, his elbow pumping back and forth in a sawing motion. Two hideous screams. One ended quickly, the other one kept going. And going.

That was the impressive thing about Bas. He could hold a note for a long time.

Way past what for most people would be the breaking point.

It was hours before he could talk, another hour after that before anything intelligible came out. Until then, it was just Bas in a corner, huddled up like a whipped dog, catatonic sometimes, shaking when he wasn't, eyes focused on nothing. Sofia held him, rocked him, reported that he felt like he'd crawled out of a cold river. Morgan and Olaf hung close, ready to help if they could, but they couldn't.

"He wanted to know," Bas said, halting every few words, "about the last album."

La máscara detrás de la cara, that would've been. *The Mask Behind the Face.*

"What about it?"

"He wanted to know where it came from."

Enrique had to let this sink in, double-check to make sure Bas had it right. Even if it explained why they'd returned him alive, Enrique still couldn't believe it come down to this: that they'd been taken by a fan who wanted to get close to the band.

"I didn't understand what he meant. I couldn't follow him. I didn't know what to tell him." Sebastián seemed unable to stop replaying everything in his mind, or stop shaking his head. "He made me look at a rock. He kept making me look at the rock. I couldn't see what he wanted me to. But he wouldn't let me look away from the rock."

It was about all they got out of him.

Things were quiet for the evening and the rest of the night, sitting in the dark with *los muertos*, the other dead. A whole new heavy black mood had settled in. Forced to butcher each other—this was an escalation nobody had seen coming, and now that it was here, how was anyone supposed to look at the person next to him without imagining which of them might end up forced to hold the knives?

None of them had overheard what Bas had said—it was too soft to hear unless you were right next to him—and Enrique wasn't going to tell the rest to ease their minds. *Go on, keep trusting one another, you're still in this together, because if it happens again, it'll only be me or Sofia holding the knife.* Yeah, that would go over great.

Just Olaf, just Morgan. He told them.

The rest? Let them live with it, the same fear they'd spent their lives inflicting on their neighbors. *This is what it takes to start paying for your sins.*

He listened in the dark as Padre Thiago ministered to the ones who decided they'd lived as wolves long enough and it was time to be lambs again. Time to let a priest pray over them, deliver them of the cruel devils that had taken them over to make them do such terrible things. If they were going to God soon, they wanted to go clean and pure and forgiven.

And there it was—the reason he'd never had much use for God. If he had to believe in a god at all, he wanted one who would really hold you to your life's choices.

When they came for him the next morning Enrique was ready for it, the only one in the room who didn't retreat to the far wall like the others. They were so used to it, these guys with their guns and their yelling, they didn't know what to make of him, that somebody would sit in the floor waiting for whatever came next. His passivity unnerved them, all eight guys peeking at each other like they didn't trust it and didn't know what to do next, afraid they were being suckered into the struggle of their lives.

"I'll go," Enrique said. "No big deal. When did fighting it ever work for anybody? I'll go."

They took him alone, him and nobody else. They escorted him around the side of the church, three days since he'd felt the ground beneath his boots and the open sky and the direct searing heat of the sun. At the end of it, the Skull was waiting, and behind him, that colossal likeness of Santa Muerte with her scythe, grim against the cloudless blue and gritting her ivory teeth at the horizon. Everything else looked baked to shades of brown.

Somebody shoved a foot into the back of one knee to drop him to the earth. He knew better than to get up. The guards backed off to give them space.

"I figured it was either you or Sebastián," the Skull told him. "Drummers, they're the heart, they're not usually the visionaries. They feel the pulse of the earth. They don't see through time. So it had to be you or him. And it wasn't him."

"I don't know what you're talking about."

"Yeah you do. You're just playing stupid."

From here, close up, it was like seeing this guy for the first time. He was more than a living skull now. Skulls didn't have eyebrows. Skulls didn't have lips. Enrique could see the way his skin moved over his actual bones, could discern the numbers and words, patterns and pictures, inked into his skin. He looked close to emaciated, either by genetics or by choice, or maybe he was an example of function creating form. He had only as much as a reaper needed, and no more.

"You keep playing stupid, I'll treat you like you're stupid. You'll make me do something to smarten you up. Is that what you want?"

"I want to be gone from here. Me and mine. That's what I want."

The Skull nodded as if this were one of many possibilities. "It could happen."

Three little words, so much hope. *It could happen.* But probably an illusion.

"Sebastián may be the one at the front of the stage, but he does what you tell him to. He's only got as much to work with as you give him. You're the architect of what you three do," the Skull said. "Tell me I'm wrong."

"It's more complicated than that. But you're not wrong."

"I get it. You need him and he needs you. You, you're not the kind of guy who'll ever be at the front of the stage. You don't have the look. But you got something better. You got the brains. You got the vision."

It was one of the more backhanded compliments anyone had given him. But under the circumstances? He'd take it.

"So . . . *The Mask Behind the Face.* I could tell, just from the title, here's someone who knows some things. Here's someone who sees. Then I listen and read the lyrics, and I think, here's someone who *understands.* How you did it, that's beyond me, I don't know how a studio works, but you managed to put together the electronics and all that other aggro shit with those ancient flutes and grinding stones and old drums, and made a sound not like anything I ever heard. An effect not like anything I ever felt. A sound, that's just noise unless you got an idea behind it. And you did. That was the thing that convinced me, whoever did this is some kind of shaman."

The Skull was pacing with the frantic movements of somebody who'd spent a long time looking for an elusive prize and was on the verge of finding it.

"It wasn't just the notes. Anybody can play the notes." He squatted, nose to tattooed nose with Enrique. "There's something in there *between* the notes, looking back out. I don't know how you captured that. But it's there. And it's a fucking monster." It was hard to tell if his eyes were desperate or insane. "How did you *know*?"

Slowly, Enrique shook his head. "I've got no answer for that. I wish I did."

"You don't leave here unless you give me better than that."

"I could make up a better lie. Is that what you want?"

The Skull peered at him from inches away, as if trying to see beneath the skin. "You got the look of the first people here. Maybe that explains it, why you and not Sebastián. You got the look of the conquered, not the conquistador. You got that blood memory in you, maybe."

He pulled back, squatting with his bony elbows on his pointy knees.

"And me, see, I know blood. I know sacrifice. I'm one of the ones they call when they really want to send a message, because I can do it and not blink." He motioned to the towering Santa Muerte, the body parts laid out before her. They buzzed with flies and gave off a stink like roadkill. "It's just another day's work to me. But that doesn't mean I don't ever think about what I'm doing. To me, it's nothing new. It's something that's come around again, part of something that goes way back. I can feel it in the knives. Their handles, man, they fucking hum."

His scrutiny turned puzzled, hungry for secrets he'd never been able to grab.

"A guy like you, you don't get your hands red the way I do. But you figured it out anyway. All I'm asking is how."

"It's just knowing some history, some myths, is all. Same shit, different century. It's just following where it leads."

The Skull nodded, eager, like they were getting somewhere. "You went straight to the oldest stories, I could tell. The people here, way before the Spaniards showed up, they had a good thing going. They had this teacher, maybe he was a god, or maybe he was something else and a god was the only thing they knew to call him. Kukulcan . . . Quetzalcoatl . . . whatever his real name was. He was teaching them everything they needed to know. These people, they were on their way *up*. The sun was theirs. And then the clouds came. It's what clouds do, right? Come in and wash things away."

The legends called him Tezcatlipoca—a dark, malevolent god who had come along and driven the teacher off.

Whatever the differences between them, he and the Skull could speak of this much like equals, at least.

These archaic figures, these events, had always felt to him like more than myth. More than his ancestors' way of trying to make sense of their failings, their hungers and thirsts, their savagery. Behind the stories was something hidden and true, and behind that, more truths that he couldn't begin to guess at. He just knew they were there.

Ever since he was a boy, seeing the world take shape around him, farther and farther from his mother's kitchen, it was hard to deny the sense that something had gone wrong here, in this land. Hundreds of years ago, or maybe thousands. Something had come down from above, or up from below, or in from outside, and convinced the people that it had a never-ending need for their blood, shed in all kinds of ways. *You see those knives? You see those chests with the hearts beating inside them? You see those skins you can peel away and wear over your own until they fall apart? Get to it, and don't ever stop. This is what it takes now, so never forget.*

It was everything he knew and nothing he could prove. All he'd ever been able to do was turn up the volume and scream into the clouds.

"Gracias," the Skull whispered, and pushed up from his squat to stand tall again. "Thank you for letting me know I'm not the only one."

They'd been friendly enough that the anger began to override the fear. "Man, everything you asked is something you could've asked me through the band's web site. Or hit me up on Twitter. People got questions, we don't ignore them. We talk back, you know."

Images flickered like flash cards. Their driver Hector, killed at the wheel. Crispin, shot out of his shoes. Guys butchered outside the window, and forcing Bas to join in. They could let him go right now, and he would never unsee these last few days. For as long as he lived, he would be waking up from nightmares.

"Did it really have to take all this?"

And look. The Skull knew how to smile. "You think this little chat is it? No, this is us getting to know each other. The next part, that's the initiation. That's the important part."

He whistled and motioned toward their makeshift prison, and three guys came out escorting Padre Thiago. He'd chosen not to fight it either. Calmest face you ever saw. Like he expected God was going to take care of him on the spot. There, there, my child, trust in me for deliverance.

"Don't do this. Please don't do this." Enrique had sworn he wouldn't beg, and listen to him now. Everybody's got a plan until the knives come out. "Did I not treat you with respect? Didn't I take you seriously? What's the point of this? You think trying to turn us into you is gonna get you any closer to answers than you got already?"

The Skull was only half paying attention as he hauled over the box of knives and the compact crate from last night. The latter was the least among his props, and with every other nightmarish thing going on, Enrique had all but forgotten about it.

He made me look at a rock. He kept making me look at the rock.

The desperation was starting to eat deeper. "It wasn't any shaman that did that album, just three pissed-off people who like to make loud noises. I don't know shit, all I'm doing is asking the same questions as you."

I couldn't see what he wanted me to. But he wouldn't let me look away from the rock.

Padre Thiago passed him then, patted him on his big round shoulder, the cruelest thing the priest could've done—absolving him in advance. It was all Enrique could do to not scream at him. *Get your hand off me, old man. Don't you know where this is going? Don't you know what he's gonna make me do to you? I don't want you forgiving me for any of it.*

From the crate, the Skull removed the artifact from last night, flat and heavy. As black as outer space, he'd thought while seeing it from a distance, not knowing why he'd made the connection. Now he remembered reading about an astronaut who came back saying that, from out there in it, space looked shiny.

Obsidian, he realized, now that he saw the artifact close up. Volcanic glass. It was shaped like an irregular rectangle, scooped out but too shallow to be a bowl, too bulky to be a plate, and polished into a black mirror. The rim was threaded with gray-green veins marbled into the stone itself, seemingly random, but nagging him with a promise that if he stared long enough he would comprehend a hidden pattern, an intentional design the earth had woven in the chaos of fire and lava.

The outer edges were rougher, designs carved around the circumference, lines that thickened and thinned, swooped and jittered and curved back onto themselves. Not Aztec, not Mayan, not Olmec, not like any patterns he'd seen before.

As he looked at it, his gaze pulled by its peculiar gravity, it caught a reflection of lumpy clouds skimming overhead, the effect like smoke drifting across its gleaming black surface.

I know what this is . . .

Except when he looked up, there were no clouds.

The Smoking Mirror—it was another of their names for Tezcatlipoca, the dark god who had chased away their teacher. They hadn't called him that because of his eyes, his face, his demeanor. None of that. It wasn't poetics, it was practical. They'd called him that because of something he'd owned and used. He would gaze into it and see things—the far-away doings of gods and men, they said.

"Where did you get this?"

"A guy in Tampico," the Skull told him. "You kill enough people, you've seen everything they try to buy you off with. But this? This was a first. Where he got it, I don't know. I get the idea it's one of those things that doesn't stay in the same pair of hands for long. It keeps on the move. It's . . . restless."

Even Padre Thiago looked drawn to it, mesmerized, until the Skull lunged at him and clocked him across the jaw with his fist. The priest hit the ground before Enrique could scramble over on his knees to catch him, not wholly unconscious but not much good for anything else for a while.

The Skull pointed at him. "He tell you why he's here?"

"He said it was for doing exorcisms, and somebody didn't like it."

"Yeah? That's what he told you? Well, he's half right." The Skull squatted before him again, voice at a murmur. "I heard about him. This priest. Still God's warrior while the Church is losing people left and right to Santa Muerte. Still out there saving souls."

It took Enrique a moment to catch on: The Skull didn't want any of these other murderers listening to what he had to say.

"So I went to him, see what he could do for me. I thought maybe this thing inside, whatever it is that's got its hooks in me, I want it out, and he's the one who can do it. Most of the time I think it's just me. But that's the lie it feeds you. There's other times I can feel it moving. Like something else has got itself lined up with my eyes."

Or maybe *that* was the lie. Anything to believe it wasn't purely him all along.

The Skull glared at Thiago with scorn. "He didn't do shit for me. Isn't that the worst thing a priest can do? Leave you the same as he found you? But I don't know why I expected more. He's still got this Old World way of looking at things. What's he gonna do for me when he's stuck chasing after some pointy-tailed devil?"

The Skull patted the bony cage of his chest.

"So I figure as long as I'm stuck with it, I might as well go all in, make friends with it. And I got *that*." He hitched his thumb at the black stone, its shiny jet surface still drifting with billows and clouds. "Only it doesn't work for me. That's all it ever does. It won't show me shit."

I couldn't see what he wanted me to.

And now, *now*, Enrique understood why they were here.

But he wouldn't let me look away from the rock.

"You? You got the vision. You got the look, like your DNA never heard of Spain. You got as far as you did figuring some of these things out on your own," the Skull said. "So I got to wonder, how much farther could you get if we juice it up for you? How much farther can you get when there's blood?"

The Skull set the black stone, the smoking mirror, next to Padre Thiago, who still hadn't come to his senses. Then he chose a knife and tossed it over. Enrique stared at it, lying in front of him on the hard-packed dirt. He gauged the distance between himself and the Skull. Looked at the guys with guns, tuning in again now that the time for talking was over.

If he wanted a firing squad, the moment had come.

"You know what to do," the Skull said. "First one, that's always the hardest. Then it gets easier. It did for Sebastián."

Enrique glanced back at the church and saw Sofia in the window, fists wrapped around the bars and everything about her imploring him to live. She hadn't watched for Bas. But she was watching for him.

He picked up the knife. The blade was long, thin, with tiny serrations along its edge. A boning knife, it looked like. It would go in easy. The Skull had chosen it for that. Enrique wiped it clean on his pant leg. Pointless, maybe, but he did it anyway.

He made himself look at Padre Thiago, at the man's droopy, stubbled face as he rolled his head to the side, gaze meeting gaze. There was already blood, leaking from a split lip swollen like a bicycle tire about to burst. The priest was coming around again, peace in his eyes as he granted permission, stupid old man lying there ready to be a martyr. This is what it takes to be like Jesus.

Fuck these guys. He didn't want to give either one of them what they wanted.

Enrique didn't think about it. He just did it. Shoved up the long black sleeve of his shirt, crusted with days of sweat and dirt, and slashed the blade across the meat of his forearm. It opened like a lipless mouth, red on the inside but nothing happening, just like he didn't feel anything yet, then all at once it hurt and welled up and spilled over hot.

"You stupid motherfucker! Why did you do that?" The Skull turned frenetic, diving toward him to snatch the knife and fling it out of reach. "Why would you *do* that?"

Somewhere behind him, Sofia was screaming too. A voice like that, maybe it should've been her at the front of the stage all along. And it was almost funny. This is what it takes to say I love you.

The Skull scrambled with him in the dirt and the blood, and he was strong, crazy strong, freakishly strong as he dragged the stone over and grabbed Enrique's arm to lay it across the shiny black surface. Because while it may have been the wrong blood, as long as it was flowing, might as well not waste it.

Black and red, red on black—it pulsed and spattered, and the Skull smeared it across the smooth glass like a kid starting on a finger painting. Enrique was already going lightheaded, maybe not so much from actual blood loss as the *idea* of losing it. He'd always been a wuss about that, seeing himself leak a reminder of those childhood beatings from guys like this, the kids who listened to the call.

Lightheaded—how else to explain what he was seeing? Stone didn't absorb blood. Sandstone, maybe, a little, but not obsidian. That wasn't how it worked. That wasn't how anything he knew about the world and rocks worked.

But the stone was a greedy thing, and it drank as if a million microscopic mouths opened wherever the blood pooled, and wanted more. His arm delivered. The Skull saw to that.

Whatever the black glass was showing him, clouds or smoke or steam, the billows and wisps began to drift apart. The space he saw waiting behind them looked shiny, shiny in a way that went beyond the glossiness of the surface. There was depth here, or a perfect illusion of it, the smooth black more like a porthole than a screen.

He couldn't tell if what he was seeing belonged to the infinite depths between worlds or the unplumbed recesses beneath the earth, only that whatever stirred there stirred alone. No, not stirred . . . *crawled*, all body and no limbs. His perspective was small, yet what stared back seemed vast, titanic in the way only something so pure and simple could be. When it raised its head, its blind face had the unfinished look of a worm.

The Skull was riding his back now, jamming his head next to Enrique's like they were both reading from the same engrossing book.

He thought of everything that lay between him and this monstrosity on the other side. He thought of altars, of ritual bowls and *chacmools*. He thought of killing fields and the steep, blood-slick steps descending the side of a pyramid. Channels and conduits, all. It didn't matter where this thing was—he sensed that much in his heart. Didn't matter how near or far away it dwelled. When blood was let, the flow found a way there. All spaces were one, a single point in time.

It drank him the same as it must have drunk millions before him, the thinnest visible drizzle falling on the flat, probing slug of its tongue. It then recoiled, as if it didn't like the taste of him. Blood was blood, you'd think, but maybe its palate was more refined than you'd expect. Maybe it could discern some difference in the flavor of him, his blood let by his own hand because he would rather do that than slaughter the man next to him.

And it spewed him from the cavern of its mouth.

The smoke billowed across the glass to obscure the gulf between once more, and the stone was only obsidian again, black glass and nothing more.

He thought it was a trick of the mind when a shadow seemed to dim the light on this patch of ground where he lay face down and bleeding. That's what blood loss did. Made your world a dimmer place.

But did it make hardened killers, bored with watching men die, shout and run?

Did it make the ground shake under three ponderous footsteps?

Did it make a sound like an enormous scythe sweeping down from above to cut the air in two?

Beside him, Padre Thiago lifted off the ground, there one instant, then gone. It took the last effort Enrique could call on to roll over onto his back, where he saw the halves of the priest's body fly away to either side of the enormous blade, and beyond that, looming far above, the bone face of their Santa Muerte, the skull he'd always thought looked much too real.

A red rain showered them all.

He awoke to heat and stillness and the lazy buzzing of flies. There were flies in Hell, weren't there? Pesky, biting, pain-in-the-ass flies that never let up tormenting the sinners. So maybe he was okay. These were just hanging around, the same old everyday shit-eaters.

The inside of his left forearm burned, but that was his own fault. Enrique found it bandaged, and beneath that, stitched. The Skull and the rest of his crew—what were they, if not a unit gone to war? It made sense they'd have a medic around.

He lay on a thin mattress atop squeaky springs, staring at a ceiling scarred with peeling paint and plaster so cracked and crumbled he could see the wooden slats above it. Some rundown room in some other building that wasn't the church. He'd slept in worse places, actually, back when the band had to take whatever it could get. Never in clothes sticky with a priest's blood, though. There were all kinds of ways to hit a new low.

Except for the flies, he couldn't hear a sound. There was no sound *to* hear.

He got up from the bed—hung over from something they'd shot him up with, it felt like—and wandered to the window. Like waking up in a ghost town. Nothing out there to see but dust and corpses and pieces of corpses. None of it seemed real. He might as well be waking up in a video game. Wounded, not a clue, and next thing he was supposed to do was find a weapon and start killing anything that moved.

Only everything was dead already. Nothing outside was moving. Just him, once he got there.

Under the hot white eye of the sun, Enrique trudged toward the bodies. They'd really cleaned house before they'd abandoned the place, hadn't they? Finished what they'd started, wrapping it up in a hurry, then bugging out fast. Maybe this was normal for them, treating places like a landfill, and when the bodies piled up too high, they moved on.

Most were hanging by their ankles, like bloody laundry, from cables stretched between poles, more than he could count at a glance. Nobody had died easy. Some had just died harder than others. More blood for the vast grave worm that tunneled through their lives, their world, their existence. And sooner or later, all the flies found their way here.

He trembled like it was twenty degrees instead of a hundred. As he scanned the rows of the dead, he looked for clothing because he couldn't bring himself to look at faces, and was relieved to see there wasn't much black, and none of it meant for a stage.

Lots of black hair, though. Except for the blond guy. Except for Olaf. Olaf the photographer. Whose real name was Oliver, he'd learned in the church, the sort of thing that came out when you were sitting around killing time waiting to see who was next to be killed. Said he got more gigs as Olaf than he ever had as Oliver—a man who knew how the game was played.

Yet here he was.

Enrique checked for a smaller body, half of it hair, but Morgan wasn't among them. He was past deciding whether something was good or bad anymore. Maybe all that was left was bad right now, and bad deferred to later.

Like that empty spot where the towering Santa Muerte had stood. Did you just pack up a thing like that and move it? Was something like that really a priority? You'd need two strong guys just to carry the scythe.

Because no way had he seen what he thought he had there at the end. That priest had found some other way to get cut in half.

He turned his attention to the church. The pair of front doors was secured with a heavy, squared-off crossbar. Before he wrestled it from its brackets, he stooped to gather what was waiting, what had plainly been placed here for him to find. Three phones, plus a charger. When he tried his own, it was dead. When he tried the others, they were dead too.

But better the phones than Sofia and Sebastián.

He found them inside huddled along the far wall. Before they saw it was him, they scurried back farther, reacting only to the opening of the door, the way you learned to live in a place like this, where a few more millimeters might mean another second of life.

No sign of Morgan, though. She was just . . . gone.

When he went to Sofia and Bas, they felt real enough, sounded real enough, even if it felt like something was missing. Everybody too far gone at this point for a show of relief, let alone jubilation. How was he supposed to bring them back to themselves? How were they supposed to bring *him* back? There were no manuals for this. There was only standing. There was putting one foot after another. There was holding hands and holding close. There was making your way back into the sunshine, in spite of what it showed.

It would've been easier if the Skull had left a note, some validation of why they were still alive. But maybe the mere fact they were breathing was all the note he would ever need: *Keep doing what you're doing. Keep looking. Like skin, there's always another layer deeper to go.*

Yeah. Like he wanted any part of that. Like he didn't want to wipe his memory clean of everything about these past few days. Like he wouldn't do anything to hit the reset switch and go back a week.

No, longer than that—go back two years, take those first conceptual sketches for *La máscara detrás de la cara* and throw them out. Hope that some intuitive voice inside would tell him *stop right now, you don't want to start looking behind that succession of masks and faces*, and hope he'd have the balls to listen.

"How are we getting out of here?" Sofia said. "They could've at least left us one of the cars."

All they could do was charge one of the dead phones, try using it to get a fix on where they were, then relay the information to whoever they could raise. Sebastián had a GPS app on his, so they put him in charge of finding the nearest electrical outlet. They would've anyway, because if Bas didn't have something to do, he was going to keep falling apart a little more at a time.

Enrique knew the feeling. You couldn't stand around waiting. You had to do something, anything. He pointed to the church's open bell tower, said to Sofia come on, they should get up there, take the high ground and see if they could spot a landmark, more than they could see from down below.

They found the roof access tucked off a hallway inside, like a closet with a ladder affixed to the wall, stuffy as a chimney the higher they climbed. A trapdoor put them topside. The bell still hung mounted on a wooden headstock, no sign of the rope used for ringing it. Sofia gave it a rap with her knuckles to summon a sad, hollow clunk.

The bell sounded as dead as everything else looked, as far as he could see.

They were on an observation deck with nothing left to observe, a seared land scraped thin across a rocky world in a dozen shades of brown, barren of everything but scattered shacks and ruins. To the east, a line of green struggled to overcome, life trying to hang on beside an *arroyo*, maybe. He wished it well.

The sky, the blue of dreams, was the only vibrant thing to see. They hadn't killed the sky yet. Give them time, and enough guns and blades and poison, and they would find a way.

Sofia saw it first, pointing it out in the distance, nearly at the limits of his vision. His soul knew what it was before his mind let him believe his eyes. Even lost amid a simmering hellscape stretching for the horizon, it towered against the rugged desert hills, crossed gullies and washes in a single step, this striding colossus with bone for a face and a scythe in its hands and hunger in whatever passed for its heart.

She was, he realized, too terrible and too true not to have been real all along. And he feared she wouldn't stop until she'd visited every square inch of this land and gathered up her due.

Something had gone wrong here. Hundreds of years ago, or maybe thousands. No wonder it had always wanted their blood. That was where the memory lingered most.

They watched until its saint passed from view, beyond the farthest hills, then turned to each other again. Sofia touched his face like she'd never truly seen it before, and when he touched hers, the thing that hurt most was knowing that under the skin, the two of them looked more alike than not, and the same as everybody else.

ALLIGATOR POINT

S. P. MISKOWSKI

When the Grand Prix stopped kicking up rooster tails of red dust at every junction Helen announced they had left Georgia behind and were officially on their first vacation. Following beat-up signs and billboards, the rest of the drive would take them further south to the Gulf Coast of Florida.

In the back seat Helen's twin daughters Julie and Debbie had been arguing for the last forty miles. The girls were out of Planter's Peanuts and Pepsi-Cola, bored with playing 'I Spy,' and sick of variations on Barbie and Francie ensembles; their eight-year-old imagination stretched to breaking over the long trek south from the outskirts of Atlanta.

The route Helen chose had little to do with scenic value. She figured the lack of notable landmarks contributed to the girls' boredom but she was willing to weather their snotty remarks and impatience, so long as it meant they could stick to back roads not found on the map. This was better than risking the preferred path of tourists and patrol cars along Highway 98.

For the eleventh time Julie asked, "Are we there yet?"

Helen shot back the brightest answer she could offer. "Where the heck is 'there'?" A glance in the side view mirror was startling: blonde bob raked back from her face and tucked behind her ears, eyes underscored by shadows, the remnant of a purple bruise not quite faded beneath makeup.

Late in the afternoon Helen pulled over and parked under a sign for a campground with the same name as the nearest town, Alligator Point. At the check-in cabin a man with a mustache so thin it might have been drawn with an eyebrow pencil, and a nametag that identified him as Dorsey Corcoran, pointed to a map. He referred to the place beside his blackened thumbnail as 'a private cove.' He reeked of tobacco and his crooked grin revealed a row of yellow teeth dotted with gold fillings. He was the kind of man Helen's husband Roy would have called a 'swamp hick.'

"Y'all are gonna be mighty cozy," Dorsey Corcoran said. "Yes ma'am. That there's a preferred spot. If y'all had come down any closer to the season, it'd be gone."

"It's fine," said Helen. She checked over her shoulder to make sure the girls were staying put in the car.

"Say, is that a '64 or a '65?" Dorsey asked, jutting his chin toward the Grand Prix outside.

Helen froze. "I don't know," she said.

"Well, you've kept it in good shape. Nice color, too. What do you call that shiny green . . . ?"

"Moss," she said. "I think it's called moss." She initialed the register and handed over cash for two nights.

Fifteen minutes later, after locating their campsite, she squinted through the dusty windshield at row after row of mangy palm trees with peeling trunks. Down the beach at the next site an elderly couple in swimsuits sat in lawn chairs staring at the brackish water. They rested silently and still with flabby arms limp at their sides, fingertips almost touching the sand.

Helen took note of the scenery and wondered if Dorsey knew the meaning of either 'private' or 'cove.' The beach formed a large C-shape and included a playground with two swing sets, all of it surrounded by the ancient, shedding palms. This tiny enclave occupied the southern tip of the larger campground where more prosperous visitors rented cabins or parked their trailers during tourist season.

"Look at us. Three gals on a spree!" Helen said as brightly as she could. "When you're on vacation, anything can happen."

The girls said nothing. Julie collected their overnight bag from the floor while Debbie gathered up their Barbie dolls and magazines.

They managed to haul the tent out of the trunk but had trouble pitching it. The fine, dun-colored sand kept giving way underfoot on the narrow beach. There were no waves, no surf, only a dull sort of gurgle each time the foamy water rolled up a few inches and back again.

Helen glanced over her shoulder while they struggled with the pole and the stiff canvas. Each time the girls caught her looking around she pretended to be estimating the space they needed.

"Smells like rotten fish," said Julie, wrinkling her nose and pointing to the shoreline.

"Stinky," said Debbie.

"Daddy wouldn't like this place at all!" Julie declared. "I bet he's glad he didn't come."

"That's how the gulf smells," Helen told them. "Y'all are here to see the sights and learn about the world and be sophisticated. Watch out. Only ignorant people complain wherever they go."

The twins took a break to drink the Pepsi-Colas she'd bought at the check-in cabin, and eat cheese sandwiches from the small portable cooler. While they ate, the girls stood as they often did, heads inclined toward one another, whispering God knows what about their elderly neighbors.

Helen stopped hammering a foot-long metal spike into the ground, and raked the hair from her eyes with her free hand. She stood for a minute and surveyed the beach with a dull sense of unease, trying to decide if the feeling was spurred by the viscous gurgle of the shoreline or the call of gulls, like chattering monkeys, overhead.

Sunset turned the shore into ribbons of royal blue and teal. Entwined clouds of periwinkle and fire-orange stretched for miles toward a crimson, falling light between the trees.

They had only two folding cots, placed at right angles inside the tent. The twins shared one of them, sending delicate snores into the air and pushing at one another gently with swimming motions, their hands and feet trying to clear an imaginary space.

Helen lay awake, staring out the open canvas flap until she saw the dark silhouettes of the elderly couple rise clumsily from their lawn chairs, clasp hands, and make their way inside their own tent. One of the two zipped the flap shut behind them.

She imagined they were on a reunion honeymoon. Alligator Point was run down, but maybe it was a relic of their youth, a hot vacation spot when it was swanky and new.

'Swanky' was one of Roy's words; it reminded Helen of their own early days. Sparkling beaches spread out before high-rise hotels painted flamingo pink, the surf so starkly blue against white she could hardly believe it was real. Roy's shocking bright smile, his black curls shiny with pomade above sunglasses so dark she couldn't see his eyes at all. He would reach over and pat her hip with one hand and ask how she'd like to spend her honeymoon in one of those *swanky* hotels.

For a while after they married she anticipated more days in sunlight that caressed her skin, more nights of dancing in clubs, her bare shoulders fragrant with coconut oil. For a long time after she stopped expecting such days and nights, she hoped for a sign that things would get better, or at least stop getting worse.

On the canvas floor beside the twins' cot she spied a couple of well-thumbed issues of *Photoplay* and *Screenland*. On the cover of one Liz Taylor and Richard Burton were photographed clinging to one another, their mouths open wide. Helen couldn't tell if they were laughing or screaming. A headline read, "Are Liz and Burton's Love Binges Killing Them?" A photo insert in the corner featured a redhead named Florinda. Another showed Taylor and Burton looking bronze, drunk, and overweight in swimsuits on a yacht.

Helen hated these magazines. The twins bought them surreptitiously at Kresge's with change begged off of Roy, and hid them in their room. She guessed they were feeling bold because they were on vacation for the first time. Or maybe they'd simply fallen asleep and forgotten. She hoped the magazines didn't remind the girls of Roy but she couldn't be sure without asking. They lay on their cot with arms crooked and entwined. She couldn't remember a time when she had slept with such innocence and abandon.

The first dream was all broken images of the twins playing: Julie and Debbie on a swing set surrounded by palm trees, their bare feet raking the sand with each pass through the air, stirring up and infuriating a line of large black ants trying to stumble to their nest with what seemed to be bits of paper and broken seashells. In the next dream Helen saw her own eyes reflected in the rearview mirror of the Grand Prix, blackened with bruises; in the mirror she watched the twins bury a bloodstained hammer in the sand. She checked the mirror again, dabbed at her chin with powder, and noticed Richard Burton approaching the car, shambling and drunk, his face filled with rage. She looked down at her hand; it was warm, wet, cupped around a pair of broken teeth.

She felt the sand between her toes and the heat rising up from the ground. One of the ants, lost and abandoned by her tribe, clambered over Helen's foot. A searing pain in her heel told her she had been stung, and she leapt from the burning leather strap of the swing seat, landing on bare feet running. Soon the burn spread from her heel to her ankle and up her calf. When she touched her leg it folded over in sections and she fell, the hot sand enveloping her until she sank to her hips. All around her the green, fishy water was rising. She saw the twins with their arms dangling over the edge of their cot, fingers dipping in the rank sea.

She bolted upright, screaming, as a tsunami swept the tent. Waves six feet high knocked the canvas sideways, tossed the twins under, and rushed over Helen. Her voice, shouting the names of her daughters, formed bubbles, and the stinking water filled her throat.

She screamed again and awoke to see Julie and Debbie sitting up on their cot, sleepy-eyed and staring at her. She ran her fingers through her hair. Her face and scalp were drenched in sweat.

"What are y'all doing? Mama had a bad dream, is all. Go back to sleep."

In the morning Helen lay on her cot with her eyes closed, trying to recall the order of these images. Each time she got lost when she pictured her eyes in the rearview mirror of the Grand Prix. Something moved in the middle distance, a long, flat body with scales and muddy green skin sweeping aside the trees as it stumbled toward her, just out of view.

At last she opened her eyes. The tent was as intact as it had been before she fell asleep. The movie magazines lay on the floor but the twins were gone.

She jumped out of bed and slapped the canvas flap aside. Her first thought, more of a frantic hope, was that the twins had gone outside to play. She glanced up the beach at the empty swing sets. She had taken for granted that the town's name was no longer appropriate, and there was no danger. But of course it was foolish to feel safe; there was always danger. Alarm rising like an approaching siren in her chest, she turned slowly, 360 degrees, careful not to miss any detail of the surrounding campsite.

When the tent of the elderly couple came into view, she gasped. There were the twins, flanking the old people who had resumed sitting in their lawn chairs exactly as they had the day before.

Helen caught her breath, a painful lump forming in her throat. She wanted to run to her daughters but she didn't want to alarm them. Just as urgently she didn't want their newfound acquaintances to question her. She couldn't answer anything they might ask.

Her flip-flops felt grimy, coated with wet sand, by the time she reached the spot where Julie and Debbie stood beside the old couple. Something different from the previous day's scene troubled her. Once she drew alongside the twins she realized the old people were not looking at the water, and not talking to her daughters. Instead their heads were tilted back, jaws slack. The woman's chin was dotted with dried saliva.

"What's the matter with 'em, Mama?" Julie asked. "Are they sick?"

"We just walked over to say 'hey' but they were sleepin'," said Debbie.

"They're not asleep," said Julie. "They're sick. They look sick."

Helen took each girl by the hand. "Come with me," she said. "Debbie's right. They're takin' a nap. Old people like to sleep in the sun, is all. So be real quiet, now. Don't make a fuss. It's time to go."

"Told you so," Debbie taunted Julie with a wagging finger.

Julie slapped her sister's hand away and said, "I'll tell Daddy you farted in the back seat!"

"Come on, I said." Helen led them away, back down the beach to the car.

In a few minutes she had broken down the tent. She rolled it roughly and tossed it into the trunk of the car with the cooler.

"Daddy says don't roll it up," Debbie reminded her, still showing off because she thought she'd won the first argument of the day. "He says you've got to fold it."

"Never mind," said Helen. "He doesn't care anymore."

"Yes, he does," said Debbie.

"He'll get mad if you do it wrong," Julie chimed in.

"Shut up, now," Helen told her. "Get in the car and be quiet."

Her daughter's dashed expression cut Helen to the quick. She softened her tone as much as she could and said, "Listen, if y'all act real nice and don't fight, we'll stop for pancakes and sausages at the first place we see in Alabama."

Both girls brightened at the idea.

"Now be good and get in the car, so we can have a nice breakfast on the road."

As soon as they did as she said, Helen retrieved the hammer from the trunk. She knew it was clean. She had washed it thoroughly before they left the house in Atlanta. Nevertheless she drew back as far as she could and pitched it high, over the beach and into the water.

She had no way of knowing how much time the old couple had paid for. Maybe they really were on a reunion honeymoon, a prelude to what they had done together, or a chance to build their courage. Or maybe they only needed the one night. Would Dorsey or some other campground employee drive by to make sure visitors didn't overstay their rental?

She couldn't risk it. She had to be on her way, well out of Florida, before anyone showed up. Back in Atlanta it would only be another day or two before somebody stopped by, most likely one of Roy's drinking buddies.

She almost cursed the old couple but thought better of it. They'd chosen this place, of all places, to die. She didn't know why and she decided it was best not to think too much more about it. Thinking never solved a thing, in Helen's experience. She slammed the trunk shut and climbed into the driver's seat.

"Are we still on vacation?" Julie asked when Helen started the car.

"Yes, we are," she said. "That's right." She checked the rearview mirror. Behind her, in the trees, something shifted sideways and then settled, as if waiting for a signal. "Three gals on a spree! Anything might happen."

DARK WARM HEART

RICH LARSON

The bite mark was wine-red on anemic-white, crenellating Kristine's bare shoulder. She moved the strap of her nightgown when Noel stumbled into the kitchen, drawn by the sizzle and clank of the frying pan, so he would be sure to see it.

"Morning," she said, sliding the sausages onto a paper towel.

"Hey." Noel stopped short, still scratching at the wiry hair up his belly. He frowned. "Did I do that?"

"No," Kristine said dryly. She dabbed at the grease. "Somebody else. While you were gone I cheated with a . . . a hyena."

Noel came closer, whispering one finger along the ruined skin. Shook his head. "Shit," he said, wrapping her waist. "*Désolé.* I didn't mean to."

"Good," Kristine said. She tipped her head back for a kiss. "I don't mind it," she decided, plucking at his hand. "See? We match."

"Yes. Lucky." Noel held up his broad hand, two of the fingers still scarred purple from frostbite. "What do you call it? An accent color?"

Kristine laughed, and gave him a small shove towards the white table. Noel sat down in his old spot, like he'd never left, while she doled out sausages and toast with margarine. The small kitchen was still crammed full with gleaming wedding gift appliances.

"So finally you had someone to laugh at your jokes?" Noel asked, sawing with his knife.

Kristine smiled. "What?"

"The hyena."

"Hm. Yeah." She watched Noel sniff at the sausage, like he'd been rescued off some island instead of from the YEG airport late last night. "And he always ate the leftovers."

Noel laughed, warm like an electric blanket, and she wished she'd told him the night before. But there had been no space for words, just skin and sweat in a bed that had been too big for too many weeks, and she'd waited this long, hadn't she?

"I'm going to start on the transcription today," Noel said, chewing.

"Already?" Kristine asked. "You aren't going to, I don't know, warm up for a day? Relax?"

"It's not so warm here either, Krissy." He nodded towards the sliding door, half frosted over, and the pinwheeling flakes beyond it. "It's snowing."

"Warmer than your igloo in NWT," Kristine suggested. "I have to run a few errands. Unless you wanted me to stay and help you. With, you know, the bilabial sounds." She leaned forward and pressed both her lips against his. They felt dry.

"I didn't sleep in an igloo," Noel said when they broke, but grinning. "All right. I'll wash up. Leave the plates."

Kristine went to the pristine bathroom, which would not be pristine for long now that Noel was back. She'd almost missed seeing his bristles in the sink. She turned the shower on, hot. The mirror fogged fast. She retched a few times over the toilet, but nothing came up, so she stepped inside the shower. After, while the curling iron was heating up, she rummaged a tube of concealer out of her vanity drawer. She shook it as she eyed the bite mark, debating.

She put the concealer back. The mark was somehow like a checked box, a reminder that Noel was real and he was home and he loved her to death, and it was nothing like the cuts up her legs she'd hidden in high school.

When she passed through the kitchen, keys jangling in her fingers, Noel was already swallowed up between Bose headphones, the noise-cancelling kind. His face looked thin and sharp and his eyes were tracking across the laptop screen, left, right, left, right.

"Don't work too hard," Kristine said, once she'd tugged one of the headphones down.

"I would never," Noel said. "Thank you for breakfast."

He brushed crumbs off his lip before he kissed her good-bye, but the sausages were still sitting on the plate, uneaten. Kristine handed him a Tupperware container on her way out the door.

Her shoulder throbbed while she was getting cash from the ATM. It throbbed when she pushed through the Grade 5/6 portable doors to pick up the worksheet she'd forgotten to photocopy, it throbbed when she shivered in the meat section of Superstore, trying to remember if Noel liked minute steaks, and it throbbed when she returned home to find him still at the table with his face sickly awash in laptop light. He'd forgotten he cooked Sundays.

"Hey, Mister Linguist, have you even moved?" Kristine asked, opening the fridge freezer. Cold billowed out as she put the steaks in, then fished for an ice tray.

"Buy me a catheter," Noel said. He gave a wan grin. "This is great shit, Krissy. Come. Listen."

"I don't speak Inuktitut."

Noel laughed, and said it wasn't Inuktitut, and then the room was quiet except for the crack-pop of ice cubes into a Ziplock. Kristine wrapped the bag in a wet cloth, still watching Noel watching the screen, and held it against her shoulder.

"All right," she said. "Show me."

"Come." Noel slipped the headphones from around his neck and held the ice against Kristine's shoulder while she put them on.

The feedback volume made her jump.

"Sorry." Noel dialed it down with a practiced finger. Kristine repositioned the headphones and listened. It was a low guttural wail, broken up by a sort of huffing. When she listened harder she could hear an uncanny melody.

"Nice. What is it?" She looked to the screen, where the spectrogram was showing the noise slither along, pitch black, undulating through the grayscale background. It made her think of ultrasounds.

"Throat-singing," Noel said. "Beautiful. I tried it, when I was up there. Very difficult." He turned the volume up slightly. "This is just the icing, though. You know, for when I get tired of the interviews. There are so many stories. Some of them, never heard in English. Never."

Kristine watched him maneuver the mouse through his crowded screen, over IPA charts and reference logs. He pulled up another audio file. The throat-singing was replaced by an old man's voice and a dialect that Noel said was all but extinct. She sat in his lap and they pushed their heads together, each using one side of the headphones, and listened.

Noel's cheek scratched her cheek and his arms ended up around her, but with the ice trickling on her shoulder she couldn't feel warm, and it wasn't the time.

It happened in the night. Noel's knee was keyed between her knees, his arm was over her arm. They'd fucked again, not so frantically this time, and Kristine was still awake when Noel plucked her hand out from under the covers. She turned in the dark and saw his eyes were not quite closed.

"Hey," she said, moving back against him.

He didn't say anything, didn't make a noise. He brought her hand up to his face slowly, deliberately, with his thumb at her wrist. In the quiet Kristine could imagine the sound of her pulse against his skin. He opened his mouth and kissed his way along her arm, teeth skimming her, making her shiver.

Kristine half-smiled. "What are you doing?" she whispered.

"Whatever I want," Noel mumbled into her skin. He gnawed at her wrist-bone, tickling her.

"I'm so glad you made it home," Kristine said. "I'm just. You know. I was scared shitless, when I heard about the storms. When you called."

Noel bit down, playful.

Kristine winced. "Easy, boy, I don't need another one."

Noel's teeth pressed harder, deeper, so she could feel each individual crown.

"Noel, stop. You're getting spit on me. Stop."

Noel pulled back a moment, tracing the indented skin with his finger, and then he bit down again, not playful, a sudden sharp snap like an animal.

"Ouch!" Kristine jerked away. "Noel! Don't!"

"Don't what?" Noel asked thickly. Kristine slapped the light on, exposing the purple bags under her husband's eyes, the sharpness of his cheekbones somehow more pronounced. "I just want . . ." He trailed off.

“Can’t you leave the transcription for like, a day?” Kristine demanded.

“Everything’s still fresh,” Noel said. “I’m, you know, I’m zoned.”

“You’re being weird. Really fucking weird.”

“You’re being dramatic.”

Kristine went to the bathroom, flicked the light on. She ran cold water over her arm. Her reflection in the mirror looked pale and sick. She prodded her stomach.

“Come on,” Noel groaned from the bed. “You don’t need a Band-Aid, Krissy.”

“Can’t you shave?” Kristine demanded, coming back. “Unpack? Call your dad to tell him you’re back so he doesn’t call *me* again?” The fresh mark was blooming on her arm, and when Noel saw it his expression was something she didn’t like. Kristine put her other hand overtop to hide it.

“I didn’t know he called you,” Noel said.

“I’m going to sleep in the study. Just for tonight.”

“I’m sorry. Look. I’m sorry.”

“It’s fine.”

“You hate the hide-a-bed.” Noel rolled up and out of the covers. He scratched at his neck. “I’ll go,” he said. “Are there pillows?”

“In the linen closet,” Kristine said.

She stopped to get them on their way to the study, and then held them against herself while the hide-a-bed unfolded with a creak and a clunk. Noel took the pillows without smiling. He tossed them onto the bed.

“Good night,” he said.

It wasn’t.

Kristine needed a swim, so she left early in the morning with the sky still dark and didn’t even open the study door, just exchanged a good morning/good-bye with Noel’s half-asleep voice. Exhaust was billowing on the cold roads like a fog as she drove, one hand on her swim-bag. She dialed her mother at a stoplight. A voice thick with sleep or Valium answered on the fifth ring.

“Hi, honey, what is it?”

“Hi, Mom.” The light lanced green through the clouds of exhaust and Kristine drove. “I just had a question about the thank-you notes, I’m still finishing up and—”

"Noel's back, isn't that right? Give him my love. Hugs. How's his frostbite?"

"I will," Kristine said. "The thank-you note for Uncle Carrow, I can't remember his girlfriend's name. Was it Sheryl?"

"No. Carol? No. Hell, I can't remember either."

"Noel's acting different."

There was a staticky pause, and then her mother's voice came edged with a sigh.

"What do you mean?"

"Just, I don't know," Kristine said, and she didn't, not quite. "Doing weird things. Not eating. Yesterday after breakfast he didn't eat anything all day. He's, like, he's obsessing over his transcription. Won't talk to me."

"Well, he's driven, you know—"

"Not like that." She dropped her indicator and turned into the Glenora parking lot, still mostly empty of cars.

"—and it's a good thing. It really is." Another pause. "A lot of things might be or look a little different now. All those little things that were nice, you know, endearing, a lot of those things look different when you realize it's for the rest of your life."

"It's not a honeymoon is over thing, Mom," Kristine said, putting the car into park. "It's been over for a while."

"I mean, your father, my God. He had his days. Weeks. Years. But it was all worth it. I never once thought of leaving him. And Noel's a good man. A really good man. It's all about compromises, isn't it? People thinking marriage is supposed to be easy? Makes me laugh. It's all about sacrifices. There were things I wanted to do, plenty of things . . ."

"I'm not talking about leaving him, Mom, I'm just saying he's acting funny and I don't know why." She turned off the engine and fumbled the key into her coat pocket. "This thing with the storm . . ."

"Sharon. It was definitely Sharon, and half his age, too. Maybe a prostitute. Look, honey, just stop worrying. He hasn't even been back for a week. Go for a swim, you'll feel better."

"Thanks," Kristine said, hefting her bag. "Bye. Love you."

"Bye, honey."

She swam longer than she'd meant to, churning up and down the lane until the water felt bathtub warm, and so she went to the school with her hair still hanging wet wires and the toothed trace of swim-goggles around her one eye like a sucker scar. But she did feel better, even though Elijah and Braden had to be sent off to the principal for the third week running.

Noel didn't answer her text, or the second one. She tried not to worry about it. She fixed a smile to her face as she climbed the stairs to the apartment, went down the hallway that always smelled like weed and Febreze, and keyed open their door. It was dark inside, but she could see Noel wasn't at the kitchen table. Kristine flicked on the lights and checked the bare sink. No dishes. She opened the fridge. Nothing touched.

"Hey, Mister Linguist!" Kristine called. "Where are you?"

No reply. Kristine remembered the noise-cancelling headphones and went looking. She was barely even surprised when she heard the computer hum from behind the study door. Cold was seeping out from the bottom of it. She eased the door open.

Noel was hunched over the laptop like an old man. The shadows hollowed out his cheeks and for a moment his eyes looked like black holes. Then he looked up with a bleary grin and pulled the headphones down around his neck.

"Hey."

"Hi."

"How were the little terrors today?" Noel slapped the laptop shut.

"Good," Kristine said. "Fine."

"That little boy, that Elijah, he didn't make trouble?"

Kristine cracked a smile. "Yeah, he did. A little bit."

"He's trying to impress you," Noel said, scooting over on the rolling chair. "He has a crush."

"Hm."

"That's why I make trouble." Noel caught her wrist, the not-sore one, and folded both hands around it. "I'm sorry about last night," he said. "I don't know what's in my head, sometimes."

"You scared me a little," Kristine said. She gave a smile. "It's okay. It's nothing. Really." Noel's hands felt like ice. The frostbite was ugly. "Why's the window open?"

"The laptop has been overheating," Noel said. "I thought, maybe, if it's colder in the study, maybe that helps."

"Hungry?"

"I found something in the fridge," Noel said.

Kristine stiffened. "No, you didn't."

"What?"

"You didn't take anything out of the fridge," Kristine said. "You didn't eat anything, did you? You've been in here all day."

"I got something at the Second Cup," Noel said, but he let her pull her arm away.

"Your shoes were still where you left them yesterday."

"You're a detective or something?" Noel was still smiling, but only with his mouth. "You photograph where in the closet I put my shoes?"

"Why are you lying about this?" Kristine snapped. "Are you on a fucking hunger strike or something? Why are you acting like this?"

"Like what?" Noel asked, still prone in the office chair, still not angry. Kristine wanted him to stand up so she could shove him back down. She felt hot and sick all over.

"Was there somebody else up there?" she asked.

"What do you mean?" Noel asked, and now his eyes were finally narrowing.

"I mean, did you fuck somebody while you were up there?" Kristine demanded. "You called once the whole time, and now you come back, you won't talk to me, you're acting so fucking weird—"

"Of course not." Noel was up, teeth bared. "Of course I didn't. Did you?"

"Oh, my God, Noel." Kristine gave a shaky laugh. "Just shut up, Noel."

They stood frozen for a long moment, Kristine's nails digging crescents in her palms. She watched Noel's face work until the grimace smoothed over.

"Maybe I have a bug," he said slowly. "My stomach doesn't feel right. I didn't want you to worry."

Kristine nodded. She rubbed her eye with the heel of her hand.

"What happened in the storm?" she finally asked. "Do you even remember calling me? They had a satellite phone in the infirmary, and you called me in the middle of the night."

"I remember calling," Noel said, cautious.

"Do you remember what I told you?" Kristine asked, remembering how she'd gone to the bathroom, flicked on the lights, pulled out the test again just to be sure. That was before she'd realized how late it was, that something was wrong.

"I don't." Noel shook his head. "I don't. I don't remember what I said, either."

"You were delirious," Kristine said, wrapping her arms around herself. The bite on her shoulder throbbed again. "You told me how you got stranded, right? Between the station and the village. One of those storms that comes from nowhere."

"Worst they had seen in years," Noel said. "They told me that later. Yeah." His voice had an unsteadiness Kristine was unused to hearing, and somehow it drained all the anger out of her. "What else did I say?" he asked.

"You said the wind felt like teeth."

"Like death," Noel said.

"The Ski-Doo broke down, so you tried to walk back to the village."

"Went the wrong way. They told me later."

"You said the mucus in your nose and the spit in your mouth were so frozen up you couldn't breathe, and the wind was like teeth." Kristine paused. "You said you lost your hands, then your feet. Like being disembodied. Like floating."

"Should've died," Noel muttered. "Should've frozen to death."

"They told me that, after they took the phone away from you," Kristine said. "I mean, it's a miracle you're all right." She shrugged helplessly. "Doesn't this feel better?" she asked. "To talk about it? Isn't this what's been bothering you?"

"What else did I say?" Noel probed.

"I don't remember," Kristine said. "You were fevered. You know, delirious."

"Did I say what I saw?" Noel's eyes were wide. "Kristine. Tell me."

"Yeah. You did." Kristine swayed, foot to foot. "You thought you saw someone else in the storm. An old man."

Noel shut his eyes now, breathing quick and shallow. "What did he look like?"

"Tall," Kristine said. "Taller than the trees. Skinny like those starving kids they show on UNICEF ads. And he was naked." She stopped. "People see things. You know. Your brain was practically, it must have been practically shutting off."

"He didn't have a face," Noel said. "Just a big dark mouth. Big black hole. I still remember it so clear. Clearer than what actually happened."

"I think you might have PTSD or something, Noel. I'm worried."

"It's nothing like that." Noel's voice was strained. He opened his eyes. Blinked. "I haven't been myself. I know. I just need to get this transcription done, and then I'll be done with it all. I'm looking for this one story. I know it's in there somewhere. Just give me the week, Krissy. Be patient for me."

"Of course," Kristine said. "I get it. Really." She put her hand against Noel's hip. It felt sharp enough to cut.

"You do?"

"Yeah. I mean." Kristine paused. "If you need to get through this transcription so you can be done with everything, storm included, and just stop thinking about it, then yeah. I get it. And then you'll be yourself again. I get it."

They embraced, and it felt like all angles. Kristine wasn't sure, but she almost thought her hands could make out the nodes of his spine under his thin wool sweater.

⤚o⤙

He said he didn't want to pass on whatever bug was in his stomach, so Noel slept in the study again. They pretended it was a sort of game, and reminded each other of the weekend Noel's French Catholic parents had stayed with them, back during the engagement, when they'd had to rearrange all their things so it looked like they slept in separate rooms.

On Tuesday Kristine stayed late at the school with her lesson plans, hoping she'd come back to find Noel antsy and missing her, something simmering on the stove, maybe his sketch-pad out on the coffee table or a comedy queued up on Netflix. That didn't happen, so on Wednesday she stayed late at the school to minimize the time between arriving home and going to sleep alone. She pretended she was married to a genius, consumed by his latest work, and she was making sacrifices.

That night, Kristine woke up cold. The shadows in her room were Baltic blue and when she nudged her phone the screen read 3:42 a.m. She pulled her feet back under the sheets, coaxing a static crackle, and rolled over.

The apartment door thunked.

Kristine sat up, clutching her phone. Half of a dream was fogging the inside of her skull. She padded into the hallway on bare feet, navigating by the light of her screen, and felt the cold coming from the study. The door was wide open. So was the window.

She hauled it shut with both hands, breathing an icy cloud, wondering about the pipes, how long it took for them to freeze in this weather. Snow was blowing in drifts off roofs and balconies, through the bony branches of a tree where a black garbage bag fluttered.

Someone was in the stairwell, feet slapping the plastic-capped steps. Kristine left the study, checked the bathroom, hoping but knowing better, and then found her jacket and keys. Her inchoate dream was dancing in the back of her head. She locked the door and circled down the four flights that had made moving such an ordeal and such a triumph. She trailed her hand on the nick they'd left with the corner of their big stupid couch.

"Noel?" she called.

The reply was the click and catch of the exterior door opening, closing. She went quickly down the last flight, zipping her coat up to her neck. The forecast had been for an overnight drop down to minus thirty, cold enough to make metal burn. Kristine felt a thrumming under her skin as she came to the glass door. Outside, the lampposts spilled yellow pools on the lumpy ice street. A disconnected shadow was crossing the empty road, going towards the park, the playground Kristine had wanted nearby even though it had seemed too early to think about kids. She opened the door and the cold bit her hard.

"Noel!" she shouted, feeling ice rasp her throat, freeze her nostrils. The shadow didn't turn around. Kristine pulled up his number by muscle memory and called him as she followed. She held her phone up like a torch, listening to the soft chime, peering into the dark. There was no pick-up, but she hadn't expected one, and now anxiety was gnawing at her stomach as she reached the park, rounded the corner of the half-painted gazebo.

Noel was ankle-deep in the snow, back turned toward her, and he was naked. In the fluorescent light from the gazebo his skin looked wax-pale, all but translucent, bruised with cold blue shadows. Kristine's eyes traced the cavities of his body. His spine looked sharp as scalpels. He was not shivering, not moving. Kristine was trembling all over.

The dream was coming back to her now. She didn't want him to turn around, because she knew what she'd see: a raw-red throat like a subway tunnel, gnashing teeth, no eyes. Her fingers were going numb at her sides.

"Noel, this isn't . . . funny," Kristine said, halting. "You're going to freeze to death. You're going to get more frostbite."

Noel turned, and it was Noel's face, heavy with sleep. He gave her a confused look. He looked down at his purple-scarred fingers.

"You're sleepwalking." Kristine took a hesitant step, then another, crunching through the snow. "Come on. You're going to freeze. Come on. You're sleepwalking, like the time in Calgary. At the hotel." She gripped his hand and tugged. He followed, stumbling slightly, red feet battered by ice. Kristine tried not to look at his ruined toenails.

They walked slowly, slowly, snow peppering their faces and searing their lips. They passed the creaking playground with its rubber swings, the ones they'd sat in, dragging circles in the snow with their boots while they looked up at the apartment complex and invented such big beautiful dreams. She tried to picture Noel pushing a tiny body, bundled in a parka, red-cheeked, but didn't manage it.

The wind picked up as they crossed the road, and by the time they reached the door it felt like teeth on Kristine's bare face.

⊸○⊷

In the morning, Kristine left before Noel could wake up and wonder about the bathtub full of lukewarm water, or the towels wrapped around him and under him on the couch. Kristine had played with the thermostat before and after eating breakfast, but the apartment was still cold. She needed the pool, the chlorine warmth of it, the lactic acid in her arms and shoulders. She threw up before she left.

She dialed her mother at the yield sign.

"Hi, honey." The voice was faux-cheery. "Sorry, I meant to return your call yesterday, it completely slipped my mind. I was over at the Blackstocks', you know how she talks."

"I don't really remember them," Kristine said. "I was, um, I was out walking last night, and I noticed some vacancies in the apartment down the road."

"Oh?"

Kristine's nails drummed the wheel. "Well, I was wondering if you're still thinking about that. You know, about moving. We talked about it in the summer, remember?"

"Too cold up there. Did we talk about that?"

"You said you wanted to be closer," Kristine said. She bit her lip. "Grandkids?"

"Honey, do you have news?"

She thought about telling her for a second, imagining how her mother's voice would turn instantly to sunshine. "No, no," she relented. "I just meant, you know, for the future." She could hear a disappointed breath on the other end.

"Too cold, honey, and besides, you know I wouldn't be able to leave this place. Not after all the work your father put into it. So much of himself, he put into it. It just wouldn't feel right."

"I thought you said the upkeep . . . ?"

"I can manage, honey. I'm sturdy. Besides, you don't need your mother hassling you all the time. You and Noel have each other now. It's normal to be, I don't know, to be overwhelmed a little at first, trying to make it as a young couple, especially with him doing the doctorate. But I know you can make it work. You're a good girl."

An SUV honked from behind and Kristine realized she hadn't moved from the yield sign. She pulled away, ending the call without saying good-bye, and wiped at her stinging eyes.

When she got home from the school she went straight to the study, rumpled card clutched in her palm. She could hear the laptop hum from under the door. She opened without knocking.

"I made you an appointment," Kristine said. "With this counselor. It's through the university."

Noel glanced up. His face was still swallowed between headphones and his eyes were strangely cloudy. He tapped something out on the keyboard.

"Aren't you going to ask about last night?" Kristine said softly.

Noel said nothing. The window was shut, but he was shirtless. His collarbones had grown a new geometry, skimming up like shark fins. Sweat was beaded under his hairline.

"You sleepwalked out into the park," Kristine said. "It was fucking forty below. You could have died."

Noel gave a fractional shrug. His eyes returned to the screen, and Kristine could tell from the swipe of his finger that the volume was going up.

"I wish you *had* cheated on me," she said.

Noel tapped his headphone to show he couldn't hear. His smile was too broad, too many teeth, a Cheshire cat grin.

"I wish I'd cheated," Kristine said, feeling a tingle up and down her back, something cold and angular in her gut.

Noel said nothing.

Kristine dropped the appointment card and left.

The next day she spent lunch-hour talking in circles with the health center. They mumbled at her about seasonal depression, flu virus. When it came time to teach ecosystems she begged someone out of the staff-room to watch her class watch YouTube clips about photovores and herbivores and carnivores. She went to the bathroom and speed-read through Wikipedia articles and WebMD links. She tried to throw up. A few people asked her if she was all right, and she nearly told them.

When she got home, the apartment was empty and Noel's shoes were not in the closet. It seemed like the thermostat had finally kicked in, because she didn't get goose bumps when she shrugged off her coat. Kristine hunted the bare counters for a note for a good five minutes before she gave up and put some Thai in the microwave.

Maybe he'd finished the transcription. Maybe if she went to the bathroom she'd find bristles in the sink, and then he'd be arriving back with clean-shaven cheeks, a bottle of white wine, take-out from the Mediterranean place they'd loved so much that first month after moving in. She would tell him she had news; he would already know. For a moment the image was so clear that Kristine nearly stopped the microwave and put the leftovers back into the fridge.

Instead, she went to the study. The door was wide open again, but the window was shut. Noel hadn't taken the laptop with him. Kristine hesitated for a moment, then plucked it off the desk and sat down on the hide-a-bed with it. Her hand kneaded the sheets while it booted up. The password screen appeared, and Kristine put in her name, clacked the enter key. The affirmative chime made her almost smile.

The transcription window was already waiting, a block of IPA symbols. Kristine tried to remember the phonetics classes she'd taken; most of the sounds she'd already forgotten. One word seemed to be recurring: wɛŋdəgoʊ. She pulled up the next window, and saw that Noel had translated a section into English. At the top it was labeled *audio48.mp3*. Kristine clicked back to the sound files and pulled the headphones up over her ears. She started to read.

the wendigo is hunger, and hunger is the wendigo. a man travelled by night. he hunted the herd. the wendigo hunted the man. a man travelled by night and through the wood, and the [blizzard] snow drove him off his trail. the wendigo hunted the man, its arms were the cold and its teeth were the wind. a man had death inside [in stomach]. the cold kills, the hunger kills. hunger is the wendigo. a man lies down in the snow. his body is given to the ice. a man travelled alone. the wendigo came to him with [singing] open mouth. the wendigo has jaws as icicles. the wendigo gives to the man a dark warm heart of human meat. a man can die, or a man can eat. a man travelled by night. he ate the wendigo's [offering]. the man lives, the hunger stays. hunger is the wendigo. a man travelled by night.

"Krissy?"

She flung upright, all her nerves sparked at once; Noel was inches away and his eyes were black as jet. The laptop crashed to the floor between them, Kristine's heart hammered in her throat. His face was gaunt, stretched thin, canvas over bones.

"Why did you write that?" Kristine whispered.

"I didn't," Noel said. The glass Pyrex pan from the microwave was clutched in his one hand. He held it out between them, arm shaking slightly.

"Bullshit you didn't. What do you mean? What do you mean you didn't write it?" Kristine stepped back and felt the cold edge of the hide-a-bed against the bends of her knees. Noel's pale face was slick with sweat.

"I translated it," he said, voice wavering. "It was already there. I knew it was there. I just had to find it. Those old men had so many stories." He held the Pyrex out again, still shaking, and Kristine took it so it wouldn't fall.

"Why are you doing this?" Kristine demanded. The glass was cold again. "Why are you fucking inventing this?"

"I'm not," Noel pleaded. "Krissy. Look."

And she had to. He held up his spidery hand, so much more bone than she remembered it, wrists like doorknobs, and planted his teeth in the webbing between thumb and finger. With a wet tearing sound, he sheared through the flesh. Kristine's lungs caught, she anticipated the spray of bright red blood, but there was nothing. Something thick and black glistened along the torn skin, and then suddenly the hand was back together again.

"It can't be me," Noel said. "I tried."

"Oh, my God, Noel."

His face contorted all at once and he lunged, his teeth suddenly canine; Kristine swung the glass dish in the same motion. It slammed against his temple with a thick crack: Noel was reeling off to the side, cursing in French, and Kristine was pushing past him, slamming the door, throwing herself against it. Her breath came in a wail. Noel's body thumped against the door once, then twice, Kristine shoved back with her shoulders, and then he stopped.

"We're going to call emergency," Kristine said, when her heart was beating again. "I'm dialing 911. There's something, I don't know, some disease you picked up up there. I know this isn't you. I know it can't be you." She couldn't keep her voice steady, it slipped away from her between words.

"Oh, fuck," came Noel's voice, raw. "Oh, fuck. I drove to the university hospital. That's where I was. Jacob. You remember Jacob. The med-student. He told me how they keep cadavers. I thought, maybe, I don't know. I couldn't get in. They called security."

"This can't be real, Noel."

He went on like he hadn't heard. "Then I thought, the morgue, maybe. Or, I don't know." He gave a broken laugh. "A graveyard. Maybe that. I have to know. I just have to. I'm going to die soon. If I don't eat, I'm going to die."

Kristine was muffling a sob in her hand, biting down as hard as she could. "A doctor," she gasped.

"This can't be for doctors. When you're wendigo, you're wendigo. Until you give in. That was what they said."

"And then?"

"I don't know. I'm sorry. I don't know." He stopped. "There are more stories. More transcriptions. Maybe if I keep going, keep looking. I don't know."

Kristine didn't reply. She sat against the door, tears sticky on her cheeks, and waited for hours. Waited for Noel's breathing to turn regular, shallow but regular, so she was sure he was asleep. She moved the bookcase in front of the study door, groaning and scraping. It was heavy. Her hands came away with deep red welts.

She was up early the next morning, wiping down the kitchen counters and stovetop with Purell so everything gleamed. When she popped the ice cubes out of their tray they skittered off the table and onto the floor. Her hands were shivering as she dropped them one by one into a plastic bag. She set her wedding ring on the counter and dialed her mother.

"Hey, honey, what's up?"

"Call me my name?" Kristine's voice came in a sob; she tamped it down.

"What's wrong, Kristine?"

"It's nothing," Kristine said, toying with the ring. "I just remembered, that cousin you had, the farmer. He lost his hand in a thresher. He just wore it on the other finger, right? His wedding ring, I mean. He wore it on the right."

"That's right, yes. On the right. I think that might be how they do it in Europe, too."

"Okay." Kristine packed more ice around her left ring finger, waiting for the numb. "I was just remembering that." She went to the counter, to the shiny Cutco knives, another wedding gift. She tried to remember the sharpest one.

"Was that all? I'm half-asleep, honey."

"When dad died, you said you'd have traded anything, didn't you?" Kristine asked. "Anyone or anything." There was a long pause. Kristine looked down at her left hand, thinking of how it cupped when she swam, how the fingers all melded together and bit the water just so. She thought about the small warm thing growing in her belly.

"I don't remember. I don't remember exactly what I said."

"Okay," Kristine said, turning the stovetop on. "Bye, mom."

"Bye, honey."

Kristine held the ice around her finger and stared at the stove element, waiting for it to turn orange.

THERE AND BACK AGAIN

CARMEN MARIA MACHADO

My mother used to love the corpse reviver. She called it the perfect cocktail. "The thing that sends you away, brings you back," she'd say as she laid out the ingredients on the dining room table before she went out for the evening. "There is only one door," she clarified once, when I looked at her in confusion. "You can go out and you can come in, but you always have to pass through the same door to get there."

I was too young to understand hair-of-the-dog as a concept, much less as an idiom, but there was some sort of clear alchemy happening on that table: the martini glass clear of smudges, the burnished aluminum shaker, the arrangement of bottles and their mysterious liquids, deep red maraschino cherries floating in a pickling jar at the end of the row. It was understood that I was not to touch this arrangement ("None of this is for little girls"), and she would know: my fingerprints on the glass would give me away. This didn't stop me from inverting the jar to watch the cherries rise like so many jellyfish, and then wiping it clean on my nightgown. But I'd only do that after she left.

And she did leave, once a week. A kiss dropped somewhere in my hair, and she'd walk out the front door and into the humid, mottled darkness.

I'd wait for her. The house felt strange when she was gone; like it'd been shucked from the thing that gave it purpose. The air hummed with her many ghosts: skin cells, perfume, the cobwebs she'd ignored from when we first moved in. I listened for hours for the sound of tires, of the front door opening, of her inky voice exchanging murmurs with a stranger.

The men and women she brought home were beautiful. The women were always dark-haired and curvy—her type. The men looked like they'd been dragged through a dewy meadow. My mother would always offer them a drink, then she'd walk past the stairs to see if I was waiting. Then her footsteps would cut a path toward the kitchen.

"On the rocks?" she'd call. My cue. I'd step into the living room and walk slowly to the body, slumped loosely on the loveseat. Their gaze was always focused on the kitchen doorway through which my mother had disappeared. I could feel them listening to the comforting sounds of ice striking glass, hope stirring through the haze of alcohol.

They were easy to eat when they were like that. Soft. Fermented, almost. And when I was done, she would collect me and take me upstairs, and we would sleep two heavy, parallel sleeps: her besotted with alcohol, me with blood and bone. The next morning, I'd always find her sitting at the table, rolling a silky glaze of absinthe around the inside of the martini glass and staring at the place where the sunlight struck the floorboards.

It was that way for many years, the two of us. And then she died and I was alone.

Learning to feed myself was hard. I've never been good with people. Perhaps that seems like a bit of a joke, but I imagine it's how certain men see the world, too: if all you want is a body, it's difficult to confront the animated spirit within.

Even when I wasn't hungry—even when I'd just eaten—it was hard to focus on the ethereal, flickering qualities that made humans individual: a smile, for example, or a voice. They were like crows—I'd been told of their intelligence, their distinctiveness, but couldn't quite bring myself to believe it.

So I was lucky that I was beautiful, that people let me come home with them even after I'd spent a date barely looking them in the eye. Which is how, a year after my mother died, I ended up at Alma's place.

I didn't mean to follow her home. That is, I tried to invite her to my place, but she'd sweetly refused, and I found myself paying closer attention to her than I had to anyone in a very long time.

"My house is closer," I said.

She smiled shyly and shook her head. I hadn't been drinking much, but she had, and every tip of her—nose, ears, cheekbones—were slightly flushed. "I'd just feel better if we were at my place," she said. "More, um, comfortable?"

In the cab she sat close to me, and a few blocks from the bar she opened up my fist—I didn't know I'd been making a fist—and gently stroked her fingers over my palm. The sensation was so intimate I nearly threw myself out the door and into the street, but then we were in front of her building, and then we were upstairs, and she sat me down on the couch by clumsily pressing both hands on my shoulders. I was still unnerved from the feeling of her fingers in my palm; I so rarely touched people with anything but my teeth, my throat.

The apartment had a curio-cabinet charm, with stone figurines and candles and intricate, draped fabrics. A preserved crocodile head sat on the bookshelf, and the smell of incense—familiar, somehow—lingered in the air. She came out of the kitchen with something amber-gold in a tumbler. I started; I'd been planning on doing it when she'd been there, but I'd been distracted. I couldn't remember the last time I'd lost focus like this. As a child, maybe.

I drank deeply. I hated seeing this apartment, the corners and tendrils of her life. I wanted to eat and then I wanted to leave.

"I hope this is all right," she said. "The drink, I mean. I didn't mean to assume, I just—I don't do this very much. Well, ever."

"It's fine. I mean, it's good. My mom used to make really complicated cocktails when I was a kid, and I took secret sips out of a few of them. Never liked them much. This is easier."

"What would she make?"

"Um, there was this one called a corpse reviver. Like, a hair-of-the-dog cocktail? Just, lots of booze with a cherry dropped in. Oh, and you had to coat the glass with absinthe, first. Really complicated. I don't even know where she learned it."

I drained my glass to the ice and set it down into darkness.

When I opened my eyes again, the ceiling rocked gently above me, like a boat bobbing against the tide. Alma's face swam into view.

"I didn't actually know if that would work," she said. "But there you are."

She stood up and stepped over me, and her voice sounded like it was coming from the end of a long tunnel. "Do you know who I am?"

I struggled to make words. "G-girlfriend of a missing person."

"Good guess," she said. "Sister of a missing person."

He'd had the smell of incense on his clothes. I remembered, now. He'd been early on, when I talked to them too much, learned too much. I didn't remember his name, but he'd talked about his older sister, whom he adored.

"He was living with me," Alma said. "Trying to get his life back on track after a bad breakup. Lonely, you know? Wanted to go on some dates. And then he went out one night and never came back."

"Loneliness is a door," I said. "You—"

I turned and retched over the carpet.

"You look like an animal," she said.

"Loneliness is a door," I said again. "You can go out and you can come in, but you always have to pass through loneliness to get there."

"What do I have to do?" she said. "Stake through the heart? Silver bullet? What the hell are you? Where is his body?"

"What sends you away will bring you back," I said. "I ate your brother. Every part of him."

"Do I have to eat you?" she said. Her voice was low and sad.

"Hunger is a door. You can go out and you can come in, but you always have to pass through hunger to get there."

She knelt down over me. She was holding a chef's knife in her hand, both of which were trembling. "I just want my brother back."

I grabbed her shirt and pulled her down close to my face. Through my disorientation, I opened my mouth wide enough, so she could see. So she could really see.

"Vengeance is a door," I said, my voice rippling through cities of teeth, forests of muscle, miles of esophagus. "You can go out and you can come in, but you always have to pass through vengeance to get there." I reached up and circled the knife's blade with my hand. "So pick your door."

⊸○⊷

She left me, alive, in an alley in a neighboring city, upright next to a dumpster. "There are always windows," she said as she got back into her car, but I couldn't tell if she was talking to herself, or to me.

SHEPHERDS' BUSINESS

STEPHEN GALLAGHER

Picture me on an island supply boat, one of the old Clyde Puffers seeking to deliver me to my new post. This was 1947, just a couple of years after the war, and I was a young doctor relatively new to General Practice. Picture also a choppy sea, a deck that rose and fell with every wave, and a cross-current fighting hard to turn us away from the isle. Back on the mainland I'd been advised that a hearty breakfast would be the best preventative for seasickness and now, having loaded up with one, I was doing my best to hang onto it.

I almost succeeded. Perversely, it was the sudden calm of the harbour that did for me. I ran to the side and I fear that I cast rather more than my bread upon the waters. Those on the quay were treated to a rare sight; their new doctor, clinging to the ship's rail, with seagulls swooping in the wake of the steamer for an unexpected water-borne treat.

The island's resident Constable was waiting for me at the end of the gang-plank. A man of around my father's age, in uniform, chiselled in flint and unsullied by good cheer. He said, "Munro Spence? Doctor Munro Spence?"

"That's me," I said.

"Will you take a look at Doctor Laughton before we move him? He didn't have too good a journey down."

There was a man to take care of my baggage, so I followed the Constable to the Harbourmaster's house at the end of the quay. It was a stone building, square and solid. Doctor Laughton was in the Harbourmaster's sitting room behind the office. He was in a chair by the fire with his feet on a stool and a rug over his knees and was attended by one of his own nurses, a stocky red-haired girl of twenty or younger.

I began, "Doctor Laughton. I'm . . ."

"My replacement, I know," he said. "Let's get this over with."

I checked his pulse, felt his glands, listened to his chest, noted the signs of cyanosis. It was hardly necessary; Doctor Laughton had already diagnosed himself, and had requested this transfer. He was an old-school Edinburgh-trained medical man, and I could be sure that his condition must be sufficiently serious that 'soldiering on' was no longer an option. He might choose to ignore his own aches and troubles up to a point, but as the island's only doctor he couldn't leave the community at risk.

When I enquired about chest pain he didn't answer directly, but his expression told me all.

"I wish you'd agreed to the aeroplane," I said.

"For my sake or yours?" he said. "You think I'm bad. You should see your colour." And then, relenting a little, "The airstrip's for emergencies. What good's that to me?"

I asked the nurse, "Will you be travelling with him?"

"I will," she said. "I've an Aunt I can stay with. I'll return on the morning boat."

Two of the men from the Puffer were waiting to carry the doctor to the quay. We moved back so that they could lift him between them, chair and all. As they were getting into position Laughton said to me, "Try not to kill anyone in your first week, or they'll have me back here the day after."

I was his locum, his temporary replacement. That was the story. But we both knew that he wouldn't be returning. His sight of the island from the sea would almost certainly be his last.

Once they'd manoeuvred him through the doorway, the two sailors bore him with ease toward the boat. Some local people had turned out to wish him well on his journey.

As I followed with the nurse beside me, I said, "Pardon me, but what do I call you?"

"I'm Nurse Kirkwood," she said. "Rosie."

"I'm Munro," I said. "Is that an island accent, Rosie?"

"You have a sharp ear, Doctor Spence," she said.

She supervised the installation of Doctor Laughton in the deck cabin, and didn't hesitate to give the men orders where another of her age and sex might only make suggestions or requests. A born Matron, if ever I saw one. The old salts followed her instruction without a murmur.

When they'd done the job to her satisfaction, Laughton said to me, "The latest patient files are on my desk. Your desk, now."

Nurse Kirkwood said to him, "You'll be back before they've missed you, doctor," but he ignored that.

He said, "These are good people. Look after them."

The crew were already casting off, and they all but pulled the board from under my feet as I stepped ashore. I took a moment to gather myself, and gave a pleasant nod in response to the curious looks of those well-wishers who'd stayed to see the boat leave. The day's cargo had been unloaded and stacked on the quay and my bags were nowhere to be seen. I went in search of them and found Moodie, driver and handyman to the island hospital, waiting beside a field ambulance that had been decommissioned from the military. He was chatting to another man, who bade good day and moved off as I arrived.

"Will it be much of a drive?" I said as we climbed aboard.

"Ay," Moodie said.

"Ten minutes? An hour? Half an hour?"

"Ay," he agreed, making this one of the longest conversations we were ever to have.

The drive took little more than twenty minutes. This was due to the size of the island and a good concrete road, yet another legacy of the Army's wartime presence. We saw no other vehicle, slowed for nothing other than the occasional indifferent sheep. Wool and weaving, along with some lobster fishing, sustained the peacetime economy here. In wartime it had been different, with the local populace outnumbered by spotters, gunners, and the Royal Engineers. Later came a camp for Italian prisoners of war, whose disused medical block the Highlands and Islands Medical Service took over when the island's cottage hospital burned down. Before we reached it we passed the airstrip, still usable, but with its gatehouse and control tower abandoned.

The former prisoners' hospital was a concrete building with a wooden barracks attached. The Italians had laid paths and a garden, but these were now growing wild. Again I left Moodie to deal with my bags, and went looking to introduce myself to the Senior Sister.

Senior Sister Garson looked me over once and didn't seem too impressed. But she called me by my title and gave me a briefing on everyone's duties while leading me around on a tour. It was then that I learned my driver's name. I met all the staff apart from Mrs. Moodie, who served as cook, housekeeper, and island midwife.

"There's just the one six-bed ward," Sister Garson told me. "We use that for the men and the officers' quarters for the women. Two to a room."

"How many patients at the moment?"

"As of this morning, just one. Old John Petrie. He's come in to die."

Harsh though it seemed, she delivered the information in a matter-of-fact manner.

"I'll see him now," I said.

Old John Petrie was eighty-five or eighty-seven. The records were unclear. Occupation, shepherd. Next of kin, none—a rarity on the island. He'd led a tough outdoor life, but toughness won't keep a body going for ever. He was now grown so thin and frail that he was in danger of being swallowed up by his bedding. According to Doctor Laughton's notes he'd presented with no specific ailment. One of my teachers might have diagnosed a case of TMB, Too Many Birthdays. He'd been found in his croft house, alone, half-starved, unable to rise. There was life in John Petrie's eyes as I introduced myself, but little sign of it anywhere else.

We moved on. Mrs. Moodie would bring me my evening meals, I was told. Unless she was attending at a birth, in which case I'd be looked after by Rosie Kirkwood's mother who'd cycle up from town.

My experience in obstetrics had mainly involved being a student and staying out of the midwife's way. Senior Sister Garson said, "They're mostly home births with the midwife attending, unless there are complications and then she'll call you in. But that's quite rare. You might want to speak to Mrs. Tulloch before she goes home. Her baby was stillborn on Sunday."

"Where do I find her?" I said.

The answer was, in the suite of rooms at the other end of the building. Her door in the women's wing was closed, with her husband waiting in the corridor.

"She's dressing," he explained.

Sister Garson said, "Thomas, this is Doctor Spence. He's taking over for Doctor Laughton."

She left us together. Thomas Tulloch was a young man, somewhere around my own age but much hardier. He wore a shabby suit of all-weather tweed that looked as if it had outlasted several owners. His beard was dark, his eyes blue. Women like that kind of thing, I know, but my first thought was of a wall-eyed collie. What can I say? I like dogs.

I asked him, "How's your wife bearing up?"

"It's hard for me to tell," he said. "She hasn't spoken much." And then, as soon as Sister Garson was out of earshot, he lowered his voice and said, "What was it?"

"I beg your pardon?"

"The child. Was it a boy or a girl?"

"I've no idea."

"No one will say. Daisy didn't get to see it. It was just, your baby's dead, get over it, you'll have another."

"Her first?"

He nodded.

I wondered who might have offered such cold comfort. Everyone, I expect. It was the approach at the time. Infant mortality was no longer the commonplace event it once had been, but old attitudes lingered.

I said, "And how do you feel?"

Tulloch shrugged. "It's nature," he conceded. "But you'll get a ewe that won't leave a dead lamb. Is John Petrie dying now?"

"I can't say. Why?"

"I'm looking after his flock and his dog. His dog won't stay put."

At that point the door opened and Mrs. Tulloch—Daisy—stood before us. True to her name, a crushed flower. She was pale, fair, and small of stature, barely up to her husband's shoulder. She'd have heard our voices though not, I would hope, our conversation.

I said, "Mrs. Tulloch, I'm Doctor Spence. Are you sure you're well enough to leave us?"

She said, "Yes, thank you, Doctor." She spoke in little above a whisper. Though a grown and married woman, from a distance you might have taken her for a girl of sixteen.

I looked to Tulloch and said, "How will you get her home?"

"We were told, the ambulance?" he said. And then, "Or we could walk down for the mail bus."

"Let me get Mister Moodie," I said.

Moodie seemed to be unaware of any arrangement, and reluctant to comply with it. Though it went against the grain to be firm with a man twice my age, I could see trouble in our future if I wasn't. I said, "I'm not discharging a woman in her condition to a hike on the heath. To your ambulance, Mister Moodie."

Garaged alongside the field ambulance I saw a clapped-out Riley Roadster at least a dozen years old. Laughton's own vehicle, available for my use.

As the Tullochs climbed aboard the ambulance I said to Daisy, "I'll call by and check on you in a day or two." And then, to her husband, "I'll see if I can get an answer to your question."

My predecessor's files awaited me in the office. Those covering his patients from the last six months had been left out on the desk, and were but the tip of the iceberg; in time I'd need to become familiar with the histories of everyone on the island, some fifteen hundred souls. It was a big responsibility for one medic, but civilian doctors were in short supply. Though the fighting was over and the Forces demobbed, medical officers were among the last to be released.

I dived in. The last winter had been particularly severe, with a number of pneumonia deaths and broken limbs from ice falls. I read of frostbitten fishermen and a three-year-old boy deaf after measles. Two cases had been sent to the mainland for surgery and one emergency appendectomy had been performed, successfully and right here in the hospital's theatre, by Laughton himself.

Clearly I had a lot to live up to.

Since October there had been close to a dozen births on the island. A fertile community, and dependent upon it. Most of the children were thriving, one family had moved away. A Mrs. Flett had popped out her seventh, with no complications. But then there was Daisy Tulloch.

I looked at her case notes. They were only days old, and incomplete. Laughton had written them up in a shaky hand and I found myself wondering whether, in some way, his condition might have been a factor in the outcome. Not by any direct failing of his own, but Daisy had been thirty-six hours in labour before he was called in. Had the midwife delayed calling him for longer than she should? By the time of his intervention it was a matter of no detectable heartbeat and a forceps delivery.

I'd lost track of the time, so when Mrs. Moodie appeared with a tray I was taken by surprise.

"Don't get up, Doctor," she said. "I brought your tea."

I turned the notes face-down to the desk and pushed my chair back. Enough, I reckoned, for one day.

I said, "The stillbirth, the Tullochs. Was it a boy or a girl?"

"Doctor Laughton dealt with it," Mrs. Moodie said. "I wasn't there to see. It hardly matters now, does it?"

"Stillbirths have to be registered," I said.

"If you say so, Doctor."

"It's the law, Mrs. Moodie. What happened to the remains?"

"They're in the shelter for the undertaker. It's the coldest place we have. He'll collect them when there's next a funeral."

I finished my meal and, leaving the tray for Mrs. Moodie to clear, went out to the shelter. It wasn't just a matter of the Tullochs' curiosity. With no note of gender, I couldn't complete the necessary registration. Back then the bodies of the stillborn were often buried with any unrelated female adult. I had to act before the undertaker came to call.

The shelter was an air raid bunker located between the hospital and the airfield, now used for storage. And when I say storage, I mean everything from our soap and toilet roll supply to the recently deceased. It was a series of chambers mostly buried under a low, grassy mound. The only visible features above ground were a roof vent and a brick-lined ramp leading down to a door at one end. The door had a mighty lock, for which there was no key.

Inside I had to navigate my way through rooms filled with crates and boxes to find the designated mortuary with the slab. Except that it wasn't a slab; it was a billiard table, cast in the ubiquitous concrete (by those Italians, no doubt) and repurposed by my predecessor. The cotton-wrapped package that lay on it was unlabelled, and absurdly small. I unpicked the wrapping with difficulty and made the necessary check. A girl. The cord was still attached and there were all the signs of a rough forceps delivery. Forceps in a live birth are only meant to guide and protect the child's head. The marks of force supported my suspicion that Laughton had been called at a point too late for the infant, and where he could only focus on preserving the mother's life.

Night had all but fallen when I emerged. As I washed my hands before going to make a last check on our dying shepherd, I reflected on the custom of slipping a stillbirth into a coffin to share a stranger's funeral. On the one hand, it could seem like a heartless practice; on the other, there was something touching about the idea of a nameless child being placed in the anonymous care of another soul. Whenever I try to imagine eternity, it's always long and lonely. Such company might be a comfort for both.

John Petrie lay with his face toward the darkened window. In the time since my first visit he'd been washed and fed, and the bed remade around him.

I said, "Mister Petrie, do you remember me? Doctor Spence."

There was a slight change in the rhythm of his breathing that I took for a yes.

I said, "Are you comfortable?"

Nothing moved but his eyes. Looking at me, then back to the window.

"What about pain? Have you any pain? I can help with it if you have."

Nothing. So then I said, "Let me close these blinds for you," but as I moved, he made a sound.

"Don't close them?" I said. "Are you sure?"

I followed his gaze.

I could see the shelter mound from here. Only the vague shape of the hill was visible at this hour, one layer of deepening darkness over another. Against the sky, in the last of the fading light, I could make out the outline of an animal. It was a dog, and it seemed to be watching the building.

I did as John Petrie wished, left the blinds open, and him to the night.

My accommodation was in the wooden barracks where the prisoners had lived and slept. I had an oil lamp for light and a ratty curtain at the window. My bags had been lined up at the end of a creaky bunk. The one concession to luxury was a rag rug on the floor.

I could unpack in the morning. I undressed, dropped onto the bed, and had the best sleep of my life.

With the morning came my first taste of practice routine. An early ward round, such as it was, and then a drive down into town for weekday Surgery. This took place in a room attached to the Library and ran on a system of first come, first served, for as long as it took to deal with the queue. All went without much of a hitch. No doubt some people stayed away out of wariness over a new doctor. Others had discovered minor ailments with which to justify their curiosity. Before Surgery was over, Rosie Kirkwood joined me fresh from the boat. Doctor Laughton had not enjoyed the voyage, she told me, and we left it at that.

After the last patient (chilblains) had left, Nurse Kirkwood said, "I see you have use of Doctor Laughton's car. Can I beg a lift back to the hospital?"

"You can," I said. "And along the way, can you show me where the Tullochs live? I'd like to drop by."

"I can show you the way," she said. "But it's not the kind of place you can just 'drop by.'"

I will not claim that I'd mastered the Riley. When I described it as clapped-out, I did not exaggerate. The engine sounded like a keg of bolts rolling down a hill and the springs gave us a ride like a condemned fairground. Rosie seemed used to it.

Passing through town with the harbour behind us, I said, "Which one's the undertaker?"

"We just passed it."

"The furniture place?"

"Donald Budge. My father's cousin. Also the Coroner and cabinet maker to the island."

Two minutes later, we were out of town. It was bleak, rolling lowland moor in every direction, stretching out to a big, big sky.

Raising my voice to be heard over the whistling crack in the windshield, I said, "You've lived here all your life?"

"I have," she said. "I saw everything change with the war. We thought it would go back to being the same again after. But that doesn't happen, does it?"

"Never in the way you expect," I said.

"Doctor Laughton won't be coming back, will he?"

"There's always hope."

"That's what we say to patients."

I took my eyes off the road for a moment to look at her.

She said, "You can speak plainly to me, Doctor. I don't do my nursing for a hobby. And I don't always plan to be doing it here." And then, with barely a change in tone, "There's a junction with a telephone box coming up."

I quickly returned my attention to the way ahead. "Do I turn?"

"Not there. The next track just after."

It was a rough track, and the word boneshaking wouldn't begin to describe it. Now I understood why the Riley was falling apart, if this was the pattern for every home visit. The track ran for most of a mile and finally became completely impassable, with still a couple of hundred yards to go to reach the Tullochs' home.

Their house was a one-storey crofter's cottage with a sod roof and a barn attached. The cottage walls were lime washed, those of the barn were of bare stone. I took my medical bag from the car and we walked the rest of the way.

When we reached the door Nurse Kirkwood knocked and called out, "Daisy? It's the Doctor to see you."

There was movement within. As we waited, I looked around. Painters romanticise these places. All I saw was evidence of a hard living. I also saw a dog tethered some yards from the house, looking soulful. It resembled the one I'd seen the night before, although, to be honest, the same could be said of every dog on the island.

After making us wait as long as she dared for a quick tidy of the room and herself, Daisy Tulloch opened the door and invited us in. She was wearing a floral print dress, and her hair had been hastily pinned.

She offered tea; Nurse Kirkwood insisted on making it as we talked. Although Daisy rose to the occasion with the necessary courtesy, I could see it was a struggle. The experience of the last week had clearly hit her hard.

"I don't want to cause any fuss, Doctor," was all she would say. "I'm tired, that's all."

People respect a doctor, but they'll talk to a nurse. When I heard sheep and more than one dog barking outside, I went out and left the two women conferring. Tulloch was herding a couple of dozen ewes into a muddy pen by the cottage; a mixed herd, if the markings were anything to go by. Today he wore a cloth cap and blue work pants with braces. I realised that the tweeds I'd taken for his working clothes were actually his Sunday best.

I waited until the sheep were all penned, and then went over.

I told him, "It would have been a girl. But . . ." And I left it there, because what more could I add? But then a thought occurred and I said, "You may want to keep the information to yourself. Why make things worse?"

"That's what Doctor Laughton said. Chin up, move on, have yourself another. But she won't see it like that."

I watched him go to the barn and return with a bucket of ochre in one hand and a stick in the other. The stick had a crusty rag wrapped around its end, for dipping and marking the fleeces.

I said, "Are those John Petrie's sheep?"

"They are," he said. "But someone's got to dip 'em and clip 'em. Will he ever come back?"

"There's always hope," I said. "What about his dog?"

He glanced at the tethered animal, watching us from over near the house. "Biddy?" he said. "That dog's no use to me. Next time she runs off, she's gone. I'm not fetching her home again."

"A dog?" Nurse Kirkwood said. She braced herself against the dash as we bumped our way back onto the road. "Senior Sister Garson will love you."

"I'll keep her in the barracks," I said. "Senior Sister Garson doesn't even need to know."

She turned around to look at Biddy, seated in the open luggage hatch. The collie had her face tilted up into the wind and her eyes closed in an attitude of uncomplicated bliss.

"Good luck with that," she said.

That night, when the coast was clear, I sneaked Biddy into the ward.

"John," I said, "you've got a visitor."

I began to find my way around. I started to make home visits and I took the time to meet the island's luminaries, from the priest to the postman to the secretary of the Grazing Committee. Most of the time Biddy rode around with me in the back of the Riley. One night I went down into town and took the dog into the pub with me, as an icebreaker. People were beginning to recognise me now. It would be a while before I'd feel accepted, but I felt I'd made a start.

Senior Sister Garwood told me that Donald Budge, the undertaker, had now removed the infant body for an appropriate burial. She also said that he'd complained to her about the state in which he'd found it. I told her to send him to me, and I'd explain the medical realities of the situation to a man who ought to know better. Budge didn't follow it up.

The next day in town Thomas Tulloch came to morning surgery, alone. "Mister Tulloch," I said. "How can I help you?"

"It's not for me," he said. "It's Daisy, but she won't come. Can you give her a tonic? Anything that'll perk her up. Nothing I do seems to help."

"Give her time. It's only been a few days."

"It's getting worse. Now she won't leave the cottage. I tried to persuade her to visit her sister but she just turns to the wall."

So I wrote him a scrip for some Parrish's, a harmless red concoction of sweetened iron phosphate that would, at best, sharpen the appetite, and at worst do nothing at all. It was all I could offer. Depression, in those days, was a condition to be overcome by 'pulling oneself together'. Not to do so was to be perverse and most likely attention-seeking, especially if you were a woman. I couldn't help thinking that, though barely educated even by the island's standards, Tulloch was an unusually considerate spouse for his time.

Visits from the dog seemed to do the trick for John Petrie. I may have thought I was deceiving the Senior Sister, but I realise now that she was most likely turning a blind eye. Afterwards his breathing was always easier, his sleep more peaceful. And I even got my first words out of him when he beckoned me close and said into my ear:

"*Ye'll do.*"

After this mark of approval I looked up to find the Constable waiting for me, hat in his hands as if he were unsure of the protocol. Was a dying man's bedside supposed to be like a church? He was taking no chances.

He said, "I'm sorry to come and find you at your work, Doctor. But I hope you can settle a concern."

"I can try."

"There's a rumour going round about the dead Tulloch baby. Some kind of abuse?"

"I don't understand."

"Some people are even saying it had been skinned."

"Skinned?" I echoed.

"I've seen what goes on in post-mortems and such," the Constable persisted. "But I never heard of such a thing being called for."

"Nor have I," I said. "It's just Chinese whispers, David. I saw the body before Donald Budge took it away. It was in poor condition after a long and difficult labour. But the only abuse it suffered was natural."

"I'm only going by what people are saying."

"Well for God's sake don't let them say such a thing around the mother."

"I do hear she's taken it hard," the Constable conceded. "Same thing happened to my sister, but she just got on. I've never even heard her speak of it."

He looked to me for permission, and then went around the bed to address John Petrie. He bent down with his hands on his knees, and spoke as if to a child or an imbecile.

"A'right, John?" he said. "Back on your feet soon, eh?"

Skinned? Who ever heard of such a thing? The chain of gossip must have started with Donald Budge and grown ever more grotesque in the telling. According to the records Budge had four children of his own. The entire family was active in amateur dramatics and the church choir. You'd expect a man in his position to know better.

I was writing up patient notes at the end of the next day's town Surgery when there was some commotion outside. Nurse Kirkwood went to find out the cause and came back moments later with a breathless nine-year-old boy at her side.

"This is Robert Flett," she said. "He ran all the way here to say his mother's been in an accident. "

"What kind of an accident?"

The boy looked startled and dumbstruck at my direct question, but Rosie Kirkwood spoke for him. "He says she fell."

I looked at her. "You know the way?"

"Of course."

We all piled into the Riley to drive out to the west of the island. Nurse Kirkwood sat beside me and I lifted Robert into the bag hatch with the dog, where both seemed happy enough.

At the highest point on the moor Nurse Kirkwood reckoned she spotted a walking figure on a distant path, far from the road.

She said, "Is that Thomas Tulloch? What could he be doing out here?" But I couldn't spare the attention to look.

Adam Flett was one of three brothers who, together, were the island's most prosperous crofter family. In addition to their livestock and rented lands they made some regular money from government contract work. With a tenancy protected by law, Adam had built a two-storey home with a slate roof and laid a decent road to it. I was able to drive almost to the door. Sheep scattered as I braked, and the boy jumped out to join with other children in gathering them back with sticks.

It was only a few weeks since Jean Flett had borne the youngest of her seven children. The birth had been trouble-free but the news of a fall concerned me. Her eldest, a girl of around twelve years let us into the house. I looked back and saw Adam Flett on the far side of the yard, watching us.

Jean Flett was lying on a well-worn old sofa and struggled to rise as we came through the door. I could see that she hadn't been expecting us. Despite the size of their family, she was only in her thirties.

I said, "Mrs. Flett?" and Nurse Kirkwood stepped past me to steady our patient and ease her back onto the couch.

"This is Doctor Spence," Nurse Kirkwood explained.

"I told Marion," Jean Flett protested. "I told her not to send for you."

"Well, now that I'm here," I said, "let's make sure my journey isn't wasted. Can you tell me what happened?"

She wouldn't look at me, and gave a dismissive wave. "I fell, that's all."

"Where's the pain?"

"I'm just winded."

I took her pulse and then got her to point out where it hurt. She winced when I checked her abdomen, and again when I felt around her neck.

I said, "Did you have these marks before the fall?"

"It was a shock. I don't remember."

Tenderness around the abdomen, a raised heart rate, left side pain, and what appeared to be days-old bruises. I exchanged a glance with Nurse

Kirkwood. A fair guess would be that the new mother had been held against the wall and punched.

I said, "We need to move you to the hospital for a couple of days."

"No!" she said. "I'm just sore. I'll be fine."

"You've bruised your spleen, Mrs. Flett. I don't think it's ruptured but I need to be sure. Otherwise you could need emergency surgery."

"Oh, no."

"I want you where we can keep an eye on you. Nurse Kirkwood? Can you help her to pack a bag?"

I went outside. Adam Flett had moved closer to the house but was still hovering. I said to him, "She's quite badly hurt. That must have been some fall."

"She says it's nothing." He wanted to believe it, but he'd seen her pain and I think it scared him.

I said, "With an internal injury she could die. I'm serious, Mister Flett. I'll get the ambulance down to collect her." I'd thought that Nurse Kirkwood was still inside the house, so when she spoke from just behind me I was taken by surprise.

She said, "Where's the baby, Misterr Flett?"

"Sleeping," he said.

"Where?" she said. "I want to see."

"It's no business of yours or anyone else's."

Her anger was growing, and so was Flett's defiance. "What have you done to it?" she persisted. "The whole Island knows it isn't yours. Did you get rid of it? Is that what the argument was about? Is that why you struck your wife?" I was aware of three or four of his children now standing at a distance, watching us.

"The Flett brothers have a reputation, Doctor," she said, lowering her voice so the children wouldn't hear. "It wouldn't be the first time another man's child had been taken out to the barn and drowned in a bucket."

He tried to lunge at her then, and I had to step in.

"Stop that!" I said, and he shook me off and backed away. He started pacing like an aggrieved wrestler whose opponent stands behind the referee. Meanwhile his challenger was showing no fear.

"Well?" Rosie Kirkwood said.

"You've got it wrong," he said. "You don't know anything."

"I won't leave until you prove the child's safe."

And I said, "Wait," because I'd had a sudden moment of insight and reckoned I knew what must have happened.

I said to Rosie, "He's sold the baby. To Thomas Tulloch, in exchange for John Petrie's sheep. I recognise those marks. I watched Tulloch make them." I looked at Flett. "Am I right?"

Flett said nothing right away. And then he said, "They're Petrie's?"

"I suppose Thomas drove them over," I said. "Nurse Kirkwood spotted him heading back on the moor. Is the baby with him?"

Flett only shrugged.

"I don't care whether the rumours are true," I said. "You can't take a child from its mother. I'll have to report this."

"Do what you like," Flett said. "It was her idea." And he walked away.

I couldn't put Jean Flett in the Riley, but nor did I want to leave her unattended as I brought in the ambulance. "I'll stay," Nurse Kirkwood said. "I'll come to no harm here."

On the army highway I stopped at the moorland crossroads, calling ahead from the telephone box to get the ambulance on its way. It passed me heading in the opposite direction before I reached the hospital.

There I made arrangements to receive Mrs. Flett. My concern was with her injury, not her private life. Lord knows how a crofter's wife with six children found the time, the opportunity, or the energy for a passion, however brief. I'll leave it to your H. E. Bateses and D. H. Lawrences to explore that one, with their greater gifts than mine. Her general health seemed, like so many of her island breed, to be robust. But a bruised spleen needs rest in order to heal, and any greater damage could take a day or two to show.

Biddy followed at my heels as I picked up a chair and went to sit with John Petrie. He'd rallied a little with the dog's visits, though the prognosis was unchanged. I opened the window eighteen inches or so. Biddy could be out of there like a shot if we should hear the Senior Sister coming.

"I know I can be straight with you, John," I said. "How do you feel about your legacy giving a future to an unwanted child?"

They were his sheep that had been traded, after all. And Jean Flett had confirmed her wish to see her child raised where it wouldn't be resented. As for Daisy's feelings, I tried to explain them with Tulloch's own analogy of a ewe unwilling to leave its dead lamb, which I was sure he'd understand. John Petrie listened and then beckoned me closer.

What he whispered then had me running to the car.

I'd no way of saying whether Thomas Tulloch might have reached his cottage yet. My sense of local geography wasn't that good. I didn't even know for sure that he was carrying the Flett baby.

I pushed the Riley as fast as it would go, and when I left the road for the bumpy lane I hardly slowed. How I didn't break the car in two or lose a wheel, I do not know. I was tossed and bucketed around but I stayed on the track until the car could progress no farther, and then I abandoned it and set myself to fly as best I could the rest of the way.

I saw Tulloch from the crest of a rise, at the same time as the cottage came into view. I might yet reach him before he made it home. He was carrying a bundle close to his chest. I shouted, but either he didn't hear me or he ignored my call.

I had to stop him before he got to Daisy.

It was shepherds' business. In the few words he could manage John Petrie had told me how, when a newborn lamb is rejected by its mother, it can be given to a ewe whose own lamb has died at birth. But first the shepherd must skin the dead lamb and pull its pelt over the living one. Then the new mother might accept it as her own. If the sheep understood, the horror would be overwhelming. But animals aren't people.

I didn't believe what I was thinking. But what if?

I saw the crofter open his door and go inside with his bundle. I was only a few strides behind him. But those scant moments were enough.

When last I'd seen Daisy Tulloch, she'd the air of a woman in whom nothing could hope to rouse the spirit, perhaps ever again.

But the screaming started from within the house, just as I was reaching the threshold.

YOU CAN STAY ALL DAY

MIRA GRANT

The merry-go-round was still merry-going, painted horses prancing up and down while the calliope played in the background, tinkly and bright and designed to attract children all the way from the parking lot. There was something about the sound of the calliope that seemed to speak to people on a primal level, telling them "the fun is over here," and "come to remember how much you love this sort of thing."

Cassandra was pretty sure it wasn't the music that was attracting the bodies thronging in the zoo's front plaza. It was the motion. The horses were still dancing, and some of them still had riders, people who had become tangled in their safety belts when they fell. So the dead people on the carousel kept flailing, and the dead people who weren't on the carousel kept coming, and—

They were dead. They were all dead, and they wouldn't stay down, and none of this could be happening. None of this could be real.

The bite on her arm burned with the deep, slow poison of infection setting in, and nothing was real anymore. Nothing but the sound of the carousel, playing on and on, forever.

Morning at the zoo was always Cassandra's favorite time. Everything was bright and clean and full of possibility. The guests hadn't arrived yet, and so the paths were clean, sparkling in the sunlight, untarnished by chewing gum and wadded-up popcorn boxes.

It was funny. People came to the zoo to goggle at animals they'd never seen outside of books, but it was like they thought that alone was enough to conserve the planet: just paying their admission meant that they could litter, and feed chocolate to the monkeys, and throw rocks at the tigers when they weren't active enough to suit their sugar-fueled fantasies.

Nothing ruined working with animals like the need to work with people at the same time. But in the mornings, ah! In the mornings, before the gates opened, everything was perfect.

Cassandra walked along the elegant footpath carved into the vast swath of green between the gift shop and the timber wolf enclosure—people picnicked here in the summer, enjoying the great outdoors, sometimes taking in an open-air concert from the bandstand on the other side of the carefully maintained field—and smiled to herself, content with her life choices.

One of the other zookeepers strolled across the green up ahead, dressed in khakis like the rest of the staff. The only thing out of place was the thick white bandage wrapped around his left bicep. It was an excellent patch job, and yet . . .

"Michael!"

He stopped at the sound of his name, and turned to watch as she trotted to catch up with him. His face split in a smile when she was halfway there.

"Cassie," he said. "Just the girl I was hoping to see."

"What did you do to yourself this time?" she asked, trying to make the question sound as light as she could. Michael worked with their small predators, the raccoons and otters and opossums. It wasn't outside the realm of possibility that one of them could have bitten him. If he reported it, it would reflect poorly on him, and on the zoo. If he didn't, and it got infected . . .

There were things that could kill or cripple a zoo. An employee failing to report an injury was on the list.

"No," he said, and grimaced sheepishly. "It was my roommate."

"What?"

"My roommate, Carl. He was weird this morning. Not talking, just sort of wandering aimlessly around the front room. I thought he was hungover again. I figured I'd help him back to bed—but as soon as he realized I was there, he lunged for me and he bit me." Michael shook his head. "Asshole. I'm going to tell him I'm through with this shit when I get home tonight. He's never been late with his share of the rent, but enough's enough, you know?"

"I do," said Cassandra, with another anxious glance at the bandage. "You want me to take over your feedings for the morning?"

"Please. I cleaned it out and wrapped it up as best I could. I did a pretty decent job, if I do say so myself. There's still a chance the smell of blood could get through the gauze, and well . . ."

"We don't need to exacerbate a human bite with a bunch of animal ones, even though the animal bites would be cleaner." Cassandra frowned. "You're sure it's cleaned out? I can take a look, if you want."

"No, really, I'm good. I just wanted to ask about the feedings, and it turned out I didn't need to." Michael's grin seemed out of place on the face of a man who'd just been assaulted. "That's our oracle."

"Ha ha," said Cassandra. "Get to work. I'll do your feedings after I finish mine."

"Yes, ma'am," said Michael, and resumed his progress across the green, seemingly no worse for wear. Cassandra frowned. It was entirely like him to brush off something as unusual and traumatic as being bitten by his own roommate, and it wasn't her place to get involved. At the same time, the situation wasn't right. People didn't just start biting.

"Classic Cassandra," she muttered. "If you can't find a catastrophe, you'll invent one. Get over yourself."

She started walking again, trying to shake the feeling that some of the brightness had gone out of the day. The sky was clear; the sun was shining; one little bit of human weirdness shouldn't have been enough to dampen her enthusiasm. But it was. It always was. Humans were strange. Animals made sense.

A tiger would always act like a tiger. It might do things she didn't expect, might bite when she thought it was happy to see her, or scratch when it had no reason to be threatened, but those times were on her, the human: she was the one who'd been trained on how to interact with wild animals, how to read the signs and signals that they offered. There was no class for tigers, to tell them how to deal with the strange, bipedal creatures who locked them in cages and refused to let them out to run. Tigers had to figure everything out on their own, and if they got it wrong sometimes, who could blame them? They didn't know the rules.

People, though . . . people were supposed to know the rules. People weren't supposed to bite each other, or treat each other like obstacles to be defeated. Michael was a good guy. He cared about the animals he was responsible for, and he didn't slack off when he had duties to attend to. He wasn't like Lauren from the aviary, who smoked behind the lorikeet feeding cage sometimes, and didn't care if the birds were breathing it in. He wasn't like Donald from the African safari exhibit, either, who liked to flirt with female guests, talking to their breasts when he should have been watching to be sure that little kids didn't jab sticks at the giraffes. Michael was a good guy.

So why was she so unsettled?

Cassandra walked a little faster. Work would make things better. Work always did.

The big cats were uneasy when Cassandra let herself into the narrow hall that ran back behind their feeding cages. They should have been in the big enclosures by this hour of the morning, sunning themselves on the rocks. Instead, they were pacing back and forth, not even snarling at each other, although her big male lion normally snarled at anything else feline that got close enough for him to smell. Cassandra stopped, the feeling of wrongness that had arrived with Michael blossoming into something bigger and brighter.

"What's wrong with you?" she asked.

The big cats, unable to answer her, continued to pace. She walked over to the first cage, where her female tiger, Andi, was prowling. She pressed the palm of her hand against the bars. That should have made Andi stop, made her come over to sniff at Cassandra's fingers, checking them for interesting new smells. Instead, Andi kept pacing, grumbling to herself in the low tones of a truly distressed tiger.

"You're not going to delight many families today if you keep hanging out back here," said Cassandra, trying to cover her concern with a quip. It was a small coping mechanism, but one that had served her well over the years: her therapist said that it was a means of distancing herself from situations she didn't want to be a part of.

It was funny how her therapist never suggested anything better. Surely there were situations that no one wanted to be a part of. What were people supposed to do then?

"All right," said Cassandra. "I'll go see what's going on. You stay where you are." She pressed the button that would close the tigers in their feeding cages, keeping them from venturing into the larger enclosure. Then she counted noses.

It was unlikely that she would ever mistake three tigers for four tigers, but it only took once. No matter how much they liked her, no matter how often she fed them, they would still be tigers, and she would still be a human being. They would eat her as soon as look at her if she caught them in the wrong mood, and then they would be put down for the crime of being exactly what nature intended them to be. So she counted noses, not to save herself, but to save them.

Always to save them.

The door to the main tiger enclosure was triple-locked, secured with two keys and a deadbolt. It had always seemed a bit extreme to Cassandra, especially since there was the concern that some zoo visitor—probably a teenager; it was always a teenager, on the news—would climb over the wall and scale the moat in order to try to pet a tiger. The number of locks involved would just keep any zookeeper who saw the incident from getting to the fool in time.

But maybe that, too, was part of the point. All it took was one mauling a decade to keep people out of the enclosures. It could be seen as a necessary sacrifice, letting the animals devour the one for the sake of the many who would be spared.

Even if that was true, Cassandra didn't want the sacrifice to involve her charges. Let some other zoo pay the price. Her tigers had done nothing wrong. They didn't deserve to die as an object lesson.

The day had only gotten prettier while she was inside, and stepping into the tiger enclosure—a place where tourists never got to litter, where snotty little children never got to chase the peacocks and squirrels into the trees, where the air smelled of big cat and fresh grass—made everything else seem trivial and small. She paused to take a deep breath, unbothered by the sharp, animal odor of tiger spoor clinging to the rocks. They had to mark their territory somehow.

The smell of rotting flesh assaulted her nostrils. She coughed, choking on her own breath, and clapped a hand over her nose. It wasn't enough to stop the scent from getting through. Whatever had died here, it had somehow managed to go unnoticed by the groundskeepers long enough to start to truly putrefy, turning the air septic. No wonder the tigers hadn't wanted to be outside. This was bad enough that she didn't want to be outside, and her nose was nowhere near as sensitive as theirs.

Hand still clasped over her nose, Cassandra started toward the source of the smell. It seemed to be coming from the moat that encircled the enclosure, keeping the tigers from jumping out. That made a certain amount of sense. Raccoons and opossums could fall down there, and the tigers couldn't get to them. If it had fallen behind a rock or something, that might even explain how it had gone unnoticed by the groundskeepers. They worked hard and knew their jobs, but they were only human.

So was the source of the smell.

Cassandra stopped at the edge of the moat, eyes going wide and hand slowly dropping from her mouth to dangle by her side as shock overwhelmed revulsion. There was a man at the bottom of the moat.

He wore the plain white attire of the night groundskeepers, who dressed that way to make themselves visible from a distance. He was shambling in loose, uncoordinated circles, bumping against the walls of the moat and reorienting himself, staggering off in the next direction. He must have been drunk, or under the influence of something less than legal, because he didn't seem to know or care where he was going: he just went, a human pinball, perpetually in motion.

From the way his left arm dangled, Cassandra was willing to bet that it was broken. Maybe he wasn't drunk. Maybe he was just in shock.

"Hey!" she called, cupping her hands around her mouth to make her voice carry further. "Are you all right down there?"

The man looked up, turning toward the sound of her voice. His face was smeared with long-dried blood. Staring at her, he drew back his lips and snarled before walking into the wall again and again, like he could somehow walk through it to reach her. His gaze never wavered. He didn't blink.

Cassandra stumbled backward, clasping her hands over her mouth again, this time to stop herself from screaming.

She had been a zookeeper for five years. Before that, she had been a biology student. She had worked with animals for her entire adult life. She knew dead when she saw it.

That man was dead.

⁂

"Now Cassandra, be reasonable," said the zoo administrator. He was a smug, oily man who smiled constantly, like a smile would be enough to chase trouble away. "I believe that something has fallen into the moat of the tiger enclosure, and I'm dispatching a maintenance crew to deal with it, but it's not a dead man. It's certainly not a dead man who keeps walking around. Did you get enough sleep last night? Is it possible that this is the stress speaking?"

"I always get enough sleep," she said, voice tight. "It's not safe to work with tigers if you're not sleeping. I slept, I ate, I drank water and coffee with breakfast, and I know what I saw. There's a man in the moat. He doesn't blink. He doesn't breathe. He's dead."

"But he's still walking. Cassandra, have you listened to yourself? You have to hear how insane this sounds."

Cassandra stiffened. "I'm not insane."

"Then maybe you shouldn't say things that make you sound like you are." The administrator's walky-talky crackled. He grabbed it, depressing the button as he brought it to his mouth. "Well? Is everything taken care of?"

"Dan, we've got a problem." The response was faint, and not just because of the walky-talky: the speaker sounded like he was on the verge of passing out. "She was right."

Dan blanched. "What do you mean, she was right?"

"There's a man in the moat."

"A dead man?"

"That's biologically impossible. He's up and walking, if non-responsive to questions. Angela thinks it's Carl from the night crew. She's going to get his shift supervisor. But he doesn't answer when we call his name, and he keeps snarling at us when we try to offer down a hook. I don't think it's safe for people to approach him. I think he might get violent."

Dan glared at Cassandra as he asked his next question: "But he's not dead."

"That wouldn't make any sense. Dead men don't walk."

"Roger. Deal with it. I'll order the path shut down. Call me as soon as you know what's going on." Dan put the walky-talky aside. "So you were right about the man in the moat. That's an unexpected twist."

"Wait." Cassandra shook her head, staring at him. "You can't be serious."

"About what?"

"About shutting the path to the tiger enclosures. People always get around the barricades. They want to see blood. You have to shut down that whole portion of the zoo. Or wait—we haven't opened yet. Can't we just . . . not open? For a little while?"

"Not open. Are you sure that's what you want to recommend?" Dan stood. "I can keep people away from that area. I can protect the innocent eyes of children. But admission fees are what pay your salary and feed your precious cats. Do you really want to risk that?"

"No," admitted Cassandra. "But the man in the moat . . . something's really wrong with him. We shouldn't let anyone in until we know what it is."

"Everything will be fine. Go back to work." Dan walked to the door and opened it, holding it for her in clear invitation. After a moment's pause, Cassandra walked out of his office.

The day seemed less beautiful now, tainted somehow, as if the stranger in her moat had cast a pall over the entire sky. Cassandra walked quickly back toward the tigers, intending to help the rescue crew, and paused when she saw a familiar figure staggering across the grass. Michael was walking surprisingly slowly for a man who had never met a path he didn't want to jog on. He looked sick. Even from a distance, he looked sick.

"Michael?" she called, taking a step in his direction. "Are you all right?"

He turned to fully face her, lips drawing back. Cassandra paused, eyes widening. His eyes . . . they were like the eyes of the man in the moat.

He was her friend. She should help him. She should stay, and she should help him.

She turned, and she ran.

The tigers were still locked in their feeding pens, prowling back and forth and snarling at each other. They were restless. Even for big cats trapped temporarily in small cages, they were restless. It was like they could smell the taint in the air, warning them of trials yet to come.

"Sorry, guys," said Cassandra, stopping in the aisle between cages, well out of the reach of questing paws. The tigers didn't want to hurt her. She was almost certain of that. They still would. She was absolutely certain of that.

Humans had intelligence, and thought, and the ability to worry about the future. It made them great at things like "building zoos" and "taking over the world," and it made them terrible at being predators. Humans could plan. Humans could think about consequences. Tigers, though . . .

Tigers existed to hunt, and feed, and make more tigers. They existed for the sake of existence, without needing to care about whether tomorrow was going to come. She envied them sometimes. No one ever told a tiger that it didn't know how to be what it was. No one ever said "you must be mistaken," or implied that there was something wrong with a tiger because it didn't want to spend its time with confusing, contradictory humans.

One of the tigers yawned, showing her a vast array of fine, sharp teeth. Cassandra smiled.

"No, I'm not going to feed you early just because you're locked in the feeding cage," she said. "We'll have you out in the enclosure in no time, and you know the guests get cranky when you spend the whole day asleep and digesting. Be good, and this will all be over soon."

As if to put an immediate lie to her words, someone outside screamed.

Cassandra was running before she realized it. A large metal hook on a pole hung on the wall next to the door, intended to be used to remove snakes from the visitor paths and animal enclosures. She grabbed it without thinking. Something about that scream spoke to the need for weapons, the vital necessity of self-defense. Whatever was happening out there, she didn't want to race into it unarmed.

The smell of decay hit her as soon as she was outside the tiger run. It was thinner than it had been on the edge of the moat. It was stronger at the same time, like it was coming from more than one source. The person screamed again. Cassandra kept running.

The tiger exhibits had their own "island" in the zoo's design, dividing the public-facing portion of a large oval structure between themselves. Cassandra came around the curve of the wall and froze, grasp tightening on the snake hook as her eyes went wide, trying to take in every aspect of the scene.

The man from the moat was no longer in the moat. The security crew dispatched to help him had obviously done so, using their own, larger versions of Cassandra's snake hook. Those big hooks were on the ground, discarded. The security team had bigger things to worry about, like the man who was even now sinking his teeth into the throat of one of their own.

She had been screaming, when he first started biting her. She wasn't screaming anymore. Instead, she was dangling limply in his arms while the other security people struggled to pull him away. For a dead man—and he was a dead man, he must have been a dead man; nothing living could smell so bad, or have skin so sallow and tattered, like he had slid down the side of the moat without so much as lifting his hands to defend himself—he had a remarkably strong grip. It took three security men to finally pull him off her.

He didn't go without a prize. The front of her throat came away with him, clasped firmly between his teeth. As Cassandra watched in horror, the security woman hit the ground, and the man chewed at his prize, still staring mindlessly ahead of himself.

This was not predation. Her tigers were predators, would eat a raccoon or a foolish zoo peacock as soon as they would look at it, but they were aware of what they were doing. There was a beautiful intelligence in their eyes, even when their muzzles were wet with blood and their shoulders were hunched in preemptive defense of their prey. Tigers knew. They might not understand the morality of their kills, but they knew.

This man . . . he didn't know. His eyes were blank, filmed over with a scrimshaw veil of decay. His jaws seemed to work automatically, inhaling the scrap of flesh he had ripped from the security woman.

The screaming hadn't stopped. It was just more dismay and anger now, as the security guards who weren't restraining the dead man tried to help their fallen coworker.

Then the man whipped around, faster than should have been possible, moving like he didn't care whether he dislocated his shoulders or broke his arms, and buried his teeth in the neck of the guard who was restraining him.

Then the woman without a throat opened her eyes and lunged for the person closest to her, biting down on their wrist. The screaming resumed, taking on a whole new edge of agony and horror. Cassandra's eyes got wider still. This was wrong. Everything about this was wrong, and she couldn't stay here any longer, she couldn't, this was wrong and unnatural and she needed to go, she needed to—

When she turned, Michael was standing right behind her.

He couldn't have been there for long; she had been working with predators for too long to be the kind of person who could be snuck up on. The same smell of putrefaction and decay that she had gotten from the man in the moat was coming off of him. Faint, as yet, but there; undeniably there. His eyes were filmed over, unseeing, unblinking.

"Please don't," she whispered.

He struck.

⊸⊷

Everything was a blur after that. Cassandra didn't know how she'd been able to escape; only that she had, because it was like she had blinked and been standing in front of the tiger habitat first aid station, with the door firmly closed behind her and the tigers snarling down the hall, still confined in their feeding pens, growing slowly angrier and angrier. Blood had been sheeting down her arm from the deep bite in her shoulder, painting everything in red. The marks of human teeth were unmistakable.

Even if they hadn't been, the fact that Michael had left one of his crowns behind would have made it impossible to pretend that she had been bitten by anything other than a human being. Gritting her own teeth, she used the tweezers to extract the small piece of white porcelain from her flesh. It was jagged where it had snapped off, and had probably done almost as much damage to Michael as he had to her. But he hadn't seemed to notice. He hadn't seemed to care.

He had been gone. Impossible as it was to contemplate, sometime between asking her to take care of his charges and their encounter outside the tiger enclosures, he had died, and kept on walking.

"No," said Cassandra. She grabbed for the hydrogen peroxide bottle and emptied it over the wound. It foamed and bubbled and stung like anything, like it was supposed to, but the feeling of rotten wrongness remained, worming its way down toward the bone. "No, no, no. No."

No amount of denial would heal the wound in her arm, or chase the smell of decay from her arm. Time seemed to jump again, taking her along with it: this time, when the haze cleared, she was applying butterfly clips to the gauze encircling her arm, sealing the bite marks out of sight. They continued to throb. Out of sight was not out of mind.

"No," said Cassandra, somewhat more firmly. She shook her head, trying to prevent another jump. What was this?

Think about it logically. Think about it like a biologist. Yes: that was the ticket. Think about it like she was back in class, like the worst that could come from getting the answer wrong was a bad grade.

Michael's roommate had been acting strange this morning. Michael had come to work with a bite from that roommate fresh on his arm. Michael had been behaving normally. Now Michael was acting like the man from the moat, and he had bitten her. Michael smelled of decay.

The man in the moat had smelled of decay when she had found him; her first impression had been that he was dead, yet somehow still standing. He was wearing the uniform of the night groundskeepers. She had seen wounds on him, but they had all been consistent with sliding down the side of the rocky wall between the fence line and the ground. What if nothing had bitten him? What if he'd just . . . fallen? It was always a risk, especially when the staff had to lean over the low retaining wall to retrieve something from the moat's edge. There had been falls before.

The woman, the security guard . . . the man from the moat had bitten her. He had torn her throat out with her teeth, and she had died. Cassandra had no doubt at all that the woman had died. She'd seen it. But after dying, she had started moving again, attacking another member of her team. So what if . . .

What if the man in the moat had died, only to come back again as something that wasn't quite human anymore? Sometime dead and terrible, that looked like a human being but smelled like the grave, and only wanted to . . . what? Feed? Bite?

Pass the . . . curse, infection, whatever it was along?

Cassandra turned to look at the bandage on her own arm. Michael hadn't died. Not like the woman. Michael had been fine. Human mouths were filthy things, but a bite wouldn't be enough to kill a healthy man, not under ordinary circumstances. She could feel the hot pulsing buried deep in her flesh, telling her that something was very, very wrong. Whatever had been in him, it was in her now too. Hurting her. Maybe killing her.

"Okay," she said, as much to hear her own voice as for any other reason. "I need to get out of here." Michael's mistake had been coming to work instead of going to the doctor. Doctors could flush the wound, could make things better. Could fix it.

She had long since accepted the fact that one mistake at her job could put her in the ground. But she wasn't going to die like this.

Feeling better now that she had a plan, Cassandra started for the door. She needed to get to the locker room, to retrieve her purse and her car keys. She would tell Dan that it didn't matter whether he closed the zoo today, because she wouldn't be here either way. She would be at the doctor's office, getting the flesh on her arm debrided and patched up, until the hot pulsing from within stopped. Until she wasn't scared anymore.

The tigers paced and muttered in their deep feline voices as she passed them, expressing their displeasure with the whole situation. Cassandra smiled wanly.

"I need to be sure the dead man isn't in front of your enclosure anymore before I let you out," she said. "If he fell back in, that would only upset you. I'll make sure someone comes to open the gates, I promise."

The tigers didn't speak English, but she had been their handler for years. Most stopped grumbling and just looked at her, staring with their wide amber eyes. They trusted her, as much as one apex predator could trust another.

"I promise," Cassandra said again, and opened the door to the outside.

The smell of decay was like an assault. Behind her, the tigers roared and snarled, protesting this invasion. She couldn't see anyone, but that didn't have to mean anything: not when she could smell them.

The zoo grounds had never seemed so claustrophobic before, so crowded with thick bushes and copses of trees. How many dead people could be lurking in there?

This couldn't be happening. This couldn't be happening. This couldn't be happening. She would get to the locker room, get her purse, and drive herself to the hospital. Maybe stop long enough to make a few phone calls, to make sure that whatever was going on at the zoo was only going on at the zoo. Michael's roommate was confined to their apartment, right? And Michael could have been exposed here, at work, picking up some . . . some novel parasite or tropical disease from one of the animals. Spillover diseases didn't always look the same in people as they did in their original hosts. This could be, could be a flu, or a respiratory illness, or something, that behaved in a new, terrifying way when it got into a human being. It could be

Cassandra crested the hill and froze, getting her first look at the zoo's entry plaza.

They had opened the gates after all. Sometime between her leaving Dan's office and coming to in the back hall of the big cat building, someone had turned on the carousel and opened the gates, letting the public—letting the dead—come to the zoo one last time. Bodies thronged around the admin buildings, moving with that same odd, graceless hitch that she had seen in

Michael, before he had attacked her. Whatever this was, it was spreading with horrific speed. Based on what she'd seen in front of the tiger enclosure, it wasn't unreasonable to think that it was spreading to everyone who was bitten.

Including her. She had been bitten. It was spreading—it had spread—to her.

Maybe that would protect her. If this was a disease, they might not attack someone who had already been infected. There was no sense in taking chances: if she got killed, who would take care of the tigers? They were trapped, penned in their little cages, without even the freedom of their enclosures to enjoy. She needed to make it back to them, now more than ever. But she also needed to see. She had to.

Carefully, Cassandra crept closer, sticking to the edges of the underbrush, where she might be ambushed, but she was less likely to be seen. When she came to one of the staff gates in the fence, she opened it and slipped through, relieved to see that the path was clear. These pathways were mostly used to transport things—food, equipment, sick animals—during the day; until the crowds got thick around noon, even the most privacy-loving zookeepers would tend to stick to the public side of the zoo. Maybe she could get to the gates without further incident.

Maybe it wouldn't matter.

The throbbing from her arm was getting worse and worse, reminding her with every step that this was how it had started for Michael. Whatever this was, it spread through the bites. If she didn't get medical help soon, she was going to become like them: dead, but still moving, still standing. Still biting. She was going to become a dangerous predator, something both more than animal and less than human.

The path ended at a slatted gate looking out over the zoo's front plaza. The merry-go-round was running, the painted horses dancing up and down in their eternal slow ballet. Cassandra stopped a few feet back, looking silently at the crowd that pressed around the classic amusement. They swayed and shambled, eyes glazed over and focusing on nothing. The smell that rose from their bodies was thick and undeniable, the smell of death, the smell of things decaying where they stood.

There had been people riding the merry-go-round when . . . whatever had happened here had happened. Some of them were still tangled in their safety belts, dangling from their painted horses, unable to free themselves as they pawed mindlessly at the air. Cassandra's stomach churned, bile rising in the back of her throat.

Soon that will be me, she thought. Soon I will be one of them.

What would happen to her tigers then? What would happen to Michael's otters, or Betsy's zebras, or any of the other animals in the zoo? Some of them were already doomed, unable to survive in this ecosystem, but others . . .

She could see the parking lot from her current position. There were dead, shambling people moving there, too. As she watched, a group of them caught up with a screaming man and drove him to the ground, where he vanished beneath a hail of bodies. This wasn't contained to the zoo. This could never have been contained.

Cassandra turned her back on the scene in the front plaza. She had work to do.

Any disease that hit this hard and spread this exponentially was going to overwhelm the city in a matter of hours: that was just simple math. One was bad; two was worse; four was a disaster. The numbers kept climbing from there, until she reached the point where the dead outnumbered the living, and there was nothing left to do but die.

If she hadn't been bitten, she might have tried to find another way. The big cat house, especially, had hundreds of pounds of raw meat stored in the freezers, just in case, and doors that were designed to stand up to a raging male lion. She could have locked herself inside with her beloved cats. She could have tried to wait it out.

But her arm burned, throbbing with every heartbeat, and she was starting to feel . . . bad. Feverish. Like she wanted nothing more than to lay down for a nap, to close her eyes and let her body finish the transition it was clearly aching to undergo. She needed to act quickly, before she was no longer equipped to act at all.

She began with the herbivores. She opened doors and propped gates, leaving the avenues of escape open for anything that wanted to take them. By the time she made her way to the aviary, there were zebras cropping at the lawn, ears flicking wildly back and forth as they scanned for danger. A kangaroo went bounding away down a side path, all but flying in its haste to get away. If there were dead people lurking in the bushes, they weren't fast enough to catch it.

The birds knew something was wrong. As she opened their cages, they flew away, wings clawing at the air, and were gone. Some of them would make it. Some of them had to make it.

Slowly, almost shambling now, she made her way back to the big cat house. The smell of decay was less noticeable now, maybe because she was adding to it. Maybe because her nose was dying with the rest of her.

There were so many doors she hadn't opened. There were so many cages she hadn't unlocked. But there wasn't time, and she didn't want to endanger her animals. Not in the end. Not when the burning in her arm had become nothing more than a dull and distant throb, like the nerves were giving up.

The tigers stopped their pacing when she came into view, staring at her silently. Cassandra pulled out her keys.

"Try . . . not to eat me, okay?" she rasped, and started down the line of cages. One by one, she unlocked them, leaving them standing open. When she finished with the tigers, she began releasing the lions, the cheetahs, until she was at the end of the hallway with a dozen massive predators between her and freedom. They looked at her. She looked at them.

One by one, they turned and walked away, heading for the open door; heading for freedom. Cassandra followed them until she reached the main door to the tiger enclosure. Her fingers didn't want to cooperate, didn't want to work the key or let her turn the lock. She fought through the numbness, until the bolt clicked open and she stepped through, into the open air on the other side.

The door, unbraced, swung shut and locked itself behind her. Cassandra didn't care.

Stumbling, she walked across the uneven ground to the rock where her big male liked to sun himself during the hottest hours of the day. She sat down. She closed her eyes. In the distance, the merry-go-round played on, a soft counterpart to the slowing tempo of her heart.

Cassandra stayed where she was, and waited for the music to stop.

HARVEST SONG, GATHERING SONG

A.C. WISE

Our first night out on the ice, we traded war stories. Reyes, Viader, Kellet, Martinez, Ramone, McMann, and me. We were all career military, all career grunts, none of us with aspirations for command. Captain Adams hand-picked us, brought us to the top of the world—a blue place all ice and snow and screaming wind—with only the vaguest idea of our mission. And none of us had cared. We'd signed on the dotted line, and had ourselves ready at 0500 on the tarmac, as expected.

The plane had dropped us at a base camp that used to be an Artic research station. We were all too restless for sleep yet, so we sat around the table and the remains of our meal, and talked.

"Why do you think Adams chose us for the mission? Why us in particular?" Reyes asked.

"To hell with that," Viader said. "What is the mission? Does anyone know?" She looked around the table.

"Extraction?" Martinez shrugged, underlining it as a guess. "We're here to get something top secret the military wants very badly."

"Okay," Reyes said. "So my questions again. Why us? None of us are anything special."

He looked around for confirmation; our silence agreed.

"My guess?" Kellet leaned back as she spoke, balancing her chair on two legs. "Because we're all fucked up."

When she leaned forward, her chair thumped down hard. The table would have jumped if Martinez and McMann hadn't been leaning on it. Kellet pointed at me first.

"You. What's your story? Syria? Iraq?"

"I was in Al-Raqqah." My stomach dropped, but I kept my voice calm.

"And?" Kellet's eyes were a challenge, bristling like a guard dog in front of her own pain.

"I was working an aid station on the edge of a refugee camp, distributing food, medicine, the basics." Under the table, my palms sweated.

Kellet leaned forward; Ramone fidgeted. Six pairs of eyes gave me their attention, some hungry, and some looking away in mirrored shame.

"I was handing a package of diapers to a young mother with a little boy on her hip, and another by the hand. Then the world turned black and red and everything went upside down."

I paused; instead of the room, the world flickered briefly, black and red.

"I was blown off my feet and ended up across the street, but I saw the second supply truck go up in a ball of flame. The first thing that came back was the smell."

"Burning hair," Viader said.

"Burning skin." This from Ramone.

I looked down. Snow ticked against the windows. Wind—cold and sharp as a knife—sighed around the corners of the research station. It sounded like teeth and nails, trying to get in. But I felt heat, the blooming fireball pushing me back, death breathing out and flattening me to the ground.

"The woman's legs were gone," I said. Silence, but for the snow. "But she kept crawling toward her baby, even though there was no way it was still alive. The other kid, her little boy, was vaporized on impact."

"You thought about killing her." Martinez's voice was soft, the intonation not quite a question. I raised my head, the muscles at the back of my neck aching and putting dull pain into my skull. "Putting her out of her misery?"

"Yes." The word left my throat raw. I'd never admitted it out loud; I'd barely admitted it to myself. Until now.

McMann produced a bottle. I didn't even look to see what it was before shooting back the measure he poured me and letting him refill my glass. My hands shook; they didn't stop as I swallowed again and again. The bottle went around, and so did the stories, variations on a theme. An IED tearing apart a market square, a hospital blown to smithereens instead of a military base; a landmine taking out three humanitarian aid workers.

We lapsed into silence, the answer to Reyes' question sitting heavy in our stomachs. Adams wanted us because we were broken. Because none of us had anyone at home who would miss us. We were expendable.

"Is that about right?" Kellet asked, looking over my shoulder.

I twisted around to see Adams watching us with her arms crossed. Her posture put a physical shape to something I'd been feeling as the stories and bottle went around. The seven of us had fallen into thinking of ourselves as a unit. Adams was outside of that—us against her. We'd follow her, but we didn't trust her. She'd drawn our pain to the surface; that made her our enemy.

"I'll tell you a story," Adams said, instead of answering.

There was one chair left against the wall. She dragged it over and turned it around, sitting with her arms draped over the back, another barrier between us and her.

"There was a map," she said. "A soldier in Kandahar sold it to me. He claimed it would lead us to bin Laden, back when we thought he was hiding out in a cave like some desert rat."

Adams snorted. Without asking, she reached for the bottle, and drank straight from the neck, killing what remained before setting it down with a heavy thunk. The wind chose that moment to pick up. The walls of the station were solidly-built, but it still sounded like something rattling and straining at the door.

"The map was hand-drawn, and we were idiots to follow it. I think my commander only humored me to teach me a lesson."

Adams twirled the empty bottle. The noise of the glass rolling against the wood made my skin crawl.

"A few clicks out from where the cave was supposed to be, our equipment went haywire. Our radios burst out with static, mixed with echoes of conversations from hours and days ago. Our compasses spun, never settling on north.

"We should have turned back. But there was a cave, right where the map said it would be, and if there was even a chance . . ." Adams grimaced.

"Ten of us went in. I was the only one who came out."

Adams pulled a small bottle out of her pocket, thick glass, stoppered with a cork. The air around it shivered, humming with the faint sound of wings. I sat forward, and saw the others all around the table do the same thing, a magnetic pull drawing us towards the glass.

"This is why we're here," Adams said.

I stared at the bottle, filled with honey, viscous and bright. It glowed. Martinez reached out, but Adams' look stopped him. He dropped his hand into his lap. Adams held the bottle up, turning it so we could watch the honey roll.

"They found me two days later, half a click from the cave entrance, or where it should have been, except it was gone. I was severely dehydrated, puncture wounds all over my body, half-dead from some kind of venom they couldn't identify. They got a med-evac copter to pull me out. Afterward, ground forces combed the area where the cave should have been, but nothing. Nada. It moves. Now it's here, so here is where we are."

We stared at her, uncomprehending, but she offered no further explanation, and her expression said there would be none, even though I could tell there was more she wasn't telling us, knowledge stored up behind her eyes. She honestly didn't seem to care whether we knew, even if it meant walking blind into the mission she still hadn't explained. The bottle disappeared, neat as a magic trick. The humming stopped, its absence so sudden my ears popped.

Adams reached into her pocket again, and I couldn't help flinching, mirrored by Reyes and Ramone. Instead of a bottle, Adams set her smart phone on the table, a video cued up.

"I had the honey with me when I came out of the cave. It saved my life." She didn't explain. Doubt flickered from Martinez to McMann to me, a spark jumping between us.

"If I'd been in my right mind, I wouldn't have told them about it. But." Adams shrugged, let the word stand. She tapped play.

The video had been shot on another camera phone, one struggling to decide between focusing on a glass cage or the rat inside it. Thin wires ran from multiple points on the rat's body.

"Lowest voltage," a voice off camera said.

"This is what happened when the doctors at the military hospital fed a rat the honey." Adams tone was non-committal, unconcerned. Only the set of her shoulders said different.

Following the voice was a distinct click like a dial being turned. I imagined the snap of electricity, the scent of ozone popping blue-white in the air. The rat showed no reaction.

"Next level," the voice on the phone said. "Sustain it longer this time."

Again the thunk of the dial, the ghost of electricity. I felt it shoot up my spine, wrapping around my bones. The rat cleaned its whiskers with its paws.

"What's the point of this?" Kellet said. "Why the hell would they feed a rat honey, then electro-shock it?"

"Because apparently I told them to," Adams said. She wasn't looking at the screen. "I told them it was the only way they'd understand."

"Maximum voltage." The camera lost focus briefly, coming back as the dial clicked again.

The scent of singed fur had to be my imagination.

"Jesus Christ." McMann breathed out.

Adams retrieved the phone as the video ended. She swiped from video to a photo and turned the screen so we could all see. Reyes covered his mouth before the screen angled my way. The rat lay on its side, one of its front limbs missing, the lining of its cage sodden and red.

"After they unhooked the wires, the rat gnawed its own leg off. It did it so quietly, they didn't notice until it was already dead."

Adams slipped the phone into her pocket.

"The cave is out there on the ice now. I can see it." Adams tapped the side of her head. There was no air left in the room; none of us could have questioned her even if we'd dared. "I'm sure it's obvious why the military has a hard-on for this honey. It's our job to bring it to them."

We set out at dawn. Thermal gear blanked our faces so we might have been the same person repeated eight times, not separate individuals. Spikes on our boots crunched against the ice, a raw sound with crystalline edges. The ice itself groaned, like bones breaking, the vast sound of massive trees cracking deep in a forest.

Trapped between the padded mask and my skin, my breath rasped. The holes to let it escape clotted with frost, leaving my face clammy. I kept my eyes on Viader ahead of me, and put one foot in front of the other. I was the tail of the party, Adams, the head.

The sky lightened, a blue so searing my eyes watered even behind the reflective goggles protecting them. Then just as suddenly, clouds rolled in, dark and heavy. Adams led us between two walls of ice, high enough to slice the sky into a thin ribbon and erase everything else. Sheltered from the wind, she called a halt, told us to eat protein bars to keep our strength up. I unwrapped mine, clumsy with my bulky gloves, lifting my mask just high enough to get the food into my mouth. Even so, the cold stung.

As I swallowed the last bite, my radio burst out in static. I jumped at the squawk so close to my ear. It was the snow made auditory, a grey-white flurry of noise. Then, in its wake, my grandmother's voice. And simultaneous with my grandmother's voice, the storm broke, howling down on us in our trench. Kellet caught my arm, and tugged me into a crouch. The others were doing their best to wedge themselves against angles in the ice.

I made myself as small as I could, pulling extremities close to the center, conserving heat while my grandmother chattered in my ear. Seven years dead, but her voice was clearer than Kellet's shouting over the storm. She sang, the way she used to while cooking Sunday dinner. I caught snatches of Slavic fairy tales, the rhythms she'd used to lull me to sleep as a child. As the storm's fury rose, she called my grandfather's name in the same high, panicked tone she used in her last days, not seeing the hospital room, but a long-ago village torn apart by war.

Martinez tapped my shoulder and I almost hit him.

"Adams says move."

My grandmother fell silent. The wind died a little, and I forced my legs from their awkward crouch. We edged forward. The fresh layer of tiny ice pellets skittering over the hard-packed ground made the going even rougher. Despite the spikes in our boots, we slid. The wind pushed at us, and the cold crawled under our clothes. Behind my mask, my teeth chattered.

"Hold here." Adams' voice cut over the storm.

Instinct made us gather around her in a half circle. The honey appeared in her hand, last night's magic trick in reverse. Everything else wavered in the dying storm, but it was bright and clear.

"It's the only way we're getting out of here alive," Adams said.

I didn't understand what she meant, but my body folded nonetheless, knees hitting the hard-packed snow. In my peripheral vision I saw Viader, Ramone, and the others do the same. Had Adams ordered us? The air hummed. I couldn't hear it over the wind, but I could feel it in my bones.

Adams didn't lower her mask, and goggles still blanked her eyes as she moved down the line. Despite the bulky gloves, her pour was deft. One by one Viader, Kellet, Martinez, Reyes, McMann, and Ramone lowered their masks and received Adams' honey on their tongues.

I should have felt frost burn immediately, but the proximity of the honey was enough to unleash the effect. I felt it sliding down my throat before it ever touched my tongue. Time bent, and the world went sideways. I had swallowed the honey, would swallow the honey, was always swallowing it. Then Adams tilted the bottle and let a drop touch my tongue.

Her limbs bent strangely, and there were too many of them. I saw myself reflected a dozen-dozen-dozen times in multi-faceted eyes. The honey was liquid fire. It was like holding a burning coal in my mouth, all heat and no taste. It was like swallowing stars. But as soon as I did it, I felt no pain.

The storm raged, but I couldn't feel it anymore. The wind became a hush, a lullaby. I thought of my grandmother, but it was someone else singing now. The words weren't Russian; they weren't even human.

Adams lowered her scarf. Her lips were cracked and bloody, but light clung to her. She was holy, we all were, and I watched in wonder as she used her teeth to pull her glove free, ran her finger around the inside of the bottle, and rubbed the last of the honey on her gums.

It should have been crystallized with the cold, rough against her skin, but it was as liquid as it had been when she'd poured it down my throat.

"Come on," she said. "Let's go."

Everything was sharp and bright after the honey. Adams walked on gravel and broken glass, fallen leaves. Each pellet of ice under her boots cracked inside my bones so I felt it as much as heard it. My blood thumped; eight of us breathed. I heard the crystals growing where my breath froze on my scarf—fractal ice patterns, branching and branching. Forming hexagons. Forming a structure like a hive. Rewriting my cells; instead of bones and blood, guts and liver, there were only endless chambers, dripping honey.

And under it all, the song. A lullaby, a nursery tale. Limbs like needles tucked me in, sealed me in wax and left me to dream. A girl with wild, tangled hair stood under a tree, its trunk lightning-struck and smelling of scorched woods. Bees swarmed the air around her, a steady hum, and liquid gold dripped down the seared bark.

Only she wasn't a girl, she was much older. Ancient. Her bones were already buried beneath the roots, her skin peeled from her ribs, her insides hollowed to make room for a hive. Raised welts dotted her skin, a secret language I could almost read. History a billion, billion, billion years old. A map. Bees hummed while her bones fed the tree and she stood in its shadow, buried and not buried, dead and alive.

All of it echoed through the song, inhuman concepts crammed into human form. The girl wasn't a girl, but a god, a seed, a splinter of history forced under my skin. I wanted to scream. Instead, I hummed, my whole body vibrating to the frequency of wings beating. I didn't feel the cold. None of us did. And together we walked, a segmented body with too many limbs, and Adams as our head.

⟜

Night fell, the sky darkening from plum twilight to deep blue-black. I didn't care where Adams was leading us. I could have walked forever. Ahead of me, Ramone stripped back his protective gear, exposing his arm to the elbow. Kellet pulled a folding knife from her pocket and cut open her palm. I listened to the blood plink-plink-plink on the snow.

The eight of us were joined, bound by an invisible cord. Reyes and McMann, Martinez and Viader, they were my skin and bone.

As we walked, something walked with us. Vast and impossible, just on the other side of a sky that was a blue-dark curtain, painted with stars. Long, thin limbs. Taller than the Empire State Building. Moving slowly. Singing. The song wanted something from me. It wanted me to change.

I wanted to.

I wanted to let the honey stitch my veins with threads of liquid gold. I needed it, more than I'd ever needed anything in my life. I wanted it to subsume me.

Al-Raqqah had been folded into my skin. The world torn apart, gone black and red; the flash-point explosion vaporizing a child. Those things lived between my bones, branched through my lungs. The honey was bigger than that. It could eat my pain whole.

Because it wasn't just honey, it was a civilization too old and terrible to comprehend. More had been lost than I could fathom. That was in the song. That was in the honey. It was too big to hold, and that gave me permission to let go.

Tears ran on my cheeks. They should have frozen, but the honey left my skin fever hot. It kept the moon from setting and the sun from coming up. I couldn't tell how far we'd gone, but it was still dark when Adams called a halt. We pitched tents from the packs we carried—packs whose weight we no longer felt—and built wind-blocks out of snow.

I watched the street in Al-Raqqah torn apart, an endless film reel flickering and superimposed on the night. I watched the mother crawl towards the burned remains of her child. I saw her other child caught in a loop of instant incineration, his mouth open in a wail. And none of it mattered.

In the here and now, I watched Reyes kneel to clear space for a fire. There was an old hunting trap buried under the snow. I saw it an instant before it happened. He put his hand into the drift, and metal jaws closed around his arm with a wet snap. Reyes saw it, too. The scene hung inverted in his eyes, playing out like the film reel of Al-Raqqah's destruction. And Reyes stuck his hand into the snow anyway.

He didn't scream. I thought of the rat in the cage, cleaning its whiskers as electricity sang through its body. I imagined teeth sunk into flesh and the rat tearing its leg off, bleeding out and at peace with the world. Reyes held his arm out, staring at torn cloth, red nerve, and splintered bone. He smiled.

Kellet and Viader moved to either side of me and together we pried the trap loose. Ramone sat by, watching his flesh redden, then go dead-white with the cold. McMann broke out the first aid kit, cleaning and bandaging the wound as best he could. Adams watched us, arms crossed, her expression saying we were wasting our time. Then Reyes sat down, still smiling, staring in wonder at the flames as Martinez built up the fire.

⟜

I don't remember sleeping. Light crept over the horizon, staining the snow pale gold and carving deep shadows in the hollows. We found Reyes' clothing, shed like skin and frozen into the ground. There were footprints, spaced farther and farther apart until they simply stopped. But no Reyes, not even his remains.

"It's like the story of the wendigo." Ramone's voice made me jump. His gazed was fixed on the last footprint, dragged long and impossibly sharp into the snow.

"It comes in the wind to snatch people into the sky, making them run faster and faster until their feet burn to ash. Sometimes, you can hear their voices in the sky, still screaming."

I didn't know the story they were talking about, but I tilted my head, listening for Reyes. I didn't hear anything except the low vibration of wings.

I don't remember sleeping, but before we woke to find Reyes gone, I woke with Adams' hand over my mouth. Or maybe it was after, or during. Time was funny on the ice.

"It's here," Adams said. "Come on."

She led me out of the tent and into the dark. I didn't ask where we were going. I could feel it—a vast system of caves under our feet, the earth gone hollow and strange. Juts of ice stabbed at the sky. I followed Adams through a maze of crystal spikes like crazed, broken teeth. There were steps cut into the frozen earth. We descended into an amphitheater for giants. One bowl below us, the other above us, the sky spattered with stars. Then we were underground.

I crawled behind Adams. Shadows moved on the other side of us. Echoes. Memories. Cracks in the real. The groove worn into the earth was a record. Adams and I were the needle, playing the sound. Occasionally, the record skipped, and we caught flickers of ancient things, impossibly out of time. Somehow, I knew: we were in the blind servants' tunnels, crawling out of sight of the masters. Wingless. Broken at birth so we couldn't flee.

There were bones in the ice around us. Australopithecus. Neanderthal. Hives hung in their ribcages, hexagons in place of hearts, dripping with honey.

"Here." Adams' voice jolted me into the present.

The ice wasn't ice anymore, but rock, a slick purplish-grey, like a thin layer of mica spread over slate, but the wrong color—night instead of gold. Or it was both. Ice and stone and rock the color of desert sand. Here and now and on a planet billions of years ago.

"Dig," Adams said.

My hands moved. I knew the patterns, written into my bones with the gathering song. I was born for this, scraping honey from the walls until my skin tore. Adams kept handing me bottles, which I filled before they disappeared into her coat, more than the folds of fabric should have been able to hold.

The cave buzzed. And all the while, the song echoed. The song like the one my grandmother used to sing while cooking Sunday dinner, calling ingredients and flavors together and compelling them to be a meal. A making song. It mellified my bones. It mummified me, rewriting me in a different language. I was the god-child beneath the tree, curled at its roots. The beginning and the end, the seed of the world. Bees thrummed the air and wrote maps onto my skin. Words. Commands, compelling me to be ancient, to be terrible, to change.

A harvest song. A blinding song. A binding song.

I obeyed.

A day later, or a million years later, we climbed out of the dark. The stars turned in dizzying motion overhead. If I kept going, I could climb right out of the world into the night. Like Reyes, pulled screaming into the sky. Adams caught me by the ankle and hauled me back down. I hit the ice, scrabbled and fought her, weeping and babbling incoherently.

She dragged me back over the snow, tucked me into my tent like a worker bee sealing up a little queen in a cell of wax. She whispered in my ear, a continuation of the song, that humming buzz, and this one said sleep, sleep.

I obeyed.

⊸

We packed our gear and left without Reyes. I thought about what we'd tell his family. We didn't have a body to bring home, no explanation to offer. He disappeared and we didn't look for him, because we knew he was gone.

The honey still sang in my veins. Had we accomplished our mission? Adams hadn't said a word about the tunnels. Only the abraded skin on my hands suggested I'd been under the earth, under some earth, gathering.

I had no sense of where we were in relation to the base camp. Like Adams' story, our compasses spun, and our GPS was useless. We'd given up on the radios long ago.

That night, we pitched our tents next to a wicked-blue crevasse, a scar in the ice so deep we couldn't see past a few feet even with our lights.

"Do you know where we are?" I asked Martinez, keeping my voice low.

He shrugged, unconcerned, and I moved to help him with the tents. I wanted to ask if he'd heard anything during the storm, or what the honey felt like on his tongue. Maybe Adams had taken him under the earth, too. Maybe she'd taken us all one by one. Maybe what Reyes had seen was too much. Enough to make him stick his hand in a trap. Enough to send him screaming into the sky.

Behind us, Viader and McMann built a fire. In the back of my mind, Reyes played on a loop, the trap closing on his arm. Each strike driving the tent peg into the ice became the snap of bone.

I smelled Viader's burning flesh an instant before it began to burn. And in my mind, the street in Al-Raqqah went red-black, and the woman crawled. I turned just in time to watch Viader walk into the flames. She made no sound. Her clothes went up in an instant. Then she stood there, eyes closed, humming. I recognized the song, felt the echo in my bones. Sparks kissed her cheek, ate away the skin and heat-cracked her jaw.

"It's beautiful," she said. Or maybe she said, "I'm beautiful."

Heat seared my cheeks, leaving salt-tracks dried to crystal. When had I started crying? I agreed with Viader; she was beautiful.

She was necessary.

Patterns had to be repeated. Viader burning wasn't really Viader, she was cities turned to ash, wax melting and the sound of wings, all the queens burning in their cells, keening, and the low, sad song as the tall creatures behind the sky moved from the beginning to the end of time.

None of us tried to stop Viader when she went to the crevasse. None of us tried to catch her as she dropped, plunging into the blue. She was a meteor, streaking into the abyss, never hitting the ground.

I woke to the sound of propeller blades, and the spray of ice and snow they whipped up as the tiny plane landed. Panic slammed through me. I couldn't hear the song over the engine, then the shouting as the team sent to pull us out hit the ground, boots too loud on the snow. Hands on me; I thrashed against them, all fists and elbows. A curse, muffled, as I landed an unintentional blow.

Three sets of arms now, restraining me. A needle snapped in my arm as they tried to give me a sedative. The ice fell away beneath me. I'd been wrestled into the plane and we were leaving. I looked around for Adams in a panic. I couldn't see her, then someone pushed my head back, strapped me down with more restraints.

A high, wild keening, like the sound of the queens in their cells as the city burned. I didn't realize until much later the sound was coming from me.

It's been almost a year since the ice.

A year of therapy, of convincing myself I couldn't possibly have seen what I thought I saw. Enough time for one honorable discharge, zero contact from Adams, and three hundred and sixty-five, give or take a few, nights of dreams—cities burning, honey dripping from bones, vast shadows crossing the sky. And all that time, the song, just on the edge of hearing. Last week, it started getting louder. Yesterday, I could feel it reverberating inside my skull.

Today, I got an email from Kellet. No subject line, all lowercase: martinez is dead. funeral at st. john redeemer, des moines, iowa. saturday 1100.

Light slanted over the church steps, leaving Kellet and Ramone in shadow as they stood in the doorway. Ramone had his empty sleeve pinned up against the wind snatching at our clothing and hair, blowing a storm of petals around our feet. I'd either forgotten or never known that he'd lost his arm after they pulled us off the ice. What had the past year been like for him, for Kellet? Had the edges of their hearing been haunted by inhuman voices, did they dream?

"What about McMann?" I asked.

"I tried to contact him, no response." A frown touched Kellet's lips, and I felt a twinge, a certainty that McMann was gone, and none of us had been there to witness it.

I didn't bother to ask about Adams.

Our footsteps echoed as we entered the church. A trio of women—Martinez's sisters? Cousins?—occupied the front-most pew on the left-hand side. A few others were scattered through the rest of the church, but the room was emptier than it should be.

"He shot himself." Kellet nodded toward Martinez's casket as we slid into a pew in the back.

A framed picture of Martinez, younger than when we'd known him, sat where his head would be. Draped over the middle of the casket, a spray of purple flowers gave off a sweet scent on the edge of rot.

I thought about Martinez in his tiny bathroom, knees bumping the edge of the tub as he sat on the toilet lid, lips puckered around the barrel of a gun. I'd never seen Martinez's apartment, or his bathroom. Certainly I hadn't been there when he died. Except I was there, now, bound as we had been on the ice. A unit. A hive.

Martinez's shoulders twitched, even as he fought to steady the gun. His cheeks were wet, the tears leaving glistening tracks in a face already carved by pain.

Shoot up. Shoot up, not in.

For a moment, I thought I'd spoken aloud. But the priest behind the lectern didn't pause, and neither Kellet nor Ramone looked at me. Were they seeing the coffin, or were they seeing Martinez's bathroom, too?

Martinez jerked, like he at least heard me. Like I was there and then, not here and now. He jerked, but he still fired and the bullet did its job, spraying blood and bone and brain onto the wall.

"I'm going to look for her," I said, as we stepped out of the church into the too-bright sunlight.

"We're with you," Ramone said; neither he nor Kellet had to asked who I meant, and of course they were coming with me. It was never a question.

"Why now?" Ramone leaned forward to be heard over the plane's engine. We'd tracked Adams to a small fishing village in the Yukon. Through the tiny windows, a network of rivers gleamed below us, the patchwork slowly resolving into detail as we descended. "Why did we wait almost a year?"

"We were scared." The engine drone swallowed my voice, but it was still just loud enough to be heard.

Kellet shot me a look, but didn't object. The look on Ramone's face was one of relief, like he was grateful someone had finally said it aloud. It was easier to breathe when I leaned back. The plane circled lower. After a year of sweat-soaked sheets and night terrors, we were going home.

We found Adams drinking in a bar converted from an old canning plant—corrugated metal walls, plain wooden furniture, the whole thing crouched on a pier jutting out over the water. It still smelled of fish, the odor laden over with sweat and beer. Peanut shells cracked underfoot. I thought of the ice cracking and tiny bones.

Adams kept her back turned, her shoulders hunched until we were close enough to touch her. Heavy cable-knit sweater, thick rubber waders, her hair cropped jagged-short. She didn't even look up when she spoke.

"I have a small plane," she said. "I can fly us out anytime."

She'd been waiting for us. Waiting while we gathered our courage. Waiting until Martinez died, the breaking point to push us into action. She finally turned, and I heard Kellet catch her breath, the smallest of sounds. Adams' eyes were gold, the color of honey, the color of fire and the stars we'd swallowed on the ice. All this time with the dreams, and she hadn't fought them. The blind things in the tunnels, the girl under the tree, the shadows, vast and slow moving behind the sky—they'd gotten inside her, and she'd changed.

The base camp Adams flew us to was smaller than the one we'd left from a year ago. Curtains divided cots set along the walls for the illusion of privacy. There was a stove, and stores, but none of us were hungry. Unlike the first base camp, the wind didn't howl outside. Only silence, the vast stretch of snow waiting beyond the walls, and the stars pricking the darkness. The ghosts were already in the room with us, the spaces of absence carved in the shadows for Reyes, Viader, Martinez, and McMann.

Kellet and Ramone retreated to their cots soon after we arrived. I was too jittery for sleep. As for Adams, I couldn't tell. I'd always found her hard to read. With her golden eyes and the new angles of her bones, it was even harder. Her impatience, her anger, seemed to have burned away. Instead, she was literally worn thin, almost flickering, like it took all her effort to stay in this world.

A fat candle sat on the table; its light sharpened the planes and hollows of Adams' face and spread the illusion of wings behind her. She retrieved a bottle of whiskey, tilted it toward me in a silent question. I nodded and watched her fill two glasses. She'd been waiting for us for a year, the strain evident in her movements. I still didn't understand why.

"What happened a year ago?" The question came out more plaintive, more broken than I intended.

Adams swallowed from her glass, lips peeling back in a grimace.

"You'll have to be more specific." Her honey-gold eyes pinned me, testing.

I didn't know how to ask about the tunnels and the gathering song. I came at it sideways.

"The mission. Did we succeed?"

"You kidding?" Adams knocked back half of her remaining drink; this time when she showed her teeth, it was wholly feral. "Soldiers who feel no pain, who keep fighting even with massive wounds, or missing limbs, soldiers who can go days without eating or sleeping? The honey was never for them. I thought you understood that."

So, she had run, when the plane came for us, and she'd never turned over the honey.

"Then why?" Why bring us on the mission at all? The map was in her head. She never needed us.

The look Adams returned was pitying. She surprised me further, covering my hands with her own. Her palms were rough, calloused, like she'd spent a year hauling nets in the cold.

"They need us to remember." Her words sparked something, a twinge of recognition. "We need them to forget."

Them. Where her hands covered mine, her skin hummed. Those things from beyond the stars, they'd fought and died and torn themselves apart. When the tall things from beyond the sky had come, signaling the end of their time, with the last dying breath of their civilization, they'd made a song. They'd flung their ghosts across the stars, casting their tattered remains into the void, hoping to find something for those echoes to hold onto, someone to remember. And like Adams said, we, the eight of us, had needed them in order to forget.

Those tall, attenuated creatures. Their footsteps extinguished stars, put out of the light of worlds. What did it mean that I'd seen them in the sky? Were they an echo of the past, or a glimpse at our future? Maybe it didn't matter. Maybe all that mattered was letting go.

I thought of Viader, falling, Reyes, vanishing into the night. Cities burning, a child buried under a tree. The seeds of a civilization that required blood and sacrifice to grow.

Adams reached into her pocket, and set a bottle on the table. Honey, the same color as her eyes. It sang, and my blood sang back. The harvest song, the lullaby. We'll seal you up, but you'll dream, and all your years of darkness will be worthwhile.

Gold dripped from my bones, written with history. I could taste it, curling my tongue with its sweetness so sharp it drowned everything else.

Adams touched the bottle with one finger. I shivered.

She unfolded a knife from her belt, and used the blade to nick the meat of her palm. Honey oozed to the surface. She didn't need the cave anymore. She licked the wound, glancing at me. I pressed a hand against my chest. Under my breastbone, a hollow space waited for a hive.

Adams stood, skinning her shirt over her head. Her dog tags gleamed as she turned around. Her back was covered in raised welts, smooth and white, old scars.

"The map," she said.

I stood, palm outstretched. The heat of her skin beat against me like a flame. Her scars met my touch, pearls stitched into her skin, the puncture wounds she'd received in Afghanistan. I traced my hands over the pattern. Stars, arranged in configurations eons old.

"It was never meant to show where we were going," Adams said. "But where they had been."

History, written on her skin. She guided me to one of the two remaining cots and pushed me down gently. The light from her eyes cast shadows on her cheeks. The bottle of honey appeared in her hand. Straddling me, Adams pulled the cork from the honey with her teeth. Liquid the color of a full harvest moon—ripe to bursting.

Adams dipped a finger in the honey and held it out to me. I pictured light leaking from her eyes like tears, seeping from her pores. The harvest song howled in the dark. Shadows bent over us, long fingers needle-sharp and venom-tipped, ready to stitch through skin and bone.

I sucked her finger clean.

It wasn't sex, it was more like farewell. Adams flickered, her translucence overwhelming her solidity. My hands closed on empty air, but the memories kept flowing through me, hers and theirs.

I was in the cave in Afghanistan. Thousands of hexagonal cells covered the walls. Needle-thin legs brushed my skin, then the first stinger entered me. My body arched, my flesh trying to escape my bones. I was being torn apart, threaded back together. Adams' map wrote itself onto me, stars burnt into my being in a pattern from before the world. But there was no pain. Bones dripped honey, skeletons embedded in the walls, but still living. They remembered. Everything. Wings beat inside the remains of their papered skin, a steady hum. A whole lost world, resurrected inside the dead, calling them—calling me—to sing.

There's a certain quality of cold where temperature becomes color. Ramone, Kellet, and I walked into a solid wash of it, thick enough to feel. I'd shown them the map on my skin, and they'd agreed, we had to finish it out on the ice where it began.

We didn't go far, just enough to be alone with the wind. Out here, we would hear Reyes when he screamed. We'd see Viader when she rose like a meteor out of the dark.

"I dream about Viader sometimes," Kellet said as we huddled around a Coleman lantern in our tent. "Her flesh is still burning. She's only got one eye. There are holes in her skin and she's holding embers in her jaws."

"Reyes came to see me," Ramone said. His right sleeve hung by his side, his left hand held a mug filled with vodka. I'd never noticed the paler band of skin on the fourth finger before.

"He came to my bedroom window. His breath fogged the glass, so I knew he was really there. His hair was all matted. His teeth were broken, and his eyes were the color of dried blood. He tapped on my window."

Kellet put her hand on Ramone's knee. I could feel myself spreading in the wind. Still here, already gone.

"I didn't know what else to do, so I let him in. He crawled under the covers with me. I thought he'd be cold from being out on the ice for so long, but he was warm. He smelled like red meat and wet dog.

"He put his head on my chest." Ramone touched his knuckles to the spot. "And then he just lay there, listening to my heart."

Ramone swallowed the rest of his drink, squeezing his eyes closed.

"The next morning, he was gone. That was the first time I tried to kill myself. I took pills, but then I chickened out and called 911."

I put my hand on his other knee. Outside, the ice sang.

"I watched Martinez kill himself," I said, my own unburdening. I'd already given the honey Al-Raqqah, everything else I had to give. This was the last thing.

"I wish we knew what happened to McMann," Ramone said.

"He's probably waiting for us," I gestured at the tent flap.

Kellet reached for my hand across Ramone's knees. She tangled her fingers with mine, and our joined hands covered Ramone's one good hand. My lips brushed the corner of Ramone's mouth. He closed his eyes again. We went soft, slow, all three of us together. It still wasn't sex. It was a map, a shared history, a surrendering of our pain.

When they left in the dark, I didn't hear them go.

I cut a bottle of honey from my veins, bled it into the glass, then drank it whole. Burning like Viader, I walked out into the cold.

My body is going up in flames, bits of me flaking away to ash. Martinez is here. I can see the stars through the hole in his skull. Reyes lopes beside me. Viader is an angel. Adams' footsteps crunch through the snow, getting farther and farther apart. Ramone and Kellet, even McMann, they're all here. We're separate, but together, strung across vast distances, never alone.

There are tall, vast shapes moving across the sky. They have no faces. Their skin blushes like the aurora borealis, studded with stars. They are the beginning and the end. They harvest the honey; they sing the song. The wind dies down, and it's the only thing I can hear. History, writing itself onto my bones. The dead being reborn.

Harvest. Gather. Change.

Open your bones, they sing. Make space inside your skin.

Let us in.

THE GRANFALLOON

ORRIN GREY

I can feel their eyes on me. I'm perspiring, a trickle of sweat itching its way between my breasts, and my face and ears are flushed and hot, like they always are whenever I have to talk in front of anyone. I rub my palms against my slacks, catch myself doing it and stop, guiltily. I'm supposed to be the grownup here, the expert, the pro from Dover. I look out over their heads, their faces, trying not to focus on any one of them, until I catch the eyes of Constance—Professor Fisher now, I guess—behind her black horn rims. She smiles at me, the same look that I'm sure she gives her students when they're giving a report in front of the class and faltering as badly as I am. I try to smile back.

"Who here has ever stood in front of the mirror, staring at your reflection, waiting for it to do something? To wink at you, maybe, or smile when you don't? To reach out a hand, or tell you a secret? Even the least imaginative among us sometimes studies our reflection in the hopes that we'll finally see what other people see when they look at us." That's how I start.

I don't understand why I'm talking to Constance's class, not really. It's not like my area of expertise really overlaps with their subject, not beyond the most basic levels, where just about everything overlaps with just about everything else. No, strike that, I know exactly why I'm here. I'm here because Constance asked me to be, and even though it's been years, and I don't know what she hopes to gain, I still can't say no to her, not any more now than I could then.

My mouth goes dry, my tongue thick. There's a bottle of water on the desk beside me, and I pick it up, unscrew the cap and take a drink, my taste buds crying out for something stronger, even though I haven't had anything stronger in nineteen months, unless you count the Coke that I drink way too much of these days.

I tell them about how ancient people believed that what we see in the mirror was not just light bouncing an image of ourselves back into our eyes, but rather our souls, our other selves. I tell them that's why vampires don't reflect in mirrors, which gets a scattered chuckle, at least, which lets me take a breath that I didn't even know I was holding. I ask if anyone has ever been in a house where the mirrors were covered after someone had died, and only two people raise their hands, but still, they're paying attention, that's something. I talk about how dead souls could get trapped in mirrors, about fetches and doppelgangers.

It all seems to be going okay, so I let myself relax a little, feel the heat starting to leave my ears, the half-an-alprazolam I dry-swallowed just before walking into the room finally starting to take effect. I walk in front of the desk—Constance's desk, I think as I lean back, feel the edge of it bite into the back of my legs, just below my ass—and then I tell them about psychomanteums.

"Since before we had mirrors, we've been using our reflections to scry. To see events that are far away, in the past or the future. To communicate with god, or the devil, with the dead, or just with our Jungian secret selves. A psychomanteum is sort of the ultimate expression of that."

I force myself to inhale again, to exhale, my breath hot and raspy in my throat, so I take another swallow from the bottle of water that I'm surprised to see is already more than half empty, but I suddenly realize that my bladder is not. "In its most basic form it could be as simple as a mirror turned to reflect only darkness, or two mirrors facing one another. You've all been in an elevator or a bathroom or a hotel lobby where you got to see the effect that can produce, right? Like an infinite hallway, stretching in both directions. Maybe you've even had the sense that you can almost look around one of those corners, or like something else is waiting there to look at you, as soon as you turn your back. Now imagine that same effect in a dark room, with nothing in your line of sight but the mirror, and no illumination but candlelight. You're beginning to get the idea of a psychomanteum."

Are they actually paying attention now? Sitting up a little straighter, their eyes a little brighter? I lean away from the desk, forward into the crowd, warming to my topic as I'm imagining that they are too, thinking, for the first time since I walked into the room, that maybe Constance isn't just devising some obscure means of torturing me, that she knows what she's doing after all.

"Some people took them farther. Not just two mirrors, but entire mirrored rooms, where every wall was a reflective surface, a thousand hallways leading off into infinity, a thousand portals to . . . well, you name it. Like that room at the end of *Enter the Dragon*, and who knows, maybe that's what Han kept that room around for. They were popular among the Victorians, during the heyday of spiritualism, but every now and then a new one turns up, even today."

When I'm finished talking, they don't clap or anything—I'm in a classroom, not a conference—but Constance comes down to the front of the room and thanks me for coming, asks me to wait a moment once class is over, as if I would leave, and then addresses her students. She says some stuff about them being grateful for me being there, and I smile and dip my head without even really thinking about it, and then she calls out a handful of them by name, reminds them of some sort of extra credit project that's happening after school. I consider slipping out to pee, but the urge is no longer as strong now that their attention is off me.

Then they're all gone in a clatter of shoes and a squealing of chairs being pushed back from desks, of backpacks being slung over shoulders and voices receding down the hallway, until the last student out closes the door and Constance and I are alone in the room that a few minutes ago felt so big and now suddenly feels too small. She smiles at me, that same reassuring smile, and this close I can see how brown her eyes are. One of my hairs has come loose from my ponytail, and she reaches up and tucks it back behind my ear, but I can see that she doesn't mean anything by it, that it's just old habits dying hard.

"Thanks for coming, Mads," she says, in a way that ends with a comma, not a period. It was always Mads with her, never Madeline or even Maddy. I try to smile back, but all my anxiety has washed me out now, and being so close to her is hard, so I think it looks more like a grimace. I want to touch her hand, her face—old habits, like I said.

"Somehow I get the feeling that I'm here to do more than give a film studies class a lesson on psychomanteums," I say, feeling like it comes out harsh when I want it to be cool.

Her hand, which has been sort of hovering between us, falls back to her side, then clasps the other in front of her skirt. She looks down at the floor, then back up at me, and her brown eyes have gotten harder, brighter, in the second they were turned away. "Have you ever heard of the Granfalloon?"

⟜

She tells me about it on the way to her house. Somewhere over the years she's traded her old Volkswagen—and I don't know how many other cars in-between—for a Mini. One of those long ones, what're they called? Country something? This is the second time I've been in it; she picked me up from the hotel before class. She also offered to give me a ride from the airport, but I opted to take a cab, just like I opted to stay in a hotel instead of the proffered guest room at her place, which didn't seem like a great idea. The hotel was themed rustic—faux log cabin, taxidermied animals in the lobby, a copy of a John Constable painting above the bed—and there was a bar with nobody in it, which was probably also not a great thing for me, but so far so good.

"Did you ever read Vonnegut?" she asks me, and I shake my head.

"I never got into him in high school, and if you don't get into him in high school then it's too late."

"Me neither," she says, "but I saw the George Hill version of *Slaughterhouse-Five* back in film school. Anyway, the word *Granfalloon* apparently comes from Vonnegut and means 'a proud and meaningless association of individuals.'"

"Weird name for a movie theater," I tell her, looking out the window, watching the houses pass by, thinking how much nicer this neighborhood is than mine, how much nicer her house is going to be than my little apartment.

"Frederick Castle was a weird guy," she replies. "Technically *Doctor* Frederick Castle, but not a real doctor, he got his PhD in parapsychology from a mail-order course. His money came from his wife, Vera Warner, whose father was a condiment tycoon, back when you could still be called a tycoon of things like condiments."

"With a name like Castle, you'd think you'd be ready-set for a themed name for your movie theater."

"You'd think that, but no, it was always the Granfalloon. Maybe that's why it never did very well, or maybe it's because Castle built it at the tail end of the era of big movie palaces, when multiplexes were already taking over. It never made it as a first-run theater; Castle mostly ended up showing revival stuff. I've got a flyer in my office advertising a showing of *Snow White and the Seven Dwarfs*."

"But you're not interested in the usual revival stuff," I say, kind of cutting her off, but not really, just jumping her forward to where I know she was headed anyway.

"No," she bites her lip in that way she always has, the way she did when she talked dirty, to delay what she's going to say, to build up suspense a little. "There were always stories, from the day the theater opened its doors. They said that Castle screened . . . rarer things, for a more select clientele during the off hours."

"Stag films?"

But she shakes her head, "No, at least, not in most versions. Early experimental movies, in some tellings, more sinister stuff in others. They say he had a sort of club, spiritualists or theosophists or something. That they screened movies by Muybridge and Mills, Bartlett and Whitcomb and Duplante."

I don't know any of those names besides Muybridge—Constance forgetting that I'm not one of her students and never really was—but I'm beginning to guess why I was actually invited here.

We met in my one and only film class, but it isn't as bad as it sounds. She was still just a TA then, and we didn't start dating until after I was out of the class anyway. If what we were doing then could really be called dating. I think we went to one movie and then some drinks and then, as we would jokingly put it later, we fell into bed together. And I guess if you can fall in that easily, then you shouldn't be too surprised when it's easy to fall back out. That's what I'm thinking as we pull up in front of her house, which is just as much nicer than my apartment as I had imagined it would be, though my imagination hadn't conjured up the suspiciously nondescript van parked in the driveway.

"Are you an electrician during the summer months?" I ask, gesturing toward the van, and she just laughs.

"If it looks like I am, then that's probably a good thing."

I don't ask what she means, because I'm pretty sure I'm already putting it together, and my suspicions only get more and more confirmed when—after we sit around the island in her kitchen making small talk and eating Chinese delivered by a college kid who's as white as I am—some of her students start showing up at her front door, the same ones she reminded about their extra credit earlier.

There's four of them, all dressed normally when they arrive, but all carrying gray coveralls, and it isn't long before they've zipped them over their street clothes and are standing in Constance's kitchen like mechanics up to no good. The kitchen's got big patio doors, and by now it has gotten dark outside, turning them into mirrors that throw our reflections back at us, albeit hollow-eyed and flanked on every side by darkness. Even Constance—who has changed into pants by now—hauls out a matching pair of coveralls and pulls them on. Only I don't get a pair. I'm guessing I won't need one.

It says something about our relationship now—and maybe even more about our relationship then—that she never actually tells me what she wants me to do, never asks me if I'm going to go. It's just assumed. When everyone piles into the van and I see that the back is full of bolt cutters and pry bars, I'm not surprised, just mad in that weird, distant, echoing way that I thought I had left behind years ago but that I guess Constance is still capable of bringing out in me after all this time, like so many other things.

The Granfalloon, when we reach it, looks almost like any other old movie theater, except that it sits alone in a wasteland of vacant lots and rented chain-link fence. The cab actually carried me by it on my way from the airport, but I didn't know what it was. Just an old building, faded and tired, waiting to be torn down, like everything around it already was. At night, though, it looks a little more ominous, or maybe that's just my dawning knowledge of our mission here.

The outside walls are painted purple, a color that I imagine was rich once but has faded with the sun like an old car's dashboard. Constance says that from the air it looks like the Pentagon, but with no empty space in the middle. Just the theater's five screens, all facing outward, like a wagon train circled for protection in an old western.

There's an unassuming car parked outside the gate of the chain-link fence when we pull up, the engine running. A guy with the look of hired security leans on the hood. He seems nervous, but like he's trying to make that nervousness resemble irritation instead. Constance leaves the van running and gets out to talk to him for maybe a minute, maybe less, and then hands him something from the pocket of her coveralls. Something that I assume is the rest of a payoff; after all, you don't take bolt cutters and pry bars to someplace you're really allowed to be. "Just lock it behind you when you leave," the guy says to her retreating back, loud enough that I can hear him in the passenger seat of the van. It sounds an awful lot like, "And remember, I was never here."

As we pull through the gate, Constance starts to talk. Though it's directed at the kids in the back, I think it's for my benefit, because they all seem to know already. She says that the theater's been closed for more than a decade, ever since Dr. Frederick Castle just up and disappeared one day. His wife apparently did the usual hoop-jumping to file a missing person's report, all that jazz, and when he'd been gone long enough she declared him dead *in absentia*. She'd never really been a movie person—that was all him—so when he was gone she let the place close, but kept the taxes faithfully paid and the bulldozers at bay, fending off several attempts at "urban renewal" over the intervening years.

"A month ago, she finally kicked off as well," Constance says over her shoulder as we come to a stop in front of the theater's gilded front doors, "and with nothing left to stop them, the city is coming next week to knock the place down."

The word is that when the Granfalloon was shuttered, Castle's wife wouldn't let anyone come in to mess with anything, insisting that her husband might come back any day, even after she'd had him declared dead. Which means that if there was anything of value here when Castle disappeared—those secret films he supposedly screened, for example—it would still be here, unless somebody else had already beaten us to it. I'm guessing that's the story Constance has fed her star pupils about why we're here.

They cut the lock on the chain holding the front doors shut, and it slithers to the ground like a heavy, dead snake. Once we're on the other side, our flashlights come on, making cones of light, illuminating clouds of dust that roll in the air like fog, kicked up by our footsteps. I've never been here before, but still the lobby looks familiar, recalling dim memories of other small movie theaters from when I was little. The same tacky carpet and concession stand. While the others discuss their plans, I shine my light along the posters in their frames that line the wall. There's one for *Son of Frankenstein*, another for *The Mummy's Ghost*.

The others head upstairs, to where the projection booths would be, and where the film would be stored, if there's any film left. Before she leaves, Constance lays her hand on my shoulder. "You know what you're looking for?" she asks, and I just nod, happy to see the pride and excitement in her smile, hating myself for how happy I am.

I wrote my dissertation on occult structures. Rooms—and in some cases whole buildings—designed to serve some kind of supernatural or metaphysical purpose. Ghost traps, psychomanteums, séance rooms. It's not as weird as it sounds, not really. When you think about it, after all, what's a church? A building built for communicating with god, right?

I think some of Constance's excitement about this is bleeding into me, or maybe I'm just excited on my own, it's hard to tell amidst the clamor of nerves and adrenaline and, yes, let's be honest, horniness. Still, I make myself take it slow, walking first around the perimeter hallways ringing the five auditoriums. What I'm doing is a kind of archaeology, and like any other archaeology, it's easy to get over-excited, go too fast, and spoil it somehow. I count the black-painted doors as I pass them; it helps get my breathing under control. One, two, three, four, five. When I'm back in front of the first door, I take a deep breath, and step inside.

The auditorium is as black as the inside of a satin bag, the beam of my flashlight creating a glowing tube in the murky gloom, much as the projector must have done when the theater was still running. The walls are painted midnight blue, with little asterisks of silver and gold and white that wink where my light touches them. I think they're meant to represent stars, but they're weirdly abstracted, as if drawn by a child playing with crayons. The seats on either side of me are red, velvety, and so are the rotting curtains that frame the big ghostly screen. The place reminds me more of the auditorium in my old high school than any modern movie theater.

The mood of the place is infecting me, working its way under my skin, and I half-expect to see something in every seat my light sweeps across, but there's nothing between me and the screen, which, as my eyes adjust, seems faintly luminous itself, as if it has absorbed all the light that poured into it over the years, and is still spilling some little bit back out. I walk up to it and raise my hand, pressing it against the fabric, reaching for the secret chamber that is waiting for me on the other side.

I've heard of stuff like this before. Not a psychomanteum in the truer sense, but more like one in reverse. A room built not for seeing or conversing, but for receiving. There's a photo that makes its rounds in my field of what is supposed to have been a Nazi experiment, mediums arrayed around a table as if in a séance, with oversized headphones clapped over their ears. In West Virginia one time, I actually got to go inside a trailer where all the walls in one room had been stacked with TVs, one on top of the other, all facing in and all tuned to different channels. I remember that the place smelled like rotting garbage and old cat litter, even though I never saw a cat.

Something like that is what I'm expecting on the other side of the big X we cut in the screen with a carpet knife. I've rounded up Constance and her students, and she's standing there in the semi-darkness, her eyes so bright they're practically glowing, her smile so big it's impossible for it not to be at least a little infectious. The others seem excited, restless, constantly moving around. And so much younger than they seemed when I was standing in front of a room full of them earlier today. Was I that young, when Constance and I first got involved? I must have been, but it doesn't seem possible.

"Wouldn't there normally be speakers behind the screen?" one of the students asks, I think her name is Erin.

Constance nods, looking around. "They're in the walls here," she says. I gather that they had some luck upstairs—an old Constantin Orlok picture in the original uncut Spanish version, a handful of one-reel experimental films by one Elizabeth Cairns—but I can tell that, for Constance, this is and always has been the real objective. Why she invited me back into her life. I almost offer to let her go first through the dark aperture, but I'm the expert here, so I'm the first one into the place on the other side.

I'm expecting a step down, but there isn't one. The floor of the chamber has been raised, so it's the exact same dimensions as the backside of the screens that compose its walls. It's also totally empty except for the chair—big and thick and bolted to the floor—and the skeleton that occupies it.

More like a mummy, really. An ossified husk in the shape of a man, the skin turned to parchment and drawn up around gaping sockets of eyes and nose and mouth. Its clothes are those of a Vincent Price villain, complete with velvet smoking jacket and cravat, appearing untouched by time.

But it isn't the skeleton that stops me in my tracks, that makes me almost drop my light. While I didn't necessarily expect to find a dead man in the room, I'm not exactly surprised, either. Frederick Castle, of course, gone mysteriously missing all those years ago.

No, it's not the skeleton itself, it's something else, something *about* the skeleton, some intangible thing that makes it difficult to look at, that pushes my eyes off it. It's that feeling you get when you've been staring at television static for far too long, so that you've started to replace the visual white noise with a thousand flies crawling over one-another.

I try to look at the corpse, but can't do it. I know what it looks like; when I'm not trying to look directly at it, I can pull up an image, clear and sure in my mind's eye. Those ridiculous clothes, those black cavities staring out at me, darker and deeper than the darkness of the room, like a black cat in a dark hallway. But as soon as I try to look I just *can't.*

A noise fills my head, like a million voices talking at once, and my eyes fill with the motion that comes from staring into pitch darkness for so long that your imagination peppers it with moving shapes, and the next thing I know I'm looking away again, at the walls or at the floor or at anything except for that body in that chair.

That's how I see the secret door, the one that would have let him in and out, bricked up now from the other side. I imagine his wife finding him here, seeing just what I've seen and turning away, as I've had to turn away, and bricking him up here and leaving the theater to stand as a tomb for him because she doesn't know what else to do. I imagine the nights that he sat here—how many?—when the auditoriums on the other side of the screens were full of people, the images flashing at twenty-four frames a second on the walls around him. What was it he expected to harness here? Adoration? The awe and wonder of the audience directed up at the screens?

I imagine his frustration, night after night, waiting for something, anything, and feeling nothing, until, finally, he felt the heart attack or embolism or stroke that killed him and then, only then, when he was no longer a man but only a shell, an empty vessel, only then to be filled with this mad buzzing emptiness that still radiates off him in waves that fill my head with noise and push my eyes away.

One by one the others file in behind me, see what I've seen, avert their eyes as I have. Constance even reverts briefly to Catholicism and crosses herself. No one is comfortable speaking, just quiet curses and half-articulated sounds in the dark, everything muted and bracketed by the radioactive emptiness that pours constantly from the corpse in the chair.

We don't really talk about what we've found. The van ride back to Constance's house is mostly silent, with each sentence spoken seeming to crack the air like a gunshot. The others get in their cars and leave, and Constance offers me a drink, then catches herself, shakes her head, smiles, apologizes.

At the door to my hotel room, Constance offers to come inside. Her hand touches mine, and I want her to, every part of me aches for her to, but I don't think it's a good idea, maybe an even worse idea now than before, so I shake my head. She leans forward and kisses me on the cheek before she goes, and I resist turning my head to place my lips in the path of hers. When she's gone, I sit on the bed and think about that empty bar down in the hotel lobby. I look at the phone and think about calling my sponsor, but I haven't talked to him in months, and I don't want to admit how tempted I am now, and I sure as shit don't want to tell him why.

So I take a shower instead, turning the water up as hot as I can stand it, baking my skin red. Every time I close my eyes under the spray, I see that room, behind those screens. My nerves are still alive and tingling, woken by the adrenaline of the night and by so much time spent in such close proximity to Constance, so I lay on the bed and masturbate furiously and frustratingly. I swallow another alprazolam and turn on the TV, turning the volume way down, letting its insensate light and noise beat against me until I finally fall asleep.

In my dream, I'm sitting in the secret chamber of the Granfalloon, with the flickering walls alive around me. All five screens are identical, and I know they're identical, even though I can really only see the three that are before me. Every screen is showing *Snow White and the Seven Dwarfs*, but everything looks wrong from this side, sinister and backward, the eyes and mouths just black spots like holes burned in the screen, like the gaping sockets of Castle's corpse, staring out at nothing.

I wake with a start, my hand reaching out of its own accord to grope for the remote and turn off the TV. I pull on some sweatpants and a loose t-shirt and stand at the door for way too long, my palm pressed against its cool surface, talking myself out of walking barefoot down to that bar, or to the liquor store down the street that my brain marked without my permission when the cab first carried me here. I press my head against the door, close my eyes, but that doesn't help, because behind my eyes I see those seven fucking dwarfs, marching along the wrong way, their eyes black and pitiless.

I open my own eyes, dig around in my bag until I locate a dollar bill, and walk down the hall to the Coke machine. The drinking may come later, but I'll be damned if it's going to be tonight.

I don't see Constance again before I leave town. She offers via text to take me to meet my flight, but I tell her I'll take a cab. On the way to the airport, I have the cab take me by the Granfalloon. In the daytime it looks less imposing, just a squat purple building alone among the vacant lots, waiting for the bulldozers to come and make way for a parking garage or a Starbucks.

The airport terminal is full of TVs, and I find myself unable to look at them for more than a few seconds. Every time I do, I see those black sockets, feel that terrible buzzing nothingness coming off the thing that was once Castle's corpse, and I can't help but wonder if that's truly what flows out of us when we sit down in the dark and surrender ourselves to the images on the screen.

FAIL-SAFE

PHILIP FRACASSI

The door was thick. The room, well-made. I knew. I'd seen. Every step.

I never heard Mother screaming in the night. I knew she was, it was obvious. I'd seen her with the cameras. Father had made me watch when I was young. Father had worried I didn't fully understand. Fully believe.

But I did.

My favorite days were when it was over and Mother was allowed to return. Mine and hers both, I imagine. She was never happier than *after*. She would hold me and squeeze me tight, and I'd laugh and she'd pepper my cheek, neck and forehead with kisses.

Father would stand by, watching, smiling, looking haggard and wistful. After giving us time to reshape our natural bond, he would join as well, hugging us both. Kissing us greedily.

I loved my parents. Loved them dearly.

Deep down, secretly, I worried I would wake up one morning and find myself alone. That the room would take them from me. I'm only a boy still, sure, only twelve. But I'm growing. Learning.

When Father first built the room I had watched. Had helped, even. In those days, Mother had been held elsewhere. By men I did not know. By friends of my father's. But she always came back, happy and healthy, hugging and kissing, just like it was after the room was built. I liked it better, having the room here. Liked her being *home*, with me and Father.

The room is not large, but it's well built. It has many fail-safes. Father explained these to me as he built them into the room's design. The walls are steel. Thick, slick, impenetrable from the inside. The door also, steel. One foot thick of it. Handle-less. Released by internal bolts that are hidden behind the metal-plated walls.

There is one light. A pair of fluorescent tubes behind a cage in the ceiling. Impossible to reach. That's what we thought.

The restraints, however, are *really* impressive.

Crafted to hold, but not hurt. That's what Father said. To keep her, and us, safe. I nodded when he told me these things. I felt I was learning, getting older, wiser. Helping.

"Then there's the gas," Father said, showing me the vents high in the walls, just below the ceiling. Far above where even her unnaturally-lengthened hands could reach them. "That's our last line of defense," he said, ruffling my hair, messy as always. "That's if all else goes to hell."

I nodded, but Father could see I didn't fully understand. He knelt down, took my arm, pressed kinda hard, looked into my eyes.

"If she gets free of the restraints," he pointed to them lying listless on the smooth concrete floor, "she still can't leave the room, see?"

I nodded again, growing.

"If she gets to the door, does some damage, then I hit a button, and *whoosh!*" He expanded his hands in a circle to show the spreading affect. "She gets the gas."

"Then what? She goes to sleep?"

Father nodded, dropped his eyes a moment, then found mine again. "She'll be dead."

I thought about this. "And we'll know she's dead because of the cameras."

Father smiled broadly, eyes sparkling with pride. "That's right, Son. The cameras."

We were standing in the half-constructed room at the time, and Father pointed to high corners where reflective orbs were tucked. I waved, saw a distorted reflection of another boy—a smeared, tiny boy—waving back.

"We'll watch her and make sure she's dead before we come in," he said, then put a firm hand on my shoulder. "She'd want us to be sure."

I knew this was true, because she'd told me so a hundred times herself. She told me to always be sure, if something were to go wrong, to always be sure we'd killed her. "I might lie," she said. "I might pretend."

"Like a game," I said.

Mother smiled and nodded, stroked my hair away from my forehead. "Like a game you must always win."

When Father and I left the room, now deemed ready, Father stopped by the heavy steel door, the shining heads of the sliding bolts poking inch-high from the edges of its frame.

"One last thing," Father said, taking off his lab coat and hanging it on a bent steel nail next to a mask and a tarnished yellow rubber suit. "And this is the most important thing of all. There's always a chance, a very, very slim chance, that Mother won't keep turning. That she'll turn once, and stay that way. Forever. You understand?"

I nodded.

"If that happens . . . or, if anything goes wrong. If I'm not here, for whatever reason . . ." He paused, because there were too many wrongs to think about. "Well. There's one last fail-safe."

I waited, thinking it silly, knowing Father would *always* be around, but willing to hear him out, to learn.

"It's a timer, see?" he said. "I start it every time your mother goes into the room. If for *any* reason, any reason at all, I don't stop or reset that timer in twenty-four hours, the room fills with gas."

"Whoosh!" I said, mimicking Father's hand gesture.

"That's right," he said. "That way, if something, well . . . if something goes amiss, then all you have to do, see, is wait it out. You don't have to do a thing. Just wait twenty four hours, and that timer will tick off, and things will be handled inside. The gas will go off, and the gas is poison. Poison that kills. You got that?"

I remembered something from my lessons. "Like the cat."

Father's eyebrows came together in confusion.

"Schroeder's cat."

Father thought a second, then laughed out loud, a wonderful laugh that filled the steel and concrete room he and his friends had just completed.

"Schrodinger!" Father bellowed, still laughing. Laughing so hard he was wiping tears from his eyes. "Schrodinger's cat. Not Schroeder. He's from *Peanuts.*"

Father continued laughing, wiped his eyes once more, and rested a hand on my shoulder, pushed me gently from the room.

"But yeah. Sure, I guess. Like that."

We tested the room many times. Mother inspected every inch of the walls, the floors, the vents, the cameras. Inspected the restraints, the heavy steel cuffs, the chains and cables that held them, the clasps that bound them fast to the wall.

The first night we were all a bit nervous.

Mother had always been with Father's friends on these nights. They were infrequent, yes, but regular. But Father seemed calm, and we both helped secure her to the new restraints. She smiled at me as I locked her wrist tight. She watched our work closely, studied the clamps around her wrists, tested them. She yanked her arms against them hard, making them clink. I took an unthinking step away from her.

"Not that testing them now matters," she said that first time, smiling sadly at Father. "I'm half the strength."

"If that," Father agreed, but nodded. "They'll hold. They could hold a mad gorilla."

Later, Father and I sat outside the room. Father watched the monitors closely. I sat on a stiff, dusty-smelling couch behind him, reading a comic book.

"There," Father said.

I set down my comic, walked over to the monitors. I watched in grainy color, like a television, as my mother turned.

Her eyes, then her skin. She looked up at the cameras, watching us watching her. As I looked on in fascination, she went still. Sort of . . . slumped. I held my breath. *A trick*, I thought.

Then she went mad. A whipping tornado wrapped in flesh, all teeth and nails, venom and fire. Her mouth spread open, chin dropping impossibly, eyes bulbous, her muscles doubling in size, squeezing against the inside of the restraints. She screamed at the pain. Pure fury. She looked so strong. She thrashed and kicked like a pale-skinned monster.

"Holding just fine," Father said, sounding relieved, and a bit proud. "Holding just fine." He turned to me and smiled.

"She won't be getting us tonight."

In the months after Mother's first night in the new room, things went perfectly. I enjoyed having Mother home more, even though some nights I couldn't see her. It comforted me because she was still *there*. Still home. Even if she was locked away.

Father's friends came over and watched the first few times, assuring themselves of the safety and security of the room. I sat nearby and listened while Father explained the fail-safes to them. He patiently explained the gas, and the timer.

The men watched, some shifted their feet. A few turned away from the monitors.

When they were all there, crowded around, I could not see Mother on the screens, but I knew she had already turned. They called it turning because she turned a little and she was one thing. But then she kept turning and was herself again. Turning and turning forever. The Great Fear was that she would turn and not turn back. It had happened to others. I always prayed it would never happen to her.

"Here," Father said, and flipped a switch.

The room filled with screams. Mother's screams. They were terrible. They reminded me of a screeching eagle I had seen on television. Screeching so loud it echoed in the room around us, swirled around our heads.

"She could talk if she wanted," Father said, raising his voice to be heard. "She could sound just like herself. But not when she's angry like this." He watched her writhe a moment, as if considering. "Not when she's hungry."

"Turn it off," one of the men said, the biggest one.

Father flipped the switch and the screeching stopped, leaving the room so thick with silence no one dared speak.

"Should he be here?" one man said, tilting his head toward me. Another man turned around to look at me, eyes narrowed, but by doing so exposed the small screen on the desk. I could see Mother, naked and twisting, bleeding from the wrists, teeth large and snapping, black tongue whipping across her lips.

Father looked at me, then back to the man, holding his eyes. The man seemed nervous and swallowed and said nothing more.

After a while they all seemed satisfied. They waited until the morning, waited until Mother was okay to be let out. Father went in, dressed her, treated her wounds. After a few minutes they came out. As always, Mother seemed tired, her skin slick with sweat and covered in a hot rash but pleased to have it behind her. Wrapped up in a coarse green blanket, she looked at me and winked. I tried to wink back—it was hard doing just one eye—but she smiled so I figured I'd done close enough.

They all talked then for a long time. I got bored and wandered across the basement and upstairs. I went outside, closed my eyes, and listened to the sounds of the neighborhood. Cars rolled by. Kids laughed from somewhere in the distance; behind a neighbor's house, maybe. I opened my eyes, saw a man watering some bushes with a hose, watching me. It was so sunny and peaceful . . . I'll never forget it.

After a few minutes I turned away, went back inside, and closed the door.

Once the routine had been established, I felt we were just like any other family.

The last evening, we sat around the dinner table. Mother had prepared fish and salad. We didn't eat meat.

I drank milk. I drank a lot of milk, because my parents assured me it would help me grow. And I wanted to grow. Wanted it more than anything. I would be thirteen in two days, and I couldn't wait. Thirteen meant manhood. Thirteen meant adult.

That night, I watched my parents eating, smiling, content. My father opened a bottle of wine, which is what parents drink instead of milk. I watched Mother closely, looking for signs. I'd been trained what to look for, although I knew it was unnecessary, because Mother always knew first, knew *way* before Father and I knew. We almost depended on her, in a way, to tell us. To let us know when it was time to go into the basement, into the room.

If she didn't tell us, it's possible we might not know in time. That's how fast it happens. One second, a loving mother. The next, death.

"Mom," I said, picking up a green bean with my fingers and biting off the tip. Mother turned to study me, cocked her head.

"You have a fork," she said.

I took another bite. She always said that about the fork.

"Do you think . . ." I said, flushed with the embarrassment of the young and ignorant. "Will I be like you one day?"

I knew there were others like Mother. Hundreds. I also knew you could become like her if she attacked you. Spread into you. Mostly people died when attacked, but some lived, and then they turned too. Like vampires or zombies, but real.

Mother's eyes went to Father, who looked at me like I'd said something sad. Their eyes met a moment while he gathered his thoughts.

"The truth is, Son, we don't know," he said, wiping his mouth with a napkin before setting it neatly down on his empty plate. "Not yet."

I finished the green bean, took a drink from the heavy milk glass they always gave me. "When?" I asked.

"Soon," he said, looking more troubled. "When you're . . . when you've become a man."

"I'm almost thirteen now!" I cried out excitedly, knocking a knife off the table with my elbow. It clattered to the floor.

"It's more than just age that makes a grown-up."

I was confused. "What, you mean when I'm a dad?"

Father laughed, and Mother smiled, but it was a sad smile, the one she used before she went into the room. The one she used when she told me everything would be all right.

"No, not that kind of man. When you are through puberty. There will be . . . signs," he said, then hurriedly added, "but it's nothing for you to worry about."

I smiled, set down my milk and burped. "Because we can build another one. Just for me," I said. "Right? We're good at it now. I can have my own room."

Father looked at his plate, set his fork down on the table.

Mother said nothing.

Later, we were watching television when Mother announced she was going to turn, and soon. She said it felt strong this time. Hours, maybe.

Father looked at her, nodded. He turned off the program, a documentary on the migration of birds.

I was sad, even more sad than usual. I sulked but knew it wouldn't make a difference. I didn't want Mother to get locked up, so I delivered my best, haughtiest frown, and walked out of the living room. Mother called after me, but I kept walking into my bedroom and shut the door behind me.

After a little while I grew bored of sulking, and anxious about Mother. I ventured back out, expecting my parents to already be downstairs. But they were there, waiting.

"You okay?" Father said.

I nodded, sniffed, wiped at my mouth. I turned to Mother. I didn't want to help that night. I wanted to be a normal boy, with a normal mother. I didn't want to see her turn. That night, I figured, I could pretend.

"Will you tuck me in?"

She set down her magazine, stood up and came toward me. I was too big for her to pick up, but she hugged me hard. I felt her hot breath on my neck. It smelled foul.

I snuggled underneath the covers while Mother stood over me, stroking my forehead. The light in the ceiling gave her a halo and left her face in shadow. Her bob of hair made her head seem bigger than it was, expanding the black shape of her head upward and outward, tiny wings at the tips.

"Will you sing me to sleep?"

She nodded, reached out and switched off the light. I felt her weight on the bed. I wondered how much time she had.

"What shall I sing?" she asked, her voice a husky whisper. "How about *Jesus Loves Me*?"

I shook my head, then realized she probably couldn't see me. Her eyes sparkled in the dark. She coughed.

"Sing the hush one."

She placed a hand on my arm, squeezed it. She sighed, then sang softly, almost in a whisper.

Hush little baby, don't say a word,
Mama's gonna buy you a mockingbird.

I closed my eyes, let Mother's voice float into my mind, fill my body with her love, her words. I let myself drift.

And if that mockingbird won't sing,
Mama's gonna buy you a diamond ring.
And if that diamond ring turns brass,

Mama's gonna buy you . . .

She stopped suddenly.

I opened my eyes. I was almost asleep, annoyed she'd stopped at my favorite part. "A looking glass," I prodded. "Like Alice."

Her hand tightened on my arm. She was a dark shape on my bed.

"Mom."

The dark shape did not move, did not speak. Her hand squeezed me harder.

"Mom."

Hours later, Father came upstairs, poked his head into my room.

"You awake?" he said.

"Sorta," I replied. I hadn't been, but he'd woken me. Like he needed to talk, to not be alone.

"I just, well, I wanted to tell you everything is just fine, Son. Nothing to worry about." He laughed, but strangely. Like pretending. "It's all pretty routine now, eh?"

I nodded, hoping it was true, and closed my eyes.

"Well, goodnight then. I love you."

I listened to Father leave. After a moment, I heard the sound of the basement door open, heard his footsteps going down the stairs.

As the sound of his steps grew fainter, then vanished, exhaustion took hold. I fell back asleep; a strange half-sleep, half-dream state. I dreamed of the cells inside my blood, forming and re-forming, clustering like galaxies, making me a universe.

I woke in the middle of the night, shaking and upset. I'd had a nightmare. I couldn't remember. The house was deathly quiet.

Father would still be in the basement, watching Mother.

My bedroom was pitch dark. There was no moonlight, no light from other houses, no light from the street. It was a small, quiet neighborhood, and late at night, like this, it was as if the whole street just turned off.

Click.

I was thirsty, and I had to go.

I went to the bathroom, washed my hands, and walked into the hallway. The lights were all off, so I stood there a moment, in the dark, the floor cold beneath my feet, waiting for my eyes to adjust. Then I went to the living room, past my parents' bedroom, which I noticed, without surprise, was empty. Then to the kitchen.

I got a glass, stuck it under the sink, let the water get cold. I filled the glass and drank down the whole thing. I never took a breath.

The door to the basement was open a little. Light came through the slit.

This was unusual.

Father always locked the door to the basement when Mother was in the room. Not to keep me out, but as a "precautionary measure." Protocol.

I stood there, holding the glass, looking at the bar of light. I listened but heard nothing. Nothing at all.

I decided to go downstairs.

At the bottom I saw Father standing over the monitors, looking tense. He turned quickly, saw me there. His eyes were wide, his face strained.

"What are you doing?"

I shrugged. "I was thirsty."

Father licked his lips, looked at the monitors again, then at the steel door that led to the room. Where Mother was.

"Dad?"

Father raised a hand. "Stay there. Just . . . stay there. Okay?"

I was confused. I was *always* allowed to go to the room. My parents never hid what happened in the room from me, hid what happened to her. They wanted me to know, to be aware, to fear *it*, but not fear her. It was the only way, they used to say. "We all have to be in this together," Mother always said. "Or we will all die."

Father pressed something on the wall by the door, and there was a sharp hiss, and a sound of metal sliding on metal, and the door clicked open, pushing outward a couple of inches.

He opened the door, I thought, hardly believing it.

Without looking back, Father pulled the door wide, peered inside.

"Dad," I said. This was not procedure, I knew that. This was not procedure in the slightest. I watched him as he stared into the room, the back of the door blocking my view. I waited.

There was no sound coming from the room. No screeching, no gurgling chatter, no panting. None of the usual sounds Mother made.

Father turned to me once more. "I was wrong. I need you." He wiggled his fingers, wanting me to come closer.

I didn't want to. I was afraid. But he needed me, and the room was so quiet, and I was almost a man. I started toward him.

"No!" Father snapped, holding up a hand once more. "Sorry," he said, wiped the hand over his face. "Wait until I'm inside. Then come over here and watch. Open the intercom if you have to, but watch the monitors. When you see me wave at you, open the door and let me out. Understand?"

I did, and I nodded.

"But only if your mother is still restrained. If she's not restrained, do not open the door. No matter what. Okay?"

I nodded again. "Because sometimes she pretends."

Father looked at me a moment longer. He looked as sad as I've ever seen him, like he had something else to tell me. He started to say it, then lowered his head. "When I wave."

Then Father went into the room.

The heavy door sealed shut behind him.

I walked slowly to the desk where the monitors and the intercom were. I pushed aside the rolling black chair Father always sat in, looked at the screens.

They flickered once, and I saw a flash and vague movement.

Then they went completely black.

I tried pressing the small power button in the lower corner of the monitors. Turned them off, then on. Off, then on. A small red light by the button proved they were on, and powered.

Then why are they black? I wondered. *And how am I supposed to see Father wave?*

I waited. I studied the steel door. My eyes went to the large rectangular black button next to it, the one Father had pressed. It was as big as my whole hand. I had pressed it before. I knew how to do it. How to open the door.

I shook off the idea for the moment, looked at the other machinery on the desk. There was the black intercom box. Next to it was the switch that turned it on, or "opened it up," as Father said.

There was a long green box with cables running out the back, toward one of the walls of the room. I knew this box controlled the gas. There was a clear plastic tab that flipped up, and under the plastic tab was a black button. When you pressed the button, the gas in the room released, and everyone who breathed it would die. Everyone, whether they were human or not.

There was a thin black screen with red digital numbers on the box. It was a timer. I saw it counting down. It was at 18:43:06. A second later, it showed 18:43:05. Next to the timer was a knob and a switch. The knob, I remembered, made it more time or less time. The switch turned it on or off.

I left it alone.

I pulled the chair over and sat down. I waited, humming to myself the song Mother sang earlier that night, hoping the screens would come back to life, show me what was happening inside the room.

I moved my hand to the intercom switch, flipped it. Listened carefully. But there was nothing. Some light static, maybe a sound of some shuffling, some heavy sliding movement. But nothing else. Father wasn't yelling for me. Mother wasn't screeching like an eagle. It was like the room was empty.

After a few minutes, I went to the couch that sat against the wall facing the steel door. I sat down, then laid down.

I was still very tired. It was the middle of the night.

I fell asleep.

"Hello?"

Mother.

"Hello? Can you hear me, sweetie? Can you hear Mommy?"

I woke up to her voice and opened my eyes, stared straight at the steel door.

Still closed.

I stood up, rubbed one eye with the heel of my hand, and walked over to the desk. I was so tired but I knew I should stay awake. Father might need me.

I sat in the black swivel chair, eyelids heavy, shoulders slouched. I looked at the green box, the one with the timer counting down.

13:22:02 . . . 13:22:01 . . . 13:22:00 . . .

There was sound coming from the intercom. Breathing, I thought. Heavy breathing. And . . . giggling? Like my parents were playing a game. I almost smiled, but realized that it didn't make sense. Not at all.

"Hello? Can you hear me?" It was Mother's voice again, coming through the intercom. There was light static, her voice sounded far away, thin and nasally. Like she was transmitting from the moon. I felt frozen. I forgot to breathe. "The red intercom light is on in here, so I think you can. Honey, if you can hear me, I need to tell you something. Listen carefully, okay?"

"Okay," I said out loud, even though I knew she couldn't hear me.

"Your father is in here. He's . . . he's hurt. But I didn't do it. It wasn't me. It was an accident. I'm . . ."

There was a pause, then a scratchy sound. It sounded like whispers.

"I'm fine. I've turned back and I'm okay. So it wasn't that. He had an accident. He came in, and he fell, and he hit his head. He needs a hospital I think. Okay? You understand?"

I yawned, looked desperately at the blank monitors. I waited, hoping they would turn back on. *The light,* I realized. *There's no light.*

Mother's voice came again, louder, as if her mouth was pressed right up to the microphone. "Baby," she said, her voice a harsh whisper. "I need you to open the door."

Later, I went up to the kitchen to look for food. I was upset, confused, but also hungry, and so very tired. Sleeping on the couch had been uncomfortable, and I had woken a bunch of times to the sound of Mother's horrible pleading, demanding voice.

I thought about calling Father's friends. The men who had taken Mother before we built the room, who had handled her. But I didn't want to call them. I just needed time to think. A man made his own decisions. Even the hard ones.

I split a bagel, put it on a plate and into the microwave, heated it for thirty seconds, then slathered peanut butter on both open halves.

There was half a jar of orange juice, and I poured myself a tall glass.

I felt better. I chewed on the sticky bagel, washed it down with cold juice, and debated my options.

I knew what Father would say. Father would say to let it ride. Wait for the gas. The gas would kill them both, and then I would be safe.

I would also be alone.

I have no other family. No relatives. I don't go to school. I have no friends from the neighborhood. My parents give me lessons every day, teach me science and mythology, math and languages.

There was no one to turn to. No one at all.

I finished breakfast and went to get dressed.

The basement was cold, and I was bored.

It was late afternoon now, almost a full day since Mother had been locked inside. Time was running out.

I sat at the desk, watched the timer ticking down. 03:34:46 . . . 03:34:45 . . . 03:34:44 . . .

The intercom had been silent, the cameras showed nothing, the monitors black as empty space. Anything could be happening inside the room.

On one hand, my parents could both be alive and well. Trapped, perhaps injured. But themselves. It was possible.

Or Mother might have turned, and not turned back. It usually took at least a day before she became herself again. But there was always the possibility it would be forever. I couldn't trust her not to pretend. Not to trick me.

I watched the timer. My stomach rumbled. I was about to get up and find more food when Father's electric voice came through the intercom.

"You there, Son?"

I froze. My mouth went dry. My eyes fell to the top of the desk. I was angry, anxious, scared. I ran a finger along the grooves in the tired old wood. My spine was itchy.

"I'm okay, Son. I was . . . hurt. I'm still hurt, but I'm awake now, and feeling better. Much better in fact."

Father's voice sounded ragged, his words coming too fast. His breathing was heavy. Irregular, he would say. Abnormal.

"Listen, I have a feeling our time is growing short in here. I don't . . . according to my watch, anyway, I'd say we have only a few hours until the gas releases. Is that right?"

I looked at the timer. *Getting close now. And it's almost my birthday.*

I was having a hard time thinking, my brain felt fuzzy, and I was so very tired. I rested my head on the desk, my ear flat against the rough wood, feet kicking air.

"Son. Please. We're fine. We . . ."

More whispering.

"Your mother is still restrained. The keys . . . I don't know where they are, but your mother is still restrained. And I'm hurt, not badly. But . . . I'm okay, you understand?"

I slipped down from the chair, walked to the room's steel door. I pressed my ear against the cold metal and listened, but I could only hear the sound of my own blood rushing through my ears. I closed my eyes. My blood sounded like waves, like wind. Like the inside of a seashell.

I banged a fist against the door. Once, twice. Father's voice came screaming over the intercom.

"That's right! Oh, thank god! Son, listen, you need to *turn off the gas*. Do you understand? Or . . ."

Mother's voice interrupted him. Loud, insistent.

"Do you want us to die, baby?" she said, sounding more and more like the eagle, high-pitched and scratchy. "Do you want to be alone? If you don't open the door, we *will* die. We will die and you will be totally alone. I don't mean to scare you but that's the truth. Please, do you hear me?"

Then there was silence. They were waiting.

I couldn't think. I didn't want to think anymore. I didn't want this to be happening. I'd never felt more alone. I pressed my palm against the cool steel door. I didn't want to make any hard decisions, didn't want to be an adult.

I missed them so much.

I laid down at the foot of the door, curled into myself, and cried.

There is no time now.

I've waited, watched the timer tick slowly down.

00:02:13 . . . 00:02:12 . . . 00:02:11 . . .

There is no way to stop the gas other than the green box. Opening the door, I know, will not stop it. The only way to stop it is by turning the little knob and resetting the timer, or shutting if off completely by flipping the small black switch. I take a deep breath. My decision is made.

I have no intention of stopping it.

I walk away from the table, cross the chilled air of the small basement toward the steel door, toward the room.

There is loud pounding from the door at the top of the stairs. Men yell savage curses.

I look to the stairs, toward the yelling. There must have been another fail-safe I didn't know about, one that alerted Father's friends. For a brief moment I panic, then relax. The door leading from the basement to the house is locked, reinforced, bolted. No one can get in without breaking it down, and it's thick, solid. It would take time, and tools.

I take a deep breath. My parents have been quiet for the past hour or so. Waiting, I know. Hoping. I don't know what's inside the room. I have some ideas, some possible outcomes, in my mind.

Mother, hideously pale skin streaked with blue veins. Anger and flaring nostrils, yawning jaw. Her teeth, her eyes . . .

Father, poisoned by her, but alive. Reborn in monstrous flesh. Waiting, biding his time. Pacing frantically, his amped-up nerve endings flexing for the very first time, the air around him feeding energy into his altered bones, his sensitized flesh. A six-foot-tall rabid dog.

If I open the door they will run at me, grab me. Tear me apart.

But I imagine other options.

They are lying in there dead. Human or monster. Maybe half-turned. Maybe half-eaten.

Or maybe the room is empty.

Or maybe the room is gone.

What do I believe?

I want to believe it will be my parents, alive and human. Just Mother and Father, tired, perhaps injured. Hungry not for flesh but for freedom. Air, food, water. They will run to me and hug me. Kiss me on the face, wipe away my tears, rub my back soothingly. Sing to me at night. Take care of me. Protect me.

Everything will be like it was, and we will be together again.

Once I open the door, once I go inside . . .

I put my fingers on the smooth black panel that releases the heavy bolts of the lock. My face is burning, there is a throbbing pain behind my eyes. The men scream and pound. I can't wait for the end. I've been counting down the numbers from the screen in my head.

. . . sixteen . . . fifteen . . . fourteen . . .

I'm tired, but I smile. I'll be thirteen soon. I will change. One way or the other.

. . . nine . . . eight . . . seven . . . six . . .

I hear the faint sound of frantic scratching on the other side of the door. I can hear it through the steel. Desperate, monstrous. My parents clawing for life, maybe. Or something else. Something I haven't thought of.

I love them so much.

. . . three . . . two . . . one . . .

I push the large black button, feel the click of the release vibrate up my arm. Metal slides on metal, the heavy door hisses.

I pull it open. The room is pitch black. Silent.

I step inside, ready for whatever waits.

There's a shushing sound. The darkness is total. I move deeper into the room, confident.

It's almost my birthday.

Something moves toward me. I lift my chin, spread out my arms.

No matter what comes . . .

I close my eyes tight.

. . . I will be a man.

THE STARRY CROWN

MARC E. FITCH

I left the university campus behind to do field work in the Deep South. I was studying folk songs from southern states that had neither a time or place of origin nor a known composer. Those old songs that just seem to rise out of cultural folklore and evangelical mysticism like steam rising from a swamp. Songs that had been sung for generations by slaves and slave owners, Baptist ministers and backwoods preachers, and whose chords had been strung by banjos and whistled on whiskey jugs. Those songs presented a mystery to me; one that seemed to be known and understood in the Deep South but eluded myself and others in the halls of academe.

In particular, I was seeking the origins of the beautiful ode in which the singer calls for all brothers and sisters, mothers and sinners to go down to the river to pray. Of most interest was a variation in the lyrics that I could not understand given its Judeo-Christian origins: the use in one line of the term "starry crown."

. . . As I went down to the river to pray,
studying about that good ole way,
and who should wear the starry crown.

More modern versions of the hymn use the words "thorny crown" to reference Christ's crown of thorns during the crucifixion. These lyrics would appear to make the most sense in the context of the song, so the use of "starry crown" in the older and possibly more genuine versions of the hymn was a puzzle. Secondly, the term presents a question of *who* should wear the crown. If this were a Christian hymn, that question should never be asked; Christ would wear the thorny crown and, one would presume, *any* crown. So the line presents a second mystery as to why and how someone other than Christ would be picked to wear a starry crown and for what purpose. I could find no relevant Biblical references to a starry crown and thus I was left with a mystery as to what its original meaning was and why it had been changed.

The earliest recognized version of the song was published in 1867 by G. H. Allan in his *Slave Songs of The United States*. But in his personal diary writings Allan referenced an earlier and heretofore unknown version of the song, recorded on paper by Llewellyn Cobb. Allan wrote that Cobb had mailed him the song in order that he might include it in *Slave Songs*, but that the version was "somewhat unbalanced" and he made changes to the music. Cobb had lived in that southern stronghold of South Carolina, long before the Reconstruction and interest in slavery's subculture developed.

I travelled to that state, driving to Evanstown, where Cobb had lived. I found residence in an old plantation home turned into a bed & breakfast, Ashcroft Manor, named after the aristocratic family that built and ran the plantation. It was an effort to immerse myself in the antebellum culture, thinking that perhaps the scenery and living situation would stir my mind to new connections and insights into this era so far removed from modern life.

The proprietors, Ted and Mary Wallstone, were an elderly couple who prided themselves on keeping the plantation as close to its original form as possible.

"We finally sprung for indoor plumbing in the eighties," Ted told me. "Can't tell you how much business we lost before then because of the outhouses, but I just didn't want to change the structure, putting holes in the walls and everything. To me, it would be like desecrating a church, ya know?"

I nodded in agreement but his relation of a slave plantation to a church, and the rheumy, wistful look in his eyes left me feeling unsettled.

I told him of my research project, leaving out the specific mystery of the starry crown, but hopeful that he could provide some direction in this unfamiliar place.

"Ah . . . that's a beautiful old hymn." Ted said. "My God! It stays with you, doesn't it?"

"It was first written on paper right here in this area," I told him.

He reflected a moment. "Doesn't surprise me."

"Do you remember when you first heard the song?"

"As a child, many years ago. Of course, back then, most people called it 'Down to the Valley,' not 'The Good Old Way.'"

I'd read this previously. There were several names and incarnations. 'The Good Old Way' was the most historically prevalent, which only deepened the mystery. "I thought this was relating to a baptism, so it'd make sense, going down to the river. But why would they go down to a valley to pray?"

He raised his eyebrows at me. "Well, most rivers are in valleys, city-boy."

"Ah, of course. Are there still river baptisms here?"

"First Sunday of every month," he said proudly.

"Where are they held? I'd like to witness one."

"Well . . . the Green River is where most congregations go. But there are lots of other creeks and rivers around here too, and plenty of smaller congregations that use them for their own services, so could be anywhere. But the Green River is probably the best bet."

I thanked Ted for his time and hospitality. He wished me luck on my search but left me with a bit of "advice":

"Careful who you question around here. People in these parts are very private. They hold their beliefs sacred and can be pretty suspicious when outsiders come asking questions. Even if it's about an old song."

He patted me on the shoulder and went about his business, maintaining a home that had previously been the site of the horrendous rites of slavery.

I slept badly that night. There were ghosts in the air.

Finding a Baptist church in the south is not a challenge. Rather, the challenge was trying to find where to start. One could throw a rock and hit a Baptist church, and the rock would bounce off that church and hit another one right next door. On nearly every stretch of road and corner there stood a large white building with a steeple, a converted warehouse with a Christ-proclaiming sign, or some old, tiny schoolhouse that reached back into the days of the colonies, but now proclaimed, "Pancake Breakfasts and Bible Studies on Wednesdays."

I began to survey each of them, explaining my project and inquiring as to their river baptismal services. The pastors and reverends were helpful and willing. Naturally, they all knew of the song but very few could point me in any direction as to its origin or meaning. Most said it was a baptismal hymn, but there was no mention of actual baptism in the verses. Just going down to a river or valley and pondering who should wear a starry crown. The reverends grew more silent when I mentioned the starry crown aspect of the mystery. None of them, for all their theology, could give me an adequate explanation as to the meaning of those words and what Biblical reference it came from.

I spent several days in the city hall's file cabinets of records, researching churches and Llewellyn Cobb's residence 150 years ago. His home wasn't in the town but in the surrounding hills that had once been cultivated with crops harvested by slaves. An elderly woman at the clerk's desk—a withered crone with fake teeth and the long, drawn-out manner of a former southern belle—asked what I was searching for, and I gave her a brief summary.

"You should go see Thomas Jeery over at First Baptist," she said.

"I feel like I've been to every church in the state at this point," I replied with a smile.

"Not this one," she said. "Thomas is one hundred and one years old. His parents were children when freed after the Civil War, and his family have lived in these parts ever since. He could probably tell you something about its history."

"Where can I find him?"

"Not around here. You have to go into the hills. First Baptist is the oldest original church in this area. It's only the size of this here room, not like all those big churches the size of airports that keep springing up. But they have the most wonderful choir. You should hear them sing at night. You hear it all through the hills. It's like hearing a lullaby sung by God."

Her eyes appeared to wane and turn in the deepened sockets of her furrowed visage and she fell silent. She was smiling, but not at me. I turned to look but there was nothing else around.

Fearing that she was suffering a stroke or some other malady, I cautiously asked if she wasn't feeling well. She did not speak but, standing before me, the old crone began humming a tune—something vaguely familiar which I could not place exactly—perhaps a gloomy bastardization of a song I knew.

"What is that song?" I asked, but she didn't answer. Instead, her humming grew louder as if trying to drown out my voice, her eyes vacantly staring beyond me.

My skin started crawling. It felt as if there was something else in the room with us, which only she could see, and it was reaching its tentacles up over my shoulders, treading lightly on the skin of my back.

I left her standing there, unsure if she was some kind of mystic or suffering an onset of dementia, but either way the creeping sensation was overwhelming me to the point of panic, and the sound of her humming voice was stirring in my head like the rising cry of locusts. I hurried out into the humid heat of the southern summer, breathing deep and heavy, the air like smoke in my lungs. The city seemed abandoned and lonely in the pastel light of day. I turned left and right. Spun myself around looking for any sign of life until I was nearly dizzy.

A single dark sedan rolled down the street and stopped at a traffic light in front of me. I could see my features in the tinted windows, distorted and twisted into some kind of monstrous being.

The window rolled down and a wizened face scowled at me from the back seat. His face seemed abnormally long and cut with deep lines of folded flesh; his staring eyes were hazy with cataracts. A pungent small wafted from the opened window, and I stumbled away from the car.

The old man continued to stare at me as the darkened window rolled back up and the sedan pulled away from the sidewalk.

I was disoriented and exhausted, and the feeling from the hall of records stayed with me into the evening as I retreated back to the bed & breakfast. Ashcroft Manor was filled to capacity. Elderly men and women mingled in dining rooms, they spilled out into the back patio which looked out on a field of grass and dark trees in the distance. I figured them for tourists but they all seemed so familiar with Ted and Mary. The proprietors mingled with the guests like old friends that hadn't seen each other in an age. They were all finely dressed, glasses of wine in their hands, laughing and murmuring in the deepening dusk.

The kaleidoscope of my delirium continued. The room seemed to spin. Ted placed a hand on my shoulder, and I told him that I thought I had too much sun. The other guests turned to stare at me, light glinting off pearl necklaces and dangling bracelets.

I saw a dress made of stars. It hung loose and breezy from shoulders of skin tanned like leather.

Beautiful music poured into my mind.

Ted escorted me to my room.

When I woke the following morning, the estate was empty of the other guests. Mary brought ice water to my room and politely suggested that maybe the climate was not suited to me. I conceded that I had been in quite a state. "I don't know what came over me."

"Seems you've been working quite a lot," she said. "Southern heat can do that to a man who isn't accustomed to it." I asked her where all the others had gone, and she told me that I'd walked in on one their monthly gatherings. "We belong to a small social club," she said. "True southern society still exists, you know."

Then I asked her about First Baptist and the clerk at the hall of records.

"Oh," she laughed quietly to herself. "That's just Ethel. She's—*ah*—a little touched in the head at her old age."

I spent the morning in my room on my laptop, searching for the First Baptist Church but could find nothing. Based on Ethel's description I wouldn't have been surprised if it were abandoned and left to rot in the hills.

Instead, I located Llewellyn Cobb's home, considered a minor historical site, and maintained by a small town historical society. It also had recently been the site of a murder investigation: the body of a young black male was found in the house several months post-mortem by some hikers. The investigation was pending and despite this turn of events in my research, I decided I should still visit Walker's house.

I followed the GPS map in my rental car out into the hills beyond Evanstown, amongst winding roads, deep bluffs, shadows, and liquid light. Everywhere were creeks and rivers. The GPS became useless as the roads turned to dirt pathways. My rented Grand Am scraped its side-view mirrors against the thickening underbrush. I was forced to stop the car and continue on foot, finding a small sign pointing toward a Historical Site.

Cobb's ancient cabin appeared as if manifested by magic from the underbrush. The forest had started to reclaim it, and any historical society that claimed to care for the property was severely negligent. The old southern shack listed to one side and brambles covered its eastern wall. The front entrance was cordoned off by yellow police tape, much of which had come unmoored and snaked through the underbrush. I climbed onto the front porch and passed through the entrance, noting a plaque that gave a brief biography of Llewellyn Cobb, a largely forgotten artist and composer. Inside was dank and dark and haunted with the smell of old meat. There was a pot-bellied stove in the living room, remnants of furniture and sleeping arrangements on the floor—an old mattress stained with blood and putrescence and tattered blankets.

I made my way through each room, trying to envision the life that Cobb had within these walled confines, with only candlelight keeping the darkness at bay, and the freezing winters huddled by the stove; fears of illness and crop shortages; loneliness to the point of insanity in the bramble forest of the South Carolina mountains. I tried to picture him running the hymns from his book over and over in his mind as he scratched out the notes onto paper.

And who should wear the starry crown . . .

In a small anteroom near the back of the homestead there was a writing desk beside a single-paned glass window that looked out on the forested hillside sloping away from the house. I sat there for a moment in the rickety chair, worn weak by age, and in the light that came through that portal I saw strange decorations made of sticks hung by twine from the wooden ceiling. They turned and twisted in the gravitational vortexes of the earth.

Forest sticks cobbled together like stars and hung from strings like something a child might fashion in school. The smell of gore wafted from the living room on a warm, wet breeze.

I spoke to the empty rooms in a moment of uncharacteristic theatrics: "So you did see stars, my friend."

I walked back out to the small front porch and looked over the sloping hillside. There was no river to be seen.

I avoided the hall of records, still frightened from the vertigo that had set in the other day and the haunting, elderly clerk.

I asked Ted about First Baptist, and he replied, "Yes . . . out in the hills. Old, old place but they haven't held services since the fifties. That old bat at the clerk's office must finally be losing her marbles."

"Can you tell me where in the hills? I'd like to see it, maybe get a picture or two."

"I wouldn't even know how to get there, son. Trust me. There ain't nothing out there that could do you much good."

So instead I conducted an old-fashioned search through the Internet for Thomas Jeery. I finally found a listing that matched the description the town clerk had given me. There weren't too many Thomas Jeerys that were one hundred and one years old. He was located way off the beaten path in what looked to be a trailer park. I made a phone call but the line was disconnected. I made the drive, instead.

Jeery's residence was located in The Willow View trailer park, so named for its looking out over a swampy area that was a breeding ground for pussy-willows and mosquitoes. In early dusk, the frogs were sounding like an ancient language of grunts and guttural consonants. It was a sad, broken looking place of rust-red dirt and busted screen doors hanging from corrugated hinges; old men sleeping in lawn chairs with bottles in their hand, and cars that had sat so long in one spot the weeds had died beneath them. My passing car elicited strange and strong stares from dark faces. I thought I heard children through my open window, but they sounded far off and as if crying. The heat was oppressive here, like the blanket-weight of history had fallen over it and would never be pulled away. This was a place to die or to never live.

Jeery's single-wide was at the eastern corner of the park, close to the bog and the swarming blood-suckers that churned in the air like a quiet storm. There was no answer at the screen door and I called out his name, peering into the darkness of the trailer. The inside was scattered with refuse and bottles. There was an old plaid cloth couch that looked like it was delivered from the seventies and a small table with a massive Bible, which lay opened beside it. I left the front entrance and began to slowly make my way around the outside of the home, catching glares from some of the residents across the dirt pathway.

I found him sitting in a chair in the small patch of weeds that looked out over the swamp. I said his name several times. He was asleep and there was a mason jar of moonshine beside him. His face was surprisingly smooth for such an elderly man, bequeathed with a solemn dignity that, even in this place as he slept off an afternoon drunk, could not be taken away. I thought for a moment of all those years—the social and cultural changes—that he had seen, that had quietly and meticulously carved their places into his memory and cast their shadows in the form of liver spots on his light brown skin.

He awoke and looked up at me as if I was expected. He sighed and then looked back out at the swamp. "You social services?"

"No." I said.

"Good. I've had about enough of them pestering me. Want to put me in a museum or somethin'. They call it a 'home,' I call it Purgatory where I wait to meet my maker."

"Isn't that the ultimate goal of the believer?" I said. "To finally meet the maker?"

He looked at me long and hard. He reached down and took a swallow from his mason jar and beckoned to me. I realized that we were communing. I took it up and had a swallow that instantly burned through my sinuses and into my brain, evaporating on my tongue before even reaching my belly.

"I used to think that I'd welcome the day when I'd meet him," Thomas said. "But now, when it's so close, you can feel death just waiting over your shoulder like . . . Well, it changes your perspective a bit. This world, I tell you, it's a terrible place. But what I fear is that the place we go to is even worse."

"You don't believe in Heaven?"

"Nah. All that's rubbish. I've seen things in my age that tell me otherwise. That tell me maybe the maker we seek is not the kindly old man we hope he'll be."

"It could even be a woman," I said with a smile.

He laughed briefly and said, "Yeah, that might even be worse for a fella like me." I sat down beside him, and he added. "So what you want, anyway?"

I told him about the song I was researching, about the belief that it may have been an old slave hymn at which point he scoffed. "Huh! Ain't no slave song, I can tell you that. Sure it sounds pretty when some lovely white woman sings it—and I've heard it sung by many a white woman—but that song should make a black man's skin crawl."

"Why's that?"

He looked at me somewhat incredulously, almost frustrated. "Where you think they'd find the slaves that run away, that was tortured and killed, huh? You think those white plantation owners gave those people a proper burial? No way. They'd take 'em down in the valley, toss 'em in the river. Where ya think the Klan did their lynchings after the emancipation? White man doesn't do nothin' out in the open. Nah. It's all backwoods and shady deals under cover of night."

He paused for a breath, working himself up. "If you was going down to the river to pray—like it says in that song—you was praying that you were only gonna come out with a beatin' and not be swinging from a tree. My mother and father were slaves just before the emancipation and they told me good. A white man wants to take you down to the river, down into the valley, you don't go down there, you run!"

"Isn't this a baptismal hymn?" I said.

"In a way, I suppose. Black man goes down into the river, he comes up into the embrace of God. Nothin' but a spirit. But, like I said, that's only if you subscribe to those kinds of notions . . ."

"What notions do you subscribe to?" I asked.

"Oh," he nodded with almost a smile, "there are other notions, son."

I looked at him closely. "What is the starry crown?"

He looked back at me with a look of quiet foreboding. "Now you onto somethin', son. Now you onto somethin'."

I went down. I went way down into the valley. Down to the river to pray for my soul, to pray that what Thomas Jeery had told me wasn't true. But it haunted me, pulled me in an inexorable flow through the muddy darkness of history.

"You want to know where that song come from," Jeery had said to me, "then you gots to see for yourself. Nobody can see it for you."

"See what?"

"The rite of the Starry Crown. There be men and women that pray to it. They pray to the crown. And they make a sacrifice."

"What kind of sacrifice?" I'd asked.

"The same kind that's made every day across this country. The same that you read about on page ten of the paper. You look at the lost black kids in this country. You look at them and you'll see the crown, all souls gone to their resting place up in the sky. What 'good ole way' you think they're singin' about anyway? The song done come out after the Civil War. Use your college-educated brain, son."

It couldn't be, though. It seemed impossible, so into the valley I went, stepping another foot in the rich loam of the South Carolina river valley. The land was flat, the earth black with tall ghostly trees that shot straight up into the abysmal night. It was dried floodland, devoid of underbrush that got swept away in the spring when the river would overflow its banks and send it all downstream. Overhead was a full moon, and its ghastly light reflected on the white bark of the trees.

Up above, standing guard over this sacrilegious land, I found the old First Baptist Church. Tiny, rotted, and being pulled down to the earth by ropes of kudzu vines. It was barely visible even in the full light of day.

"Once that church was gone," Jeery had said, "it was free reign for the Starry Crown again. They wanted their sacred ground back, and they got it. Land deals, real estate prices, offers of big, brand new churches down in the town proper. It wasn't the congregation's fault. No one knew. No one remembered."

"Except you," I'd said.

"Except me. I warned 'em. But I'm just an old fool, see? The congregation took a deal for a brand new church down in Evanstown, and the realty company took hold of First Baptist's land more'n twelve years ago."

"What are they doing with the land?"

"Well, that's what you want to find out, isn't it?"

He looked out at the swamp and took a sip from his jar of white lightning. "They haven't come for me yet," he'd said. "They just letting time run her course. Nobody believes an old fool anyhow."

After my visit with Jeery, I'd returned to the town hall of records and looked up the land purchase for First Baptist Church. The crone was gone that day. In her place were fat and friendly clerks with teased-out hair and big, white Jesus-lovin' smiles. They showed me to the proper files and I dove in for some tedious reading. First Baptist was purchased by Old Pride Realty in 2002 for an extravagant amount of money plus the building of a new Baptist church in the city of Evanstown, just as Jeery had said. Old Pride Realty was actually a collection of real estate agents, owners, and attorneys throughout the state that pooled resources to purchase land and historical sites considered part of the Antebellum South's heritage. They owned and operated estates and manors, plantation homes and historical sites clear across the south from Illinois to Florida and west to Arkansas. It was a new Confederacy, a quiet Civil War, and Old Pride Realty was buying back the south in one of the largest private land grabs since the Homestead Act.

Down in the valley, standing before the moonlit First Baptist Church, I thought again of what I'd read. Nearly all of Evanstown and the surrounding counties belonged now to Old Pride Realty, including Llewellyn Cobb's crumbling house. The smell of that place came back to me. The blood-stained mattress, the stars made of twine, and sticks turning in the light.

The First Baptist Church—the first black church that had been erected after the Emancipation—and the adjacent river valley seemed to move around me, to spin in the ghost light of southern high-summer night.

"They got that land again, they's coming out of the shadows," Jeery had said. "Now they got that river and that valley, the sacrifices been happening again. They found who should wear the Starry Crown, all right."

Halfway down the list of real estate agents and lawyers that made up the governing body of Old Pride Realty had been Theodore Wallstone, owner and proprietor of Ashcroft Manor Bed & Breakfast. I didn't return to my room that night. Instead I drove down into the valley, directly to the forgotten, black land of First Baptist.

I walked from the church to the river, its banks still muddy from the spring rains. I could hear it flowing up ahead. And then came a music, a beautiful music from behind me in the darkness. It sounded like it was emanating from the kudzu church itself, as if a forgotten choir had broken in and begun to sing. I stopped and listened to the dirge: solemn and reverent, growing in tone and intensity. Ahead of me the river glinted moonlight across its slow waters. I glared into the darkness, searching for the source of the low hymn.

Then lights began to appear. Flickering flames of candlelight dancing between the trees; first one, then two, then a multitude growing in number and intensity. At first they seemed apparitions, will-o'-the-whisps that were beckoning for me to touch them, to become enchanted. But the dirge grew heavier and more intense. My momentary flight into fancy turned suddenly terrifying as I returned to my senses and realized that these were candles being held by people, hundreds of people, and they were appearing out of the darkness like ghosts of Confederate soldiers passing across Gettysburg.

They were all-too real, walking amongst the thin trees of the river bed with candles, chanting a vaguely familiar rhyme that was beginning to worm its way into my brain.

Panic set in. Jeery was no old fool. He told of those infernal rites of the Starry Crown taking place on full moons, of a cult finally able to again practice on their most sacred ground.

I was trapped between the hundreds of moving bodies and the turbulent river beyond. I considered running under cover along the river bed, but I was overcome suddenly with the urge to *know*. So much of anthropology, archeology, and folklore is guess-work and estimation, tall-tales, and fabrications gleaned out of cultural cloth. It was my only chance to witness. It was my one chance to see, even if what I saw was horrifying.

I found a thick tree with branches low enough that I could shimmy up the trunk and grasp them. I pulled myself higher and higher, dripping sweat and choking back my straining breaths till I was confident I was out of eyesight. Like Zaccheaus sneaking a glimpse of Christ, I was trying to catch of glimpse of some secret satanic messiah.

The lights began to pass beneath me, flames held in lanterns by white-robed men and women who walked serenely toward the waters chanting their hymn, a strange version of "The Good Old Way," but sung in low octaves, the rhythm and meter changed so that the soul of the song transformed from a quiet, heartfelt prayer to a dark, unrelenting march.

My first thought was that this was some kind of Ku Klux Klan rally but this was so different, so much more reverent, quiet and insidious. It wasn't the hooded back-woods abortions that light fire to crosses and wave flags, croaking protests in bad English. This was organized, religious. Its darkness contained a certain beauty and ancient depth that even modern Christianity had difficulty recreating. I could make faces out in the glow of the candlelight. They were pale and serene, well cared for, bright and clean. They appeared to be from the upper echelons of society and, based on my research into Old Pride Realty, I had a feeling that these worshippers were of a class much higher than your typical Klansman or Neo-Nazi.

The number of robed men and women still continued to swell, a sea of glowing candles that spread out beneath me, stretching to the river's edge. They deftly raised their voices to some dark god that I did not know, growing louder and louder as one in resonant chant until suddenly stopping as if a switch had been thrown. Everything along that river had turned silent.

There appeared a figure on the river's other side, seemingly clothed with light. He stepped out from the trees, glowing with a luminescence that radiated from his robe like a lunar aura. He was adorned with a great crown upon his head that reached many, many fingers up to the starry sky. The gathered crowd stood silent and unmoved, but below me in the mud and patches of river-grass, terrified small animals scurried away.

Then the radiant creature came, gliding across the surface of the river without ever setting foot in the water.

And he was tall, much taller than anyone there. The stars on his crown glowed with a pulsing brilliance, and though his face resembled a human's, it were as if carved into an old oak tree—some product of psychological pareidolia—rather than the face of flesh and bone. The creature's mouth opened long and wide and was hollow with darkness while he remained suspended in the air inches above the muddy bank.

The crowd met him with bowed heads and silent reverence.

And then there was a boy. A black boy who was brought to the front of the horrid congregation by a man in a robe. I recognized the old, wizened visage as he led the boy before the creature with the starry crown. I had seen his face before in my delirium outside the town hall of records glaring at me from the back seat of a dark sedan.

There was no other sound but for the boy crying: an adolescent, I estimated, by his voice and build. The glowing figure moved to him through the air, and the boy screamed in terror. A great and terrible blade was handed to the starry king, and it was raised up over the screaming boy and brought down into him over and over again.

The boy's body was dumped in the river. Baptized, like Jeery had told me, where no one would see his blood in a river of black.

The sun was rising over the eastern mountains when I was finally able to come down from my tree and make my way to the car. On the hood was placed a single lantern, its candle burned down to a nub. A warning.

I snuck into my room at Ashcroft Manor. I gathered my computer with all my work, dumped my clothes into my suitcase, and made my way back down the stairs.

"You heading out already?" Ted stood at the reception desk, neatly dressed, clean and pressed from head to toe, friendly and warm smile on his face. "You weren't going to leave without checking out, were ya?"

I smiled but I was sick in my stomach. "Of course not."

I signed his ledger and signed for the bill. Ted crossed his arms and looked out the window at my rental car. "That's a nice car they gave you."

I only kept smiling.

"Should get you back to New York without a hitch," he said. He clapped a meaty hand on my shoulder and escorted me to the door. "Y'all come back now, ya hear?"

I nodded but kept my head down, unable to bring myself to make eye contact. I saw the residue of dark river mud on his boots.

I returned the rental car to the nearest return lot and took a different car home. I drove without music, only my thoughts streaming through my head, dark and churning and winding their way to an ocean of reality. I could not remove from my mind the glowing figure with its crown pointing to the stars and its impossible parody of Christ walking on the Sea of Galilee. I could not shake off Ted's smile and the sensation of his touch on the back of my shoulder. This was something larger than any one man could comprehend, too fantastic to be believed. I would be laughed out of every PhD review hearing and torn to shreds in a culture awash in skepticism. My story would be discarded as either the rantings of a lunatic or lies by an attention-seeking folklorist in an age of racial strife. My story, though I had lived it, would be banished to fiction.

Those people had my address, my phone number, email, and even my credit card number. But they didn't need to kill me. If I spoke I'd be relegated to the swampy backwaters of society like old Thomas Jeery, a man to be laughed at and ridiculed, left to die in a trailer park.

I did not stop.

I did not sleep.

I drove through the night till I reached the safety of my apartment.

I sat down and erased my dissertation, and in the darkness began a new work that would surely be called fiction by all those who could not and would not ever see: *I left the university campus behind to do field work in the Deep South . . .*

EQALUSSUAQ

TIM MAJOR

As Lea had predicted, Peter threw a tantrum the instant he opened the front door to find her standing on the step. As she scooped him into her arms, he shuddered against her. She had imagined that he would be taller, visibly older, in the twelve weeks that had passed. If anything, he seemed to have become lighter.

"Don't fret, now," she said. "Mum's back."

Peter buried his face into her shoulder, depositing mucus onto her cardigan. More like a newborn than a six-year-old. His blond hair had begun to sneak over the tips of his ears.

With her usual tact, Lea's friend Karen had already stepped soundlessly into the lounge, leaving mother and son to their reunion. Lea closed the front door with her hip and entered Karen's house. Peter regained his calm but still said nothing. He wriggled free of Lea's embrace to sit close beside Karen on the sofa. Anyone might have assumed she was his mother, not Lea.

"So. Tell me," Lea said.

Karen wrinkled her nose. "I won't lie. It was tougher this time. But we had our fair share of fun. Didn't we?" She rubbed Peter's head, but he shrugged her away in order to glare at Lea.

"And at school?"

"Worse. More biting. Poor Daphne's parents said they'll call."

Lea winced. Stains marked Peter's cheeks, though he wasn't crying. Old tears.

"Peter, listen," she said, "What did we agree, before I left? About how you treat other children?"

Peter only shook his head. Based on past experience, it would take days for him to thaw. Until then, he would be impenetrable. An iceberg.

"That's not all," Karen said. "I couldn't think how to tell you by email. Last week, Thursday, he ran away. I was frantic." Her hands began to tremble. Lea glanced down and saw that her own hands shook a little, too. "The whole island helped me search for him. We found him in one of the refuge huts out on the causeway. He'd been trapped there for hours, Lea."

A shudder ran through Lea's body. She felt chill sting her skin, then seem to penetrate to her bones in an instant. "Thursday? The fourteenth?" she said, her jaw tight to stop her teeth chattering. "You're sure?"

Karen shrugged. "Pretty sure."

Lea examined her friend's expression. There was concern there, but it was directed at Peter, rather than Lea herself. The news mustn't have reached Britain yet. Or maybe the media didn't judge the story as dramatic as it had seemed first-hand.

She glanced at Peter. What was the appropriate parental response to the news about his attempted escape from Lindisfarne? A mother ought to know, instinctively.

On the fourteenth of September, when she had slipped beneath the water—perhaps for the last time ever, she reflected now—the cold had seemed more absolute than it ought. She had felt a sudden shock of fear then, during that solo dive, easily comparable to the fear she experienced during the incident later that day. Perhaps it had been a response to danger back at home. Perhaps she had a maternal instinct, after all.

"You understand, don't you?" Karen said. She was choosing her words carefully, too. Forcing herself not to scold Lea in front of her son. "He wasn't trying to get away, so much as he was trying to get closer to what he wanted. He was trying to follow you."

Lea made her excuses to Karen, with vague arrangements to meet later in the week. As she stepped over the threshold, Karen gripped her arm.

"I know it was an important trip for you," she said. "I understand why you went. And it's not that I mind having him here. You're closer to me than my sister, and Peter's like a son. But three whole months, Lea, and not a single phone call from you . . . I can't do that again, okay? Not for a while."

Lea nodded and shuffled into the street with her shivering child.

It was only when Peter had finally fallen asleep that Lea had the chance to check the contents of her duffel bag. She pushed aside the thick parka and dirty laundry to retrieve the hard black case beneath. Inside, six portable hard drives made a neat row. Throughout the journey, she had suffered from paranoia; all those weeks of work contained within something so easily lost. On the bumpy flight from Ilulissat she had woken shouting from a doze, certain that some atmospheric phenomenon had wiped the drives.

She booted her computer, slipped out the first drive, and ran a backup. She exhaled fully for the first time in days. Safe and sound.

When all of the backups had finished, she glanced towards the staircase. No sounds from Peter. Guiltily, she slipped on her headphones. If he yelled now, she wouldn't hear it.

She selected a file at random and clicked play. A waveform appeared onscreen, reassuring in its dark fluidity. Her eyes narrowed as she concentrated on the skittering sound. Onscreen, a dark peak broke up and away, matching a corresponding sound in the headphones. She smiled. The call of a black-legged kittiwake. Her thighs had ached terribly after she had crouched for hours with her rifle mic pointed at the nest.

She chose another track. Instantly, her headphones filled with a burping, chuckling noise. She checked the filename against the handwritten description in her notebook. Earless harp seals, slithering on the ice as they huddled together.

She settled into the swivel chair, sipping wine as she browsed through the tracks. Her hands shook only a little now, the lingering fear subsiding. The tracks were all pristine. A month of good work.

The most recently-used drive was easily identifiable, as its surface was scuffed and scratched. When she had awoken in the hut on the fifteenth, she had insisted that it be found and brought to her immediately. When she had finally made herself understood to the Inuit guides who watched over her, and they had relayed the message to her colleagues, and the hard drive had been located, she had cursed at Nils for allowing it to be handled so roughly. The look on her producer's face as he handed it over was easy to read. *After what's happened*, his expression said, *you're worried about the work?*

She had earned her reputation as a killjoy early on in the expedition. Of the seven-man team, she was the only one who refused to play along with the in-jokes about the island where they had been based for the first fortnight, insisting on using its Greenlandic title, Qeqertarsuaq, rather than the anglicised Disko Island. She had asked for the Earth, Wind and Fire to be turned down during the jeep ride from the airport. She had complained to Nils when someone had scrawled DISKO SUCKS in Tippex on one arm of her wetsuit. And when, on the first day of work proper, her first hard drive of sound recordings had been replaced with another containing only one track, a repeated twenty-second loop of the Bee Gees singing "Staying Alive," she had thrown a tantrum that would have awed her six-year-old son.

She didn't care then and she didn't care now. She had the files.

She hooked up the most recent hard drive and selected the first track, labelled *14Sep16_001*. Her two glasses of wine had left her a little drunk. She raised her hands like a conductor as the track played.

It began with a gulp. The sound of her own body slipping into the water, probably. She shivered now. Hadn't the thought passed through her mind, at that moment, of Peter's fate if she were to freeze there in Baffin Bay? Even at the time, she had recognised the thought as uncharacteristic. If she was being honest, she hadn't thought about Peter a great deal, up to that point in the expedition. But being alone in icy water, far from assistance, might make anyone behave oddly. From underwater she had looked up at the towering iceberg above, its edges knife-sharp from its recent calving from the Jakobshavn glacier. Refraction had made it bend towards her. She had felt impossibly fragile.

Bubbling sounds followed. Her last exhalation before she had settled herself into position. As the bubbles ceased, the background sounds became more easily audible. Lea leant forward to turn up the amp.

The creaking sound reminded her of her grandmother's rocking chair against wooden floorboards. Except there were layers beneath, too. A sighing, a throb of life. The quiet belch of bubbles released from somewhere in the depths and pushing along the underside of the iceberg before finding freedom at the water's surface. The rumble and snap of the iceberg itself as its regions thawed or refroze. An embrace of womblike warmth that eclipsed the physical memory of the water's icy chill.

It was good. A beautiful, living sound in its own right, as well as fulfilling producer Nils' brief of demonstrating the rate of thaw for the TV documentary. Lea sipped wine and conducted the orchestra of creaks and burbles. It was good.

Even back then, floating twenty feet down, she had had the distinct thought, *This is the best yet.* Then, as she had stifled her shivers in order to hold the microphone tight and to track the fast-moving iceberg, *This is the best work I might ever do.*

At the time.

By lunchtime, during the team meeting at the tiny base situated north of Ilulissat, a new opportunity had presented itself. An achievement that might easily surpass the glacier groans.

The second camerawoman, Reeta, was first to notice the change in the Inuit guide, Sighna. She interrupted Nils' summary of footage gathered that morning to rush over to Sighna and steady him, preventing him from toppling into the open brazier in the centre of the hut. Lea and the others watched on in silence as Reeta tried to grasp Sighna's hands. He wrenched them away and pressed them to either side of his head. He shook as though he were trying to squeeze his skull. He hissed a word, again and again and again. *Eqalussuaq*.

Nils tried to speak to Reeta, but she waved him away. He returned to stand next to Lea, his arms folded. He had never been good at inaction. Some other members of the team moved away from Sighna and Reeta, too, similarly embarrassed.

"Eqalussuaq," Nils whispered.

"What does it mean?" Lea asked.

"It's a name," Nils said. "Or two names, depending how you think about it."

They watched as Reeta helped Sighna to sit and gathered rucksacks to make a cushioned throne.

Nils continued, "I read the name first in a book of Greenlandic legends. Kind of a cute one. Some old woman washed her hair in urine—I know, go figure—then dried it with a cloth, which then sailed away on the wind, into the ocean. It became Ekalugsuak, and its descendants, Eqalussuaq."

The first-unit director, Terence, was listening. He stuck out his tongue. "So what's the significance of this progeny of a piss-cloth, then?"

"It'll be of interest to you, Terry, professionally speaking," Nis replied. "Eqalussuaq is an animal. The Greenland shark."

Lea saw Terence's eyes widen. He turned to Reeta, still kneeling beside the Inuit guide, whose lips were moving even though his voice had quietened. "Hey. Hey. Ask him why he's saying that word."

Sighna looked up blearily as Reeta asked the question in Greenlandic. He lifted his hands from his ears, only for a moment. He spoke in a voice too low for Lea to hear.

Reeta turned. "He says it's close. No, that's not quite the word. I don't know. Exalted? High up."

"Shitting hell," Terence said. "Meaning the Greenland shark is close? Does he know that for a fact?"

The guide was still speaking to Reeta, his lips trembling as he spoke. Reeta frowned and nodded, her palm raised to the man, perhaps as a signal for him to remain calm.

"What's the deal?" Lea whispered to Nils. "What's so exciting?"

Nils pressed his hand on his face, drawing it downwards until his jowls bounced. "It's the biggest bastard out there. Twenty-plus feet and with the oldest living to two hundred years. It's notorious, but partly that's just because of the toxicity of the flesh—remember in the port bar last night, I told you the natives use the phrase 'shark-sick' to mean drunk?"

Reeta stood up. She glanced at Sighna, who had slumped back into the pile of rucksacks. "It's all a bit of a jumble. My translation skills—" She blinked, perhaps registering the expressions of her team members. "Sighna says the shark coming close always affects him in this way. Says his head hurts, it's hard to concentrate. I'm not sure I'm getting this right, but he's complaining about something loud. Shouting. Maybe screaming."

Terence held her by the shoulders. "And the shark? He thinks it's nearby?"

"He's positive. Although I don't know why you'd treat that as—"

"Where?" Terence was already packing gear into a bag. He whistled to get the attention of the assistant director and another of the cameramen, who were deep in conversation at the far side of the hut.

"All the way back where Lea was this morning," Reeta said. "Right at the foot of the Jakobshavn glacier."

Terence and Nils exchanged glances. After a few moments, Nils shrugged his approval. "I'll buzz the boat crew. We'll meet them as close as we can get."

Lea started gathering her kit, too. "I'll show you the way down to the water." She turned to Nils. "So this shark's a catch, right? A rarity?"

Nils' face had turned pale. "Like you wouldn't believe. They almost never show their ugly faces. If one's come close to the surface—"

She was first in the jeep, turning over the engine and gesticulating orders for the other team members to hurry.

Lea pulled off her headphones and listened for Peter. Still no sound. She scrolled down the filenames on the hard drive. The file size of the final track was enormous. Whoever had been operating it remotely from the boat must have let the recording run on, afterward, while she was being hauled out of the sea. Her index finger paused over the mouse button. She turned in her swivel chair and lifted the phone.

The call went to voice mail. She hung up and tried again. This time, after several rings, Nils answered.

"It's Lea. I need to see it."

"Lea? It's—what time is it?"

"I don't know. Late, I guess. Can you send me the footage?"

"Jesus. Are you alright?"

"I'm just not tired, that's all. Got back this afternoon."

"That's not what I meant and you know it. How are you? I thought they were going to keep you in longer."

"It was only concussion, and I couldn't bear it any longer. It was so cold. Hospitals are never cold." Lea shuddered at the thought of her bare feet against the cold, tiled floor of the ward at Queen Ingrid's Hospital.

A pause. "Have you spoken to anyone?"

"I'm not a talker. You?"

"Yeah. I mean, of course. My wife, kids, my two best friends. I spoke to Carl on the phone, too, as soon as I got home. Two days too late to be anywhere near the first to offer commiserations, of course, but—" Abruptly, the phone line hummed with static. It took a few seconds for Lea to realise that Nils was sobbing. "Fuck. Lea. Carl was—I don't know. He refused to blame me. Said I'll be welcome at her funeral. But . . . Reeta was part of my team. She was my responsibility. If it wasn't my fault, then I don't know who. And then there was almost you, too."

"Almost." Lea tested the word 'blame' in her mind, holding it up against herself and her own actions. "But I'm okay. I am."

"I'm glad," Nils said, sniffing. "I'm so glad. If you ever need anything, Lea . . ."

"I just need you to send me the footage."

The jeep skidded to a halt at the coast. Lea leapt out, jogging to the shore, scanning for corpses. Terence ran at her side, barely able to contain his glee at the prospect of discovering a bear or seal, evidence of one of Eqalussuaq's rare forays above the surface. During the jeep journey, Nils had pulled up Google image results of seals found with rips that corkscrewed around their bodies. As she had glanced at the photos, Lea's only thought had been to wonder what the attack must have sounded like.

They found nothing but the waiting boat. Its three crew members took Nils aside to speak to him, before allowing any of the production team on board. Even then, they remained far quieter than usual.

For three hours, the boat bobbed in the waters at the foot of the Jakobshavn glacier. After the first hour, Lea's eyes grew tired of staring at the roiling waters and her stomach ached from leaning over the rail. She gazed up at the glacier and imagined that she could make out its creep, pushing across the sea towards the boat.

When Reeta volunteered to go below the surface, Lea stood at her side and insisted that she should go too. She held the microphone before her like a staff, as if to demonstrate her strength. Nils protested, of course, but Lea made her case again and again. If Eqalussuaq wasn't down there, then she could simply gather more iceberg and background recordings. And if it was, then wouldn't it be a crime to have video footage but no sound?

Lea refreshed her inbox until the email appeared. She followed the link to the fileshare site. While she waited for it to download, she darted upstairs to fetch a blanket, then drank another glass of wine huddled within it. It was getting colder all the time.

She opened the final sound file, *14Sep16_044*, then clicked the pause button before it started.

The video finished downloading. She set it running. The video was far from broadcast quality, as it was the backup from the remote feed the rest of the team had viewed on the boat, rather than the master files. After a dizzying flurry of pixel artefacts and indigo bubbles, the image cleared a little. She saw herself, barely recognisable in her wetsuit, identifiable only by the Tippex marks on her shoulder: DISKO SUCKS.

Onscreen, she held up three fingers. Here, now, Lea copied the pose, then two fingers, then one. Then she clicked the play button on the sound file.

Suddenly, the bubbles produced by her scuba equipment were accompanied by gulping sounds through the headphones. Lea leant close to the screen, trying to judge whether sound and image matched. The underwater Lea tapped on the microphone, twice, producing dull thuds. Perfect sync.

It was as she remembered. Reeta's camera swung smoothly around, performing a three-sixty turn to end up facing Lea again. Lea gesticulated and Reeta spun quicker, losing her balance. Lea shook her head. She hadn't meant to suggest that she had seen anything that should be filmed, she had only meant to tell Reeta to point the camera somewhere other than towards her.

The gurgling sound increased in volume, the only clue that Lea had allowed herself to descend further. Reeta's camera dropped, too, and the indigo screen darkened. When the bubbles lessened once again, Lea could hear the low grumbles and creaks of the icebergs above.

It was difficult to remember how long they had floated there, searching the darkness for signs of the shark. Even now, watching onscreen, Lea lost track. Her eyelids drooped. If it hadn't been so cold, she might have slept.

A flurry of bubbles alerted her. The video artefacted again as Reeta bounced the camera around. When it stabilised, Lea could see herself once more, in the bottom left-hand corner of the screen, barely visible against the blackness of the lower depths. This tiny Lea was looking up and away from Reeta's camera.

And then there it was.

Eqalussuaq.

Lea felt a swell of disappointment. Even with its entire length visible, the shark seemed squat and small, making a horizontal stripe across the centre-left of the screen. Its tail was only a few pixels in height. She tried to judge the distance between her and it. Ten feet? Five? Both of them seemed to fidget, an effect of the camera shaking.

The shark seemed to hover before Lea, maintaining a consistent distance. The effect was as though it were tethered to her like a balloon. Onscreen, Lea stretched out her arm, pushing the microphone towards the thing. New sounds came from the headphones. Whooshes and hisses. Its fins as it adjusted its position.

Then, both Lea and the shark seemed to grow. Reeta was moving closer. Brave girl. For the first time, Lea felt a stab of guilt about what happened next.

It would be any second now.

The shark edged backwards—she hadn't realised that at the time—before it leapt towards Lea. Her arm lifted to protect her face, producing loud gulps as the weight of the water pushed back against the microphone. Then, onscreen, Lea's head raised to look directly at the shark as it came.

She remembered the sequence of events clearly, up to a point. Her memories filled in what the grainy footage had failed to capture.

She remembered seeing the thin threads that trailed from each of its eyes. Nils had described them during the jeep journey—parasites that itched and blinded the shark.

She remembered the moment in which the shark seemed to travel above her, rather than towards her, before its jaw dropped open.

She remembered the distinct difference between its two sets of teeth: broad and square below, thin and pointed above. An ugly phrase had repeated in her mind: *seal ripping.*

She remembered opening her mouth just as the shark did, releasing her grip on her scuba mouthpiece, and letting loose a storm of bubbles that almost, but not quite, obscured Eqalussuaq, and she remembered shouting at it. The recording failed to capture the words, but she spoke them aloud, again, now.

"Not me! Take her!"

Abruptly, a squall of sound shrieked through the headphones. Lea spasmed and one arm knocked the glass from the worktop, spraying red wine onto the screen. She ripped the headphones from her ears.

Onscreen, the open jaws of the shark shuddered, as if the shriek came from within.

What was *that*? Instinctively, she glanced at the waveform. Its shape was smoothly bulbous, without peaks.

She bent the headphone cup to listen with one ear. The shriek began again, even louder than before. Even with the amp dialled down, she could hardly bear to hear it. Now she could make out a guttural growl beneath the shrill static.

She flung the headphones down again.

Onscreen, silent, the shark turned. Now it faced the camera full on.

Perhaps Reeta wasn't so brave, after all. At the moment that it was clear that Eqalussuaq was accelerating towards her, she let go of the camera. The blue light of the screen flashed bright and dark, bright and dark, as the camera spun and dropped down, down, down.

Upstairs, Peter began to howl.

She slept badly, imagining herself in the depths along with the abandoned camera. Something was down there with her, sinuous and sleek. It was a bad joke, she thought when she woke. Eqalussuaq, of the family Somniosidae. *Sleeper shark.*

The bulky headphones comforted her. As she strode towards the island's coast, she listened to the live recording stream from the binaural microphones fixed to the exterior of the earphone cups. Her footsteps redoubled in her ears, lagging fractionally behind the real world, as if following her.

Lindisfarne could be defined by its sounds. The wind tumbling from the sea and up the rock outcrops. The cries of the gulls and the whip of their wings. The dense, tactile calm within the oasis of the priory ruins. Captured and suitably arranged, it all belonged to Lea.

Her pace quickened as she headed through the sand dunes to the pebble beach, putting distance between herself and home. The Arctic recordings weren't scheduled to be delivered to Nils for another week, after Reeta's funeral, and indexing the sound files would involve only a handful of hours of work. That morning, when she had returned from delivering Peter to school, she had lingered in front of the computer, unable to bring herself to boot it up. Eqalussuaq's shriek had still echoed in her ears.

She had decided to distract herself by concentrating on other projects. Her record label had shown only muted interest in her proposal of manipulated ambient recordings from Lindisfarne, but they hadn't heard even the raw audio yet. Following post-production work in the studio, the tracks could be wonderful.

She was still crouching beside an abandoned boat, leaning in with the binaural mics to capture its dull scrape against the pebbles, when she noted the time. All those weeks away from home had left her insensitive to the timing of the tides. She would have to rush to make it across the causeway and back before the sea made it impassable.

As she turned from the shore a faint sound registered in her headphones. She turned to the boat again. Had its hull made that screech? She turned her head from side to side to locate the direction. It was coming from somewhere out at sea. Shrill. As the high-pitched noise grew in volume, she heard a deep grumble beneath, and she thought of icebergs. She stared out at the water, half-expecting to see a disturbance, something cutting through the waves as it approached.

Nothing. At least, nothing visible.

But the volume increased, all the same. The screech and roar became more insistent. Louder.

Angrier.

After another ten seconds she could no longer bear the shrieking. She pulled off the headphones and sprinted back towards the dunes.

Lea sat opposite Peter at the melamine table. He hadn't touched his burger. There were dark shadows beneath his eyes. After the awkwardness of the apology to Daphne and her parents at the school gates, Lea had brought him to a McDonald's in Berwick, but her desperation to maintain the pretence that it was a treat was wearing thin. Peter was a smart six-year-old. He understood that her delay on the island, and the high tide that now covered the Lindisfarne causeway, meant an enforced wait of four hours before they could return home.

"What if you'd got lost when you were away?" Peter said.

Lea flinched. Once again, she imagined herself freezing in Baffin Bay. If she'd found herself trapped down there, would she have prayed for Peter or would her final thoughts have been of her precious recordings?

"I had maps and people to show me around," she said. She noted the petulance in her own voice.

"But you were far, far away."

"Eat your food."

Peter pushed away the greasy container. "Daphne said you weren't coming back."

"And that's why you bit her?"

"I bit her because she's a bitch."

Lea sprung from her seat. "Don't you *dare* use that kind of language!" She hovered beside him. What was she going to do, hit him?

Peter slumped further into his chair.

Lea sighed. It was fruitless to wonder where he'd learnt the word. She had no idea how he'd been living for the last three months. She would never have thought him capable of running away from home.

"Look," she said, "I was far away, you're right. But I found my way back to you, didn't I?"

Peter's sullen expression changed to one of quiet hope. "Like I've got a homing beacon? So you can always find me?"

"Exactly. I zoomed across the seas, from Greenland all the way back to here. And I won't leave you again." Instantly, she regretted the last part.

That night, after Peter had bathed, he insisted that Lea bring the portable radio into his bedroom. Karen, it transpired, had taken to leaving a radio on low volume, following a phase of interrupted sleep. The mutter of Radio 4 voices was unintelligible but soothing nonetheless, despite the static that wouldn't quite abate, no matter where Lea tuned the dial.

Shadows in the depths. Smooth skin and sharp points.

Lea woke in a panic.

That shriek again. It pulsated, echoing around the walls and in her head.

She burst into the corridor and down the stairs. Behind her, Peter's shouts mingled with the scream that seemed to come from everywhere at once.

The shrill sound was even louder as she neared her studio at the back of the house. She staggered with the pressure of it as she entered the room. The huge bookshelf speakers emitted waves of piercing white noise.

Lea lunged up at them. Once they were turned off, her body slumped in delayed shock.

She ignored Peter's wails. In the kitchen she turned on the radio, then flicked it off as the squealing sound began again. The TV in the lounge gave the same result, though the picture was unaffected.

It was everywhere.

With shaking hands, she booted up the computer. She opened one of the iceberg sound recordings at random.

She saw what had happened immediately. Instead of a smooth waveform, the sound editor showed a single block of black, with only occasional slices missing, like shards calved from an iceberg. Tentatively, she lifted the headphones and pressed play. The scream was unbearable, even with the headphones held at arm's length. The plastic buzzed and shook with the force of the sound.

She opened more and more sound files. They all appeared identical—masses of noise, black blots on the screen.

All of the recordings were gone. All of the sounds, eclipsed by a single shout. A shriek. A scream.

"No," she whimpered. "Please. Anything but this."

She staggered backwards. The loss of the recordings felt like grief.

She remembered how the sound had approached as she had stood on the shore of the island. A phrase from the day before echoed in her mind.

. . . across the seas, from Greenland all the way back to here . . .

She thought of Sighna, the Inuit guide, his hands clamped over his ears.

She thought of Eqalussuaq, its jaws wide. Its silent scream, back then. Its shriek, on the recordings.

Whatever she had picked up on her microphone, it hadn't been a sound, not in the usual sense. It was something else. Something that she had trapped, or that had—what was the word? Hidden? No . . . burrowed. Torn and ripped and burrowed, hiding itself within her recordings.

And she had brought it home.

The bookshelf speakers began to rock. Lea shuddered. She could still hear the sound, though only faintly. She pulled the plug from the wall. The sound only grew in intensity.

Anger.

She felt an icy chill all over her body. The sound grew and grew and grew, dizzying, nauseating. It no longer came from the speakers. It seemed to be emitted by the walls, the air, her own skin.

"Stop!" she shouted. "Whatever you are, stop! Leave me alone!" Another phrase, the same one she had used when she had first encountered Eqalussuaq, pressed at her. "Not me!"

The scream stopped.

Lea waited. The calm felt like deafness. Tentatively, she plugged in the speakers and turned them on. Nothing.

Safe and sound.

With shaking hands, she booted the computer, then scrolled down to the first recordings of that final day in the sea. She selected the first file. A low, warm, creaking sound came from the speakers. The song of the iceberg had returned, pristine and ethereal, its wheezing groan continuing without interruption. No screaming, no anger.

She selected another recording made that same morning, then another. All were unimpaired, the clean, clear sounds matching the smooth waveforms on the screen.

Breathless, she gathered recordings together in the sound editor, overlaying and overlapping them, until the orchestra of soft moaning sounds grew into a single, overwhelming, glorious song. Bubbles rose around her. She felt warmth despite the chill. She danced slowly as if underwater.

Only one unwanted, alien sound penetrated through. Lea finally registered Peter's complaints from upstairs.

As she entered his bedroom, her son reached up blindly with both hands.

"It's okay," Lea said, rocking him against her chest. "It's gone."

Peter said nothing. Tears trickled down his cheeks, making twin spots on her pyjamas. His open mouth worked from side to side. Lea remembered making the same motion herself, as the plane touched down and she tried to restore her hearing.

"Stop shouting," Peter murmured.

Lea frowned. Was he dreaming?

But then he looked directly at her. His voice sounded far away. "It hurts so much, Mum. Make it stop."

She watched him writhe, his hands pressed against his ears and his face pushed into the pillow. She felt a sudden certainty that it wouldn't help.

Peter's body was slack in her arms as she made her way downstairs. She stood holding him, before her computer, watching the undulating shapes of the waveforms on the screen. The iceberg recordings continued playing. Warm and heavenly.

She hesitated for several moments before laying Peter down on the battered studio sofa. Her hands wavered over the computer keyboard.

Peter's mouth contorted with pain, a thin white line pressed tight as if withholding something trying to force its way out.

It felt like a choice. Save the recordings, or Peter. Eqalussuaq was demanding that she choose.

She understood that her hesitation was unforgivable. She understood that she would spend her life attempting to rationalise the fact that she had even considered the alternative.

She looked at her son.

She chose.

14Sep16. Select all.

She wept a little.

Delete.

Peter whimpered as Lea smoothed his hair, then pressed his head further into the sofa cushion. His body shivered and shook. Clearly, he was still in agony.

She yanked out the plug to the computer and clawed at its case.

In the lean-to beyond the kitchen she found a hammer and chisel. As she cracked through the casing of the computer she shouted and wailed, a sound almost as feral as the scream on the recordings. The chisel revealed the internal hard drive, then fractured it. Once it was in pieces Lea turned her attention to the portable drives. In her desperation she shattered them all.

If anything, Peter appeared to be suffering even more now. His knees pulled up to his chin. As he rocked back and forth, his entire body spasmed.

Then his white lips trembled. They parted, showing his teeth.

The scream of whatever had followed Lea from the Arctic burst forth. Peter's head rattled from side to side with the effort of restraining himself against the force of the sound.

Lea gripped his hands. She pleaded.

But she understood. Destroying the recordings wasn't all that Eqalussuaq demanded.

"It's not him you want," she said in a whisper. "It's me."

Peter's eyes opened.

Lea gripped the wooden arm of the sofa.

It hit her. Creaking limbs, something bellowing, screams that knifed through the water.

She clamped her hands over her ears, without any effect. The shriek took swipes at her head and torso, threatening to send her toppling. Her body convulsed with the cold.

Peter recovered within hours.

Lea's tinnitus would be permanent, the doctor said, though over time it transitioned from excruciating to deafening to a persistent, wavering drone.

She stood on the rock outcrop at dusk, facing out to sea. She watched a flock of gulls, concentrating on the shifting shapes that they formed, at first a ribbon, then a fat arrow, then a winding river.

She stretched her body upwards, tracking the flock, then winced at a pain in her stomach. She pulled her cardigan and T-shirt up. The thing had left her, but it had also left its mark. If it had ever been a real wound, one might have said it was healing fast. It was clear that the scar would remain, though—a single line of ripped, raw, pink flesh that corkscrewed around her abdomen.

A wave curled into existence and bundled itself towards the shore. Once she might have worn her binaural microphones to capture the sounds of the wind and waves, but the ringing in her ears interfered with the recordings. Now the sounds of the Island served only as a temporary mask over the hisses and shrieks.

Above her, for a few seconds, the flock of birds formed a new shape—something sinewy and snub-nosed. It flexed and flicked its tail as it swam across the darkening sky.

LOST IN THE DARK

JOHN LANGAN

TEN YEARS AGO, SARAH FIORE'S *LOST IN THE DARK* TERRIFIED AUDIENCES. NOW, ON THE ANNIVERSARY OF THE MOVIE'S RELEASE, ITS DIRECTOR HAS REVEALED NEW INFORMATION ABOUT THE CIRCUMSTANCES BEHIND ITS FILMING. JOHN LANGAN REPORTS.

I

Pete's Corner Pub, in the Hudson Valley town of Huguenot, is a familiar college-town location: the student bar, at whose door aspiring underage patrons test their fake id's against the bouncers' scrutiny, and inside which every square inch is occupied by men and women shouting to be heard over the sound system's blare. Its floor is scuffed, its wooden tables and benches scored with generations of initials and symbols. More students than you could easily count have passed their Friday and Saturday nights here, their weekend dramas fueled by surging hormones and pitchers of cheap beer.

During the day, Pete's is a different place, the patrons older, mostly there for its hamburgers, which are regarded by those in the know as the best in town. A few regulars station themselves at the bar, solitary figures there to consume their daily ration of alcohol and possibly pass a few words with the bartender. Between lunch and dinner, the place is relatively quiet. You can bring your legal pad and pen and sit and write for a couple of hours, and as long as you're a good tipper, the waitress will keep warming your cup of decaf. The bartender has the music low, so you can have a conversation if you need to.

This particular afternoon, I'm at Pete's to talk to Sarah Fiore. To be honest, it's not my first choice for an interview, but it was the one location on which we could agree, so here I am, seated in a booth at the back of the restaurant. The upper half of the rear wall is an unbroken line of windows that curves inward at the top, for a greenhouse effect. I'm guessing it was intended to give a view out over the town, but the buildings that went up behind the bar frustrated that design. Still, they provide plenty of natural light, which must save on the electric bill.

It's Halloween, which seems almost too on the nose for the interview I'm here to conduct. Already, small children dressed as characters from comic books, movies, and video games wander the sidewalks, accompanied by parents whose costumes are the same ones they wear every day. I see Gothams of Batmen, companies of Storm Troopers, palaces of Disney princesses, and MITs worth of video game characters. There are few monsters, which saddens me, but I'm a traditionalist. In a couple of hours, the town will host its annual Halloween parade, for which they'll close the lower part of Main Street. It's quite a sight. Hundreds of costumed participants will assemble in front of the library—just up the street from Pete's—and process down towards the Svartkill River, which forms the town's western boundary. Once there, they'll turn into the parking lot of the police station, where they'll be served cider and donuts by members of the police and fire departments, accompanied by the mayor and other local officials. I find it quite sweet.

In the interest of full disclosure, I should add here, while we're still waiting for Sarah Fiore to arrive, that she and I know one another. Specifically, she was my student twenty-one years ago, in the first section of Freshman Composition I taught at SUNY Huguenot. She was in her mid-twenties, settling down to pursue a degree after several years of working odd jobs and traveling. She was a big fan of horror movies, wrote several essays about films like *Nosferatu* (the original), the Badham *Dracula*, and *Near Dark*. We spent fifteen minutes of one class arguing the merits of *The Lost Boys*, much to the amusement of her fellow students. After the semester was over, I occasionally bumped into Sarah in the hallways of one building or another, which was how I learned that she was transferring to NYU for their film program. I told her she would have to make a horror movie.

Eleven years later, when *Lost in the Dark* was released, I remembered our exchange. I hadn't seen Sarah since that afternoon in the Humanities building, had no idea how to get in touch with her to offer my congratulations for her good reviews. "A smarter *Blair Witch Project*" that's the one that sticks in my mind; although the only thing Sarah's film shares with Eduardo Sànchez and Daniel Myrick's is its reliance on hand-held cameras for the faux-documentary effect. Otherwise, *Lost in the Dark* has a much more developed narrative, both in terms of the Bad Agatha backstory and the Isabelle Price main story. The sequels did a lot to perpetuate the brand, and helped to add Bad Agatha to the pantheon of contemporary horror villains. Sarah's involvement with these films was limited, but she pushed for J. T. Petty to direct the second, and she reached out to Sean Mickles to bring him in for the third. As a result, you have a trilogy of horror movies by three different directors that work unusually well together. Sarah's sets up the story, Petty's explores the history, and Mickles's does its weird meta-thing about the films. While her name is on the fourth and fifth movies as producer, that had more to do with the details of the contract her agent worked out for her. Recently, there's been talk of a *Lost in the Dark* television series. AMC is interested, as is Showtime. There have been a couple of tie-in novels, and a four–issue comic book published by IDW.

Truth to tell, I think a good part of the continuing success of the *Lost in the Dark* franchise has to do with its Halloween connections. It didn't hurt the original film to be released Halloween weekend, and whoever thought up giving away Bad Agatha masks to the first dozen ticket buyers, was a promotional genius. Plastic shells with a rubber band strap, they were hardly sophisticated, but there was a crude energy to their design, all flat planes and sharp angles. An approximation of the movie's makeup, the masks captured the menace of the character. It's the eyes that do it, especially that missing left one. The bit of black fabric glued behind the opening gives the appearance of depth, as if you're seeing right into the center of Bad Agatha's skull and the darkness therein. The last I checked, one of the original masks was going for four hundred dollars on eBay. The versions that have been released with each subsequent *Lost in the Dark* installment have varied in execution (though a colleague said that the mask she received was the best thing about the fourth movie), but they've become part of the phenomenon.

Throughout this time, Sarah Fiore has kept herself busy with other projects. She wrote and directed two films, *Hideous Road* (2009) and *Bubblegum Confession* (2011), and was director for *Apple Core* (2012). She wrote and directed the 2014 Shirley Jackson documentary for PBS's *American Masters*, which was nominated for an Emmy. With Phil Gelatt, she co-wrote an adaptation of Laird Barron's "Hallucigenia" that John Carpenter was rumored to be considering. Yet none of these movies or scripts has attached to her name the way the *Lost in the Dark* series has. For the most part, she's borne this with good grace, expressing in numerous interviews her gratitude for the films' success.

While not inevitable, it's hardly surprising that, in today's short-term-memory culture, any work of art with staying power is going to be milked for all it's worth. In the case of the original *Lost in the Dark*, this means a celebration of the movie's ten-year anniversary. There's a special-edition Blu-ray with an added disk full of bonus features, screenings of the film in select theaters, and a new batch of Bad Agatha masks. Plus, the announcement that Takashi Shimizu has signed on to direct the sixth *Lost in the Dark* movie, which is supposed to herald a bold new direction for the franchise. None of this is especially remarkable; much lesser films receive much grander treatment.

What is of note lies buried within the fifteen hours of new footage on the Blu-ray's bonus disk. There's a forty-minute group interview during which Sarah, and Kristi Nightingale, who was her director of photography, and Ben Formosa, who played Ben Rios, sit around a table with Edie Amos of *Rue Morgue* discussing the origins and shooting of the movie. It's the kind of thing film geeks love: behind the scenes of their favorite film. There's a pitcher of water on the table, a glass in front of each participant. Sarah sits with her elbows on the table, her hands clasped. She's wearing a black linen blouse, her long black hair pulled back in a ponytail. Kristi leans back in her chair, the mass of her curly brown hair springing from underneath an unmarked blue baseball cap. A black and white Billy Idol, circa *Rebel Yell*, sneers from the front of her white sweatshirt. Ben has shaved his head, which, combined with noticeable weight loss, gives him the appearance of having aged more than his former companions. The red dress shirt he's wearing practically glows with money, an emblem of the success he's enjoyed in his recent roles. Edie sits with a tablet in front of her. Her oversized round glasses magnify her eyes ever-so-slightly.

The conversation flows easily, and the first fifteen minutes are full of all sorts of minutiae. Then, in response to a question about how she arrived at the idea for the movie, Sarah looks down, exhales, and says, "Well, it was supposed to be a documentary."

At what she assumes is a joke, Edie laughs, but the glance passed between Kristi and Ben gives the lie to that. She says, "Wait—"

Sarah takes a sip from her water. "I'd known Isabelle since NYU," she says, referring to Isabelle Router, who plays the ill-fated Isabelle Price. "She was from Huguenot, which was where I'd done my first two years of undergrad. We kind of bonded over that. She knew all about the area, these crazy stories. I was never sure if she was making them up, but any time I went to the trouble of fact checking them, they turned out to be true. Or true enough. That's why she was at school, for a degree in Cultural Anthropology. She wanted to study the folklore of the Hudson Valley.

"Anyway, we kept in touch after we graduated. I landed a position working for Larry Fessenden, Glass Eye Pix. Isabelle went to Albany for her doctorate. There was this piece of local history Isabelle wanted to include in her dissertation. She'd heard it from her uncle, who'd been a state trooper stationed in Highland when she was growing up. Sometime around 1969 or '70, a train had made an unscheduled stop just north of Huguenot. This was when there was a rail line running up the Svartkil Valley. Even then, the trains were on their way out, but one still pulled into the station in downtown Huguenot twice a day. This was the night train, on its way north to Wiltwyck. It wasn't very long, half a dozen cars. About five minutes after it left town, the train slowed, and came to a halt next to an old cement mine. A couple of men were waiting there, dressed in heavy coats and hats because of the chill. (It was only mid-October, but there'd been a cold snap that week. Funny, the details you remember.) No less than five passengers said they witnessed a woman being led off the very last car on the train by one of the conductors and another woman wearing a Catholic nun's veil. None of the passengers got a good look at the woman between the conductor and the nun. All of them agreed that she had long black hair and that a man's overcoat was draped across her shoulders. Other than that, their stories varied: one said that she had been bound in a straightjacket under the coat; another that she'd been wearing a white dress; a third that she'd been in a nightgown and barefoot. The woman didn't struggle, didn't appear to notice the men there for her at all. They took her from the conductor and the nun and, guiding her by the elbows, steered her toward the mine opening. Before anyone could see anything more, the train lurched forward.

"I suppose that might've been all, except one of the passengers was so bothered by what she'd seen that she called the police the minute she walked in her front door. The cops in Huguenot didn't take her seriously, told her it was probably nothing, the engineer doing someone a favor. This was not good enough for our concerned citizen, who went on to dial the state police, next. Their dispatcher said they'd send someone out to have a look. Isabelle's uncle—what was his name? John? Edward?"

"Richard," Kristi Nightingale says. She is not looking at Sarah.

"Right, Richard, Uncle Rich," Sarah says. "He was the one they sent. It was pretty late by the time he reached the old access road that led to the mine. He told Isabelle he didn't know what to expect, but it wasn't a pair of fresh corpses. He stumbled onto the men ten feet inside the mine entrance. One had been driven forward into the wall with such force his face was unrecognizable. The other had been torn open."

"Wait," Edie says, "wait a minute. This is real? I mean, this actually took place?"

Sarah nods. "You can check the papers. It was front page news for the *Wiltwyck Daily Freeman* and the *Poughkeepsie Journal* for days. Even the *Times* wrote a piece on it: 'Sleepy College Town Rocked by Savage Killings.'"

"Well, what happened?"

"Nobody knew," Sarah says. "The whole thing was very strange. Apparently, the dead men were the same guys who had met the woman from the train. It turned out they were brothers who came from somewhere down in Brooklyn—Greenpoint, maybe. I can't remember their name, something Polish. Neither of their families could say what they were doing upstate, much less why they'd been waiting at the mine. Nor was there any trace of the conductor or the nun. All of the convents within a three hour radius could account for their residents' whereabouts. The conductor who had been working that section of the train was a new guy who didn't return the next day, and whose hiring information turned out to be fake. Of the mysterious woman, there was no trace. The police searched the mine, the surrounding woods, knocked on the doors of the nearest houses, but came up empty-handed.

"There were all kinds of theories floating around. The most popular one involved organized crime. There used to be a lot of Mafia activity in the Hudson Valley. They had their fingers in the locale sanitation businesses. Great way to dispose of your rivals, right? The story was, they also used some of the old mines and caves for the same purpose. In this version of events, the woman had been brought to the mine to disappear into it. Whoever she was, she or someone close to her was guilty of a particularly grievous trespass, and this was the punishment.

"But then what? How had she turned the tables on her captors and killed them? Not to mention, in such an . . . extravagantly violent manner. You could imagine adrenaline allowing her to overpower one of the men, seize his gun and shoot him and his partner before they had the chance to react. Crushing a man's skull against a rock wall, cracking his friend's chest open, were harder to believe. Plus, neither one showed evidence of having been armed.

"Maybe the woman hadn't been there to be murdered; maybe she was there to be traded. She'd been kidnapped, and the mine was the place her abductors had selected to return her to whoever was going to pay her ransom. Or she was a high-class prostitute, being transferred from one brothel to another. Either way, the scheduled meeting went pear-shaped and the men died. It didn't explain why they had done so in such a fashion, but the cops liked it better, it felt more probable to them.

"There were other, wilder explanations offered, too. The dead guys were Polish. This was the end of the sixties, the Cold War was in full swing, and Poland was slotted into the Eastern Bloc. Were the brothers foreign agents? Was the woman a fellow spy who had failed in her duties? Had she been sent here to be liquidated? Then rescued by other spies? Or were the brothers working for the US Government, and the woman a captured spy who had to vanish? These weren't the craziest scenarios, either. *Rosemary's Baby* was pretty big at this time, which may explain why some people picked up on the detail of the nun who stepped off the train. Could it be that the woman had been carrying the spawn of the Satan, or otherwise involved in diabolical activities? It would account for the savagery of the brothers' deaths—the Devil and his followers are pretty ferocious—if not for what the men had been doing at the mine in the first place. It's been a while since the Catholic Church sanctioned anyone's murder.

"In the end, the investigation dead-ended. Officially, it was left open, but in the absence of any credible leads, the cops turned their attention elsewhere."

Sarah drinks more water. "Within a year or two, the local kids were telling stories about the woman in the mine. Some of them portrayed her as criminally insane, delivered to the place to be kept in a secret cell constructed for the sole purpose of confining her. Other accounts made her a witch, dropped at the mine for essentially the same purpose, imprisonment. Whether she was natural or supernatural, the woman escaped her bonds, slaughtered her jailors, and was now on the loose, ready to abduct any child careless enough to allow her too close. A few years later, when *The Exorcist* was released, the narrative adapted itself to the film, and the woman became demonically possessed, transported upstate for an exorcism, which obviously had failed. It was one of the peculiarities of the story, the way it shaped itself to the current cultural landscape. The woman morphed into a teen with dangerous psychic abilities, an alien masquerading as a human, even a vampire. For older kids, venturing into the mine, especially at night, and especially at Halloween, became a rite of passage. After the railroad stopped running in the seventies, high school and college kids would drive to the access road and hike to the entrance to build bonfires and drink.

"A similar process happens all over the country—all over the world. Something bad happens, and it hardens into the seed for stories about a monstrous character. This was what Isabelle's dissertation director said. There was nothing unusual about the woman in the mine, as the local kids called her. Isabelle disagreed, said she had additional information that distinguished this narrative from the rest. Once again, it involved her uncle, Rich, the cop.

"Ten years to the date after he answered his first call about the mine, he received a second. A group of high school seniors had been partying outside the entrance, and one of them had gone into it on a dare. That was three hours ago, and there had been no sign of him since. A couple of the other kids started in after their missing friend, but could find no trace of him as far as they dared to go. Everybody panicked, and eventually someone who was sober enough drove home and phoned the police. The Huguenot cops were busy with a costume party at one of the university's dorms that had gotten out of hand when someone spiked the punch with acid, so the call was booted to the state troopers. Rich suspected a Halloween prank, probably by the missing kid on his friends, possibly by all the kids on the cops. Despite that, he drove to the access road and made his way on foot to the spot.

"There, he encountered a dozen teenagers, all of them more or less sober, so sick with worry he decided they must be telling the truth. Flashlight in hand, he set off into the mine to search for their friend. He wasn't nervous, he told Isabelle. Sure, he remembered the bodies of the men he'd discovered a decade before, but he'd seen a lot worse than that in the meantime. The dark had never bothered him, nor did the thought of being underground. He was more concerned about the debris littering the floor: rocks of varying sizes, dusty boxes, rusted bits of old machines, the occasional tool. His feet crushed fast food containers, kicked the bones of small animals, clanged on an empty metal lunchbox. There was one good thing about the clutter—it allowed him to track the missing student without much difficulty.

"He came across graffiti farther inside the mine than he would have expected. He read names of people, sports teams, bands. He saw hearts encasing the names of lovers, peace symbols, even the anarchist A. He stumbled through a heap of beer cans, whose musical clatter wasn't as comforting as he would have liked. Finally, he came upon the portrait."

"Portrait?" Edie says.

"A woman's face," Sarah says, "done in charcoal on a patch of rock about head level. Whoever she was, Rich said, she was striking. Long black hair, high, strong cheekbones, full lips. Her left eye had been smeared, which made it look like a hole into her skull. The artist had given the picture a force, a vitality Rich struggled to define. He said it was as if she were two seconds away from stepping right out of the rock.

"By this point, he was pretty far in. Any sounds of the high school students had long since ceased. He was grudgingly impressed that the kid had traveled this distance. On the right, the tunnel he'd been walking opened on a shallow chamber. He swept his light across it, and stopped. There was a bed in there, its metal frame spotted orange with rust from the damp, its mattress black with mold. Lying half on the bed was a long piece of clothing—a straightjacket. He entered the room, lifted the restraint to check it. Mold blotched the material. What wasn't mold was covered in writing, in symbols. He saw rows of crosses, stars of David, crescent moons, other figures he didn't recognize, but assumed were religious, too. He held up the straightjacket, passed the light over it. The right front side and sleeve were stained with what he was certain was blood. He replaced the garment on the bed, and heard a footstep behind him.

"It was some kind of miracle, Rich said, he didn't spin around gun in hand and shoot whoever was there, or at least brain them with his flashlight. Of course it was the missing student, who'd gotten himself good and lost in the mine's recesses and had only come upon Rich through dumb luck. 'Why didn't you call for help?' he asked the kid. Because there was someone else down there, the kid said. A woman. He'd seen her at the other end of one of the tunnels, right before the torch he was carrying guttered out. There was something wrong with her face, and when she saw him, her expression made him turn and run as fast as he could. The student couldn't say how long he'd been hiding, listening. He'd thought Rich was *her*, and had debated fleeing further into the mine before she saw him. Now that he'd found Rich, it was imperative the two of them exit this place without delay.

"Had he heard the kid's story outside, Rich told Isabelle, beside the fire he and his friends had built, he would have taken the tale with a block of salt. This far into the mine, the only source of light his flashlight, facing the stone cell with the weird straightjacket, the tale sounded less incredible. The student was all for bolting for the entrance, which Rich nixed. They needed to pay attention to their surroundings, he said, or the kid would find himself lost again, and he didn't want that, did he? 'No way,' the kid said.

"The walk back to the surface took a long time. Rich did his best to remain calm, not let the student's hysteria affect him, but there was a stretch of tunnel, about halfway to the exit, in which he was suddenly certain he and the kid were not alone. The hair on the back of his neck lifted, and his mouth went dry. For fear of spooking the student, he didn't want to stop, but the echo of their feet on the walls made it difficult to decide if the sound he thought he was hearing, a whispering noise, like fabric swishing over rock, was more than his imagination. He didn't want to put his hand on his gun, either, though the spot between his shoulders itched, as if something was stalking him and the kid, just a handful of footsteps behind them in the dark. The kid picked up on it, too, and asked him if there was someone else there with them, if *she* had found them. Rich heard the panic rising in the student's voice and said no, it was only the two of them. If the kid suspected him of lying, he didn't say anything.

"At last—at long last, Rich walked the student out of the mine and into the waiting arms of his friends, who were overjoyed at their reappearance. It was all he could do, Rich said, not to look back into the mine. He was afraid he'd see a woman standing inside it, something terribly wrong with her face."

There's a moment of silence, during which both Kristi and Ben fidget. Finally, Edie says, "That's . . . incredible."

"Isabelle thought so," Sarah says. "A couple of years after that, the stories about the woman in the mine gained a new detail: the left side of her face was scarred. Whether the student Rich had retrieved told his story, or other kids ventured into the mine and discovered the drawing he'd seen, that became part of the description. It didn't hurt that the first *Nightmare on Elm Street* was released around then, with its disfigured villain. The point is, there was something interesting going on, and Isabelle already had enough information to justify further research and analysis. She told me she was planning to make the woman in the mine the center of her dissertation, an instance of the way traditional folk story was affected by the presence and pressure of newer narrative forms. The professor overseeing the project disagreed. She more than disagreed, she told Isabelle her idea was a non-starter. Instead, she wanted Isabelle to go south, to Kentucky, where there were reports of a lizard monster that had been spotted during a local disturbance at the end of the sixties. It wasn't that Isabelle wasn't interested in the lizard monster, but she had done a lot of work on the other topic, and she didn't want to drop it. Her professor's attitude left her unsure what to do, scrap what she had and start over, or look for another director who would be more agreeable to her plans. Either way, she was watching the completion of her dissertation recede into the future. Which happens, but is still a bummer.

"Enter me. Through five years of busting my ass, I had convinced Larry that I could and should be trusted with a camera and a small crew. We were searching for the right project. I read a lot of scripts; nothing clicked. I tried writing a couple of screenplays, myself, but they weren't any better. Then one night, I'm talking to Isabelle on the phone. We spoke every couple of weeks, caught up on what each of us was doing. She'd been telling me about the woman in the mine forever, since undergrad. I must have heard the story a thousand times. This particular night, the thousand and first time, things fell into place, and

I realized I had my movie right in front of me. I would take Isabelle's research project, and I would put it onscreen. I would make a documentary about the woman from the mine, about the whole weird thing. Isabelle had assembled a huge archive. There were audio interviews with twenty people. There were hundreds of photographs. There were maps. There were police reports, train schedules, articles about mining. Before I even started, I figured I had a good portion of what I needed for my movie. Production costs would be relatively low, which is never a bad thing for a beginning filmmaker. Sure, a documentary wasn't exactly the most exciting debut, but I planned to jazz it up by filming an excursion to the mine. We'd take a look around inside, see if we couldn't find the drawing Isabelle's uncle had described. If we did—or better, if we located the straightjacket—it would give the film an added *umph.*

"Isabelle didn't need much convincing. She saw the documentary as a middle finger to her professor, a way of demonstrating exactly how wrong the woman was. I doubted it would matter to her; her head sounded as if it was pretty tightly wedged up her own ass. But the idea led Isabelle to sign on with me, so I didn't argue."

"Hold on," Edie says, "hold on. Did you make this? Are you telling me *Lost in the Dark* is a documentary?"

"No," Sarah says, "no, it's—it's more complicated than that." For the first time in the interview, she is flustered. Both Kristi and Ben appear to be barely containing the impulse to bolt. "We went to the mine—this was after Isabelle and I had put together a rough introduction, twenty minutes laying out the story of the mysterious woman. Her Uncle Rich was retired in Tampa, but we interviewed him via phone and he repeated everything he'd told Isabelle. I had arranged for a professor from SUNY Huguenot who specialized in folklore to sit down for a conversation with Isabelle about the woman.

"First, though, I wanted to shoot our trip. I planned it for Halloween, because how could I not? That was when everything had started, when kids built their bonfires outside the entrance, when Rich had ventured into its tunnels. I had my crew: Kristi on camera, George Maltmore on sound, a couple of film students who'd agreed to do whatever we needed them to. The barest of bones. And Isabelle, who was our guide. I gave George and Isabelle handheld cameras and Priya and Chad a camera to split between them. I wasn't expecting anyone to catch anything remarkable; I liked the idea of having shots from other perspectives.

"At dusk on Halloween, we entered the mine. I was certain we'd run into kids partying there. In fact, I was counting on it. I wanted it as an illustration of an annual event, a local ritual. But there was no one there. As far as setbacks go, it wasn't bad. After filming the mine's exterior, we walked into it."

Edie waits a beat, then says, "And . . . ?"

"And we came out again," Sarah says. "Eventually."

II

A synopsis of *Lost in the Dark* is simple enough: an academic leads a film crew into an abandoned mine in search of a mysterious woman who disappeared there decades ago. While in the mine, the crew is plagued by strange and frightening incidents, culminating in a confrontation with the missing woman, who is revealed to be a supernatural creature. After she brutally murders most of the crew, the others flee deeper into the mine. The movie ends with the survivors proceeding into the dark, pursued by the woman.

The devil lives in the details, though, doesn't he? After all, you could make a terrible film from such a plot. There are three scenes, I think, on which the movie's success depends. It seems to me a good idea to pause here a moment and consider them. The IMDb listing for *Lost in the Dark* features what has to be one of the most thorough descriptions of any film listed on the site. At twenty-three thousand words, it's clearly a labor of love. In the interest of not re-inventing the wheel, I'd like to quote its summaries of the scenes I'm interested in. This is how the movie begins:

Synopsis of *Lost in the Dark* (2006)
The content of this page was created directly by users and has not been screened or verified by IMDb staff.
Warning! This synopsis may contain spoilers.
See plot summary for non-spoiler summarized description.

Professor Isabelle Price (Isabelle Router) is being interviewed in her office. Thirty-five years ago, she says, on Halloween night, a woman was brought by train from Hoboken, New Jersey, to a spot north of the upstate New York town of Huguenot. As she speaks, the screen cuts to a shot of 1960s-era passenger train speeding across farmland, then back to her. The woman's name, she says, was Agatha Merryweather. The screen shows a graduation-style portrait of a young woman with dark eyes and long black hair. The image switches to a large blue and white two-storey house. In a voiceover, the professor says that for the previous four years, Angela Merryweather had been confined to the basement of her parents' home in Weehawken, New Jersey. During that time, neighbors reported frequent shouts, screams, and crashes coming from the house. The photograph of the house is replaced by one of police reports fanned out over a desktop. The Weehawken police, the voiceover continues, responded to one hundred and eight separate noise complaints; although only at the very end did they actually enter the house. The camera zeroes in on the report on top of the pile. When the Merryweathers opened the front door to their house, Professor Price says, the police saw the living room in shambles, furniture upended, lamps smashed, a bookcase tipped over. They also saw Agatha Merryweather, age twenty-one, crouched in one corner of the living room, wearing a filthy nightdress. The screen shows a photograph of a middle-aged man and woman, him in a brown suit, her in a green dress. Agatha's parents, the voiceover says, assured the officers that things were not as they appeared. Their daughter was not well, and every now and again, she had fits. The police thought the couple was acting strangely, so they entered the house. One of them approached the girl. The screen shows an open door, its interior dark. The other officer, Professor Price says, was drawn to the door to the basement. As the camera focuses on the darkness within the doorway, she says, He noticed that the door had been bolted and padlocked, but that the bolt and the lock had been torn loose when the door was thrown open, apparently with great force. There were no working lights in the basement, but the officer had his flashlight. He went downstairs, and discovered a bare, empty space, with a pile of blankets for a bed and a pair of buckets for a toilet. The walls were covered in writing, row after row of crosses, six-pointed stars, crescent moons, other symbols the cop didn't recognize. The smell was terrible.

The screen returns to Professor Price, sitting at her desk. From behind the camera, the interviewer (Gillian Bernheimer) asks what happened next. The answer to that question, the professor says, is very interesting. While the police were going about their business, Mrs. Merryweather was on the phone. As you can imagine, the officers were certain they had stumbled onto a case of child abuse. Before they had finished questioning Mr. Merryweather, a black car pulled up in front of the house. Out steps Harrison Law, the Archbishop of Newark, with a couple of assistants. The film shifts to a clip of a heavyset man wearing a bishop's mitre and robes and holding a bishop's crozier, greeting a crowd outside a church. The officers were surprised, the professor says, and even more surprised by what the Archbishop said to them: This woman is under the care of the Church. She is suffering from a terrible spiritual affliction, and her parents are working with me to see that she returns to health.

The screen returns to the professor. The interviewer asks how the police reacted. Professor Price says, They were very impressed. This was when the Church still commanded considerable respect. For an archbishop to intervene personally in a situation was unusual. The cops were willing to give him a lot more leeway than they would in a similar situation today. Although, she adds, to his credit, one of the officers still wrote a fairly extensive report on the incident, which is how we know about it.

The interviewer asks if there was any follow-up. The professor shakes her head. She says, The report was filed and forgotten. However, she was able to track down one of the Merryweathers' former neighbors. This person, who did not want to be identified, said that the morning after the police made their incursion, they watched Agatha Merryweather led down the front steps of her house by a priest and a nun. She appeared to be wearing a straightjacket. The priest and nun helped her into the backseat of a black car. The black car drove off, and that was the last the neighbor saw of Agatha. Professor Price says she asked the neighbor if they remembered the date of Agatha's departure. As a matter of fact, the neighbor said, they did. It was Halloween.

What were the priest and nun doing there? the interviewer asks. The professor says she can only guess. She's been in touch with the Archdiocese of Newark, not to mention, Harrison Law, who currently holds a position at the Vatican. Neither was any help. The Archdiocese claims to have no record of contact between the former Archbishop and the Merryweathers. Harrison Law says that the assistance he offers those under his pastoral care comes with a guarantee of utter discretion.

The interviewer says, It sounds like the Church was a dead-end. Which leads me to ask, How did you learn about Agatha Merryweather in the first place? And what led you to connect her to the woman who left the train outside Huguenot?

Professor Price says, Bear with me. She holds up a photocopy of a drawing. It shows the face of a young woman with dark eyes and long black hair, and bears a strong resemblance to the photograph of Agatha Merryweather. She says, This was made by a police sketch artist in Wiltwyck, New York, after several of the passengers who were on that train called the police to express their concern. All of their reports agreed that the woman was wearing a straightjacket, and was accompanied by a priest and a nun. The professor lowers the piece of paper. She says, The passengers also agreed that Agatha and her companions were met by another pair of men, also priests, outside the entrance to the mine formerly run by the Joppenburgh Cement Company. The police might have passed off the reports as not worth more than a call to St. John's in Joppenburgh to ask if their priests had met someone off the Wiltwyck train. However, one of the reports came from a local judge, who insisted on a more thorough investigation. This, Professor Price says, is how they found the bodies.

Bodies? the interviewer asks. The professor is replaced by a series of black and white crime-scene photographs. They show a pair of naked men lying side by side next to the wall of a cave. Their legs are together, their arms are at their sides, and their eyes are shut. Their throats have been torn open, down to the bone. There are long scratches on their faces and their arms. The wall beside them is splashed with blood, as is the floor near them. In voiceover, Professor Price says, These two were found by the officers who were sent to check the site. As you can see, their clothes, any jewelry they might have been wearing, whatever might have identified them, has been removed. The evidence was that they were killed after a brief, fierce struggle. Obviously, the cause of death was the wound to each man's throat. The medical examiner said their throats had been ripped apart by a set of teeth, most likely human, though he noted irregularities in the bite marks upon which he failed to elaborate. After their deaths, the men were stripped and positioned together. Whoever had tended to the corpses had been careful to leave no traces of themselves. As for the assailant: a scattering of bloody hand- and footprints were found near the top of the tunnel wall, nearly twelve feet up. They retreated into the mine for twenty-five feet, and stopped.

The professor returns to the screen. The interviewer asks her what exactly she's saying. Professor Price says she doesn't know. For eight days, the police conducted a substantial investigation. The murders were front page news in papers up and down the Hudson Valley. They were the lead story on all the local TV news broadcasts. There was a lot of concern that a homicidal maniac or maniacs was on the loose. One of the local papers speculated that the killings might be the work of a Manson-style cult. Huguenot was quite the counterculture mecca at this time. After a few days, the story moved from the front page to page two or three, but it was still very much news. A couple of the passengers on the train thought the dead men were the priests who had helped Agatha Merryweather off the train, but none of the local clergy admitted to knowing them. The sketch I showed you was published in the paper, shown on TV. This was how Agatha Merryweather was identified as the woman on the train. A couple of her former neighbors saw the sketch and called the local police to say they recognized her. The police went to the Merryweathers' house but it was empty, the couple nowhere to be found. None of the neighbors had seen them leave. Apparently, the police did some kind of follow up with the Church, but they don't appear to have had any more success than I did.

The professor says, In Huguenot, the police searched for Agatha in surrounding homes and buildings, and turned up nothing. They brought in dogs in hopes they might discover something. Two of the dogs pissed themselves, then started fighting with such ferocity their handlers needed help separating them. A third dog went into the mine a hundred yards, sat, and started to howl. The police had dismissed the bloody hand- and footprints on the wall as some kind of red herring; although they hadn't been able to explain why the false lead had been placed in such an outlandish place. Now, they decided to search the mine. They broke out the flashlights and set off into its tunnels in pairs.

The interviewer asks if they found anything. Professor Price says, They did. In one of the mine's side passages, the police came across what was left of a straightjacket. It was stiff with dried blood, and had been ripped open by its wearer. More officers were brought in to assist in the effort. Several reported hearing sounds ahead of or behind them, footsteps, mostly, though one pair of officers described something growling close to them. The police said they were concentrating their efforts on the mine, which was where they were reasonably certain their suspect was hiding. And then . . . nothing. The search was called off.

Called off? the interviewer asks. The professor nods. Why? the interviewer asks. The professor says, No one knows. The mine remained the best lead. There was no trace of Agatha Merryweather anywhere else. When they heard about it, the local papers tried to get to the bottom of what had happened, but the police stonewalled them. It didn't take the papers long to move onto other stories. Since that time, no more has been done to determine Agatha Merryweather's fate.

Really? the interviewer asks. The professor says, I've made a pretty through search. There are stories the local kids tell, legends, but nothing in the way of formal investigation. Oh, Professor Price says, but I did learn one more odd fact in the course of my research. The bodies of the murdered men that were left at the mine's entrance? Three days after they arrived at the county morgue, they were claimed, by a John Smith, of Manhattan. The interviewer says, An alias? Professor Price nods. She says, I haven't talked to every John Smith who was living in the city at that time, but I'm pretty confident whoever came for those corpses did so under a fairly blatant pseudonym. Why? the interviewer asks. The professor says, That question comes up a great deal, doesn't it? If we're going to answer it, then I think we need to start with the place where Agatha Merryweather was last seen. We have to go to the mine.

The second scene occurs two-thirds of the way through the movie. By this point, we're well into the mine. In addition to Isabelle Price, we've met Carmen Meloy, the director; Kristi Fairbairn, the cameraperson; George Slatsky, the sound person; and Ben Rios and Megan Hwang, the interns. We've passed the entrance, with its remnants of parties past, its scattered garbage, beer cans, and bottles, random articles of clothing, and graffiti, including the warning about "Bad Agatha," a name everyone in the film crew, with the exception of Isabelle, picks up. Following the old map of the mine Isabelle has folded into her knapsack, we've descended the main tunnels, running across strange, rusted pieces of machinery, shovels and other tools, a dusty copy of *Playboy* that's been a source of temporary amusement. Along the way, we've had snippets of Isabelle recounting the story of Agatha

Merryweather, as well as moments of the crew reacting to the tale. We've encountered the portrait of Agatha's face, split between a normal right and a cadaverous left half; we've flinched when Ben touches it and jumped in our seats when he starts screaming, only to laugh with nervous relief as his outburst dissolves into laughter, and Megan calls him an asshat.

We've worked out some of the relationships among the crew, as well. Ben and Megan are involved; she's worried about how her parents will react to her dating someone who isn't Korean. We catch the tail end of a couple of heated, whispered exchanges between them. George is short-tempered, preoccupied with his ten year old daughter, for full custody of whom he's locked in legal combat with his ex-wife. Kristi is unhappy from the start with this project, a sentiment exacerbated by a mild case of claustrophobia. Carmen spends much of her time checking in with the others, consulting on technical matters, touching base on personal ones. Isabelle is focused on searching the mine with an intensity that's unnerving; she gives the strong impression of being in possession of additional information she has not shared with her companions.

(A pause here to say that Isabelle Router deserves credit for a remarkable job of acting. Granted, her part is based to a large extent on her actual background, she nonetheless delivers an exceptional portrait of a woman struggling to maintain her composure in the face of pressures external and internal.)

On the soundtrack, sounds that started as background noise, barely distinguishable from the clamor of the crew proceeding, have increased in volume substantially. Some are identifiable: a low, weak sobbing, the kind that comes at the end of hours crying; the rattle and click of a small rock being knocked across the floor into another rock. Some are harder to place: a metallic ping, and a sudden, deafening roar that sends the film crew into wide-eyed panic, racing headlong through the tunnels as the sound goes on and on.

This is what brings them to a low opening on their left, into a small cave where they spend a solid minute shouting, cursing, and screaming, until the noise drains away and we're left with their mingled panting. Only now do they notice the chamber they've entered. Overhead, the ceiling slopes down into darkness. To either side, walls that are marked with rows of unfamiliar symbols stretch to join it. Directly in front of the crew, a narrow trench bisects the floor, running away into blackness. The bottom of the trench is streaked with blackish-red liquid. Despite the warnings of the others, Ben Rios kneels and extends a hand to the substance. When he raises his fingertips to his nostrils, he pulls his head back, lips wrinkling in disgust. "Blood," he says, as we knew he would.

While the others digest this news, Isabelle Price is on the move, sweeping her flashlight over the weird figures on the walls. Geometric shapes—mostly circles within circles—punctuate long lines of characters that appear almost hieroglyphic. She directs her light to the floor, and picks out something scratched on the rock, a rectangle the size of a dinner tray. YES is incised in its upper left hand corner, NO in its upper right hand corner. The letters of the alphabet line the inside of the rectangle, beginning with A below the YES and Z under the NO. A series of lines, some more recent than others, loop from letter to letter to the flat stone positioned at the rectangle's center. The lines seem to have been drawn in blood. Isabelle lifts the flat stone and turns it over, revealing its underside smeared with shades of red. Rock in hand, she crosses to the trench, where she kneels to dip the rock in the blood there. As the crew members exclaim and ask her what she's doing, Isabelle returns to the primitive Ouija board and replaces the stone within it. She beckons Ben and Megan to join her, but Ben refuses. After a brief debate, George says he'll take part in the professor's little séance. Passing his equipment to Ben, he lowers to his knees to Isabelle's right; Megan is on the left. There's a whispered exchange off camera, Kristi asking Carmen what the fuck is going on, Carmen telling her to keep shooting.

Here's how the IMDb entry describes what happens next:

Professor Price says, Rest your fingers on the stone lightly, like this. She places the tips of her fingers on the stone. Megan and George do the same. The professor says, Good. Now, clear your minds.

Megan asks, How are we supposed to do that? Have you seen where we are?

Just do the best you can, Professor Price says. You can close your eyes, if it helps.

Megan shakes her head no, but George shuts his eyes. He says, All right, what next?

The professor closes her eyes. She asks, Is anyone there?

Nothing happens.

Professor Price says, Is anyone there?

Slowly, the stone scrapes across the floor. Megan screams, but keeps her fingers on it. George says, What the hell? The professor says, Easy. Stay calm. Keep your hands on the planchette.

Megan says, The what?

George says, The stone.

Right, Professor Price says, the stone. Her eyes are open. The stone settles on YES. The professor nods. She asks, Who is there?

The stone slides from YES to the letter A beneath it. Then to G, back to A, to T, to H, and back to A. Professor Price says, Agatha.

Kristi's voice says, Holy shit. Ben Rios crosses himself.

The professor asks, What happened to you, Agatha?

The stone spells out T-R-A-P-P-E-D.

Professor Price says, Trapped? You were trapped here, in the mine?

The stone moves to YES.

The professor asks, Why?

The stone spells B-A-D.

Professor Price says, You were bad.

The stone spells B-A-D.

The professor frowns. She asks, How were you bad?

The stone does not move.

Professor Price says, How were you bad, Agatha?

The stone spells out B-L-O-O-D.

The professor says, I don't understand. How were you bad, Agatha?

George says, Seems pretty obvious to me. She was doing something with blood. Ben says, Maybe she was drinking it.

The stone slides to YES.

Professor Price says, Please, let me do the talking. What were you doing with blood, Agatha?

The stone moves to NO.

The professor says, All right. Who trapped you here, in the mine?

The stone spells K-L-E-R-O-S.

Megan asks, Who is Kleros? George shakes his head. Professor Price says nothing. Ben says, I think it's Greek. Carmen asks, Greek? Ben says, yeah. It's like the root of clergy.

The professor asks, Where are you from, Agatha?

The stone moves to NO.

Professor Price repeats the question.

The stone does not move.

The professor exhales. She asks, Can we help you, Agatha?

The stone does not move.

Professor Price waits for an answer. None comes. She asks, Are you still there, Agatha?

The stone does not move.

Megan asks, What happened? George says, We lost her. He sits back, lifting his hands from the stone. Megan does the same. The professor maintains contact for a few seconds more, then she sits back, too.

Kristi says, What the fuck was that? Carmen says, Yeah, Isabelle, what's going on?

Isabelle Price starts to speak, but her answer is interrupted by George shouting, Shit! and scrambling backward. Megan screams and stumbles to her feet. The professor raises her hands, startled.

The planchette stone is bleeding. All over its surface, drops of blood appear, swell, and collapse into streams that trickle to the edges of the stone and spill onto the floor. Kristi shouts, Fuck! Megan turns and collides with Ben. Blood pools around the planchette stone. Professor Price stares at it. Carmen says, Isabelle, what the fuck is happening? Blood spreads over the words and letters of the Ouija board. Ben mumbles something. George is praying, Our Father, Who art in Heaven. Blood flows to the edges of the trench in the center of the cave and slides into it. Kristi says, What is this? What is this? What are we seeing? What? Carmen tells everyone to move away from the blood, to come over beside her. The crew does, except for the professor. Carmen says, Isabelle. Come here, Isabelle.

Professor Price turns around. Her face is blank. Her left eye is red, blood pouring from it down her cheek.

⊸

The third and final scene is, of course, the movie's climax. By now, the movie's title has been realized, as the film crew has emerged from the cave to discover that their panicked flight has carried them off Isabelle's map. Despite following several seemingly familiar paths, they have remained lost. Their complaints have grown more hysterical.

In the meantime, Carmen has succeeded in coaxing Isabelle out of the trance-like state into which she fell. The sclera of her left eye is still stained red with hemorrhages, but it's no longer actively bleeding. Prompted by Carmen and Kristi, she has revealed some of the secrets we've suspected her of harboring. Her research on Agatha Merryweather, she says, led her to a website that's kind of a clearing house of weird information. There was an entry for the Bound Woman of the Mine that sounded as if it might connect to the information she'd already gathered. The site kept crashing her computer, so she wasn't able to read all of the listing, but the portion she finished was intriguing. It concerned a fourteen year old girl who had been responsible for a series of terrible murders in northwestern New Jersey during the early nineteen sixties. This was farm country, near the Pennsylvania line. For some reason, after her apprehension by the sheriff, the local Catholic priest was brought in to consult on the case. This led to another pair of priests being summoned, an older man and a younger one, whose accents no one recognized. They said they were members of a small order, the Perilaimio. Eventually, the girl was released into their custody on the condition she remain confined to her house. At some point thereafter, she, her parents, and the priests were discovered to have fled for an unknown destination. There was talk of a search for her, but it came to nothing.

When Kristi asks what any of this has to do with anything, Isabelle reveals that the website gave a name for the girl: Agatha Merryweather. Obviously, with the assistance of the Church, she and her family fled east, where they were resettled in Weehawken. The question was, why?

This Agatha was possessed, George says. That's where the story is heading, isn't it?

That is what she thought, Isabelle says, until she looked into the order to which the priests belonged, the Perilaimio. It's an old, old group, maybe older than the Church itself.

What is she talking about? Megan wants to know. How can there be a part of the Church that came before it?

Like Christmas trees, Ben says, or Yule logs. Pagan things the Church folded into it.

That's it exactly, Isabelle says. The Perilaimio were charged with managing the *Keres*.

Which means what? Kristi asks.

Death-spirits, Ben says.

Death-spirits? Megan says. How does he know this stuff?

He took Greek in high school, Ben says.

Does he mean ghosts? Megan says.

Sounds more like devils, George says.

No, Isabelle says. These are beings of the primordial dark, beyond the Church's sway. They depend on blood to maintain their presence in this world. They can't be cast out, or destroyed, only contained.

Which is what happened here, George says. Agatha Merryweather was brought to this place to imprison her.

That's the theory, Isabelle says. At first, she read this entire story as a case of a mentally ill girl subjected to a prolonged victimization by religious maniacs. The mine, she assumed, was intended as a jail, primitive but low profile. Most likely, the men who transported her to upstate New York planned for her to die in these tunnels, of malnutrition or disease.

Why would they have thought this? Kristi says. Didn't Isabelle just say the death-spirits couldn't be killed?

It's complicated, Isabelle says. The *Keres* are fundamentally violent; they can't be killed by violent means. However, if their host dies of natural causes, they lose their hold on it.

This makes no sense, Kristi says. How does any of this make sense?

The point is, Carmen says, Isabelle thought they were dealing with a crazy person.

Honestly, Isabelle says, she was sure Agatha had been dead for years. The most she expected was to find her remains.

Instead, Kristi says, they have . . . this. What they have.

"Us," George says, "lost. In the Dark. With a monster."

Their wandering has brought the crew to another unfamiliar location, a small chamber whose rough walls recede at regular intervals to what appear to be doorways. This is the IMDB summary of what ensues:

⊸

Ben shines his flashlight on the recess furthest to the right. It shows solid rock. He swings the light to the left. The next recess opens on a passageway. He swings the light to the left, to the recess directly across from him. It is solid, too, but there is something on the rock at approximately head level. It is the same portrait the film crew saw at the beginning of the expedition, a woman's face, the left half a skull. Megan shrieks. Kristi says, What the fuck? Ben says, It's only another drawing, and crosses to it. He reaches out his free hand to touch it. He says, See?

His flashlight goes out. Megan shrieks again. Carmen says, Ben? George says, Now is not the time for screwing around, kid. He aims his flashlight at the recess.

There is a flurry of motion. Ben screams. George's flashlight beam swings from side to side, trying to keep up with the action. Kristi shouts. Carmen points her flashlight in Ben's direction. She says, There! There! Ben continues screaming. There is someone grabbing him from behind. White arms wrap around his neck and chest. White legs encircle his waist. A head with long black hair presses against his neck. Ben grabs at the arms. He slaps at the head. He stumbles back into the wall. Megan screams, Someone do something! Professor Price shouts, Agatha! Agatha, stop!

Agatha growls and tugs her head back. There is the sound of flesh tearing, followed by a hiss as blood sprays from Ben's open throat. He drops to his knees, slaps at Agatha's hands, and falls forward, Agatha still clinging to him. She drops her head to his neck. There is the sound of her slurping his blood. Kristi says, Holy shit. Megan screams, You fucking bitch! and runs at Agatha, raising her flashlight as a club. Agatha ducks her swing and leaps onto her. She knocks Megan onto her back, and rips her throat out. Kristi says, Jesus Christ.

George says, We have to get out of here. He runs from the chamber. Agatha jumps off Megan onto the wall. She hangs on it like a spider. Professor Price shouts, Agatha! Please! Agatha! Agatha scrambles up the wall and out of the light. Carmen sweeps her flashlight around the ceiling. Kristi shouts, Where did she go? Where is she? The professor shouts, Agatha! Please!

Agatha drops onto Carmen. Her flashlight spins away. She screams. Agatha growls. Kristi and Professor Price scramble out of the way. There is the sound of Carmen struggling. Kristi shouts, Come on! Let's go! Now! Carmen shouts, wait! Help me! Kristi says, I'm sorry, and runs through the passageway Ben discovered. Carmen shouts, Kristi! Agatha snarls. The professor says, Agatha, please, then follows Kristi. Carmen screams.

The screen goes black.

After five seconds, there is a clatter and the screen fills with Kristi's face, illuminated by the camera light. She says, I don't know why I'm doing this.

There's no way either of us is getting out of here. I can hear her—Agatha. She's coming closer. Kristi begins to cry. She says, I just wanted to say, I'm sorry about Carmen. I couldn't do anything about Ben and Megan. Maybe I couldn't have helped Carmen, either, but I'm sorry. She wipes her eyes with the back of her hand. She says, And George, if you make it out of this place, and somehow see this, fuck you, you chickenshit piece of shit.

The camera turns to show Isabelle Price's face. Kristi says, You never told us everything, did you? Professor Price shakes her head. Kristi asks, Anything you want to say now? Isabelle shakes her head. Kristi says, You know this is all your fault. The professor nods. Kristi says, We're going to leave this camera here, in hopes that someone will find it. Which is about as stupid as all the rest of this, but hey, why stop now? She sets the camera down, turned to light the tunnel she and Professor Price are headed down. She says, We still have a flashlight. We'll hold off using it as long as we can, to save the batteries. Professor Price starts along the tunnel. Kristi follows. When she is almost out of view Kristi stops and turns. She says, I can hear her. Hurry.

The women disappear into the darkness. For the next three minutes, the credits roll over the scene. Once the credits are finished, the camera light dims. There is the sound of bare feet slapping stone. Agatha's face fills the screen. Her features are those of a young woman, covered in blood. Her eyes are wide. Blood plasters her hair to her forehead and cheeks. The screen flickers. Agatha's left eye is an empty socket, her left cheek sunken, her lips on this side drawn back from jagged teeth. The screen flickers again, goes to static, then goes dark.

III

It's the teacher in me: I can't help wanting to discuss all the things *Lost in the Dark* does right. The opening, for example, which imparts a substantial amount of background information to the viewer without sacrificing interest, as well as the Agatha Merryweather narrative, itself, which taps into the enduring fascination with the Catholic Church and its secrets (which, if I felt like being truly pedantic, I would point out is one of the ribs of the larger umbrella of the Gothic under which the movie shelters). Or the way the film suggests there's even more to the Agatha narrative than we've been told, than anyone's been told. Only Isabelle Price knows the full story, and to the end, she keeps back some portion of it. By making her the model for the portraits of Agatha the crew encounter, a similarity no one mentions, the movie visually suggests a connection between the women, which contributes to the audience's growing sense that the characters are in a situation that's much worse than they understand. (It's one of the enduring conceits of the film that the identity of the actress who portrays Bad Agatha has never been revealed. The credits assign the part to Agatha Merryweather. I'm of the camp that would wager money Isabelle Router played the monster; it fits too well with the portrait ploy not to be the case.)

Were it not for Sarah Fiore's interview in the Blu-ray extras, this article might address itself to exactly such a critical analysis. That interview, though, changed everything. According to Sarah, the trip into the mine to shoot footage for Isabelle Router's documentary lasted much longer than they had planned, almost twenty hours. During that time, the crew became lost, wandering out of the mine into a series of natural tunnels and caves. While underground, they had a number of strange experiences, about half of which at least one member of the crew caught on film. They returned to the surface with a couple of hours of decent footage that was not what they had been planning on. After a rough edit, Sarah sat down with Larry Fessenden to watch the film. He loved it. He also thought she had abandoned her plan for a documentary in favor of an outright horror movie. Thinking quickly, Sarah responded to his enthusiasm by saying that yes, she had decided to go a different route. Fessenden offered to produce a feature-length version of what he'd seen, on the condition that Sarah revise the script to give it a more substantial narrative. Since there was no actual script at that moment, his request was both easier and harder to fulfill; nonetheless, she agreed to it. She also agreed that she should keep as much of what she'd shown him as they could in the longer film. This turned out to be about forty minutes of an hour and forty minute movie. Isabelle Router was willing essentially to play herself, as were Kristi Nightingale and George Maltmore. The interns, Priya and Chad, had no interest in taking part in another expedition to the mine, so they were replaced by a pair of actors, Ben Formosa and Megan Park. Rather than juggle the roles of director, scriptwriter, and actor, Sarah hired Carmen Fuentes to play her. The rest is cinema history.

If we're to believe Sarah, *Lost in the Dark* was built from another film, a piece of fiction constructed using a significant portion of non-fiction. I use the "if" because, as soon as word of her interview got out, the question of its authenticity was raised. After all, this was a filmmaker who had started her career with a faux-documentary. What better way to mark the ten-year anniversary of that production than with another instance of the form, one designed to send audiences back to pore over the original movie? By those who took this view of Sarah's revelations, she was variously praised for her cleverness and decried for her cynicism. I've swung back and forth on the matter. I did my due diligence. The narrative Sarah relates, of the mysterious woman who stepped down from the train to Wiltwyck, the murdered men at the entrance to the mine, is true. You can read about it online, in the archives of the *Wiltwyck Daily Freeman* and the *Poughkeepsie Journal*. Confirming Isabelle Router's uncle's story proved more difficult. Richard Higgins died in Tampa three years ago. I located one of his former colleagues, Henry Ellison, who confirmed that Rich had gone into the mine to retrieve that dumbass high school kid. Of any more than that, Rich never spoke to him.

Still, there's sufficient evidence that Sarah Fiore was telling at least some of the truth. This doesn't mean there was a documentary shot between her discovery of this information and *Lost in the Dark*. Once again, I did some digging and came up with contact information for all but one of the members of the (supposed) original crew. Wherever Chad Singer currently resides, it's beyond my rudimentary sleuthing abilities to locate. Of the remainder of those involved, Priya Subramani listened to my introduction, then hung up and blocked my number. Kristi Nightingale told me to go fuck myself; I'm not sure if she also blocked me, since there didn't seem much point in calling back. George Maltmore instantly was angry, demanding to know who the hell I thought I was and what the hell I thought I was playing at. Despite my best efforts to reassure him, he became increasingly incensed, threatening to find out where I lived and show up at my front door with his shotgun. Finally, I hung up on him. Somewhat to my surprise, Larry Fessenden spoke to me for almost half an hour; although he did so without answering my question in a definitive way. Sure, he said, he remembered the film that Sarah had brought to him. It was a terrific piece of work. Was what he saw a documentary? I asked. Ah, he said, yeah, that was the story making the rounds, wasn't it? He couldn't remember Sarah saying that to him at the time, but it would be something if it turned out to be true, wouldn't it?

Yes, I said, it would.

Even more unexpectedly, Isabelle Router agreed to talk. Once *Lost in the Dark* was done shooting, she and Sarah had an argument which resulted in a falling out that has lasted to this day. Isabelle returned to Albany, to work on her Ph.D. at the state university, only to leave after a single semester. For the next few years, she said, she was kind of messed up. She moved around a lot, did . . . things. Eventually, she pulled herself together, settled in Bolder, where she became a yoga instructor. She asked me if I had spoken with anyone else, and what they had said. Isabelle was particularly interested to know if I'd talked to Sarah. That I had been her teacher was of great interest; she wanted to know what Sarah had been like as a student. When it came to the question of the documentary, her answers grew vague. Yes, they had done some preliminary filming in the mine. In fact, they'd gotten kind of lost down there. Did I know that the idea for the movie, for all of the supernatural stuff, was hers? It came out of the research she'd been doing for her dissertation. You did shoot a documentary first, I said.

"I don't know that I'd go that far," Isabelle said. "We were just lost in the dark. Sarah got that much right."

Nor could I coax any more definitive statement from her. There was enough in Isabelle's words for me to take them as supporting Sarah's claims, but not enough to settle the matter. Not to mention, the more I paged through the notes I'd taken from all of the interviews, the less certain I was that I wasn't being played for a sucker. The extremity of Priya, Kristi, and George's reactions—their theatricality—added to Fessenden's bland non-answers and Isabelle's ambiguous replies, seemed intended, *scripted*, to give the impression that not only had the documentary been filmed, it had recorded an experience singularly unpleasant. On the other hand, quite often, the truth looks glaringly untrue; as Tolstoy said, God is a lousy novelist.

In the end, I would need to speak with my former student. Rather than a phone conversation or e mail exchange, Sarah suggested we meet in person. Halloween, she was scheduled to attend a special late-night screening of *Lost in the Dark* at the Joppenburgh Community Theater. Why didn't we get together before that? She'd bring her laptop; there were clips she could show me that would prove interesting. I agreed, which has brought me here, seated at the back of Pete's Corner Pub, while trick-or-treaters make their annual pilgrimage.

IV

Sarah Fiore enters the bar as she used to enter my classroom—walking briskly, head down, oversized bag clutched to her side. The heels of her boots knock on the wood floor. She's wearing a hip-length black leather coat over a white blouse and black jeans. With her head tilted forward, her long black hair curtains her face. Before the hostess on duty can approach her, she's crossed to where I'm sitting and slid into the bench across from me. Since I didn't meet her until she was in her mid-twenties, I don't see as dramatic a change in her as I often do with my former students. That said, time has passed, which I've no doubt she notices in the tide of white hairs that has swept both sides of my beard, and is washing through what brown remains on my chin. We exchange greetings, Sarah orders a martini from the waitress who's hurried to the booth, and she slides a gray laptop from her bag. She places it on the table in front of her, unopened. Hands flat on either side of it, she asks me if I've talked to the other members of the original crew.

With the exception of Chad Singer, I say, I have, and relay to her abbreviated versions of our conversations. She smirks at Kristi Nightingale's cursing, drops her head in an attempt to conceal a laugh at George Maltmore's furious show. Larry Fessenden's non-committal response receives a nod, as does Isabelle Router's remark about them being lost in the dark. "She was intrigued to learn that I had been your teacher," I add, but it draws no further response from Sarah.

The server returns with Sarah's drink, asks me if I'd like more coffee. I decline. If you need anything, she says, and leaves.

"All right," Sarah says after tasting her drink. "How should we do this?"

"Why don't we start with a question: why now? Why wait ten years to reveal this new information? Wouldn't it have been simpler to do so back when the movie was first released?"

"Possibly," Sarah says. "I don't know. At the time, Isabelle and I weren't on speaking terms. We still aren't, but then, it was new. We'd had this massive fight—things didn't just turn ugly, they turned hideous. Everything felt pretty raw. Part of me did want to go public with the documentary stuff, but it was mostly because I thought it would hurt Isabelle. She was back at graduate school, trying to pull together a dissertation. If word got out that she'd been part of this crazy documentary project, I figured it would make her study less pleasant.

"For once in my life, though, I listened to my inner Jiminy Cricket and did the right thing. For a long time after that, I was so busy, I didn't have time to think about the footage. Really, when I sat down for the interview with *Rue Morgue*, I had no intention of mentioning any of that stuff. It just . . . came out. I don't see the harm in it, now. I mean, Isabelle left her doctoral program, didn't she? Isn't she a massage therapist or something?"

"Yoga instructor," I say. "But you have to admit—"

"The timing is highly suspicious, yes. I can't blame anyone who thinks that. It's what I would say."

"You, however, have the original documentary."

Sarah nods. "I do." She raises the laptop's screen. "The problem is, we're living in an age where it's easy to fake stuff like this. If you have the resources, you can put together something that would fool everyone up to and maybe including the experts. Although, why would you want to?" She lifts a hand to forestall my answer. "Yeah, publicity, I know. It's a case of diminishing returns. If all I was after was to generate interest in the movie, I would have ended my story saying that the original footage was lost, wiped when my computer crashed. It wouldn't be worth whatever meager spike in sales you might project for me to go to the trouble of creating a new fake film."

"Which is exactly the sort of thing I'd expect you to say, if you were trying to pass off a fake movie as authentic."

"Yeah," she says, sweeping her fingers over the computer's touch pad to bring it to life. "The thing is, if you want to believe something's a conspiracy, you will. No matter what I say, one way or the other, it'll be evidence of what you're looking for."

"Fair enough."

"Okay." She taps keys, and turns the computer ninety degrees, allowing me a view of the screen. The window open shows a woman's head and shoulders foreground right, the entrance to the mine background left. It's Isabelle Router, her face burnished by the same late afternoon sunlight that paints the rock face behind her bronze. "This is how we began," Sarah says.

"Isabelle standing in front of the mine, reciting the history of the mystery woman. We could watch it, but you already know the story, right?"

"Right."

"Let's . . ." She fast forwards ten minutes. We're inside the mine, rough rock walls and ceiling, scattered trash on the floor. To anyone who's seen *Lost in the Dark*, it's a familiar shot, although the voices are different. Somewhere off screen to the right, Chad Singer is saying, "Am I going to have to carry this for very long? Because it is *heavy*." From what sounds as if it might be behind the camera, George Maltmore is muttering about the acoustics of this damn place. Much closer, Kristi Nightingale says, "Eww," at the desiccated carcass of a small animal, likely a mouse. "We had to swap out the soundtrack for something more atmospheric," Sarah says to me. "Plus, Chad had left, so we couldn't use his voice." She pauses the video. "There's plenty more of this kind of thing I can show you, if that's what you want." She advances five minutes, to the crew encountering a piece of Jack-Kirby-esque machinery the approximate dimensions of a refrigerator, its yellow paint faded and flaked away in patches, the large round openings in its sides strung with cobwebs. A leap of another six minutes brings us to the comic relief of the ancient *Playboy*, its cover and interior pages crumpled. The crew's jokes approximate those in the later film. Ten minutes more down the dark tunnel brings the first surprise of the interview, the portrait of a woman's face on the rock wall. It's exactly as it appears in *Lost in the Dark*. Despite myself, I flinch, say, "Jesus. This is for real?"

"It's what we found," Sarah says.

I stare at the waves of the woman's hair, the lines of her cheekbones and nose, the weird smearing on the right hand side of the drawing, which gives the left half of the face a roughly skeletal appearance. I fight the urge to reach my fingers to the screen. "I assumed—I mean, I know Isabelle's uncle mentioned it in his story, but I figured he invented it."

"Me, too," Sarah says. "It seemed hard to believe, didn't it? Like something out of a horror movie."

"Who did it?" I can't stop looking at the portrait, which is in some ways no different from what I've seen previously, and in other ways has been fundamentally changed. Stranger still, the portrait's resemblance to Isabelle remains as strong as ever. "I mean, did Isabelle have any friends who were artists?"

"She swore it wasn't her," Sarah says. She lets the movie play. The camera pans from the tunnel wall to Isabelle, who is not pleased. "Very funny," she says.

"What do you mean?" Kristi says.

"You think I don't know who this is?"

"Isabelle," Sarah says, "we didn't do this."

"Yeah, right," Isabelle says.

"Seriously," Kristi says.

"You think we had something to do with this?" Priya Subramani says.

"Obviously," Isabelle says. "How else do you explain it?"

"Um, someone drew it," Chad says. "Someone who isn't one of us."

"Are you sure?" Isabelle says.

"Yeah," Chad says. "When my friends say they didn't do something, I believe them."

"What would be the point?" Sarah says. "Why would we do this, and then lie to you about it?"

Doubt softens Isabelle's features, but already, she's invested too much in the argument to yield the point. Plus, she doesn't want to contemplate the implications of the crew telling the truth. She says, "Whatever," and turns away.

The camera swings to Sarah, who blows out through pursed lips while rolling her eyes.

"Probably should have omitted that last bit," she says, tapping the touch pad and freezing the screen. "After we returned from the mine and were going through the footage, Kristi suggested that maybe Isabelle was responsible for the drawing. I told her there was no way, she was being ridiculous. Had she not seen Isabelle's reaction to the thing? When the group of us met to screen what Kristi and I had put together, she asked Isabelle about the portrait point blank. I didn't stop her. I'll admit: I was curious. Isabelle acted genuinely surprised at the accusation, enough for me to believe her. Although, when I think about her performance in *Lost in the Dark*, how well she acted, I wonder."

"Why would she have done that?"

"To back up the story that had brought us there in the first place," Sarah says.

"I don't know," I say. "That seems like a little far to go."

"Well." Sarah brings the movie ahead another ten minutes, hurrying the crew through a pair of large spaces whose flat ceilings rest on rock columns the girth of large trees. In the second chamber, their flashlights pick out a shape to the right, a dark mound like a heap of rugs. Flashlights trained on the thing, they cross the space towards it. As they approach, the mound gains definition, resolving into the carcass of a large animal. When they reach it, Sarah returns the film to normal speed.

"—is it?" Chad is saying.

"I think it's a bear," Sarah says.

"No way," Kristi says.

"There are bears here?" Priya says.

"Yes," George says, "black bears." He steps away from the group to circle the remains.

"Be careful," Priya says.

"Yeah, George," Chad says, "watch yourself."

"Relax," George says, "this fellow's been dead a long time." He crouches next to the bear's blunt head, playing his light back and forth over it. His eyes narrow. "What the hell?"

"What?" Sarah says.

"What is it?" Priya says.

"From the looks of things," George says, "something tore out Gentle Ben here's throat."

"Is that strange?" Chad says.

"What could do that?" Kristi says.

"I have no idea," George says. "Another bear, maybe. A mountain lion, I guess."

"Hang on—I want to see this," Kristi says. The camera moves around the animal's prostrate form to where George sits on his heels, his flashlight directed at the bear's head. Its eyes are sunken, shriveled, its teeth bared in a final snarl. The right canine is missing, the socket ragged, black with blood long-crusted. What should be the animal's thick neck is a mess of skin torn into leathery ribbon and flaps, laying bare dried muscle and dull bone. "Jesus," Kristi says.

"Should be more blood," George says. He sweeps his flashlight over the floor around them, whose dust and rock are unstained. "Huh."

"What does that mean?" Priya says.

"Could it be, I don't know, poachers?" Chad says.

"Black bear isn't protected like that," George says. "You're supposed to have a license, but if you shot one by mistake, you wouldn't need to go to this amount of trouble to hide it. Not to mention, I don't know what gun would inflict this type of wound."

"Maybe it was shot," Chad says, "came in here to escape, and another bear got it."

George shrugs. "Anything's possible. Doesn't explain the lack of blood, though."

"I do not like this," Kristi says.

"Hey," Priya says, "where's Isabelle?"

Sarah pauses the movie.

"What happened to Isabelle?" I say.

"She . . . wandered off," Sarah says.

"In a mine?"

"Yeah," Sarah says, "that was what the rest of us thought."

"Where did she go?"

"All the way to the end of the mine, and then further. There's a network of caves the mine connects to. We spent most of the shoot searching for her—about fifteen hours." The next twenty minutes of the film advance in a succession of scenes, each of which leaps ahead another half hour to hour and a half. The expression on the crew's faces oscillate between irritation and worry, with intermittent stops at fatigue and unease. Sarah says, "We hadn't brought much in the way of food or drink; we hadn't expected to be down there for more than a couple of hours. We ran out of both pretty quickly. Not long after, Chad floated the idea of turning around, heading for the surface, where we could call for help, bring in some professionals to find Isabelle. Kristi was aghast at the thought of abandoning her here. The others agreed. We kept on moving further underground. Isabelle had left enough of a trail for us to follow; although there were a couple of times we really had to search for it. Finally, we arrived at this spot."

She taps the touchpad. The screen shows the tunnel dead-ending in a shallow chamber filled with junk: rows of rusted barrels, any identifying marks long flaked off; cardboard boxes in various stages of mildewed collapse; shovels and pickaxes, mummified in dusty cobwebs; a stack of eight or nine safety helmets leaning to one side.

"Shit," Sarah says.

"What do we do now?" Chad says.

"Go back," George says, "see if we can pick up the trail again at that last fork."

"Hang on," Kristi says. The view moves behind the row of barrels closest to the wall. As the camera's light shifts, so do the barrels' shadows, swinging away from the rock to reveal a short opening in it. "Guys," Kristi says, bringing the camera level with her discovery. Manhole-sized and-shaped, the aperture admits to a brief passage, which ends in darkness.

"What is it?" Sarah says.

"Some kind of tunnel," Kristi says. The opening swims closer.

"What are you doing?" Sarah says.

"Wait," Kristi says. The screen rocks wildly as she crawls through the passage.

"Hey!" George calls.

Kristi emerges into a larger space. Curved walls expand to a wider exit. The camera scans the floor, which is strewn with an assortment of stones. A rough path pushes through them. "Guys!" Kristi shouts.

The film jumps to Priya scrambling out of the tunnel. Chad helps her to her feet. To the left, George says, "Is everyone sure about this?"

"No," Chad says.

"I don't know," Priya says.

"Do you want to abandon Isabelle down here," Kristi says, "in the dark?"

"It's worth checking out," Sarah says. "We'll go a little way. If we don't see any sign of her, we'll turn around."

"What the fuck is she doing here?" Priya says.

"When we find Isabelle," Sarah says, "we'll ask her."

Another cut, and the crew is standing in blackness that extends beyond the limits of their flashlights. Ceiling, walls are out of view; only the rock on which they're standing is visible. Chad and Kristi shout, "Hello!" and, "Isabelle!" but any echo is at best faint. "Where are we?" Priya says. No one answers.

In the following scene, an object shines in the distance, on the very right edge of the screen. "Hey," Kristi says, turning the camera to center the thing, "look." The rest of the crew's lights converge on it.

"What . . . ?" Priya says.

"It looks like a tooth," Sarah says.

"It's a stalagmite," George says. "Or stalactite. I get the two confused. Either way, it isn't a tooth."

"It's not a stalagmite," Chad says. "The surface texture's wrong. Besides, you usually find stalagmites and stalactites in pairs, groups, even. Where are the others?"

"So what is it, Mr. Geologist?" George says.

"It's a rock," Kristi says.

It is; though both Sarah and George's identifications are understandable. Composed of some type of white, pearlescent mineral, it stands upright, three and a half, four feet tall, tapering from a narrow base to a flattened top the width of a tea saucer. Halfway down it, there's a decoration, which, when the camera zooms in on it, resolves into a picture. Executed in what might be charcoal, it's a face, the features rendered simply, crudely. In the scribble of black hair, the black hole of the left eye, it isn't hard to recognize the repetition of the portrait near the mine's entrance. "What the fuck?" Kristi says.

"What is this?" Priya says. "What is happening here?"

"Um," Chad says. The view draws back from the face to show Chad standing beside the stone, in the process of picking up something from its flattened top. Frowning, he raises a thin, shriveled item to view. "I think this is a finger."

"Jesus Christ," Kristi says. "Are you sure?"

"No," he says, replacing the digit gingerly, as if it might shatter.

"What the hell is this?" George says.

"We need to leave," Priya says. "Right now, we need to leave."

"I think she might be right," Kristi says.

"Just a little further," Sarah says. "Please. I know this is—this is scary, I know. But please . . . We can't leave Isabelle here. Please."

"What makes you think she's even in this place?" George says.

"I do not want to be here anymore," Priya says. "We have to *leave*."

"Sarah," Kristi says.

Without another word, Sarah walks past the strange rock in the direction the crew was heading, her flashlight spreading its beam across the floor in front of her.

"Hey!" Kristi says.

"What is she doing?" Chad says.

"Making a command decision," George says.

"Are we going to follow her?" Chad says.

"What choice do we have?" Kristi says. "We already lost Isabelle." The camera moves after Sarah.

From behind, Priya says, "This is so unfair."

After the next cut, the screen shows Sarah a half-dozen steps in front of the crew, trailing her light through blackness. "Sarah," Kristi says. "Wait up." The others join her in calling Sarah's name, urging her to slow down. "Come on!" Priya says.

When Sarah stops, it isn't because of the requests directed at her. Her light slides over the cave floor to her left, illuminating a low line of dark rocks. As she changes direction towards it, so do the others, aiming their lights at her destination. "What now?" George says.

Less than a foot tall, the line is composed of stones fist-sized and smaller. They're black, porous, distinct from the rock on which they're arranged. At either end, the row connects to a shorter line of the same rock, each of which joins another longer row of rocks, forming a rectangle the dimensions of a large door. The space within it sparkles and flashes in the lights. Chad kneels and reaches into the rectangle, towards the nearest piece of dazzle, only to snatch his hand back with a "Shit!"

"What is it?" Priya says.

"Glass," Chad says, holding his fingers to display the blood welling from their tips. "It's filled with broken glass." He sticks his fingers into his mouth.

"Fuck," Kristi says.

"What does this mean?" Priya says.

"Yeah, Sarah," Kristi says, "what the fuck is this?"

"I—" Sarah starts, but George interrupts her: "Shh! Hear that?"

"What?" Kristi says.

"I do," Priya says.

"What?" Chad says.

"Over here," George says, waving his light at the blackness on the far side of the stone rectangle. "Listen."

Everyone falls silent. From what seems a long way away, a faint groan is audible.

"Is that Isabelle?" Chad says.

"Who else would it be?" Kristi says. "Come on." Now she takes the lead, skirting the edges of the stone design as she heads in the direction of the moaning. "Isabelle!" Kristi shouts. "We're here!"

In the middle distance, the cave floor shimmers white. This is not the crystalline fracture of broken glass; rather, it's the flat glow of light on liquid. "What the hell?" Kristi says. She is approaching the shore of a body of water, a lake, judging by the stillness of it surface. Given the limited range of the camera's light, the lake's margins are difficult to discern, which gives it the impression of size. This close to the water, the groaning has a curiously hollow quality. The camera swings right, left, and right again. "Isabelle!" Kristi shouts.

The rest of the crew catches up to her. Exclamations of surprise at the lake combine with calls to Isabelle. Flashlight beams chase one another across the water, roam the shore to either side. "Where . . . ?" Kristi says.

"There," Sarah says, pointing her flashlight to the right. At the very limit of the light's reach, a pale figure stands in the water, a few feet out. Camera bouncing, the crew runs toward it.

Arms wrapped around herself, Isabelle Router stands in water ankle deep. Her eyes are closed, her mouth open to emit a wavering moan. Priya splashes into the lake, at Isabelle's side in half a dozen high steps. When Priya touches her, Isabelle convulses, her groans breaking off. Her eyes remain closed. "It's all right," Priya says. "Isabelle, it's all right. It's me. It's Priya. We're here."

"Priya?" Isabelle's voice is a hoarse whisper.

"Yeah," Priya says, "it's me. Everyone's here. We found you. It's all right."

Isabelle opens her eyes, lifts her hands against the lights.

"Isabelle," Sarah says, "are you okay?"

"You're here," Isabelle says.

"We are," Sarah says.

"What happened to you?" Kristi says.

"You're all right," Priya says.

Isabelle drops her eyes, mumbles something.

"What?" Priya says.

Her gait stiff-legged, Isabelle sloshes toward the shore. She does not stop once she's on dry land; rather, she continues barefoot past the crew, the camera tracking her. "Wait a minute," Kristi says, "where are you going?"

Without looking back, Isabelle says, "Out."

"That's it?" Kristi says. "We go to all this trouble and . . . that's it? 'Out?' Really?"

"Kristi," Sarah says.

"No, she's right," Chad says.

Priya steps out of the water. "She's obviously freaked out," she says.

"She's obviously a pain in my ass," Kristi says.

"Guys," Sarah says, "could we have this discussion while we're keeping up with Isabelle?"

"Yeah," Chad says, "it'd suck to lose her a second time."

"Shut up, Chad," Kristi says.

Three quick scenes show the crew traversing the darkness that lies between the subterranean lake and the tunnel to the mine. Even after she cuts her right foot on a rock, leaving a bloody footprint until the others catch up to her and insist on bandaging it, which George does, Isabelle maintains a brisk pace. She does not let up after they have reentered the mine; though the comments from the others shift from complaint to relief. Throughout, Kristi continues to return to the question of what happened to Isabelle, asking it at sufficient volume for her to hear; Isabelle, however, does not answer.

Not until they have reached the portrait of the woman nearer the mine's entrance does Isabelle stop. Immobile, she stares at the artwork as the rest of the crew gathers around her.

"What now?" Kristi says.

In reply, Isabelle screams, a loud, high-pitched shriek that startles everyone into stepping back. The scream goes on, and on, and on, doubling Isabelle over, breaking into static as it exceeds the limits of the recording equipment. While Isabelle staggers from foot to foot, bent in half, her mouth stretched too wide, the soundtrack cuts in and out, alternating her screaming with an electronic hum. The members of the crew stand stunned, their expressions shocked. Tears stream from Isabelle's eyes, snot pours from her nostrils, flakes of blood spray onto her lips and chin. The audio gives up the fight, yielding to the empty hum. Finally, Priya runs to Isabelle, puts her arms around her, and steers her away from the drawing, toward the exit. While she remains doubled over, Isabelle goes with her. Chad and George follow. For a moment, Sarah studies the portrait, then she, too, turns to leave.

The camera remains focused on the wall, at the weird image that so strikingly resembles Isabelle Router. It zooms in, until the half-skeletal portion of the face fills the screen. As it does, the soundtrack recovers. Isabelle is still screaming, the sound echoing down the mine's tunnels. The picture goes black. "Directed by Sarah Fiore" flashes onto the screen in white letters.

"And that's it," Sarah says, freezing the film.

"Huh," I say. I'm suddenly aware that in the time I've spent viewing Sarah's video, the sun has dropped behind Frenchman's Mountain, hauling night down after it. The autumn light has slid from the windows at the back of the bar, leaving a tide of blackness pressed against them. I can hear the shouts and shrieks of the trick-or-treaters, somewhere in that darkness. It's absurd, but after spending the last hour immersed in the film's subterranean setting, I have the impression that the blackness of the mine has escaped into the night. I swallow, say, "That's something."

"Larry was worried it was too oblique," Sarah says. "He liked it, but he thought the film needed developing. I was—it was surreal, you know? I had this documentary I'd put together that showed . . . I don't know what, and here was this filmmaker I respected treating it as if it was fiction, and I realized, *Yeah, you could watch it that way*, and then I thought, *Wait, was that what it was*?" She shakes her head.

"Did you ever think of telling him the truth?"

"For about half a second, until he started throwing around budget numbers, talking about possible distributors. All of it was extremely modest, but compared to what I was used to—that, and the chance it represented for me as a director—well, it wasn't much of a decision.

"My biggest concern was Isabelle. She was in pretty rough shape after we exited the mine. Priya drove her to the ER in Wiltwyck right away. She had stopped screaming not long after Priya took her away from the portrait, but her throat was a mess. She was exhausted, dehydrated, and there was something wrong with her blood: the white blood cell count was too high, or too low; I can't remember. Anyway, she was in the hospital for a couple of days. I assumed she'd have no interest in a return trip to the mine, to put it mildly, but I felt I owed it to her to fill her in on the new plan."

"And?"

"And she was completely into it, which was a surprise. She offered to help me with the screenplay, and she had some great ideas. A lot of the Bad Agatha stuff came from her." Seeing me opening my mouth, Sarah holds up a hand to forestall the inevitable question. "Yes, I asked her what had happened while she was on her own down there. She shrugged off the question, said she'd gotten lost and freaked out. Okay, I said, but what made her leave us in the first place?

"She heard something, what sounded like someone calling her name. She already thought the rest of us were pranking her with the woman's portrait; she assumed this was more of the same. Her intent was to find whoever was saying her name and kick them in the ass. Instead, she lost track of where she was, and then she had a little bit of a breakdown, and that was all she could remember clearly until she was in the hospital."

"Did you believe her?"

"Yes," Sarah says, drawing out the word, "but I was pretty sure there was more she wasn't telling me. I couldn't figure out how to persuade her to let me in on it. She told me she was fine with returning to the mine, but I was pretty nervous about it. Honestly, I would have been happier if she'd refused. The problem was, Priya and Chad had already bowed out, which meant we couldn't use as much of the documentary footage as I wanted. If Isabelle hadn't agreed, then we would have had to shoot an entirely new film, which might have exceeded our meager budget. So I went with her, and I have to admit, she did a terrific job. For all the years I'd known her, I had no idea she was such a convincing actress."

"What caused the two of you to fall out?"

Sarah frowns. "Creative differences."

"Over?"

"A lot of things." As if she's just noticed the night outside, Sarah says, "Holy shit. What time is it?" She closes the window on the laptop and squints at the corner clock. "I better go," she says, folding the computer shut. While she slides it off the table into her bag, I say, "Anything else you'd like to add?"

"It's funny," she says, easing out of the booth, "there have been moments when I've thought about posting the video online, putting it up on YouTube with no fanfare, letting whoever discovers it make of it what they will. Except, I knew people would view it as a publicity stunt, some old footage I'd stitched together to generate new interest in my movie. I had no plans to mention it on during the interview for the anniversary edition, until there I was, talking about it. Once I started, I figured, why not?"

"And people still thought it was a hoax."

"Yeah. What are you gonna do?"

The walk from the booth to the bar to pay the bill is no more than twelve or fifteen feet, yet it seems to take us an hour to make it. My thoughts are racing, trying to fit what I've heard and seen this afternoon with everything else I know about Sarah and the film. After all, I'm the horror writer; it's why the editors of this publication have asked me to conduct this interview. I'm supposed to judge the veracity of Sarah's footage and, assuming I accept it as true, trace its connections to *Lost in the Dark*, explain the ways in which the fiction refracts the facts. It's a favorite critical activity, isn't it? Especially when it comes to the fantastic, demonstrating how it's only the stuff of daily life, after all. The vampire is our repressed eroticism, the werewolf our unreasoning rage. The film Sarah has shown me, though, isn't the material of daily life. I don't know what it is, because to tell you the truth, I'm more of a skeptic than a believer these days. Strange as it sounds, it's one of the reasons I love to write about the supernatural. The stories I tell offer me the opportunity to indulge a sense of the numinous I find all too lacking in the world around me. But this movie . . . I can't help inventing a story to explain it, something to do with an ancient power captured, brought to a remote location, and imprisoned there. Those dead men at the entrance, maybe they were there as a sacrifice, a way to bind whatever was in that nameless woman to the mine. The stuff inside the tunnels, the caves beyond, was that evidence of someone or someones tending to the woman, worshipping her? And Isabelle Router, her experience underground—was the movie she co-wrote an act of devotion to something that found her in the dark? I half-remember the line from Yeats about entertaining a drowsy emperor.

None of it makes any sense; it's all constructed with playing cards, waiting for a sneeze to collapse it. I pay the bill, and we walk out of Pete's. The sidewalks have filled with a mass of children and parents making their slow way up Main Street to the library to assemble for the Halloween parade. Zombies stagger along next to Clone Troopers, while Batman brings up the rear. Clown parents carry ladybug children. Frankenstein's bride towers over the Hobbits surrounding her. Witches whose pointed green chins are visible beneath the broad brims of their black hats talk to fairies sporting flower crowns and wings dusted with sparkles. There's a kid costumed as a hairy dog, an adult dressed as a boxy robot. The Grim Reaper swings a mean-looking scythe; Hermione Granger flourishes her wand. Vampires in evening dress walk beside superheroes in gaudier colors. A few old-fashioned ghosts flutter like sheets escaped from the clothes line.

A number of Bad Agathas are part of the procession, one of them quite small. This diminutive form darts through the crowd to where Sarah and I are standing. The mask the girl tilts at us is too big for her. It's an older design, the features angular, the left eye socket a black cavern. Sarah's eyebrows lift at the sight. The girl raises her right hand. She's holding a Bad Agatha mask, which she offers to Sarah.

Sarah hesitates, then accepts the mask. Apparently released by her act, the girl sprints away into the costumed ranks. Sarah considers Bad Agatha's stylized face, as if studying a photograph of an old acquaintance. She turns the mask over, tilts her head forward, and slides bad Agatha's face over hers. She straightens, turns to me. Whatever witty remark I was preparing dies on my tongue. Without another word, Sarah turns and joins the parade.

For Fiona

HONORABLE MENTIONS

Allan, Nina "Four Abstracts," *New Fears*.
Arkenberg, Megan "But Thou, Proserpina, Sleep," *A Breath from the Sky*.
Balázs, Thomas P. "Waiting for Mrs. Hemley," *Horror Library Volume 6*.
Barron, Laird "Swift to Chase," *Adam's Ladder*.
Benedict, R. S. "My English Name," F&SF May/June.
Campbell, Rebecca "On Highway 18," F&SF Sept/October.
Clark, Stephen J. Out of Bounds," (novella) *Murder Ballads*.
Dowling, Terry "The Other Séance at Kenmyre," *The Night Shop*
Dowling, Terry "Still Life, with Stranging Glass," *The Night Shop*.
Edelman, Scott "Faking It Until Forever Comes," *Liars, Fakers, and the Dead . . .*
Evenson, Brian "Sisters," *Haunted Nights*.
Ford, Jeffrey "The Twilight Pariah," (novella) Tor.com Books.
Ford, Jeffrey "Witch Hazel," *Haunted Nights*.
Hand, Elizabeth "Eat the Worm," *Mixed Up*.
Hand, Elizabeth "Fire," *Fire. Plus*.
Headley, Maria Dahvana "The Orange Tree," *The Weight of Words*.
Hodge, Brian "I'll Bring You the Birds From Out of the Sky" chapbook
Jakeman, Jane "In the Rigging," *Supernatural Tales* 36.
Johnstone, Carole "The Eyes Are White and Quiet," *New Fears*.
Johnstone, Tom "How I Learned the Truth About Krampus," chapbook.
Jones, Stephen Graham "Alis," *Mad Hatters and March Hares*.
Jones, Stephen Graham "Dirtmouth," *Haunted Nights*.
Jones, Stephen Graham *Mapping the Interior* (novella) Tor.com Books

Kassel, Mel "Weavers in the Cellar," Interzone 268, Jan/February.
Khaw, Cassandra These Deathless Bones," Tor.com, July 26.
Kiernan, Caitlín R. "Tupelo (1998)," (novella) Sirenia Digest 132.
Lanchester, John "Signal," *The New Yorker*, April 3.
Little, John R. "The First Lunar Halloween," *Haunted Nights.*
Madron, Suzanne "The Water Shed," *Shadows over Main Street volume 2.*
Malik, Usman T. "The Fortune of Sparrows," *Black Feathers.*
Mills, Daniel "The Christiansen Deaths," *Looming Low.*
Nevill, Adam L. G. "Little Black Lamb," *Darker Companions.*
Nix, Garth "The Seventeen Year Itch," *Haunted Nights.*
Oates, Joyce Carol "Great Blue Heron," *Black Feathers.*
Rickert, M. "Everything Beautiful is Terrifying," *Shadows and Tall Trees 7.*
Royce, Eden "Sweetgrass Blood," *Sycorax's Daughters.*
Royle, Nicholas "Jizz," *Ornithology.*
Salmonson, Jessica Amanda "The Ice Maiden of Snow Lake," (poem) *Anthony Shriek*
Samuels, Mark "Moon Blood-Red, Tide Turning," *Terror Tales of Cornwall.*
Schaller, Eric "Smoke, Ash, and Whatever Comes After," Black Static Jan/Feb 56
Schwader, Ann K. "Pothunters," *Black Wings VI.*
Sharma, Priya "The Crow Palace," *Black Feathers.*
Slatsky, Christopher "The Carcass of the Lion," *Darker Companions.*
Slatter, Angela "Run, Rabbit," *Mad Hatters and March Hares.*
Taylor, Lucy "Sweetlings," Tor.com, May 3.
Vaz, Katherine "Moon, Memory, Muchness," *Mad Hatters and March Hares*
Warren, Kaaron "Whither," *Darker Companions.*
Williams, Conrad "Succulents," *New Fears.*

ABOUT THE AUTHORS

Inna Effress is a former speechwriter who emigrated from Ukraine as a child. Her fiction appears in the *Santa Monica Review*, *The Wrong*, and the *Nightscript* anthology. She writes in LA.

"Liquid Air" was originally published in *Nightscript III* edited by C. M. Muller.

Marc E. Fitch is the author of the novels *Paradise Burns*, *Dirty Water*, and *Old Boone Blood*. His short fiction has appeared in publications such as *Nightscript*, *Whispers from the Abyss 2*, and *The Big Click*.

Fitch is also the author of *Paranormal Nation: Why America Needs Ghosts, UFOs and Bigfoot*. Marc lives and works in Connecticut with his wife, four children, and three goats. For more information visit www.marcfitch.com, and he can be found on Facebook and Twitter.

"The Starry Crown" was originally published in *Horror Library Volume 6* edited by Eric J. Guignard.

Philip Fracassi, an author and screenwriter, lives in Los Angeles and works full-time in the film industry and on his writing. He is the author of the novellas *Fragile Dreams*, *Sacculina*, and *Shiloh*. His short horror fiction is collected in *Behold the Void*. His feature film, *Girl Missing*, is currently available on demand via iTunes and Amazon.

His stories have been printed in numerous magazines and anthologies. You can visit his website at pfracassi.com for more information. You can also find him via social media on Facebook, Instagram (pfracassi), and Twitter (@philipfracassi).

"Fail-Safe" was originally published in his collection, *Behold the Void.*

Stephen Gallagher is a Stoker and World Fantasy Award nominee, winner of British Fantasy and International Horror Guild Awards for his short fiction, and is the author of fifteen novels including *Valley of Lights, Down River, Rain*, and *Nightmare, With Angel.* He's the creator of Sebastian Becker, Special Investigator to the Lord Chancellor's Visitor in Lunacy, in a series of novels that includes *The Kingdom of Bones, The Bedlam Detective*, and *The Authentic William James.*

"Shepherds' Business" was originally published in *New Fear*s, edited by Mark Morris.

Orrin Grey is a writer, editor, amateur film scholar, and monster expert who was born on the night before Halloween. His stories of monsters, ghosts, and sometimes the ghosts of monsters have appeared in dozens of anthologies, and have been collected into *Never Bet the Devil & Other Warnings* and *Painted Monsters & Other Strange Beasts.* He is also the author of various licensed work and *Monsters from the Vault*, a collection of his essays on vintage horror cinema.

"The Granfalloon" was originally published in *Darker Companions: Celebrating 50 Years of Ramsey Campbell* selected and edited by Scott David Aniolowski and Joseph S. Pulver Sr.

Brian Hodge is one of those people who always has to be making something. So far, he's made thirteen novels, around 130 shorter works, and five full-length collections.

He'll have three new books out in 2018 and early 2019: *The Immaculate Void*, a novel of cosmic horror; *A Song of Eagles*, a grimdark fantasy; and *Skidding Into Oblivion*, his next collection.

He lives in Colorado, where he also likes to make music and photographs and trains in Krav Maga and kickboxing.

Connect through his web site (www.brianhodge.net), Twitter (@BHodgeAuthor), or Facebook (www.facebook.com/brianhodgewriter).

"West of Matamoros, North of Hell" was originally published in *Dark Screams Volume Seven*, edited by Brian James Freeman.

Carole Johnstone is a British Fantasy Award winning Scottish writer, currently enjoying splendid isolation on the Atlantic coast of the Isle of Lewis in the Outer Hebrides. Her short fiction has been published widely, and has been reprinted in Ellen Datlow's *Best Horror of the Year* and Salt Publishing's *Best British Fantasy* series.

Her debut short story collection, *The Bright Day is Done*, and her novella, *Cold Turkey*, were both shortlisted for a 2015 British Fantasy Award.

"Better You Believe" was originally published in *Horror Library Volume 6*, edited by Eric G. Guignard.

John Langan is the author of two novels: *The Fisherman* and *House of Windows*, and three collections: *The Wide, Carnivorous Sky and Other Monstrous Geographies*, *Mr. Gaunt and Other Uneasy Encounters*, and *Sefira and Other Betrayals*.

With Paul Tremblay, he co-edited *Creatures: Thirty Years of Monsters*. One of the founders of the Shirley Jackson Awards, he serves on its Advisory Board. Currently, he reviews horror and dark fantasy for *Locus* magazine. He lives in New York's Hudson Valley with his wife and younger son.

"Lost in the Dark" was originally published in *Haunted Nights*, edited by Ellen Datlow and Lisa Morton.

Rich Larson was born in Galmi, Niger, has studied in Rhode Island and worked in the south of Spain, and now lives in Ottawa, Canada. Since he began writing in 2011, he's sold over a hundred stories, the majority of them speculative fiction published in magazines like *Asimov's*, *Analog*,

Clarkesworld, *The Magazine of Fantasy and Science Fiction*, *Lightspeed*, *Omni*, and Tor.com.

His work also appears in numerous Year's Best anthologies and has been translated into Chinese, Vietnamese, Polish, Czech, French, and Italian. His debut novel, *Annex*, was recently published, and his debut collection, *Tomorrow Factory*, is forthcoming in October 2018. Find more at richwlarson.tumblr.com and support him via patreon.com/richlarson.

"Dark Warm Heart" was originally published on Tor.com, April 12, 2017.

Rebecca Lloyd is from the south of England. Her short stories have been collected in *Mercy and Other Stories*, which was nominated for the 2014 World Fantasy Award, and *Seven Strange Stories*, *The View from Endless Street*, *Whelp and Other Stories* which was a finalist for the 2014 Paul Bowles Short Fiction Award, and *Ragman and Other Family Curses*.

Her story "The Ringers" was short-listed in the Aestas Short Story Prize 2016, and her novel *Oothangbart* was published by Pillar International Publishing. She is also the author of the novellas *Woolfy and Scrapo* and *Jack Werrett, the Flood Man*.

She recently finished *The Child Cephalina*, a Gothic horror novel set in 1851.

"Where's the Harm?" was originally published in her collection *Seven Strange Stories*.

Carman Maria Machado's debut short story collection, *Her Body and Other Parties*, was a finalist for the National Book Award, the Kirkus Prize, *LA Times* Book Prize Art Seidenbaum Award for First Fiction, the Dylan Thomas Prize, the PEN/Robert W. Bingham Prize for Debut Fiction, and the winner of the Bard Fiction Prize, the National Book Critics Circle's John Leonard Prize, and the Crawford Award. In 2018, the *New York Times* listed Her Body and Other Parties as a member of "The New Vanguard," one of "15 remarkable books by women that are shaping the way we read and write fiction in the 21st century." Her essays, fiction, and criticism have appeared in the *New Yorker*, the *New York Times*, *Granta*, *Tin House*, *The Believer*, *Guernica*, *Best American Science Fiction & Fantasy*, and elsewhere. She holds an MFA from the Iowa Writers' Workshop and has been awarded fellowships and residencies from the Michener-Copernicus Foundation, the Elizabeth George Foundation, the CINTAS Foundation, Yaddo, Hedgebrook, and the Millay Colony for the Arts. She is the Writer in Residence at the University of Pennsylvania and lives in Philadelphia with her wife.

"There and Back Again" war originally published in *Mixed Up: Cocktail Recipes (and Flash Fiction) For the Discerning Drinker (and Reader)* edited by Nick Mamatas and Molly Tanzer.

Tim Major is co-editor of the British Fantasy Society's fiction journal, *BFS Horizons*. His novels and novellas include *You Don't Belong Here*, *Blighters*, and *Carus & Mitch*. In 2018, ChiZine will publish his first YA novel, *Machineries of Mercy*, Luna Press will publish his first short story collection, *And The House Lights Dim*, and Electric Dreamhouse Press will publish his non-fiction book about the silent crime film, *Les Vampires*.

Tim's short stories have appeared in *Interzone*, *Not One of Us*, *The Literary Hatchet*, and numerous anthologies. Find out more at cosycatastrophes.wordpress.com.

"Eqalussuaq" was originally published in *Not One of Us #58 October*.

Seanan McGuire lives, works, and occasionally falls into swamps in the Pacific Northwest, where she is coming to an understanding with the local frogs. She has written a ridiculous number of novels and even more short stories. Keep up with her at seananmcguire.com. On moonlit nights, when the stars are right, you just might find her falling into a swamp near you.

"You Can Stay All Day" was originally published (under the name Mira Grant) in *Nights of the Living Dead* edited by Jonathan Maberry and George A. Romero.

S. P. Miskowski is a three-time Shirley Jackson Award nominee, and is the recipient of two National Endowment for the Arts Fellowships. Her stories have been published in *Supernatural Tales*, *Black Static*, *Identity Theory*, *Strange Aeons*, and *Eyedolon* magazine, as well as in the anthologies *Haunted*

Nights, *The Madness of Dr. Caligari*, *Autumn Cthulhu*, *Darker Companions: Celebrating 50 Years of Ramsey Campbell*, *Tales from a Talking Board*, and *Looming Low*. Her books are available from Omnium Gatherum and JournalStone/Trepidatio.

"Alligator Point" was originally published in *Looming Low Volume 1* edited by Justin Steele and Sam Cowan.

Mark Morris has written over twenty-five novels, among which are *Toady*, *Stitch*, *The Immaculate*, *The Secret of Anatomy*, *Fiddleback*, *The Deluge*, and four Doctor Who books. His short stories are collected in *Close to the Bone*, *Long Shadows*, *Nightmare Light*, and *Wrapped In Skin*. His fiction, articles, and reviews have appeared in a wide variety of anthologies and magazines, and he is editor of *Cinema Macabre*, for which he won the 2007 British Fantasy Award, its follow-up *Cinema Futura*, two volumes of *The Spectral Book of Horror Stories*, and *New Fears*. He has also written audio dramas.

His recently published work includes the official movie tie-in novelizations of *Noah* and *The Great Wall*, the novellas *It Sustains* and *Albion Fay*, and his Obsidian Heart trilogy.

Forthcoming in 2018 is *New Fears 2*, a new audio adaptation of the classic British folk-horror movie *Blood on Satan's Claw*, and the first publication of Mark's first ever, previously unpublished novel *The Winter Tree*.

"Holiday Romance" was originally published in *Black Static* #58, May/June.

David Erik Nelson has become increasingly aware that he's an "unsavory character" in other people's anecdotes. His stories have appeared in *Asimov's*, *The Magazine of Fantasy & Science Fiction*, *Pseudopod*, and elsewhere.

In addition to writing stories about time travel, non-Euclidean houses, and carnivorous lights, he also writes nonfiction about synthesizers, guns, cyborg cockroaches, and Miss America. More of his writing can be found online—as can he—at davideriknelson.com or twitter.com/squidaveo.

"Whatever Comes After Calcutta" was originally published in *The Magazine of Fantasy and Science Fiction*, November/December.

Sarah Read is a dark fiction writer in the frozen north of Wisconsin, where she works in a library in a castle on an island. Her short stories can be found in *Gamut*, *Black Static*, *Lamplight*, and *BEHOLD! Oddities Curiosities and Undefinable Wonders*, among other places. She also writes numerous articles about crocheting and fountain pens. She is the editor-in-chief at *Pantheon* magazine and an active member of the Horror Writer's Association. When she's not staring into the abyss, she knits. To learn more about Sarah, you can visit her website at inkwellmonster.wordpress.com.

"Endoskeletal" was originally published in *Black Static* #59, July/August.

Kelly Robson's book *Gods, Monsters and the Lucky Peach* was recently brought out by Tor.com Publishing. Her short fiction has appeared in *Clarkesworld*, Tor.com, *Asimov's Science Fiction*, and multiple year's best anthologies.

She was a finalist for the 2017 John W. Campbell Award for Best New Writer. Her novella "Waters of Versailles" won the 2016 Aurora Award and was a finalist for both the Nebula and World Fantasy Awards. "A Human Stain" was nominated for the Nebula Award.

Kelly lives in Toronto with her wife, fellow SF writer A. M. Dellamonica.

"A Human Stain" was originally published on Tor.com, January 4, 2017.

Kaaron Warren is a Shirley Jackson Award Winner who published her first short story in 1993, and has had stories in print every year since. She has lived in Melbourne, Sydney, Canberra, and Fiji. She has published four novels (*Slights*, *Walking the Tree*, *Mistification*, and *The Grief Hole*, which won all three Australian genre awards) and six short story collections, including the multi-award winning *Through Splintered Walls*. Her next short story collection is *A Primer to Kaaron Warren* from Dark Moon Books.

You can find her at kaaronwarren.wordpress.com, and she Tweets @KaaronWarren.

"Furtherest" was originally published in *Dark Screams Volume Seven*, edited by Brian James Freeman.

A. C. Wise was born and raised in the Montreal area, and currently lives in the Philadelphia area. In addition to short fiction appearing in publications such as *Clarkesworld*, Tor.com, and *The Year's Best Dark Fantasy and Horror 2017*, she has two collections published with Lethe Press, and a novella, *Catfish Lullaby,* published by Broken Eye Books. Her work has been a finalist for the Lambda Literary Award, and won the Sunburst Award for Excellence in Canadian Literature of the Fantastic. She contributes a monthly short fiction review column to *Apex* magazine, and her Women to Read and Non-Binary Authors to Read columns appear monthly at *The Book Smugglers.* Find her online at acwise.net.

"The Stories We Tell about Ghosts" was originally published in *Looming Low Volume 1* edited by Justin Steele and Sam Cowan.

"Harvest Song, Gathering Song" was originally published in *For Mortal Things Unsung* edited by Alex Hofelich.

ACKNOWLEDGMENT OF COPYRIGHT

"Better You Believe" by Carole Johnstone. Copyright © 2017. First published in *Horror Library Volume 6*, edited by Eric G. Guignard, Cutting Block Books. Reprinted by permission of the author.

"Liquid Air" by Inna Effress. Copyright © 2017. First published in *Nightscript III* edited by C. M. Muller, Chthonic Matter. Reprinted by permission of the author.

"Holiday Romance" by Mark Morris. Copyright © 2017. First published in *Black Static* #58 May/June. Reprinted by permission of the author.

"Furtherest" by Kaaron Warren. Copyright © 2017. First published in *Dark Screams Volume Seven*, edited by Brian James Freeman, Cemetery Dance/Hydra). Reprinted by permission of the author.

"Where's the Harm?" by Rebecca Lloyd. Copyright © 2017. First published in *Seven Strange Stories*, Tartarus Press. Reprinted by permission of the author.

"Whatever Comes After Calcutta" by David Erik Nelson. Copyright © 2017. First published in *The Magazine of Fantasy and Science Fiction*, November/December. Reprinted by permission of the author.

"A Human Stain" by Kelly Robson. Copyright © 2017. First published on Tor.com, January 4, 2017. Reprinted by permission of the author.

"The Stories We Tell about Ghosts" by A. C. Wise. Copyright © 2017. First published in *Looming Low Volume 1* edited by Justin Steele and Sam Cowan, Dim Shores. Reprinted by permission of the author.

ABOUT THE EDITOR

Ellen Datlow has been editing science fiction, fantasy, and horror short fiction for almost forty years. She currently acquires short fiction for Tor.com. In addition, she has edited about ninety science fiction, fantasy, and horror anthologies, including the series *The Best Horror of the Year*, *Fearful Symmetries*, *The Doll Collection*, *The Monstrous*, *Children of Lovecraft*, *Black Feathers*, *Mad Hatters and March Hares*, and *The Devil and the Deep*.

Forthcoming is *Echoes: The Saga Anthology of Ghost Stories*.

She's won multiple World Fantasy Awards, Locus Awards, Hugo Awards, Stoker Awards, International Horror Guild Awards, Shirley Jackson Awards, and the 2012 Il Posto Nero Black Spot Award for Excellence as Best Foreign Editor. Datlow was named recipient of the 2007 Karl Edward Wagner Award, given at the British Fantasy Convention for "outstanding contribution to the genre" was honored with the Life Achievement Award given by the Horror Writers Association, in acknowledgment of superior achievement over an entire career, and the Life Achievement Award by the World Fantasy Convention.

She lives in New York and co-hosts the monthly Fantastic Fiction Reading Series at KGB Bar. More information can be found at datlow.com, on Facebook, and on Twitter at @EllenDatlow.